CATCHERS IN THE SKY

MISSION: KOREA

a novel by

Jonathan Damien

BookSurge Publishing

This is a work of fiction. All of the characters, names, incidents, organizations, and dialogue in this novel are either the products of the author's imagination or are used fictitiously.

ISBN: 1-4196-6995-8
ISBN-13: 978-1419669958
ISBN: 1-4196-7241-X

Library of Congress Control Number: 2007933575
Publisher: BookSurge, LLC
North Charleston, South Carolina

Visit www.booksurge.com or Amazon.com to order additional copies.

For additional information, please visit with Jon at jonathandamien.com

Dedication

This book is dedicated first to my wife, Literature Herb,
secondly to the long-separated people of Korea, and finally to
the men and women of the Air Force Research Laboratory.
May they someday find the Grail of 'Peace Through Light.'

On Korean names

The Korean language has a complex honorific grammar. Names are
also highly honorific and interwoven with functional titles, especially
for those of age and rank. Translated to English, such names feel
lengthy, bureaucratic, and aloof. To give the reader equal access to
all characters, I address Koreans as I do Americans, using given or
family names—with occasional titles—as appropriate to the story.
When required, I attempt to convey the true feeling of a Korean
language exchange by the –nim (highly respected), –ssi (respected),
and –ya (boy) suffixes, and hopefully the reader will intuitively sense
and enjoy the added intimacy or stratification. Likewise, I have taken
some latitude with place names, locations, Korean spellings, and
military projects and organizations to clarify the story.

CHINA

RUSSIA

MANCHURIA

NORTH KOREA

East Sea
(Sea of Japan)

★Pyongyang

Namp'o Harbor

Pyong-son

Kansong

Panmunjom   DMZ

★Seoul

Ullung-do Island

Osan AB

SOUTH KOREA

West Sea
(Yellow Sea)

Pusan AB

Korea Strait

JAPAN

RUSSIA

Khabarovsk

Pyongyang

NORTH KOREA

JAPAN

Tokyo

CHINA

Beijing ★

Seoul

SOUTH KOREA

Kadena AB, Okinawa

map illustration by Barbara Bastian

Foreword

At the dawn of the 21st Century, science fiction depicted lasers as a standard weapon of future warfare.

In fact no laser weapons existed.

Yet.

Who, then, will be The First Laser Warriors?

What will be their story?

The Air Force Research Laboratory Project Officer's Ten Commandments

Book 1. Come to work each day willing to be fired.

Book 2. Do any job needed to make your dream come true, regardless of your job description.

Book 3. Find people to help you.

Book 4. Be true to your goals, but be realistic about the ways to achieve them.

Book 5. Follow your intuition about the people you choose and work only with the best.

Book 6. Work underground as long as you can—publicity triggers the corporate immune mechanism.

Book 7. Circumvent any order aimed at stopping your dream.

Book 8. Remember, it is easier to ask for forgiveness than for permission.

Book 9. Never bet on a race unless you are running it.

Book 10. Honor your sponsors.

Prolegomena to a Future War

Prelude North Korea

The 1ˢᵗ of September

NAMP'O HARBOR – NORTH KOREA

The man waiting in the moonlight on the end of the dock, surrounded by a soft swell shimmering with swarming plankton, had a frightening face. Asian, aging, and fierce—with a strangely lumpy jaw line—the face seemed to be a cross between a Samurai, a Chinese warlord, and Genghis Khan.

In fact, this crude geopolitical triangulation placing him between the Shogunates of Japan, the Forbidden City, and the Steppes of Mongolia was accurate in many ways. Not only did he share genes with these illustrious if bloodthirsty compatriots from the ancient surrounds of Northeast Asia, he was of high martial status: he was Marshal Song Il-Moon, First Vice Chairman of the National Defense Committee and second in command in North Korea.

With a frigid intensity, from a face like a stone, Il-Moon's eyes stared across this inlet to the Yellow Sea, or as he called it, the West Sea. He seemed not to see the huge harbor with its miles of military piers, naval warehouses, darkened fortified islands, and half-submerged entrances to Special Forces installations.

Nor did he seem aware of the tough-looking North Korean frigate, the *Inchon*, at the pier's side. Portholes lit, the *Inchon* lay at the ready, props roiling the water, smoke wisping from her stacks, radars turning briskly. Nor did he seem to care, out in the harbor, that four small sleek naval craft—Internal Security Forces fast torpedo boats—patrolled in paired circles in apparently open water.

He sniffed the sea air; he could almost smell change. How long had he waited? He smiled wolfishly, his misshapen dentures sharp, when 'One hundred years' came to mind. After two thousand years of the glory of independent Korea, he had not been sorry to see the 20ᵗʰ century pass. During that century, invaders had occupied, enslaved, decimated, and humiliated them. Now, on the ozone of the sea breeze was carried the tang of a new time.

Next to him, a respectful pace back despite his almost eighty years, his personal aide, Aide Park, stood holding the distinctive circle-trapped-in-a-square box of a 70 millimeter movie reel. They both appeared to wait, standing on the quay's quiet end.

It had not been quiet long. Hours earlier, before he'd set a foot on this pier, his personal security detachment—Guard Command bruisers in full battle dress uniform, three hundred strong—had arrived in ten new Zil trucks. They swarmed the dock, snooped every leaf and can, searched the frigate, the water, took up positions at high points, and cordoned off the entrance to the pier. When all was secure, they lined up for Il-Moon's arrival. Row after row of Guard Command now stood stiffly like drab terra-cotta statues along the white cement pier.

The only movement was the spinning radars of the frigate *Inchon* and the tight patrol circles of the Internal Security craft.

Il-Moon looked broodingly down at the water. An elongated blob of oil lay softly undulating on the swell like a slowly-rolling worm. *There it was again, that fragment of half-remembered English poem:*

> 'The invisible worm
> That flies in the night...'

His shark-like lumpy mouth smiled grimly at the memories floating up from the classical reference. He'd gotten a good European education—a sadistic Russian Political Officer had beaten it into all the boys at the Soviet detention camp in Khabarovsk just over the Korean border during the Great Patriotic War[*].

The Guard Command Chief ran up, saluted, and spoke to Aide Park, not daring to look at Il-Moon. Aide Park reported to Il-Moon, "Great Vice Chairman, the harbor is clear."

"Call them."

COL KANG

The harbor was not, however, clear.

Along the shoreline a mile away across the harbor, a husky soldier crouched among the tides sucking at the massive stanchions of a mini-submarine base. Col Kang wore the battle fatigues of the North Korean Special Forces, or as they termed themselves, Combatants. His shoulder rank was full colonel, and incongruous to his fatigues, from his breast pocket hung the Gold Medal of the Hero of the DPRK. He panned the ungainly military night binoculars carefully, shielding the optics from a possible revealing flash to those on the pier.

Col Kang was tough, disciplined, and—it was widely acknowledged—never made a mistake.

Into his past stretched an endless string of one hundred percent scores on his

---

[*] The North Korean term for World War II

Special Forces tests, in his Political classes, self-criticism sessions, on the firing range, in physical training, and in his on-the-spot decisions during exercises and maneuvers. He had been—for as long as anyone could remember—nothing short of perfect.

Crouching by the soft tides swishing into the concrete pens, Col Kang skillfully studied Il-Moon on the quay, then the circling Internal Security boats.

Behind him in the murky shadows, hidden in a minisubmarine pen, was a military cabin cruiser. Its low flying bridge was black and rubbery, and its gunwales were faceted rather than smooth. Around it, a furtive group of other Combatants, two officers and an ensign, lugged what appeared to be heavy ash cans from under nearby shoreline debris. Wading into the water on either side of the cabin cruiser, they hung the ash cans along the prow.

One of the officers broke away, came and shared Kang's binoculars. He looked across the harbor to the lighted pier and over the inky water beyond. Major Tam Ho handed the bulky binoculars back to Col Kang. "Any sign?"

"None. But they will not keep him waiting long," Col Kang murmured, watching again. He heard the music clearly across the water, knew just where to look. "There."

IL-MOON

Il-Moon saw the small ferry boat appear and chug toward the pier from out in the dark swells. Engines burping smoke, all along the ferry's sides, lights suddenly flickered on. The railings were now trimmed with strings of festive lights. Loudspeakers came on, pumping out tinny martial music.

"They are coming." Aide Park shifted his film case to under his arm.

Despite the ferry looking like nothing so much as a South Florida party boat, Il-Moon and Aide Park seemed unsurprised at its strange appearance.

The party-boat pulled along the pier, a big '27' emblazoned on it below the off-centered-star flag of the Korean People's Navy. The center of the boat had an open hole in the deck going right down to the water. The boat stewards wore party hats although they were in stiff wool KPN uniforms. They laid the boarding plank out and Aide Park followed Il-Moon onto the ferry.

In unison, bowing deeply to Il-Moon, the ferry stewards chorused, "Welcome, Great First Vice Chairman!"

Aide Park replied, "Take us to Mansion 27."

COL KANG

Across the water, Col Kang saw the ferry take on its two passengers. He looked at the party lights, listened to the music floating brightly across the water, and waited until the ferry took on its heading.

Maj Tam Ho said, "Colonel, we are ready for inspection."

They walked to the cabin cruiser, where the attached canisters formed a necklace around the prow.

Col Kang walked into the freezing water alongside the boat. He ran a finger over the wiring, pulled at each installation until he was satisfied with all eight. He touched the sealed containers. *Strange how something so small will make so great a difference. These few, and how the world will shake.*

The men watched him nervously. Once he was done, he climbed from the water, squeezed out his fatigues, and shook hands firmly with Tam Ho. "Go, now. It is time."

"Very well. May the forces of the Revolution and Juche be with you." Tam Ho held the docking lines as the three crew—Col Kang, Lt Han, and an ensign—heaved themselves over the gunwales onto the cabin cruiser. Lt Han watched with respect as Col Kang broke off the GPS antenna on the boat's roof, and dropped it into the cabin below, saying, "We will not need it, we cannot risk it."

No one could navigate a boat without GPS except Col Kang, thought Lt Han. Confident, the men clambered down into the cramped cabin and pulled the hatch to. Inside, Col Kang, Lt Han, and the ensign took their stations at the helm, weapons, and engines.

Tam Ho pulled loose the bow and stern lines and tossed them up on the bank. Silent electric engines swung the boat free from its mooring. Once free, the cabin cruiser strangely did not motor away, but rather began sinking. The boat sank until the roof of the cabin submerged. The last thing to disappear was the stub of the broken-off GPS antenna. When the boat had sunk a meter beneath the water, it was in infiltration mode—and nothing showed on the surface but a mirage-like image.

Maj Tam Ho watched the ghostly submerged image turn and swing slowly after the Party Boat.

IL-MOON

The Party Boat chugged out into the empty harbor, heading into the pool of inky ocean. Il-Moon and Aide Park stood quietly as the boat approached a pair of large buoys in the middle of the empty harbor. Alongside the boat, underwater lights shimmered as the pilot positioned the ferry between the buoys.

A glass elevator—like a huge phone booth—suddenly popped up, foaming with water as it rose through the hole in the middle of the ferry deck. Unruffled,

Il-Moon and Aide Park entered the glass elevator. It dropped back down into the water.

As the elevator descended, the source of the surface lights became clear. Il-Moon saw again, without emotion, an extraordinary site on the seabed.

Below them, eighty feet down on the harbor floor, floodlit and shining, almost an illusion, stood a complete Parisian mansion.

THE UNDERWATER MANSION

The Underwater Mansion had been the 27th mansion of Dear Leader Kim Jong-Il. Built as the last and most sumptuous of his party mansions, the former dictator of North Korea completed it just before his unexpected and sudden death. As inherited, it now belonged to his first son and ascendant to the throne of North Korea, Dearest Leader Kim Jong-Nam.

The Underwater Mansion was a replica of a famous grand Parisian house on the Avenue Foch. From its massive front door, porticos, and huge picture windows in beautifully crafted casements, to its four stories topped in Mansard roofs with gabled dormers, to its spot-lit yard with submerged folly walkways, gardens, and gazebos, it was, as its designer Architect Su was fond of saying, the eighth wonder of the world.

As Il-Moon and Aide Park's elevator dropped toward the front door, they could see through the dozen huge front windows—brilliantly lit from within by crystal chandeliers—to inside the main ballroom. Among the antique French furniture was going on a truly high class party: uniformed generals and tuxedoed North Korean elite—all men—drank and smoked and laughed with provocatively-gowned and showgirl-accoutered beautiful women.

First State Architect Su, who had designed the mansion, had done so with style. He had spot-lit the windows from without, attracting fish and strange creatures of the deep to swim by the casements for the enjoyment of the partiers inside.

Il-Moon and his Aide Park entered the airlock through the front door and came into the velvet and gold brocade glory of the Underwater Mansion's main banquet hall.

The booze was flowing, the cigars were smoking, the caviar heaping. On a big stage, a jazz orchestra enthusiastically blew accompaniment for a chorus line of incredible North Korean beauties high kickin' it to a number from *Show Boat;* dancers from the "Joy Brigade."

Il-Moon patiently shooed away other nubile Joy Brigade escorts who rushed up, slipping arms into his and Aide Park's, entreating the men to accept their favors.

Their beautiful faces soured as if from a bite of lemon at the rejection—Il-Moon would have been the greatest honor to please. The girls whined attractively as the two men moved past the grand staircase and into the splendid French banquet room full of partying elite among painted ceilings, Ormolu clocks, Rodin statutes, and 18th century French and Italian oils.

The cult of the Kim family regime had completely rifled the pockets of the North Korean economy. Unique as it was, Mansion 27 represented only a fraction of the hundreds of millions Dear Leader Kim Jong-Il had spent on himself every year for birthday parties, perks for his family and friends, luxury cars, yachts, racehorses, wine cellars, cooks, prostitutes, palaces, and monuments—thirty thousand statues of his father, 'the Great Leader,' alone.

During his life, Dear Leader had nurtured many bizarre and god-like tastes. The top rooms of the mansion had been set aside for his specialized services. In one room, two dozen young women with chopsticks sorted rice grain by grain. Dear Leader would eat—as suitable to a god—only the most perfect rice, each grain of which was hand-selected. The Rice Grain Maidens were chosen for their manual dexterity, beauty, intelligence, family, and maidenly virtue. After a grueling acceptance process, each Rice Maiden underwent three months of intensive physical, political, and spiritual indoctrination. Besides techniques for properly sorting rice grains, daily exercises and ping pong for reflexes and to build strength, they were also trained in CPR, first aid, and emergency procedures.

In the corridors around the Rice Maidens were Dear Leader's sumptuous playrooms, which he shared with his friends. Besides a spa, Love Hotel rooms, and a dungeon for bondage with a variety of trussing materials, there was—its back seat accoutered for lovemaking—a sumptuous Rolls Royce Silver Shadow. These apartments were where the Joy Brigade really earned their keep, and even with thirty girls on duty tonight, the upstairs rooms had a two hour waiting list.

Il-Moon glanced at his watch, then his eyes searched the party for the key people who should be here. Among the hostesses, hustling uniformed waiters, and tables loaded with extravagant displays of delicacies, he saw them. *General Chon and Premier Yu. Good.*

Everyone it seemed was partying and laughing, except a spry portly man in a beautiful silk Japanese business suit. The young Dearest Leader of all North Korea sat solemnly in a cushioned gold-brocaded window-well. Behind him—outside the window in the floodlit sea—strange shining-eyed squid whiplashed their tentacles, propelling themselves in manic circles as they chased tiny fleeing fish. Dearest Leader caught Il-Moon's eye, waved him over with his cigarette holder.

Il-Moon and Aide Park, still carrying the film suitcase, crossed the room toward Dearest Leader.

COL KANG

In the cramped cabin of the infiltration craft, Col Kang and Lt Han navigated submerged.

Col Kang had the helm of the craft—designated the XF/210 Infiltration Boat by the U.S. Intelligence Services. Despite its appearance as a crude military cabin cruiser, its differences were major: designed to deliver Combatant Special Forces to missions in South Korea in the event of war, the faceted upper deck was coated with radar absorbing paint for stealth, the entire boat could cruise slightly submerged, the upper deck just below water with only the whip antenna above—if you didn't break it off like Kang did—and maintain a running speed of six knots beneath the surface for several miles.

Kang looked out through the front windows over the submerged prow. He could see the canisters clinging to the forward railing like baby spiders piggy-backing on their mother.

Indicating the windows, Kang ordered, "The lights should glow in this plankton-filled water. Look for the lights."

IL-MOON

Il-Moon swept up to Dearest Leader respectfully. "Welcome to my pitifully small party for you. Is your mansion not the height of amazement?" He waved his arm at the party, the furnishings, the Joy Brigade, the generals. "Unequaled in all the world. The best of Korea!"

Dearest Leader greeted Il-Moon with a short bow, his cigarette holder gripped elegantly. His hair was cropped ascetically, he wore tiny chic designer glasses, and despite his chubby frame, his obvious energy and engaged features made him look nothing like his father, the fat aging playboy; he was more a chubby Korean James Dean.

To the great celebration of the whole world—minus some of North Korea—Dear Leader Kim Jong-Il—party animal, film enthusiast, nuclear weapons coveter, extreme militarist, dictator passionate to maintain his power and god-like status while simultaneous killing his own people—had died unexpectedly. Whether the death, variously rumored as choking to death on an excess of food, having a stroke, or being strangled while he slept, no one, including Il-Moon, knew the real story—except Dearest Leader, who had been there at the end.

What the world did know was, following his father's sudden death, with an amazing speed and agility, Jong-Nam had seized the throne. As head of the merciless and brutal State Security Department—the highest North Korean secret police—he was perfectly positioned to quickly purge everyone in his way.

With his years-in-the-making alliance with Il-Moon, which had been costly but invaluable, few even considered resisting. Younger siblings, competing family members, pretenders, and old cronies, all were dealt with quickly though mercifully—exiled to China or to the far provinces. These energetic and focused actions, within the last four months, had consolidated Jong-Nam's power and he had now replaced his father completely. Following the daisy chain of titles starting with his grandfather as "Great Leader," then his father as "Dear Leader," the son adopted the sobriquet of "Dearest Leader."

Dearest Leader smiled warmly at Il-Moon. "Ah. Song Il-Moon, my father's best friend. So it is you who is throwing this party for me?"

"You asked for something modest."

Dearest Leader spread his arms to the room, "Modest? This is modest?"

"For your father's last birthday we had more than one million people march and wave flags in unison in Pyongyang."

"An unnecessary expense, I fear," Dearest Leader replied evenly. "Such money is better spent on roads or energy. Did you know yesterday, even for my birthday, I could not light Pyongyang for the whole night?" He sighed, disgusted. "What could this mean? We have not enough electricity for our capital?"

Il-Moon replied, graciously, "There is indeed enough power. Much of it, as you know, must be fed to the army's power grid for their readiness in case of invasion. It is exactly the policies of the Enemy State to the South, the so-called Republic of Korea, which forces us to be ever vigilant in the protection of our glorious North. Otherwise, the American Imperialists and the Puppet State would try to enslave us—"

Dearest Leader interrupted gently, "Yes, Il-Moon, many thanks. I had hoped for something more...appropriate to the times—"

A waiter ran up on the double, two brandy snifters on an elegant carved jade tray so thin that light showed through the crystal. Il-Moon took the bulbous snifters, held one out. "Dearest Leader, so serious! You must try this. Your father's favorite. From the monastery at *Crecis*. A bottle is $500 U.S.! You know," he laughed proudly, "Your father habitually bought the monastery's entire yearly output!"

Dearest Leader took the snifter, paused to ceremoniously inhale the bouquet. *I cannot tell this from any of the others.* He himself preferred *Soju*, the Korean rice-wine vodka.

Il-Moon raised his snifter. "For Korea, the best of France!"

"Korea is One!" Dearest Leader said, echoing the reunification slogan, and took a miniscule sip. "Exquisite, Il-Moon. Your taste, as usual, is stratospheric."

The Joy Brigade finished their number with a final fanny flip of their short dresses and tittered like Broadway veterans as they hustled off stage. Dearest Leader politely applauded. He noticed Aide Park's 70mm film canister. He raised his eyebrows. "Movies, however, are something else!"

Il-Moon bowed slightly. "I have obtained a museum quality surround sound print of James Cameron's *Titanic*."

Dearest Leader said, smiling. "Only James Cameron would make a museum copy of his own film! 'I'm King of the World!'" He laughed. "As you would say, Il-Moon, the best of America!"

"Indeed." Il-Moon stood, waited for Dearest Leader to lead. "Let us adjourn to the theater. Your father put in the 70mm projector and IFX digital sound. But did you know he also added a thirty meter Cinespark IMAX screen? Japanese! For you, Dearest Leader, the best of Japan!"

INFILTRATION BOAT

Rubbing the condensation from the windows, the crew of the infiltration boat tried to look into the water below them, but the windows were for negotiating harbor entrances to land Special Forces, and had little look-down for submarine work.

Kang checked his watch. "We missed it." The submersible had little navigation prowess without GPS. "Turn in an arc, head 131 and slow."

At the submersible craft's weapons station, Lt Han wished they had the GPS so they could navigate accurately, but Col Kang must be right—he was never wrong—that the harbor defense radars would have spotted the antenna. Still...

The ensign obeyed Kang's orders and they turned. Now the flaws in the submersible were becoming apparent. The air inside was throat-burning caustic from smoldering electrical wires, the windows were fogging up, and the lights cut on and off. Yet there was no surfacing—above them they could hear the Internal Security boats and the *Inchon* had good radar.

Lt Han suddenly was sure he saw in the back window the lights of the Underwater Mansion. "I see them! Off to the right side, behind us."

"No," Kang replied, and hunching to look out the front window. "It is only the reflection of the moon. We must go on."

DEAREST LEADER'S SCREENING ROOM

The heavy leather-padded soundproof door of the mansion's exotic theater swung shut behind them, and Il-Moon and Dearest Leader entered a room appointed like the Paris Opera House's boxed seating with gilded wood Rococo cupids, and paintings carefully copied from San Marco.

Waiting for the film to be loaded in the projection booth, they sat in the central Leader's box.

"My apologies, Dearest Leader." Il-Moon stiffened to attention. "The movie is not *Titanic*. Instead, I have much grave news."

"Ah! What is it now, Il-Moon?"

"I'm afraid things have reached a critical juncture."

"Critical? You mean, affecting our cash flow from the outside?"

"Exactly. If we review our sources of hard currency, I will show you how each one is being squeezed by the Americans."

Dearest Leader shook his head at this. "We have given them every diplomatic reassurance—on arms shipments and so on."

"Yes, however they label these other issues as criminal, and not diplomatic; a specious distinction, you will agree? First, our key source of independent funding from our great friends of the Chongryon," referring to the General Association of Korean Residents in Japan, North Korea's shady political and financial support organization in Japan with ties to the *Yakuza*. "Their patriotism in sending Pachinko funds has been our bedrock. Just this week, the U.S. again froze the assets of our Macau transfer bank. Not only is the Japanese government pressuring the Chongryon, but our funds are being held ransom."

"We have other methods of getting cash."

"Since you have stopped our counterfeiting of U.S. $100 bills, we have lost a huge source of hard currency."

"Il-Moon, that money is far more damaging than valuable. We make the bills so well we cannot tell them from the real thing. Our own people print extra and buy hard currency items from us! We cannot afford to sell our few valuable goods to ourselves for free! No, Il-Moon, that operation has done us a huge amount of harm. We'll be the first country to have our own black market collapse."

Il-Moon ignored this. "We have also curtailed at your request our drug operations."

"I especially never liked the drugs."

"The Chinese do it, the Indians do it, the Afghanis do it. If the Japanese scum and sick white people wish to kill their souls with drugs and dreams, why not? Did they not force opium upon us once as the best cash crop they could find? Is it not fitting?"

"Still, I ordered it halted."

"This has other consequences. A second freighter of ours has been confiscated. It is impounded in Bahrain, freezing tens of millions of dollars worth of exported arms, after the discovery of fifty kilos of heroin which was not even ours."

"Not ours?"

"Some fools in the People's Navy running a sideline operation. You see, the more we at the top squeeze, the more the entrepreneurs and criminal element are forced to seize the moment."

"What about the loan issues from the Tumen River Development Project?"

Il-Moon indicated to Aide Park in the projection booth, "Play the movie," and the screen flickered on. The soundtrack was inappropriate martial music.

Over the blaring marches, Il-Moon continued, leaning close to Dearest Leader's ear. "Regretfully, I must report to you the failure of the Tumen project." The screen showed huge partially-constructed concrete factories, blighted windowless office buildings, half-finished piers, and silent piles of looted construction kit.

"It cannot work?"

"It can work," Il-Moon said angrily. "It is stopped. The financial credits have been withdrawn following the recent progress inspection. It is too far north, too far from electricity supplies and so on."

"What about our other operations?"

"You mean, our manufacturing of alternate supplies of luxury timepieces—"

"Counterfeiting Rolexes...must we?"

"We have always copied. In the South, many is the merchant who made his fortune copying things."

"What about our indigenously produced products?"

"The most profitable would be to sell more missiles to the oil-rich Arabs."

"This makes the whole world unhappy."

"It is a legitimate product. It violates no international law. Do not the Americans sell whatever they want, the Russians, the Chinese, the Europeans? Is it not the height of shame that the world's foremost exporters of arms think somehow we should not be allowed?"

"Still, they cause us great pain and trouble."

"Then how do we have the funds to survive?" The screen showed giant Hwasong missiles, three stories tall, being loaded for export into a container ship. "The Americans illegally stopped us on the high seas again this month. Although they cannot halt the shipments of missiles, they use it as propaganda, calling us renegades, when in fact they lead the world in just such exports."

The film continued and showed starving North Korean children and people waiting for handouts from international aide workers in what must have once been a handsome village.

Dearest Leader jerked around to the booth, irritated by the sickeningly inappropriate martial music. "Off. Turn the sound off!" The sound died, leaving the screen to continue in pantomime.

The unmistakable camera angles and drab color of documentary propaganda films lit the huge screen, making the scenes viscerally real. "If the American stranglehold were not enough, natural disasters continue to destroy our crops." The screen panned across scenes of famine in North Korea. A farm team walked among dried corn rows. Emaciated families held out empty rice bowls. An armed guard at a grain warehouse shouted at people waving empty forage tins.

"What can we do for our people?"

Il-Moon continued quietly, respectfully. "We in the army have been working with the central committee to maintain order, and to distribute the food provided by you, Dearest Leader, for all the people."

Jong-Nam looked at porridge being ladled into cups as spiritless villagers numbly waited their turns. The portions were pitifully small, and of rough grains—maize and barley—instead of decent rice or wheat. "This does not seem right, Il-Moon."

"We have done what we can to increase the portions given to our main political base. We have continued the 9-27 camps, following the Great Leader's directive on 27 September 1993, as you know, for those unable to be productive enough to feed themselves—"

"Il-Moon, do you think that is wise? Because they are starving, we starve them more?"

Il-Moon sighed histrionically. "You do not understand. The commitments from the world are forgotten. The few we do have are tenuous and conditional."

Dearest Leader got up, pacing, the film-light catching him in shadows and gleams. "I thought we had arranged help. I thought we could move on from these things to address the shortages and yet keep our own form of government."

"The Japanese and Americans are delaying their promised supplies. They withhold, ask for humiliations in other areas like missiles before they will feed our peasants. They again hold us hostage." Il-Moon paused. "On the good side, the last 500,000 tons of grain from the Americans have been used wisely. The army remains strong, provisioned for months of war, even though a few of our peasants who do nothing to contribute to the DPRK's wealth and status, except goldbrick on their duties to the State, are starving."

"I am sure all these things can be solved if we would just trust the Americans. They can be shamed into restoring to us reparations for their imperialist wars and compensation to rebuild ourselves. They can help us mightily. The Japanese will help as well—they owe it to us for their occupation."

"The Japanese only help if you beg—and if you kowtow. Would I not, if I knew it would help, lick a Japanese boot? Bah! They will only develop a taste for it."

"I tell you Il-Moon, the Japanese are just an American lapdog. It is the Americans who can solve our problems."

"Not all our problems—and not the Americans." On the screen, there was now no sound, so Il-Moon provided a narrative in a low voice. "One of the jobs of the army is to maintain an understanding of the political tensions in the nation."

Jong-Nam bristled. "That is the business of the State Security Department."

Il-Moon slipped in, smooth as silk. "That is all very well, Dearest Leader, and yet you still have to contend with our own *friends*—and the treachery of the Americans."

A grainy intensified video showed a night scene where people approached and furtively entered a grim apartment block. Faces buried in collars and under hats, the video camera still captured the fearful, guilty, and familiar gaits.

Dearest Leader jumped up in recognition, as Il-Moon called to the projection booth, "Sound on!" Il-Moon gestured at the screen. "Here are your *friends*." The video was now inside the apartment. Looking out of a heating vent, the video was grainy and shadowed, but the voices were distinct: an American man, with the tired suit and patient eyes of a spy, sat with the North Koreans. "We can provide you what you need. Aide and assurances. But you must cut to the root." A tall Korean general responded, "We here agree. Dearest Leader must be removed if the country is to survive."

Dearest Leader leapt to his feet, the movie beam catching his face. "Premier Yu and General Chon!"

COL KANG

Col Kang saw the lights of the mansion, and referring to a sketch of the mansion layout, steered in over the mansion's faux gardens and toward the front door.

Invariably flawless in duty, Col Kang proceeded to the first of three mistakes he would commit this night. "Weapons officer," Kang ordered, "Set for twelve meters."

Lt Han, the son of one of Kang's oldest friends, looked up from the weapons station, surprised. His Confucian obedience kicked back in. "Sir. Arming," the boy said nervously and with trembling hands flipped the correct switches.

Kang took them in over the front walkway of the floodlit mansion, lined up the infiltration boat's prow, and ordered: "Away Number 1!"

"Number 1 away, Sir!"

Without breaking the surface, the infiltration craft loosed the first canister. It sank as Kang took the boat away in a sharp turn.

Depth Charge Number 1 silently fell away in the glimmering murk toward the floodlit gabled roof of the Underwater Mansion.

UNDERWATER MANSION

"Premier Yu and General Chon!" Aide Park flipped on the lights as Dearest Leader stormed to his feet and struggled against Il-Moon's restraining grip. "It cannot be! Call them, they are here! I will have it from their faces now!"

Col Kang's first depth charge reached twelve meters depth—and detonated.

In the theater, the walls and floor shook ponderously and a thunderclap of sound crashed around them.

Dearest Leader froze. His mind was not weak and yet Il-Moon's military mind seemed a million times faster, instantly reacting to the thunderclap even as Dearest Leader could only sputter, "What is it?"

Il-Moon let his brainstem take over, "Assassins!" as he ran with his Aide Park to the theater doors. Il-Moon opened the door a crack, letting in screams and the sounds of glass shattering in the main banquet hall.

Il-Moon commanded Aide Park: "Go and help. See that General Chon and Premier Yu use the elevator to safety. For the rest," he handed him a key, "Get them into the Hermit Room and lock the door behind you all!"

"Sir!" With his orders—which were essentially a death sentence—the spry old man ran out the door betraying not the slightest flicker of worry or hesitation.

Il-Moon bolted the door. He found Dearest Leader behind him. "How could this be!" moaned Dearest Leader. Muffled screams came through the padded theater doors. "What about the others, the generals, the Committee?"

"I have sent my Aide to help. He is skilled, and yet that path has too little likelihood of survival. This way."

Dearest Leader resisted. "There is the Joy Brigade, the workers in the kitchen, the attic."

Il-Moon finally managed—half dragging, half carrying him—to run Dearest Leader across the theater and out a small door under the huge movie screen.

INFILTRATION BOAT

Unfortunately for Col Kang, whose luck would turn poorer still, depth charges produce a steam bubble shock wave to shatter and split a ship's metal hull. The Underwater Mansion, on the other hand, was not a hull. In designing a dacha to take the pressure of one hundred feet of water yet without the mobility requirements of a ship, First Architect Su and his Paektu-san Academy of Architecture Special Bureau—in light of certain and lingering death should the design leak, let alone breach—found it simplest to over-engineer the building by a factor of ten. The outside concrete shell only partially shattered. The inside walls held fast.

Water burst through an attic window, but the cupolas were mostly for show.

The water flowed into the tiny room but trapped air slowed the incoming flow, and the hall doors bulged but did not breach.

For about one second, the Joy Brigade was unsure how to react. Not wanting to look bad, they continued dancing in feathers and skimpy bikinis. But at the frozen fearful reaction of their audience, paintings falling from the walls, and the sounds of things breaking, the Joy Brigade burst off the stage in an explosion of panic, scratching, and collisions.

Then they ran for the back door.

The fifty North Korean leaders looked desperately around. The elevator only held a few, and was already carrying up Premier Yu and General Chon. Although the walls had not cracked open yet, one truly effective explosion and the mansion would become their watery graveyard.

IL-MOON

Once through the back door out of the theater, Il-Moon dragged a fuming Dearest Leader down a flight of concrete stairs.

Dearest Leader was babbling, "Do they not know I love Korea? Would they kill the true prophet of their future?"

Il-Moon pulled him along. "Come! There will be time for contemplation later."

Then they were in a concrete-walled and well-lit subbasement with high ceilings, piping—and two elephant-sized minisubs hanging from winches above a launching pool.

Il-Moon smiled in satisfaction. The North Koreans build anything involving paranoia with extreme tenderness and empathy. Tunnels, tank traps, prisons, nerve gas, half-live anthrax, and underground facilities were all crafted exceptionally. In one of the most highly-engineered and paranoid obsessions of them all, their personal mini-submarines were marvels of engineering.

Il-Moon called, "Hold on. There will be more explosions," and began to maneuver one of the minisubs down onto the calm sea-green eye of the launching pool.

COL KANG

Col Kang cursed as he saw the effect of the first charge. The mansion's lights still burned and few bubbles escaped the shattered gable. It was clear he'd had little effect.

Meanwhile, at the first depth charge explosion, the frigate *Inchon* had burst into life—galvanized into action when two of the circling patrol boats were blown up in a waterspout of spume and wreckage. The *Inchon*'s crew, half in pajamas, ran to stations. Missile launchers spun up wildly, engines revved, targeting officers panicked, unsure of what had happened, punching commands into the consoles and pressing alarms in contradictory ways. Sirens, searchlights, and panic.

The prow of Kang's submerged boat—and the depth charge canisters—were again over the mansion on the harbor floor below.

Kang ordered his second mistake. "Arm for nine and thirty meters!"

"Sir!" Lt Han looked up suddenly at Kang, not understanding. That seemed wrong.

"Do it!" yelled Kang. "I do not tolerate insubordination!"

The boy, this time, with the explosions and choking cabin smoke, did not hesitate. He entered the fusing. "Sir!"

"Away 2 and 3," Col Kang said.

"Away 2 and 3, Sir," said the boy.

The two charges dropped from the forward railing and fell away into the coruscating plankton over the eerily floodlit house on the *Avenue Foch*.

The first of these charges was fused for a shallow blast. It blew just as Premier Yu and General Chon were making their escape in the elevator as helped by Aide Park. The glass walls of the ascending elevator splintered and exploded inward. Glass shrapnel speared into the riders, riddling them—then subsided back out in a gush of red-stained seawater.

This charge also blew out two of the windows in the main ballroom.

The second charge missed the mansion and dropped to the sea floor, landing right above the subbasement where Il-Moon worked feverishly to launch the minisub. The charge detonated, its blast directed downward.

UNDERWATER MANSION

In the ballroom—after his initial success with getting General Chon and Premier Yu into the elevator—Il-Moon's Aide Park realized his rescue mission was doomed.

His key problem was the Joy Brigade. At the first explosion, they had merely panicked and stampeded away into the house. When they realized they could not just flee out the back door, the trampling herd of them had come screaming back.

They arrived just in time for the next explosions. The thirty Joy Brigade girls went quiet for three long seconds while they contemplated the blown-in banquet room windows: two obscenely long green tongues of seawater poked into the ballroom—and began flooding the floor.

The Joy Brigade went berserk.

Chosen for their beauty, size, physical strength, and kept in top shape, they had no real skills beyond providing dancing, sexual gymnastics, and withstanding being trussed up and hung from a ceiling for the Joy of the North Korean elite. They were magnificent specimens who had never developed the slightest ability to think for themselves. Smashing furniture, fastening onto people, scratching faces, kicking up freezing seawater into eyes, and all the while screeching wildly, these thirty extremely strong and panic-stricken females had turned Aide Park's lifesaving mission into a shambles.

In the seawater filling room, Aide Park could make no headway shepherding his fifty crucially important leaders to shelter. In the midst of the mass-panic of the banquet hall, Aide Park paused to look around. *Seventy-eight years of life only to fail at my greatest duty.*

Shame slammed him. *Everyone here is going to die.*

IL-MOON

In the basement, Il-Moon—using the crane and winch—had just managed to line up a minisub over the launching pool when the blast of the next two depth charges blew the launching pool up in a monstrous wildcat gusher of seawater.

The pillar of water smashed the minisub hull into Il-Moon, who instinctively didn't resist. The metal hull and wall of water pushed him back and then fell away.

A tidal wave of freezing water rocked across the room. The wave caught Dearest Leader and swept him backwards flailing, mouth filling with acid seawater, shocking him as its huge power overwhelmed him. He'd never felt a power he couldn't resist; known anything to stop him ever. The wave swept him into a grid of iron piping. Hit on the head, torso, air knocked out, his left forearm slipped between pipes.

In the surge of the second wave—in a fireworks explosion of pain—his forearm bone snapped.

Dearest Leader screamed.

COL KANG

Col Kang could immediately tell from the lack of huge air bubbles and still functioning underwater lights that the mansion was still only breeched minorly.

Col Kang carried out his next to last mistake. "We can't see! Surface! Prepare to fire! Surface!"

Lt Han looked at him again. *Surely, they dare not—*

"Do it!" Kang yelled to the petrified boy. "We must see this done!"

UNDERWATER MANSION

It was The Rice Grain Maidens who turned it around for Aide Park.

At the first explosion, they remained in their fourth-floor post, eyes down on their rice sorting, unwilling to acknowledge any emergency since this would be an insult to Dearest Leader—despite the freaked generals running past from the Joy Brigade rooms in their underwear. The expression of alarm on their matron's face—she got her job through pure cronyism and was dumb as a stick—drove the bravest of the girls to speak, only to be rebuffed. After the next explosions and the smell of seawater entering the room, they all begged their matron to let them see if they could be of assistance. The matron succumbed and the two dozen Rice Maidens raced down the three flights of back stairs.

Halfway down the grand staircase, they immediately understood: the Joy Brigade was a herd of thirty wounded moose rampaging through the wrecked and flooding banquet hall, while in the middle, Aide Park was to them a beacon of calm.

The Rice Grain Maidens knew exactly what to do. Following Aide Park's commands, they formed a human corridor leading to the Hermit room while chorusing in their singing un-panicked voices: "This way please, gentlemen. This way please," and held on tight as the Joy Brigade careened into them from behind, even trying to climb over them. Not one Joy girl broke through the cordon, so strong the Rice Maidens' hands and grips and wills were.

Aide Park yelled, "Yes, girls. Keep calling!" and together they began to funnel the North Korean leadership down the length of the human corridor and into the Hermit Room.

COL KANG

The instant the infiltration boat popped up in the middle of the harbor, the *Inchon's* radars were at such point-blank range they caught the few nails of the stealthy boat and their console alarms shrieked. Radar operators yelped and reacted. Searchlights probed toward Col Kang's boat. Sirens wailed, enemy sighted! Missile batteries swung like swiveling puppets and the remaining two Internal Security launches spun around toward the intruder.

On the surface, Col Kang seemed to panic. Perhaps it was the nearby security boat. Perhaps as he said at his trial, it was because he was trying to kill someone whom he had worshiped since birth. Perhaps he over-estimated the readiness of the *Inchon*'s missile batteries, sure they would vaporize him in seconds. Whatever, things would have gone differently had he continued to bombard the mansion methodically and waited until the last minute before dooms-daying it.

Instead, he jogged his boat forward until he was almost directly over the mansion lights—and ordering his last mistake—dropped his remaining five depth charges straight down.

Il-MOON

Il-Moon watched as the wall of water swept Dearest Leader across the subbasement, certain he would be fine in the narrow contained space. No matter what, Il-Moon could reach him in a few steps. Il-Moon even smiled as Dearest Leader's arm caught and snapped in the grid of pipes.

Perhaps now he will awake from his silly slumber. Back to work.

Il-Moon intently worked the winch, almost crushing his fingers under the cable, but still moving forward. *There is little time left.* Finally freeing the minisub, he swung it on its hoist down to float in the launching pool. He pulled open its side hatch.

"What is the point of this pathetic boat?" screamed Dearest Leader, half-hysterical from the shock of his broken arm.

"Dearest Leader, this is a North Korean AIM-2 submarine. Our Special Forces equipment is the best and will take us to safety." Il-Moon gently helped Dearest Leader stabilize his broken arm, getting him to hold it against his chest with his other hand. "Come, we must hurry."

Like royalty of old, and today's children of the mega-rich or celebrities, Dearest Leader had never been hurt, nor did he know about pain and suffering like the man in the street. He had never been hungry, suffered more than a cold, and had lived a life in which everyone praised even his bowel movements. The fall into the pipes and the snapping of his arm bone overwhelmed him with pain. Pain as he'd never felt. With the pain came a terrible sudden deep awareness of the world—and what it could take from him.

Dearest Leader would not move, resisting Il-Moon's push toward the hatch, crying out, "How could this happen? To me, who has the greatest love for the Korean people!"

If Il-Moon ever cursed out loud, this would have been the moment. Instead, he gang-heaved Dearest Leader's considerable unwilling bulk into the sub, scrambled in after him, and slammed the hatch shut. "Here, there is safety. And morphine."

"I do not need morphine! I demand to know who did this!"

UNDERWATER MANSION

Col Kang's five depth charges, silently dropping in a ring toward the roof of the mansion, like a finale of a grand fireworks display, simultaneously exploded.

Again, Col Kang had miscalculated. Although the depth charges were indigenously developed by North Korea from copies of the Russian BB-1 and were standard HBX explosive canisters, the North Koreans had fitted them with precision fuses from Bofors in Sweden. The timing on the Bofors fuses was so precise that the five depth charges went off within microseconds of each other. The circular pattern of five falling charges blowing off simultaneously produced a completely different effect than had they been staggered explosions. Like a giant lens formed by several mirrors, the five explosions cancelled in some directions, and in one, they phased together and focused into a precise point charge. Rather than blowing up across the entire foundation, the point charge struck just below the top floor at the gable line of the mansion. The Mansard roof covering the whoring rooms cleanly sheared from the building as a lid peels back from a sardine can.

The Rice Grain Maidens had been the last to leave the seawater-filling ballroom, never pausing in their duty until the cooks, servants, jazz band, and even their childish compatriots of the Joy Brigade had been evacuated.

Now, with everyone in the Hermit Room—a huge hermetically sealed steel box meant for fire or other emergency—Aide Park locked the door. The leadership of North Korea and their minions felt the *Crump!* of the last salvo. The room shook sideways, noses burst blood, and ears rang. The room tilted and the Joy Brigade screamed in terror. *The floor, the floor is rising up and tilting under our feet!*

Explosive separation charges fired. The Hermit Room snapped free of the now roofless Mansion 27 foundation. Intact, like some giant bug collection box, the room rose, spinning slowly as it ascended—exactly as First Architect Su had planned in the event of a catastrophe.

At the surface, the pressurized box split open and spilled the North Korean leadership, the Joy Brigade, and the Rice Maidens—along with one hundred flotation pillows—out into the gentle swells of Namp'o Bay.

COL KANG

Col Kang's infiltration boat rose briefly from the final blast's steam void directly beneath it, and splintered. He was the only one on board to survive, as he was already halfway out the hatch. The shock bubble from below tossed him end over end into the foaming explosives-acrid water just as the *Inchon* reached the scene and heaved-to, spotlighting the water around the shattered boat. Bleeding from the scalp and arms, Col Kang fought to find his service automatic. Around him in the water there seemed to be hundreds of people swimming and struggling. Their cries surrounded him even as the *Inchon* launched every rescue boat they had aboard. Col Kang groaned and pulled his pistol's action back to cock it, put it to his head as a spotlight found him. A bullhorn voice came down sharply from the frigate: "Surrender! Do not kill yourself or your family will pay the ultimate in suffering. They will suffer forever. Surrender and your families will not be harmed!"

Col Kang let his pistol go and it dropped away into the deep water below him. He raised his arms high and let a rescue boat pull him from the water.

IL-MOON

Il-Moon had just managed to get Dearest Leader stuffed into the minisub and clamp the door shut when the five charges gang-exploded. The overpressure smashing through the mansion pushed a huge bubble of air ahead of it and down into the subbasement.

The blast rocked the two inside the minisub. Dearest Leader screamed in agony as his broken arm flapped loosely against the meters and valves in the jam-packed minisub interior.

The pressure walls of the mansion finally collapsed with an enormous crack. The force blew the minisub out the exit tunnel.

First Vice Chair Il-Moon and the Dearest Leader of all North Korea, spinning over and over in the minisub as if inside a demonic clothes drier, cleared the ruins of Mansion 27.

Gradually stabilizing, the minisub righted itself deep under the cold clear water of Namp'o harbor. Slowly it rose toward the surface, which coruscated in searchlights and the dappling reflections of the moon.

DEFENSE INTELLIGENCE AGENCY – OSAN AB, SOUTH KOREA

One hundred meters below Osan Air Base forty miles south of Seoul, in the 'Ant Colony,'—a maze of underground tunnels and rooms dedicated to keeping the DIA safe no matter what the situation was like above—Senior Airman Teresa Valenzuela sat calmly watching as troop movements, aircraft radar calibrations, radio testing, and sea-coast security information flooded in from intelligence assets all over Korea.

Despite the late hour, her gaze moved methodically over one row of monitors, up to the next row, and down to repeat the sweep. A bleat from a corner monitor, a SBIRS-Low missile-launch detection satellite, jolted her. Infrared images flashed past. First, a wide misty space image of North Korea, then zooming in on a hot spot in the center of Namp'o harbor.

Airman Valenzuela grabbed the STU-III secure phone, punched the button for the Air Force 50th Space Wing at Schriever AFB in Colorado Springs. A voice answered with the Black World's favorite phone greeting, "Hello."

"Let's go secret," she said. A grunt from the other end, they both inserted their encryption sticks, and a distorted Donald Duck voice said, "Satellite Network Ops."

Airman Valenzuela said, "This is the DIA duty officer at Osan." She looked back at the SBIRS-Low monitor. A huge new explosion bloomed. "Wow." As the explosion's aftermath settled, she saw the unmistakable flotsam of a destroyed naval vessel. A tough-looking frigate came racing toward the detonation's swirling center. "Some kind of North Korean ship at Namp'o just went bye-bye. Blew up completely. Can you get a recce bird over the site?"

Deep within the 'Black Cube,' so named because the 50th Satellite Control Network was housed in an onyx-shiny box building, the Ops Group duty officer glanced up at the ready board for the Air Force Satellite Control Network. Schriever was the national center for satellite operations, controlling not only the hundred or so Air Force satellites, but most other U.S. government satellites as well, including 'National Technical Means,' the euphemism for the NRO's prized imaging birds. "I see something we can use. Will send the images along real time."

A minute later, Airman Valenzuela awoke Col Kluppel, who was cat-napping on a cot. While drinking coffee, they watched the NIA—New Imaging Architecture—infrared satellite overpass of the harbor. Hampered though the optical sensor was by nighttime conditions, from the thermal images it was clear there was a mass of floating debris and a large naval rescue operation underway. Tiny bright figures—seemingly people—were being pulled from the dark water into a variety of vessels. "What kind of ship was it?" Airman Valenzuela asked.

The colonel, restlessly pressing his coffee mug between large hands, half-thinking ahead to his TWIX, mused. "Not a ship. An underwater facility of some sort."

Under pressure to have an analysis on the wires ASAP, the colonel soon quit replaying the IR satellite pass, went to the Comm room, and with a phone in each ear to incoming INTEL officer calls from across Northeast Asia, began pounding out his TWIX:

// TWIX generated by /GPXUDF - DIA Detachment 22 - OSAN AB
TOP SECRET – NOFORN – NOCONTRACT

WNINTEL – Warning: Protect for Intelligence Collection Methods

ROUTING:
/DUCFO – Air Force Satellite Control Network - Schriever AFB
/GUFXX – National Reconnaissance Organisation Central Dispersing
/DPWUX – Joint Intel Clearinghouse - CIA Reconnaissance Distribution
/PFUXJP – AMEMBASSY Seoul, South Korea
/DUTXX – Air Force Space Command - Space Warfare Center
/DUPRX – White House Situation Room
/DPRGU – Air Force Research Laboratory
/GFXXO – Marine Corp Intelligence Activity
/GFVCD – Kadena Air Base - Air Force Intelligence Service

TEXT FOLLOWS: RE – DPRK NAMP'O HARBOR EXPLOSION

In an apparent accident, a small underwater North Korean military facility appears to have exploded. Located in Namp'o Bay near a collection of military installations including Korean People's Navy (KPN) largest naval station, the explosion took place at 2100Hrs KST. Sources at South Korea's NIS and the Japan Defense Agency suggest the facility was engaged in Special Forces training with mini-submarines as common to North Korean military doctrine. Nighttime IR imagery within one hour of the incident revealed high thermal signatures of personnel being rescued from the water, suggesting many were still living, as body temperatures were unreduced despite Namp'o's cold water. Weather is predicted to be cloudy in the morning, so there will likely be no coverage by SPOT-5 or commercial imaging satellites. Higher resolution pictures will be provided on subsequent overpasses. Since nothing is publicly acknowledged about this facility, it is likely a secret military installation with probable naval purpose. The large number of surface craft used for the search and rescue indicate a high level of Kim family regime interest.
// END TRANSMISSION

Col Kluppel carefully proofed the TWIX. He turned to Airman Valenzuela. "Remember that Treaty Ops guy came through last week? Sean? Where was he from again?"

She pulled a yellow sticky from the corner of her desk. "I've got his address here," holding out the sticky. "Sir, what do you think it really was?"

He answered, as many would do in the coming month, "I'm not sure. That's DPRK Special Forces turf there. A training accident; most likely nothing will come of it."

He would, in hindsight, admit he had been dead wrong.

The colonel pushed a button and sent the TWIX on its way to the other side of the world after he'd added a final address: AFTAC Treaty Operations – Patrick AFB – Attn Major Sean Phillips.

Prelude USAF

The 2nd of September

AIR FORCE TECHNICAL APPLICATIONS CENTER (AFTAC) – PATRICK AFB – SATELLITE BEACH, FL

On the barrier island just south of Cape Canaveral and beyond the Indian River, the small town of Satellite Beach clings to a narrow spit of land, barely wide enough for itself, the 1A1 highway, and Patrick Air Force Base. In some places, the entire island is only a few hundred yards across and when landing the first time, pilots often remark that between the white sand beach on one side, and the Indian River on the other, it seemed the narrowest runway in the world.

The pilot, banking over the tiny ribbon of runway, had been pushing an Electronic Intelligence plane bristling with antennae for twenty hours and wanted down soon. Besides the normal desire to get home, there was a going-away ceremony none of the crew wanted to miss. The pilot quickly landed, braked harder than usual to make the closer taxiway, and drove the big plane right at the speed limit across to the high tech support buildings which served the treaty monitoring service of the Air Force, AFTAC—the Air Force Technical Applications Center.

The flight-suited crew hustled out and headed at a run for the large command building, yelling to the ground crew that they'd be back later to do the paperwork.

Inside the quickly-filling AFTAC ceremony hall, USAF blue-suiters, NCO's, and civilians packed the seating, noisily chatting.

Just off stage, Maj Sean Phillips stood relaxed, waiting. From any distance, Sean's quick manner and passion came through. He loved what he was doing. On his chest were a few decorations, and instead of wings, a missile pin. He was of the cerebral Air Force, not a carefree fly boy type, although under the uniform his frame was athletic.

The Mistress of Ceremonies, Sergeant Nannette Vigil, went to the podium, tapped it, and called, "Everybody! Commander's Call will begin. General Ostend."

Everyone rose to their feet in a rumble and rustle of rising to attention.

Hands curled at the sides in attention as the honor guard and flag bearers marched up the central isle carrying the USAF and American colors. A trim General John Ostend followed the flags onto the stage.

After the flags were posted and saluted, and the honor guard retired, Sergeant Vigil called out in her announcer's voice, "Major Sean Whittier Phillips."

Sean stepped up to the podium, exchanged sharp salutes with Gen Ostend. Together they stood, Sean at attention, facing the audience.

Sergeant Vigil laid a document on the podium, and began reading it aloud to the crowd: "Attention to orders! Citation to accompany the meritorious service medal, third oak leaf cluster." Behind her, a video came to life, showing Sean during his assignments at AFTAC: Sean in cramped sensor-filled airplanes, walking through frozen mud at a Russian ICBM field, on a storm-tossed intelligence ship pointing a strange gizmo at a Russian missile frigate. "While serving with Air Force Technical Applications Center, Patrick Air Force Base, Satellite Beach, Florida, Major Phillips worked tirelessly for the non-proliferation division. He worked at the Nuclear Arms Control branch, was the Integrated Product Team lead for weapons of mass destruction, then led the On-Site Treaty Inspection Team. After chairing the Iran Nuclear Reactor study group, he was appointed to lead on the OSIA—"

Gen Ostend spoke up suddenly, deadpan. "The man can't hold down a job!" and winked at the audience. They laughed, partly at Sergeant Vigil's somewhat scandalized, "Sir!" to the jocular interjection.

With a mock frown at the general, Sergeant Vigil continued, "Major Phillips represented AFTAC at the Chelyabinsk-70 SS-19 X-ray facility, and perfected the Meso-scanner for transshipped illegal nuclear materials."

"The boy likes a toy!" Gen Ostend said.

"Please, Sir," Sergeant Vigil begged. "Major Phillip's new assignment is military inspector to State Department Treaty Operations in Korea."

"Wonder how long he'll last there?" The general joked.

Sergeant Vigil just shook her head. "The actions of Major Phillips reflect great credit upon himself, and on the United States Air Force." She motioned for Sean to step forward. General Ostend pinned the medal on Sean's tunic, handed him the framed citation. After they shook hands for the official photo, the general turned to the audience. "Seriously, Sean, we're sorry to lose you. We'll miss your fresh face and your sense of how things fit together. Try not to forget you have a ton of friends here, and you are always welcome back. So go to Korea and keep the North Koreans honest. But always remember: for us here at AFTAC, you were the greatest thing since sliced bread."

Sean stood forward, asked, "You ever wonder what the thing to be greater than was—before there was sliced bread?" Everyone laughed at the Sean-ism they all expected.

The audience eagerly waited for Sean to go on. He looked them over—it was hard leaving everyone you had gotten to know so well. Parting was not a sweet sorrow for the military—rather a constant ripping and healing that left you with many friends in many places, and yet somehow, still left you... He actually did for a moment want to tell them how he felt, but he'd seen too many moving leaving speeches, and he'd rather die than go out moist-eyed.

His face suddenly changed, grew strained and sad. He struggled, choked up, falling toward that farewell brink of tears. The audience worried, wondered, *Was he really going to cry?*

Sean's voice was tight and his eyes gleaming as he said, "It would be so incredibly hard to tell you all the feelings and emotions I'm having; to tell you how much you've all meant to me..." Sean suddenly grinned. "Luckily, I'm not here to do that! I'm here instead to tell you something that will embarrass you, hopefully even humiliate you!"

The audience cracked up, clapped, and when they quit, Sean added, "Seriously, I'm gratified to go to Korea. Professionally, it's where I've always wanted to be; where a better future world can and is being forged. But for me personally, Technical Applications, you've been more than family. I can't decide whether to meld with you forever...or to kick your butts in a last board game of World Peace Keeper!"

The audience applauded, started to rise. "Hey!" Sergeant Vigil called. "Wait for the general."

General Ostend waved grandly. "Let's party. And that's an order."

Sean's farewell picnic was at the beach across 1A1 on the sparkling white sands of the Florida coast, but still part of the base. The enlisted cooked, while everyone lined up for chow, stood, sat, chewed, and talked. Meat smoked while INTEL aircraft took off in the background. Under the scanty splayed shadows of a couple of palm trees, Sean had indeed succeeded in kicking butt in their favorite board game, a local Treaty Ops version of Risk, the board game of World Strategy. Another major, Marsha Teg, was the only one left standing as armies, piled high on the board all around Asia, fought in a major roll-off dice battle.

Sean growled, "Korea, again! Let's go."

The dice rolled. He won, plucking Marsha's armies from the board with zeal. "Again!"

Marsha whined, "The United Nations will hear about this naked aggression. These aren't just markers. They're people with families, kids, debts, worries."

"Next time don't attack Korea. Korea is my life."

"You mean Korea is your wife."

"Same difference," Sean removed Marsha's armies as he grabbed his dice. "Thank you. Quit crying and roll."

Gen Ostend strode up, without his partying face on. "See you a moment, Sean? A TWIX from Korea. Oddly, it's marked for you."

Sean was up and gone toward the vaults in a flash.

Marsha called after him, "I'll play both sides and see if you still can win then."

Prelude SECAF

The 3rd of September

VISITING OFFICERS QUARTERS – VANDENBERG AFB, CA

In the VOQ, fifty years old and feeling it, Jeanette DeFrancis woke up, disoriented in her Spartan suite. "Where am I?" she asked herself, wonderingly, and for a moment realized she really didn't know. Then streetlights, mingled with the night-darkness outside, filtered through the curtains and silhouetted the outlines of the suite's simple furniture: Formica table, small ironing station, and ancient wet bar—and she remembered.

Her battered leather travel alarm glowed green, showing the time as 4:30 a.m. *May as well get up. It isn't much early anyway.*

She dug down just a little for the tingle of the day to come. The on-the-road-again and a million-frequent-flyer-miles exhaustion fell away and with a slight *shudder* of excitement she rose from bed. "Oh yes."

Jeanette's room in the Vandenberg VOQ, although their best VIP suite, wouldn't have gotten any Marriott awards. The bed sagged, the blankets were itchy, she'd had a centipede to deal with in the shower, and last night after jogging she'd put her pink Nike's up on the coffee table and one of its corners splintered. She was used to this official luxury; it was the lighting that was always the hardest.

In the harsh and unforgiving cheap fluorescent lights of the garishly tiled bathroom, she calmly applied her makeup, grimacing at her puffy face even as she was cheerful. Gradually her face worked its way from sleepiness to grace.

From the single wire clothes-hanger in the closet, she pulled off and slipped into a patterned Santa Fe crumple skirt—they could be stuffed into your roll-on and look great when pulled out; better even. Black flats, a new silk blouse, and she looked herself over in the mirror, checking. *Great!*

Outside of the VOQ, dawn was coming over the craggy California hills off to the east, just lighting the sky and bleaching out the stars when Jeanette, elegant and feminine, exited the VOQ moving fast, dragging her roller board. Her exec Major Dave Zeret opened the door of a waiting black Jeep Grand Cherokee. In D.C., it would have been a black stretch limo with seals and flags, but an operational Air Force base didn't have the stomach for that kind of frippery. The Air Force Reg says no one may have a dedicated vehicle asset, and half the time the Base Commander was driven around in a four-year-old Plymouth.

Dave smiled, "Good morning, Dr. DeFrancis," using more formality than usual since the junior officer driver was present.

"Good morning, Dave! You have the wine?"

He nodded and their driver, the Base Commander's young fresh-faced Exec, closed their door and motored the Cherokee off slowly into the breaking morning darkness and out of the populated section of the base with its sleeping ranch houses, office buildings, flight line, and satellite dish clusters. Past the base theater, the plastic lettering of the name of the base's cut-rate movie of the week slightly askew, the BX, and a few museum-pieces, old Titan and Minuteman launchers on display stands. Once on the highway to the far reaches of the base, the Exec, chattering to Jeanette about possible next assignments, ran the Cherokee up to the forty-five mph speed limit, and headed for an island of white floodlights out in the dark distance of the sea-foggy desert base.

In the slight lightening from a rosy dawn just diffusing over the rugged hills to the east, Jeanette looked out at the rough gravel and brushy chaparral as they followed the bluffs of the seacoast, and mused to Dave, "The day is finally here."

"All but one. Let's hope this weather holds."

SPACE LAUNCH COMPLEX-6

At the launch complex gate, Air Force SP's—Security Police—said good morning, checked their passes and saluted them toward the gantry. They wove around a giant white cube-like rocket prep building, from which a sea-fog-damp American flag, many-stories-high, hung soggily. They passed vast concrete structures, huge empty herringbone parking lots, and locker-like outbuildings until they came to a smaller side complex.

They pulled up to a launch gantry supporting a slender saucy ten-story Taurus launch vehicle topped in a mysteriously shrouded payload. It looked almost beetle-like, the shadowy bulk under the shroud. The Cherokee stopped at the back of the small crowd gathered around the gantry. The crowd consisted of more engineers and nerds and fewer officers than one might expect at a missile launching.

Jeanette stepped out of her Jeep limo and smiled warmly at everyone.

From a small platform near the launch vehicle, a protocol sergeant called over the PA, "All stand for the Honorable Jeanette DeFrancis, Under Secretary of the Air Force for Science and Technology."

Dr. Jeanette DeFrancis, with her civilian rank of Senior Leader-3—equivalent to a Major General—stood in the quiet dawning, and looked up at her baby. She felt groomed, pert, and still somehow—after all the trials, and smiles, and frequent flier miles; the meetings and greetings—like someone you could count on. She still had her principles, her Senior Executive Service slot, and her enthusiasm, she thought, if not her chance for children, or her shot at a challenging professorship she now knew she would never find the time to giddyup and win.

She nodded to Dave, "Go ahead and pass it out, please," and he moved toward the back of the Jeep while she turned toward the gantry and the rocket.

She tilted her head up to look up the sleek missile body with its cloaked payload.

It was like her child feeling, she supposed. What would their christenings have been like? There, atop the missile's sleek white tower was her baby. Such things were to be her children, just as the people crowded around the gantry here were her family—in addition to her sisters and nieces, and her quiet retired husband who spent his time cultivating their boutique organic farm near Great Falls.

This was what she had instead, feeling the warming California wind rustle the wheat-like golden summer grasses around her, carrying with it the smell of the cold sea she could hear roaring below the cliffs, knew her rocket would soon launch over. Was it the same, enough like a child so she would grow old satisfied? Technology was what she birthed—and projects and people and the occasional party. She shook it off, calling herself back. *Why did this come up now?* She was at peace with it, wasn't she? *Yes.*

General Paulus, a dapper man with impeccably shiny shoes and a head to match, took his place at her side. "Good morning, Bob," she said, and he smiled back, motioned to the platform alongside the rocket.

Jeanette and the general climbed the stand and stood by the rocket's towering column. Everyone silently watched the general hand Jeanette a bottle of Champagne.

She smiled to the crowd; recognizing so many faces, the sun peeking over the mountains low and slanting, picking up the lines in the faces where there had not always been such.

She spoke clearly, melodiously, to the waiting crowd. "When I told the President you all believed an electro-magnetic satellite could do new peacekeeping missions, we hoped he would be excited. When he said, "Go do it!," we all went "GULP!" But you took it on. You made the choice. The choice to miss evenings and weekends with your families. To spend half your time on travel. To eat your dinners out of Styrofoam. To wake in hotel rooms not knowing where you were. If you'll allow me, it brings to my mind a poem, one I think which sums up who you are and what you have chosen:

"'Once to every man and nation, comes the moment to decide,
In the strife of truth with falsehood, for the good or evil side.
Some great cause, some great decision, offering each the bloom or blight,
And that choice goes on forever, 'twixt the darkness and the light.'

"Tomorrow, thanks to your choice, the world will have a lot less darkness and a lot more light."

She held up her paper cup, "Everyone have one?" The crowed murmured ascent, and when Jeanette continued, her voice warmed. "Anyway, thank you all for coming. Although the launch isn't until tomorrow and many of you are now off and doing new projects, I thought after five years of effort we should all get together for a send-off party." She raised the Champagne bottle. "Everybody?" The crowd below held plastic cups high.

Jeanette swung the bottle at the rocket, but rather than smashing it against the towering body, she instead touched the bottle gently to the behemoth, and then waved it at the shrouded payload above. "I christen thee 'Radiant Outlaw!'"

She popped the cork, and gave a hoot of joy! Everyone took up the cheer, as among the crowd the many bottles she'd brought were popped. Sparkling wine splashed into plastic cups. Everyone quaffed the bubbly while workmen nearby unfurled a banner: 'Long Live RADIANT OUTLAW!'

Jeanette sipped her drink and looked up at her satellite. The last earthly time she or anyone would see it. Soon it would begin circling far above, returning to earth only when its orbit finally decayed in perhaps ten thousand years. She grinned to her nearby well-wishers and friends. "Again, good work! Congratulations! Good luck tomorrow." She turned to General Paulus. She had been at Vandenberg less than eight hours and yet work called her urgently from across the country. "Bob, I'm afraid I have to get back," and in a giving-and-taking of congratulations, she made her way through her crowd of friends and on toward the long trip home.

Crossing the crowd, so many faces. Not any of them getting younger. Many who should be here, yet had already finished their careers and were now enjoying their well-earned retirement, grandchildren, families, and memories.

As she passed through the crowd, whirling to converse almost in a do-si-do of old friends and new, saying "Good luck tomorrow!" and "Thanks for all the extra effort!" she passed an old friend from Space Vehicles Directorate, years on the project, who asked, "Aren't you worried she won't make it?"

She smiled. "Well, are you?"

"No atheists in Missile Control. Team Vandenberg will get her up there for you."

She patted his arm. "You will, I know."

Moving toward her Jeep limo, her escorts opening the back door, she turned for her *now this was it* last fleeting glimpse. Although it was superstition-forbidden to even *feel* your satellite would make it into orbit—and she'd seen plenty of her own birds go into the drink—for some reason, this time, she was sure.

Radiant Outlaw is on the loose! She felt a pleasure in her body, a sudden surge. *Most satisfying. Like dining when famished, but more...* She suddenly did feel hungry. "Dave, perhaps a snackeral on the way to the flight line?"

"The O'Club is just opening," her Exec replied, climbing in beside her.

She nodded enthusiastically, "Perfect." *Oh! I must remember to stop at the O'Club shop and get those 'Spacetown' sweatshirts for my nieces like I promised.*

Prelude Airborne Laser

The 4th of September

THE AIRBORNE LASER (EXPERIMENTAL) – AIR FORCE RESEARCH LAB – KIRTLAND AFB, NEW MEXICO

The taxiway lights in the dusk caught and brightened the coat-of-arms, a vibrant multi-colored shield, hand-painted on the smooth gray gunmetal fuselage of the jumbo jet. The special unit shield was a USAF emblem with an attitude: coiled around a cloud, a colorful flying rattlesnake reared to strike—spitting laser fire to explode an enemy missile. Under the shield was lettered the motto: 'Airborne Laser (X). Peace through Light!'

Engines whined and the giant plane began to taxi. The Airborne Laser coat-of-arms slid away into the dusk. As the hulking military Boeing 747 jumbo jet rolled past, its battered paint was that of a workhorse, not a show horse. Following the Airborne Laser shield was the Missile Defense Agency's logo with a green and blue earth below an intercepting missile, and the Air Force Research Laboratory's stars-and-launching-rocket shield. The shields slipped away and the lettering 'U.S. Air Force' scrolled past over a fuselage lined with strange antennae and weird structures. When the giant aircraft paused before the start of the runway, from its nose bulged an exotic bulbous turret—its laser beam director.

The bizarre gargantuan plane, running lights flashing, engines idling, held at the end of the taxiway.

There were only a few windows to compromise the structure of this behemoth—until close to the front a large almost picture-window in the forward fuselage shone with dim light, illuminating the interior. Sitting in the window, her pretty face looking out reflectively into the gloaming, sat Airborne Laser (Experimental) Chief Scientist Dr. Emily Engel.

She had a strong feminine face, post-graduate and then some. A face used to understanding things, to knowing things—to being right and therefore getting its way. Under her carelessly-worn tightly-clamping military earphones, her raven moppet of hair was bound up into a French-braided coronet.

Inside Airborne Laser (X)—or ABL as everyone on the project called it— Emily, in USAF flight suit, sat at her console with its computers and monitors in her own special seat by the window, hands lying loose on a lapful of technical papers.

Her flight suit was wrinkled and worn, free of unit symbols or rank—except for Fellow pins from the American Physical Society and The International Society of Optical Engineering, and ABL's laser rattlesnake logo.

Emily's left ear was itching like crazy under the heavy headphones. She pulled one headache-tight earpiece off and clamped it on her temple, leaving the headphones half-on.

She stared out across the runway, over the jumbled cubist buildings of the Air Force Base to a distant desert horizon on which lightning struck. *In every sense, what am I doing here?*

Her headphones clicked and Airborne Laser's pilot—call sign 'Slammer'—spoke. "Laser One, this is the Flightdeck. Wicked lightning tonight."

Emily reined in her thoughts, secured her papers into a pouch on her console. "You want fair weather, Slammer, sign onto the Love Boat. I say we go."

"You're the boss, Laser One. Coming up, one twilight dinner cruise. Ready?"

Emily looked around the Airborne Laser's Tech Area. It was the command and control as well as the science and technology heart of the plane, home to the key crew. High-tech gear arranged at consoles filled the wide-body cabin. Her crew, seven military and civilian scientist types, sat strapped in at their consoles listening on their headsets and all eyes were on her. There was no science-fiction feel to the plane; just the very real U.S. Air Force at the dawn of the twenty-first century.

Her crew looked to Emily apprehensively.

Emily said, formally, "Flightdeck, this is Laser One. Tech Area is ready," and muttered to herself, "We can always dream."

Airborne Laser turned onto the runway. Lightning struck the far mesa horizon in a dazzling web of forks and flare-offs. The crew felt the lightning, saw the flash in Emily's window. A breath-catching moment, then the four huge non-noise-suppressed General Electric military jet engines wound up into a howl that rattled everyone's teeth.

From the flightdeck, Slammer murmured a low benediction into the crew's headsets. "The lightning strikes, and the thunder *rolls*."

The engines went to full screaming power, ripping thunder. Airborne Laser's brakes released. The hulking 747 Jumbo airframe jolted forward.

And the big ol' junkyard dog of a research plane, engines smoking, rumbled down the runway and into the darkening sky.

Catchers in the Sky

BOOK 1

"Come to work each day willing to be fired."

The AFRL Project Officer's First Commandment

Chapter 1

The 1st of October

PYONG-SON MISSILE RESEARCH ZONE – NORTH KOREA

The high grim hills seemed to resent the shiny polish of the black diplomatic limousines bumping slowly up their muddy road and into their secret hushed valley.

The motorcade, ignoring the grim travail of the gorse and heather of the infertile hillside, moved slowly up the flanks of the mountains toward the pass into the valley.

The three Benz limousines were in the lead of the convoy. Trailing out behind them were a dozen vehicles. First rumbled three heavy canvas-back trucks, Russian KRAZ-260 turbocharged 6x6 all-wheel monsters—the new expensive transport used for the all-important North Korean face-saving. The trucks' back flaps were tied open, and from each stared out thirty hard-faced Guard Command troops in full battle gear.

Following the Guard Command were two incongruously brightly-colored American Chevy Blazers, each flying small American bumper flags, and shadowed by three beaten-up bulbous Chaika sedans jammed with black, blue, and gray-Vinalon-suited DPRK State Security Department watchers.

Bringing up the rear was a North Korean BTR armored personnel carrier coming on heavy—there was to be no dallying by the wayside to smell even the few woebegone flowers.

Dr. Emily Engel rode in one of the big Blazers with 'Treaty Verification Team' stenciled on the side. Among the serious-faced professional treaty inspectors in the van, she stood out with the natural curiosity of the born scientist; her dark ringlets and milky skin out of place in the company around her of button-down diplomats and professional soldiers.

She took in the bleakness of the northern Korean peninsula with wide idealistic eyes, noting the harshness of the landscape. She thought back to New Mexico, where she'd been just a short few hours ago before being jerked into this assignment. The land was harsh there too, but the forbidding feel of this forsaken valley with its ruined rice paddies and mosaics of cracked mud streambeds was a new level of forlorn.

She wasn't used to treaty operations, and wasn't sure she liked them. She'd rather be home, keeping ahead of her pressing schedule on Airborne Laser. An exotic overseas trip wasn't a joy ride. She'd simply return to New Mexico that much farther behind; there would be many weekends and nights to pay for doing this favor to her old mentor. *Sigh.*

The motorcade crested the pass; the cars slanted down—and below was the remarkable site of Pyong-son complex.

The rugged mountains almost seemed to cradle the muddy remote military R&D complex. Amidst camouflage nets, blast walls, anti-aircraft guns, and troop fortifications, lying half-buried were four hundred buildings—shadowy blockhouses, launch pads, missile gantries, and laboratories.

Emily lost all thought of New Mexico, and leaned out the window to stare at the complex. In the center of the valley, by an enormous abstract statue symbolic of scientific might, was a smooth white windowless building the size of a football field. Nearby, the missile gantries were old and rusting, but the angular structures of cooling towers and fuel assembly points were gleaming.

"The opposite of ground zero," Emily mused to herself. This is where it started; she usually worried about where it ended.

The motorcade lumbered through the usual single fence line of a DPRK military facility—much cheaper given their resource shortages, and nothing more was needed due to the very closed and therefore secure society—before parking at the big white building.

From the lead limousine emerged an upright American wearing the dark suit and beige overcoat uniform of the high-level DoS—Department of State. His strong features lost nothing even as his graying hair receded. The intentness of his eyes and the aristocratic curves to his nose made his action of raising his head slightly to sniff the air like he was seeing into the future.

This, Emily knew, was chief negotiator Ambassador Harold Hakkermann. It had taken her only a microsecond to assess him. Here was a man sure of his place in history—or of his desire for a place in history.

The North Korean contingent of diplomats and treaty-inspection-minders waited confidently—they knew their job perfectly. Unlike the dabbler Americans, whose careers spanned diverse assignments, this was their only and forever job. Emily was amused at the North Koreans' clear hierarchy: the elegant Foreign Minister was dressed in a Seville Row suit and wore hand-made shoes from Jermyn Street in London, the well-fed Pyong-son Zone Manager had on a good off-the-rack suit and Japanese shoes, while their bony Technical Liaison—whose hair looked like it had been trimmed with a bowl—wore a terribly-cut cheap Chinese suit and the almost-cardboard shoes they manufacture in North Korea.

Before Il-Moon emerged from the middle limo, his one hundred Guard Command protectors formed up nearby in rows. A dozen stood close, watching for any threat to Il-Moon as he stepped from his limo. Despite wearing the Marshal's uniform of the Korean People's Army, with its anachronistic khaki wool cloth and Imperial Japanese Army sartorial heredity, his almost eighty years seemed not to weigh on him. Energy radiated from his every controlled movement. Only the mask of his face held the North Korean leadership's single-minded love of power and position. It was a look implanted in the face muscles permanently, setting them into a chilling display of frigidity toward all of humanity. Emily was appalled by his palpable coldness. *He's going to be the first human icicle.*

Now here is a person more interesting. USAF Maj Sean Phillips jumped from the Blazer. She'd met him only briefly over their formal breakfast. Unlike the rest of the party who were stretching and wondering about the chance of coffee, Sean immediately paced to the fence. On his light middle-linebacker frame he wore, as the others did, a coverall-like flight suit, but with 'Treaty Ops' stenciled in white on the back. She looked for his unit patches. The main one said 'Caught you in the Act!' with a logo of Felix the Cat grabbing a launching missile—nor was it worn discreetly. Even without the patch, as a USAF civil servant of many years, she instantly recognized Sean as technical Air Force, with all the criticality of that canny breed, although with his pacing and intelligent gaze he seemed pretty darned physical too.

Hakkermann huddled his people just out of earshot of the minders. He waited patiently until everyone was looking only at him. "You all know what's expected of you. Look hard, cover your notes, and no open discussion. Keep communication line of sight only."

The Ambassador's eyes, darting from face to face, stopped on Sean. Hakkermann reached over and tugged at Sean's 'Caught you in the Act!' unit patch. The patch peeled off noisily with a Velcro ripping sound. Hakkermann handed it to Sean and watched, school-teacherly, until Sean zipped it into a pocket. "Major, you are going to stay very very cool. We are here to make history. Not break it."

Sean nodded briskly, and turned toward the white building. "Major Phillips?" Hakkermann inclined his head a millimeter toward Emily. "A tech advisor. She stays with you." He favored the rest of the team with a slight smile. "Let's move, *mes enfants.*"

When the Americans reached the North Korean leaders, Hakkermann shook hands warmly with Marshal Il-Moon.

A sudden explosion *boomed* through the air. The Americans flinched, ducked, looked around, unsure if it were a threat. A mile away against a mountainside, a dust cloud blossomed.

Sean rattled off some quick Korean to his stone-faced North Korean minder. The man shot back a few sharp words, and Sean translated ironically, grinning at Hakkermann, "He says he didn't hear anything."

Hakkermann smiled back pleasantly, Il-Moon watching him like a stoat. "Forgive my associate, First Vice Chairman Il-Moon. I translated it to be 'It's nothing. Just some worker dormitories being constructed on the hill over there.'"

Sean joked back, but so quietly only Emily heard, "Right. How could I have messed up the verbs so?" Turning, Sean gave Emily a piercing glance, caught the instrument case, the non-sensible clogs for shoes, the mop of dark curls against the milky complexion of the indoor scientist type. He quit analyzing. "I'm Sean. I didn't get your name; your organization."

Emily's oversized mouth smiled good-naturedly. "True. Call me Emily. What now?"

As each of Hakkermann's group moved toward the white reactor building, a pair of taller than average North Korean treaty minders stepped into their personal space, and followed them, dogging their every footstep.

Sean moved in the opposite direction, looking at the muddy tracks, the rundown old Frog-7 missile systems mounted on decaying Soviet 8x8 chasses, the tires half mired in mud. He used a small electronic camera, recording what he saw, then surreptitiously snapped a full face shot of thoughtful Emily as she pulled a small hand scanner from her case. She turned it on and sensed the launchers, the ground, the surrounding area.

Sean recognized her scanner as some kind of radiation isotope detector. "I thought we weren't supposed to have nuke sensors."

"Well, they have their approach, and I have mine," Emily replied as she jotted in a small notebook.

Workers, ignoring them, were flooding a small rice paddy right next to them, the shoots green and succulent in the muck. Sean studied the missile trucks intently, then his eyes drew toward the ridge where the tracks went. Emily seemed more interested in the rice paddy. Sean saw her toting up numbers in a notebook.

They stood next to each other for a moment, Sean shaking his head and kicking angrily at a dried muddy tire track.

Emily whispered to Sean, "Perhaps there's the waste of a few hundred reprocessed fuel rods cooling under this new paddy."

"Would you like to warm up your hands?" Sean murmured back. "Mine are freezing."

The day was pleasant, and the air fragrant and warm. "Yes, autumn in North Korea can be that way."

As their minders stood by, Sean climbed into the Blazer's driver's seat while Emily got in shotgun. Sean turned on the engine and they sat pretending to warm their hands.

Sean said, "This place has been scrubbed. SS-1c's or something heavy has been moved recently. You're sure about the reprocessing waste?"

Emily glanced down at her scanner, as if confirming her comments. "Krypton isotopes, et cetera." She looked up at Sean, the intelligence in her gaze startling him. She nodded toward the nearby hill that had drawn his eye. "Yes, and there's something more just over that far ridge." *He takes it so seriously, as if it were a treasure hunt rather than a duty tour.* Even she, a rube to Treaty Ops, accepted that this was how it was played. She couldn't resist teasing him. She leaned over and whispered in his ear: "Just over the ridge. Just beyond your reach. Tempted?"

Sean dropped his hands as if to his lap, and casually put the Blazer in gear. He slammed on the gas. The Blazer fishtailed away up the muddy road toward the crest.

"We'll just take a look over that ridge! I know Il-Moon's cheating."

Emily was so surprised she instinctively glanced back at the compound. So much the scientist was she, this unexpected event was mediated by an enthusiastic childlike interest; a sort of 'So that's what rat poison tastes like' kind of happy disembodied musing. So although her heart skipped a few beats, it soon settled, and she was herself wondering what was over the ridge—and what Hakkermann and Il-Moon would do. She looked back at the motorcade cars parked along the fence. The inspection teams were freaking! Hakkermann and Il-Moon yelled, pointed, and then ran toward their vehicles. Then everyone was jumping in and a motley crew of limos, trucks, and the BTR revved their engines and came zooming after Sean and Emily.

Sean drove breakneck up the crude road, jolting Emily totally. She held on, grabbed Sean's loose notebooks before they could fly away, and managed to ask innocently, "If we have suspicions aren't we, uh, supposed to file a written report?"

"I've always preferred Orals."

"Perhaps you're over-reacting?"

"In my job, I can't afford to under-react. Cities turn to rubble. People die."

Emily glanced back at the rabid U.S. and Korean pursuers. "Your approach is, shall we say, *interesting*?"

"By which you mean stupid." He grimaced as the Blazer's tires churned up the mud like a berserk cake mixer whipping chocolate batter. "Sometimes you just gotta get down and do it in the dirt."

Then he had his hands full. The Blazer bucked over the top of the ridge and they both saw a huge North Korean cargo container. Mounted on truck wheels, the container sat at the edge of a flat dead-looking lake.

"Get ready," Sean called. "I want to know what you see when we get there."

Emily readied her scanner as Sean slammed on the Blazer's brakes and its rear end fishtailed and the front wheels slipped into the muck of the lake. A strange-looking one, given its stark and infertile feel.

"What is it?" asked Emily.

"A brand new rice paddy," and as they jumped out, Sean growled, "OK, do the estimate. What do you see?"

Emily, working with her scanner, looked, calculated, and started carefully writing down numbers in her small notebook.

"Can't you do it in your head?"

"Better this way. Documented and can be verified," although Sean had a point in that they were going to get tackled any moment based on the roar of cars coming up the hill. "I'd estimate the waste from the Plutonium extraction of another, oh, two thousand reprocessed fuel rods have somehow found themselves under this brand new rice paddy."

"Two thousand! You're sure?"

"I'm rarely sure of anything. How could I be? It's just well-educated speculation."

Sean looked around. There was nothing but the big shipping container semi-truck all alone by the paddy. He grabbed the lug wrench from under the Blazer's back seat and ran to the trailer. Emily, now in the spirit of the chase, sprinted to the truck behind Sean, the sound of their motley cavalcade of pursuers roaring nearer.

The big side door of the container truck was barred and locked. "Something's not right here," Sean said as he twisted and tested the large official seals on the cargo door.

"Diplomatic seals." Emily gently pulled Sean's hands away. "You break those, inside you'd better find Hitler singing at a grand piano."

Sean raised the lug wrench. She lightly stayed his arm. "I'm just asking. You're certain you'll find something really remarkable?"

"You mean, really *interesting*? Yes, I do." Sean brought the lug wrench down violently and the lock—and the diplomatic seals—broke away cleanly.

A rumbling sound. The trailer door fell open and a cascade of huge missile bodies came rollicking out like logs off a log truck. Sean tackled Emily under the truck, barely escaping the bowling-pin crushing masses of the rolling missile frames. Tackled to the ground, Emily found Sean covering her, the moment almost intimate, his hard-muscled body enveloping hers.

As pleasant, oddly, as that moment was, she pushed herself up from under him enough to peer down the hill.

It was an awesome sight. The freed missile bodies had rolled down the road, heading straight for the pursuing vehicles. The drivers, seeing the on-rolling missile frames, panicked, jerking their steering wheels, spasmodically propelling their cars off the road and into ditches and fields. At a curve in the road, the rolling missiles missed the turn, and whammed directly into a low wall of rock. White hot fire leapt in a spire, and sound boomed and echoed across the sullen valley as the hillside erupted as missile fuels sparked and exploded.

Emily carefully counted the cars, and reassured that everyone seemed unhurt, she looked to Sean. "Just standard missile components. Nothing really remarkable."

"Remarkably unremarkable."

Emily moved to him, unzipped his flight suit to the waist. He felt her arms go in around his chest. "Kinky! But your timing..."

Emily grinned and slipped Sean's notebooks, her pad and scanner into his flight suit at the small of his back and brusquely *zipped* the suit closed, encasing them. "We might need our hands free."

When the furious Hakkermann and Il-Moon and entourage converged on Emily and Sean, Il-Moon, purple with rage, screamed, "The outrageous behavior of Major Phillip continues! We are a sovereign power. These missile types are not restricted under any treaty."

Sean pushed right up into his face, and yelled back. "Legal missile components don't need diplomatic seals. You son of a bitch! You were laying for me."

Hakkermann, quietly and in control, spoke respectfully to Il-Moon. "Vice Chairman Il-Moon, I am desolated."

"I'm telling you, Harold, there is high-level waste here, this new paddy—" but Sean got no farther, for Hakkermann nodded to his aide Sandy standing behind Sean. Sandy swung violently, clobbering Sean with his leather attaché case. Sean fell forward, bloodied and stunned.

"Harold!" Emily shouted, furious at the cowardly violence, and interposed herself between the prone Sean and Sandy.

Hakkermann ignored her. "First Vice Chair Il-Moon, you have my complete apology. This renegade no longer represents the United States." He turned to the two U.S. Army guards in his entourage and spat an order: "Get Major Phillips out of here! Put him—and I mean put him—on the next plane east!" Eyes down, he held out his hands to Il-Moon. "First Vice Chairman. You will please accept our most sincere and humble retraction of everything Major

Phillips has done here."

Il-Moon, stiff and seemingly counting to twenty, considered the stunned Sean. Then to Hakkermann, "Very well, Ambassador. I accept your apology. Come, we return to our important work."

Emily pushed back the army guards, knelt beside Sean and checked a pupil. The hazel pupil contracted in the light, and then the eye blinked. She gently pulled the bleeding major to his feet and brushed him off. The guards stepped in, held him lightly by the arms, waiting for him to come fully around. "Sorry Ma'am," one of them said to Emily. "He's heading back to Osan."

Emily moved close up against him, took Sean's hand, and looked him in his dazed but clearing eyes. As she did, she managed to press his dropped camera into his nerveless hand. She felt his fingers slide over hers as he palmed the camera.

"Good-bye, Sean. Working with you was *interesting* but good."

"Thanks," he laughed. As he slipped the camera unseen into a coverall pocket, she felt the intense proximity of his hurt but handsome phiz, so close; he took several long seconds to look full into her open face. "We'll be even better next time." From a foot away he looked directly into her eyes as if, inside her, he saw infinity.

She was tingling. *He's just the perfect height...the perfect...* "Sadly, it's unlikely we'll get the chance—we live in different worlds. So long."

Sean smiled. "So long," and shook off his guards' grip so that even though they were stepping him away, he no longer let them touch him.

Chapter 2

The 2nd of October

CHOSUN LUXURY TOWERS – SEOUL, SOUTH KOREA

Abbey Yamamoto was showering in her luxury high-rise flat in the chic Changdam-dong district of Seoul when the phone rang.

The flat was not at the truly high-end of the Korean elite, and yet it had five rooms, overlooked the majestic heavy-flowing Han River to sparkling downtown, the parking circle below was jammed with BMWs and Lexus, and not a flower or leaf was out of place across the *Dong* for as far as you could see from her stunning high-floor view. Abbey was old money—Japan style.

She heard the phone's waspish buzz from the living room despite the Japanese financial network on the TV blaring the morning market news through the flat.

Abbey didn't answer the call because, even at 6:00 a.m. with a beautiful fall day dawning, she had nothing to hope for. The pain of her banishment from Reuters Japan, her firing from the Reuters Seoul desk and demotion to Financial—just last week in an acid-drenched knock-down drag-out screaming argument, fueled by pre-lunch alcohol, with the Seoul Reuters' station chief—was still bloody and raw.

In addition, Abbey was in the position so many Asian professionals find themselves after fifteen or so years on the hard-drinking nighttime work circuit. She was still fooling herself that the drinking didn't matter, that her classic Japanese beauty, the gleaming-black raw-silk hair, the hardness of her body to the touch—its easy athleticism that made her lovers, admittedly none for some time, touch her musculature in wonder at its firmness—and her sharply-crafted journalist's copy meant she was still queen. But last night's angry binge drinking translated to a sick and bitter morning.

Instead of answering the phone, she let the latest stomach flip-flop subside, and turned the shower to as cold as she could take. She drank thirstily from the shower stream while simultaneously bowing her legs and urinating directly into the shower drain.

She finally felt better enough to shut off the water. Toweling her hard body, she stalked through the halls into the bedroom to dress.

Except for the impeccable expensive Japanese clothes in her closets, her apartment—which was never entered by another human being—was a wreck.

Last night's burned canned supper, after boiling over onto the Japanese luxe ceramic-topped stove, had in some kind of a drunken dream been placed on the fridge where it gushed, lava-like, all over the white surface. It joined many similar dinners and their spilled burned guts lying on almost every windowsill, countertop, table, and in the corners of the living room. The rugs were torn and stained, the walls smeared. Crud crusted the appliances and furniture.

She managed to dress quickly but the remains of the glass of Suntory whiskey she'd thrown at the wall last night was still slick enough on the tile so when she slipped in it and ripped her clothes, she had to change her signature miniskirt and black fishnet stockings in a rage of panting and cursing.

At the door, she checked the peephole—no neighbors passing. All she could see was the hall's elegant table with fresh blue delphiniums in a cut crystal vase and some bird feathers over a mirror. She popped open the door, reached through the burglar door bars and grabbed the pile of six morning newspapers from all over the world. Slamming the door shut, she flipped through the papers. Nothing breaking, nor on CNN.

She again checked for passersby in the hall, and then darted out quickly. In dark miniskirt, satin blouse, and black fishnets over exquisitely muscled legs, she double-locked her apartment door and the steel burglar bars from the outside, and stalked to the elevators while digging out a cigarette.

Even as the elevator doors opened in the lobby, Abbey was scanning out through the building's front glass doors to big upscale Apkujong Boulevard for that rarest and most fought-over of early morning resources in Seoul: a free taxi. Spotting one, she made a 2-iron straight off the tee drive for it, her peripheral vision catching the blur of a competitor—*no fucking way and you are going to be hurting you keep it up*—coming in hard from just off her port bow. It was a young Korean man in a business suit and he just managed to get the door slightly open before Abbey, having flicked her cigarette away to keep from getting burned in the collision, bowled him out of the way. It was unnecessary to even reason or be conscious of it, for Abbey had quickly adopted the Korean social calculus of politeness only to those to whom one had been formally introduced; the others were nothings—not that she was nice to people to whom she'd been introduced either.

Abbey was fast-twitch-muscle heavy and very strong. Her push was ferocious, yet even as the nothing man seemed headed for the gutter, he was amazingly agile. He took the push with a wrestler's aplomb and rolled up from the curb in a recovery that slipped him inside the cab even as she was slamming the door, his sunglasses un-displaced.

From behind the sunglasses, as dark and opaque as black granite, the young man bowed respectfully to her, and spoke to the driver in Korean, "Jongno Square, Reuter's building," then to her, smoothly switching to ultra-polite high Japanese: "As is the desire of Greatly Respected Reporter Yamamoto."

A curse and splayed fingernails, Abbey's gut reaction and main procedure for dealing with her current world, rose from deep in her solar plexus—until he spoke her name in such sophisticated Japanese. Her more basal reporter's instinct took over. Her strong golden hands calmly took from her purse a pack of Mild Seven cigarettes.

The driver shot an angry glance back at the cigarette and dual fare, but his heart stopped when he saw Abbey's eyes. He grunted, accustomed to fisticuffs for the single ride in the back, as well as the occasional armistice—whoever won, won. He pulled out suddenly into the Seoul traffic to the usual accompaniment of a quartet for four screeching tires and a serenade in five angry horns.

Abbey had to wait just a fraction of a second before the man snapped open a gold Sarome lighter and held the flame to her cigarette. She inhaled deeply on the Mild Seven and blew a thick stream of smoke in the young man's face before responding disrespectfully in guttersnipe Japanese. "So what is this, stink girlie?"

The man was unaffected by the smoke or her insults. He produced and proffered her a bulky envelope with the respectful presentation flourish that can only be perfected when one is raised Japanese. "Some mutual friends offer information in which they felt you might have an interest."

As she took the big envelope she did not look at it—although she instantly weighed and measured its bulging thickness with her quick fingers and noted his gloved hands. Instead she studied the handsome face. She saw his pedigree as could only a native Japanese. Of Korean stock, yet softened by three generations in Japan, the face was that of a favored son raised in the sacred fishing grounds of the Pachinko parlors of Japan: it was the face of a gangster; the face of the Korean underbelly of the *Yakuza* back home.

Her innate xenophobia and distaste for all things Korean made her curt, and she continued in street Japanese. "Why me, pretty boy?"

"Your reputation for fairness and your understanding of Asian matters make you a perfect ally in disseminating the truth."

She bumped her Japanese up a notch: "Where the hell did you learn to speak like that? Is the High-Oyabun of Osaka now sending his foot soldiers to college? Look, I know who *you* are. Whom do you represent?"

Behind the sunglasses, the man chuckled. "I offer information. Unsullied. Uncorrupted. Truth. Let's say it is the brave forces of freedom and humanity. We think you would be invaluable in making sure the media coverage of certain events have an honest Asian face and presentation."

Abbey kneaded the envelope for texture and thickness. *Documents. Plastic badges.* "What the hell kind of information could such as you have?"

"*Ichiban* information, Respected Reporter Yamamoto. *Agi Ichiban.* Very First Rate."

"If your sources are so great, how come you don't know I got fired?" It made her stomach heave to say it and her pharynx tasted of bile but she sure as hell wasn't going to toss it with this guy watching. She swallowed her biley gorge.

"You were not fired. Laterally moved, one might say. The financial desk is a perfect place from which to work this."

"What am I supposed to do with what you've given me?"

"Whatever you wish. If I may give you my assurances?"

"Pardon fucking me, but what are your assurances worth? How about I take your assurances in the form of some ID?" She nodded to his gloved hands. "No? I didn't think so. What about restrictions?"

"None. You will know best what to do." He removed his sunglasses, and for a moment she saw the worry lines she wouldn't have expected to be there for another twenty years. He added carefully, "In the course of time, you may have more information than you might prudently use. Whatever you receive, perhaps it is better not tacked up on the bulletin board at Reuters. Use it wisely, Highly Esteemed Reporter Yamamoto."

"No ID, nothing, and you expect me to front you? What about a contact number?"

In Chinese characters, the young man jotted a phone number on her cigarette pack. At the next light, he bowed politely as he opened the door and moved off into the crowds surging across the huge pedestrian zone at Namdaemun Market. For a second, the young Korean's posture and confident way of moving stood out from the slightly work-weary and trudging masses, then he merged magically into the crowds of the pedestrian zone and was no more.

Abbey ripped open the envelope. Inside was an announcement, dated three days hence, for a press conference at the Joint Security Area at Panmunjom on the DMZ. Next were VIP press passes into the inner sanctum of exactly those Panmunjom negotiation facilities lying astraddle the border of North and South Korea. Amazingly, the passes were also pre-dated three days, with current ID photos of her and her videographer partner, Akiru Takahashi, already affixed. Yet no story of an event had popped. Not a peep in any morning newspaper or CNN.

This news conference doesn't even exist yet.

The other sheets were U.S. State Department legal documents, eagle seal and all; a high-level policy memorandum on official letterhead. She was shocked to see emblazoned across the top of the documents in bold letters was **TOP SECRET**.

Heart skittering, Abbey read the memo title. 'On developing possibilities for the confederal reunification of the Korean peninsula: Peace Treaty initiation procedures.' And then she could read no more—her breath caught short and the following adrenalin rush was so sudden and intense that her eyes spun over the document's paragraphs in a blur of meaningless symbols. Her fingers seemed palsied as she tried to steady her hands. She looked down at the paragraphs. They floated into a kind of meaning for her: something gigantic this way comes—and the news had come to her first.

Despite the driver's angry look, she lit yet another cigarette. It only dizzied her more, and her thoughts were already dizzy. If she tried to file this story at work, her supervisor would take the credit—and her source. Besides, it wasn't financial news and she was stuck in Financial with strict orders to clean herself up to the norm—and in a place as full of damaged and alcoholic people as the average wire service office, such a command was extreme unction.

The young Korean *Yakuza* had said she would know what to do. She could take a chance. File it independently over the Internet. Get the credit and bypass the station chief. Or go talk to CNN.

Suicide. She grimaced. *No, it would be Seppuku. At stake was a point of honor.*

On the other hand, she had the source. *Even if you were fired?* She could always go to a big Korean news agency like Chosun-Ilbo.

That won't get you back to Reuters Tokyo.

Abbey looked vaguely out the window. Her vision sharpened as up ahead she saw a big Internet café emblazoned with that unique Korean creature: Turtle-Serpent. In the strangest mix of character, turtle-serpent was a shelled being who was also an aggressor. It symbolized more North Korea's world attitude than the South's—but here it was just the name of an Internet café franchise. *Alright then.* She grinned for the first time in weeks. *Seppuku it is.*

She spoke sharply in Korean to the taxi driver. "Here. Stop."

BASE OPS – OSAN AIR BASE – SOUTH KOREA

The enormous American airbase at Osan, America's main air defense outpost in Korea, forty miles south of Seoul, was as always, cooking.

Sean had arrived under armed escort at the sprawling base, been checked in through the Korean-street-vendor-surrounded Osan main gate—and was now headed out the back door to America.

At the moment, he was pacing the cement hardstanding just outside of the Base Ops building in the Transport Area—the military equivalent of the waiting lounge at the airport—praying that Col Kluppel at the Osan DIA detachment had heard about Pyong-son, and would come so Sean could give him a fast out-brief before he got booted out of Korea.

Sean looked out across the huge 7th Air Force air base. A hundred buildings clustered busily along one side of a wide runway almost three miles long. Arranged along the runways were three enormous diamond-shaped operations areas formed by aprons and taxiways. All along the sides of the diamonds were hangars, ammo bunkers, scoot-and-hide covers, unit headquarters' buildings, arming sheds, emergency vehicles bays, security detachment ready areas, machine shops, aviation fuel tank farms, radar anti-air artillery, Patriot missile batteries, and machine gun bunkers for base defense—and the hardened base command post.

The flight lines were hopping, aerial hot shots of all sorts coming and going and messing around. A-10 Warthogs with their mad-dog pilots, pioneering and scouting planes, big ELINT planes and U-2's for surveillance of the border, F-16's, electronic attack planes, and dog-eared transport.

Yet all this military plant was within easy striking distance of North Korea. Not only were they on the prime hit-list for massive assaults by Combatants in stealthy transports and helicopters, but even the antiquated air forces of North Korea—let alone their MiG-29 fighters—could take off from airfields under mountain fortresses, and within six minutes be over Osan unloading their ordinance. Similarly, salvos of cruise missiles were just five minutes from launch to impact. It all meant high-explosive and fragmentation—and possibly chemical and biological—warheads bursting on the bustling flight line, hospital, and happy families in the base housing area. If the balloon ever went up here, for everyone involved, the work would be extremely wet and reddish.

It was small comfort to him to see the amazing air base activity, which he usually would have enjoyed. He cursed himself for the hundredth time for falling into Il-Moon's hands. *I was so sure. The paddy size, the radioactivity over the ridge, that amazing woman Emily.*

He suddenly stopped, secretly touched his flight suit. She had saved his camera—and both their notebooks. Amazing foresight, for the notebooks contained months of work and were his major worry even when he was being clonked. He felt a tremor of excitement thinking about the strange girl. She was almost nun-like in her purity, and yet...his bitter feelings re-surfaced. It was doubtful even with what she had given him that he had enough to placate Under Secretary Jeannette DeFrancis.

Col Kluppel from DIA had indeed heard about the Pyong-son mess, and was walking out on the apron even as Sean watched in depression as a C-130 Hercules, his low-luxury flight to Yakota, Japan, wheeled into place out on the tarmac.

Although Col Kluppel was breaking procedure in showing up, he was a man who knew his job. The INTEL business demanded of its leadership initiative and persistence and prescience. A few minutes with Sean now was worth a hundred hours later. Especially because something had gone wrong—and wrong was always to be noted.

He indicated Sean to the guards, and they stiffened trying to decide how to respond. An order from any officer on the spot had to be obeyed, although if it contradicted a higher order, there was room for, if not argument, let's say manipulation. The officer giving the new order had to take responsibility, and it was good practice to casually mention under what orders you were presently operating. However, one look at this particular colonel and they let him walk to Sean.

Col Kluppel said, "Heard there was a misunderstanding."

"Rather more than that." Sean felt his sore skull where he'd been clonked. "The skids are under me, at the moment."

"Sorry, Sean. What did you think of the inspection?"

Sean gave him a quick rundown on Emily's assessment.

"Who was she?"

"'Emily' is all she would say."

"Was she a nuke?"

"I don't think nuclear engineering was her specialty. She just seemed to have a way with the numbers, natural." Sean thought back, ran his impressions past again, verbalizing to clarify them. "You know how it is. Not the bossy insistence you get from people who are brilliant but unconsciously unsure and are offended by your questioning of their estimate. She was naturally confident; took a look, guessed based on the isotope density and size of the paddy it was the reprocessing waste from about two thousand fuel rods."

The colonel whistled, "If she's right, about the Plutonium for four to five nukes." He looked at Sean's guards watching them attentively. "What did you *actually* find?"

Sean frowned. "A few Hwasong SCUD parts. A diplomatically sealed truck. Harold wouldn't rescan the area although that new rice paddy was big, and I'm not sure what else was nearby."

"What was your assessment? About what's really going on at Pyong-son?"

"I don't know. It's a triangle of confusion. It looks like war or the usual posturing for intimidating the south, and yet," Sean leaned closer and without moving his lips, said, "Hakkermann actually asked me for a draft of a PT."

Col Kluppel absorbed this like a body blow. He glanced around, making sure this security breach—speaking of highly classified facts outside of a vault—in referring to a peace treaty was unnoted. A peace treaty initiative for the Korean armistice, even the idea of the possibility of the notion of one coming up, would be a highly classified State Department matter, Special Compartmentalized Information—SCI—access only. Even acknowledging the existence of such could get you hung up by your patuttis—tortured and shot and then fired. The colonel mused, "He often does that. Did in Africa, I recall. It's effective. Gets various parties to draft up their wish lists, then he mulls it into his version. You gave him something?"

Sean smiled. "Wouldn't you? Chance of a life-time, I'd say."

The colonel and Sean shared a moment where they knew it was, for Sean, most likely the last of *his* lifetime. "You stuck it to 'em?"

"You betcha. Trust but verify. I was, though, very nicely spoken about it."

The colonel thought it over, what he could use. "Did you get to keep something concrete? Pictures, site notes, documents, anything?"

Sean chuckled, feeling the notes and scanner under his flight suit back. "My email on the SIPRNet is my first name dot my last, plus aftac.af.mil. Send me a note and I'll send you *billets-doux.*"

"If you even *have* an email account when Jeanette gets through with you," adding apologetically at his insensitivity, "Sorry, Sean."

Sean grimaced. That was truth. *Don't spatter us all with mud, Sean. We need you there—and to get you in place with State we had to climb out on a thin high limb.*

The Hercules was revving its engine, and the small train of army and air force taking the jump to Yakota started filing up the back ramp into the four engine transport.

Col Kluppel looked to where the windowless amenity-less crude turboprop was gearing up its engine tests. "Looks like you're getting the VIP treatment." It would be a long harsh bumpy dark ride to Tokyo.

Sean assessed the soldiers tramping up the boarding ramp. "At least my poker chances look good."

The colonel put out a hand, gripped Sean's firmly. "Hope to see you again soon."

Neither of them thought it likely given Sean had just blitz-offended the person who was likely to be, for the foreseeable future and beyond, the most powerful American in Korea.

Sean saluted, the colonel punched him on the arm, and looking around at

Korea for the last time—given the transport had no windows—he crossed to the waiting Hercules.

The guards escorting Sean stopped, finally, forty feet from the plane and left him to cross the hardstanding, relieved of their duty now certain the C-130 was taking Sean to Japan and on toward the CONUS.

Failure gnawing at him, Sean stepped onto the transport and the door swung up behind him.

Chapter 3

ROOFTOP – KORYO HOTEL – PYONGYANG, NORTH KOREA

Forty-five floors up, on the rooftop of the twin towers of the luxury Koryo hotel for foreigners, tourists, diplomats, and hard currency users, the Dearest Leader of all North Korea took a deep breath of the autumn evening air and looked out over his Pyongyang.

It was a monumental city. Against the backdrop of some distant but very respectably pretty mountains, the huge memorials, statues, buildings, boulevards and bridges of his capitol city were lightly immersed in the early evening haze. It looked, he reflected, somewhat like an imposing Imperial Roman city as idealized in a painting by Sir Lawrence Alma-Tadema. A city of memorial and triumphal arches, and this impression was reinforced by the single small lights burning like oil lamps here and there throughout the colossal buildings. It helped too, that the darkness hid the stains and wear.

Jong-Nam could see to the east, perhaps only a quarter-mile away, the park-like beautiful spread of the thirty-acre compound he was raised in and had now inherited: the Magnolia Palace, the White House of North Korea. Pyongyang's Forbidden City, the enclave for the most privileged of North Korea, was on the surface a gorgeous garden. It was also ground zero for American cruise missiles and bombs. Hiding below the giant square marble Magnolia Palace, surrounded by temples, sculptures, and raked-rock Zen spaces, was an underground complex of steel-reinforced concrete bunkers hiding housing and streets of baronial size and luxury.

Under those steel and concrete slabs, in the florescent lighting of this buried city, he had played his hopscotch and learned to ride his bike. Occasionally when the summer sun was high, he would be permitted up into the light. He and his friends would run in the gardens and play Parcheesi while the sun wheeled joyously overhead and the birds sang in the bushes—while his grandfather and father remained below, deep underground, deep in their machinations. When called, young Jong-Nam had never ever wanted to leave the light and sky to go back down into the bunkers.

Now, remembering his childhood's few moments of pleasure, he was angered at the worn lines and failing infrastructure of his city this evening. He did not want to notice the rust and rot.

Instead he thought back to his diplomatic coup downstairs at the Koryo banquet hall; remembering how he—the Dearest Leader of all North Korea—had dropped in unannounced on his own Foreign Minister Kong and Hakkermann.

In his surprise meeting with Hakkermann, he'd timed his entrance to be totally unexpected. His own top diplomat Kong had almost spewed his dentures into the blancmange. Oddly, Hakkermann—especially for someone perhaps conspiring against him—reacted smoothly, slipping the reins of customary diplomatic restraint and diving directly into substantive interaction.

In their brief encounter, Hakkermann had impressed him. There was no sign of treachery—instead a directness and a hunger. Not desperation, nor fear, but a longing. The past was falling away, and in front of them a door seemed ready to crash open to infinity. Yes, infinity and forever were in the air. Palpable. Hakkermann had assured Dearest Leader of his great respect and belief they together could make history. *So, he feels it too.*

He'd concealed his broken arm from the assassination attempt in the underwater mansion under his evening clothes, and it seemed of only passing interest to Hakkermann as they agreed on a joint press conference soon at Panmunjom. It was also interesting that immediately following their talk, Hakkermann paid $5,000 in cash per hour for a KPAF—Korean People's Air Force—helicopter to chopper him down to Panmunjom on the DMZ, and motorcaded to his embassy in Seoul to request permission to proceed.

Yet despite Dearest Leader's pride at shaking up the diplomatic process, at being a mover and shaker, at out-styling even his skilled grandfather Kim Il-Sung, the rooftop view was a piquant reminder. The luxurious spread forty floors below at the Pyong-son inspection reception, or even the meals in front of the foreign diners just across from him in the rotating restaurant atop the opposite Koryo tower, were in stark contrast to the million Pyongyang-ers around him—his people—who were going to bed tonight at least slightly hungry. His thoughts moved to the south.

Pyongyang became not what it was but what it could be; sublimed into another city, majestic, beautiful, bustling. His thoughts carried him to Tokyo. To a clattering subway car, and a young woman rising like the Lady of the Lake from the mist...

He came back to Pyongyang. It was so magnificent, and yet so dark. Strangely, on his birthday just a few weeks ago, he had ordered the city to stay lighted all night, but when he went out into the street—which almost gave his security detail apoplexy as no DPRK leader had ever walked the streets spontaneously for pleasure—the sidewalk was so dark he didn't realize people were passing until he heard their low murmurs right at his elbow.

His Guard Command security contingent was calling to him now—having given him a circular space of a respectful twenty paces. They called for permission for Vice Chair Il-Moon to approach inside the cordon.

Il-Moon passed the Guard Command bodyguards, came up to Dearest Leader, and looked out with him over the city. Il-Moon loved the view, the glory of what they had done—with this child's grandfather of course. *A whole city.* Il-Moon remembered when there wasn't one brick left standing on another; the city completely leveled in the Fatherland Liberation War* by the American Air Force. The Americans had sworn it would take a century to rebuild, but they had done it in seven years. The Americans had bombed Pyongyang far more thoroughly, he bitterly thought, than they had the non-yellow German people when they were leveling their cities. Even against Japan they had spared cities, in particular Kyoto because of its irreplaceable cultural value. Against communist North Korea, the Americans had no such compunctions; they leveled every city. Il-Moon knew the Americans had eventually dropped more bombs on North Korea than they had in all of World War II. Yet now, it had blossomed into this spread of glorious concrete and unique structures, houses, factories, athletic fields, train stations, and boulevards. A whole city; a jewel and a gem.

Il-Moon nodded to the skyline. "The city is beautiful, is it not? Unique in the world."

Dearest Leader paused, put away his previous musings, and answered, "Shall I tell you how it makes me feel? Beyond, what you see down there, in every direction, North Korea is a prison. The prisoners are not just those beyond us; it is you and me! Don't you ever want to travel, see the world? To shop in London, smoke cigars in New York, try the French brandy you like so much at a country inn in *Provence?*"

"I have no taste for tourism. My life is service to *Juche,*" using the word for North Korea's policy of self-determination and self-sufficiency—their right to be a superpower all their own.

"But what about the others? Besides, such contact does not contradict Juche: you could come to the world as a welcome guest! As a self-sufficient country's representative. You would be rich far beyond what you are now. You could have a peace treaty with the USA. The world would love you, and you could go anywhere you wanted."

"Like *Disneyland?*"

Dearest Leader flushed at the spiteful reference, but he had been reading self-help books on the Internet and avidly watching satellite TV every day as American TV psychologists dished out the afternoon life-advice. He'd learned a

---

* The North Korean term for the Korean War

thing or two about how not 'to engage in destructive behavior.' "Yes! A thousand times yes. We, Il-Moon-ssi, you and I, could be the darlings of history. We could have the world, if we just let go of our chains. Think of history! You and I could become *Tangun**."

Il-Moon thought of history. For him the past was the time of the Great Patriotic War, the thundering hooves of Imperial Japanese Army cavalry as they ran him down, a mere boy, on a hardened mud road these more than sixty years long gone. It was a filthy basement where he choked on and vomited his own blood and begged for mercy and got none. It was the Russian military camp in Khabarovsk as a boy: the eye-stinging smoke of the filthy huts, the cries of the sick and dying, the constant beatings, the eating of putrid rice and any vermin they could catch under the floorboards and in the outhouses. It was living underground for a year while the Americans *drenched* North Korea in napalm, firebombing every city into ruins and death. Most of all, it was a sweet-limbed young schoolgirl walking unresisting with her companions up into the back of a covered truck...

The memories were of nothing but subjugation and enslavement. He felt again something inside him bite teasingly; an invisible but somehow crimson worm, seemingly feeding on his passion. "They do not mean us well! It has gone too far. Did not the assassins at the Underwater Mansion show you this: Kang admitted the Americans were behind his attack—in fact your friend Hakkermann. Yet now you talk to him as a comrade? If you go with him we will not survive—by which I mean *live*—to create this new paradise you talk of."

"Yet the paradise we have is rotten in many ways, and stifles and imprisons us all."

"It is the world around us that imprisons; a prison only because we are surrounded by enemies." Il-Moon paused, waved. From atop the forty-fifth floor of the Koryo hotel, named for the ancient dynasty and the land that had been Korea for four thousand years, the world seemed to curve beyond them. "Looking south, just one hundred forty miles away, is the line. The demarcation line of the Demilitarized Zone. Behind that line are 690,000 South Korean puppet troops of the United States backed with every modern weapons system and just waiting to invade. To the west and east are two very unreliable allies: China to the west, Russia to the east. They once were everything to us; the promise of help and economic aide and protection from war and attack. Now they wait to fall on us when we stumble. To the south waits the mad dog Japanese—and beyond them lies American troops and aircraft, great military forces aimed like daggers toward our heart: B-1 and B-52 bombers based in Guam and Japan, a force in Alaska, a

---

* Legendary first unifying leader of Korea, circa 2000 BC

huge base near Seattle, a fleet of carrier battle groups, not to mention Kadena on Okinawa, and Osan only a few miles from here."

"I know all this, Song Il-Moon," Dearest Leader said forcefully. "But since you mention it, you could see how I look at it so differently. To the west, China: our old ally and helper, without whom we could never have maintained our thousand-year dynasty. They still continue to send us a fifth of our food and 80% of our oil—at the *friendship cost* of $4.50 a barrel of oil, and rice similarly.

"To the east, Russia. It was they who helped found the People's Republic. They then pulled all their troops out by 1949, leaving promptly, no thought of occupation. They supported us through the Fatherland Liberation War, and later with years of help, funding, and political support. Now, they continue to take every opportunity to engage us as a market and a partner. They are extending the Trans-Siberian railway to our east coast, perhaps an oil pipeline as well. Do not forget, for decades, they sent us so much money our standard of living was even higher than the south. Yes, a strong good ally, and one uninterested in our domination."

He paused, brightened almost feverishly, threw an arm wide. "To the south, I see, the world!" He paused for a moment. "Look at your Juche paradise," and he spread the other hand wide to Pyongyang. He waved to where just below them sat a stained and decrepit oblong building with a crumbling folly dome. "Our magnificent train station. Absurd. Have you seen Shinjuku station in Tokyo?"

"I have not, as you know, traveled widely outside our Paradise."

"Well, Il-Moon-ssi"—using an intimate vocative form—"I proclaim to you Shinjuku is a beautiful soaring temple surrounded by golden and sapphire skyscrapers. I have seen it—and know we are squatting in a hut here."

Il-Moon's fury grew as he spat his words with disgust. "The Japanese. *Shinjuku.* 'Japan's Times Square'! Built with the blood of Koreans."

"Which Japanese? Do you mean the ones who enslaved us in the Great Patriotic War? They are all dead! I tell you there is not one person there of any fit age who even remembers the war except for our harping upon it. What Korean blood? That of my dead father and grandfather—or the millions of innocents of North Korea? You are talking about ghosts. The Japanese people gave Korea billions of dollars in reparations money."

"To the South! Without an apology! To the puppets of the Americans. Not to the legitimate government—"

"We could have had it too. My grandfather refused to take the money unless it were ten times more, and he could spend it as he pleased."

"He wanted nothing from the Japanese unless they apologized."

"South Korean President Syngman Rhee got a billion dollars and he let them slip by on the apology. Why not? He knew he needed the money more than a few useless words. He knew he could create a prosperous South Korea with it—and he did!"

"The lack of apology isn't a matter of useless words. It is central to the continued Japanese pattern and plans for domination and repression. Germany freely admitted her guilt in the Holocaust. She paid and pays reparations generously, is adamant about not burying the past, but atoning. The Japanese are bad actors in this matter. They have never paid a yen to the Koreans they had enslaved who died in Hiroshima—or to those worked to death here and across their genocidal empire. They have never apologized to even the Chinese for their inhuman crimes."

"Yes, let alone to the tens of thousands of kidnapped women—" Dearest Leader stopped short at Il-Moon's expression, quickly switched tack. "Still, Grandfather got nothing, because he couldn't bring himself to do something selfless for his people."

"He knew what was best for the people."

"Perhaps that was true before the Fatherland Liberation War. Once he faced defeat, he never forgot how much he wanted to stay in power. He told his own people he was a great anti-Japanese guerilla who personally drove the Japanese from Korea. He arrived here on a Russian ship months after the Americans beat the Japanese, and the Russians opportunistically invaded the North after declaring war six days before Japan fell. You yourself know well he spent much of the war in Russia in comfort. How many others did he purge and execute who really did carry the fight honorably to the enemy occupier? Because they threatened his power, he killed dozens of patriots!"

If his grandfather had known the snake of his own blood he had hugged to his breast. "He was a great inspiration and standard bearer. The Soviets recognized his genius and backed him completely."

"Even the Soviets told Grandfather to invest in light industry for export. To not try to be independent, but rather to find ways to make money from the world. Grandfather would have none of it—inventing Juche, the path of total self-reliance and independence—building tractor factories and steel mills when they could never compete with the outside world, while ignoring toys and telephones and trinkets like every other economy in Asia from Japan and Taiwan, to Indonesia and China—even Vietnam."

"We are the greatest experiment in self-determination ever tried by mankind!"

"An enormous source of pride, admittedly. Even the Americans with their almost infinite homeland resources would never try what we did. Regardless of the great thing we have accomplished, are our citizens better off than those in the Puppet State to the South? We are thirty years behind even China. We are so bankrupt, what can we even offer the South in reunification?"

"We offer our iron will, extreme discipline, and unflinching and indomitable dedication to Korea."

"There is much truth there." Dearest Leader said, stopping when he saw Il-Moon's look, and did not add the South had fabulous wealth, world political stature, and a vibrant sports, cultural, and artistic life to bring to the table. North Korea's contribution was only their indomitable dedication Il-Moon spoke of. He continued more gently, "Yes, our people are what will make Korea a superpower. Yet, that goal is not yet reachable, nor can we afford to be picky." His voice went to his most convincing, most sincere, "We are counterfeiting Marlboros and Rolexes—for piddling profits. Do you know I have figured out what our chief export is? We export instability! This the west then imports, paying in negotiated inducements for us to stop threatening everyone. We export fear—when instead we should be exporting cars! Did you know Toyota invested more than $16 billion in new plants in the USA this year and bought more than $25 billion in supplies from American manufacturers for a total of $40 billion? Forty billion is our entire GDP! Japan invests in the USA, who beat the pants off them in the Great War and where it is not even economical to invest but where it is smart to. Just think what we could do in the car market. Do you realize North Korea represents for the Japanese several years of automobile production? We are a market for $9 billion in cars in the next five years. Three million cars easily. And we are cheap and dedicated. I do not want us to be a regional drug supplier for Japan and Australia—I want us to make cars! We have people far more skilled, far more dedicated then the softening Japanese! You have said we have an indomitable will—with it we can finally take our place in the world above the Japanese—and they will pay us to do it."

"Yes? It is exactly those Japanese—with the U.S. and Europe—who have all but cut off heavy oil shipments as well as food. Only China continues to send us oil and food, and even then not enough, for the army requires the bulk of it. You might reconsider the idea the Japanese are going to help us."

Dearest Leader shook his head. "There, Il-Moon is Pyongyang. A rust-stained bucket leaking water—"

"And whose fault is that? It is exactly the Americans and the Japanese who have given us the bucket leaking dirty water that the people are forced to drink! They fail completely in their promises to us such as heavy oil shipments and peaceful nuclear power plants and are somehow shocked that we feel they have voided whatever we have promised as well. They negotiate by insisting we meet all their demands before they will even agree to talk. They call us names to our faces such as 'evil' and 'repugnant.'"

Jong-Nam felt great agreement, flashing anger at the spites against their love of Korea, yet shrugged it away. "Let me tell you what I see out there. As my father's oldest friend, and my grandfather's comrade, I tell you if we really want a paradise here, it is there for the taking." His eyes burned and he swept his hand out in the air and grabbed as if plucking up treasure. "Instead of having this wreck of a third world city, people in those apartment blocks going to sleep hungry, we could have a jewel." He paused to see what Il-Moon was thinking. He was impossible to read. "And they would pay us to do it. They would pay us and rebuild it all for us."

"The imperialists?"

"No. Yes. Who cares? Talking about imperialists, did you know Grandfather started the Fatherland Liberation War?"

Il-Moon looked back at Dearest Leader's State Security Department bodyguards. *I could toss this young popinjay off these forty-five floors. They might not reach me in time.* "Propaganda! Lies."

"You mean because American sources say so? It isn't just there. It's everywhere! It is all over the Internet. You can read the actual documents. The only place you can find a different story is in the bookshops right below us. There is nothing in those shops except books on North Korea tourism and titles like *The American Imperialists started the War.*"

"Do those truthful documents also say that it was neither one nor the other? For two full years before we finally ran out of patience we had pitched battles against intrusions involving thousands of troops from the South in full fledged attacks. Bah! They were just as much to blame. War was inevitable."

"He still invaded. The South's forces were far smaller and ill-equipped because the Americans didn't want them to start a war. The Soviet documents show Grandfather traveled to Moscow and asked eight times before he got Stalin's permission, then was ordered and got permission from Mao. You can read the telegrams. It's in the Russian textbooks! It's in the Textbooks of Uganda!"

How was it the world twisted the truth so? "The south wasn't adequately armed? Very sad! If you bullyrag, you must be prepared to spar. What legal right did the Americans have to interfere in a civil war? What gave them the legal right to firebomb our every city into rubble?"

"Nevertheless, I have ordered the books removed. After all, we are going to be dealing with the Americans now. How can we forge a decent agreement while they call us 'Despotic' and 'Evil', and we publish books calling them 'warmongers'? How can Korea ever become whole if we let our people see not so much as a packing slip let alone a foreign newspaper?" For a moment, despair took hold of him at Il-Moon's icy stare. "You yourself know every six-year-old in the DPRK can answer the question, 'What is the Internet?' Their memorized answer is, 'The International Network,' and yet they have never seen it, know nothing of it. An American six-year-old doesn't know what 'Internet' means—but he can surf the net, daily uses a computer. Every month our children are falling farther and farther behind, and not just technically." His voice became pleading. "It does not matter what we negotiate in money: if we continue to teach them lies about the Americans and to hate the world, they can never join it." Dearest Leader struggled to find a way to reach Il-Moon. "Il-Moon-ssi, we love the people down there…" They both looked over Pyongyang. In the low light, citizens still went about quickly in the quiet streets, moving home from their jobs, doing a last bit of shopping for dinner. Dearest Leader's voice dropped into silence. Down below in the train station square, in the warm evening, waiting travelers had chosen to sit outside. They sat chatting quietly by their small bundles of rags; here a card game, there someone smoking. In the stillness, the clear notes of one traveler playing a small flute carried up to them high above; the sad folk song melody of love-lost 'Arirang.' How amazing they were, his people! To suffer as they had for more than sixty years, and still to chat, enjoy their families, to play a flute despite the darkness. He motioned to the waiting travelers below. "So, you say they are about to be destroyed by the U.S.?"

"Yes."

Dearest Leader sighed. "You are sure there is no other way out?"

"You heard the assassin and traitor Col Kang at his trial and even at the moment of his death, did you not? From his own mouth—and you know many of his officers feel the same. Would you rule North Korea and bring in your revolution, or feed the worms? If we ourselves wish to remain, we must find a way to move forward so that we are not conquered by the past. We must do so immediately; any delay could be fatal. The armed forces are ready. If we act now, we can settle this thing in weeks!"

Dearest Leader was surprised. "Il-Moon, you are indeed a man of action. A few weeks sounds very short."

"With the assassination attempt, the lack of ability to raise cash, the real Korea does not have long. We do not have long." Il-Moon gestured to Dearest Leader's broken arm. "Soon, another assassination attempt will be successful. Once we have the peace treaty, things will not be so easy for our enemies. For one thing, our army will either occupy Seoul or be dissipated to the northern borders. We will not be assailable. Should someone try to occupy our offices, they will be illegitimate and will be defeated by the world—including America. Until we have the peace treaty, we could die at any moment. Most painfully."

Dearest Leader flushed at the reference to his scream upon the breaking of his arm. "I am not afraid to die. Even painfully."

"Dearest Leader-ssi," Il-Moon's tone softened in a slight joke by using a presumptive appellative which for a moment placed them almost as equals. "It is neither pain nor our deaths which we fear. It is the death of our dream for a great new Korea."

"How can you be so sure of Hakkermann? He seems sincere in his proposal of a peace treaty."

Il-Moon barked a laugh. "Not a month after trying to kill us? He is an American bastard and merely a beast wearing clothes. He talks of confederation, but he means absorption. He plans for us nothing but enslavement—and his Treaty is the chains."

"I shocked him tonight, sprang on him a proposal with no notice—and there was not the slightest hesitation. I struggle to see him as assassin." At Il-Moon's furious face, Dearest Leader paused, finally asked heavily, "So if I am being fooled, you have an alternate plan to ransom Seoul and the south for Korea's long term rebirth and survival?"

"Yes. We will be prepared to strike and make our own peace if they try treachery."

"We would then force a peace treaty recognizing us, compensating us for the crimes of the Great War and the Fatherland Liberation War and our people's suffering—and pushing us into the world of today?"

"Yes."

"Can this be shown convincingly?"

"You have great respect for Architect Su, yes? Would you believe his assessment?"

"He is a very capable man. Yes, I would accept his assessment."

On the cooling night air, a sweet young woman's voice floated up as she sang a few lines to the flute player's accompaniment. "Arirang. I looked for you, my love, in our secret spot / You were so beautiful and superior / I was so crazy and blind and willing to bleed.'" Dearest Leader shook off the piquant memories from the song. He chose his next words carefully. "You and I are the future leaders of Korea. You and I thus hold the Mandate of Heaven to promote harmony and the well-being of those beneath us. If we lose the Mandate...?"

Il-Moon rumbled sarcastically, "When we lose the Mandate of Heaven, our ancestors will arise, will train the forces of nature on us to bring us down in a storm of thunder and floods and lightning."

"That is true. It is good to remember we are stewards. Very well. Arrange for Architect Su and offer Hakkermann more—and move the process forward."

The Dearest Leader of all North Korea looked back over his monumental and yet heart-rending city, only a few guttering lights pinpricking the gloaming, the silent ghosts of pedestrians walking the dark streets. "I will have my freedom from this vile slough. This prison of the past. You and I will reunify Korea. I will have my peace treaty or you will have your war. Either way, we will bring back *Tangun*—and Korea shall again be One."

AMEMBASSY – SEOUL

In the American Embassy, the Honorable Harold Hakkermann, former— and therefore for life—Ambassador, and currently Chief Negotiator for the United States for all things Korean, stared hungrily at the wet bar in the corner of the embassy ready room. His main aide, Sandy Denton, was on the line coordinating—against heavy skepticism—their report to the State Department Operations Center at Foggy Bottom.

It had been a rough helicopter ride down to the DMZ from the Koryo hotel, and even a motorcade escort from the border couldn't do much for Seoul traffic. It was a lot of hours of transport and he was glad to see the slightly dilapidated tiers of the beige concrete high-rise that is the U.S. Embassy Seoul, the Ambassador to South Korea waiting in his dressing gown, so late it was...

He thought out aspects of the treaty terms while waiting for the T+12 hour briefing on the inspection at Pyong-son from the grouping of IAEA inspectors, and feeling damned impatient about it. "Did you find anything?" "What do the inspectors say?" were his constant interruptions to their discussions.

The IAEA were all looking beat, and Hakkermann as usual was bent on keeping even the junior ones prisoner until the whole briefing was done. At the wet bar, a strange feeling of lightness came over him and he changed his mind, suddenly waving them out with a smile and a thanks. He took their draft report; it was all he needed. Il-Moon was clean. The inspectors left looking surprised and happy. Hakkermann wasn't so bad, but he could slave-drive far past the point of need.

Hakkermann watched the team leave, and remembered Sean. *What a freak. What a fiasco.* He admired the boy for his energy and knowledge, but he had 'big fricking dangerous non-diplomatic approach' branded on his forehead. The point of the State Department was diplomacy without war. The point of the Pentagon was diplomacy with war. When they came together, it could be a circus. He again turned over in his mind the things he was the most surprised about, the cleanness of the site; even more how *nice* Il-Moon was.

He thought back to the sudden meeting with Dearest Leader. Sandy had already reported the broken arm, perhaps important. It had looked recent and painful. Yet Dearest Leader was amazingly urbane and fresh. Maybe it was the Vicodin that was loosening the old boy up.

Despite Foreign Minister Kong's unruffled exterior, such a battle-hardened diplomat still couldn't hide his surprise. So Dearest Leader had wanted to size him up, without any preparation time. It was interesting how he did it; he was clearly curious about Hakkermann.

Harold went to the bar and looked at the bottle of branch water brought all the way from some gracious holler in Kentucky. He touched the clear hard glass of the water flask. The American embassy might technically be on U.S. soil, but if you asked any DoS employee on overseas assignment, they all spent a good amount of time reminding themselves of that uncertain and non-apparent fact, so surrounded one was by the *otherness*. But this water, this water was really...

Sandy said a last few irritated words and hung up the phone. He noticed Hakkermann musing, touching the bottle. He himself was less pensive. He'd been answering some hard questions from State Ops Center and felt on edge. He cleared his throat. "Suppose Sir, it's all a set up? We could look pretty darned foolish getting horrifically diddled."

Harold looked up from the bottle, its hard glass still cool under his fingertips. His mouth twisted in pleasure. "Do you know what is the most righteous sentence in American literature?"

"Tell me, Sir."

Hakkermann was from the Midwest of the USA, and when he spoke, as had his mentors Truman and Acheson, he often peppered his speech with homilies and stories from those never-forgotten and long-loved plains. "It's when Huck Finn says, 'All right, then, I'll go to hell.'"

"Sir?"

"Huck had to decide whether to turn the slave Jim over to the authorities, or help him run away. Huck loved Jim, but knew society was right in expecting him to turn Jim in—so it was a choice between right or best. Huck was willing to pay the ultimate price—hell—to make his own choice. 'All right, then, I'll go to hell.' He didn't turn Jim in, and instead they headed off down that great big river of life. So what do you say, Sandy? Should we turn Jim in, or head down the Mississippi?"

Sandy joined him at the bar, now pensive himself. Taking the branch water bottle and a pair of cut-crystal tumblers, he mixed two strong Yellowstone bourbons with branch. He handed one heavy tumbler to Harold, suddenly smiled, held out his glass.

As they clinked, Sandy said, "All right, Sir, then we'll go to hell."

Chapter 4

The 4th of October

PENTAGON CITY – PENTAGON

Sean walked out of the Residence Inn at Pentagon City, the early morning heat and haze already obliterating the transitory night freshening of the air by the nearby Potomac. After Korea, the huge Pentagon City Mega Mall up the street, the droning hum of the I-395 freeway between him and the Pentagon, and the long-suffering weeds and grass at its flanks seemed alien and unreal. Crossing Army-Navy Boulevard at a big intersection, he marched through the long low narrow pedestrian tunnel under the I-395 overpass and out onto the edge of the huge Pentagon parking lot, the sea of paving surrounding the world's largest office building. He'd arrived last night, found his billet at the Residence Inn set up for him, and thus had no need of a car or an apartment for the near future. His orders gave no clue except 'Assignment Pentagon.'

Joining the streams of cars and people crawling through the Pentagon parking lot, heading down the walkways sluicing the workers into the giant building and to their posts, Sean felt almost as if he were entering some huge correctional institution. For him—a field operative with a decade of technical treaty operations—this was as close as you could get to prison.

The Blackberry on his belt buzzed. His news service, programmed for any breaking news of Korea, was pinging him. Standing among the streaming crowds passing him on the Pentagon walkway, he painstakingly read the just-breaking byline as it scrolled past in the low-resolution Blackberry reader:

> Reuters Seoul – Abbey Yamamoto – Reuters has learned that a major new diplomatic effort between the United States and North Korea may be underway. This effort bypasses the Six Party talks, with the U.S. apparently conceding to the direct bilateral negotiations sought for over fifty years by the North Koreans, despite the U.S.'s long commitment to its multi-party approach. Because this diplomatic position of the U.S. has been the major stumbling block to replacing the armistice that in 1953 ceased hostilities while still leaving a state of war on the Korean peninsula, this appears to be more than simply a new diplomatic effort: it is an embracing of the new Kim regime and its many positive indicators by systematically changing the underlying approach to finding peace to the longest-lasting war of

recent centuries, and from there to rapprochement and reunification. This reporter expects soon to have public comments by the chief negotiators, Ambassador Harold Hakkermann of the U.S., and Marshal Song Il-Moon of the DPRK. Ambassador Hakkermann is well known in the region as a previous sitting ambassador in several Asian countries, including Korea and Japan. "Hakkermann seems to have far greater discretionary powers than anyone we've ever dealt with," a South Korean official said. Foreign Ministry officials who know Hakkermann also believe that he enjoys more trust than any previous American chief negotiator since Dean Acheson. He is apparently reporting directly to the U.S. President and has orders to bring in a major agreement any way he can in light of the new regime's positive attributes. Given the extent to which U.S. strategy hinges on the issue, Hakkermann may have even greater room to exercise his discretion provided Pyongyang agrees, as there are hints it will, to the core demand of unconditionally giving up its nuclear program and to inspections of its missile sites. On the North Korean side, Marshal Song Il-Moon is the highest-level official ever to participate directly in negotiations. He is a veteran of the Korean War, the second-highest member of the reigning National Defense Committee, and a key architect of the North's 'Military First' policy.

"Il-Moon!" Sean cursed at the name, rubbed his jet-lagged and Blackberried eyes, and shook his head in surprise. Things usually leaked, but this story was amazingly well researched for a pop-up. He wondered about this lucky reporter—Abbey—who'd figured it out. Still, things leaked, and it was just one more reason to be depressed; eight thousand miles and thirteen time zones from where he should be. *Son of a bitch Il-Moon. Someday, if the crusty bastard doesn't die of old age first, may we get to meet again—this time Marquis of Queensbury rules.*

The Pentagon's limestone gleamed white and cheerful, although Sean felt his body bow as he followed the legions of day-workers entering through its heavy varnished wood doors. He forced himself to brighten. *The day will improve.* He passed the preliminary scanning stations and called his contact.

Lt Jack Schaeffer was a hairy guy with arms hanging low and muscled along his bulky body. His beetled brow and follicle-ly challenged dome made him seem like a medieval ferryman, as he in-processed and conveyed new people into the huge depths of the Pentagon. He arranged Sean's Pentagon photo ID, and when they passed security and up the escalator and through the bright shops of the Concourse, Jack asked, walking down the D-ring corridor so quickly Sean was half a step back, "Your billet OK?"

"Fine. Is there any message for me from Jeanette?"

"You mean Under Secretary DeFrancis? I'd guess she'll know where to find you."

"Where is that?"

Lt Schaefer pushed open an older stairwell door. "This-a-way."

They followed D-ring for several blocks, ducking through the connecting corridors into the inner rings, ending up in B, then following several poorly-illuminated halls until they plunged down into a file-box cluttered subbasement with an amazingly low ceiling. At the end of a corridor lined with dead TWIX machines and exposed phone lines, Sean and Jack entered an old door, labeled BAY 829(1)-K, with pebbled glass runny enough to have been installed in the Pentagon when it was built in 1943. The whole place, furniture and walls alike, was painted yellow-green. The old ceiling fluorescents lit the few other colors with a greenish tint as well. In fact, Jack's skin took on a Frankenstein-like hue from the ancient lighting, and Sean suddenly realized the whole office seemed to have a curious kind of pea-green smell to it.

Jack hurried Sean back past several empty offices—they were all empty!—and finally showed him into a tiny decrepit windowless room in the back. Jack smiled, as though a pleasant attitude could disguise this end-of-the-line hovel for anything but a hard-time desk job. "Here you are. Logistics Efficiency Evaluation Center. Staff meeting 0900 in C-Ring, 5th floor corridor 4, bay 209 is at least thirty minutes away, so it's usually not worth walking over. Perhaps in a few weeks, they'll assign someone to show you the ropes."

Sean ignored the claustrophobic purgatory. "What about my request for an appointment with the Under Secretary?"

The lieutenant sniffed and brushed petulantly at a green paint chip that had attached itself to his cuff, as if this forgotten corner of The Building were somehow trying to get him. "Well I don't know, but I wouldn't hold my breath." He drummed fingers on some files on Sean's desk. "And here we have some *good reading*. Air Force Logistics Instructions. Duty hours are 0800 to 1700. You're expected to be available here. Enjoy."

After the lieutenant left, still picking at the paint on his uniform sleeve, Sean turned and prowled his cell. Without a glance, he threw aside the pile of paperwork on his desk. Sitting back in his ancient wooden swivel chair with cigarette burns, he took out his camera from the Korean inspection. He laid down in a row Emily's scrawled notes, her little scanner, and his camera.

He carefully played back all his pictures from Pyong-son. Something he'd missed, something perhaps would be useful.

Flipping the pictures, he stopped on his full face snapshot of thoughtful Emily absorbed in using her little scanner.

Sean fired up the computer, found he could still log onto his AFTAC email account, and the old HP printer actually worked. He propped the camera up on the desk. Zoomed the picture in until the cropping was just around Emily's pretty face. He hooked the camera into the computer, and a full-face photo hummed into the printer tray.

Sean picked up the photo of Emily and plinked the edge reflectively. "Who are you, exactly?"

SANDIA HEIGHTS – ALBUQUERQUE, NEW MEXICO

Dr. Emily Engel's Delta flight from Seoul terminated in Los Angeles rather than all the way home at the great savings to the government of $110, but she did it anyway because that was the Reg. It meant, however, that her price-chopper Southwest flight from Los Angeles came in through Las Vegas at 1:00 a.m. Despite the lateness of the hour, Emily felt a surge of happiness to be home as she walked the empty adobe-like Albuquerque International Sunport building with its Native American rug-patterned tile, high open-beamed ceilings, and dramatic oil painting mountainscapes. Emily got her own bag and equipment case from the baggage conveyor, although she found a porter to help her with the luggage because it had been twenty hours since boarding the flight from Korea. Even though the government voucher she would file tomorrow—well, when she got the chance in the press of the next few days of catch-up—wouldn't reimburse her, it was an excellent economic and personal exchange.

The taxi drove her up to her house in Sandia Heights on the foothill slopes of the southern Rockies. The Sandia Mountains glowed cathedral-like in the almost full moon, lighting the wilderness-landscaped neighborhood. Her house was surrounded by a yard of pleasantly plant-dotted desert. A couple of jackrabbit eyes gleamed as she dragged her luggage up the travertine pavers to her big Sante Fe Territorial modern house, its huge windows facing the city lying in the tubular valley below.

Her cat Quark was waiting, having endured a week of cat-door freedom and neighbor's feeding. Emily was pleased because between the hawks, the owls, the coyotes and the roadrunners—even with the netted back patio to flee to— it was no picnic being an outdoor cat up here on the flanks of the southern Rockies. Even a small lapse in judgment could be a cat's last.

She dumped her bags inside the tiled entryway, and turning on lights through the house from the master panel, she looked up the stairs to her aerie above.

She wished she could call up; call to a special somebody waiting. Quark nuzzled her leg. Emily picked her up and carried her as she ran upstairs.

She went out into the exercise room, a big rumpus room. From up here out the floor-to-ceiling picture windows, Albuquerque spread a glimmering sequin stream of lights down the valley on either side of the distant dark streak of the Rio Grande. She started up the Jacuzzi in one corner of the room, got on her exercise bike, and began cycling, looking out over the golden lights of Albuquerque where all those innocents slept below her.

This was her favorite room, with its view over the lights of the sleeping city below. She set the clock on the exercise bike for thirty minutes and pedaled hard to get going, to shake off the jet lag and the cramped muscles from the long flight. Emily thought back to Sean. Boy, was he nice and fun and she imagined him again with her in bed, talking, her hair loose and on the pillow for once, his warmth against her side. *Stop it! But it's been so long. I mean it! He's gone!* She pumped her legs harder on the machine to wipe out the desire, the loneliness that only spiced and worsened the longing. She said angrily to herself, *This is the life you chose! Get used to it!* She got what she wanted when the immediate aerobic reaction to the pedaling made her see red. When the rush finally wore off, she was safe again. She tucked Sean away into a mental file: unfinished business, probably never to be reopened.

She was now her solid self and she said aloud what she always said up here, pedaling, looking over the glimmering sleeping city.

"You have a catcher," and she settled into her workout.

* * *

Dawn was only a few hours later and Emily left early enough to miss even what traffic Albuquerque called rush hour on I-25 south. She passed onto the sprawling Kirtland AFB and skirted the huge 14,000-foot runway the Air Force base shared with the commercial Albuquerque International airport at the far end. The ABL hangar complex was on the far side of the runway on a stretching piece of desert bordering a ravine which gave it a little more security—and removed the day-to-day science operations from the inflexible regulations within the flight line. The morning sun as usual poked straight into her eyes as she followed the last bend around the end of the runway and saw the rough complex of hangars and Butler temporary buildings. Home for her was just beyond the ALF—the Advanced Laser Facility—in the Air Force Research Lab's facilities and offices around the working apron for its large experimental aircraft.

Set out on a flat stretch of desert sweeping to foothills several miles away, in the early morning light the desert was fresh, the sky a bluewashed iridescence. She shrugged off the cobweb memories of the nightmare place North Koreans called home, and her world held out the unbreakable promise of a sunny day.

Emily caught a glimpse of her plane, Airborne Laser (Experimental), docked as usual into its support structure, known as 'the White Elephant,' because of the hulking legs and trunk look of it. From the White Elephant's structure, cranes, and calibration shacks, the big jumbo freighter was festooned with umbilicals, feeding hoses, electronics support, power cables, and laser fueling hoses.

Parking along the side of the huge maintenance hangar, and in her usual flight suit and clogs, Emily clomped past the picnic ground to where dapper Chief Master Sergeant Augsburger—'Chief' to his crew and 'Auggie' to everyone else—was just firing up the power to the giant ABL. Auggie, sharp as a razor, his hair slicked back and his tie as always seemingly tacked to his chest, was exuding Emily's favorite let's-get-it-done attitude.

Emily, sucking on a huge cup of Fair Trade organic Italian roast, leaned on the airstairs and chatted with a strong smooth-faced Asian-American USAF officer, Capt Matt Cho, who was dressed in a business suit this morning for a class he was teaching across town at the University of New Mexico. While they waited for Auggie to unlock the passenger door to ABL, they stood enjoying the fall desert morning, the possibility of afternoon thundershowers absent now in the coruscating pure deep blue of the sky.

WYNDHAM HOTEL – ALBUQUERQUE AIRPORT

The spy, while at a distance of more than a mile away in his perch in his room on the top floor of the Wyndham hotel, lucked out. Although he was surveilling across both the airport terminal and the long runway, for the moment the air was cool and the heat mirages to come later in the day weren't an issue. Through his twenty-inch Questar telescope, set up to look sideways over the top of the airport parking structure, the view to ABL was breathtakingly clear.

The huge 2000mm focal length telescope lens was hooked up to a new Hasselblad 39-megapixel camera. He zoomed the magnification up as far as he could. There, as usual, on the airstairs of the giant plane, was the science-boss college-girl with her moppet hair and creamy skin—*What a piece of ass! Would I ever like to drop the F-bomb on her!*—and his shutter clicked again and again as he shot the plane and the girl. *This morning light is perfecto.*

He stopped. His face grew hot as he saw the features of the man she was talking to. He knew the look of the Korean in the black business suit—a foreign government official. He connected the dots with what he'd read in the paper this morning. *Koreans! On our sovereign soil!*

It took him some time to find the phone number. He had to dig through the filthy clutter of his 'hunting stand' hotel room. Pawing aside aerospace magazines, an Air Traffic Control radio scanner, beer cans, take-out food wrappers, a burlap sack of green chili, and jugs of non-fluoridated water, he finally found his wallet in the minibar fridge. *How did that get there? Here's her card. I tell her about this, she'll see the situation gets blown apart.*

Chapter 5

The 4th of October (Korea)

MINISTRY OF PEOPLE'S ARMED FORCES – PYONGYANG

Ordinarily, First Chief State Architect Su Hyok, known to the elite of North Korea simply as Architect Su, would have enjoyed the buildings and monuments as his Benz whisked him through the spotless, straight, wide streets of Pyongyang.

After all, he had designed or consulted on almost every aspect of the city's rebuilding after the American bombing in the Fatherland Liberation War. Despite an undercurrent of concern about his cityscape's real aesthetic quality, he never settled back in his seat when he could press his thin mild face to the window. He loved to look at the buildings, the road net, the people. He'd laid out the boulevards so they ran straight ten lanes wide; parkway connected to avenue, traffic circle to plaza; vista after vista of monuments, bridges, fountains, squares, stadiums, cultural centers, and gardens. Even the huge apartment blocks were tiled on the outside to give them sheen and scope. The city was unequaled in Asia, a unique urb in a unique quarter of the world. Its streets were the cleanest as well. Architect Su had put in bus washing stations, so that extra dust was not brought into the capital. In addition, from single families all the way up to whole apartment blocks, teams of residents scoured and cleaned the streets of the slightest debris or dirt. There was no litter because nothing was thrown away. Everything in this extremely constrained environment had to be reused, be it paper, plastic, metal, or human waste. There was no trash; in North Korea it was all resource.

Much as he loved the cityscape and its people, today as he neared the huge Ministry of People's Armed Forces—the Pentagon of North Korea—Architect Su felt, deep in his spry but aging bones, worried.

He was not concerned by his summons to the MPAF from Il-Moon and Dearest Leader. Although Dearest Leader was new enough so no pattern was established—in fact was clearly on track to be different—Architect Su was frequently called to the MPAF. After all, he was much more than an architect these days: he was Chairman of the all-powerful 2nd Economic Committee, the highest fiscal organization in the DPRK, subordinate only to the National Defense Committee. The 2nd Economic Committee took the yearly fiscal requirements from the armed forces and the civilian quarter, and then reconciled them with the available resources of the nation. Architect Su essentially ran the whole enchilada of the economy of North Korea and—within the constraints of the extreme poverty of their country—he did it superbly.

Of course, his position of power meant he was always at risk of arrest. To allow such a competent and incisive mind near the throne was a necessity. Dictators only remain in power when they are effective. Indeed, the main drawback to a crony-based system such as North Korea's was that it encouraged incompetence since only the Great Leader, or now his heir Dearest Leader, could be all-knowing. People selected for loyalty were rarely the most skilled executives. Even the hard working ones couldn't do the Allan Greenspan kind of work. For that, you needed genius.

Genius was needed, was valued, and yet it was also a threat and must be watched carefully. All of Su's activities—as with every other important person in the DPRK except Il-Moon and Dearest Leader—were recorded and sent directly to Dearest Leader on a quarterly basis. Everyone in the DPRK had their loyalty and political reliability monitored and judged. The reports—and Dearest Leader's judgment—formed the basis for everyone's future fortunes, privileges, and perks—or their and their family's fateful trip to the firing squad or re-education camps.

Su glanced out the back window. His usual watchers were following him in a beat up Chaika. Architect Su laughed as he noticed again—it had been about a week or so since it started—a new Benz now followed his watchers. Another set of watchers now apparently was watching them! *Sed Quis Custodiet Ipsos Custodes?* 'But who will watch the watchers?' The Juvenal quote brought a slight smile to his face.

No, he was not worried today about his watchers.

Nor was Architect Su's anxiety connected to the rumored debacle at Mansion 27. Not only had his Underwater Mansion taken direct hits and not collapsed, but his emergency systems had functioned like a thing of beauty. The only people of importance who had died—Premier Yu and General Chon— had not used his safety egress system. Architect Su felt a funny tingle of pride at being part of something that worked for a change—unlike the economy and so many other aspects of this hurting country. It was sad though, he reflected, that their creation was gone: the world's only Parisian mansion on a seabed was now a thing of the past. He shrugged off his dream of recent nights in which he stood on the pier jutting into Nampo's black waters; on the dark swells floated a muddy burned window tassel.

No, today, none of these things worried him. Not the summons, not the economy, not the watchers, not the attack on the mansion.

Today he was worried because his unmarried twenty-year-old granddaughter had just failed a compulsory virginity exam.

The routine physical exams, meant to guarantee the virtue of the flower of Korean womanhood in the DPRK, were so irregular or bribable the daughter of a high-level official could risk it—but the foolish girl had triggered an immediate special exam when, without thinking about it, she had changed addresses. She then seriously compounded her error by actually appearing for the exam, and now there were written records.

She had wanted to live near the boy she loved who was at Kim Il-Sung University for the next few years and was not allowed to marry. Architect Su—and his whole family in fact—very much liked the boy as well. Now, First Architect Su, at the pinnacle of North Korea, was going to be further indebted to the Second Vice Chair of the General Political Bureau and that could be costly. On the other hand, should he allow his granddaughter to be publicly declared maiden no more, her chances of marriage would drop to zero—and bring about the death of all her hope and joy. Even her own boyfriend would be unable to marry her, such would be the pressure on his family to forbid it. Unfortunately, saving her would create just one more vulnerability for him. The records were filed, copies here and there. For this simple small act of intervention, should he indeed use his influence, he might someday face a firing squad. Should someone want to renounce him, such an act would strongly support a charge of suborning others in the DPRK's paradise; the written record of his corruption would be invaluable evidence for use at his trial.

And it was not just *his* trial. His whole family to three generations would be stripped and broken. There would be the moment when their houses would all be violated, searched in such a rough way as to destroy everything the police didn't want. Possessions would be divided up in front of the families and carted out as booty and reward for the arresting agents. The children would be slapped around, and the wives—always the easiest family members to terrify—forced to sign confessions that they were all guilty. The families would then be dragged downstairs and shoved into waiting sealed trucks.

From there, it would get worse. Much worse...

We made the ceilings too low, Architect Su sighed as the monotonous rhythm of the cramped blank windows of a big white tiled apartment block thrummed past. *Where is all the laundry? It used to make the city so lively, the laundry hanging out. Then there was a law...a law about laundry. Where was the law about beauty?*

The car's wheels suddenly hummed as they ran onto the metal bridge over the Taedong River—he was very near the Ministry now—the silty waters looking so chocolaty rich he brightened. *Well, as least she's taking some pleasure along the line.* For without love, the days—much like his architecture, unfortunately—could be very gray and grim and empty in the life slough of the Democratic

People's Republic of Korea.

A block away from the massive MPAF building, his car turned into the tunnel entrance for the elite. Five stories down, the tunnel ran through security checks before letting him off at the deep underground lobby of the command center and from there he was escorted to his meeting.

In the simple large meeting room with extended table pointing toward a display board for briefings, besides Il-Moon and Dearest Leader, Architect Su was more than a little surprised to find seated at the long polished table the highest leaders of the North Korean armed forces. The best military minds in North Korea were rarely assembled together for security and political reasons. They were the ruling clique—and the arms and legs of State Control—and they were very impressive. None of them had gotten here without hundreds of dead and ruined colleagues, purges, tough assignments, and physical work levels that would have sent any other armed forces command on the planet into open rebellion. There was diminutive General Kwon, Missiles and Artillery; tough General Kim, Naval and Special Forces; avuncular General Park, Armored Corps. There were also civilians, Minister Lee, Internal Security, and Minister Wan-Koo, Korean Workers' Party. These were the seven members of the National Defense Committee, who reigned supreme over the DPRK.

There was an empty chair, and for a moment Architect Su wondered if indeed he were to be purged, for a lone open seat was always reserved for the unfortunate's last meeting. Yet there were only pleasant greetings all around, although the water carafes and snacks were untouched, a sign of tension.

Wall maps and diagrams displayed the usual Armed Forces plans for the invasion of South Korea. Army, Special Forces, Artillery, Missile Forces, and Navy movements were all marked.

After the greetings, Dearest Leader spoke, waving to the war plans. "First Architect Su, we would like to listen to your thoughts on our plans for a reunification war."

Architect Su was shocked and could not hide the fact.

"Now, now," Dearest Leader said, "It's not all that bad. However, in preparation for updating our plans for the glorious reunification, we need an outside expert; one who will be honest with us about how all this would work. Tell us your thoughts on the standard plan."

Architect Su forced himself to calmness. From his work on the 2nd Economic Committee, he was in fact the greatest expert on the Armed Forces of the DPRK. He knew every facility, unit, ship, weapon, and project—from missiles to bunkers to rice storage. He funded nothing without good purpose—for every dollar taken from the civilian side was a dagger in his heart—and his architectural genius instantly grasped military functionality to a depth impossible for anyone else. His was the last word on military projects, and perhaps his greatest contribution to the state was the wisdom he gave freely when requested by these men here around the table, his old friends.

Architect Su recovered, and when he spoke politely, everyone listened intently. "Comrades and Leaders of the great Juche effort and to our still present President for Eternity and his son Dear Leader for Eternity." The room nodded approvingly to this punctilious opening. "As the Great Leader said in his bold speech of 5 November 1972, 'It is wrong to try to avoid the struggle against imperialism under the pretext that independence and revolution are important, but that peace is still more precious.'"

The generals were as usual shaken by Su's ability to pull the most apposite Great Leader quote from the rabbit hat with zero notice, and there were bemused glances around the table as Su continued. "This effort requires the utmost diligence, and such a plan must pass the test of Juche—complete self-reliance—to succeed. First, let us review the issues and attitudes we have toward the glorious reunification of the Fatherland. This of course is the plan entitled 'The One Blow Non-Stop Attack.' It is," and he went to the blackboard and spoke as he wrote:

1. Breaching the DMZ and annihilation of forward deployed Puppet State ROK and U.S. forces.

2. The isolation of Seoul and consolidation of gains within the forward areas.

3. Pursuit and destruction of any remaining ROK and U.S. forces.

"These phases must receive the utmost in self-criticism. First, the annihilation must be limited. Seoul destroyed means our job is much more difficult. The goal of the encirclement and capture of Seoul should be to seize it intact. Therefore, the artillery's purpose must be renewed and rejuvenated to include only the necessary bombardment of forward stalling points. For example, in the corridor from Kaesong to Munsan—the main approach to Seoul—we may well have to blast our way through. Such areas—where the Americans are fortified as well— cannot be spared. Anyone of Korean blood who has chosen to live so close to the DMZ knows the risks.

"However, I council you my Dearest Comrades, let us strike and yet not kill our brothers. Let us negotiate and reach an agreement which somehow puts few troops in our way, and those that are, we shall deal with. Yet the people of the Puppet State to the South, even to their politicians, must be preserved if we are to truly win the day. This will also remain true for Combatant attacks on the political structure."

Dearest Leader jumped up. "My Comrades, let me add to Architect Su's comments a most hearty foot-stomp!"

The room looked at him, confused. His westernized phrases from the Internet and international popular fiction, when translated directly to the Korean, were often jolting. "That is, I give these sentiments my heartfelt applause," and the generals relaxed at the explanation, although Il-Moon thought *he is such a pansy*.

Su continued. "Further, Seoul contains a quarter of the population and 50% of the GDP of South Korea. It must be captured intact so that we may not just use it, we must harness it for all citizens of The One Korea.

"Now, we must find entirely new approaches to this effort. Even our courageous troops backed with armor will not prevail unless we employ to the fullest a way to stay the enemy's strengths. You are all aware of the Energizer Bunny? The Americans are the Bunny." This produced a feeling of merriment around the table, and the generals who sometimes went months without smiling, hitched their belts and let their faces do the strange and unfamiliar. Architect Su paused to let them enjoy their pleasure at his joke, then continued. "To keep the Bunny from going on and on, we must pay attention to communication, communication, communication. We must think long and work hard on what is required to stop the Bunny.

"Now, on the last point, the annihilation of the Americans, we can give no quarter. Their airbases, especially Osan, must be brought to their knees immediately. The casualty rates of Americans must be over 10,000 or they will not become sick enough of war to allow our reunification plan to work."

Dearest Leader broke in, "Yes. It must be with a minimum of Korean blood shed. The very minimum."

"Very wise, Dearest Leader. War is simply the most straightforward application of politics, its sorry stepchild, and yet it is in the end, politics."

"We will have a good political plan. War may never be necessary."

"Comrades, there will be ways to fight smarter and faster. Should you open your military facilities for inspection and cataloging, I will, with your support, bring you a plan, an architecture if you will, for this undertaking."

Il-Moon spoke for the first time. "Thank you, Comrade, for your exceptional wisdom. We will expect the report in a week."

Architect Su went suddenly cold. "A week—"

"A week," continued Il-Moon bullying past the worry in Architect Su's face. "Everyone here will open their information banks directly to you. I suggest you start immediately. Comrades, our meeting is ended."

*　*　*

Outside in the hallway, as Architect Su shakily walked toward the exit, he was intercepted by his burly blue-suited senior State Security Department watcher. Although Su let this man spend every night in the anteroom of Su's home—instead of like most watchers, miserably left outside to watch from a car—here, the agent was extremely formal: "A minute of your time, Respected Comrade First Chief State Architect."

Su nodded and followed him. In a side room, Dearest Leader and Il-Moon waited, silently, until Su's watcher left the three alone.

Dearest Leader asked, "And your final assessment, please?"

Architect Su, recognizing the format of the meeting—the leadership letting him know exactly what official policy was—went to the table and poured a glass of water before answering. His granddaughter's joyful face on the family's outing to beautiful Mount Kumgang only a month ago bubbled up. Her pinkie had entwined with her boyfriend's in a slightly forward gesture as the two fell behind during the hike. Her joy had been smilingly acknowledged and secretly delighted the whole family. He felt a flash of anger. *Who were these men he had known and served so long, that they would hurt his family so?*

Oddly, Dearest Leader spoke before Su could answer. "Apropos not of this, I see there was quite an error made by the Political Bureau's medical committee. Apparently, they mixed your youngest granddaughter's records up with another girl's. I have personally seen the file corrected and the careless doctor has admitted himself to Yondok Camp for re-education. The matter is settled well, I believe."

A threat. A very real threat. The record would always be there, waiting. Anytime, in the years until she was married, if he were unresponsive, she could be called back for another exam. For a moment, Architect Su found his anger suddenly rise in him to almost homicidal.

Dearest Leader's eyes sparkled behind his small chic glasses. "With such a mistake, such an injustice, the Great Leader's University rules' committee has met. A waiver for your granddaughter's marriage is arranged. Next Tuesday, at the People's Hall. I will of course be present, as our friendship is of such old date."

Architect Su dropped his gaze in almost a swoon, could not respond until the electrical jangle of anger and relief passed. He was moved beyond words. His family would burst with happiness when they heard. Dearest Leader at the wedding! He, like everyone else during a regime leadership change, had to feel their way along, intuit what support to give, what safety nets to preserve. At this moment, he realized which camp he was in: he would, for better or worse, follow this man to hell and back. "I shall endeavor with all my heart to find some truly helpful avenues of approach, Dearest Leader-nim."

Dearest Leader's voice sharpened again, and was now critical. "That is not, First Chief State Architect, exactly an answer—and I request an exact answer—

to the question you were asked."

Architect Su sipped more water, thinking at lightning speed until he was clear. Then he pulled out three chairs and set them into a rough triangle. He motioned politely for Dearest Leader to sit first, and he and Il-Moon took the other chairs. Su drew his chair closer to Il-Moon's, knees almost touching. For a moment, Su leaned back and looked at Il-Moon fondly. "Il-Moon-nim, when you and I as boys ran the streets of Manchuria as messengers for the patriotic Korean freedom fighters, under the very noses of the stupid Imperial Japanese Army, do you remember how you would beat me for my dreaminess?"

Il-Moon, although his lumpy dentures made the smile shark-like, grinned with true pleasure, for rarely had they time for reminiscence. "You were eight-years-old, and very impressionable, Su-ssi. I did not wish you to be captured and tortured—or grow up to be a dreamer."

"You were ten, and yet you took my education seriously." Su reached over and patted Il-Moon's knee chidingly. "Thank you. And yet are you not now the dreamer yourself? Surely, Il-Moon-ssi, you have more than you showed me. There must be some advantage we have, something most of the MPAF are not aware. Otherwise, your plan is like the dreams you used to beat out of me. The Americans may look soft, but they are in fact the most vicious killers ever seen upon this world."

Il-Moon grinned again. "You forget how we fought them! How we beat them before!"

Su did not go outside the permitted bounds, reminding Il-Moon of the night the Americans had—in a move calculated to starve North Korea into defeat—systematically bombed their every major irrigation dam, flooding virtually all their arable land, ruining the year's harvest, and plunging the entire country into famine. Su and Il-Moon had been together that night, and as the news trickled in of the apocalyptic magnitude of the destruction, hardened as the two young army officers were, they had held each other and wept at the mercilessness of their foe.

Instead Su said gently, "Perhaps we won. Perhaps it was a draw. Perhaps, if you look at the casualties, it is not so clear. The Americans lost 37,000—while we Koreans lost one million and the Chinese one million more. Indeed, Mao Tse Tung's only son volunteered for the war and was killed by an American air strike, crushing his father's hopes for an heir. Further, if you look at our economy you will see just how thoroughly the Americans won the surrounding field as well. Not only here, but in all Northeast Asia. They broke the mighty Japanese—who sat on Korea for thirty years and almost conquered China—into no more than their lap dog! They have almost strangled us without even sweating. Realize, it is their kid gloves that fool. They use their stock exchanges and their IMF and 'free' markets to dominate the world with apparent professionalism, empathy, and reasonableness. They thus appear soft. It is not the case. They are simply expedient. Yet as things are, they will find a way to stop us perhaps even before we start."

Absorbing his amazingly blunt words as if they were resonant, Dearest Leader looked at Il-Moon expectantly, who murmured, "We will be negotiating the withdrawal of the 7th Air Force. Should that occur, we will have an overwhelming military advantage."

Dearest Leader corrected, "Should they withdraw, however, we will be in a good position to reunify the Fatherland politically, so do not worry, Architect Su. It will not come to war. Unless there is no other way and the Americans intend war anyway."

Su studied the man. *Could it be you are the answer to our boyhood dreams? Can you make Korea whole again? You appear to be Tangun—and yet, should I go with you?*

Su stood. He bowed deeply to Dearest Leader. "If they intend war, I will prepare us for war."

Il-Moon stood also. "Yes, Su-ssi. Prepare as though war is our only option."

"I will endeavor greatly to that end, Il-Moon-nim. What more then do you have for me to even the fight to come?"

Il-Moon's reply betrayed no hesitation as he had always out-thought Architect Su. "I invite you both to meet me at Pyong-son. You can examine the facilities. Then, First Chief State Architect Su-ya, you will finish your report—with the Pyong-son portion only to us."

'THE PIT' – REUTERS OFFICE – SEOUL

The taxi dropped Abbey Yamamoto at 6:00 a.m. in front of the Reuters' offices in downtown Seoul. The Seoul oriental megalopolis here was a mixture of extreme high-rise buildings seemingly mortared into place with crumbling tiny buildings in the cracks.

Ignoring the ironic backdrop of a huge ball of garish plastic vegetables—a sphere bursting with giant vivid cauliflower, peppers, tomatoes, and tangled green onions (the sculpture required by law at every tall building in Seoul and whose main function is to mystify pedestrians)—Abbey bitchily paid the cab and, feeling the adrenaline come up on her, stalked into Reuters.

She would have liked to be, for the next day, anywhere else. But she had to go in. She had no other option. If she stayed AWOL, at any moment the station chief would fire her and void her office entry card and computer account. She would be hugely less effective without her Reuters status and locked out from her resource base at the wire service office.

Her peace treaty news release had gone out twenty-four hours after the taxicab encounter with the Korean *Yakuza*. First, she had checked the Reuters' database from the Internet café. Then she spent the day doing research, calling around town discreetly. With the documents she had been given she knew exactly who in Seoul's embassies, Ministries, and news agencies to treat for lunch, cocktails, and dinner—and exactly what questions to ask. Reporter she was first and last and by the next morning she had her facts lined up and was certain the documents weren't a hoax. Just after dawn, she was back at the Internet café. She logged onto her Reuters account and posted a routine—and therefore unchecked—wire service release. Within a few moments, at every Reuters' office in the world, her byline and story came zipping into terminals, clacking out on telexes, and had been posted on-line as a for-sale item to Reuters' subscribers. The rabid sales reaction to her piece triggered automatic emails to the station chiefs of key nerve-centers such as New York, Paris, Tokyo, and London. CNN and print media picked it up instantly. She smiled when she thought how Hakkermann and Il-Moon, when they saw it, probably almost popped their gaskets. Fun fun fun. Except...

The story had broken while she'd hidden with her cameraman in a bar for the entire day. This morning, she was about to pay the consequences—and not just the hangover. The Reuters' station chief was almost insane with rage judging from his unreturned messages on her cell phone. Luckily, half-crazed angry was his normal state so Abbey hoped he would still be able to negotiate should she not be able to sneak past him or his guards. Abbey wasn't, however, about to back down with her bulldog jaws on this particular bone, and if that shithead of an editor jumped her, he could kiss her ass. Or she would hop to CNN. *Maybe. Risky.* Normally, she would just take a Reuters' satellite-link van and scoop the still-unannounced press conference at Panmunjom big-time. Except her van keys had been confiscated when she was kicked down to Financial—a slight disagreement about what blood alcohol level you should have while driving madly around Seoul in a company vehicle. She had to figure out how to cover the press conference and not get caught until she had too much momentum to get fired.

Reuter's main wire service room filled a whole floor of a sky-scraper, windows to windows. Across this huge open arena, cluttered with desks and cubicles, she cut between obstacles toward the financial side of the room and into its separate space. This circular cluster, with its workstations, teletypes, and servers, was a nerve center of the Reuter's International information marketing machine. 'The Pit' was connected to every Reuters wire service, news, and financial reporting network on the planet. The Pit was in operation 24/7 and was never unattended. Abbey's walk became surreptitious as she sneaked up behind the almost drowsing-off Hugh Levine. Hugh was the new guy, barely through his twenties, and as usual, the fresh meat was apprenticed to The Pit's grave shift. They were expected to monitor all lines, acknowledge receipts of anything interesting, direct developing stories to the appropriate desk, and condense everything coming in so that Reuters could sell it by the story on the open market or offer it to their subscribers in the enormous database of world events. From town chess matches in Nigeria to amateur fashion shows in New Delhi, from wars to elections, the graveyard shift coverage spanned the globe's human interest, financial, political, and international news—and was a nightmare that was painfully and unsuccessfully juggled by every Pit apprentice until they either broke, or fresh fodder arrived.

Hugh was doing a brave job of not nodding off over his terminal when Abbey pounced. "Where are last night's condensed stories?" she snarled.

Hugh jumped. "Abbey. Can you believe, after your story the Korea Exchange was up 7% yesterday, and if you look at the electronic after-hours last night—"

"What about the damned condensed stories?"

Hugh blushed. "I couldn't do them all, Abbey. I picked these."

Abbey sneeringly shifted through the piles of documents that were his night's work. "You condensed information from some kook holed up in a hotel calling about something called Airborne Laser, while ignoring the Brady Bond Index drop in Paraguay? Honey, you are a moron."

"I didn't know, Abbey. The guy sounded important. He saw your story. He met you in New Mexico. He said he trusts you."

"Yeah, it's my morning for trust," Abbey quickly ran back in her mind, remembering the ugly mountainous country near the Texas-New Mexico border, when strangely she found herself on assignment—another one during which she was sure her boss was insane—talking to white supremacists. There actually had been a bond of sorts when she made it completely clear to—what was his name? *Spiney*—what she, as no slouch of a racist herself, thought of Spiney's race and how they should stay the hell away from her.

It was thus only half-heartedly that Abbey yelled at Hugh, mostly for form: "Spiney was a racist pig who asked me if my pussy slit went sideways like my eyes! Why the hell would he want to give me anything, let alone help or trust?"

"Well," Hugh pulled up the few wits he had left, muzzied as they were. "He wanted money wired to him. Three hundred dollars. Could it be, he perhaps sees cash in it for himself?"

"Christ, boy! Three hundred wouldn't keep his operation going for a day and Spiney thinks the mongrel races should fight it out and destroy themselves..." She slowed, stopped abruptly. *Yes, he did. Now for some reason, Spiney wasn't below enlisting her help—with pictures of the mongrel race...*

As she mused, she picked back up yelling at Hugh: "Don't you dare show anything from him to anybody, you understand! Except me. Someone sees you condensing this, they'll think I'm training an idiot. Save it for me, got it?"

Hugh, puppy dog-like, nodded avidly.

She took the fuzzy pictures of the strange aircraft and the Korean official standing beneath it, and dismissively threw an arm wide to the room. "Get those fucking stories condensed and out on the net now! And do the damn Brady Bond drop first! Only a moron would ignore Paraguay."

"I don't know from Paraguay, Abbey. I came here to be your cameraman; not a reporter. They promised me—"

"I have a cameraman who was filming firefights in Vietnam before you were your father's worst idea. And he can condense stories. God, how will I ever get back to Tokyo working with a loser like you?"

Akiru Takahashi, Abbey's cameraman, came into The Pit. Wiry and small, in his fifties, he was aging poorly as do so many overseas cameramen. He looked at Abbey, "You still are planning to cover the news conference? What about Roy?"

"We'll just go and do it."

"We will need cameras and a Sat dish—or you will be talking to yourself."

Abbey got an idea, barked at Hugh, "What's the girl's name in motor dispatch, the Korean cow always mooing over you?"

"You mean Kimkim? I don't want to raise her expectations, Abbey—it's not fair."

"Fair? Oh, *fair*. Let me put *fair* to you like this: is it *fair* you sit here night after night condensing stories? Or that you don't get to do video work? No?" Abbey went sweet. "You want to be a cameraman, here's your chance. Get me a Sony camera, a satellite-ready dish, and the van, and you can do some shooting." *The van they'll notice immediately.* "Forget the van. Get me the Land Cruiser and you can tape a whole episode."

Hugh stuttered, "I'm not sure she'll—"

"You've told her your dream about being a cameraman? Tell her here's your chance. Get me the fucking keys!"

Abbey's tirade made the first Reuter's workers who were bringing The Pit to full morning life glance up. Abbey snarled at them, "What are you looking at? Butt out."

None of them felt like messing with the wolverine in their living room, so they looked away as Hugh, cowed, pulled himself together and walked unsteadily toward the elevators. Abbey lit a cigarette, stretched like a cat, sat down to wait, calling after him, "You look like shit. Go wash your face!"

Akiru looked at the morning energizing of The Pit through hung-over eyes. "Rightly do they call it The Pit."

"Here," Abbey said and blew smoke in his face. He inhaled thankfully. "How come it feels like I quit this week, but it has been twenty years?"

"It's Korea, Akiru. It's like a disease."

The phone rang and she automatically picked it up. "Yamamoto."

She cursed under her breath in response to the audible squawking of the Reuters' station chief. Then she yelled back, "The treaty is so financial news. I'll do any fucking story that screws with the markets...and if it goes big, I want Tokyo. Tokyo, you understand me? Columbia? You can't take me off the treaty! The Pit? Don't you hang up—"

She slammed down the phone and turned to Akiru, who was shuffling through the papers on his desk. They both looked at the bustling Pit.

Akira waited, silent.

"We're off the story. Assigned to The Pit. We may not leave until we tell them who our source is."

"He's threatened before."

"This time he says he'll transfer us both to Bogotá."

Even Akiru paled at possibly the most miserable Reuters posting in the world. "Perhaps we should tell him."

"Not on your life."

"Aren't you surprised Roy wouldn't come down here and throttle it out of you personally?"

"It'll dawn on him soon," and she jumped up and paced fretfully.

Hugh returned carrying a set of keys and a camera case. Abbey grabbed the keys and cursed when she saw it was the small Hyundai 4x4. "Fuck! The Hyundai!"—she hated what she saw as an inferior Korean-made SUV—"I told you the Land Cruiser."

"I did my best. Now can I come on assignment, Abbey?"

Abbey yanked the camera case from Hugh and gave it to Akiru. "Next time, you'll get a nice chance. Now get back to those stories."

Hugh exhausted, said, "Abbey, I've been up all night. Got to sleep."

Abbey shouted, "Sleep under your desk. Don't you leave until these are done. Then do Akiru's too."

She was about to add something, but ran out of steam when the lack of breakfast and her hangover suddenly swooped in on her. She looked about desperately, seeing the 7:00 a.m. Pit through a wave of nausea as Hugh collapsed on the floor to sleep under his desk.

Akiru shook his head in pain. "Oh, my head hurts—and all my stories to condense."

Abbey pulled out Hugh's ABL write-up and pictures, and dumped Akiru's pile of work onto Hugh's desk. "The kid will do yours, Akiru."

She took a pink memo, wrote on it, 'Wire Spiney $300,' and taped it to sleeping Hugh's forehead.

We've got to get out of here. Abbey scooped up the Hyundai 4x4 keys, the fuzzy pictures of the weird plane, and looked at the press passes for Panmunjom. *A day to kill.* Her solution arose pre-consciously: "Com'on, Akiru, let's go get a fucking drink."

PENTAGON – NATIONAL AIR AND SPACE INTEL CENTER

Sean had—knowing the outcome in advance—walked over to Jeanette's office in E-Ring's SecDef area high over the Pentagon's River Entrance. He was made to wait by her receptionist for hours until Jeanette came out of her office. He mentioned Emily's notes and Jeanette had brusquely taken them and, gold eyes flashing, commanded: "You are hereby cast back into outer darkness where there is weeping and wailing and gnashing of teeth. Do not return to us until you are called!"

Sean, unwilling to return to his cell deep under B-Ring, prowled the Pentagon's oblong linoleum halls, wishing he could do something. It was unlikely that he could get his hands on the latest INTEL from Korea, for he had no need to know, and he had no idea of the status of his clearances since the debacle at Pyong-son. He did know, however, people in the community, and so perhaps he could keep a hand in the game. If there weren't too many questions, he could waltz around the need-to-know. He couldn't very well send in a visit request from Logistics. Done in person, it might work.

On the top floor of E-Ring, he followed the outermost of the five ring halls around toward NASIC, the National Air and Space Intelligence Center, at least where he remembered it being. He suddenly came to a dead end. The corridor was completely sealed by an unattended and apparently unused vault door leading to a limited access area. Trying to keep a mental map of where he was, since in the Pentagon no corridor runs to compass points and each ring has a variety of stairwells and interlocking office corridors, he backtracked to the nearest stairwell, dropped a couple of floors only to find himself stopped at a door guarded by a pair of serious Marines. With the entire building in constant renovation, his path was a mess of short-circuited corridors, vaulted areas, and no-go zones. He remembered the Pentagon song, sung to a ukulele, which was the equivalent of 'Get Charlie off the MTA' where some poor sod had been lost for weeks.

A half-hour later, he finally found the front entrance to National Air and Space Intelligence Center. There was a small lounge with reception desk for people waiting to be admitted. Beyond, vault doors led into a Sensitive Compartmented Information Facility—a SCIF—a specially sealed and electronically-isolated top secret vault.

Sean borrowed the receptionist's phone, and within a few moments, he was being escorted inside the vault by Steven Goddard—although red lights strobed along the hall to indicate an uncleared person was in the vault and secret conversations were disallowed.

Steven was a handsome man, especially in the bureaucracy arena where the standard civil servant in Intelligence was thickening at the waist beneath his beige raincoat and dark blue suit, sported a scruffy beard peppered in gray, and stared suspiciously at the world from within an over-worked face. On top of his vigor, Steven had four children of active age and a wife who missed Florida—a home was so much bigger with Florida's coast just outside the door.

Sean had known him from AFTAC before he was forced to leave the comfort of raising a family at Patrick AFB in sunny Florida, where life was simple, if somewhat lacking in sophistications such as schooling and culture. D.C. offered those things—along with long commutes, winter storms—and a three bedroom tract house in Virginia, a hard slogging hour's commute south.

They had gotten along well. Steven's sophisticated political sense ran interference for Sean's more damn-the-torpedoes approach. Steven brightened when he saw Sean. "Great to see you, what are you doing here in D.C.?"

"I thought this was the place to be. Power, influence, money. Isn't that what they told us?"

"Yeah, and how soon do you leave to catch the van pool for two hours home, and the kids doing soccer and all that stuff."

Sean made a decision. "I'd like to ask you for a favor." He hurried on, incredibly embarrassed at making a request that no INTEL officer could grant, and would have to both curtly rebuff—and report. "There was a TWIX came out of DIA Osan, a copy to me. About that explosion at Namp'o. I really think I need to look at the supporting INTEL, really feel like there's something to it. Something we don't understand. Something we missed."

"Don't you have a job?"

"Logistics. But I can work it in."

Steven looked grave, putting his hands into his dark suit pockets. "You think this would be a good idea? Me letting you use one of the NASIC workstations and looking over the data?"

Sean couldn't say anything. His mouth just wouldn't move.

"I mean, you're not even in those SCI compartments." SCI was the acronym for Sensitive Compartmented Information—Top Secret programs. Nothing was generic Top Secret. All top secret information was held within programs, each of which were compartmentalized from all others. Compartmentalization, or SAR—Special Access Required—was the only way of keeping things truly secret. The Top Secret clearance was nothing; everyone with a good clean nose could get one. The only mojo that counted in INTEL lay in the 'tickets' to the compartment. So, while Secret was the clearance itself, Top Secret was all about need-to-know.

"There is something really wrong out there, Steve. Put me on it, I'll get you some good things for the NIE." Sean was as close as he had ever come to begging.

"I didn't get a clearance or visit request. Maybe missing a small item like your 'need-to-know'?"

Sean was embarrassed, face flushing. "I didn't send a visit request."

Steven said gravely, "So you're asking me to let you, while you are working Logistics, to have SCI access without a need-to-know?"

Sean paused for a long moment. "No, I don't suppose I am."

"Well, that's good because it isn't necessary. Jeanette sent yours down this morning."

"Really. I wasn't sure she remembered."

"Yes, I don't suppose you thought she'd do it—after what happened at Pyong-son."

Sean grimaced, shot himself in the foot with a finger-gun. "Good news travels so quickly."

"For what you did, buddy boy, 186,000 miles per second is far too slow for us to hear about it."

"Oh, you two are such rats!"

"Careful, sonny. I could always lose Jeanette's letter."

BOOK 2

"Do any job required to make your dream come true, regardless of your job description.

The AFRL Project Officer's Second Commandment

Chapter 7

The 6th of October

MPAF INTERNET VAULT – PYONGYANG

For more than forty years Il-Moon had never been alone. Ever since his ascendancy into the upper strata of North Korea, even in the toilet or in bed—even early in his career before he tired of it when every night he hammered one or several of the Joy Brigade—someone always stood near to help or protect. When he was outside his apartment or the Armed Forces Ministry building he was swarmed. Besides Aide Park, he was always accompanied by ten other aides and at least a hundred Guard Command soldiers.

Now, in the space of three months, he was destined to be completely alone twice.

The first time had not been so difficult. However, that had been only few minutes—and inside the MPAF.

I will have to find a way to be alone again—this time out in the Real World and for several hours. He knew this would be much more problematic.

Il-Moon thought back to the last time he was alone—just two months ago. It had come as such a shock to Aide Park, Il-Moon had almost laughed.

It had been a web surfing session. Perhaps Aide Park had imagined Il-Moon was sampling pornography or *The Washington Times*—same thing—which he could only enjoy in private.

Il-Moon was not. He had traveled enough of the world to know it was uninteresting—only the DPRK held his love. He loved Korean food and landscape and North Korean power, and the feel of the seasons and the harsh bounty of the land; it was all he'd ever loved since that drumbeat of hooves on the rice paddy road now seventy years gone past...

The privilege of surfing the Internet was available to only a few hundred people in the DPRK, all of whom had the highest security clearances and the most impeccable political reliability. Even in overseas embassies, Internet access was restricted. In all of Pyongyang, there were only a few dozen terminals, mostly for collection of intelligence and for the MPAF to study foreign militaries, hardware, and personalities.

Il-Moon and Aide Park took the executive elevators—made by Hitachi; most luxury goods in the DPRK were made in the hated country of Japan—down to a deep MPAF basement and through a cave-like corridor to the Internet vault.

In his private booth was a terminal for the MPAF Intranet—a secure fiber-optic link between the various commands of the Korean People's Army, Navy, and Air Forces. Based on the idea of the Internet, spreading out from Pyongyang was a centralized fiber optic control and communications system that was buried and hardened against air strikes and impervious to jamming and most interception. Almost all the armed service functions—artillery, control of ballistic missile launches, infantry, re-supply of petrol and other critical war materials—were directly controllable from Pyongyang.

It was not for the MPAF Intranet that Il-Moon had come. The other terminal was his PC for surfing the World Wide Web and the only terminal in the DPRK—except Dearest Leader's—immune from monitoring by the State Security Department.

Aide Park brought the system up and opened the Google search engine. He was shocked by Il-Moon's order to stand outside the room and not return until summoned.

"Perhaps you would permit me to help you surf, Great Secretary?"

Il-Moon would ordinarily been furious at the disrespect. The invisible worm in his belly however, gave a small nip, urged him on. *Lose no time.* "It is very important you keep your objectivity. I do not want you polluted by what I must look at."

Aide Park nodded. He did not want to see Il-Moon humiliated if he couldn't manage to surf the net himself, nor could he sit by without extreme discomfort while his boss needed help. Nevertheless, he had raised his one barely-permitted objection.

With Aide Park outside the closed door, Il-Moon tried to Google.

His fluent English was fine for putting in his search terms. The enraging thing wasn't the search, it was the results. Thousands upon thousands of pages of minimal interest and dubious value spread across the page. "Like a cancer," he thought grimly. It took him more than an hour of brain-hurting reading to learn which of the sites were the most promising. He found despite his distaste that the American professional organizations were the best. He had been at it for an hour when he was jolted. He reread carefully this time, puzzling over the words as the still half-remembered poem flickered by in the back of his mind:

> *'The invisible worm*
> *That flies in the night,*
> *In the howling storm,*
> *Has found out thy bed...'*

Il-Moon had been glad Aide Park was not in the cubical. For, when he realized he had found his answer, he involuntarily gave out a long dark growl of anger and anguish.

NASIC INTEL ANALYSIS VAULT – PENTAGON

Sean was surrounded by the wreckage of a hard day's—and evening's—worrying work: notes, Coke cans in the food and drink box across the room, document printouts, correlation reports, and images; always images. Panchromatic, color, stereoscopic, infrared, hyper-spectral, and radar. He was swimming in images. Piled in stacks, shuffled around, marked with stickies; of the perhaps four hundred images, in several hard hours of work, he had managed to know what each one seemed to purport, and where it was in the piles. They were a strange series of documents: Il-Moon and Dearest Leader watching, while a colonel—Sean could see the shoulder insignia—who was being executed, ran and climbed the walls until trapped and killed. The images of the North Korean execution were odd, although maybe taken by themselves, an officer freaking out during an execution could happen. But how many executions did Dearest Leader attend? Then there was a concomitant execution in the nearby work camp. One image was of a seven-coffin-catafalque leaving the North Korea camp, while another showed the coffins being interred in a grave area nearby.

Then there was the explosion at Namp'o harbor. Sean looked at the images more closely for the thousandth time. Again, what leapt out at him were the huge billowing white patch, the strange people in the water, the feel of how important it was from the response of the Korean People's Navy—whose efforts were nothing short of superhuman.

The South Korean NIS—National Intelligence Service—analysts, and the National Reconnaissance Center had messed with the imagery. With the additional image processing, they got a whole bunch of different things out the image: the white patch could be a sea monster eating a giant marshmallow, a white bulldozer plowing into a huge pillow...Sean finally went back to the original image.

He put calipers across the screen, and played the video frame by frame until the object was stretched out on the water to its fullest extent. The real-time images sparkled like sequins. Huge, the object was almost...thirty meters long! No one knew what it was, amazingly; the tagged footnote references in the images contained a few half-hearted tries.

Dawn, the girl-next-door type who spent most of her waking hours in the vault, came up to Sean. "Sorry, Sean." It was way after work hours, she had stayed as long as she could, and now she was closing the vault for the night—and the two person rule applied here. No person could be alone in the vault.

Sean gathered his notes. Skipping the laborious paperwork process of creating a new SCI top secret document set with its numberings and controlled copies, he instead wrote across the bottom of each page, 'Working Papers/Top Secret/ Destroy or Permanently Reclassify within 60 days,' followed by his name, the date, and the required descriptive triad for this TS compartment, YNG. The joke was—since it was Korean INTEL—it was short for Ying-yang.

"Would you mind double checking my lock-up and all the safes?" Dawn asked. "We're the only ones left."

"No problem, Dawn, if you'd file these, I'll check your lockup in just a moment."

Sean handed her his documents and looked back at his image analysis station. In a moment, he would log off and the surveillance satellite image on his console—of the March 1st Prison with the North Korean colonel dying— would disappear.

He could hear Dawn opening the safe to pop his documents into his temporary folder in the big filing cabinet. His eyes drifted up from the prison image on his LCD screen to the sign someone had taped on the console: 'Intelligence Satellites have no Intelligence! So you have to!' Sean leaned back.

The image on the screen was telling him something. *What had gone wrong? What did it mean?* He closed his eyes, and tried to imagine the execution.

FLASHBACK – 6 SEPTEMBER – DPRK PRISON OF 1ˢᵗ MARCH, 1919

Inside the football-field-sized prison courtyard, three hundred North Korean officers of Regiment Koguryo of the Combatant Corps stood in formation. The squads were composed of soldiers of the same height to emphasize a de-individualized solidarity. Against the high walls, their anachronistic uniforms— replicas, strangely, of those of the hated Imperial Japanese Army—were identical daubs of drab color; the men as unvarying and stiff as the eagle emblems on their peaked almost bird-beaked hats. Their faces were impassive as granite. A small cheap-suited group from the State Security Department—the watchers of the military and civilian power structure—stood carefully noting everyone's posture, demeanor, and zeal.

The courtyard was enclosed by rough stone walls twenty feet high. Pyramids of variously-sized rocks, from small to big—as if workers had carelessly left piles of unused materials—stood between the units of officers.

The trial had followed the standard North Korean military format. In a private court, with only the most senior unit officers in attendance, at a long table sat the prosecutor and judges—all uniformed except for the People's Service Bureau chief, who represented the Korean Workers' Party. The charges were read and the confession also. Col Kang then endured epithets, the naming of co-conspirators, was made to publicly and loudly denounce his own corruption—and that of his American puppet-masters.

Kang, after three days of truncheon beatings, ice water drenching, and electrical shocks and drugs, had finally divulged six names—and received a promise of amnesty for his father, mother, mother-in-law, wife, and his three children in return for his full confession. Usually the torture would have lasted weeks. Luckily for Kang, the brazen attempt on no less than Dearest Leader's life brought a frenzy of irrational anger to the torturers. In their fury and desire for a full confession they lost their usual patient sadistic composure and had soon—but not too soon—broken him and gotten everything they wanted. Besides, Marshal Il-Moon had demanded the information immediately.

The prosecutor, supremely confident, proved Kang's guilt to the judges, and got signatures for the warrants for the other conspirators. The judges then moved through the standard incensed questionings of the guilty, furious denouncements, and livid harangues—restraining themselves with difficulty to only an hour—and pronounced sentence.

Within scarcely two hours of appearing in the docket, Col Kang—face bruised and one ear almost sheared off—was marched out into the enclosed stone courtyard to face his fellow officers.

Looking down from a parapet, out of sight of the rank and file below in the courtyard, Il-Moon stood with Dearest Leader, who was complaining. "Is this really productive? Us coming here merely to see this assassin?"

"Dearest Leader, six days ago this man nearly killed us both—and he is not merely an assassin, but highly respected as you know. His was the third assassination attempt this year. I felt you should see the trial; was it not very enlightening?

"Perhaps, although I think it is questionable not to further study this man."

"The best move we can make is to destroy the other conspirators immediately, and show the officer corps the swiftness of our justice."

Col Kang crossed the paving stones of the courtyard, the sky like a blue roof above him, and even the tall walls could not shut out the surrounding beautiful up-swept Korean mountains. He could hear birds twittering, arguing over a morsel, and he smiled—even as he marched the courtyard toward the execution pole.

For Kang, things were very clear in the cold air, and he felt and saw and thought as he never had before. For a moment, his wife's face came to him, the horror etched on it as he laid on the dungeon flag stones before her for the forced apology which was his one true regret.

He marched toward a small cement circle, now passing the lines of officers. To him, they were beautiful; the crowning achievement of Korea—his men, his unit, the finest. Nothing could make him prouder than how they would now carry out their orders.

The officers each in turn stepped out, spat on him, screamed at him.

First, "Defiler of our dream!" The next, "Betrayer of the People!" and the screaming and spitting fused into a long gauntlet of sputum, epithets, and ostentatious hatred.

Many of the officers were Kang's friends. Their harsh Combatant features betrayed no trace of sympathy; only in the depths was there confusion, pain, or regret. State Security agents noted on a numerical scale each officer's enthusiasm in spitting and screaming.

From the sea of furious faces, Maj Tam Ho—his friend—stepped out, spat copiously. "Besmircher!" Tam Ho was suddenly right on him, eyes wild with fury. He grabbed Kang's blouse and pulled him close, slapped Kang in the face. Under the closeness of the blow, Kang looked into the eyes of Tam Ho—and saw the almost imperceptible shake of his head.

Kang knew his family had been officially liquidated.

He continued on for five steps, as if Tam Ho had said nothing. With Tam Ho now behind and past, Col Kang went wild.

He jumped aside from the line of officers, suddenly tall and strong, shouted to his regiment, "How long must your families starve? How long must you truckle to that Beast of Korea we jokingly call Dearest Leader!"

The officer corps froze. Kang pointed up to the parapet. "Dearest Leader! I know you are up there! I can smell you! You who are no better than a bastard pig and stand in the way of the Great Korea!"

Il-Moon jumped to the parapet, swelling to huge size as he overlooked the shocked troops. He pointed down to Tam Ho. "Major Ho! Show the worm Kang how we deal with traitorous vermin!"

Tam Ho jumped to the command, pulled up a stone from one of the piles, and whipped it straight at Kang.

Kang ducked the stone. "Dearest Leader it is you who are betraying us! Regiment Koguryo will never let you live or give you the honor of our love!"

"Fulfill the sentence!" Il-Moon shouted commandingly. "Stone him!"

To these officers, Il-Moon was both God and Satan. Tam Ho cried, "Kill the traitor!" and the regiment swiftly moved to grab rocks.

Kang ran for the high stone walls, yelling to his regiment. "Let Korea take its rightful place in the world! Rise up, Comrades! You have nothing to lose but your chains!"

The regiment quickly closed in on Kang, trapping him against the high stone walls of March 1st Prison. Kang began to scale the rough wall, still yelling treasons.

Almost to a man, Regiment Koguryo threw. A cascade of smaller rocks laced into Kang. He hung on for a moment, then fell back to earth. Tam Ho, a huge stone held high over his head, ran to Kang's prone body. He hurled the boulder down and crushed out Kang's life.

Kang's body was then kicked the fifty feet back to the cement execution-circle where he was supposed to have stood during the stoning.

Within moments, the regiment was marching past Kang, forced to kick him, spit again on his body and yell something. They were however, quieter now, and over the wall could be heard the chirping birds. The State Security Agents could hardly take notes, so shattered was their world; none had predicted Kang as this kind of traitor—and heads were going to roll.

Dearest Leader moved back from the parapet, from the ugly words and the stoning. It wasn't cowardice or fear. It was the sharp pang of the words: *you will never have the honor of our love!* going into his heart like a dagger.

Il-Moon motioned to the officers degrading Kang. "Look. Your elite officer corps do not think he is a traitor."

Dearest Leader took a glance at the lackluster kicking and spitting. "What of his family?"

"They were removed to the February 27th Work Camp and have all been liquidated."

Dearest Leader, with years of experience as chief of the State Security Department, which routinely dealt out interrogation, torture and death—a necessary part of the Kim Family Regime's rule under Kim Jong-Il—was taken aback. Dearest Leader had not simply inherited his father's leadership. He had served his father ably, showing himself to be a ruthless and skilled security manager—with several thwarted treason plots to his credit. Purposely only partially hiding his anger, he snapped, "Was this wise?"

Il-Moon replied, "It is the only way to slow the officer corps' traitorous thoughts. They now know there will be not the slightest mercy for their families."

Dearest Leader reflected, "It is not so simple, Song Il-Moon," he said formally using Il-Moon's full name without title. "The co-conspirators with Kang. Where are they?"

"Across Korea, they are being arrested and will share Kang's fate."

"I think not so quickly," Dearest Leader spoke sharply. "Isolate them. I want none of them executed, understand? I will think upon this."

Il-Moon shook his head. "We must face the fact that due to American aggression and our encircling enemies, our regime is coming to an end. Soon, it will be us down there." He crossed to Dearest Leader, spoke urgently. "If we do not stabilize the situation, within one month we will be overthrown. Let me take action."

Dearest Leader thought and then spoke. "Leave the traitors alive for now. Meantime, the Committee will meet tomorrow in Pyongyang. We will discuss all this and see if your plans appear feasible."

After Dearest Leader left, Il-Moon walked to the parapet and looked down where Col Kang's shattered corpse lay smeared in spittle and blood. His regret was piquant and bitter. *Such a valiant officer; having to die this way.* He had been an honorable officer, one of the best Korea had known. *Sleep well, for you have done more than your duty.*

*   *   *

Sean awoke with a start as Dawn touched his shoulder. She laughed, "Welcome home, Christopher Columbus! Where were you?"

"Some place hideous. Let's do that lock-up and get you on the road home. What time does the vault open in the morning?"

"I can be here 0600 Hours. See you then?"

Chapter 8

The 7th of October

PANMUNJOM VILLAGE – THE JSA ON THE KOREAN DMZ

Abbey was pensive, letting Akiru drive their purloined Reuters' Hyundai 4x4 out of bustling Seoul. Again and again, she went over what she would ask at the press conference, how she would comport herself. Occasionally, she reached into a small birdcage between Akiru and her and petted the little white dove within. For the first half-hour of the drive, she furiously chained smoked. Finally, Akiru reached across and plucked away her pack of cigarettes. "If you keep it up, at the press conference you will be bright green around the gills, and the dove and I will be dead of second-hand smoke."

Abbey relented, eyes still fiercely looking out the windshield, her mind in turmoil as they drove up Freedom Highway along the broad Han River estuary with its strange lumpy islands, mudflats, and artillery posts. Along the river bank was strung extensive razor-wire as well as around the freeway overpasses—there to slow DPRK Special Forces' infiltrations. On the other side, distant dramatic mountains had their fall colors coming on. In the myriad valleys rolling out to them, rice paddies were drying, ginseng shrubs dotted the cleared hillsides, and it seemed the Koreans were fall-planting everything they could think of under white plastic greenhouses, the crops under their covers presaging the coming of winter.

At Grand Unification Bridge, the Imjin River-crossing and checkpoint for Panmunjom, Abbey and Akiru showed their press credentials to the big U.S. and ROK guards, and wove the tank traps of the small road running the two kilometers to the center of the DMZ. Here, entering the Joint Security Area—the JSA—they pulled up at the combination tourist-trap and armistice-control-center for the Korean Peninsula that is popularly called by the name of the nearby now-defunct village, Panmunjom.

The main Panmunjom buildings were robin's-egg blue—United Nations blue—and sat astride the boundary between North and South. In the negotiating buildings, the actual border ran down the middle of the rough tables so one could harangue one's counterparts without ever leaving the comfort of one's home country—even if the cushion-less seats were brutally uncomfortable.

Although at the press conference Abbey was to ask only four questions—not counting a couple of prompts to a CNN reporter she befriended—after the conference, no one would ever doubt she had framed the picture unforgettably.

On alighting from the Hyundai, Abbey fought her way through the scrum of reporters, and guessing her seat at the press conference was reserved—courtesy of whomever gave her the press passes—she made a bee-line for the CNN news van. After convincing the CNN news director—who knew she'd broken the treaty story—to assign her feed to one of his monitors and use it as he wished, she and Akiru raced to set up in front of the more-comfortable side-building where she alone knew the treaty was being discussed. From here, the negotiators would emerge to walk to the main press conference building.

Looking into Akiru's camera, Abbey started her broadcast. Her face was open and honest, and her voice silky and warm. "This is Abbey Yamamoto of Reuters Seoul. We're here at Panmunjom for the opening ceremonies of what we believe will be the most historic treaty talks ever."

When Hakkermann, Il-Moon, and entourage emerged behind her, Akiru nailed them face-on as Abbey called, "Ambassador Hakkermann, is it true these talks have been named the 'The Agreed Peace Treaty and Confederation Framework'?"

Hakkermann's face in the extreme close-up betrayed just a twitch. "The talks will be discussed at the conference; however, I think you are onto an excellent title there."

Abbey turned, widening her large eyes to the camera. "Peace treaty? Confederation? Is that like reunification?" In his van, the CNN news director, who had barely cut in time to Abbey, was rewarded with this mini-scoop, and so kept on her feed as Akiru shot some beautiful following video of the official entourage entering the press conference room. When Akiru panned the global dignitaries and representatives of the other parties most interested in North-South Korean détente—China, Japan, Russia, and South Korea—the CNN director was sold. He just went with Akiru's camerawork documenting the key negotiators at the podium and the other dignitaries at a long table with expensive biscuits, drinks, miniature flags, and table decorations of small Korean dolls in native dress.

Eschewing the elite press corps of Yomiuri, Chosun-Ilbo, and the Korea Herald, Abbey positioned herself intimately close to a dashing CNN reporter, establishing a quick camaraderie with an arm-squeeze and a whisper. Akiru caught Abbey's Asian beauty in profile against the handsome CNN Caucasian male—the image almost a cameo of the unfolding East-West event.

Hakkermann planted himself at the podium microphone, posed, and orated. "In the darkest days of World War II, when tyranny ruled Korea as it did so much of the world, and both North and South Korea and we Americans were striving to make a new world order, President Roosevelt spoke for all of us, and I paraphrase slightly: 'Mindful of the enslavement of the people of Korea, the good powers of the world are determined that someday, Korea shall be free and united!' Thanks to all Korea's good friends here," and he inclusively waved to the six party dignitaries, "and in particular to my friend First Vice Chairman Il-Moon, this promise may soon be fulfilled."

Il-Moon added, "Yes, together we are truly seeking a just and right future for all parties, compensation for the past, and a united Korean people."

Before the posturing stopped and the questions even started, Abbey managed to get in the opening shot, although her voice was velvety: "Marshal Il-Moon, are you on behalf of North Korea truly offering the Korean people—both North and South—their dream? Are you promising reunification?"

Il-Moon brought forth his answer with gravitas: "As you know, the DPRK has always held the key to peace is for the United States to enter into bi-lateral negotiations to end the war. This being accomplished today, we can approach a confederation agreement—"

At the revelation that reunification was really on the table, the room erupted in yelled questions, while Hakkermann, feeling due credit and clarification was needed, tried to add over the shouting, "These talks are indeed a framework for a unified Korea," while Il-Moon appended pedantically, "A confederal Korea, of course. Two systems, one country."

After a few misdirected questions from ill-prepared reporters, Abbey managed to get in, "Marshal Il-Moon, but what of Japan? Isn't that the longest standing issue?" Abbey's voice was even softer now, her sympathy clear. "Reunification would require financing and support from Japan. Have you, Vice Chairman Il-Moon found it in your heart to *forgive* the Japanese for their occupation?"

Il-Moon looked like he'd bitten into a rotten salmon, but got control within a few seconds. "Indeed, there is a shared feeling among the parties these negotiations differ from those in the past."

The CNN man, prompted by a whispered crib from Abbey, put in a solid shot with: "Ambassador Hakkermann, what about the Agreed Framework, the South-North Joint Denuclearization Statement and many others which are theoretically still in force—but completely failed. Are you admitting these are really dead and if so, don't those failures haunt you? Don't they point this time as well to failure?"

"We will deal, rather than with particular policies or old stumbling blocks, only with those issues which are key to immediate peace."

After a fumbled interjection by Chosun-Ilbo about the South Korean position, Abbey politely asked, "Ambassador Hakkermann, you mention key issues for immediate peace—surely one of them must be the long-standing concern the DPRK has with the 7th Air Force, nearby at Osan, as representing a threatening offensive force. Are you considering such a U.S. withdrawal from Korea as a gesture?"

Hakkermann grunted as Il-Moon took advantage of this to grand-stand: "The 7th Air Force is of course a powerful offensive force, and represents a dread to all Koreans. Perhaps such a small gesture would be worthwhile, considering the reunification of Korea?"

Hakkermann nodded, hitting back sagely, "Perhaps in return for a token DPRK withdrawal from the DMZ, in particular the 820th Tank Corps, which is most forwardly-deployed, and consists of the most capable North Korean armored divisions?"

The negotiators were glowering slightly at each other, each having their strategy tweaked to the world. Hakkermann tried to pour on soothing oil: "The key point at issue is to first end the war, which implies withdrawing all forces from the DMZ, as it makes no sense for a single country, unthreatened, to maintain offensive capabilities along an internal or confederal boundary."

Il-Moon pressed his point. "Certainly, many offensive systems and capabilities would be unnecessary in a dual state. And this should most likely include those currently in place."

Hakkermann, trapped, added uncomfortably, "Perhaps a strategic withdrawal of U.S. forces to show good faith and that we are not truly an offensive force."

Abbey last question was, "First Vice Chair Il-Moon, would you not expect the U.S. to ask for permission to inspect nuclear or missile sites in returns for such a concession? Would Pyong-son be on the table?"

Neither Hakkermann nor Il-Moon were looking particularly happy, and they ignored the question, as Abbey gave a last whisper into the ear of the CNN reporter, who asked loudly, "You both implied several times 'immediate peace.' You make it sound like this deal is a matter of weeks!"

Il-Moon and Hakkermann exchanged glances, and Il-Moon leaned carefully into the microphone. "We believe if we move rapidly with good principles—those of peace and prosperity and recognition of all persons' rights on the Korean peninsula—we can soon achieve a peace treaty with productive results for the future of the entire peninsula."

This brought cries for clarification, while the negotiators motioned instead to end the conference. Instead of pressing forward with final questions, Abbey sprinted for the door, leaving Hakkermann and Il-Moon to shake hands and chat with the other diplomats. Akiru and his camera followed her—and so did the CNN director. He wasn't about to miss her next move, even as Akiru skillfully framed her between a bronze Korean lion-beast and the North Korean buildings across the DMZ fence.

Opening up the F/stop so he could focus on both the background and Abbey's intense face, Akiru worked to project her, as if bodily, into every living room, bedroom, bar, and office watching around the world. Citizens around the globe—and especially in South Korea—leaned in to hear her every word, spellbound.

Abbey seemed to search their faces, then spoke quietly, warmly. "After all the heartache and broken dreams, the years of living in terror and separation, today the deepest hope of all Koreans has been given a great breath of life."

Akiru zoomed in until her face filled the whole frame "Every once in a long while, we news people have more riding on the story than a paycheck. We too, are part of the news and share with all of you the dream of world peace."

She took from under her coat the small white dove, held it up high, poised on her fingers. "From me to each one of you—and especially every Korean— this is Abbey Yamamoto of Reuters Seoul, wishing us all that the dream—as in all our hearts—on this amazing day, has taken flight."

The little bird sprang from her fingers, and fluttering madly, rose into the bright sunlight.

Akiru's camera followed the white dove spiraling up into the afternoon sun. Guessing the dove would head toward the nearest water—a pond just past Reunification Village on the North Korea side—Akiru had set up to catch the sun-flash on the bird's wings as it swooped across the DMZ fence.

Abbey's voice, choked with emotion, came in over Akiru's images. "Take flight, dove! Take flight, take flight, and follow the light!"

Across the world—and nowhere more so than across South Korea—at her words and the little bird's flight, whole rooms of watchers jumped to their feet.

A collective shout of approbation rose up in a million throats across all the realm of the earth.

* * *

Striding away from the press conference, Hakkermann was still shaking his head, remembering the interview and seeing Abbey's dove-launching replayed on a screen just outside the press room. Sandy had to race to keep abreast as Harold demanded, "Who the hell is this Yamamoto woman?"

Sandy chuckled, "Isn't it time for a Midwest quote? As Bobby Knight would say, 'She came to play!'"

Hakkermann chuckled as well, but ruefully. "It wasn't you up there dealing with her."

Sandy already had Abbey's bio, and while they strode handed it over to Hakkermann. "Her thing has always been the world financial impact of news, disasters, wars. Degree in finance, Tokyo U. Couple years at London School of Economics for polish. Worked all over the world. Reputedly a great-granddaughter of Admiral Yamamoto of Pearl Harbor fame—"

"And she deigns to work in Korea?"

"Not voluntarily. Probably goes to sleep every night with Tojo's autobiography under her pillow. She's in Korea because, believe it or not, she was once hot shit but is now totally in disgrace at Reuters. Fired from Tokyo, kicked out of New York for—get this—screwing the brains out of the Reuters' chairman's college-age son and then breaking his heart for fun; in public. Seems he didn't tell her who his father was—until after."

"Oops, I did it again." Harold stopped, looked right at Sandy. "Doesn't tally with what we saw back there."

"No one ever said she wasn't complex—or a smart one."

"I'm not sure anyone is this smart. Who could be using her?"

"South Koreans, Japanese, Chinese, Russians; we have a lot of pissed off friends in the six party talks. Just about any one except the North Koreans—she really stuck it to them. Did you see Il-Moon's face when she asked him if he *forgave* the Japanese?"

"A classic, agreed. Well, if she's a loose cannon, she should be our loose cannon. Figure out a way to open a channel to her—without letting her know who we are—and say we want to talk."

"Maybe we could leak our treaty terms; skip a lot of the posturing and nonsense we usually go through."

"Arrange a conference. We need to know what she can offer. And get me on the President's calendar for a thirty-minute phone chat as soon as you can."

"We'll wake him up with the glorious news..."

"He's probably already awake and watching replays of that damned bird stunt. The flight seen round the world."

POTOMAC JOGGING PATH – GEORGE WASHINGTON PARKWAY

During the interview, Sean—even as he was intent on Hakkermann and Il-Moon—was drawn to Abbey's face. The huge eyes, the classic Japanese features, the expressive voice, the soft sensitivity with an amazing honesty. She'd asked all the right questions, and nothing slowed her. Her cameraman was pretty amazing too; always knew when to get close up, when to cut to something else—and nailed the dove-flight. No one in their right mind, Sean realized, would bet against this diplomatic effort's momentum, and it was with bulls-eye accuracy that Abbey had brought this out—as well as the 7th Air Force being on the table.

It meant things were moving fast and dangerously. After the interview, Sean knew he had better take what he had and go with it.

He changed in the gym in the old subway station in the Pentagon's basement, and emerged into the October sunshine. He jogged over the little entrance ramp that arched across the buzzing 110 Expressway, and under the car-whizzing George Washington Parkway to emerge in the strip of park along the Potomac with its running paths.

He saw Jeanette's signature bouncing red-gold pony tail and white sun visor up ahead a mile, jogging along, chatting with a junior officer accompanying her. Many of the Pentagon's high rankers ran together, but Jeanette more often was to be seen along the Potomac with the lower ranks, which was useful for both of them—the younger officers for their chance to brush with power, talk, complain, and ask advice; while Jeanette got to hear what was going on several ranks below her General Officer status.

She had at least a mile on him. Sean poured on the coal and a flash came to him that this was how it was supposed to be.

He caught up to Jeanette and her jogging buddy. In response to her warning glance, Sean said, in a jogging air-deprived voice, "The white object floating in the Namp'o satellite images is a movie screen."

"Go on," Jeanette panted in her jogging voice.

"This particular movie screen was almost ninety feet in diameter. Embedded with high tech diamond sparkles, it cost a million dollars—and is designed exclusively for 70mm cinema projection."

"You say 70mm cinema?" Jeanette slowed. "I am still very angry with you. Let's walk, Dave, if that's OK," she said to her jogging partner. "Something else?"

Sean continued, "Our mutual high muckity muck friend from DoS reported to State Ops that when he met Dearest Leader, on his right arm he was wearing a cast. A fresh cast."

Jeanette dismissed Sean with a nod and a change of pace. "Alright, I'll see you at my office at 7:00 p.m.," and speeding up she turned to her running partner as Sean reversed around back toward the Pentagon. "OK, Dave! Let's pick it back up!"

MAGNOLIA PALACE – THE NORTH KOREAN WHITE HOUSE

Perhaps the one person most affected by Abbey's broadcast was Dearest Leader.

When she first came on, there was a murmur of surprise—matching his own—from his wife Yong-Sok. They looked at each other in wonder.

It was not Abbey's wonderful manners, or how well-prepared she was, or her huskily modulated voice, or the dove-flight. It was her face; it was a shared memory.

An hour later, in the luxuriant garden outside North Korea's White House—the Magnolia Palace—Dearest Leader walked alone, pondering on Abbey. Such a classic Japanese face! Dearest Leader and his family all remembered one just like it once on a subway forever ago—saving them...

Chapter 9

Flashback — April 2002

BEIJING – NARITA – TOKYO – A NIGHT ON ARIRANG HILL

The JAL jetliner at Beijing International had been the color of pure milky marble, and was exactly on time leaving for Singapore. The long flight was over a wilderness carpet of trees and rivers and seas so terrifyingly huge it made Jong-Nam—the future Dearest Leader—nervous. The world was so big!

His plan was all in place and surely his father Dear Leader—traveling to Russia on his special train (he would never travel any other way because of the well-known statistic of dictators most frequently dying in air accidents) spending his days trading gold on-line through Zurich and Cairo and his nights carousing and eating—would not miss him.

Jong-Nam had managed to get the false passports, despite the problems.

Money wasn't the problem, since his Visa card had a $8 million limit; secrecy was. As head of the State Security Department where espionage and false entry were routine, he had access to expert passport forgers. But the whole Agency was so full of snitches he would be found out instantly. So in Moscow a month before, he had a Russian FSB contact—happy to cultivate an incredibly high-level friend in Jong-Nam—arrange to secretly mint four elegant new République Dominicaine passports.

The green and gold covers were beautiful as Jong-Nam handed them to his wife Yong-Sok and Olathe, the Japanese nanny, who also took his son Jong-Jo's. The women tucked them happily into their Luis Vuitton handbags, and looked pleased with their matching small roller bags that were their only luggage. They were reassured by the new passports because—while they had every interest in Seeing the Elephant—it was scary as well, even if the marvelous destination beckoned brightly in all the literature.

He had booked all the flights on the Internet himself, paying considerably more to use JAL, the one Japanese carrier where they wouldn't have to switch carriers in transit. He was very proud of himself, although he hadn't really thought out the details of back-to-back nine hour flights with a transit time of five hours as well—but they just couldn't go direct.

If he had any doubts, they were dispelled by the magic the instant they boarded the flight from Beijing, and the friendly Japanese stewardess helped them with their seatbelts, found a baby-seat for Jong-Jo, and the world opened up below him.

The flight was a dream, passing over the rich countryside of southern China until Hong Kong was a teasing slap in the face with its enormous energy of a people as industrious as the Koreans. It was evening when they flew back out of Changi airport and past the sparkling beehive towers of Singapore. After the five hours of transiting and several more hours on the flight to Narita, Jong-Nam's party was wearing down and he was beginning to be unsure of himself. He worried Olathe, when confronted by her native country, would find herself so torn she would abandon or betray them, for perhaps deep inside her was the memory of being kidnapped off a beach in Japan with her mother. Yet he was counting on her. His own Japanese was mediocre, although he could read the signs in Chinese.

In the terminal at Narita, Jong-Nam and family had no idea what to do. The women were panicky in the alien airport, Jong-Jo was exhausted and crying, and Dearest Leader could only numbly follow the crowd and hope.

The immigration inspector was suspicious of their new unstamped passports—but it was 2:00 a.m., his shift was ending, and this party of overseas Koreans was so woebegone and confused—and when he heard their destination he had to grin. Also, Olathe's excellent Japanese humility reassured him. He electronically scanned their passports for the Interior Ministry, and waved them into Japan.

Past the Japanese police and out into the freedom of Japan passed the leader-to-be of North Korea. To keep from panicking Olathe more, he took the helm in finding transportation. He explained to the taxi driver where he wanted to go, but did not understand his reply. Too late, after driving only a few miles, it turned out the driver had said their destination was too far, and he could only drop them at a train station.

At the light rail station, Jong-Nam, for all the wracking of his brain, couldn't find their train. Olathe struggled to read the schedule board, since most destinations were in Kanji that she didn't know. When she did decipher a few cities like Urayasu-shi, they meant nothing to them. Jong-Nam asked tentatively at a window and was sold four tickets with grunted instructions that were very long. He could feel his fear building—he had no idea what to do next.

At the train platform he hoped for the best—and when the next train stopped he helped everyone in. The collection of people inside looked like workers, and the train stood in the station for what seemed like a long time. His fear was contagious, Olathe looking wildly around, Yong-Sok with her arms folded and withdrawing. It was into this mess that Jong-Jo awoke and started to scream.

Just as the doors were hissing closed, Olathe deciphered the PA announcement of their train's destination. She repeated, eyes growing huge with horror, "This train is the express for Shinjuku Station. No stops between here and Shinjuku!"

Olathe froze and Yong-Sok gripped his arm in panic. They were heading into the heart of Tokyo two hours away.

A well-shod foot in a blue leather pump shot out and just caught between the closing doors. The doors hissed back open. Jong-Nam looked up into the concerned face of a woman with classic Japanese features—he later would realize she seemed the *twin* of Abbey Yamamoto.

The woman smiled at them. "Are you sure this is the right train for you?" and she held the door open, much to the irritation of the other riders, who started bellowing in Japanese things like, 'What are you doing for Pete's sake we'll be a minute late you keep this up.'

"Come," she said, and helped Yong-Sok and Olathe onto the platform. As the night express to Shinjuku pulled away, Jong-Nam saw the woman glance back in regret at the departing train—he realized she was not likely to find another soon.

"Well," the woman said, patting Yong-Sok's arm, "Let us see where you want to go and get you over there, shall we?"

In the end, she corrected their tickets, walked them under a long tunnel to the correct train link, and waited with them for the right train.

His last image was of her smiling on the platform, waving.

He would never forget the kindness of that face.

* * *

The Abbey twin had been a life-saver, for within thirty minutes they were straggling into the Tokyo Bay Hilton. Jong-Nam's mean-machine-looking Visa card, the diamond-encrusted $50,000 Rolex on his wrist, Yong-Sok's pearl choker, and the boy's designer clothes made the concierge take advantage of their exhaustion and inexperience—besides, it was really right for them—and put them into the $3,000 a night Deluxe Suite on the top floor with huge bedrooms, a spacious living room, every convenience, and fresh flowers. Their passports were duly noted to be sent to the Interior Ministry in the morning.

The concierge and a manager took them up the elevator with a special key opening directly into their suite, and they were bowed into a set of rooms with a view out the windows of what seemed to Olathe and Yong-Sok an unearthly blaze of city lights unlike anything they'd ever experienced in Pyongyang.

The concierge showed Jong-Nam the bar, and then insisted on having the chef whip up a snack of Bul-go-gi right before them over a portable burner, with fresh fruit juices and pickled vegetables. It was late when all alone, Jong-Nam—his women and child safely tucked in bed and smiling in anticipation of tomorrow—sat with a Scotch at the window looking out over the lighted festival sprawl of fantasy and folklore that is Tokyo Disneyland.

* * *

Their passports were accumulated electronically with many others from Narita that night, and by 5:00 a.m., the server, separating them by country into the proper desks, batched them over to the Ministry of Interior for filing.

First thing in the morning, an alert civil servant noticed the République Dominicaine passports. He frowned as he saw the total lack of stamps of entry. It would be almost impossible to travel from the West Indies to Japan and not pick up an entry somewhere. It smelled funny. He picked up the telephone and called Narita. An hour earlier in Seoul, a Japanese reporter, who had been up all night playing cards with a Russian journalist stationed in Pyongyang, had learned that there was a scuffle about the location of Jong-Nam. As he was a highly-placed North Korean member of Dear Leader's inner family, there was a rumor of defection, and Japan would be a natural place to attempt this. The reporter called a friend at the Japanese Security Service. The security man thanked the reporter and called to alert Narita.

The boss of Customs at Narita told the security man they had not seen a single Korean man enter the country, but would watch for it. He then got a call not ten minutes later from the Interior Ministry asking *why on earth* had they passed the République Dominicaine Koreans?

Within an hour, the Japan Intelligence Services had issued a bulletin for a Korean man traveling with two women and a boy toddler. Their passport photos were provided by the Interior Ministry and disseminated up to politicians, civil servants, and police agencies at the highest levels. Although there were no photographs extant of Kim Jong-Nam—so they could not be sure it was he—everyone was informed that the Justice Minister, Cabinet Secretary Teijiro Furukawa—and Prime Minister Junichiro Koizumi—were expecting results.

The Japanese National Police scrambled and began a massive manhunt.

* * *

Mr. Fukuoka loved his job as a guard at Tokyo Disneyland. Although there were more than a million Koreans in Japan, as with most of them, he had on the surface assimilated and only his fellow Korean guards knew he was Korean. Many years ago—fifty years before 1939 when Japan started forcibly expatriating Koreans to work in Japan—his parents had emigrated to Japan for economic reasons. After the war, they had stayed as they had no place really to return to. The children had been raised in Japanese schools and the family had taken on a Japanese name for all but the most intimate family rituals of ancestor worship and genealogical recording; the Japanese policies toward Koreans were benign provided you were invisible. Mr. Fukuoka loved Japan and also felt a special attachment toward Korea as well. He was active in the Japanese Korean Association, a pro-North Korean organization that dreamed of a reunified Korea that would be a homeland to them if they ever chose.

How did it come that he recognized Jong-Nam, as there were no photos since he was a boy of ten? However it happened, something in the bearing of the confused Koreans waiting so diligently, stiff-spined as diplomats, caught his eye. Looking closely at the watches and jewelry, and at the discomfiture in the women's faces, he suddenly knew.

Mr. F hurried over to them, and bowed very low. He saw their shock and fright and opened his hands softly and gently as he spoke to them.

Speaking in careful Korean using only the most formal tenses of respect dredged up from his memory of classes in Korean grammar forty years earlier—and the slaps on the head as a child when he incorrectly addressed an elder—"Greetings, greetings. Respected Top Person, should I not be somewhat concerned that you are here in the open public?"

The man replied in Korean so fast he almost couldn't follow. It was beautiful. Korean as Mr. F had not heard in thirty years: "Alas, we are here as ourselves, and not anyone special."

"I must then ask you to come with me, as this is too uncomfortable a place to tarry." He managed to tug them along to a corner of the entrance tunnel where he knew there were no surveillance cameras.

Mr. F told them his Korean name, and said that perhaps they would come with him and leave the park before...trouble. He needed at all cost for them to avoid the humiliation, the calumny, the loss of face when the Japanese learned who he was—for there was no love in Japan for the son of a man who kidnapped Japanese off the beach and took them away never to return. Jong-Nam's father was a child-eating devil in Japan. There would be no mercy for them here.

Jong-Nam seemed so unhappy at the idea of leaving, that Mr. F's heart went out to them when he said, "You mean leave the park when we have not even started?"

"Yes, I'm afraid that you must be identified, and it will be very unpleasant."

"How so? Can they prevent us enjoying the park?"

"Exposure, even should you be fairly safe, will draw such a crowd you will be unable to breathe. It will grow and grow—and bring great unpleasantness."

Jong-Nam looked up the concrete ramp to where the sounds of organ grinders and electric trams hummed against the bright vibrant colors of Tomorrowland, happy activity almost bursting from the scene. "I cannot leave, having come so far. We will not be recognized. Thank you for your help, but we must go on."

Mr. Fukuoko thought furiously; this could only end in disaster, humiliation, shame beyond his wildest dreams of shame. He looked across the park. Even if they could make it to Fantasyland, which offered the most security and had other Korean guards, and he brought them to the front of the lines, there was still the problem they were just so...royal.

He noticed how his presence seemed to soothe the women, who were looking at him like a savior.

He knew he couldn't leave them—and they couldn't do it alone. Mr. F accepted his duty, apologized profusely.

Mr. Fukuoko bowed his head. "Perhaps a ride or two. Perhaps this and you will let me take you to a better place?"

*　*　*

By this time, the Japanese police had decided Jong-Nam was in Japan to visit the local wildlife—he must have headed straight for Tokyo's sin city of Soapyland. Hundreds of police units descended rabidly onto its five square miles of massage parlors, brothels, and steam baths with such force as to scare the pants onto a thousand sex workers and their freaked clients.

The Japanese National Police were furious as time passed and the quick catch eluded them, while all morning the Justice Minister paced his office, shouting at anyone who approached, "Why haven't you got him yet?"

Then the North Koreans' passport numbers came in.

Leaving most of the available manpower to continue the Soapyland roust, several elite units raced to raid the Tokyo Bay Hilton.

The Commissioner General of the National Police and the Superintendent General of the Tokyo Metropolitan Police both took to the air and choppered over to meet their troops at the Hilton—and see if they could help pick up the scent.

*　*　*

Working with what he could find at nearby stands, Mr. F proceeded to fashion disguises for the Koreans. Mickey ears for the nanny and child, wings and a princess halo for the wife.

Jong-Nam was the biggest problem, for with his regal posture, he stood out like a squid on a butter cookie. Finally Mr. F found a pineapple hat that was so ridiculous most people were simply too embarrassed to even think of looking closely at the wearer.

Looking over his handiwork, he still had a sinking feeling. *Just a few rides...*

Jong-Nam had smiled in agreement, Mr. F in his uniform clearing the way. Jong-Nam noticed with relief that this official escort immediately reassured the women, and both Yong-Sok and Olathe seemed—as if following a tour guide—ready to have fun.

Mr. F felt a small tugging at his pants. Olathe and Yong-Sok smiled as Mr. F picked up the squealing, wide-eyed, thrilled child of four, to whom heaven had just descended to earth and was now all around him.

Jong-Jo said, "All that!" and pointed (to the great trepidation of Mr. F) not just to the nearby Mr. Toad's Wilde Ride—but to the myriad of wonders whirling and swooping beyond.

* * *

By the time the Japanese National Police got to the Hilton suite, they were panicked enough so as soon as their Commissioner arrived they just kicked in the door. In the middle of ransacking the place and finding nothing, a frantic radio report came in from Soapyland.

On seeing the hunted man's passport photo, one sex worker named Sonoda—described a few days later by her Tokyo tabloid interviewer as having long hair and voluptuous curves, and being 'The star attraction at Bathhouse Y' (one of the area's more deluxe establishments charging visitors 80,000 yen for two hours of sudsy revelry)—was quoted as saying, "I thought my heart would stop when I found out who he really was! I know him! He always wore a diamond Rolex, a polo shirt under a vest, and had a gold Korean chain around his neck."

Because she neglected to mention the incident she barely remembered was several months ago, this lead inspired the police to even more headstrong action.

The Commissioner General of the National Police was standing at the window of Jong-Nam's suite—fuming and looking over Disneyland—when he heard the report. He turned from the view of the amusement park and yelled at his men, "He has got to be at Soapyland. Tear the place apart!"

*   *   *

Mr. F looked out at the swirling primary-color-splashed world of Disney Tokyo. He knew the day was going to be terrible. There was disaster written all over the flowing bubbling rivers with paddleboats full of exuberant people, the swirling sparkle of the mad tea party ride, and the laughing baby elephants of the Dumbo merry-go-round.

While Mr. F saw ahead of him only a day of utter catastrophe—for the North Koreans, it was *epic!*

With every one of their nerve-endings tingling, completely over-stimulated, ears buzzing, satisfyingly stuffed with rough new foods like a squid pizza and endless sticks of sweet succulent yakatori, their noses sunburned, and hanging on for dear life in what most of the world would consider fairly mild entertainment park fare, they were in Heaven. If their backs were sore from the rollercoaster turns and their eyeballs and minds zooming at the speed of light, their souls were in nothing short of Nirvana. It was when Jong-Nam insisted on a third time through 'It's a Small World' and was mopping his tears unashamedly at the beautiful song—and noting that Korea needed a much much bigger presence—that they reached the zenith.

Jong-Nam looked at Mr. F and realized, though a fog of adrenaline and endorphins, that Mr. F was shaking and sweating and approaching a nervous breakdown.

At 4:00 p.m., the North Koreans finally allowed Mr. Fukuoka to drag them from the park.

*   *   *

It was lucky they left when they did, for by the afternoon the National Police had finished tearing the Hilton and Soapyland apart to no result, and someone—based on Jong-Nam apparently having brought to Japan something that resembled family—finally overcame the Confucian proscription against daring to suggest to his most senior Commissioner that he might be wrong by off-handedly mentioning—perhaps—they should search the park.

They narrowly missed actually catching the future Dearest Leader. But they not only missed the North Koreans, they also missed many guards from the early shift who had seen Mr. F acting mighty strangely. Of the few guards left, several were Korean and covered for Mr. F, knowing the score. When the police tried to find the off-duty guards by phone, understandably many of them couldn't be reached. When there were enough sightings of Jong-Nam and yet he clearly was no longer in the park—it took them several hours to search it—the policed fanned out into Tokyo to interview the guards.

They were further hampered by the fact that many guards lived hours away. They would not raid Mr. F's house until 5:00 a.m.

With the many reported sightings of Jong-Nam in the park, the Commissioner finally called a halt to 'Operation Soapyland.' By that time, his police had rousted the bathhouse area so thoroughly they left the whole *Cho* in shock—and blasted into red-faced fury and embarrassment a large number of very influential businessmen and politicians.

It was a day the Commissioner of the National Police and the Superintendent of the Tokyo Metropolitan Police were to rue for many a year.

*　*　*

It was a thing of beauty, Jong-Nam reflected. Mr. F had borrowed a Disney van—convincing Jong-Nam not to return to the hotel but instead—it was all he could think of—to come to Mr. F's house in Nan-to Cho. As the van crawled through downtown Tokyo, Jong-Nam soaked up the megalopolis. Past partying Roppongi and the luxe shopping of Ginza, then on through the soaring beauty of Shinjuku and the neon and spectacle of the Times Square of Japan, Jong-Nam was so far away from Pyongyang's dankness and darkness where the walls of his Agency ran in blood and the beauty of human achievement was to build forty thousand statues of two men. This, now, was a city a man would be proud to build.

When they finally arrived at Mr. F's small flat, Mrs. F immediately bustled the women into the kitchen. Their neighbors—all Koreans and to a person members of the Korean Association in Japan—began to spread the news and a trickle among them approached tentatively to visit.

Yong-Sok and Olathe were happy to find themselves in a much safer environment than the raw excitement of Disneyland. They got to hear first hand from the other women about pesticides and why you have to soak cabbage overnight to remove them, the cost of garlic in Japan, the difficulty of getting really good but cheap Korean red pepper, and how the women's maternity hospital system worked.

The trickle of Koreans from the neighborhood turned into a deluge. Overseas Koreans living in Japan, dying for a word from home, came to pay respects to their amazing hero who was fighting for the freedom of all Korea, the One Korea. All evening long, the procession continued until the pile of gifts such as $100 melons and Ginseng roots and chocolates throughout the house was seriously cutting into the party's maneuvering space.

After a good meal, Yong-Sok insisted everyone crowd into the living room. This was contrary to custom, where the women were relegated to the kitchen for the evening, but being royalty, Yong-Sok could have what she wanted. For the future Dearest Leader, he later remembered this best: a poor high-rise flat in a forgotten neighborhood of Tokyo where the struggle for a decent life was almost as hard as in North Korea.

As he sat in the chair of honor, feeling these things, the daughter-in-law of the house was called. She sat, strummed the dulcimer-like geomungo, and tears came to his eyes as she sang:

> Arirang Arirang Arariyo
> Arirang all alone, I am crossing Arirang Hill.
> If you leave me, my love, if you leave me, my love,
> Your feet will fail you before you have even walked
> Ah, even walked ten steps.

> Arirang Arirang Arariyo
> Arirang I believed you when you told me
> We were going to Arirang Hill for a spring picnic.
> With a bottle of rice wine hidden under my blue skirt,
> I looked for you, my love, in our secret spot,
>   in Odong, Odong forest.
> You were so beautiful and superior,
> And I was so crazy and blind and willing to bleed.

> Arirang Arirang Arariyo
> Arirang; give me my love back, on Arirang Hill.
> Arirang; give me my love back, on Arirang Hill.

*   *   *

The North Koreans left before dawn. Mr. F's son drove the van, while he himself could only fit in the very back lying on the luggage. His son had found a flight to Beijing on the Internet, and though expensive, it was agreed after phone calls from other Korean guards at Disneyland that time was not on their side.

Jong-Nam remembered coming into Narita, meaning 'Becoming Rice Fields.' It was indeed becoming rice fields compared to Tokyo. He looked out at the impossibly fertile Japanese paddies, a level of agricultural richness only dreamt of in Korea whose shallow rocky basins of fertilized land were created, not indigenous. Why, here just around the airport was almost the rice production of a huge part of North Korea. The cyclone of jumbo planes, even this early in the morning, coming in for landing on either side of them, was exhilarating. Pyongyang airport was complete dead; it had exactly one flight per day.

"Yes," said Mr. F, "The airport would be even busier, except they are unable to get the land to expand onto."

Jong-Nam noticed big red buses idling on ramps, looking as if they might roll down onto the airport access road any moment. He asked about them, and Mr. F's son laughed, called over his shoulder in English, "Shit happens."

Had Mr. F been able to reach his son, he would have slapped him on the head for his rudeness, but instead explained gravely. "There are sometimes terrorist attacks on the airport. In the event of an attack, the buses block the road and seal the airport."

Jong-Nam absorbed this. "Terrorists?" and he got the scoop from Mr. F. A tiny number of people dissented in this society, in this case farmers who did not want Narita to expand. "They refuse to sell their land to the government, for any price."

Jong-Nam struggled with this. "The airport is severely overcrowded...and yet the government cannot take the land to use for the people?"

Mr. F smiled. "When the Americans ruled Japan after the war, they seized all the big land-owners' holdings—almost 90% of the land. They gave this land to the share-cropping farmers who had worked for the land-owners. When the Americans left, the Japanese decided they never wanted the government to be able to take land again." He grinned suddenly from his perch on the luggage. "And now the rice farmers, to whom the Americans gave the land, are fighting the importing of American rice!"

"It is all very strange," said Jong-Nam.

"People are very strange," said Mr. Fukuoko, adding with excellent English intonation, "People: you cannot live with them, and you cannot live without them!"

The future Dearest Leader thought this was the funniest thing he had ever heard. He made Mr. F teach him over and over again until he himself could say it with just the right ironic tones. Then he asked, "What does it mean, 'Shit Happens'?"

* * *

Insisting Mr. F drop them off outside, within thirty seconds of entering Narita terminal they were arrested. "What will happened to Mr. F?" Yong-Sok whispered as they were rudely hustled along by the police. Jong-Nam whispered back not to worry, although he knew from the treatment they were getting—being in the security biz himself—that Mr. F was *fucked*.

There was on-and-off interrogation all day, and when asked who he was, Jong-Nam replied he was Kim Jong-Il's son, and he and family were just visiting Disneyland.

The newspapers—who were told the family had been arrested upon entry at Narita—eagerly picked up the story, reporting that the family spent the night separated in the detention facility for illegal immigrants in Ushiku near the airport. Jong-Nam was housed in the standard male quarters with his son, and ate the same meals as others detained at the facility. Apparently, he talked with the other detainees, everyone liked him, and when he left he shook hands with the warden and said, "Thanks for taking good care of us."

While the Narita Police were questioning him, a bitter fight raged in Tokyo. The National Police Commissioner—who had personally looked like an idiot while his forces raided Soapyland to no effect and also humiliated the Metropolitan Police by demanding their help (and then got laughed at by the third-rate Narita security who got the credit)—was spittle-spraying angry and insistent on an arrest. The meeting ended, failing to reach a consensus on whether to arrest the detainees—or simply deport them.

When the fierce debate picked up the next day, Prime Minister Koizumi settled it—knowing full well he had no interest in arresting a possible future head of state who might one day be sitting across the Sea of Japan with nuclear-tipped missiles and bitterness in his heart. Koizumi sent word through Cabinet Secretary Furukawa to deport Jong-Nam, saying "His identity does not appear confirmed."

The Justice Minister, furious at the kid-glove treatment afforded the prisoner who had run them all ragged and made his Commissioner extremely unpopular with certain politicians who'd been in Soapyland—and further insulted their investigative prowess by claiming they hadn't even identified the man!—excused himself and was followed out by his aide, who knew exactly what his boss wanted, but could never do. From a stall in the gents, the aide made a cell phone call to Nippon Television.

Within an hour of the deportation decision, the Chinese embassy liaison in Tokyo showed up at Narita and certified a visa for four unnamed persons of unknown origin clearing them to enter China.

But before Jong-Nam and family could board the prepping JAL flight to

Beijing, a news team from Nippon TV got onto the tarmac at Narita where the North Koreans were waiting for their flight. The news team got good clear shots of the lovely wife and nanny—and the chubby bespectacled future Dearest Leader—before they entered the 747 where the entire upper cabin had been reserved for them.

The Japanese journalist who had given the original tip had now spent more than forty-eight hours continuously drinking and playing cards and waiting and was close to collapse when he finally got his payback with a tip from the security man on Jong-Nam's flight to Beijing.

The news team he called in Beijing was less fortunate than Nippon TV. On the way to the airport a big white Benz limousine expertly ran their van into a ditch. Coincidentally, a few moments later, it was a big white Benz, one of twelve in the motorcade, which entered the diplomatic gate at Beijing International and whisked the wayward family away unseen.

*   *   *

Mr. Fukuoka did not lose his job at Disneyland. After being questioned at length by the police—who were unable to charge him—they vindictively sent his boss at Disneyland a demand that he be fired. On the day Jong-Nam returned to Pyongyang, two polite Korean *Yakuza* visited the boss's wife at home. Whatever they said, Mr. F was at once demoted to garbage man. Three months later he was quietly reinstated as a guard.

For Dearest Leader, a long month passed before his father Kim Jong-Il would talk to him—and it was not pleasant. On the other hand, Jong-Nam was not at all the same man who had left ten days before on a runaway trip. Before the trip, Jong-Nam had been restive, perhaps anxious, about the future, the outside world. The Japanese were—however nice their country—rude and arrogant and the enemy. Now he realized what Korea could become.

His father finished yelling at him about the humiliating news stories, ending up with the intended crushing blow: he had changed his will. When he died, he would not leave the country to Jong-Nam.

Jong-Nam didn't worry. He told his father that he, Jong-Nam, was a foolish boy. Having seen the deplorable state of the world outside the sacred borders of the DPRK, he would now rededicate his life to the paradise that was North Korea. He requested, no, demanded, that his father assign him to a clothing collective in a northern province. "Father, my desire to leave is gone. It is as the Great Leader said: the key to history is not the struggle of the worker with the oppressor. It is that human activity can transform history. I wish now to take action."

Within a year, he was back in Pyongyang, again head of the State Security Department, which monitored and watched all the citizens of North Korea—including Il-Moon, whom he cultivated carefully. If his father Dear Leader thought he would not be next, he would be wrong.

When the Dear Leader Kim Jong-Il, affectionately known by his foreign kitchen staff as 'Pork Chop,' was years later struck down at his Fragrant Mountain Dacha with a stroke, Jong-Nam had the machine of State Security purring along for himself—and no one was ever more ready to use it for a good cause.

His father's case of apoplexy luckily happened during an argument with Jong-Nam, who let the stroke go untreated: when Kim Jong-Il clutched his head, falling, Jong-Nam locked the door. During the next two days he let no one into his father's room—especially the doctors. Jong-Nam sat on the bed by his father, neither drinking nor eating until his father's labored breathing hitched—and stopped. It was justice of a sort. Jong-Nam knew Dear Leader had similarly sat by his father the Great Leader for the two days it took him to die of his untreated heart attack—and so had similarly come to the throne. As badly as Jong-Nam felt about it, there was a kind of closure in it.

No one who had been in the dacha for those two days survived the following purges. On the return to Pyongyang, the two lead choppers of doctors and nurses accompanying his father's body in the rear chopper suddenly and mysteriously crashed. The rumor was they actually were blown out of the air by two SA-7 guided anti-air missiles. Dearest Leader was not truly ruthless; it was more that he was clear-headed. He had a dream and he would not pale from any necessity. Further purges were coordinated and carried out with Il-Moon—at a price which cemented their bargain—until finally Dearest Leader had truly assumed the throne.

As Dearest Leader's consciousness returned from his reminiscences he remembered Abbey's face and those moments in Tokyo. He had seen a vision of beauty and its name was Japan. He knew that anything Japan could do, Korea could also. He went inside from his gardens to his bed under the Magnolia Palace, smiling at the beauty of the dream he was about to bring home.

Chapter 10

The 7th of October (USA)

PENTAGON E-RING – USAF UNDER SECRETARY (S&T)

Promptly at 7:00 p.m., Sean walked into Jeanette's office high up in E-Ring above the Pentagon's River Entrance.

Home to the military's highest executives, such offices looked out over the Potomac to the D.C. side and beyond to the layer-cake government buildings, the tidal basin monuments, and the White House. Jeanette had a straight shot across to the Washington Monument. More than once Sean had watched the lights on it blink off, signaling that midnight had come while he and Jeanette worked late in her office.

In such SES—Senior Executive Service—offices, no posters or replicas of art were allowed. The only acceptable forms of wall ornamentation were mounted awards and original oil paintings. Jeanette had oils of Army Air Force planes flying missions over Europe, future aircraft not yet off the drawing board, and a portrait of Dr. Theodore von Karman, her mentor and founder of NASA's Jet Propulsion Laboratory and the first scientific advisor to the Air Force.

The waiting room was large, paneled with gleaming wood, and the office furniture was polished teaks and mahogany. Sean calculated out of the twenty thousand offices in the Pentagon, only perhaps one hundred were furnished like this.

Sean always wondered where the luxury furniture department for this high-end stuff was. Deep under the Pentagon, in some sub-subbasement was a stash of very beautiful antique office furniture and oil paintings, right down to teak coffee tables and Cloisonné lamps and silk flowers and cherry sideboards.

Such furniture was part of the process of political appointments—for all of the offices high in E-Ring were political jobs. When the change of guard inevitably happened, new appointees would rudely barge in during the remaining days of the old administration, walk right past your—the incumbent's desk—look out the window and say, "Sorry, I'm picking an office."

There you were, a seasoned senior political appointee in your wonderful office you had chosen—what, about four years ago when your champion had won the race? You barely remember now—with all the blood since spilled, the wear and trauma of the eighty-hour work weeks, and the constant crises—what those first halcyon days had been like.

Now here's your first indication it is finally over. Suddenly, looking out your window is the new Appointee. Dressing sharp and looking sharper, s/he comes in, glances with dissatisfaction at your interior decoration, your secretary, your visitors' book, your paintings, and without even really noticing you, looks out into the parking lot you haven't had the time or the energy to eye-ball for years, and says, "Not a bad view. Better than so-and-so's. How do I get new furniture?"

Sean had expected to find Jeanette buried, busy, and behind schedule. Instead, she was at the window, pensive, looking out over D.C. Perhaps she was thinking ahead to the relief of just that moment when the next tenant—the next Temp—reported for duty and showed her the door.

Jeanette wore a creamy fluffy blouse and dark skirt; her red-blonde hair was in a chignon, and her silk dress jacket on her roll-back leather chair.

She looked up at Sean and although there was still a trace of anger in those golden-brown eyes, she said, "You know Dave, right?"

"Hello Dave." Sean shook hands with the major, a new guy. Jeanette preferred to work with a single more junior exec, although she did have Colonels and Lt Colonels answering phones and keeping her calendar.

Jeanette motioned them to the conversation grouping of chairs and sat, waving Sean to a seat next to her. Dave brought them coffee. She said, "I was talking with the Secretary, and he said he would be interested to know what you have come up with."

Dave signed for Sean's couriered Top Secret working papers, and acknowledged they were now in his care, and closed the door. With the door secured, Sean flipped through his charts on the low polished cherry table before them. Skipping over the mess of the treaty inspection, as Jeanette and Dave exchanged pained expressions, Sean hurried on to Emily's estimates of the unaccounted processed nuke fuel rods.

Jeanette's hand flew up to her mouth. "Who was this science person?"

Sean admitted he had looked everywhere, and couldn't find her.

Jeanette chuckled politely, "You don't even know your source?"

"Actually, forgetting about my slight difficulties there, I went back and started all over with the unexplained explosion in Namp'o harbor. You heard about this?"

"It was in the NIE"—National Intelligence Estimate—"this week. It's considered an accident."

Sean produced the DIA Osan Detachment's T+2 hour brief. He flipped to an infrared satellite image of the water with a large white object floating in it. "Several image analysts have gone over this, and post-processed the images—

the originals were too blurry or degraded to really see well."

Dave remarked, "Well, they didn't improve the clarity. It looks like Casper the Friendly Ghost chewing on a hunk of Mozzarella."

Sean smiled, "Exactly. They got carried away with the edge sharpening. Even though you can't identify the object, you can measure it to be exactly thirty meters across with proportions of 6.3 to 2.4. Further, look at it sparkle in the searchlights. This is a Cinespark 2001 movie screen. Fewer than one hundred of these have been made, each costing almost one million dollars. For use in 70mm cinema entertainment systems."

"What would a cinema screen be doing in Namp'o harbor?"

"The only explanation is that it was in a huge high-class underwater movie auditorium."

"It makes no sense for there to be a theater under Namp'o Bay," said Dave. "Most people think a submarine or naval vessel we didn't see blew up. The screen could have been on a boat, being transported."

"There were no big surface craft near at the time of the explosions. Their subs are tiny. After the explosion, I counted more than seventy people in the water." Sean pointed to the waspish looking vessel in the picture. "The only North Korean ship with a crew of that size is their frigate *Inchon*—and it's right here in the midst of the rescue operation. Also—note the people being rescued look to be wearing uniforms and Tuxedos."

Jeanette pushed on small reading glasses, studying the pictures while Dave looked unconvinced. "Tuxedos? You can't tell from these alone, can you?"

"True. Except there was also an incredibly high-level emergency response to the disaster. What would make them scramble so many ships in such a panicked mode? The SIGINT data showed the North Koreans reacted as if they had not one second to even worry if they were being monitored. No radio discipline at all. You know, radio discipline is the first thing to go when the excrement hits the flinger. Completely unlike if it had been a training accident. Someone very important was in the water."

Sean continued, "So now we have seventy important Tuxedoed people in North Korea watching a movie at the bottom of Namp'o Bay—in the military part of the harbor. Given the love Dear Leader and his son Dearest Leader have for cinema, I can draw no other conclusion than that this screen and other debris is flotsam from Dear Leader's legendary Underwater Mansion."

Jeanette, who was ahead of him, nodded, while Dave whistled. "One of his supposedly most expensive and fantastic extravagances. But we don't really know anything about it first hand, as you say it's legendary—not confirmed."

Sean handed over a picture of a barge hoisting a car from dark water. "I had a trained INTEL guy confirm my ID of this car. Far too valuable to leave under Namp'o." In the photo, the elegant silver car hung like a dead fish from a crane swinging it up onto a barge. "From the wreckage site, they're recovering a mint-condition Rolls Royce Silver Shadow sedan." He paused, watching Jeanette think.

Jeanette meditatively answered, "You know, I've always wanted to make love in the back seat of a Silver Shadow."

Her exec Dave looked slightly shocked, while Sean—who knew her silly streak pretty well—grinned.

"Alright," Jeanette said. "You're the swing vote," with a questioning head gesture to Dave, who slowly worked through it out loud. "The underwater mansion would be part R&R spot, part business center, and part official whore house—hence the Rolls at eighty feet below."

"Exactly." Sean nodded. "Every luxury hotel should have a Rolls in their Kinky Suite."

"So what happened? An accident?"

Sean shook his head 'no,' showing the missile launch detection satellite data. "There was a series of three separate very hot explosions."

"You mean, like boiler or a magazine going up?"

"No. It was ordnance detonating—and not by accident or inside a hull. It was a well coordinated attack on the mansion, probably by a surface vessel."

"You're guessing."

Sean nodded slightly to acknowledge this truth. "Hakkermann in his report to State Ops said Dearest Leader had a freshly broken arm."

Jeanette put aside her small reading glasses. "So, Sean, how do you read it?"

"Someone tried to sink Dearest Leader in as audacious an assassination attempt as there has ever been. Further, they likely succeeded in killing a good number of his friends."

"There are other problems with that," Dave mused. "Getting a boat in undetected over the mansion would be impossible, they would have a thousand security forces—literally—everywhere. If they did blow the mansion, why are all those people in the water alive? In particular, how did Dearest Leader escape? I can't imagine a group competent enough to get this far and not pull it off."

Sean put down images of Col Kang climbing the walls before dying in the bungled execution. "Six days after the Namp'o incident, there was a big assembly of Special Forces and a stoning. Not that unusual, but I was puzzled because such executions usually go off pretty simply. The officers in the assassination attempt would have confessed to save their families—everyone in Korea has family to protect. It started normally, calm and controlled, then suddenly the officer went bananas; yelling, running."

"Why would he go crazy?"

"In the execution battalion, somehow during the processional, he must have learned something and freaked." Sean flipped to another page, "So I looked around, and found," he showed Jeanette and Dave, pointing a finger at satellite images of a crude cortege of coffins. "Dawn the day before, at the February 27th Work Camp. Seven coffins, three children's. The officer would have confessed at his trial to save his family, but they butchered them anyway. Terrorizing your officer corps won't keep you in power long. The regime is about to crumble."

Jeanette leaned back. "You mean, there are still more conspirators out there."

"Yes. Who knows what is going on in the ranks. Not just fools, either. Il-Moon must know there is a highly capable bunch gunning for him, and being pulled in a fishnet from the bottom of Namp'o Bay would be enough to wake up anyone. Now, boom, within a couple of weeks, peace treaty talks? How could those things be unconnected?"

Dave shook his head negatively. "That makes no sense either. You don't have a public funeral for the family. First, you want to motivate confessions. If you go after the families, you have no leverage and you turn your enemies into suicide attackers—they have nothing to lose. Also, even if you do kill them, why display the fact with the coffins in broad daylight? Why not cremate them and shovel the ashes out with the rubbish?

"Further, why even kill the family? Unless they knew something, what would be the point? They are no threat. Yes, they would be 'crossed out' in terms of normal North Korean society, but that is a far cry from killing family. They are supposed to suffer as an example anyway. Even more, Dearest Leader hasn't shown himself to be that kind of ruthless. There is every indication once his power is consolidated, he will be admirably reasonable—for a North Korean leader."

Sean knew these were major problems. "You want people to know, is all I can think. I don't know. But the number of conspirators must be increasing. If I were Il-Moon, I'd be seriously watching my back—and he may be desperate."

Dave interrupted, "But what is the connection?"

Sean said, "With several kilograms of Plutonium kicking around there, with the peace treaty so sudden after the assassination attempt—bottom line, Jeanette, you know this peace treaty proposal is bullshit. Having Il-Moon as peace negotiator is like having the Marquise de Sade as your physical therapist. Whatever he's up to isn't peace."

"I'm not sure it's proof, Sean. But I agree it's very worrying. So, you want us to do...what?"

"Get me back to Korea. Get me on the inspection team."

Jeanette's gold eyes flashed, although her velvety voice roughened only a trace. "Korea is Hakkermann's ballgame—and you've struck out."

"Then let me go in with a Special Ops team. I'll get you proof!"

"Oh, highly likely. I'd need presidential approval and I somehow don't see it forthcoming. He likes Hakkermann. A lot of us do, within limitations. He's the chief negotiator. An Ambassador at Large. Do you know what that means?"

"He's politically connected."

"A resounding understatement. His rank in this matter is essentially presidential."

"So I'm supposed to sit this one out?"

Jeanette would never remind someone it was their own fault. Instead, she moved on. "I have something else for you," and handed Sean a photo of a jumbo Boeing 747-400F freighter with an odd looking nose and strange unit symbols and gear. "One of my programs for future warfare technologies. Airborne Laser."

"I'm up on the program." Sean said. "A-B-L for short. Anti-missile planes. They patrol near a hostile country. If ballistic missiles are launched, ABL smokes them with a laser. None of it works yet. Missile Defense Agency has the SPO going, but it's years away from completion."

Jeanette smiled, said, "The official project, yes. This is Airborne Laser (Experimental) or ABL(X). It's our little secret, my lab prototype, and it's almost finished. I just need someone to go get them past being *almost* operational."

"Great work, Jeanette. But I belong in Korea."

"You know missiles, you've worked technology transition."

"I'm not going to baby-sit some partially-baked project while my country goes wrong."

"Sean, you are one of the few people who know how important this might be in Korea. Theater missile defense would be a place you could contribute, even if you aren't on the ground in Treaty Ops."

"Almost operational?"

"They're close, but I don't know. I hear rumors. Would you go for a few weeks and get them back on track?"

Sean shook his head. "A complex weapons system, a laboratory prototype, no ConOps, no testing, no procedures, no nothing—no chance."

"Just a lookey-loo from you, and they'll be turning cartwheels in days."

"I hate to destroy your pathetic faith in me, but unless I see them in real action it'll take weeks just to learn the basics."

"Well isn't this just serendipity! In two days I'm part of Roving Sands war-games. How about you play in that?"

Sean knew Roving Sands. A huge theater-scale war-game in the American southwest, with an emphasis on missile defense. He shook his head 'no.' "I'm Treaty Ops."

Dave, into the silence that followed, innocently asked, "So, how are you enjoying Logistics?"

Corralled. Sean took a long moment without replying. The light he had hoped was still on had burned out long ago; and yet he saw a glimmering. "You get us into Roving Sands and I'll go play project officer. If I get Airborne Laser operational, I know you want it in Korea. So promise me Korea."

"No promises, Sean. Except that you will get a fair chance at doing whatever is best once this is done. So, go and do the job—and without telling anyone you would like to deploy to Korea. That must come later."

BOOK 3

"Find people to help you."

The AFRL Project Officer's Third Commandment

Chapter 11

The 8th of October

AIRBORNE LASER COMPLEX – AFRL – KIRTLAND AFB

The waspish C-38 Learjet with the seal of the Secretary of the Air Force banked, and Sean caught sight of rugged mountains with pink granite faces overlooking the pointillist desert, vast suburbs, and shiny new downtown that is Albuquerque on the Rio Grande. Along the river, the neat furze of the *Bosque*—the Spanish term for the river-bottom bramble of salt cedar and Russian olive under ninety-foot cottonwoods—was still lime-green, softly edging the muddy ribbon of river against the spreading desert.

Below in the spacious wild desert south of the city lay Kirtland Air Force Base. Hemmed in by rugged mountains and Indian reservation, the eighty square miles of open land was home to a big science community, varied wildlife, and all kinds of unique test facilities. Sean had transited through Kirtland many times, and along the huge 14,000-foot runway, besides the F-16's of the Tacos—the local Air National Guard—he could make out Sandia National Laboratories where he had teamed up with various technical groups on treaty Ops. On the west side of the base, the domino tiles of the Air Force Research Laboratory—The AFRL—clustered in a set of geometric offices, domes, chemical facilities, and laboratories. Just off the end of the flight line, on the far less populated south side of the base, he made out a huge hangar. Alongside it was an oddly equipped white 747-400F freighter, which must be his destination...

Jeanette's SECAF Learjet taxied off the far end of the runway to the flight line gate out to ABL's apron. The Learjet stopped and let Sean, carrying only a duffle bag and a laptop, down to the tarmac. He walked the few remaining yards to where waiting Security Forces police rolled ABL's big flight line gate open a crack to let him walk the taxiway to ABL.

The taxiway ran a hundred yards across a highway to an apron with its enormous attendant hangar. Alongside, Airborne Laser sat docked to a big support structure hung with umbilicals carrying power, chemicals, communications, and fuels.

As Sean crossed the hangar lot, he could see more details of the big aircraft. The big bulbous nose held a huge optic, a glittering mirror as tall as a person. Other instruments stuck out along the body of the aircraft, and he could place only half of them. Painted along the upper fuselage was a row of unit shields:

the flying winged sword of Air Combat Command, the Missile Defense Agency logo, and the stars and launching spaceship of the Air Force Research Laboratory. Separately, apparently hand-painted locally, was the Airborne Laser's individual unit shield of a flying rattlesnake shooting down a missile.

The shields caught the afternoon sun, giving Sean a pleasant tremor as, dwarfed, he walked under ABL, and strains of Rock and Roll came to him just as he smelled barbecue.

Marine Captain Jay 'Jarhead' Hull, ABL's Air Defenses officer, worked the guts of vicious-looking Gatling guns mounted in ABL's belly. He was late twenties, smooth-faced, squared jawed, and had the easy athleticism of someone to whom grueling daily workouts were routine. Greasy-handed, Jarhead saluted Sean. Seeing the duffle bag and the hundred-yard stare of an officer showing up for a new assignment, he added, "Abandon hope all ye officers who enter here."

Sean smiled, returned the salute. "Major Phillips. Sean. Those look like Phalanx Gatling guns. Usually, for ship air defense close-in."

"For this particular mission, we need a concentrated inner-ring air defense. We had some weight margin...I trimmed back the mounts some...I thought... so we'll see..."

Sean slipped into Marinespeak. "So, was it a GOBI?" *General Officer bright idea.*

"No, it was a BOGSAT." *Bunch of guys/gals sitting around a table talking.*

"So now it's up and running?"

"Right, we're just doing a FAWCIT." *Fuck around, we'll call it training.*

Sean waited, but the marine clearly had run out of things to say, so Sean nodded and stepped out from under the massive ABL to see a USAF family picnic. Children ran and barbecues smoked. ABL crew in flight suits munched, chatted with spouses, and tended babies. From their demeanor and grooming, despite the flight suits, Sean could see many of the crew were not officers but rather USAF civilians.

Nearby, a scrum of crew and children of all ages were playing touch football—and doing it quite badly. Sean caught sight of a willowy young woman bobbing, weaving, and going out for a pass right toward Sean. Raven mop of hair flying, graceful and yet unskilled—

Emily! The Emily of the North Korean inspection!

Sean dropped his bags and cut into her pass pattern. Neatly, he timed the quarterback's throw and intercepted her pass.

Given the state of the defense—a dozen children all under ten—Sean ran in slow motion up the field, dodging the kid tacklers as if moving through honey. Suddenly, he was really bogged down as a child glommed onto his leg. Slowing to a galumphing walk, *Bam!* someone much larger than a kid—the firm curvy feel of Emily!—had jumped onto his back. The rest of the Airborne Laser kids swarmed over him and they all went down in a laughing pile.

Sean helped the kids and Emily up, she shaking her head in wonder. She wore her moppet of black hair in a rough French braid secured with a scrunchie, a faded flight suit with few badges, the top of the suit rolled down to show a clingy angora sweater over her svelte outline. She squeaked, "Sean?" then coughed and got back her usual husky voice, "Sean?"

For some reason, his eyes involuntarily darted to her left ring finger. He jerked them back to her opalescent gray eyes.

Her reaction was for the hand to fly upwards and cover her wide mouth as if in surprise. "Sean?"

No ring. Sean cleared his own heart out of his throat. "Emily? ABL Chief Scientist Emily? So Korea was you checking out the real world. Any of these yours?"

Emily stooped, pulled a child off unsteady legs and picking her up, cuddled her, replying, "Bring kidlettes into a world where I'm spending my life fighting ballistic missiles?"

Sean was startled again, pushing his brain to react smoothly, managed, "It seems pretty nice here. Besides your new anti-missile weapon—"

"—I try not to think of Airborne Laser as a weapon," Emily interrupted gently. "To me, it's a defensive system."

"We wear the white hats, remember?"

Emily cocked her head; put the child down to run free and hugged herself as if cold. "Here I was worried we might be the kind of heartless people who'd develop a secret weapon of mass destruction and then unthinkingly drop it on some defenseless Japanese city."

Sean looked at her in surprise, trying to think of an answer. "Anyhoo, thanks for the help in Korea. I owe you, although I'm not sure how I'm going to repay it."

Nearby, the picnic area, a couple dozen people watched them, glued to every move.

Emily smiled sunnily. "It is already paid. Best damned science ride—I mean inspection—I was ever on."

"*Interesting?*"

She thought about this, and somehow the word made her look around and she noticed his duffle. "Hey, I knew you liked me; I didn't think you'd find me like this."

"Maybe running into you at the donut machine in the Pentagon?"

"I don't eat donuts. Well, I was expecting you'd find me somehow through DIA, tap my phone, read my email, get to know what latte flavor I like, whether I'm a dog or cat person, then just turn up casually—surprisingly, enchantingly, completely compatible with me—'Just thought I'd return your scanner'...isn't that the Sparrow's way?"

"The Sparrow is the female entrapping spy. The male is the Sparrow Hawk."

"The male version then."

"Contrary to your inaccurately low opinion of me, I'm as pleasantly surprised as you. I am not a spy. I'm Korea Treaty Operations."

"Still?"

"Well, no."

"Then if I haven't drawn you to the Land of Enchantment," using the tourist slogan for New Mexico, "what are you doing in my pass pattern?"

"I hate to say it—I'll be a nice as I can about this—I'm your new project officer."

"You are?" Sean could almost see a kind of a shudder run up her spine and tingle her brain. "Following your minor lapse of diplomatic *savoir faire,* I thought you'd be banished to outer darkness."

"So you know Jeanette, too? She gave me this assignment."

It was Emily's turn to grimace, then she laughed. "I need a tiger team. Jeanette sends me a very large twelve-year-old."

"I make a wonderful twelve-year-old tiger. *All I Really Need to Know I Learned in Kindergarten* is my favorite book if that's a help."

Emily looked apprehensive, worried, one more surprise. Actually, Emily was thinking, *I can't believe I'm already wanting him.* "Walk with me," and she moved toward ABL, putting a little distance between them and the curious stares of the ABL families and crew.

As they walked toward ABL, Sean noticed little yellow flags on wires stuck around a prairie dog hole. "A tripping hazard?"

"Oh, it's a family of New Mexico burrowing owl. They're endangered and so we don't disturb them, see?"

Sure enough, when Sean looked closely, three small owls—Mommy, Daddy, and Baby all dressed in their desert camouflage of golden speckled feathers—sat atop the open burrow looking right at him with wide shiny eyes.

"Don't you have to kill the rattlers that come around?"

"I'm a pacifist," Emily said with deep seriousness. "We've defanged all the snakes for a mile around."

"What?" Sean managed.

Emily grinned, "You really are out of your depth here," touched his sleeve, moved into his space, looking him in the eyes. "Did you know this burrowing owl is one of the very few owls whose visual acuity is the same day and night?"

Her eyes were a little owlish, and he let himself go into them. "I want to know about the snakes."

"Oh, we relocate the curious ones to across the arroyo," pointing to the deeply water-scoured gully running behind the hangar.

"You don't have return customers?"

"Only one. You'll meet later."

They stopped on the airstairs up to the 747's passenger hatch, and in the more private space, Emily and Sean leaned against the railings on opposite sides. Emily finally spoke, "As project officer, I hope your qualifications aren't that you go ballistic every time you smell something funny. Oh. Sorry," hoping he didn't think she was referring to the Korea incident. "I mean, I didn't think Jeanette could find an officer crazy enough to come down here. We've had kind of a high attrition rate. Not our fault, mind you."

"I'll try to live down to your expectations. Meantime, I'm also the bearer of good news: we have orders to fly, in two days, in Roving Sands war-games."

WYNDHAM HOTEL – ALBUQUERQUE AIRPORT

Through the telescope, the science girl's reaction to whatever the tall straight guy had said was so sudden her motion affected the big auto-focus mechanism and it whirred and whined, trying to compensate for the suddenly blurred image.

Spiney had immediately picked up on the arrival of the SECAF Learjet. He knew it well as a C-38A, the militarized version of the intercontinental Astra SPX business Learjet. He always monitored the radio traffic of the ATC tower and so knew a VIP was flying in. When the sleek swept-wing jet landed right past the terminal, he got a good shot of its tail number and blue and gold emblem. He knew this plane was mainly used to transport DV's—Distinguished Visitors— the official designation for the most senior civilian government officials.

The SECAF Learjet surprised Spiney by not pulling in at Flight Ops. Instead, it taxied to the far end of the runway near the ABL hangar. Because the C-38 was in high demand by VIP's, flew farther and faster than the old C-21, could hold up to eight passengers very comfortably, and with its range of 3,600 miles had a U.S. coast-to-coast capability under virtually any weather conditions, Spiney was doubly surprised when the Learjet, before wheeling around and immediately taking off, deplaned to the ABL flight line gate only a single young officer.

A grunt, obviously. Not even any decent luggage—only a brief case and shapeless duffle bag. *What's a jazzy bird like that doing delivering a single Gomer?*

Now, he studied the pictures flying by from the big Hasselblad on continuous exposure—high quality electronic stills showing the virginal college girl's arms fly up and her profile sharpen for a moment. Her passionate reaction to whatever the straight ramrod of a guy—*what a Gomer!*—made her look sexy as hell and Spiney's lower brain kicked into a new gear. *I'd like to see this college girl gone wild....*

Spiney saw the Gomer working to sooth the science girl. He was still watching a few minutes later when, together, the college girl and the Gomer scrambled the crew.

AIRBORNE LASER – AIRSTAIRS

Sean had waited patiently until Emily stopped storming around. She finally ran down, sat on the bottom step of the self-contained air stairs that folded down from under ABL's passenger door, and squinted at him. "You don't believe a thing I've told you, do you?"

"I believe you, but it doesn't change how it's a big honor to be selected and we've got our orders."

Emily chewed her braid for a moment, looking out across the runway at the distant jumble of cubey cream buildings that were the Air Force Research Lab's main offices. "Boy, I know we're not meeting our milestones and I realize we're not everyone's favorite failing project. But sending us into war-games without warning is just being plain mean about it."

"Emily, you know Jeanette. One of her first rules is 'Don't be mean.' She has her needs, and is just reacting to strong pressures on her."

"Sean, ABL is totally not ready for war-games. We have science issues, we have laser problems, we have beam control problems, we've got a mice infestation. Let's punt."

"I assure you, it's worth it and we'll get a fresh perspective."

"That's it?" She looked at him carefully. "What's the hurry? There are other war-games out there; why push so hard when we're not ready? We're not even supposed to shoot down a missile for another year or so."

Sean's brain rocked back. Jeanette had made it sound like ABL(X) was struggling, but close to operational. "You can't shoot a missile down?"

Emily loosened her piled crown of hair, pulling her braid free of its scrunchie. Glossy in the sun, her hair tumbled over the shoulders of her flight suit looking *very* non-regulation. "Well, theoretically, we might be able to shoot down a missile.

Sure, probably. I don't know. We certainly never have—or even tried. We're in the science phase of things. If you go after a missile, everyone is watching, and if you fail, well, I'm up in D.C. for a month trying to explain it away. So, you want to manage risk, walk before you run, and not display your embarrassing unreadiness in front of the world unless you have a pretty good idea you can get away with it. Since none of these things here obtains, why the rush?"

"I suppose Jeanette has her reasons."

"That's it?" she asked incredulously.

Sean hesitated. "Let's take one thing at a time."

"Is there any connection between our Korea thing and you being here?"

"I was fired. I needed a job. Jeanette...We'll have to have a talk in a different place." Sean used the standard oblique reference—and standard subtle evasion—to a Top Secret discussion that was disallowed outside an approved vault.

Emily was not entirely satisfied. "There isn't enough time to get ready."

"I wish we had more time. But Roving Sands only happens once every two years—and it's a great way for me to learn Airborne Laser faster."

Emily moaned, holding her head, "What is he thinking? Learning Airborne Laser during war-games is like putting your mouth over a spraying fire hose nozzle."

"C'mon. Please don't send me back to Jeanette. Besides, don't you owe me a ride?"

Emily, silent, considered him. "I do at that. Well, although we are totally unready for war-games, I suppose we'll give it a shot. Your funeral, true? We'd better run a system check and get the crew going." She shouted loudly, waved her arms at the picnic area. The ABL crew looked up, started moving toward them.

Sean wasn't sure how he felt letting her take the lead—he didn't think it was a personal snub—after all, up till now they were her group.

The crew gathered around the airstairs, and no question they were looking at Sean a little slantendicular. In the New Mexico sunlight and clear air, the open desert stretching behind them to blue sky and the family barbecue still smoldering nearby, they were, Sean had to admit, a nice looking group. Good gene pool, a little more diverse, far more female than he expected—yet the faces were both innocent and wise, and without question focused.

A few stood out. Jarhead the MC Captain with his square crew-cut head, working Goop into his square muscular hands to remove Gatling gun grease; a buxom wavy-haired blonde with a frankly sexual stare who looked like she'd be at home in any trailer park in Texas; the cerebral Korean-American USAF officer he'd heard called Capt Matt Cho; some serious dapper senior NCOs and a few grooming-challenged younger enlisted. Then there was a general assembly of Air Force family types. The two pilots with their wings on their chests and carefree handsome miens were at the back, sucking on their beers and looking in-the-moment.

Overall, the crew didn't look difficult, but Jeanette's words came back to him. "Did I mention ABL is a challenging assignment? Most of the crew are civilian specialists whom you cannot fire—you need their special skills—and yet they won't listen either. You'll be the fourth project officer I've sent this year. Try to play nice."

Emily used the airstairs alongside the enormous plane as an elevated pulpit, and it was clear as the crew looked up at her attentively, they were hers first and last.

Emily relayed, with under-whelmed enthusiasm, the great honor of ABL's selection for the Roving Sands war-games. Everyone kind of looked around nervously, although Jarhead called out "Hooyah!" His shout of affirmation and its enthusiasm was shared by perhaps 50% of the crew. The rest groaned at the set of headaches they knew were coming on. Emily asked everyone to clean up their stations and load in the latest software and make sure configurations were frozen for the war-games. "Everyone, this is Sean Phillips, our new project officer. He's family now, so feel free to abuse him." Everyone smiled, and, when Emily gestured she was done, they all pounded past Emily and Sean, sprinting up the airstairs and into ABL. Trying to find something positive, Sean thought, *Well, running is a good sign.*

Emily, about to give him 'The tour,' saw his face as the crew mounted up. She blocked him on the stairs. "Before we go into the Tech Area, I feel I should warn you."

"About what?"

"The technology isn't the strangest thing you're going to see on the plane."

"You have to be a little crazy to be on ABL, right?

"Ground truth? My people *are* a little eccentric. That's what works here. We're feeling our way along. I encourage creativity. You know, in some ways we don't even really know what ABL is yet."

Sean almost exclaimed, "Are you crazy?!" but instead asked, trying to keep his voice even, "You don't?"

"Be reassured we're using every skill we have and working as hard as we can. You know the questions. 'What are we?' and 'How could we be coalesced into something significant?'"

"Ground truth? How long will it take to get operational?"

Emily smiled, brushed some dirt off Sean's shirt. "I have no idea. I'm a scientist. I have my own internal clock."

"Dream your way onto the battlefield and someone will eat your cookies."

"And that doesn't apply to Treaty Ops?"

Sean bit his lip. "Fair enough."

Emily stopped for a second and Sean saw her heart pulse in her milky neck. Her eyes were so clear and direct, opalescent gray, and the whites without flaw or even the tiniest blood vessel. It was kind of awing. Every gene was replicating perfectly from its ideal destiny—and this was a woman under extreme stress in charge of a giant aircraft project at the peak of human achievement, living with who knows what other family sorrows, worries, and personal demons.

In her silky neck, just a flutter, and he felt an answering flutter in his own. *My luck to like her. This is going to make it ten times harder.*

Emily leaned close. "I would like this to work. Frankly, I..." *Couldn't we just make love a lot and enjoy that early part where everything is great, you are just so happy, and there are no problems and only bliss?*

As she paused, clearly about to say something personal, an answering prickling ran up Sean's spine. He'd never thought about the women he knew in the Air Force this way. Of course, the usual proscriptions didn't apply, as she was a civilian and not up or down his chain of command...

Whatever she was about to say, Emily seemed to change her mind, turned and ran ahead of Sean, her impractical clogs clomping up the airstairs and into the main door of ABL.

Of all the experimental military aircraft on all the Air Force bases in all the world, I walk onto hers.

He followed her.

AIRBORNE LASER – TECH AREA

Although ABL's main door was like a normal passenger jet, there the similarity ended. Upon entering, one immediately was in a big room filling the whole forward cabin.

Overhead, almost a cathedral ceiling. The rear half of the traditional upstairs 747 First Class cabin had been removed to make a high-ceilinged spacious work area.

The Tech Area's high ceiling was then carried forward, until the remains of the First Class section stuck out in an upper deck behind the cockpit. This upper deck overlooked the whole Tech Area, much like a loft in a ski lodge. Sean saw ladder-like stairs running up to the loft, which served, besides the entrance to the flight deck, as a galley, for the corner of a kitchenette peeked out.

The Tech Area was bulk-headed off from the much larger aft part of the plane, which Sean supposed held the laser. The Tech Area looked like an explosion in a Radio Shack: there was no passenger seating; instead, jammed into two rows across the wide-body cabin were eight consoles, each loaded with monitors, computers, blueprints, electronics, and racks of equipment. Sean had been trained for treaty inspections to enter a human work space and instantly assess what it was used for. He now quickly identified the stations and their functions as science, military, or C3I—Computers and Comm.

Up front hung a huge liquid crystal TV. This big screen was set to display items of common interest to the whole Tech Area like images, data, and maps. The other notable feature was a fat pipe running through the Tech Area and into the nose of the plane. It disappeared into a kind of closet right below the cockpit. Sean imagined this was where the laser beam, generated in the rear of the aircraft, shot out the nose.

Other than a few portholes, the fuselage was continuous, with one big exception: opposite the door, a big almost picture window gave a view out to the airfield. Next to it was a console of computers and monitors that just screamed Emily.

Emily was suddenly at his elbow. "This is the ABL Tech Area."

Sean had already assessed the two rows of tech consoles, each with a function, each with a captain's chair with serious safety belt harnesses for takeoffs, landings, and rough weather—yet could swivel for comfortable general seating if not in operation. "Looks like Battle Management."

"We weren't meant to be a combat system. Are you OK with 'Tech Area'?"

Sean was nothing if not affable early on in assignments, and so he nodded 'fine' and instead noted Coke cans on consoles, food, general mess. There were also a dozen ABL guests wandering around, kibitzing. *I can see a lot of their troubles.*

Emily excused herself to talk to a VIP, and Sean took a moment to guesstimate who were the key crew from the layout of the Tech Area consoles.

Emily's station must, of course, be next to the big picture window. Neat, orderly, and designed for intense brain work and comfort. There was a jade plant, for god's sake, sitting on the side of the desk. *Please, no picture of the cat.* Instead, he saw a neatly-lettered sign tacked up, 'Oh, dammit! Did we forget the silent prayer?'

Her station was positioned to take in the whole Tech Area with ease, and have direct eye-contact to the nearby key consoles. Next to her must be C3I, then, laser radars. Besides these key consoles, there was Air Defense, Radars, and some kind of navigation. The crude console just in front of Emily was run-down, with older headphones, a sheepskin seat cover, the sign of a USAF officer type, and emergency indicators for fire, cabin pressure loss, oxygen problems, engine failure, and other calamities.

Ops! Operations. This would be home sweet home plate for Sean.

Sean walked to the scientific consoles nearest Emily's, where the big blonde he'd noticed eyeing him inappropriately earlier clacked her long nails on the keyboard. She was a young forty or so, her flight suit peeled down to her waspish waist to expose a skin-tight T-Shirt. Emblazoned across her splendidly augmented breasts was 'Gentlemen, Start Your Engines!'

As he passed, she said without looking up, "You're supposed to be learning, 'Kay?" She turned to him, leaned in, and provocatively pushed up a ream of printouts under her more than ample chest. "So, how do these data look?"

Sean faked a languid look down. "Those data look wonderful!"

Lorrie laughed at his speed, and said, more seriously, "I'm Lorrie. Lorrie O'Leary. I'm C3I—mostly computers. You want *anything*, Sean, see me."

The gal at the next station, with complex screens and a computer with some serious horsepower, was a creamy-skinned svelte flaming redhead of about thirty, laughed sarcastically, "Lorrie, doesn't he look a little top-shelf to go for the welfare mother type?"

Lorrie instantly bit back: "Red, you lame bitch. I wasn't on welfare but a year and had two babies to feed. If I'm such a bad mommy how come both my boys are army officers, serving in Korea?"

Red leaned over and offered Sean a firm hand. "I'm 'Red.' I run Laser Radars for precision tracking and remote sensing of chemicals. So to answer Lorrie's question, do you go in for the welfare mother type?"

Lorrie yelled at her, "I have a degree and everything!"

"Yeah, they even give you your diploma on the same matchbook you got their number from."

No love lost between these two. As the senior officer on board, Sean was deciding how to react to this interpersonal tension when a pilot-type—a captain—passing, play-punched Sean's arm. "The madness will take its toll. Please have exact change."

Sean glanced at his wings, his flight suit name tag. It said 'Schumacher.' "You're the pilot of the Airborne Zoo?"

"None other, call sign 'Slammer.' But don't tell the crew I'm a pilot. They think Airborne Laser is a bus and I'm the bus driver. Welcome aboard. Stop up the flightdeck way and visit when you get half a moment."

"Thanks, Slammer," Sean grinned, tossing a salute.

Emily returned, saw the expressions on Red and Lorrie's faces, and said to Lorrie, "That is an old joke and not funny. Do you just flirt automatically?"

Lorrie, hurt, eyes downcast as if she really felt the error of her ways, said, "Sorry.

He's cute and it's fun."

Red laughed, mocking, "Wow, another great cerebral quote for 'The Slut's Progress.'"

"Redhead, *fermez la bouche*! And you're a Ph.D.!" Emily shook her curls in exasperation at Lorrie. "Is this all you two do all day?"

Lorrie bit her lip, humiliated. "Here's Major Phillips's email account patched in." She handed Sean a slip of paper. "This is your temp password for the ABL Ops console. You should be able to get to your Pentagon email—NASIC is it?—where I found you, and just use that for now until I get the VS computer center to move you to our organization. You can use the SIPRNet* when you sign here that you've been trained. Just realize when that door you came in is closed, we're a vault, and Secret is 'Kay. Sign here."

Sean signed, pleased. "Have I been trained?"

"You seem very well trained to me." She looked directly at him with china blue eyes. "My degree is from New Mexico State—it has a great EE department."

"Go Aggies," Sean grinned. Her efficiency, directness, and conscientiousness had caught him off guard. He'd have to watch O'Leary.

Emily took Sean to the jade plant console. "Here's Laser One, my home so to speak. I'm Physics. I develop the science, calculate the performance degradation for various errors. Mostly atmospherics, since that is our main challenge. During testing, I control and shoot the Attack Laser—its Air Force designation is the YAL-1A1. Here's you on Ops."

Emily pointed to the run-down console he already had identified near her nice one. Sean logged onto his new email. There was plenty there, nothing urgent. Airborne Laser fell under the AFRL Directed Energy Directorate, and after the morning INTEL brief tomorrow at 0730, the Director, Ms. Canthor, and Sean's Division Chief wanted to meet him. Also, the VOQ had a nice room waiting for him tonight, and the custodian of the test equipment he'd lost in Korea was wondering if Sean would kindly return it—or should they start the lengthy report-of-survey process to assign Sean the financial responsibility for the missing equipment? Sean sighed and looked back up at Emily. "How come you rate the window seat?"

"On the happy day I quit ABL, you're welcome to it."

Sean was puzzled again. She was obviously extremely talented, could certainly choose among a hundred other places to work. Instead, here she was with Excedrin headache number 10^{10}, 'What do you mean my billion dollar laser aircraft project is full of cats and dogs and doesn't work?' What *was* this

---

* Secret Internet Protocol Router Network, The DoD SECRET Internet

strange vibe coming off the whole Emily thing? "You're leaving?"

"As soon as I can. I'm dying to be finished," she blurted out, then blushed and Sean decided not to pursue it. He had his own agenda, and this was neither the time to advance it nor question hers.

AIRBORNE LASER – GALLEY

Sean asked if there were any quarters on the plane, and Emily nodded, said they were minimal. She led Sean to the forward end of the Tech Area to the slanting ladder-stairs that went up to the upper level loft behind the flight deck.

Sean followed as Emily expertly scaled up the ladder, and into the small galley just behind the flightdeck. The six sleeping bunks, head, shower, and tiny kitchen with table looked incredibly inadequate for the dozen crew.

Strangely, when she got to the upper deck, Emily leaned over the railing and called down to the Tech Area below, "In the galley for Diablo check. Ten minutes."

Sean didn't follow this, but Emily just went on, motioning, "The galley, our amenities. With extra flight crew and aerial refueling we can stay on patrol indefinitely. We rotate bunks. You'll alternate shifts with me. We'll fight less."

Sean saw a thick coiled diamondback rattlesnake lying watching them from a hanging cage. "Like the one on your unit shield."

In passing, Emily brushed her fingers on the cage bars by the snake's face. "How dost thou, little crocodile?" The rattler buzzed softly. "Our mascot Diablo. He's the one who wouldn't stay away from the owls."

Sean threw his duffel bag onto one of the rude beds. "I'll bunk here, all right?"

"It's going to be inconvenient for you." The crew would hear of this, think he was crazy. Chief Master Sergeant Augsburger—Chief Auggie—was pulling something from a nearby supply cupboard and said they would leave the power on for him at night, but Sean replied, "Waste to power her up all night unless someone is working. So cut everything you can. And Chief?" Auggie turned. Sean said, "Don't stop any work on the plane if I'm sleeping. Just play on through."

"Yes, Sir." Auggie sized the new commander up and, although it was a no-hat no-salute area, snapped off a quick illegal salute before sliding down the ladder to the Tech Area.

From a wire-enclosed bookshelf Emily began pulling out manual after manual, documents, books, binders, and reports. She dumped them on the bunk across from the one Sean had claimed. The pile made a three foot high pyramid. "ABL

Program briefs on requirements, Ops, laser, beam control, drawings, logistics, doctrine, schedule. Welcome aboard. You are now on the periphery of life."

Sean flipped through the pile, looking. Pilots often had to memorize tremendous amounts of information, alternate targets, returns, and procedures; the requirement for intelligence was extremely high. To master this entire aircraft weapons system was nothing less than stratospheric. "Thanks. Perfect. Emily, this is good. I'm really looking forward to working with you on this."

Her face sharpened, and she looked dubious as Sean added, "Although I don't see a few items: safety files, security, training, environmental impact statement, equipment accounts, contractor case files. I'll also take care of attending division staff meetings and your branch suspenses too. I'll do the beans and bullets part of Airborne Laser. You concentrate on the physics."

Emily cocked her head, surprised. "You really want to do the scut work?"

"Sure."

She seemed embarrassed, and he asked, "What?"

"We usually don't turn those files over to the Project Officers because...when they quit or get fired in a month, the Tech Area people just have to pick it back up. Really disruptive. It's easier to keep it with the science people."

"I'm saying it'll be better if I do it."

As they stood looking at one another in silence, Sean heard people in a group coming up, one after the other, climbing into the galley. In a moment, the whole crew seemed crammed in around them, all looking expectantly at Emily.

Emily took down the cage with the grouchy rattlesnake and put it on the small dining table. "Diablo," Emily nodded to the thick rattlesnake. "He doesn't bite if you tell the truth—if your intentions are pure. Want to see?"

Sean couldn't tell what the heck she was talking about—then his heart suddenly pounded as Emily opened the cage door and put her hand in just inches from the viper's heavy head. She said, "Everyone here is completely dedicated to this project." Diablo sensed her hand, his triangular head cocking and rising above the thick coil of his patterned body, his infrared sensors blooming with the heat of Emily's hand. His tail buzzed furiously—yet he did not strike. "So, are you here to help us—or are you here to put us into Roving Sands so we fail and they shut us down?" Diablo hung, almost seeming to wait.

Everyone watched Sean, expectantly. He moved to stand by Emily; he felt his hand instinctively resist. His muscles creaked and little nerve pulses twitched in his arm as his hand froze outside the cage.

Emily took his hand. Hers was cool and dry and firm. She gently led his hand in, held it only inches from the viper's powerful head.

Diablo seemed to rear up higher, tense. Sean felt the heat and firmness of

Emily's body against his as she said, "Say it."

Sean looked around at the crew, catching each pair of eyes and then moving to the next, ending with Emily. "I'm not here to shut down ABL. I'm here to help in any way I can."

Diablo seemed to relax and Emily pulled their hands clear. "OK, people," she said to the group, "He'll do," and the crew grinned. "Back to work. It's an early day tomorrow. Seat check at 0800."

After an afternoon with the manuals and a long run across the base—it went for miles out into high desert vistas and foothills—Sean showered at the Eastside gym and walked the dirt jogging path the mile back to ABL under a million bright stars. Up ahead across the dark desert, huge Airborne Laser was silhouetted against constellations that in the clear New Mexico air shone even at the horizon. Her few portholes were lit and golden.

Home. With snake.

Sean changed into jeans and T-shirt as pajamas, and lay down on his miniature bunk.

The lights flickered and dimmed as the NCOs outside began closing down the plane for the night. Chief Auggie came up. "Goodnight, Sir. Everything mostly should work on aux power. Except the A/C, but it won't get too stuffy in here just overnight. Anything you need, Sir?"

"No, Chief, I'm fine. As long as I have a little power for the reading lights."

He thought the Chief was going to say something more, and then decided not to. "Welcome aboard, Sir."

"Thank you, Chief. It's a pleasure." He had a thought. "Auggie, does Diablo have fangs? I mean, does he ever bite?"

Auggie grinned, "Only if you're Navy, Sir."

Sean sat heavily on the bed, turned on the reading light, and opened one of the manuals from the big stack and started to read the story of the inner life of Airborne Laser. Strangely, in the quieting plane, there was the sound of scampering tiny feet.

He felt hatches slam somewhere in the rear of the aircraft. The big plane sat back on her springs, settling.

The motion swung Sean—and Diablo—slightly. Across the cabin in the low light, seemingly watching Sean, the snake's eyes gleamed as he lay in his swinging cage.

FARMERS' MILITIA – PYONG-SON MISSILE COMPLEX

The battalion of the Workers' and Farmers' Red Guard Militia—the lower level reserve army of North Korea—arrived at Pyong-son airstrip and the adjacent missile complex areas in the dark at 0400 hours. The nine hundred militia were drawn from not too distant villages, each of which formed a company that drilled together one day a week for civil defense and rear-area security. The battalion came by forced march from their assembly point ten miles away in the valley below. They were, as the least well-fitted North Korean reserve army—although the biggest at four million strong—older and somewhat beaten up despite their superb toughness and lifetime conditioning. The constant food shortages and famine were taking their toll, and in the farmers' chests you could have counted every rib.

Each farmer had served at least seven years in the Korean People's Army, yet now they wore only threadbare hand-me-down KPA uniforms without insignia. They had no weapons as these were only irregularly issued for training—and they each fired exactly three rounds per year for certification purposes. In any case, firearms were strenuously disallowed for this duty. The Farmers' Militia had not been fed breakfast but were promised a soup lunch and perhaps even a bowl of barley for dinner—although none of them thought this likely.

The farmers surreptitiously gawked at the sights of Pyong-son. This was not farming land, such an isolated mountainous area, and seemed alien to them. They were awed by the large North Korean military complex in the lonely valley—it frightened them as well. The ghostly moon that tore through the night's clouds, outlining the threatening terrain of buried bunkers, gantries, and pillboxes, heightened the fear. Even more frightening, there were strange egg-shaped domes set into the rock along the ridges, and tubular microwave beam directors pointed to the sky. None of them had ever worked on such a project. They knew top-secret construction such as this was done by prisoners condemned to death or life in prison. No worker who had constructed the tunnels and interiors on any such military site was allowed to leave captivity alive; most were summarily executed at the end of the job. It made them instinctively nervous even to go anywhere near the walkway to the giant steel entryway into the mountainside.

Due to the 'creative idea' of the main political officer of the State Security Department in charge of the preparation for Il-Moon and Dearest Leader's visit, each Farmers' Militia member was issued three brand new white towels, assigned to the airstrip, roads, or walkways into the missile complex—and given orders to literally mop the entire area clean.

Company Leader Tong-Hu took his towels and briskly followed his Battalion Leader to the assigned walkway to the entrance into the bunker complex. The smell of cabbage soup brewing in several oil drums a couple of hundred meters away made his stomach wrench. His body was wiry and strong, as he had spent many years—as all North Koreans did—in the grueling physical army training that in any other army would have resulted in open rebellion. That wiriness was now slowly, under the assault of malnutrition, fading into a gristly toughness that was the only thing holding him together. The day felt cold even though it was warm autumn, so few calories had he available to burn.

Tong-Hu was proud to be part of this operation. Today, he might even see Dearest Leader, and his heart swelled as he carefully and perfectly scrubbed at the walkway his Dearest Leader would tread upon—even if it did lead toward the ominous bunker doors into the mountainside.

At 0800 hours, with solid rain clouds now darkening the sky, three hundred of the Guard Command—the unit charged with Dearest Leader's and Il-Moon's personal security— arrived in full battle gear aboard a dozen new Russian Zil trucks. They arrogantly pushed the Farmers' Militia off the clean runway and onto the grass ten meters off the airstrip, and proceeded to roughly body-search every one of them.

Tong-Hu was nearest the walkways and was one of the first to be searched. Several of the Guard Command soldiers handed down metal trash barrels from the trucks, and the Guards commenced to pull from the farmers' pockets all their meager personal possessions. When even the smallest 'illegal' item was found, like pocketknives or nail clippers, the Guard confiscated them and threw them into the barrels. Later, they would raffle them off for their own pleasure. The farmers complained bitterly, but the brutes of the Guard Command just laughed and punished with a blow anyone whose comments rose over a low volume.

At 1030 hours, a motorcade of ten Benz sedans with a sky blue Cadillac limo in the middle drove up, and Architect Su, Il-Moon, and Dearest Leader got out of his Cadillac—a present from his father when he was six for going to the dentist. In response to the cheers and shouts of "Long live!" from the farmers, Dearest Leader smiled and waved broadly at them. They immediately moved forward to get a better look and to see what the fellow was really like, having heard and worshipped him from his birth.

The Guard Command reacted violently, and Tong-Hu found himself, like many others down the line, struck in the stomach with a rifle butt and knocked breathless to his knees.

The man next to him yelled, "Do the bastards of the Security Service believe they alone are powerful?" and was immediately slapped to the ground and viciously kicked.

Along the line, there were more farmers' calls of "Bastards! What do they think of us? Do you not think all of us are servicemen too?"

A sergeant major in the Guards sneered back, "We think all are the same servicemen. But you are the third rate ones!"

North Koreans are little different from you or me; insolence, pride, jealousy, anger, and love—all the strong human feelings—are just as real. The difference was they only very rarely gave vent to them. In addition to the Confucian admonition for self-control of emotions, complaining, let alone dissenting, invited a trip to a re-education camp or the firing squad. No, instead your only hope, no matter how poor the likely outcome, was to seek refuge and help from the collective. So every North Korean, almost always, got up each morning and did the miserable things their government asked of them.

But here anger and hunger mixed in a potent brew and, bent on repaying the insults, the line of farmers began pushing back angrily. They were all tough as tendon, and outnumbered the Guard more than three to one.

The sergeant major looked quickly to where Il-Moon and Dearest Leader had already walked to the sunken blast doors into the mountainside. Nervous, he didn't want to be seen in conflict with the farmers, nor did he want to retreat until he'd taught them a lesson. Nevertheless, allowing anything to appear to jeopardize Dearest Leader's security ring was awful to contemplate.

He took too long, for the insults and blows angered the farmers, while the loss of their pocketknives and fingernail clippers—items both difficult and expensive to replace—enraged them. When the Guard Command pushed back, the farmers surged forward in battle order—after all, they'd trained together for years. Guards began going down, pushed to the ground, kicked, and spat on. Caught between the angry farmers and with their backs to Dearest Leader, many of the young guards panicked, knowing they had no live ammo in their AK-47's.

The sergeant major saw Il-Moon turn at the complex door to look for the source of the unpleasant commotion. Il-Moon spoke sharply to Dearest Leader, nodding to the brewing rumble.

The sergeant major gave a quick low howl for retreat, and his Guard responded immediately. In broken order they fell back to ring the motorcade and the Pyong-son missile complex entrance. The sergeant major, however, found himself knocked onto his back and swarmed over by angry farmers.

The farmers gave a shout of triumph at the bullies running away and from the safe distance of the airstrip edge they called, "We think all are the same servicemen, but the Guard Command are the third rate ones!"

Dearest Leader moved decisively and jogged lightly toward the fracas. Il-Moon started after him, and then stopped, as his crimson worm nipped him warningly in the stomach.

He watched furious as Dearest Leader broke quickly through the ring of guards and shouted, "Attention!" to everyone. This froze everyone in their tracks.

Apoplectic with rage and fear, the sergeant major got up, almost spoke—an unpardonable breach—so he clamped his mouth shut. Dearest Leader barked gravely, "Tell me the meaning of this disharmony! You there!" He pointed to Tong-Hu, reading his nametag aloud. "Company Leader Lee Tong-Hu!"

Tong-Hu now had gotten his close look at Dearest Leader, and it was frightening and yet his face was different from the statues. A pleasant face with tiny chic designer glasses and a spry portly frame in a beautiful Japanese silk business suit. Taking courage from this surprisingly human embodiment of his god, he managed to choke out honestly, "We wanted to get a better look at you, Sir! We have cleaned well and worked hard. The Guards were rough—"

The sergeant major could not control himself, "Sir, these rabble were a threat—"

"Yes, I see that," Dearest Leader said, saluting him. "Excellent work, Sergeant Major, excellent work at security. You are to be commended. Consider yourself promoted to Lieutenant."

Tong-Hu's face fell as he heard this, for the jaws of the Re-education Camp abruptly yawned wide.

Dearest Leader turned to him, "You are a fine fellow Company Leader Lee and we understand completely. Beautiful job of cleaning. Of course, these misunderstandings happen. You have no complaints against your brother Guard Command now?"

"None, Excellency, Sir," and yet he could not help himself—he had his company to think about after all. "Except perhaps our nail clippers?"

Dearest Leader almost smiled at his brave insolence, noted the barrels, and nodding at them, seriously turned to the former sergeant major. "Lieutenant, I feel you have made it quite safe here so perhaps you shall return the personal items to your brother servicemen?"

The newly-minted lieutenant bowed low. "I shall see to it immediately, Sir!"

Dearest Leader announced in a booming voice, carrying over the huge crowd of soldiers, "Thank you all! Five kilos of rice and a large bowl of hot grain for everyone to take home!"

There was a cheer from the Militia ranks, ecstatic, and they began to yell, "Praise him! Praise him!" at which Dearest Leader signaled emphatically for them to quiet. The Farmers' battalion commander hurriedly gave orders; the dinner bell sounded; and the one thing enormously more important than anything, including some friendly jeering at the humiliated Guards—lunch—pulled every single farmer toward the fragrant barrels of soup, and beyond, to home.

Tong-Hu soon found himself, as did the other Farmers' Militia, strangely, with a stomach full of warm cabbage soup, a five kilo bag of rice over one shoulder—and carrying home to his family a big can of beautiful steaming barley.

PYONG-SON UNDERGROUND MISSILE COMPLEX

Architect Su smiled broadly at Dearest Leader when he rejoined them at the bunker door, and chuckled. "Open Sesame!" Dearest Leader laughed, "You mean, Open Barley!"

Il-Moon's thoughts were unprintable as he turned and led them in through the blast doors and into the mountain caverns of *his* Pyong-son complex.

Inside the door, Dearest Leader told his escorts to wait, and only he, Architect Su, Aide Park, and Il-Moon continued down the corridor.

A hundred meters into the complex, the corridor opened into a huge chamber with vaulted ceilings. To the left, the chamber was so cavernous its dimensions could barely be guessed at in the low light. An enormous rusting assembly line hundreds of meters across stood abandoned and dusty, around it the metal fragments and detritus of a huge heavy manufacturing operation.

Il-Moon motioned. "We have built our facility under the signature of the 12th of November Underground Tractor Factory. Of course, you will not find it in the Guinness Book of World Records, and yet it is the largest underground facility ever built. How many of our other accomplishments does the world not acknowledge? Now, as you can see, the factory has finished production of its fifty-thousandth tractor, and a good number of tanks as well."

Their eyes left the rust belt, to the newer concrete on the other side of the room. A small railroad, its tracks gleaming and small electric engine shiny, was lined up to drive straight into a tunnel into the mountain. It was clearly a special subterranean train, its electric engine pulling open passenger, freight, and rock cars. "We built a railroad through the mountain, so all the debris from digging out our facility can be dumped on the far side. This facility is unknown even to those who study Pyong-son. They know there was the tractor factory here, but not that we have set up under the abandoned section."

Against the far wall were six tunnel openings. Il-Moon pointed to six video monitors hung on a display. Each of the six showed an isolated rock chamber, hollowed out, and in each stood a complete missile gantry holding a waspish ballistic missile. The missiles pointed up launching tunnels, almost like vertical torpedo tubes. In the video, technicians swarmed over the missiles gantries, fitting, testing, and tinkering. The missiles were clearly approaching operational; the technicians' work merely final preparation.

Amazing. Architect Su, who loved anything amazing and functional, moved eagerly to see the missiles. While he'd funded this effort, he'd no idea it was so far along. Il-Moon had clearly managed the tech effort to a fare-thee-well. Entering one of the six tunnels at almost a jog, the others following, he came into one of the missile-launching chambers. He could see immediately they launched straight up. *Up two hundred meters of launching tube through solid rock. Clearly, undetectable from above.* To the side, he saw the all-important rocket engine plume diversion cave, directing the burning inferno of combusted rocket fuel out the side of the mountain so the missile wouldn't self-immolate or parasitically ignite one of the other missiles when this chamber was sealed from the main cavern.

The enormous three-stage Taepo-Dong 2 missile looked slick and ready, and the machining, the ceramic covers, and the painted DPRK flag—with its off-center star and inspiring red, white, and blue colors—were completely beautiful.

It is hard to appreciate the strength of feeling Koreans have for their country and, especially, how her accomplishments simply overwhelm them with pride. One South Korean described how, at his first sight of the newly Korean-created Hyundai sedan, he literally fell to his knees and wept. It was so for Architect Su. Il-Moon and Dearest Leader watched his reactions carefully. Here was the foremost mind among them. All the words and promises of generals involved in Missiles and Artillery, Navy and Special Forces, Internal Security, and the Korean Workers' Party, who had won and held their posts through cronyism and luck and hard work, were as a child's opinion compared to Architect Su. He was the real thing: the one mind in North Korea competent and honest enough to tell them what everything meant.

It was with feeling Su turned to Dearest Leader and Il-Moon. "Your missiles are indeed most beautiful, Il-Moon-ssi."

Given his reaction, Dearest Leader looked closer at the missile himself. They were awing indeed; a *frisson* of pride and respect tingled his loins and armpits.

Il-Moon said, "Yes. No other country isolated by the world could have mastered such technology. Technology to make history with."

"And yet, still, are they ready for real use?"

"See for yourselves. They will be ready for launch within days."

Architect Su replied, demurely, "Launching says little about the precision of their delivery. Without testing, are the missiles likely to be accurate?"

Il-Moon replied, "There is, in this case, no need for accuracy."

RADIANT OUTLAW – SPACE – ABOVE KOREA

Asia from space is a thing of beauty. With its verdant lands, other-worldly mountain chains, vast deserts, checkerboard valleys, fertile watercourse plains, rich silt-laden rivers, endless fractal coastlines and varied bountiful seas, when the cloud patterns boil up over this gorgeous panorama, the look can be transcendent.

Today, below Radiant Outlaw, a cloud-dotted Korea glistened. Radiant Outlaw, cruising, was a strange beast. Unlike any satellite you are likely to have seen, with its unique mission and heritage, it looked like nothing so much as a metal beetle in flight. Its carapace of Kevlar wings folded back, its long slotted-boom antennae swiveling, below its thorax-like structure hung extensive maneuvering engines, including huge tanks of rocket fuel for rapid orbit changes.

The giant bug of unknown purpose hung in space over Asia, listening to the chatter of commands coming from over the limb of the earth.

At Schriever Air Force Base outside of Colorado Springs, the 50th Space Wing satellite operations noted Outlaw's activity with interest. The satellite operator announced to the observers clustered around the command monitors, "Outlaw is scanning Pyong-son, North Korea."

Radiant Outlaw rolled. Its antennae seem to pincer Korea. Green pulses shot through the antennae, but it was only invisible radiation that beamed down into cloudy Korea. The laser-driven UHF radar beam passed through the clouds, interrogating the complex mountains and facilities of Pyong-son.

PYONG-SON UNDERGROUND MISSILE COMPLEX

In the domes above the missile caverns, a North Korean technician let his radar antennae sweep the sky one more time before sending an urgent call down into the complex below. Aide Park took his report by phone, said aside to Il-Moon. "Great Chairman, Dome 1 reports the approach of an American satellite."

Il-Moon said, "Under these clouds we are invisible. Nevertheless, we will be exacting. Underground we are invulnerable. Withdraw all surface structures and seal the ports."

The exposed missile silo ports and microwave domes above dropped into the ground. Rock slabs slid to cover portholes. The domes, radar antennae, and transmitters disappeared from sight.

Il-Moon said to his group, "Come, Comrades. I will show you the missile command areas."

As he and his friends crossed the huge underground military facility to the Command Section, Dearest Leader asked Architect Su, "So, then. You have the main idea? Can you give us enough to synergize with these so that it will work?"

Architect Su produced his notes, and small pair of reading glasses as they walked, spoke to Dearest Leader. "We can do an immense amount toward evening our odds. And in the end, if everything is in balance, it will be the South Koreans who agree, as they are sovereign indeed, to merge with us at terms more favorable to us."

"Quickly, " Il-Moon said. "It must be quickly."

Su paused in silence. Architect Su loved North Korea, and yet he knew her fragile infrastructure well. "May I suggest that your ultra-fast timetable is indeed the way to proceed? The dangers of delay are many. Discovery is the main one. We must give the Americans no warning. No warning."

Dearest Leader said heartily, "Well, all this is theoretical, since the Americans—if they are not lying—will withdraw their 7th Air Force, and we our tanks, and we will have a great confederal system without bloodshed."

Architect Su nodded. "You may return full force to the negotiations, knowing what you must have, and asking for it."

Il-Moon said, "My bargaining is of course crucial."

As they crossed back to the control center, Aide Park moved next to Il-Moon, murmured to him alone, "Our sensors show an American satellite illuminated us with a UHF radar of unknown type."

"Conclusions?"

Aide Park's eyes were down, awaiting the outburst of temper. "We do not know, Great Vice Chair."

Il-Moon only murmured back, "Get me the details. Everything they have from all the sensors." He moved on to show his compatriots into Pyong-son control center. A large airy room with clocks, monitors, and computer terminals. "Here the missiles are launched and controlled. We receive varied and full information from our detectors about what INTEL is being collected on us."

Architect Su was polite, but questioning. "The missiles alone will not constitute an attack. There must be a way to add the additional assets I am assembling. Without central coordination, it cannot be timed and therefore it will be of doubtful success."

Il-Moon pointed to a separate set of terminals. Dell computers sat in a line as if at an Internet café. "The North Korean Armed Forces have, as you know, an extensive buried fiber optic network; the MPAF Military Intranet. This Intranet has a main terminal center here, one in the auxiliary leadership war bunker north of Pyongyang, and one under the Magnolia Palace. All the MPAF forces—missiles, Special Forces, navy, air forces, artillery, and armor—can all be controlled as needed from any of these Intranet centers."

RADIANT OUTLAW – SPACE – ABOVE KOREA

The data returning to Radiant Outlaw was conceptual now, a mere stream of energy. It needed to be processed, turned from data into information.

Radiant Outlaw, after its orbit over Korea, began sending its data through a set of MIMIC—Microwave Monolithic Integrated Circuit—boards and processors. On-board data crunching was needed since even the MILSATCOM Comm downlinks could never handle the immensity of raw data. Once reduced, the data would be beamed to Ka'ena Point telemetry station on Oahu, then cross the Pacific on fiber-optic lines to satellite command at Schriever in Colorado.

The cloudy-day data from Radiant Outlaw's pass over Pyong-son began to make its way east toward Washington D.C.

Chapter 13

The 10th & 11th of October

AIR FORCE RESEARCH LABORATORY – KIRTLAND AFB

Sean spent the next two days up to his armpits in ABL. To participate in the Roving Sands war-games, ABL had to be electronically integrated into the exercise command structure. This integration was of two types, both of which were invaluable in helping him get a grip on the giant aircraft and its complex interleaved weapons systems.

First, there was the matter of ABL's Comm being tied into central war-game operations back at Norfolk, Virginia. In the age of instant global communications, war-games were commanded through satellite links and fiber optic networks from whichever command post was appropriate given the order of battle, and where war-game Comm infrastructure was already in place. In this case, the ties were into Norfolk and these had to be connected to ABL's C3I system. Then video, voice, and data could run freely between the giant aircraft and headquarters, who would talk to them when they wished, and monitor their actions. It was fairly straightforward for Sean to put these patches in place, with the help mostly of Lorrie—today's T-shirt said across the breasts, 'No pictures please'—and Chief Auggie, who had twenty years of military experience and smoothed out the wrinkles with the NCO's doing the link-up back in Norfolk.

The second task was trickier. It involved tying all the radars, lasers, and weapons systems in ABL into a general digital war-game model. In a battle between exercise-adversaries—for example, combining the virtual attack parameters of an incoming anti-air missile, the electronic response to that missile from ABL's anti-missile systems, along with the relative positions of ABL and the anti-air attacker—Norfolk's war-game computer would then analyze the opposing capabilities, and determine in this interaction who was victorious and who was dead.

For the Roving Sands' tie-in, Sean quickly figured out the key tech crew were a different group than the science weenies. These were the more pointy-edge people, most of whom were so busy preparing they only waved hello. There was the airborne radars lead, J-Stars, a middle-aged experienced African American, and really young 2nd Lt Eila Coast, at 'Strikeback,' who coordinated fighter air defense and their strikes back at missile launch sites. Eila gave him a quick safety look-over, saw his Air Force ring. "You're Academy? Me too, but can't wear any metal or rings on ABL, 'cuz of electrical hazards, does that make sense?"

Emily then dragged Sean across the teaming Tech Area, moving fast amongst the chaos. "Coming through. We put in every new idea in E&M, that's electromagnetics, we could think of for peacekeeping in the next decades. Also, strategically placed ultra-light explosive reactive armor. Shielding for EMP and nuclear bursts. We'll never need it, but for air defense: two Phalanx chain guns, radar-controlled. And one Marine officer, Jay Tull, un-controlled."

Jarhead looked up from messing with his Air Defense Fire Control console. "Semper bang bang, Herr Doctor. The major and I have met." Sean could tell Jarhead was also ABL's INTEL officer by the maps and signals traffic on his monitors.

Sean was amazed to see a howitzer sitting in the Tech Area, its barrel weirdly silvered and poking out through the ABL's side like a cannon at the gun port of a man-of-war. Sean stared at the cannon—and nearby ammo—as Capt Matt Cho looked up from soldering electronics on the barrel. Matt stuck out a solder-smudged hand, and shook with Sean. "Matt Cho, X-Weapons. That is, unconventional weapons like explosively-generated microwaves. This is an EMP cannon; this is your brain on microwaves."

"Those are bagged artillery charges!" Sean exclaimed.

"You want explosively-generated microwaves, you need explosives."

"Christmas! Lock that stuff up."

"It's bad enough they won't let me shoot it. Now I have to put away the ammo?"

Sean's brain was on fire. *I can't believe this plane. How are we ever going to do this?*

Of all of them, Sean immediately liked and understood Jarhead. Jarhead could tie his Phalanx system to the war-game computers himself. Therefore, unfortunately, the one person Sean was most comfortable with didn't need him—nor did he get to enjoy his company either.

At least Matt Cho's tie-in was easy: because his weapons were all considered so experimental, the computer simply assigned the probability of their success or failure in any interaction as 50%, and left it at that.

YAL-ATTACK LASER

The attack laser—and Emily—were a lot more problematic. First, no one really knew how to assess the laser, and it either really worked or it really didn't when it was assigned to shoot. Yet in the fuss, he enjoyed being next to Emily if nothing else, and watching her work. Her mind was lightning fast and even in simple matters like refueling and magazine emptying rates and so on, she far outstripped his own mental calculations. It was kind of an icky feeling, he reflected, like driving along in a Model T and getting blown past by a Porsche. He liked and needed talent, but experienced up close, it gut-level shook you.

Sean spent a difficult time learning about laser weapons, although when Emily lectured, with whiteboard marker accidentally daubed on her face, eyes flashing with passion even about some point which to her was a baby-level concept, it was really pretty fun. He began to wonder, if maybe, all their problems would simply disappear. He reminded himself: *you know how you always are sure it will work, but then there are a million little failures and huge amount of pain until it finally does.*

The laser area took up the whole rear three-quarters of the jumbo. At the door, Emily handed Sean a pair of laser goggles. Above the door, a flashing light warned, 'Danger: Laser Radiation,' with the international symbol for a laser, a starburst with a single line shooting out its center. They waited until the door was opened, bolted as it was from the inside as the Reg required.

Entering the laser section, Emily said, "The YAL-1A1 attack laser." The rear tube of the aircraft was stuffed from front to back with the attack laser. Plumbing, electronics, optics, mirrors, lenses, huge tanks, and wiring spread everywhere. *This attack laser is really a mess!* Emerald light zipped around the maze of laser optics, seeming to add, to the quiet din of fans and pumps and transformers humming, the song of a zillion pulsing excited molecules.

Dr. Marty Carreras, a grizzle-bearded Hispanic in his forties, was the chief laserjock, one of five laser crew working on the Big Mess of the YAL-1A1. Up to their armpits in laser, they all waved hello but no one stopped because they were in a critical alignment phase—a condition Sean came to realize was unceasing.

Emily pointed out laser components, talking loudly over the noise of hoses, piping, and pumps. "Here's the laser fuel, where the chemicals are mixed. It's a real bear trying to keep it going all the time." Then she pointed out the beam path. "The oscillator 'seeds' the laser amplifier which is like a chemical furnace. Low-energy beam in; high-energy beam out! Beam-control is key, as you have to then get the laser energy down the beam-train tube to the beam director in the nose, where it— "

"Gets directed to the target. What if the airframe flexes? The laser hits the beam tube?"

Emily pointed to ganged laser fuel bottles. "The laser magazine. Holds one hundred missile-killing shots. A ton of energy. The beam gets loose...can you say 'catastrophic airframe failure'?"

ABL COCKPIT

Sean walked through the upper floor galley, past his bunk, and into the busily prepping flightdeck. There was the usual pair of 747 pilot seats and room for a Nav on a swivel chair behind the pilots.

There was every button, switch, and display you could think of, including the set of four identical rows of switches for all the engines—and many extras for avionics, payload, and fuel balancing.

The pilots gave a glance over their shoulders as Sean came in. In the left seat, Maj Terrance 'Bozon' McMillan was running a checklist. An African–American with narrow face and crows' feet from a ton of time in the air, Sean later asked him where his call sign came from. "Don't you know the Bozon? The only particle can be in two places at the same time!"

The wiry flight-meister Slammer was hot and heavy into the checklist. "Welcome aboard, major. No shaking hands just now."

"May they never shake," Sean replied.

As things got a little less worrisome, and Bozon stopped to tally the checklist, Sean said to Slammer, "I used to fly 'Island Girl' for treaty monitoring. She was just like this."

Slammer nodded. "She's ABL's sister ship. We were 'Bering Maiden' till some Senator's wife said using girls' names was sexist."

"Yes, it's going the way of aircraft nose art, unfortunately." Slammer showed Sean some of the differences in this 747, and in particular, how the laser safety system was programmed into the autopilot. ABL definitely wanted to avoid shooting off her own wing.

"What's it like flying her?" Sean asked.

Slammer laughed, shaking his head. "Tons of beam director fore, and tons of explosive laser fuel aft? She's a flying dumbbell with the aerodynamic sleekness of a Port-O-Potty and the operational safety of the Hindenburg."

It was Sean's turn to laugh. "You like it."

"You betcha, but she ain't no eagle."

"You mean she ain't no falcon."

Slammer replied seriously, "She ain't neither one. She's pure warbird. As pilots, we live to shoot things down. Can you imagine shooting down a bunch of giant launching ICBM's? What a trip!"

The crew pulled themselves up from the sheepskin seats, and Bozon opened the hatch below the cockpit. They apparently liked this exit, "Keeps us in trim," said Slammer. "We're outta here. Early mañana," and the flightcrew flamboyantly exited through the floor hatch and slid down the ladder straight to the tarmac.

Chapter 14

The 10th & 11th of October (Korea)

SEOUL TOWER – BREAKFAST BUFFET

From five hundred feet up in the Seoul Tower on wooded Namsan hill, Abbey could see down over the rugged forest park below to where downtown Seoul began abruptly, golden and white beehives sparkling in the early morning light. She smirked as her eyes zoomed in on the Reuters' building—and the fifteenth floor where she was supposedly officially imprisoned. Did her boss have the guts to fire her now? She had demanded to be cut loose as special reporter to the Treaty Talks. All he'd done was swear and yell.

The towers of Seoul flowed between the hills in all directions, and the glory of Korea was that both its terrain and cities were dynamic. The early autumn meant the mountains were in full leaf-turning spate, gorgeously cradling the skyscrapers. With city parks everywhere, the buildings seem to float in a sea of goldening green.

She could imagine Hugh below at Reuters, holding down all the desk traffic in Financial, getting screamed at by Roy as a substitute target for herself. She wondered how long before Hugh had a nervous breakdown. Meantime, several top South Korean officials were eyeing her, deciding if they should approach. That was why she'd come to this power breakfast—to rub elbows with the high muck-a-mucks.

So far, she'd gotten nothing new. There seemed to be a pall over her previous efforts. *A story is like a shark, it has to keep swimming or it will die.*

It seemed everyone was thinking peace was bustin' out all over, and Abbey was perfectly happy to see the two Koreas go down the toilet or not—as long as she got the story. She had talked to the Minister of Finance at the buffet. She was also managing to eat a very respectable miso breakfast with kippers; usually mornings were impossible her stomach was so sour. She got nothing from the Minister—and now she found herself frowning viciously into her third cold sweet Mimosa cocktail. Akiru was not helping much, for despite the beautiful fall morning he was already slightly drunk, getting morose, and it was catching.

Abbey muttered, "We have got to find a way to keep this going and get back to Tokyo."

"After what you did in New York? They will never call us home."

"How could I know he was the chairman's son? He had his mother's name, the pussy," Abbey responded angrily. "There has got to be something. Some angle."

Akiru went on dejectedly, "We will have to get a job working for some bottom-feeding paper, and then we will die here."

"I'm telling you, this is our break. We just need an angle."

Since the only thing giving Abbey any pleasure was being fancy free while Hugh was eating shit down at Reuters, she was angry when she saw him happily padding, puppy-dog-like with his briefcase, across the revolving tower restaurant toward them.

Akiru groaned. "I don't think I can take The Moonbeam before a couple more drinks."

Abbey waited until Hugh was close, then held her Mimosa glass for a vigilant waiter to get her a refill, said to Hugh, "I'm sorry I can't offer you breakfast, but there just isn't money in expenses." Abbey stifled a belch politely. "A real shame. Now, what the hell are you doing away from your desk? We could get a call any minute."

"I can't drink anyway, Abbey. I'm an alcoholic, remember? Thanks for offering, though. Why I'm here, I think you're missing—"

"Son of a bitch!" yelled Abbey, and everyone looked up. She was slightly mortified to realize one person looking at her was the Minister of Finance. She recovered by pulling Hugh down violently into a chair and leaning close and hissing, "I don't miss anything. Now why is your sorry ass here?"

Hugh looked around worriedly. "Tell you here?"

"Yes, here and now."

With obvious surreptitiousness, Hugh dug into his briefcase and pulled out ABL pictures, laying them out for Abbey who didn't react. He began speaking in a conspiratorial voice. "I've been talking to this Spiney character. You asked me to keep this to myself and I have, but it's pretty interesting."

It was done in such a spy-like manner that Abbey winced. *Anyone can see we are having a secret meeting. Well, maybe that's good thing,* as her reporter senses tickled the light hairs on her neck. People were indeed watching her. *Yes! I am mysterious!* She came back to Hugh's pictures.

Hugh pointed to a sequence of photo-documented events. "First, a Korean official is spotted visiting this special 747 called Airborne Laser. Then this USAF officer is delivered by no less than a SECAF Learjet—and he starts *living* on the plane. The next day, the 747 is an ant hill getting ready for something. Spiney says this woman is the chief scientist, you know, the brains. The new officer—

the Gomer he calls him—is clearly now in command. He must be connected to this SECAF person who owns the Learjet." Hugh pulled out an official SES web Bio, its photo of a pert groomed smiling woman with friendly eyes in front of an American flag. He tapped a fingernail her. "Dr. Jeanette Suzanne DeFrancis—Under Secretary for Science and Technology. Some Pentagon heavy hitter. One of her projects is Airborne Laser. Do you know what kind of project that is?"

Abbey stabbed a Jimmy Choo stiletto heel into Hugh's foot. He gasped in pain as she growled, "Don't ask me stupid questions."

Hugh recovered from the spiking, managing: "It's an anti-ballistic-missile system. One of its intended missions is to fly patrol just off Korean air space, and if anything launches, shoot it down."

Abbey tried to hide her excitement by digging out a cigarette. She managed to get it lit, and said, "What the hell are you suggesting?"

"I'm saying, this plane is getting ready to come to Korea. The Americans are trying to have it both ways! They're running with the peace treaty while sending over an anti-missile plane—secretly."

Abbey dragged in a hot lungful of smoke and looked at Hugh's pictures. Something about the Gomer looked familiar. She'd have to show it to someone military; someone would know.

Hugh was, she knew, making sense. The U.S. military did not trust the North Koreans one inch, and were trying to sandbag the process. Since she didn't want it sandbagged—the best opportunity of her life as a reporter was at stake—she mulled how to view what had been data and was now intelligence. Absently, she told Hugh, "Alright, you've said your piece. Get back to the financial desk and I'll call you."

"You'll call me?" Hugh asked, excitedly. "I'd like to do some videoing."

Abbey pointed a long nail at the elevators down from the tower. "Out!"

As Hugh left, limping, Akiru watched Abbey stand, and knowing her well, asked, "Are you sure you know what you are doing? We shouldn't pull the trigger until we know our angle."

Abbey shook her silky mane of hair in frustration, "I'll just have to see what kicks loose."

"Be careful, Missy-san."

Abbey grinned. "Get the table cleared and a couple more drinks."

Eschewing her cell phone—so easy to trace and tap—she moved past the swinging door of the restaurant kitchen to the relative privacy of the phone alcove. On the way, she banged her hip into a table. She righted herself, said sternly to the fallen table, "I do not bruise."

At the phones she dialed the number jotted down by the Korean *Yakuza* in the taxi.

In response to the soft Japanese hello, "Konichiwa?" Abbey said, "This is Reporter Abbey Yamamoto. I wish to make arrangements to speak to Marshal Il-Moon."

There was a soft chuckle, like water past a hull. "Respected Reporter Yamamoto. We hear from you so soon."

"Ah, pretty boy," she replied, laughing harshly. "You are so hard up for a date you just wait by the phone all day?"

"I'm not sure I can accede to your request. I am, after all, a neutral party. What makes you think I can help you talk to the Marshal?

"As a neutral, don't you have access to all sides?"

She heard the mirthless tightening around the young man's voice. "If you had a question, perhaps within a day I could find the right someone to answer it."

A little petulantly, Abbey waved a hand, frustrated, "I am not sure what I want." Then: "OK, you've got twenty-four hours. Otherwise, I'm going out with the story."

"What story?"

Abbey smirked as she said, "Would Marshal Il-Moon like to comment on a secret American anti-ballistic-missile system being readied for Korea?"

Chapter 15

The 10th & 11th of October

AIR FORCE RESEARCH LABORATORY – NEW MEXICO

Weapons-class lasers, at the dawn of the twenty-first century, had more than their share of problems, burdens, and challenges. To understand the immense difficulties in creating 'bullets of light,' you must first realize: from a laser there is no kinetic impact, blast, or heat convection. The only mechanism by which lasers can deliver weapons energy to their targets is by transfer of heat using light.

Weapons-class lasers are called HEL—High Energy Lasers—and are a subset of DEW—Directed Energy Weapons.

To understand just what a truly impressive object a HEL DEW is, one must understand that for destructive power, the light beam must be hot enough to melt steel. Imagine a search light so bright that when you put a bar of iron in front of it, the bar instantly melts. Same with the laser. There are no kinetics of mass impact of the artillery or gun projectile, nor the thermobaric heat wave of chemical explosion, nor the flame of gasoline, nor the shock wave of high explosive. No, each little particle of light, each photon, must be extremely energetic, reach the target, and there must be a humongous number of them.

Consider also that this 'energy transfer over a distance' can do no more than take the energy you have on hand, convert it to light energy—and then beam it on over to the target. Thus first you need to have a huge amount of readily convertible energy. That is, the HEL weapon 'shot' must be stored in a magazine. This magazine—containing chemical, electrical, nuclear, or solid state energy—must be contained, stable, and convenient. It must also be of incredible density since it must be miniaturized to keep the overall weapon size and mobility reasonable. You can't very well have a power generation station hooked up to a laser artillery piece.

Any Directed Energy Weapon faces the same issue. So whether it's a laser, a Star Trek phasor, or a 'photon torpedo,' behind each weapon must be an immense energy source, but miniaturized and instantly-available.

You must then, upon demand, convert this intense miniaturized energy supply, with some unavoidable loss, into usable energy, stuff it all into the laser (known as 'pumping the laser cavity'), take the resulting sizzling-hot beam traveling at the speed of light out of the cavity without getting torched as you manipulate it, and send it out the equivalent of the gun muzzle. Then, you must keep this ferocious beam on the target for a long enough time so that the target gets hot enough to melt, blow up, or ignite. This entire process is further complicated by that fact that you will be going up against the strongest elements of the enemy's defense; the usual targets in wartime are the most robust and hardened and protected forms of metal, armor, steel-reinforced concrete, explosively-reacting armor, and stealthy faceted surfaces designed to spoil heating. The heat capacity of a modern main battle tank is pretty high. You can't just train a thousand degree spot on it for a few seconds and get much response—except for it to send a HE round back at you at 3,000 feet per second.

As an example, the bottom line for a DEW to blow up a bunker, is you must engineer a system which takes the energy of a bunker-buster bomb, place all this energy in a stable miniaturized magazine, then on quick order, pump this bunker-buster's worth of energy straight into the laser cavity—without destroying the laser itself or the pipes for the energy—get the resultant light to come out as a good straight-shooting spotlighted beam hot as a detonation, track the target while holding the beam on boresite until the target is destroyed. It is a wonder that anything gets toasted at all.

All this being said, DEW is not completely impossible. If anyone could do it, it would be the Americans, with their tech base, optimism, and sense of the future. For, what lasers lack in convenience as weapons, they make up in their surgical precision, their pinpoint force, their versatility, their uniqueness—and their desirability: they have stealth, instantaneous effect, a muzzle velocity of 186,000 miles per second—and the potential not just for war, but to keep the peace.

Take enemy missiles, for instance. In those precious few minutes of their boost phase, no interceptor rocket could ever reach them. For you must stretch out hundreds of miles in a few seconds, and strike a fatal blow. But they are vulnerable on takeoff, slow and filled with fuel.

This is where lasers come in. They can reach, they can kill. Of course, there are so many things that have to be just right. Yet when they are all right, something perfect happens: the enemy ICBM goes down in flames over its own the country. Chemical, biological, or nuclear weapons fall back on the aggressor country. And the planet is the better for it.

As the technology barriers begin falling—albeit with more historical difficulty than previous generations of military systems—a new era of peace could begin.

History is being made as humankind brews up something new—truly new—under the sun.

* * *

NORTH KOREAN WEDDING – TI SU'S HOME – PYONGYANG

The bride wore brilliant red, and Architect Su had never seen any young woman so radiant. The groom—of course no one cared what he was wearing—at least was impressively and completely smitten. As usual in the DPRK, it wasn't just the obvious—his good fortune to be marrying without the years of tedium and frustration normally imposed on his class. And, it is impossible for someone not raised in North Korea to know what it is like having Dearest Leader walk up to you and shake your hand. It would be as if President Lincoln appeared suddenly, touched your arm, and said "Good work!"

Then too, the groom was ecstatic because of the avoided shame.

When he'd first made love to Ti Su, they had pledged their commitment. Yet an icy-cold hand had lain on his neck since that day—the fear of not only discovery, but the discovery of the cover-up and deception—these were not light matters in the People's Paradise. His sleep had been poor and his grades were suffering. He knew Ti Su had been physically examined—and their *corruption* uncovered. Any moment, an agent of the Political Bureau, sent by Ti Su's grandfather, might stride into his university self-criticism session and point an accusing finger. He'd been tempted to confess he'd slept with his fiancée, yet somehow each time he came back from the brink—luckily. No, his heart was in the sky, and as they walked the courtyard as was traditional, up the steps for the civil ceremony, Architect Su read his face as easily as a scroll of calligraphy hanging on a wall.

Architect Su, slightly sadly, contemplated the young groom. It was clear he was partly joyous at the wedding because he'd been so fearful of the consequences of his seduction—Ti Su being much younger, less schooled, and in the very powerful Su clan (whose head, Architect Su, could crush him like a bug, literally)—and what he had to lose. Su's own fear was a long-conquered beast, buried decades ago as an eight-year-old boy guerilla courier in Manchuria who ran the streets despite the murderous Japanese military police putting a rising price on his head. *You are being unkind. Perhaps we raised them in fear, and so that is why they are fearful. They know only the threat of the loss of their houses and careers—not the real fear for Korea.* Like many a patriot, he knew that in building the new state there was a price they had not agreed to pay—yet was now being exacted.

Architect Su had taken the young man aside before the wedding for a fatherly talk. In Korea, he had reminded the young tyke, a marriage was not between two persons. It was marriage between two families. The boy had nodded respectfully. Su added, watching him carefully, "In time, I may have need of you. Promise should this be so, you will come to me and fulfill your duty—to our family." The boy had passionately sworn his loyalty, leaving Su partially reassured as he watched the wedding vows read at Ti Su's home, as was traditional. Su smiled, savoring the words as they were, in the prescribed fashion, spoken by the bride and groom simultaneously: "Praise our President for Eternity the Great Leader, and his son Kim Jong-Il, the savior of all mankind. Praise Kim Jong-Nam! May their greatness never leave us. Praise them! Praise them! For they have given us this day, and our very lives, to commit.

"We pledge our devotion to Kim Il-Sung and Kim Jong-Il—may they remain for eternity showing us the way—and to the Greatly Respected Top Person Kim Jong-Nam. May he live forever! We will strive to be as a cell of the Party and DPRK society, offering to follow with diligence their leadership for our family, placing our trust and reliance on each other, and walking the single path of revolution together."

Su felt a glow. *Ah! Life is good!* He watched as, at the feast table, Korean drinking glasses were shared between Ti Su and her groom. After their exchange of wedding bows, the ceremony ended with the pouring of drinks and offering of rice cakes to the parents of both families—and Dearest Leader made some remarks that no one understood since they seemed to have nothing to do with the Great Leader, and everything to do with his hopes that the Bride and Groom would *Progress* and create a new *Future* for Korea.

Afterward, Su handed the groom the traditional *Three Keys* (to a new car, a new apartment, and the family offices), and there followed photographs at the Magnolia Palace temple, the Party Foundation Commemorative Tower, the 5.1 Stadium, and especially the Tower of the Juche Ideal as required for the happy new household. These architectural sites, with their fine decorations of flowers and banners, would make for a set of beautiful pictures, Su thought.

Su let it all go, enjoying the gorgeous weather and the vermilion gown on the luscious bride so satisfying to the soul. All over Asia, scarlet was the color of marriage and white the color of death. It was the flash of a white shirt, a foreigner across the river at Kim Il-Sung Square, which made Su realize. He looked around after the flash; there was something missing.

Marshal Song Il-Moon was nowhere to be seen.

IL-MOON – VILLAGE SUNAN-RI – PYONGYANG EXURBS

Within moments of receiving the transcript of Abbey's telephone call, Il-Moon knew he would have to be alone again soon. It would be the second time, he reflected, in almost forty years, and after it, he might never be alone again.

This time was more difficult for it was not just in the Internet vault at the MPAF. This time, he needed to reach the village of Sunan-ri undetected, spend an hour, and return. Moreover, he had to find a time when Dearest Leader would not miss him. Were there to be a summons or emergency or simply a whim, and Il-Moon's whereabouts uncertain, he would face the ruin of all his plans.

It was not the State Security Department watchers he had to worry about. In the agreement to support the purges for Dearest Leader during the change of regime—and in particular to arrange the quick exile of Dearest Leader's competing brothers, more difficult because they were high up in the security services—Il-Moon had moved himself into the rarified atmosphere of the North Korean hierarchy. Previously, only the Great Leader and Dear Leader had been exempt from the State Security Department watchers. Now, as reward for arranging the banishment to Beijing of Dearest Leader's competing relatives, Il-Moon had exacted this same exemption for himself. Even so, he was still never alone, his aides and others always in attendance. He also enjoyed constant Guard Command security. He'd killed many a man and woman whose friends or relatives were biding their time, awaiting the chance to return the favor.

Il-Moon had been considering his options, and saw one window of opportunity: The wedding of Architect Su's granddaughter. All the key admirers of Dearest Leader and many in the MPAF would attend the service. It would also take hours, with the pre-wedding reception, the ceremony, and afterwards, the traditional photos; both the political ones in front of the Great Leader's statue, and then those at a Korean temple; the mantelpiece ones required for every wedded couple in all Korea. Il-Moon could excuse himself from the wedding, claiming exigencies of time and task. Everyone knew he was sleeping fewer than four hours a night, tirelessly negotiating on the treaty and attending other crucial responsibilities.

He looked over the transcript of the call from Abbey for the fourth time. The message from the Japanese reporter was clear. "Would Marshal Il-Moon like to comment on an American anti-missile system deploying to the Korean theater?"

He would need to be ready before he called her back. *Now, how to reach the suburbs without detection?*

Of all the amazing feats of the North Korean construction, one of the many untold stories—for reasons of paranoia it couldn't be a badge of honor—was the escape route from Pyongyang for the North Korean leadership in case of war.

Longer than the 'The Chunnel' connecting England and Europe at thirty-one miles, and longer than Japan's Seikan tunnel of thirty-three miles connecting Hokkaido to Honshu, the North Korean leadership had constructed the longest underground railroad tunnel in the world.

Buried directly beneath the Magnolia Palace, the leadership could walk down to the train station below, enter the electric train, ride for forty miles completely underground to a distant safe haven under mountains north of Pyongyang's suburbs. The lessons of the American bombing in the Korean War had convinced the government—and it was still the same people sixty some years later and they had not forgotten—that no place on the surface of the earth was safe.

It was under the guise of checking this tunnel and the facilities at the Leader Bunker that Il-Moon excused himself from Architect Su's granddaughter's wedding.

The rock walls roared past as Il-Moon idled over reports. At the big Leader Bunker, he called up the staff, berated them for slovenly habits despite the bunker's spotless condition, and left the workers standing at attention to contemplate their errors. He then diverted to the surface and emerged with only Aide Park. A dark-windowed Benz limo was waiting. Aide Park took the wheel. They soon were skimming a big six lane highway. Nearing the village of Sunan-ri, they left the main freeway. The local road was lined with bundle-carrying people walking. The main mode of local transportation in North Korea was by foot. Even bicycles were for the elite. Aide Park steered into the village and parked the car at the only gas station.

Gas stations in North Korea were considered strategic assets—and as such were always disguised. This one was camouflaged as a rice store. Aide Park entered and demanded a battery for the Benz. The manager, having none of course, was sent scurrying to get one from the next town. Il-Moon stepped from the car and into an alley. His greatcoat covered his uniform, and although it seemed as heavy as wet felt in the warm afternoon sun, he needed the coat to conceal the gun.

He walked the alley to the back door of a small hut with a large luxuriant vegetable garden. He had not called and yet his boyhood friend, now a retired high-level state physician, nevertheless showed no sign of surprise.

"My great older friend," said Doctor Pak Gil-Yon, bowing him inside. Gil-Yon served Ginseng tea and they sat for long minutes in silence, both looking not at each other, but out the windows. The garden was beautiful with its ripened vegetables, maturing gourds, and now reddened peppers. Bordered by Korean flowers, medicinal herbs and spices, an interwoven fragrance carried in to them on the atomizing rays of the warm sun.

They sat comfortably for several minutes, breathing together, enjoying each other. "I have been wondering," Il-Moon said at last, "If you would do me a kindness."

Gil-Yon nodded without replying. The sunlight in the room was indubitably golden, and the silence as well. He finally rose. "If you would come, I have a small surgery here. For the village, I am still a resource."

"We must continue to provide services to the revolution as long as we breathe."

"Even after we have stopped breathing, our example is important. Let us go."

In the tiny examining room, occupied mostly by a wooden herbal chest with Chinese characters on its drawers and a small bench for medical exams, Gil-Yon sat Il-Moon on the bench still wearing his coat.

Il-Moon began, "Lately, a friend of mine has complained of being fatigued. Now, it seemed there is a hardening here. I do not need a diagnosis, merely some comments for my friend."

Gil-Yon looked over Il-Moon's face, checked his pulse, tapped here and there. He felt under the coat, to Il-Moon's abdomen. The hard lumps near the surface were the size of plums.

"If you wish to tell your friend, he is right."

"What will be the progression?"

"Weakness and nausea. The inability to eat well. Pain, both localized and general. Soon, a loss of mobility."

"My friend feels very well. Perhaps it is only some casual malady. The gentle nip of time."

"There has been a slow progression?"

"Almost nothing. Perhaps some slowing, and yet some sense of a precipice."

Gil-Yon face betrayed more to Il-Moon than his words. "Some people feel very well for a time, weeks. Gradually, they do not look well. They often jaundice. I can give your friend something for that. From your friend's symptoms now, over the next month, the effects will increase. There will be a swelling of the abdomen. This can be drained effectively perhaps only once."

"Then?"

"The onset will nevertheless come."

"How?"

"It is usually quite sudden. One day, you are running up the stairs. The next, you cannot rise from your bed."

"When will this moment come?"

"One month, two at the most. Perhaps—even in such a state without clear external signs—three months is highly unlikely." Gil-Yon moved to his medicine chest, using a small chopsticks and a hand scale, he calmly ground several herbs together with mortar and pestle. He slipped the remedies into two envelopes, and wrote 'Tea' and 'Spice' on them.

Gil-Yon lay the medicinal packets to his side on a table. Gil-Yon was facing the garden window, could not see Il-Moon. "The tea three times a day, a gram or so of the spice every evening."

Il-Moon looked at the back of the old man's head, the hair left only in patches. Il-Moon knew he had to kill Gil-Yon. From under his coat, he pulled out and raised the pistol. The heavy gun butt would snap the old man's neck instantly.

Gil-Yon's wrinkled face remained turned to the window. He said softly, "Do not worry. I am an old man, and have lived long. You and I have made Korea blossom from the mud and blood of the war. See, there is even a patch of just dirt that I keep to remind myself." He pointed out to where in the garden, a bare patch of plowed dirt sat weeded and furrowed—and unplanted. "Remember when all Korea was just dirt? Nothing could grow under the occupation, so destitute was the land. There is the patch to remind me how you and I celebrated the Japanese and Americans fleeing and life returning to Korea in full measure. If you ask me, 'Is it enough?' I will tell you: 'It is enough.'"

Gil-Yon's wrinkled face still looked over the garden. A face Il-Moon had known unwrinkled when as boys they had often shared such treats as the lucky meal of a centipede caught in the Russian detention camp's garden—or inside the punishment boxes when they were bad. Always full of light and now still so, Gil-Son had partially chewed the centipedes for starving Il-Moon, whose teeth, that hard first winter in the camp, were ruined and unusable.

"My village practice and garden are my greatest pleasures, except for the occasional visit from an old Comrade and friend. I do not mind if one such visit is my last, should it be necessary for what we have accomplished."

I am making a mistake. Il-Moon pocketed his pistol. "No one knows I have visited."

Gil-Yon nodded. "You did not visit," but as Il-Moon rose brusquely to go, the old doctor reached out, turned him back. "And yet," Gil-Yon smiled as his eyes lingered on Il-Moon's face, "Thank you for letting me see you again."

Il-Moon grimaced a tight grin. He quickly stepped out the door and into the lush garden. Stopping amidst the sun-splashed rows of greenery, completely alone for just this moment, he squatted by the sunny yellow squash lying on the rich warm earth. He scooped up a handful of the warm soil. *Ah, there it is at last. The Blake poem wholly remembered:*

> *'The invisible worm*
> *That flies in the night,*
> *In the howling storm,*
> *Has found out thy bed*
> *Of crimson joy,*
> *And his dark secret love*
> *Does thy life destroy.'*

Il-Moon sifted the warm dirt through his fingers like sand through an hourglass.

He was an extreme Korean Nationalist—and this was not a sham for the outside world. The love of the place almost overcame him.

He realized suddenly he could not get up from this crouch; for a moment he was sure he would collapse the feeling was so dark, so primitive.

He touched his dirt-dusted fingers to his mouth, and it brought back the memory in a rush.

He was running again, just a boy, running in that ramshackle inefficient way before manhood, arms flying wide, panicked-hurrying, sprinting toward his sister's school to warn her before...he had run until his lungs were raked by fire and his vision kaleidoscoped with lack of oxygen and pain. He had made it to her street, to her very street and running almost blind hadn't seen the amused Japanese soldier— one of many around the school building—gently swing out his rifle. The gun barrel tripped him up and he sprawled face first into the dirt. The earth rammed into his gasping mouth.

Yes, it was the taste again, just as it was when as a humiliated boy he had laid choking on the ground, mouth jammed with dirt—and through his impotent tears saw the young schoolgirls in their uniforms filing obediently up into the trucks, among them his delicate fifteen-year-old sister.

His strength flowed back at the taste of the dirt, and he easily rose from his crouch. The mere idea of weakness was again unthinkable. He swallowed the dirty saliva in his mouth.

He placed a handful of the dirt in his uniform jacket pocket. He turned and walked back to find his car 'repaired' and slipped into the back seat. Ahead was the bunker where everyone would still be at attention for his inspection. He had just one small bit of business with the Bunker Chief, and then the train ride home. The wedding was still going on. Time to think of how to do it, how to make them pay; time to think of a way....

Aide Park started the car and Il-Moon was once again in the company of someone who loved him, and his armor shielded him perfectly.

AMEMBASSY – SEOUL

"A month!" bellowed Harold Hakkermann again, and his aide Sandy grinned because their lifestyle of career-strained marriages, round-the-clock work, and 10,000 volt high-tension stress was—at this moment—a heck of a lot of fun.

Sandy said, "I'm telling you, Il-Moon personally pulled me into a side-bar and told me he's positive the reactionary 'counter-revolutionary ding dong element' will screw us peaceniks if we don't do the treaty like right now immediately."

Harold went to the wet bar, mixed himself a short one, and enjoyed an adrenalin surge as if the beauty of the hunt were upon him, and he was sighting on the twenty-point trophy. "Man, what kind of protocols would we need?"

"Nuclear powered ones," Sandy said immediately, then on reflection, brightened. "Of course, the main problem with negotiations usually is that one side—mostly them—is faking it. We never really had a situation where they wanted anything to happen. Can you imagine a negotiation with North Korea where they are honest, cooperative, and productive?" He giggled at the novelty of the idea.

"Pinch me, I'm dreamin'!" Hakkermann laughed in agreement. "We never had anyone actually cooperate. Quite a fresh idea in diplomacy. What do you recommend?"

"Well, one way to do it is to adopt a prior protocol—like say the Paris ones we've already negotiated—everyone agrees, we push a few weeks out of the way."

"Get their negotiation points, and give them ours. When Il-Moon sits down to negotiate, we'll cut right to it."

Sandy grinned. "That won't stop them from giving us eight non-stop hours of pointless Juche cant before we get there."

Hakkermann smiled in return. "Yes, but I won't have to sit through it, knowing the outcome."

Sandy said, play-ruefully, "You don't care that I will have to endure it?"

"Courage under fire, my boy! Dean Acheson once sat through a Soviet speech in the UN that lasted sixteen hours and advanced not a single new idea or proposal."

"I read about that, Sir. He couldn't leave because the Soviets would have called a key vote and flummoxed him."

"So there we are. You are, I mean."

They both laughed, and Sandy felt immensely privileged. He busily gathered papers from the desk. "Well, I have a gourmet meal and a sexy date and a hot tub evening waiting for me," referring to an all-nighter in his hotel room over a smoking laptop with a room service supper.

"I envy you," said Hakkermann. "I'm going on the forty-hour health-spa immersion program complete with vibrating message chair and full-on aromatherapy," referring to the two-day trip back to D.C. under cramped, stuffy, and unsleeping Learjet conditions. "With all the fun we're going to have, we need to keep up the healthy chow, regular hours, and Pilates workouts."

Since people of their caliber in the civil service worked for shockingly low wages compared to what such talented and driven people would make at Exxon or Slumberger or Berkshire-Hathaway where their private sector equivalents worked, a civil servant's main badge of honor could not be money earned. Instead, there was a subtle jousting about who was working the longest toughest hours, who was sacrificing the most. Never mind the not-so-distant long-shot of a best-selling memoirs.

Sandy picked up the phone and quickly arranged the fast jet back to Washington D.C. for Hakkermann. With State's Gulfstream IV at his disposal, Hakkermann could make the flight in an international record-tying eighteen hours, see the President the moment he arrived—night or day—and be back in Korea in less than forty hours.

Hakkermann looked over the treaty inputs from his team; surprised at finding Sean's on top.

Amazing kid, really. He had the names right, a good feel for what was important, and some truly great ideas on keeping everyone happy while letting things really start to open up. He almost wished the kid were still around.

Harold chose pages from Sean's, as well as from others that he liked. He laid them out, looked them over, adding his own notes.

His draft of the peace treaty—really ending the armistice under a confederal agreement—was suddenly starting to come along really well. From his briefcase he dug out his favorite fountain pen. He always thought better in long hand. He mixed himself a Kentucky Yellowstone bourbon, as his heroes Dean Acheson and President Truman would have, and set to work.

Like his heroes, he knew only that history was in the making. When you were living it, it was like a piece of flesh and blood. It breathed and lived or struggled and died. History was the past becoming flesh—with all its weakness and glory.

And the past became flesh and dwelt in the present. Hakkermann smiled, and picked up his beautiful fountain pen, a Parker. He turned it in his hand, looking at the fine tortoiseshell barrel, "We're living history," he said out loud.

Sandy, going out the door, stopped. "You mean, we're living through history?"

"No, we ourselves are the living body of history. The past is only prologue. We've been at this game for a long time. Time enough."

As Sandy left, Hakkermann unscrewed the top of the fountain pen. He put the nib to the paper and started to scratch the opening lines of his treaty, longhand, just because this moment of historical progress needed to be cherished and felt in the skin, your hand, your body. There was nothing like a real fountain pen between your fingers for a document like this. It just felt so damned good.

Chapter 17

Harold Hakkermann &
Song Il-Moon's Treaty

THE AGREED PEACE TREATY AND CONFEDERATION FRAMEWORK BETWEEN THE UNITED STATES OF AMERICA AND THE DEMOCRATIC PEOPLE'S REPUBLIC OF KOREA

Panmunjom, October 31ˢᵗ

Delegations of the governments of the United States of America (U.S.) and the Democratic People's Republic of Korea (DPRK) held talks in Panmunjom from the 15ᵗʰ to the 31ˢᵗ of October of this year, and negotiated an overall resolution to the long-standing state of war and division of the Korean Peninsula.

In accordance with the noble will of the entire Korean people, who yearn for the peaceful reunification of the nation, both sides agreed to attain concretely the overall objectives of a lasting peace, security guarantees for all parties, and a nuclear-free zone within a re-unified state of Korea.

I. Both sides declare an end to the state of war in the peninsula, and hereby agree to bring about a political reunification of Korea under a confederal state.

1.) In accordance with the October 15ᵗʰ letter detailing the founding of a unified Korean confederation, in recognition of both the vision of the Great Leader's 10 Point Reunification Plan, and the Republic of Korea (ROK) Official Reunification Path, we declare:
- As of the date of this document, a state of war no longer exists on the Korean peninsula.
- In recognition of the lengthy separation of the Korean people, and to emphasize their unity and establish a sense of the inevitability and permanence of Korean unification, the nation shall be henceforth known by the single title of 'Koryo.'
- To recognize this historic moment and the struggles of the last two centuries of both North and South toward a free and independent Korea, the nation of Koryo will consist of two federations with respective historical titles. The northern federation, formerly the DPRK, will henceforth be known as Koguryo, and the southern federation, formerly known as the ROK, henceforth will be known as Shilla.

2.) In accordance with the October 18th letter of assurance from the U.S. President, the U.S. issues a Security Guarantee to the former DPRK, effective upon the signing of this document.

- The U.S. guarantees that no use of force, including the threat or use of nuclear weapons, by the U.S. would be allowed or contemplated by themselves or their allies indefinitely from the date of this document, provided there is no attack from the former DPRK on the U.S. or its allies.

- The U.S., prior to the signing date of this document, will remove their most mobile air forces from the Osan and Pusan Air Bases to Japan.

- The U.S. assures the DPRK of its security, provided it withdraws 15% of its offensive forces from the DMZ by the date of this document, followed by, upon confederation, the withdrawal and integration of all armed forces, both the former ROK and DPRK, into an Armed Forces of Koryo. All armed forces to be withdrawn within three months of the date of this document, and the army consolidation within the framework detailed in the Armed Forces paragraphs below within one year.

- In recognition of the decades-long defense relationship between the U.S. and Korea, and the continuing need for training and cooperation in humanitarian aide and regional security operations within new Koryo's international sphere of responsibility, the U.S. will establish with Koryo a consolidated rural base (With liaison offices in Seoul and Pyongyang) in the southeastern Korean peninsula for all U.S. forces, at a location to be agreed upon within one year of the date of this document.

- In order to provide security guarantees to the rest of Northeast Asia, Koguryo and Shilla will open all nuclear facilities immediately to the IAEA, and enter into the full NPT (Nuclear Non-proliferation Treaty) regimes within the context of the state of Koryo. The U.S. and Koryo will then conclude a new bilateral agreement for cooperation in the field of peaceful uses of nuclear energy. Off-sets of any loss of energy within Koguryo will be replaced and supplemented as delineated within the Koguryo resource paragraphs below. Expert-level technical talks on the integration of Koryo nuclear efforts between Koguryo and Shilla will commence within three months of the date of this document.

3.) Koryo will be recognized internationally as a single neutral nation, and its representation within international bodies updated to reflect the membership of the entire Korean Peninsula.

- Because the geography and balance of power in Northeast Asia has always made Korea a point of political contention, Korea will declare itself a neutral country, based on the model of Sweden. It will maintain diplomatic relations with all parties surrounding it, tolerate no foreign troops within its borders (with the historical exception of a single U.S. base), and declare all nations to be the equal friend of Koryo.

- The U.S. will establish bilateral relations to the Ambassadorial level immediately, with full normalization of political and economic relations with Koguryo and Koryo within three months of the date of this document.
- The U.S., China, Russia, and Japan will sponsor a joint resolution to make Koryo a single entity in the United Nations in place of the current ROK and DPRK. Within six months of the date of this document, United Nations representation shall recognize Koryo as a single country and sole representative of the Korean Peninsula's polity.

4.) Koguryo and Shilla agree to follow the basic principles and inspired guidance of the Great Leader's 10 point Confederation Plan and the ROK's Proposal for Reunification. As soon as possible following the date of this document, Koguryo and Shilla will hold expert talks on confederation issues within the following agreed guidelines:

- Koryo shall have combined army, national security organization, and foreign policy bodies.
- No internal borders will exist within Koryo. In particular, the Military Demarcation Line will be maintained as a preserve, although immediate openings of roads and railroads between Pyongyang and Seoul will be accomplished.
- No repatriation of land, houses, property, or industrial plant in either north or south will take place. Deed is to the occupant, industrialist plant to the organization currently in control. For Koguryo army units with industrial concerns, those units will transition to commercial enterprises with joint ownership of the assets by the whole unit.
- Land reform in the North is to deed land to the tiller man.
- There will be no requirement for 'Cash on the Barrelhead' for industrial plant or capital assets taken over by management who has the demonstrated intent to run the plant for the good of the workers and Koryo. Instead, responsible units organized with effective plans for revitalization of industrial plant, construction, utilities, distribution networks, transportation, consumer markets, or similar economic entities, will be selected based on the most productive use of the capital assets.
- Each side will open a liaison office in the other's capital following resolution of consular and other technical issues through expert level discussions, and reduce any barriers to trade and investment.
- The university systems of Koryo shall be integrated to allow attendance throughout the principle, and to invest in the facilities as required in either Koguryo or Shilla.

II. The two sides will move toward implementation of economic integration, with the following assistance from the world community:

1.) The U.S. will organize under its leadership an international consortium to finance and supply Koguryo with the necessary resources to fully integrate and compete as it moves to take its appropriate place as a leader in the international sphere.

- The U.S., representing the consortium, will make best efforts to secure the conclusion of supply contracts for Koguryo within three months of the date of this document for the provision of support energy and foodstuffs. Contract talks will begin as soon as possible after the date of this document.

- Energy and foodstuffs: Until the per capita GDP of the Koguryo confederation exceeds $5,000, the U.S., representing the consortium, will deliver to Koguryo 500,000 tons of heavy fuel oil per year, and provide 1,000,000 tons of rice and 500,000 tons of coarse grains, and 100,000 tons of cooking oils, to be distributed equally to the population of Koguryo per capita.

- The consortium will guarantee a cost of living payout to citizens remaining in Koguryo of $50 dollars per month. Any DPRK currency of record can be converted at the rate of 1,700 Won per dollar. For mothers of record with children under 6, they will be guaranteed an additional $20 dollars per month and 1Kg per day of rice for themselves and each child.

- The consortium will improve the Namp'o and Wonsan harbor facilities for receipt of supplies, and build 5,000 Megawatts of new thermal power plants within two years.

2.) The Japanese will establish an 'Investment bank of Chosun' for the express purpose of investment in Koguryo, 50% in infrastructure and 50% in commercial ventures. The available balance shall be $20B over 5 years. The bank's primary purpose is Japanese investment in the confederation of Koguryo for the upgrading of utilities, ports, roads, infrastructure, health care, and manufacturing. The bank will also fund Japanese management and cooperative work.

3.) The Chinese will establish an additional energy fund of 500,000 tons of light crude oil, more fully integrate the rail and road nets of the two countries, and reinvigorate the Sinuiju Economic Zone.

4.) The Russian Federation will complete the Siberian-Korean railroad link to below the DMZ at the highest possible speed.

5.) The EU, to prevent difficulties with international banking organizations for these joint activities, will pay off the outstanding international debts of the DPRK, approximately $7B, and reestablish Koguryo's credit standing among international organizations such as the World Bank and IMF.

III. Both Koguryo and Shilla will work together to establish political freedoms and rights for all Koreans.

1) Within one year, a preliminary constitution will replace this document.

- The two sides will remove any barriers to trade, investment, and cultural exchange, including restrictions on telecommunications services, financial transactions, artistic, and sports exchanges.

- All Koreans, (those of at least ¼ Korean ancestry) are citizens of Koryo, with all those rights appertaining, and within 1 year, a standard passport will be developed and issued to any citizen if requested.
- Human rights will be respected according to the norms of Amnesty International and the Swiss Red Cross, and all purely political prisoners will be released from both federations.
- There is a free flow of persons north and south. For two years, for documentary purposes, visas will be required to move south and north over the former DMZ. Visas shall not be denied for any reason other than criminal intent or fraud. Visitations between relatives is sufficient visa reason.
- There will be an immediate search for, and Japanese passports issued to, Koreans of Japanese descent living in Koguryo and Shilla so as to determine their own future.
- So as to make available to every living Korean this historical agreement, and to encourage debate on its shortcomings and virtues, within one month of the date of this document, this complete agreed framework treaty document will be freely available throughout Koguryo and Shilla. It will be printed daily as an appendix, in both Korean and English, in the Rodong-Sinmun and Chosun-Ilbo newspapers.

2.) The security aspects of this document will remain in force permanently between the U.S. and Koryo, while articles I and III will be replaced with a constitution as written by Koguryo and Shilla within two years. A constitutional congress will be convened within six months of the date of this document.

IV. Both sides will work together for a smooth and considered transition of the armed forces of the Korean peninsula to a level as required to maintain a strong national defense and to provide for international peacekeeping, disaster, and humanitarian efforts, while employing the undoubted capabilities of the current organizations for the good of the confederation.

1.) Koryo will maintain an integrated army of approximately 200,000, with centers of operation in Kaesong and Pusan.

- The model for the Koryo armed military, within 2 years, will be an all-volunteer force, with only a core of professionals, based on the Swedish model.
- All military forces, including American and UN, will be withdrawn from the DMZ. For a period of 1 year, three divisions of former ROK and DPRK troops can be posted around the respective capitals. Within 1 year, no military force may have plans, equipment, or strategies which include defense from the other federation.

2.) Due to the changing nature of the armed forces personnel structure, to prevent dislocation and discomfort, the following steps will be taken to assure efficient use of the current organizations and prevent dislocation and discomfort.

- The overall KPA structure will be maintained for the next 10 years to help in the reconstruction of areas of economic necessity and to provide services and manpower within a solid organizational structure. This tasking area of responsibility will decrease over the next 10 years, and in any case, this organization will retain no force of arms capability separate from the Armed Forces of Koryo.
- There will be immediate cash payments made to all high ranking DPRK military persons, as compensation for their services to Korea and to help with transitioning to a smaller armed forces.
- For those who have planned a career in the Armed Forces, no forced retirement will be enacted. Those interested in a continued career within a structured national service will be retained, although their units may be transitioned to a civilian service with responsibilities in construction, management, or operation of economic entities as required by the federations.

3.) The limitations on the Armed Forces and general guidelines are:

- No military use of civilians will be permitted in Koryo.
- The Joint Security Area will be immediately civilian-operated, and turned into a border crossing point and museum within 1 year from the date of this document.
- The large amount of military hardware in place in both Koguryo and Shilla will be recycled for civilian purposes and not sold in the international market. All recovered material will be the property of the federations.
- Within three months of the date of this document, all conventional weapons, including artillery tubes and armored vehicles of any sort, will be withdrawn to 100 miles south and north of the DMZ, and parked in the open where they can be monitored prior to recycling.
- All landmines are banned on the Korean Peninsula, and any currently in place will be removed and destroyed within a year of the date of this document.

Harold H. Hakkermann
Head of the Delegation of the
United States of America,
Ambassador at Large of the
United States of America

Song Il-Moon
Head of the Delegation of the
Democratic People's Republic of Korea,
First Vice-Chair of The National
Defense Committee of the Democratic
People's Republic of Korea

Chapter 18

The 11th of October

ALBUQUERQUE – SANDIA HEIGHTS & AIRBORNE LASER

Emily rose from the Jacuzzi in her big living room overlooking the lights of Albuquerque. She wrapped a towel around herself to walk to the bedroom, but wasn't able to make it; she finally lay on the couch, sleep washing over her after the exhausting preparations of the last two days. She felt whipsawed between seeing Sean again so suddenly and preparing her jumbo jet in what she was pretty sure would be a fruitless attempt to contribute to tomorrow's war-games.

On the couch, she stuffed a Zia-patterned pillow under her head, propping herself up so she could see down the valley to the lights of planes on approach to the airport. In the pattern of blue and white light clusters demarcating the Air Force base, she could almost see Airborne Laser under the floodlights, the NCOs still prepping for tomorrow. The moon was a waxing crescent hanging over the city lights and far dark mesas. She watched as over and over, a plane lifted from the airport and headed out toward some far land, while—in an odd conservation of coming and going—others landed from a similar distant realm.

Down at Airborne Laser, Sean felt grimy. He was layered in desert dust from non-stop days of sweaty aircraft work and the Jet-A and oil fumes from the flight line clung to him. The kind of clean-up he could get in the tiny ABL galley was starting to become severely inadequate. He kicked everyone out early, calling for an 0400 seat check for the start of Roving Sands the next day. It was a couple hours after sunset when he finished memorizing the ABL ConOps and missile shot scenarios, jogged the mile to the eastside gym, got a good workout—and finally scrubbed up well there with a shower and shave.

The hard workout and clean-up clarified his mind. When he walked the desert mile home, climbed the flightdeck ladder to his quarters in the galley, and lay down in his tiny bunk, Sean was sure they were ready.

Tomorrow—in Roving Sands war-games—*his* Airborne Laser was going to take names and kick ass.

SCUD MOUNTAIN – KUMGANG-SAN REGION – DPRK

In contrast to Sean and Emily, who were thinking hard and working harder getting ready to *defeat* SCUDs, it was precisely the opposite for Architect Su. He'd been preparing SCUDs for use, crisscrossing the whole of North Korea—doable because the few six-lane freeways were almost completely empty. (In a way they were worse than empty, the only other vehicles were those of the international aid workers shuttling food around the country. *Humiliating.*) Since North Korea was about the size of New York State, such trips were mostly day-trips. Only the mountain chains slowed things up, forcing the occasional over-nighter. The freeways were, however, made from concrete rather than macadam, because limestone was something that was abundant in the DPRK, while the all-powerful triad of POL—Petroleum Oil Lubricants—were scarcer than Phoenix's teeth. This meant sleeping was difficult as you rolled over the joints between the poorly poured plates. It was a kind of washboard thrumming, and it took its toll on Su's eighty-year-old body. Yet SCUDs, and their bigger No-Dong and Taepo-Dong derivatives, were so important, Su had dedicated several full days of back-breaking road-work to working out his plan for them.

Here in SCUD mountain, Architect Su looked up at the big Hwasong—a North Korean reverse-engineered version of the Russian SCUD B—and sighed. It was a work of art, in many ways a more difficult technology than a nuclear weapon. Of course, it helped that many brilliant Russians had themselves used the V-2 rocket as a start toward good guidance, engines, and control systems. It could not be said the North Korean version was as good as the Russian. Such technology, especially the control systems, were just too subtle to copy perfectly. In several of the tests with their Iranian friends, the delivered missiles barely functioned and many were completely ineffective. Nevertheless, even if only one in four missiles actually worked, the Iranians needed missiles, partly to flummox the USA. They were willing to spend hard currency, and this was the one place they could buy them.

These SCUDs were also used as the stages for the more powerful Taepo-Dong missiles, and they and the dozens of No-Dongs here were long-range missiles and capable of reaching the main home islands of Japan and even America's Kadena Air Base at Okinawa.

Like the smaller SCUDs, some were set to launch from underground silos, some were on railway cars, and others hidden cunningly: prowling the roadways of North Korea on TEL's, parked in barns, railroad tunnels, and garages; or poised hidden in hospitals, factories, and schools.

But here in SCUD Mountain was the biggest and most accurate collection of them—perhaps two-thirds of the DPRK's eight hundred long-range missiles.

Su knew these SCUDs were the best thing he had available for possible strategic use. This capability was their chance to really limit America's powerful Japanese supply line. If the main air bases in Japan were out, it would be a completely different fight on the Korean peninsula.

Architect Su had a limited trust in Il-Moon's big Taepo-Dong rockets, especially the three-stage Taepo-Dong 2. Even having seen the Pyong-son complex, he knew these big missiles alone would not be effective. He needed something with real offensive oomph if he were going to back a thirty-division armored attack on Seoul.

No, the backbone of the whole thing—not withstanding the great idea Il-Moon had for his big missiles—were these SCUDs.

Su looked at his notes. He had enough of a war plan to go back to the National Defense Committee.

He would remind the Committee of just how effective these SCUDs would be—and not worth husbanding. They must shoot the whole bolt of them—even if only 30% were operational—at the U.S. air bases and Japan.

If three hundred SCUDs loaded with high explosives, chemical nerve gasses, and biological agents couldn't slow down the American air bases, what would?

ROVING SANDS – AMERICAN SOUTHWEST – TEL 'GORBY'

The huge missile TEL—Transporter Erector Launcher—truck roared along the unpaved rough desert road in almost total darkness. The driver, wearing night vision goggles, had enough light to see out of the snubbed-nosed cab, but even with the giant 8x8 suspension computer-adjusting each tire independently, the ride was rollicking, and any mistake was sure to defeat their mission. The driving was made considerably more challenging because the giant SS-1c SCUD missile carried on the top of the launcher weighed more than thirty tons. The complex weaving of the road through the canyon mouths and dry flood-channel *barrancas* in the broken rugged territory of Canyonlands made it all the more treacherous. The driver kept up his speed. They needed to be in position long before dawn or when Roving Sands started, their ground motion would immediately get picked up by a Joint-Stars radar plane—and they would get clobbered.

On the side of the TEL was its nickname, 'Gorby,' next to a painted likeness of Mikhail Gorbachov, complete with map-of-Russia-birthmark on his bald head, his happy face as usual smiling.

It was one of the SCUDs bought at the end of the Cold War for hard currency, and was a working model in every way.

The USA had spent the money so their missile defenders could get operational experience with these very nasty buggers the Russians sold throughout the world. In North Korea it had been copied and sold for export as the Hwasong. Iran re-labeled it the Shahab 6. In the Sudan, Ethiopia, Cuba, and so on it had its other names. For despite the smiling Mikhail Gorbachov, the capability of the missile was every bit as deadly as it had been when the intermediate nuclear arms treaty made Russia get rid of a passel of these monsters.

The U.S. hadn't only bought the MAZ-543 8x8 all wheel drive TEL launcher, they had also bought dozens of the actual missiles. The U.S. operated them perhaps better than any other country, even where they were actually deployed as weapons systems.

Capt John Harshbarger, jammed shoulder-to-shoulder uncomfortably into the correctly-named six pack seating—three in front and three in back in heavy Russian rocket-launching suits—was being constantly jolted by the bad back road he himself had picked.

He had chosen this road through heavy sand and deserted streambeds for a reason. It was a good idea—provided it worked.

SCHOOLYARD – FRENCHMAN'S FLAT, NEVADA

A few hundred miles away at Frenchman's Flat, Nevada, a man tied a motionless child into a swing in a desert playground. The child seemed stiff, unwell. The harsh desert abruptly washing right up to the playground was like a raft of thorny plants floating on a sea of grit. Beyond, this dirt sea undulated into a pre-dawn distant landscape of brutally barren and rugged mountains.

Wires trailed from underneath the child and ran away into the sand.

TEL 'GORBY' – CANYONLANDS

Capt. John Harshbarger felt the big front tire on the TEL slump off the road-edge. Suddenly, gravel crunched and the huge vehicle slipped over the shoulder and down the embankment.

"Hang on!" yelled his corporal, double declutching while trying to keep the top heavy TEL from rolling into the sandy mesquite below.

"We are!" and the six-pack of men inside the big cab bounced around like bugs in a box.

The big long TEL and its load of SCUD missile, its center of gravity high enough to totally throw off the vehicle steering, rollicked down the side of the hill like a bronco-angry centipede, finally got its legs back, and galumphed to a halt in a dry streambed.

Everyone OK?" called John.

"Sure, right, perfect," came from the crew with assorted degrees of sarcasm as they climbed out.

The TEL support truck behind them ground to a stop on the road, and the crew got out and looked down at them. The TEL was somewhat lopsided, its missile payload precarious. They all stared, assessing, frustrated.

"You'll have a hard time getting back up on the road."

"We could launch from here, I suppose."

John dug a heel into the sand. "The ground is pretty soft. Let's get the re-inflate going."

He thought back to the local maps he had memorized. Where could he set up that was survivable, yet effective for a missile launch?

For one thing, he knew the terrain analysis software Blue Team would be using took into account the TEL's weight, size, and space requirements for launching, quickly reducing the number of possible launch locations to only a few—and they would be watching those. Further, there were Unattended Ground Sensors listening along many of these roads for the sound of vehicles. They would quickly relay the type and direction to Blue Team INTEL, who would vector a strike aircraft right to them.

"Get out the camouflage and cover both vehicles. Maybe we can fool the over-fly birds until we can move."

They all looked at him. It was 100% clear the TEL was never going to get back up on the road.

"Hey," said John, as he started to jog away into the darkness, trying to get a grasp of the beetling canyons to either side of them. "We have a schoolyard to destroy. Get with the program."

The crew of TEL Gorby went to work.

SCHOOLYARD – FRENCHMAN'S FLAT

The unseen man finished tying the motionless child into the swing. After checking his handiwork, he looked around him at the silent playground within the desert town of bombed-out and brand new buildings. Nearby, more unmoving children sat in other swings, wires trailing.

ABL COMPLEX – TAXIWAY

Sean woke when Airborne Laser's front hatch was pulled open. His alarm said 2:00 a.m. He swung his feet out onto the cool metal floor and walked to look down from the galley into the Tech Area. Below, Lorrie was flipping on the lights despite the fact that seat check—when everyone was required to be present and afterwards could not leave their duty stations—wasn't for hours.

Her flight suit was peeled down to her waist as usual and today her shirt had lettered across her high breasts, 'My boyfriend is out of town!'

She caught Sean reading it, crinkled her eyes, "A little too early in the morning for that, Flyboy, but OK." No matter how tired, drunk, or exhausted she was, it seemed she never came in to work without perfect makeup and she always washed her hair everyday even if she had to do it in a sink—and she was always joking.

Sean replied, "I'm just getting the range on the safety hazards. Wouldn't want to get an eye poked out on a pointed object."

"Ooo. Fast. You got the morning coffee on the IV drip again?"

"What are you doing here so early, O'Leary?" Sean asked, pulling on his flight suit over his olive green underwear and sliding down the ladder to the Tech Area.

"Oh, tit and tat." She was dismissive, nonchalant in her answer, but Sean wasn't fooled.

He moved to stand behind her, pressuring her. "Then maybe I'll just watch your monitor over your shoulder while you do this and that."

Lorrie shrugged, and her long nails—French manicure with jewels embedded—clacked the keyboard at high speed without pause. "So, when you met Emily before, did you two fuck?"

Sean reddened. "Straight up, you expect me to answer that?"

"She's been acting a little crazy since she went away—that special crazy you get when that thing has happened between man and woman. That thing you can't ever take back, changes everything. Did you fuck and run?"

"Lorrie, I don't fuck. Or fuck and tell. Why?"

"Not just 'cuz love without sex is like the worst hell. We'd all be lost without her, you run her off."

"Not in my plans."

"'Kay." She seemed somewhat mollified. "You just watch yourself with Emily, Mister, or you'll answer to me 'cuz from where I'm sitting it's good odds you'll be the one ruins it for everybody."

This plane was bass-ackwards, thought Sean smiling at her brass. Lorrie was pretty junior to hassle him. But the INTEL was good—even if it ripped him in two trying to figure where the hell to go with him and Emily. "So, tell me what you are doing and I'll leave you alone."

"'Kay. Versionizing software. Emily really needs to know exactly what version we're using, in case we got a problem and need to go back to a previous version that didn't have that problem."

"You mean, configuration control?"

Lorrie stood up and stretched provocatively only inches away from him. "You think you know everything about what Airborne Laser is, don't you?" then she swayed to the door. She looked back over her shoulder as if in a sexy teasing. "You'll find out, Major know-it-all." She raised a big graceful hand and smacked herself on the butt with a loud *crack*.

"Airborne Laser has a paddle for everyone's ass."

TEL 'GORBY' – CANYONLANDS

While his crew worked to re-inflate the squashed tires on the MAZ-543, John Harshbarger jogged up the dry streambed, stopping in the starlight to peer up each canyon to see if TEL Gorby would fit.

He finally found what he was looking for. He checked the geological maps.

Without having to get back onto the road, they could corkscrew up this steep-walled canyon. The radar shadow of the canyon would hide them, and perhaps even provide a good hiding place after launch. The TEL's enormous tires and articulated suspension could handle off-road flat desert almost as well as a tracked vehicle. But still, this would be dicey; the canyon mouth was strewn with rocks and riven with pits of deep soft sand.

The crew had the tires re-inflated and the load re-balanced.

Darryl the NCO, banged sand off his coveralls and dusted his hands. "We're going where? Sir?"

"Be optimistic, my boy!" said John Harshbarger. "Either way, our target is a dead duck. Suicide missions are part of our training, remember?"

"Yes Sir, after you, Sir!"

John walked ahead. TEL Gorby's huge diesels roared to life, and slowly, the TEL crawled after John along the dry riverbed and up the canyon.

SCHOOLYARD – FRENCHMAN'S FLAT

Airman Welsh finished wiring up the children, while Airman Reba watched.

The light had come up enough so the whole playground and surrounds were visible. Beyond the school—with its child dummies—lay a small isolated desert town of bombed-out and brand new buildings.

"Oh, I love the look of Gound-Zero town in the morning," said Welsh.

Reba shook his head, looking from the schoolyard to the town, where in various spots children and adult dummies sat propped up and wired. "These weapon-effects dummies are too creepy. Why'd they have to make them look like people?"

"Who knows? Next year it might be out of fashion. For now, helps us relate to the threat."

The town also had a creepy paint job. Everything was marked in unique patterns of stripes and squares, each building lettered and numbered with codes so after an explosion the debris could be analyzed. "Every year we rebuild the town. Every year they try and protect it. Every year it gets wasted." They both looked at the jigsaw-numbered buildings, the explosion sensors wired to the child dolls. "Maybe this time...I heard there was this new anti-missile technology, some plane?"

The dolls, almost alive, seemed to stare back at them, frightened.

Reba shivered as Welsh said, "Stop ICBM's? Sorry, boy. The missile will always get through."

THE WHITE HOUSE – WASHINGTON D.C.

For the second time in ten days, Ambassador Hakkermann found himself back in D.C. from Korea. Even though the State Department's big C-20 Gulfstream IV had staterooms and stand-up toilets, it was still a rough service.

The C-20, however, could hold twenty-six people, so it was decently roomy and he could travel with company, and Harold had told the pilot to try to beat the Korea-D.C. transiting record. He came very close; they covered the eight thousand miles to D.C. in under eighteen hours, and despite the time change, Hakkermann felt marvelous as they landed at Andrews. He reviewed his notes for the meeting with the President. He had to deal directly with the President because Dearest Leader's comments weren't something he could relay except in person.

Deplaning, the D.C. fall weather was beautiful if hot, and he was amazed how similar it was to Korea. *Almost the same latitude. The Horse Latitudes.*

It was, if anything, the opposite of that image of stagnation—it was movin'. But he needed permission—much as he hated to admit it—to negotiate the pull-out of the U.S. 7th Air Force from Korea even as the final seal-the-deal negotiation point. This was precisely the last thing any American would consider doing since it would leave South Korea essentially on its own. The North considered the South—perhaps unfairly—to be a military pygmy except for the U.S. presence. Going all-in like this was a 'nads issue, and had to be pressed in person.

In the Oval Office, he pitched it this way to the President: for a moment, we may be unguarded. For a moment, they could decide to strike. If they do, it will end the stalemate on the peninsula, and the ROK had an incredible force in place to deal with it.

There was no question who would win—and further—the 7th AF wouldn't be all that far away at Okinawa. So, let's do it. It's a gamble, and if we lose, we'll simply take our lumps. In either case—and this would be a miracle like The Promise after The Flood—we would have removed one of the most deadly governments left on the planet, and freed millions to seek their full potential. No longer would militant Middle East countries be able to buy increasingly sophisticated missiles and missile technology. No longer would cheap AK-47's ship into Bangkok and Indonesia and Somalia by the freighter load—flooding deadly state-of-the-art small arms into every trouble spot in Asia, Africa, and the Middle East. No longer would there be a growing nuclear threat, and no longer would Iran have an ally in lies and hate. In fact, there would then remain for the world only one true problem state—and as such Iran would be much more isolated.

And, Harold was sure, Dearest Leader was the kind of man who only comes along once a century. They should embrace his humanity and decency or what the heck did we stand for anyway?

It was a great speech, and Harold himself was almost amazed, as if it had come from somewhere up there—until at the end of his meeting, the President called in Jeanette.

The President was young and visionary, and he was sold on Harold's bombast—it never hurt to keep your ideals shined up. Introducing Jeanette DeFrancis to Harold, the Chief Negotiator smiled, slightly ironically. "Yes, we've met; we have a mutual...troubled acquaintance."

Jeanette nodded politely at the reference to Sean, and the President told Harold that Jeanette had seen some troubling things in North Korea as Jeanette handed Harold a sheaf of images. "Our new satellite Radiant Outlaw has a ground-penetrating radar imager. It shows that beneath Pyong-son are assembly and launch areas for ICBM's."

Hakkermann said, "Ms. Under Secretary, our intelligence sources disagree. We have a wealth of information. None of it points to North Korean treachery."

Hakkermann's science advisor, after studying the picture added, "These Radiant Outlaw images look ambiguous. And unconfirmed. INTEL community guidelines require two sources. One source must be an approved sensor—which this is not—and the other HUMINT."

Jeanette murmured, "That is a *difficult* requirement in North Korea, where there is virtually no spy network on the ground. Often, decisions there have to violate the rules."

Hakkermann was shaking his head. "I have pressed the flesh with Dearest Leader. He wants to be the Gorbachev of his people. He understands the historic opportunity. He wishes to press it for all it's worth."

The President asked, "Could he be acting?"

Hakkermann was almost impatient. "Man, the guy came to us and said, 'Let's do it!' and with a pretty concrete proposal for a confederated system where, sure, he maintains a lot of power—but the troops on the DMZ and elsewhere in the country are going to get gone! People are going to be able to cross the DMZ for the first time in sixty years. The Japanese have pledged $10 Billion if the missiles and nukes go—and that's just a start. If this is all just pure subterfuge, then he's going to war anyway and I say we call his bluff. It might be cold, but it's South Korea's problem today, or ours and Japan's in five years. I mean, did you know the guy likes Disneyland?"

Everyone smiled. The rumors had been unclear, but everyone knew something human had happened to Dearest Leader—he liked traveling abroad if nothing else.

"Instead of icing his competition," Harold continued, "he exiled them to China to get educated. He's sending back Japanese spouses of Koreans, talking to us like people. He has an improving human rights record. He's released a good number of people from camps, and pulled those ridiculous books like 'The Americans Started the Korean War' out of the bookshops in the whole country. None of these have even been discussed before. I mean, I ask you, Ms. Under Secretary?" the emphasis a slight insult since to Harold, Under Secretary was a low rank.

Jeanette didn't blink. "Pyong-son looks to us like a threatening new missile complex. What about our troops, Japan, Hawaii?"

"I'm from the 'Pre-Launch-Phase Interception' school of missile defense. I'll put Arms Inspectors back into Pyong-son if you'd like. The treaty is huge and we shouldn't hold back based on speculation."

The President went and sat heavily at his desk, and swiveled to look out at the Washington Monument. "I wish you could have heard my conversation today with South Korea's President. The treaty is worth great risk. I'm afraid, Jeanette, I have to side with Harold here."

Jeanette said, "Understood, Mr. President. I'm suggesting just in case, we deploy anti-missile technology like Airborne Laser somewhere not too near Korea. Just in case—and in secret."

Hakkermann said roughly, "You are compounding my difficulties. These North Koreans have been around. An anti-missile plane shows up anywhere in Northeast Asia, they will find out. They *will* be pissed—and no treaty."

The President mused, asked Harold, "Can you press the flesh one last time with Dearest Leader? Speak to him personally and get his word? You think you can tell if he's lying?"

"I have a built-in lie detector in my head. If he's lying, I'll know it."

Jeanette was thinking a good actor could fool anyone's head-detector, but she said nothing. It wasn't her place.

"Get his word—and give him mine. Tell him if this goes, I'll meet him any time, any place."

The President rose. "Thanks, citizens." He walked to Harold and touched his shoulder warmly. "Harold, you are green-lighted all the way. Come back with your treaty or wrapped in it. Jeanette, would you stay?"

ROVING SANDS – AMERICAN SOUTHWEST

For several thousand square miles of military reservations, air bases, and testing ranges—like an enormously-scaled game of hide and seek—across the southwestern United States, Red Units fanned out with shock troops, Ballistic Missile TEL's, anti-aircraft units, and terrorist squads. Their objective was to destroy American units, cities, military installations, and seek to remain operative as hostile units for seventy-two hours.

As John Harshbarger put it, "It's going to be a helluva three-day weekend." The Blue units—Air Force RECON planes, Unmanned Aerial Vehicles with experimental intelligence and targeting pods, fighters of all descriptions, Joint Stars ground battle control, NRO reconnaissance satellites, Patriot missile batteries, and a plethora of already-sunburned patsy scientists with their pampered gizmos were ready. The object was to test these mature and infant systems in the quest to detect and nail SRT's, Strategically Relocateable Targets, or more simply, 'missiles and their launcher support.' The Airborne Laser was flying as part of an Advanced Technology Transition Demonstration, even though no one believed it was anywhere near even prototype operational.

The Red Team was looking to sock it to 'em—and they knew they held the odds.

For these three days, it was to be simulated war at its sharpest. Anyone left standing at the end was going to get citations and the joy of victory—and of course, bragging rights. That's how the soldiers looked at it. The scientists were hoping they could contribute, knowing they probably would get ignored, and being used to it, just planned to try to shake up the establishment. But everyone was committed to showing that they could find SRT's and deal with them. They were in a way still chafing from the Desert Storm and later wars, where they were unable to locate, let alone destroy, a single TEL or SCUD Launcher—and most of the missiles got through.

This weekend, in their own backyard, with a new generation of anti-missile systems, everyone was going to try again.

AIRBORNE LASER – FLIGHTDECK

Long before the sun rose and brightened the land, it brushed pink streamers and rose petals across the sky. The desert birds were chirping up a storm and the air was fresh as a mountain stream and clear as gin. The spectacular growing dawn made Sean wonder if he'd ever seen anything as pretty. In the distance, the sheer rock faces of the Sandia Mountains towered up into a lost horizon of mist, going from grey rock to golden sky.

In all the dawns and departures of his soldier's life—and Sean had had many across the globe—for some reason, right now was the most beautiful morning he had ever seen.

Slammer turned and spoke to Sean, who was sitting behind the pilots for takeoff. "She puts on a great dawn, doesn't she, New Mexico?"

"Enchantment Inc. One of God's best light shows," Sean agreed.

In the mission pre-brief, Sean and the pilots had decided, given their targets to protect—which were scattered over Nevada, New Mexico, and Utah—to take up position close to the Four Corners region.

Sean had briefed: "Our mission is Theater Missile Defense. We patrol above the clouds in a racetrack pattern, watch the battlefield for missile launches. We ID anything coming up. If it's a hostile we smoke it with your ray gun."

"You make it sound trivial," Emily said. "No one's done it yet because the science isn't right. Turbulence will dissipate the beam, and the laser hardware is temperamental."

"Well, let's give it our best shot."

Auggie now called up on the intercom, "Ground to Flightdeck. All umbilicals off. Airborne Laser, you are free to taxi."

The engines whined up. Ground crew waved their batons. The muttering between the flightdeck and tower commenced as Sean felt ABL wheel along the taxiway from their hangar complex over to the main runway.

Lt Eila Coast broke in, "Flightdeck, this is Strikeback. We will pick up fighter escort at 0830, approximately the Colorado border. I'll know more when Combined Air Operations Center assigns someone to us."

Bozon replied, "Thanks, Strikeback. Laser One, are you good to go?"

Emily: "ABL, this is Laser One. All stations call off please."

Lorrie: "This is C3I, Ready."

Red: "Laser Radars. Ready."

Eila: "This is Strikeback. Ready."

Jarhead: "This is Air Defense and INTEL. Ready."

J-Stars: "This is Radars. Ready."

Marty: "This is Attack Laser. Ready."

Matt Cho: "This is X-Weapons. Ready."

Emily: "Flightdeck, this is Laser One for Ops. ABL technical crew and Tech Areas are secure and ready for takeoff."

Slammer answered: "Roger that, Tech Area. Hold on tight, *girls*."

TEL 'GORBY' – CANYONLANDS

TEL Gorby's big tires had finally gone to spinning and throwing up clouds of sand, and John Harshbarger accepted they were high enough up between the cliffs so a radar would have to be right over them to see them—until they launched.

The TEL crew jumped out and began to camouflage the TEL and SCUD, making them invisible, while John went to the launch console. He began to key in the long sequence of commands—in Cyrillic—into the Russian computer that would work out the impact point hundreds of miles away. He called out as he entered the data, "Target is Frenchman's Flat schoolyard. Frenchman's Flat will be flattened."

AIRBORNE LASER

As ABL rumbled off the runway, Sean unbuckled and went into the Galley. Looking down into the Tech Area, it was a beautiful sight. Everyone was at their terminals bringing up their systems, there was no talking, and Lorrie already had the big screen tuned to the Command Center in Norfolk. In the video feed, generals, admirals, and DV's sat monitoring all the action from a gallery of tiered seats. A podium waited, empty, for the War-game Commander. "The kick-off is coming in," Lorrie called up to Sean, and he slid down the ladder and walked to Ops.

On the big screen, General Washer came on from Norfolk, and interspersed with his comments were patched in live video feeds from across the Roving Sands theater. Sitting with flags behind him, in dress blues, General Washer sounded off: "Greetings Roving Sands warfighters! Welcome to the largest ever anti-ballistic missile war-game. Red Team will attempt to inflict massive damage upon the United States. Come out killing! The enemy will do his best. We expect the same from you—even if you are Navy."

He motioned, and video rolled of Red Team prepping. Huge TEL's loaded with missiles rumbled through the desert; anti-air missile batteries dug in, Navy F-18 Hornets banked on patrol, red marks on wings.

Gen Washer continued, "Blue Team will attempt to locate, engage, and destroy the missile units of Red Team."

Blue Team was the other side of the coin. AWACS planes with bulbous domes flew level patrols, Patriot Missile Batteries set up in blowing sand, and a group of blue-tagged Japanese F-15's taxied in a tight group.

Suddenly, on came a live feed of Airborne Laser taking off! Her huge white fuselage was menacingly lined in antennae, her alien beam director nose seemingly charged with potential. The images sent a *shudder* through the watchers all across the war-games.

General Washer announced in a special voice, "Flying today with Blue Team is Airborne Laser. For the first time in history, mankind is fielding a laser weapon."

"Defensive system," Emily noted primly.

Sean yelled "All Right!" and indeed the tech crew's faces were rapt as they watched Gen Washer.

The general continued, voice rising up to a crescendo. "Laser Warriors, we salute you! You are authorized live fire on ballistic missiles. Lassies and Geronimos, Roving Sands is on!"

Sean bellowed over the intercom until he heard some ABL crew join in, as Airborne Laser surged upward toward its first battle station.

TEL 'GORBY' – CANYONLANDS

In the narrow canyon, the huge MAZ-543 8X8 vehicle huddled against one rock wall, John Harshbarger signaled for the NCOs to start erecting. The thirty ton SCUD C ballistic missile began its slow rise to vertical for launch. He didn't want to risk the motion being detected later by a ground moving target indicator radar and blowing their cover. So he was getting it up now. The next motion from the TEL would be the launch, and then it would be too late to stop them.

While John finished working the launch checklist, one of the NCOs brought out a bunch of brush hooks and snow shovels, and looked around hopefully for volunteers. In an hour or so, they'd be ready. The enlisted set out some cheap beach chairs. When the SCUD was in launch position, the unit went into watching mode, chatting, smoking, eating, enjoying the quiet desert awaking to a new day—and waiting, as always, for the order to launch.

COL HAREDA – JAPAN AIR SELF-DEFENSE FORCES (JASDF)

As Airborne Laser pushed through blue skies and puffy clouds over American deserts far from home, Sean sat looking out Emily's window. Two Blue Team F-15's flew up, wings emblazoned with Japanese Flags and the Kirin Dragon emblem.

Eila radioed, "Ops, this is Strikeback. Blue Team fighter escort is here. It's squadron Kirin."

Sean was surprised, "The Japanese are here for Roving Sands?"

The Japanese had been pretty resistant to missile defense—until Dear Leader launched a three-stage ICBM right over the Japanese homeland to a splashdown in the Pacific Ocean. After that, with nuclear and more missile tests, they joined up with the U.S. in Missile Defense. They imported batteries of Patriot Missiles, Aegis Cruisers, and in every other way—from research at their defense universities, to participating in ballistic missile war-games—the Japanese were now deeply involved in ballistic missile defense.

Still, they had nothing that could deal with the big ICBM's out of Korea, and they needed operational training in anti-missile work. So, it made sense they would become participants in Roving Sands.

Sean recognized the F-15 call signs. He motioned to Eila to let him speak, opened a mike. "Kirin 1, this is ABL Ops. Major Sean Phillips. Is that Colonel 'Mulligan' Hareda?"

Col Hareda replied, "Major Phillips. How nice we meet again. It has been a long time since the All-Military golf tournament. However, I believe the concept of Mulligan is Irish, not Japanese."

Sean chuckled at this reference to his background. "Either way, in war—"

The F-15's did loop-de-loops and fell in alongside ABL as the crew drew breaths at the crack maneuver. Col Hareda said, "In war, you do not get no Mulligans."

RED TEAM F-18 HORNETS

The pilot and wingman of the Red Team F-18 Hornets had several things in common but the most interesting was their call signs. The Pilot was 'Ripsaw' and his wingman was 'Hacksaw,' and they'd flown together for years.

Just out on Red Team patrol, they had run across ABL and were now trying to figure out what to do about her. The bulbous nose and the strange gizmos unsettled them. Watching her with an occasional mono-pulse of their radars— they didn't want be too obvious—they slowed their speed down to conserve fuel and match her course. They were up at almost forty thousand feet and were keeping Airborne Laser about fifty miles off the beam as they pondered.

Hacksaw, the wingman, called over to Ripsaw, "How about we try for the laser plane? Be a great thing to bag."

Ripsaw, the lead, replied, "Look at that thing. It's got more ugly stuff growing on it than a warthog. Creeps me out. Who knows what they've got on there— besides the laser."

They weren't discussing real weapons, simply their virtual weapons within the war-games computer; the electronic and human referees who resolved what a particular skirmish meant war-game-wise in terms of damaged, dead, and wounded—who was still in the game and who was out.

Hacksaw said, "You think they're allowed to target us?"

"In war-games, they try and the Ref is likely to say, 'Hey, good fun different out-of-the-box move, and we'll be smoking rubble at forty thousand feet. Besides, look at those Eagles." They took a moment to examine the fighter picket between them and Airborne Laser. "That fighter screen? We'd be out of the game in a minute. Let's bide our time. It's early hours yet."

AIRBORNE LASER – TECH AREA

Emily by this time had kicked off her clogs, put her feet up, and was getting slightly sickened on a whole carton of Ben and Jerry's cookie dough ice cream. It was a sign of stress, she knew, for her diet was usually exemplary. The rest of the ABL crew ignored Sean's admonitions to sit alert in their seats. Only Lorrie and J-Stars were constantly at their stations, methodically scanning for activity.

Sean realized after a time the crew was right. You just couldn't really sit at the consoles for all those hours with nothing to do. You quickly burned out. So, he just people-watched as the crew chatted, ate, and walked around.

Emily was wearing small ruby earrings today. Sean was surprised as her ears were un-pierced. She modeled them for him. "Once, someone told me lasers were a good idea looking for an application. So, I made these lucky earrings, ruby semiconductor lasers." The gemstone sparkled as Emily held one up, blinked on the tiny ruby, the laser flash so bright Sean saw spots. "Tell me lasers don't have a use!"

Sean settled in with J-Stars, whose radars were overlaid onto the battlespace map. On it, Sean could see units across the Southwest USA as the war-games raged. Dogfights, Special Forces attacks, fighter patrols, unmanned vehicles of all sorts, and overhead satellite patches.

Sean saw J-Stars' X-band radar making blips near ABL, "Who's this?"

J-Stars smiled, "Red Team F-18 fighters. Eighty clicks out. They're lookin' at 'cha. Lickin' their lips."

Sean growled, "Let them try. I'll fry them out of their flight suits!"

J-Stars said, "Keep on with the ideas, Son. But planes are off-limits for the laser."

TEL 'GORBY' – CANYONLANDS

John Harshbarger put down the radio from the Red Team HQ, and his men jumped up and ran to their stations. When this beast blasted off, even though they'd worked with brush hooks and shovels to clear every plant they could find, in about twenty seconds there was going to be a firestorm hereabouts when the rocket engines ignited every remaining bit of flammable dust and dirt.

John signaled "Go!" The countdown started while they all ran for the small shelter they'd erected a hundred yards away.

Rocket engines ignited. Liquid-fueled inferno roared and spat from the SCUD C as the huge three stories of missile left behind the little canyon and roared up into the sky.

John breathed, "Good-bye, Ground-Zero Town."

AIRBORNE LASER – TECH AREA

Ten hours on patrol, the novelty is gone. Everyone was bored, walking around, eating, chatting. Sean couldn't really blame them. They had two full days of patrol ahead and they weren't really expecting anything in broad daylight. So, he wasn't about to be hard on them.

The fun of being in the Tech Area was the big screen. Lorrie kept the huge liquid crystal display up front lively with video from all over the battlespace. There were also PowerPoint slide presentations running automatically: a constant stream of all kinds of statistics on the Blue Team; order of battle, logistics, and attacks were all there for the seeing.

On the big screen battlespace map, a dot *flared.*

J-Stars called out, "Kettledrums! Kettledrums! Suspicious ground motion at Antelope Wells."

Sean radioed, "Flightdeck, this is Ops. Bearing 355 and level battle course."

"Ops, Flightdeck," Slammer said. "Backatcha on that," and ABL banked steeply and any unready crew, talking or munching, found themselves skidding and falling before getting up and running for their stations.

Lorrie, being C3I and the main croupier for all comings and goings, called out, "Beam director acquiring. Red, Laser Radar prepare for coordinate hand-off."

The big bulbous beam director nose of ABL, with its single big optic, cranked around looking. "Ops, C3I," Lorrie said. "Long-range video and Laser Radars up."

On the big screen, Lorrie's video showed the towering plume of a distant missile launch, so far away it was only a climbing gray-white streak.

From the cockscomb laser pod on top of ABL leapt a narrow ray of emerald laser light. It jumped across the space between them and tagged the missile at the tip of the smoke column.

Red called, "Wideband Doppler hits! Missile motion and location coming in."

Lorrie looked, called, "Missile velocity fifteen meters a second."

Emily radioed, "Attack Laser, where are you?"

In the laser area, Marty, up to his armpits in laser guts, radioed back, "We need more notice than that! Klystrons coming up. Fuel is still being mixed."

Sean yelled, "You're supposed to be ready!"

On the big screen the SCUD arced higher, trailing fire. Lorrie called out, "Velocity thirty meters a second, rising."

Sean took up a position behind Emily, watching her every move. He wanted to see the actual weapons system, to learn it himself. He looked over her moppet of raven curls, seeing her screen and flying fingers on the keyboards. On her sensors, through the full aperture of the beam director, the image was very close, and the missile—or something anyway—filled the high magnification screen.

Sean looked at the splatter on the monitor in amazement.

Emily glanced over her shoulder and saw his consternation. "You like?"

He didn't. What Sean expected to see in the targeting monitor was a nice crisp image of a picture-perfect gleaming missile rising on a plume of fire, clear and bright in the afternoon sun—and perfectly framed to aim at and blow away.

He got no such thing. What he did see was a shimmering chaotic cloudy jumping mess. "Where is the missile?"

Emily, through gritted teeth said, "That is the missile!"

"What's wrong with your system?" Sean was shocked by the broken-up speckled shaking banshee, unfocused and gibbering so hard it double-visioned all over the monitor. "Why does it look like that?"

"You ninny! It's the atmosphere!" Emily snapped out, hands totally full as the laser beam did not stabilize on the shaking missile, but rather jumped around, lost track, fell off the missile. She got it back on, barely, looked up. "Sorry. I'm slightly tense." Then dove back in working.

"What do you mean? The atmosphere? I can't even read the lettering on it or ID it!"

"You were expecting maybe an Imax movie? Consider: the missile is moving at Mach-oh-my-gosh, it is two hundred miles away, there's a ton of rough air and clouds between us and it, and we're flying in a different direction at six hundred miles per hour in an aircraft whose wings are flapping in the turbulence. You want to know what the lettering on it says? It says, 'You can't see me—let alone touch me.'"

Outside, another laser, this time golden and from the beam director, shot out and tagged the missile. Lorrie called, "Tracking Laser guidestar on!"

Emily said to Sean, "This golden laser creates an artificial star right at the missile. Then we follow the star. It's much brighter than the missile."

"Oh."

"Tracking guidestar loop closed!" Lorrie yelled, excitedly. The blobby speckled missile image snapped to the middle of the monitor, although to Sean it still looked like a flaming marshmallow freshly fallen into the campfire.

At least it was held in the center of the monitor. Sean said, "It's better, but we'll never get a positive ID on the missile and be allowed to knock it down."

Emily grimly smiled, "Oh no, we'll soon know exactly who this bad actor is— and exactly where he's going."

TEL 'GORBY' – CANYONLANDS

The TEL crew worked like lightning breaking down the TEL camp, tossing things, stripping camouflage. They had only moments to escape—in theory to hide and reload.

Although going up higher into the canyon was impossible, backing down was much easier. John had already found another canyon just a mile away, and he was sure they could hide there pretty well.

His crew jumped into the TEL. It rumbled away, escaping.

AIRBORNE LASER – TECH AREA

Sean, waiting, feeling useless, turned, said, "Strikeback, Ops. Eila, what about the launcher?"

"I'm working it! Laser Radars, what is origin and target?"

Red replied, "I'm thinkin' on it," which was, besides a break in intercom protocol, not really true since she was working like crazy. She called out, "Laser radar has ID, trajectory: TEL launched SCUD C. Impact point is Frenchmen's Flat, Nevada."

Eila yelled, "Ops, Strikeback. It's a hostile! A SCUD targeting Frenchman's Flat. Wow, look at it go."

Emily called out, "Ground-Zero Town. I should have guessed. Lorrie, can we get a picture of Frenchman's Flat?" She turned slightly to Sean. "Don't you have something to do?"

Sean jumped to his console and called the Command Operation Center. "COC, this is ABL Ops. We have Positive ID of a SCUD C, NATO designation SS-1d, launched offensive strike at Frenchman's Flat, Nevada. Request weapons release to us."

He waited for the answer while watching Lorrie get the long-range video up of Frenchman's Flat. She zoomed in to see the estimated impact point.

At high magnification, Lorrie nailed the playground. She adjusted focus and in the video, tied into their swings, the weapon-effects dolls swung gently.

Everyone in the Tech Area saw the schoolyard, the dummies looking just like children playing...

Emily blanched. "Back on the missile!"

This wasn't any better. The SCUD was like a mad Horseman of the Apocalypse riding his fiery steed down upon his prey.

Red called, "Eila, the GPS for the launcher is coming over machine-to-machine."

Eila checked. "Machine-to-machine didn't work. I've got to go manual." She opened her radio link and sang out. "Kirins, this is Strikeback. Launcher location is 15.43.1, 34.22.55. Go get 'em! Both of you!"

Airborne Laser's F-15 fighter escort peeled out for Antelope Wells—and her GPS hack.

Sean, surprised, looked up from getting weapons permission from the COC. "Hey, that's our air defense screen."

RED TEAM HORNETS

In the Red Team Hornets, watching from out beyond missile range, Ripsaw and Hacksaw both saw Airborne Laser's fighter escort break away.

"Ripsaw!" called Hacksaw, "The bad guys have made a mistake. The laser plane's ass is hanging out! Let's get her!"

The lead man, asked, unsure, "Even if it's a war-game, you wanna be the first pilot in history shot down by a laser?"

Hacksaw retorted, "Just pretend they're gonna barbecue your home state, what is it, New Hampshire?"

"You're right!" Ripsaw yelled, and threw his afterburner switches. "Live free—and unbarbecued—or die!"

Twin afterburners on both big jets blew carbon, and the Hornets looped over sharply.

The two F-18's accelerated into a missile attack run straight at Airborne Laser.

AIRBORNE LASER – TECH AREA

Sean had no time to worry about the F-15's being called away, for before he could yell to Eila to call them back, Emily shouted to him, "Sean, what the heck does COC say?"

As usual, under pressure the first thing that went out the window was radio protocol.

"Laser One, Ops. You got permission. Go!"

The missile—although like rice grains bouncing around on a drumhead—was at least being held in the center of the screen.

Sean asked, looking at the hideously ugly but centralized missile, "Now what?"

Emily said, "We turn on the magic mirror." And she set to work on something that looked like a fishnet flopping up and down on the screen. "Our friend the atmosphere, again" she said, and Sean wondered what the hell she meant.

The golden guidestar continued to shimmer on the side of the missile.

Lorrie was calling off meaningless numbers, "Greenwood frequency, three kilohertz. Two kilohertz." Lorrie noticed Sean's look. "It's the frequency of the atmosphere, how fast it's boiling. Lower is better. One kilohertz! Go!"

Emily pressed the bottom marked, AO Loop. "Adaptive Optics loops closing," and suddenly, the missile looked clear...well, it was more recognizable. No question, it was not a cinematic image, nor was it in color. But now, except for the shimmering around its body, it was clearly a missile.

Sean asked Emily, "What happened?"

"The adaptive optics is taking out the atmosphere—"

"—you ninny."

Emily grimaced, trying to keep her mouse hand right and still be civil. "I was going to ask, have you read *all* the manuals yet? Ha ha."

"Looks great!" Sean said, mentally lowering his standards as all tech managers are forced to do in the heat of battle.

RED TEAM HORNETS

The Red Team F-18's came ripping in right for Airborne Laser.

AIRBORNE LASER – TECH AREA

J-Stars yelled, "Kettledrums! Kettledrums! Fighter attack! Targeting radars trying for a weapons' solution on us."

"Air Defense, this is Ops. What about it?"

Jarhead looked, replied, "Red Team Squids coming in just under Mach 1 and getting ready to launch missiles."

"What kind?"

"Likely Phoenix extended range radar missiles. They carry two each for this exercise and they're fast and deadly as hell—even from forty miles out."

J-Stars said, "Fighters' targeting radar has a weapons solution."

TEL 'GORBY' – CANYONLANDS

By the time the F-15's were overhead looking for them, TEL Gorby was wedged up in another narrow canyon. Although John Harshbarger knew he would never get it back out, he also knew in a real military scenario there would be recovery teams to rescue and refurbish a still functional TEL.

He had won—the TEL would live to launch another day.

AIRBORNE LASER – TECH AREA

Marty called, "Attack Laser almost ready."

Lorrie said, "Thirty seconds to pop-up. You're losing the window. Hurry!"

Jarhead, looking at the electronic read-outs of the simulated battlespace, said, "Hornet missiles launched! Four Phoenix anti-air kicking off right at us. Fragmentation warheads."

"Air Defense, this is Ops. Can you take them?"

Jarhead shook his head. "That's a lot of missiles. They are so fast—and four of them—I couldn't get them all at once even they are in range. I'll try, but it's not going to work."

Matt Cho spoke up. "Hey Sean, I could knock them all down with a shot of the EMP cannon."

Emily looked up long enough to yell, "Don't do it! The EMP spatter will mess up the laser and my beam control!"

Sean yelled back, losing his patience, "We're going to get clobbered! We've got to do it!"

Emily said, evenly, "Don't you dare! You'll probably crash every computer in the place."

"You morons; it's all virtual anyway," Red called over. "Why don't we just not do it, and say we did?"

Sean said, "Matt?"

Matt fake-pulled his EMP cannon lanyard. "Boom!"

Sean called out, "Referee, this is ABL Ops. We have fired our EMP cannon and knocked all the Phoenix missiles out of the air."

"Say what?" The referee asked.

"We might not have the network connection to you worked out completely, so you can't see it, but we certainly blew every missile's brain away with EMP. Give us a break." He let his voice drop, a plaintive note in it of 'Give me liberty or give me death.' "We've only had two days' integration time—SECDEF orders."

The Ref went off the air for a moment. He returned and said, "OK, ABL. We flipped a coin and you're right." He patched in the Hornets, "Red Team Hornets 1 and 2, your Phoenixes are all downed."

"What!" yelled Ripsaw and Hacksaw together.

"Some gizmo, turns the missiles' brains into goop. They're toast."

"We is being robbed!" moaned Ripsaw.

"Hornets, you know the rules," the Ref rebuffed them. "No sniveling."

Sarcastically, Hacksaw asked, "How's about if we ram them, will that satisfy you?"

Back in Norfolk, the referee—handpicked partly on the basis of unflappability, as it could get pretty angry and competitive in war-games—replied after a second of static hiss, "Hornets, you are cleared to strafe."

"Strafe!" yelped Ripsaw and Hacksaw, again in unison. "You gotta be joking!"

"Suit yourselves, Hornets," came back the prim reply.

Across the few meters of air between them, from one cockpit to the other, the two F-18 pilots looked at each other. As one, they banked together toward ABL. The backs of their windscreens were fluffing white with sonic boom compressed air, and it was at a pretty speed...

The Hornet fly-boys laughed.

Afterburners shot flame. Heading straight up the Mach meter, they started their run toward Airborne Laser, forty miles distant. Within moments, the fluffy shock-compressed air built up and clung like cotton candy to their canopies as they approached the sound barrier—the cotton candy clouds blew away as they boomed through Mach 1.

AIRBORNE LASER – TECH AREA

Sean gave a whoop of triumph when the Phoenix missiles were downed, and turned to see the laser beam director sending out a violet burst of light, scanning over the SCUD. He looked back at the laser people and asked, "Why haven't you shot yet?"

Red said, "Remote sensing laser radar measuring warhead chemical composition."

Sean said, "Screw its composition, knock it down."

Emily said, "This isn't just war, we need the science data. Besides, if it's biological you might not want to blow it up."

Lorrie called, "Tropopause pop-up ten seconds. Come on, you guys. It's getting away."

Red and Emily frantically worked the data until Red looked up and said, "Warhead shows traces of Triple Superphosphate. It's a simulated nuke—actually just a ton of high explosive."

COL HAREDA – SQUADRON KIRIN – ANTELOPE WELLS

Although Col Hareda and his wingman in their F-15's had gotten to Antelope Wells in just five minutes, they and their radars saw nothing down below in the riveted and broken browns of the rock and scrub of the desert. When they checked Eila's GPS hack, it was a rocky area where a SCUD could not have been launched.

In a few moment, realizing they could not find the target, they called back in. "ABL Strikeback, this is Kirin 1. We do not see Bandits. No bandits sighted."

Eila came back on. "Sorry, Kirins. I was mistaken on those coordinates. It was point 34, not point 35."

"Ask Major Phillips if he would like a Mulligan."

RED TEAM HORNETS

The Red Team Hornets roared toward ABL, this time no targeting radars locked on. They opened their M61A1 20mm cannon gun ports—they were on a strafing run.

As they got closer, Ripsaw yelled. What the hell is that?" In his zooming video camera, he could see weaponry sticking out of the belly of ABL.

"Is that a Phalanx gun on the belly?" Hacksaw asked.

"Sure looks like it. Kind of amazing, really. Range is almost exactly same as our M61A1's."

Hacksaw yelled, "Let's jump them from overhead where the Phalanx can't reach us!"

Ripsaw pulled hard on his stick. "Alright!"

The Hornets steepened their angle of attack. By the time they were in range, they would be above ABL.

The fighters climbed.

AIRBORNE LASER – TECH AREA

The SCUD on the big screen was a flaming arrowhead roaring like a demon toward Frenchman's Flat and the schoolyard.

Marty said, "Attack Laser is ready."

Lorrie said, "Five seconds to pop-up. Hurry!"

J-Stars yelled, "Kettledrums! Kettledrums! They're coming again—and fast!"

Jarhead said, "I've got them! Red Team Squids coming in at Mach 2!" He studied the radar for a moment, "They're on a strafing run; going to bounce us from over top. I can't get the elevation for them. I need twenty degrees."

Sean said, "Flightdeck, this is Ops: emergency bank right twenty degrees! Bank! Bank!"

"Slammer, this is Emily. Do not bank. We'll lose the SCUD."

Sean yelled, "What about the fighters?"

Emily said, "Shut up! Just shut up! That's a game. This is real. Laser guidestar on."

"Broil the fighters with the laser. The war-game computer will accept it."

"There are people in those planes. Do you know how many treaties that violates? This laser is for missiles."

"We are not going to live to see it!" yelled Jarhead, while Sean let go of the pressure of the airborne attack coming at them and barked, "OK, then at least smoke the missile!"

"Tracking loops not closing all the way," reported Lorrie. "Main laser window is..."

"Excrement," Emily exclaimed, "We didn't clean the damned window."

"Can't you shoot?"

"It's not clear enough. We'll never get enough power. We have to hope we get a clearer atmosphere, less turbulent."

Jarhead stormed around, "Then give me an effing shot!"

AIRBORNE LASER – TECH AREA

Ripsaw's voice came into Airborne Laser crew's headphones over the Command line and razzed them. "Your big old ugly laser plane is going down down down."

Sean ignored him, watched the separation of the booster. Matt Cho said quietly, "We've lost the last stage. We can't kill the boost vehicle now."

"What about that, Emily?" Sean asked.

"We can still cook-off the warhead before it hits. It's a little harder, but we can try maybe."

Just in front of the rocketing SCUD, the laser focused to a pinpoint, the guidestar spot blindingly golden.

Marty called on the intercom "Laser fire control to you, Laser one!"

Emily's hands hovered over her console. "Guidestar target loop closed. No. It won't work."

The missile warhead, now heading lower and lower toward the ground was shimmering and dancing again on the big screen.

"What's happening?" Sean asked.

"Close to the ground the turbulence is much worse. It's too late."

Sean said, "Do it! Shoot! Just shoot now!"

Emily hands were frozen, unable to get herself to fire the laser, while the crew, hands gripping their consoles, watched helplessly as the SCUD rocketed toward the schoolyard.

At Frenchman's Flat, the frightened dolls stared out at them, almost human.

Lorrie was crying her makeup. "Missile going terminal."

The huge SCUD warhead ripped in on the mock children in the playground. Its thousand-pound high-explosive warhead slammed into Frenchman's Flat— and detonated.

The explosion took out the half the town, the school—and blew the playground all to hell.

Emily and the whole Tech Area stared in shock at the inferno of the town. Blast debris roiled so high over the annihilated town there was simply nothing left but smoke and flames.

Just then, the Red Team Hornets reached Airborne Laser—and blew past at Mach 2. Their Mach shock wave boomed through ABL with a roar like a passing locomotive.

Hacksaw called over the command channel, "And your *precious* laser plane is *cold meat.*"

The words struck Airborne Laser Tech area like a blow. Everyone looked each other, suddenly even more depressed.

Sean jumped up on his chair and yelled, "That's right, people! You feel really bad when you die in a war-game." He let his voice drop, still angry, "Yet it's nothing compared to the real thing."

They all got to feel bad for just a moment, then they felt worse when on the big screen Gen Washer's face replaced the fiery ruins of the schoolyard.

Jarhead muttered, "*Ave atque vale.*" *Hail and farewell.*

Gen Washer, restrained, his shaven head slightly bowed, considered his words carefully as they were going out to everyone on the command circuit. "Laser Warriors, hail and farewell! The town you defended suffered 100% destruction, the launcher escaped, and the war-game computer shows you have been shot down. However, a valiant effort. We are confident some future day the battle shall be yours."

Emily laid her head on her console. *Defeat.*

AIRBORNE LASER – HEAD

Sean never dwelt on failure, rather always looked for something to *do*. He pulled Emily to her feet, prodded her up the galley ladder and into the tiny head.

Crammed into the tiny room, Emily looked at Sean for several long seconds in silence, and then sank against him. Gratefully, she allowed Sean to hold her for a moment, shushing her.

Sean said, "That was our one shot. Why didn't you fire?"

"It was too late. That close to the ground—you saw the display. The missile was just a spattering of speckles, the laser beam would have been smeared all over."

"You still could have shot."

Emily pushed away, eyes closed, head tilted up until her crown of her head leaned against the mirror. "And risk burning the main window for nothing? We just haven't tested it enough—"

"You've tested plenty. Why?"

"I saw the numbers, the beam loading wasn't enough. Maybe for this low probability shot, we might have blown out the million dollar laser window."

"Explain."

"It's highly technical."

"There's more than technical here."

She was silent, then, "I hate being in the war business. Everyone who develops something like this always creates a monster."

"Ten thousand dollars a flight hour up here and you've got moral qualms?" Sean said bitterly. "I should fucking arrest you."

Perhaps it was the obscenity, Sean's first to her, for Emily suddenly cracked, screamed at him. "Fucking arrest me? *Fuck you*, for coming in after all the work and judging me! *Fuck you*, for forgetting the five years I have sweated inside this testosterone-stinking tin can of a plane! *Fuck you*, for all your whining when you are incapable of even conceiving a plane like this let alone building it! *Fuck you*... what am I saying? I quit. Oh, that felt great. I really quit."

Sean, you blew it. Sean tried to think of an angle, some leverage. All he could come up with was, "What about those years of sweat? What about your dreams of ballistic missile defense? You're so close."

"If we're so close, you finish it."

"You know I can't. No one can but you. You and the people you've got here. Help us, please."

"Screw you." Emily yanked open the door and went out to where the galley loft overlooked the Tech Area. She yelled down at the upturned faces of her crew, "Everybody? I Q-U-I-T! I repeat, I quit!"

Following her out of the tiny head, to Sean it suddenly smelled of toilet bowl cleaner and the metal of the sink seemed battered. Sean mumbled aloud to himself, "Weeks like this, you start thinking maybe the Silver Star is the least of your worries."

PAEKTU-SAN ACADEMY OF ARCHITECTURE – PYONGYANG

It was ironic, Architect Su thought, that the group should meet this time, instead of at the MPAF, at his Paektu-san Academy of Architecture.

After all, if he had any true center for his life, it was somewhere here in his Chairmanship of the Academy, his students and projects, his pleasant corner office looking out of his giant building to a sensual park he'd designed in a hilly corner of Pyongyang. Here, unlike the MPAF, he could bring family members, play with children, and savor life. Military and 2nd Economic Committee business he always did elsewhere. That was work; the Academy was, well, his true life.

It was at the Academy that Su had done the happy work of reconstructing Pyongyang, and the more personal work of designing the dachas, mansions, and palaces for Great Leader, Dear Leader, the generals, and the leadership clique. Perhaps, should things go well with the treaty, from the Academy he would soon work with Dearest Leader on redoing the whole DPRK—but this time, doing it right!

His specialties had passed through various phases. Right after the Fatherland Liberation War, the cities had been flattened. With millions homeless, there were huge constructions of housing to be done. Su had argued vociferously for copying many of the things the Russians had done with their housing: celebrate the worker and give them some ceiling space, some comforts, some extras. After all, on the giant scale they were going to work, it wasn't that much harder to put bathrooms on every floor, instead of on every third. The Great Leader, however, looking ahead at the concrete projections and the safety limits on building heights, had denounced the Soviet idea of freeing the proletariat and giving them their due as being "retrograde," and "recidivist," and not respecting "the local values and aesthetics of the Korean people." This was code for, "I don't want to pay for eight-foot ceilings and lots of toilets; the commoners will have to live with six-foot ceilings and we can pack on many more floors and use a lot less concrete."

Sadly, not only were the living spaces they created simply huge log cabins with door jambs that the newer generation hit their heads on, but even from afar, one saw that the construction was shoddy; the plumb-lines of the balconies hung crookedly.

His limo was passing the hulk of the 104-story Ryugyong hotel with its three never-revolving restaurants. Triangular in shape, the building was the twentieth-tallest in the world, almost as tall as the Empire State Building. Although inspired by Stalinist skyscrapers, the Ryugyong's pyramidal shape had the unmistakable visual effect of displaying the Pharaonic ambitions of the Kim leadership. Although more than twenty years old, the hotel was still only a shell, its crocked elevator shafts and bad workmanship dooming it. Neither a single restaurant, nor one of its 3,000 rooms was completed, their windows just gaping holes. It would now never be finished; a failure of gigantic proportions visible across Pyongyang. Su smiled wanly. *At least I was not involved in the design—and told the Great Leader the project was inadvisable.* But the South Koreans had just finished building the world's tallest hotel in Singapore, and the Great Leader needed to answer this thrown-down gauntlet. Architect Su managed to halt the project after the shell was done, and honor was at least visually satisfied—and it was clear to all continuing was folly. *At least its presence is amazing.*

With the bombing over, Architect Su had gotten a clean slate to work with, and he laid in the river-bridges arrow-straight and gorgeous, the boulevards were the widest in the world, and from vista to monument to park to glorious Korean-roofed palaces for the People, the Phoenix of a new ideal rose from the DPRK's charred napalm-smelling ruins.

The cities built, Architect Su had then passed on to monuments and plazas. He'd done many of the squares, and literally thousands of statues of North Korea's leaders. For example, he had designed an enormous statue of Dear Leader to stand in front of Pyong-son, which made the Statue of Liberty look like a dwarf. Later, he turned to special shrines, mansions, and parks. These days, when he had some moments to himself, it was to human living spaces he turned his current passion, to the likes of the Underwater Mansion.

Now, heading to his Academy, he looked out of his Benz's windows at the suburbs of Pyongyang. *They are beautiful,* he thought, emphatically trying to see the good. It was easy, looking out at the moldering cityscape to instead feel depressed. He remembered his first contact with an American ex-architect who was on an agricultural exchange team and passing through Pyongyang. The American architect had laughed politely when asked what he thought of Pyongyang, Architect Su's pride and joy. The visitor had had far too much to drink, and so without the cultural translation necessary for an appreciation of his insouciant observation, he was honest. "If you imagine Minsk or some other godless Soviet era construction, and give in to the desire for truly going in for the socialist decorative look, then partially clean it up, shrink the already tiny living spaces, throw up a multitude of huge concrete statues of Monkey-gods, forget everything about human joy and aspiration, and behold, you have Pyongyang."

It was not true at all, of course, the city could be beautiful and distinct from every other city in Asia, and in fact on earth. "You must admit," Su had countered, "It is an amazing city, distinct and full of monuments of perfection, should you not agree with them, even the form you must admire."

"Yes, it is amazing. It is an achievement. It's just has no humanity."

"Why? Even the people of the city are especially beautiful."

The visitor took another of many swigs. "Sure. Carefully sorted and chosen. You've banished anyone under five feet tall to the outer provinces, and forcibly removed any handicapped, mentally challenged, chronically diseased, feeble, old, and ugly people. The government castrates dwarves. Of course your Pyongyang-ers are beautiful. They're hand picked! You only allow the elite to stay in the capitol of the People's Paradise. Architecture is supposed to be about all the people, the interaction of public spaces and the needs of the people, and yet in the People's Paradise, you declare many of them to be unfit. It's easy to architect for the ones who don't defecate. You don't need handicap access, stairs can be massive, doors can be huge. There can be nowhere to really sit. What about the real people, the ones given the half-empty rice bowls and yet all the real feelings?"

"It is because of the Americans! Their threat!"

"You mean, no mentally challenged people in the capital because of America? My friend, form follows function, and the function here is to make North Korea look like something it is not."

Su bit his lip. He knew what the architect meant and it hurt him deeply.

After this, Architect Su managed to finagle a few trips to foreign Consulates, and managed some subscriptions to forbidden trade magazines from the USA, Asia, and Europe. When he finally had a good look at the world, he was appalled. He could barely finish his current projects—especially when his last minute inspirational changes were slapped down in icy silence by the building committees. When in Manhattan, Phillip Johnson put a saucy Chippendale top on his new AT&T building—a crown on a seemingly socialist-themed skyscraper—Architect Su walked onto the bridge over the Taedong in the dead of winter, hoping he would find the courage to jump into the icy river. The State Security Department car, following him, quickly disgorged several agents who assisted him back home. The self-destructive urge passed, he came to grips with his place in the world, and in the design of his dachas he had found some solace.

Ahead Su saw his Academy, the green park rising behind. The large buildings looked almost perfect in their white tiled exterior and neat rows of windows—until you got close and saw many of the small windows were broken open because the air conditioning never worked. Besides the lack of electricity, the cooling fluid had long ago been stolen and couldn't be replaced.

He passed through the lobby. When there were no official visitors it was empty, the lights and heat off. A huge model of Pyongyang sat in the center of the room, but the windows were too small to light it and the model was sunk in a darkness as real as true evening in Pyongyang. He passed under the single light bulb which lit the corridor. Few people worked here now, so tight was the budget. In the first area along the hall, his young men and women graduate students in architecture were working hard at assembling air conditioners for export—ironically, given the propped-open windows of their own work room.

There was little support for architectural study. When Su had put it to the students they could stay and work, studying only in the evenings, they had all opted to work. Here, all day, his grad students put together the pieces Su managed to obtain from a few still-working local plants. Here in plain sight, there was less thievery of valuable parts such as compressors. Done under Su's supervision, the money went to the students; no distant institute or army unit could strip the profits along the export railroad to China.

In his office down the hall, for a happy moment, he enjoyed the quiet of the huge empty building as he flipped through the idealistic design sketches of his students—until he came across an old drawing.

It was a source picture for his design of the Underwater Mansion; a color lithograph on some happy bygone autumn afternoon of the real *Mansion Parisian* on the *Avenue Foch*.

The huge guardian horse chestnuts lining the front of the mansion spread their broad branches of green-goldening leaves over the arched entrance to the grounds, and the clear fall sunlight bounced off the pickets of the black wrought iron fencing seemingly surrounding the secrets of the full lives within the house.

As in his dreams, again the death of his mansion came to him in the image of a burned and floating window treatment, a ruined muddy tassel. Instead of time dulling his grief, the pain surged at the memory of his murdered architectural child.

* * *

The National Defense Committee members came singly, so as not to be noticed, and although most wore their KPA uniforms, they entered at the back and moved quickly out of sight.

By evening, they were all in the building. In the auditorium, First Architect Su delivered his report two days ahead of schedule and only five days after they had all met at the Ministry of People's Armed Forces.

Now, they had met for hours, the room tense. Wall maps showed the plans for the invasion of South Korea. Army, Special Forces, Navy movements marked, and yet the room was skeptical. Although most of them preferred war to the constant poverty of the land, and believed they could win—they still needed to be sure they had no other choice.

Dearest Leader indicated Architect Su. He stood, weighing all the years and times they had had together. As Chair of the 2nd Economic Committee he had dealt with all their requests for coordination of filling the most important need in North Korea—the Armed Forces requirements. They trusted him and liked him. When Su had presented his slides, the generals looked pleased. Architect Su had indeed, again, come through for them. With his plan and strategy, if required, they were certain to win over the South in short order.

Only one last brow furrowed. General Kwon said, "What about the American 7th Air Force at Osan? What if they are not withdrawn? If we do need to invade, they could stop us."

"Not in time," Il-Moon said. "Seoul holds a quarter of the population and 70% of the economic base of South Korea. If we take Seoul we will have millions of hostages and most of the wealth of South Korea. With the help of new technology and your forces we can easily annihilate the Americans and take Seoul."

General Kwon persisted, "What about Desert Storm? And Kosovo?"

"The lessons of campaigns near Europe or in open desert Kingdoms do not apply to our heavily-fortified country six thousand miles from their shores. In both cases the American preparations took months. Even air strikes took weeks to start."

General Park said emphatically, "My armor can smash across the DMZ and take Seoul, a mere forty miles away, and its population intact within two days, perhaps within one day! Then we dig in and start peace negotiations. Even the Americans admit we can take Seoul. They will not dare use nuclear weapons. Would America destroy Korea to save it?"

Il-Moon agreed. "We are reunifying Korea. We are on our sacred soil. Do the Americans have the will to put hundreds of thousands of their boys in some far away place that is unimportant? If so, we will make it painful and we will make it bloody. Once we have Seoul, they will accept peace negotiations as inevitable. We will have reunified Korea."

Dearest Leader looked at them all carefully. "It will not come to war. I believe we will prevail in the treaty talks and peacefully obtain a confederal system with all of us still in power, and yet many great improvements. You have all looked at the terms? Everyone here will have total amnesty from all the past—and much money and power. Come, who would not wish to play on the bigger chessboard of the One Korea?"

The generals fiddled with the bankbooks Dearest Leader handed out, looking at sums in dollars equivalent to their salaries and perks for one hundred years.

"That being said," Dearest Leader continued, "You have planned the details for fifty years. Refine them later. You know you can win. If our negotiations fail, who votes for war?"

Slowly, all seven of The National Defense Committee raised their hands.

Il-Moon said, "Comrades, Korea shall be one. Begin your preparations."

CLOAK ROOM – PAEKTU-SAN ARCHITECTURAL ACADEMY

Architect Su, at the meeting's end, requested that Dearest Leader review plans for a huge statue in Kim Il-Sung Square to honor his father. There were...*difficulties*... of color, theme, placement. It was all very...*difficult*. Would he mind?

With twenty Guard Command soldiers outside in the hall, Su outlined his issues to Dearest Leader, who seemed impatient about his father's statue, until Su said, "It will take the better part of a year's supply of copper from the Yondok mines to make the statue."

"I believe my father would not want this. After all, the electrical cabling company must then import expensive copper. No, my father would not mind waiting for a time for his statue."

Architect Su enjoyed the tug of a suppressed smile. If old Kim Jong-Il heard this he would not be merely turning in his hermetically sealed tomb—he would be spinning like a top. The country having to sacrifice was unimportant compared to his needs. Su remembered—in perhaps an encapsulation of the difference between Confucian and Western ways—Ecclesiastes: 'The dead know not any thing, neither have they any more a reward; for the memory of them is forgotten. Also their love, and their hatred, and their envy, is now perished; neither have they any more a portion for ever in any *thing* that is done under the sun.' This was surprisingly untrue for the Kims, for, even more than Mao, they held dominion despite their deaths. Their love, their hatred, and their envy lived on; their mortal passions *were* the life of many of their citizens.

Su looked at Dearest Leader, who was enjoying the fall colors of the park. He hoped he was not being overly familiar. Nevertheless, the strange grief at the loss of his mansion was sharp now, and he pushed on: "As I know you a little better, Dearest Leader, perhaps I could ask you about the end of the Underwater Mansion."

Dearest Leader jerked his eyes back from the park. Showing weakness was the most serious weakness, and as the former Director of the State Security Department he knew even acknowledging an assassination attempt made the leader look victimized, human, and humiliated. It opened the nightmare box, and released the hitherto unthinkable.

"How dare you presume?" Dearest Leader jumped to his feet, looked daggers at Architect Su, and spun on his heel.

In his anger, he exited out Su's door toward the public lobby. Because this direction had not been secured for him by his Guard Command, there was shouting, running, the kicking-in of doors as his security contingent got ahead of him and took down anyone they saw.

Suddenly, over the smashing of doors and bellowed threats of the Guards—and the ringing shame in his brain—Su heard Dearest Leader bawl: "First Chief State Architect Su!"

Architect Su realized the Dearest Leader's Guard Command, running ahead down the uncleared halls ahead of him, had seen the students in the air conditioning manufacturing room and taken them all down as security risks to Dearest Leader.

Architect Su—his old sore joints creaking—came running. Dearest Leader pointed through the glass to where the Guard Command had rifles at the heads of a dozen terrified spread-eagled boy and girl students amidst their architecture drawing tables and half-built air conditioners. "This is the strangest student study area."

Time to face the music. Architect Su sighed. No one seemed to understand what it took to keep the doors open... "As the Great Leader said in his famous speech of April 13, 1968, 'Youth must become the vanguard on all fronts of our economic and defense construction to bring our revolution to final victory.' For my own graduate students here, they not only study hard, they want to help bring in a few dollars for the State."

"But what are they doing?"

Su explained how he obtained locally-made parts, while bartering North Korean fish meal for cheap coolant from India. "So, the students can manufacture competitive units here between their studies. We have orders for several thousand units for China, where in the outer provinces they are becoming wealthy enough to want air conditioning—and yet cannot afford Japanese or Chinese models."

"So, you are actually making things for export?" Dearest Leader suddenly clapped him on the shoulder. "Good work, Su-ssi." He motioned to the Guard Command to release the students. "Let them get back to work." Taking Su's arm, he led him back toward Su's office. Once there, Dearest Leader asked, "What makes you inquire about Mansion 27?"

"It is perhaps personal, but there is a sadness; it was our creation you see. I wanted to know of its end. Much like a father grieves and wishes to know how his child died."

"I will allow you a few questions."

'I understand there were explosions. How many were there?"

"First there was one. Not so bad, and your mansion held up admirably."

Su nodded and waited. "Then there were more? From where?"

"Two more followed. They came as if dropped on our heads."

"How much time later? What had happened in the meantime?"

Dearest Leader described Aide Park's efforts, and his own escape in the minisub with Il-Moon.

Architect Su hid a small grin as he allowed himself a moment's pleasure at Il-Moon and Aide Park's superb mastery of the disastrous situation, then mused, "Perhaps five minutes. Then?"

"We were in the minisub when the final detonation occurred. We were shoved out of the mansion, and the walls did finally break."

"Was there ever an investigation?"

"Of course, there were culpable persons. The conspirators were led by General Chon and Premier Yu. Il-Moon convincingly showed me their corruption."

Architect Su said mildly, "This surprises me. They would have been the last people I would suspect. Why did only they die?"

Dearest Leader stood, looked at his watch. "It is a mystery to me. I saw the movies of their treason, but I was never able to speak to them."

"Even more puzzling. If they were part of the conspiracy, would they be at Mansion 27? They would know they were likely to die. And the assassins?"

Dearest Leader described Kang's trial and execution, leaving out only Kang's more hurtful words.

"Colonel Kang? I-Pong Kang?" At Dearest Leader's nod, pain rushed into Su. "I am beyond shocked. I served his grandfather in Manchuria when I was just a boy runner for the freedom fighters. He was a true Hero of the Revolution." Su stopped when he saw Dearest Leader's face. He too knew Kang's family was special.

"I am well aware of Colonel Kang's grandfather's service to the DPRK, and his friendship with my grandfather," Dearest Leader said in a warning tone. "We were all shocked."

Architect Su sat for a moment in stunned contemplation. He could not imagine the ramifications. *If I-Pong Kang had lost faith, who among us is worthy...* "And the outcome?"

"The interrogations were effective. The whole story was revealed, and it was well-documented the Americans and Puppet South were behind it. Colonel Kang was very explicit with names, rendezvous, and so on."

"You are convinced of Hakkermann's perfidy?"

Dearest Leader looked up at Su's crumbly cement office ceiling, considering. "They talk to us of peace—and yet it is still talk. Your defensive work remains our most critical backstop." Dearest Leader flicked back a silk sleeve and looked at his Rolex. He was punctual to a fault. "I must go. I have many people to brief on the financial and political arrangements for the post-Treaty world."

Su was still reeling, his heart pumping hard as if full of viscous fluid; the thick sluggish black blood of deepest betrayal. He had held baby I-Pong Kang in his arms; played round-about-mouse with the little tyke until they both were dizzy. "And the fate of the others?"

Dearest Leader turned back at the door. "Only Colonel Kang of the culprits was executed. The others remain imprisoned."

"And the basis for this mercy?"

Onto Dearest Leader's face slipped a narrow confused smile. "I suppose I had my reasons."

"Might it be possible for me to see the files, to talk to these individuals?"

Dearest Leader shrugged, "Of course, it is *possible.* I specifically ordered them held, although Il-Moon was in charge of the details." He avoided looking at Su. "I do not know where they are, but you may discuss your *sadness* with the officer who conducted the interrogations." *Be careful, Su-ssi.* "The interrogating officer will know the whereabouts of the prisoners. His name is Major Tam Ho."

AIRBORNE LASER – TECH AREA

Lorrie spent the first half of the return flight in desperate begging with Emily, but by the time they passed over Four Corners and into New Mexico airspace, she had given up. Emily was not going to change her mind, nor was there a point in trying. The fulfilled time in Lorrie's life, the time where she'd become someone thanks to Emily, was over. Her past, however, was filled with sadness and even tragedy, and so the guilty part of her brain accepted this as simply one more brass knuckles in the face: she'd always known it was coming. She didn't deserve this good a life. *You're scum, O'Leary, that's why this happened. That's why Pa killed himself. You could have prevented it. You could have prevented this just like you could have walked into the bedroom and stopped him. Except you're worthless and you deserve this—and everything else shitty that's going to happen to you.*

After giving up on Emily, who sat staring out her picture window and not responding to anyone, Lorrie cried herself out at her console.

Red for once was careful with her words, wisely, since not only did Lorrie outweigh her by forty pounds and had a strong if tattered sense of honor, but she had been victor in not a few cat-fights. Red, knowing all this, just pretended to ignore her crying. She herself felt at sea at the prospect of no Emily. Distractedly, Red searched her computer for her last resume. She was startled when she realized she hadn't updated it since Emily hired her. Never once had she considered leaving, the years so rich and endless spreading out before her. *Emily's the only one I can talk to. She's the only one who knows anything about remote sensing. Without her, I won't be able to figure it out. We're all D-E-A-D.* She couldn't wait to land and run away from this mess. *I knew this whole thing would never work.* She started updating her resume.

The rest of the crew was numb, most hoping it would blow over. Meanwhile, their jobs were flashing before them. Someone else besides Emily in charge? How would this person manage the work? Who would keep their jobs? What would the new management do with the current contractors and government personnel? After the comfortable years of Emily's tenure, it was all too alien to think about.

When Lorrie had cried herself out, she hid her face in a towel as she walked through the consoles of the Tech Area. She climbed the ladder to the galley loft awkwardly and locked herself in the head.

She was too crummy to have Emily forever as she'd prayed every night since Emily had hired her almost off the street—but she had to concede, as she washed her raccooned mascara face, that Emily had the right to give up.

Lorrie might have been crushed, but she knew her duty. She cleaned herself up, then popped open her cell phone and made the calls some crewmember always had to make under these circumstances.

AIRBORNE LASER – HANGAR COMPLEX

Airborne Laser landed down the tire-scarred white runway in the desert sunshine. As usual after landing, she taxied to the end of the miles-long Kirtland runway and rolled onto the apron extending through the flight line fence. As usual, Chief Auggie had the big gates open and the traffic on the highway road-blocked. ABL rumbled across the highway and, dwarfing the Advanced Laser

Facility office building, trundled past to where the waiting ground crew flagged her to a stop against the White Elephant.

ABL TECH AREA

The tech crew, carrying ropes, sneaked up behind Emily as she unbuckled, stood, and cried out, "My last flight. Stanford here I come–"

The crew pounced on her. She struggled as they hog-tied her, yelling, "Chief Scientists don't get washed out!"

Emily was strong and well-built, but the crew had her roped in a second, then carried her down the airstairs. The ABL crew yelled and whooped as they watched Emily unceremoniously dumped onto the tarmac.

From nearby, there came the moaning wind-up of sirens.

Around the corner of the ABL hangar, emergency and headlights flashing wildly, zoomed a huge yellow USAF flight line fire truck. In the fore and aft turrets, the crew was already manning the water cannons.

The whole ABL family, alerted by Lorrie's calls, were hooting and calling out as struggling Emily rolled to try to get to her knees, bound as she was at ankles, knees, arms, and chest. Fighting to get off the ropes and untie herself while lying on the tarmac, she managed to get partially erect before the fire truck—only twenty feet away—opened up with the forward water cannon!

The heavy jet of water caught Emily kneeling and knocked her sideways onto the tarmac. The second cannon came on and the jets of water rolled her over and over, pounding her into a sodden mass in her 'last flight washout.'

Sean stood aside from the mêlée, numbly watching the crew laugh, take photos of whacked Emily, who still worked madly to get the ropes loose. Washout knots are of a special kind which will fall away with the right trick. But in the freezing hard fire hose spray, it seems impossible. Lorrie ran to help Emily.

Emily, who secretly had the ropes loose enough, grabbed Lorrie and pulled her into the stream. They screamed and laughed and cried in the slamming jets of water until the fire truck quit spraying. It tooted its air horn, brakes hissed, and the big yellow truck turned and rolled away.

"Good-bye, Airborne Laser. Hello, Stanford," Emily yelled, and exhausted, rolled over to get to her feet and saw—looking down at her—a concerned Jeanette DeFrancis.

"Emily, are you all right?"

Emily froze. "Oh, no!"

Sean walked over, pulled Emily up, whispered to her, "I thought you liked her."

"She's the Princess of fricking Darkness!"

For a moment they formed a tableau: Airborne Laser, Emily just risen from the tarmac, Sean and Jeanette facing her.

Beyond them, across the airport, glowered the distant high-rise Wyndham hotel.

WYNDHAM HOTEL – ALBUQUERQUE AIRPORT

If the hotel room had been pitted out before, it was now approaching buzzard cage territory. The only things impeccable were the Questar telescope with its mounted Hasselblad camera and the laptop hooked up to the hotel Internet. Spiney looked over the photos on his laptop viewer. He found the best ones of Emily's washout. So little human company had he, Spiney often talked to himself. Looking at the tableau in front of Airborne Laser he muttered, "Limo woman, Pussy Galore, and the Gomer. What a party. This is going to make me a killing."

AIR FORCE RESEARCH LAB – SCIF VAULT

As Jeanette, Sean and wet-haired Emily waited, Ms. Canthor, the Directed Energy Chief—for Airborne Laser (X) fell under the Directed Energy Directorate—touched her proximity card ID to the vault lock and green lights flashed. Sean pulled open the heavy door and they walked through a tight file-cabinet lined hall and into a cramped conference room.

As they walked, Ms. Canthor asked conversationally, "So how do you like our Airborne Laser, Sean?"

"There are two things you don't want to watch being made: sausage and science."

Jeanette laughed. "Other than that, Mrs. Lincoln, how was the play?"

"First rate. Airborne Laser will revolutionize warfare."

Emily, toweling her hair, muttered, "Your mutual admiration society has five seconds to makes its point before I tunnel out of here. I have a date with the out-processing office."

In the conference room, a beige room like all the others in the government, there were pictures of famous satellites and aircraft on the walls.

Jeanette's Exec was projecting a Vu-graph briefing. The first slide was clearly a surveillance photo of a North Korean mountain valley and its now-familiar outbuildings—except overlaid on the surveillance photo were the outlines of strange complex structures and whorls like cancerous growths. "This is a satellite image of Pyong-son," Jeanette talked to the picture, "while overlaid on it is a radar image taken by Radiant Outlaw of what is below ground."

Sean dragged Emily up to the screen for a closer look at the above-and-below-ground picture. Jeanette said, "You see why we're all so worried, Emily?"

"We? No one believes you, do they? You always promise technology you can't deliver. This is a synthetic ground-penetrating radar image. It requires you to guess the physics of the ground, like emissivity and conductance. Guess wrong and you get bogus images like these."

"Just because we're not sure, doesn't mean we shouldn't do something!"

"You're not a scientist anymore, Jeanette. You've become a prophet; and you're a stranger in your own land."

Sean pointed at several features. "Emily, here is warhead integration, telemetry, launchers. It's a hidden—and unacknowledged—ballistic missile complex rigged for war."

"We could make sure those missiles stay home and dry," Jeanette added, "if Airborne Laser were operational and deployed to Japan. We could watch over Korea, Emily."

"*Good morning!* Wake up and smell the burnt toast. The city we defended today got obliterated and we got our own asses zotzed out of the sky. Who would be stupid enough to ask us to defend a real country?"

Jeanette held out the few rough pages of square black type on cheap paper that are USAF orders. "For the two of you. Personally signed by the President." She read from the text: "'You will secretly deploy Airborne Laser (X) to Japan to defend against surprise ballistic missile launches from North Korea when our forces are withdrawn before the treaty signing.'"

Emily shook her head at the patent insanity of it, asked mockingly, "What did you tell him? That we'd be operational in Korea by last Friday?"

Jeanette said gently, "You'll be very proud of me. I actually did refrain from promising you can time travel yet."

Sean felt he had to interrupt. "One problem, Jeanette. That plane shouldn't go to Korea. It should be court-martialed. Ops are chaos, the attack laser is unreliable, managing the crew is like herding cats, and the chief scientist is a freeze artist."

Emily laughed sarcastically. "You were a great help. Imparting worldly wisdom by yelling in my ear 'Smoke the fucker!'"

Jeanette looked at them until they each looked to her. "Emily, you have a passion for protecting the innocent. Sean has operational experience."

"I've done my part. I'm going to Stanford."

Sean, in a low voice, said, "A million innocent lives in jeopardy."

Ms. Canthor added quietly, "You know they will never ever make it in time without you, Emily."

Emily whispered, "I just don't think I can do it."

Jeanette looked Sean and Emily for a long quiet minute. "Did I ever tell you I always really wanted to have children? When grad school and getting a job were done, Peter and I tried and tried, but it was not to be. Some nights, it's 3:00 a.m., looking at myself in the mirror and I wonder why go on? Then I think how I have you. And you. I smile at myself and go on."

The room seemed to ring with the silence of the vault. Then Emily said, "Only until Airborne Laser is operational."

Sean jumped in, "And deployed to Japan for this operation."

As they were leaving, Jeanette reached to swing the vault door open. Sean stopped her with a motion, and said, "We still didn't settle how we're going to do it. I say we deploy immediately and train in Japan."

Emily snorted, "Deploy a non-working system six thousand miles from home? Do you know what the turbulence is like over Korea? Without a bad-weather wavefront reconstructor the laser beam will break up from air eddies. Science fixes first. Then Ops. Then deployment."

"We need the focus, the team cohesion that comes from being in the field."

"Technical is all that counts. If it's not technically right, it's not right."

Sean looked at Jeanette. "I'd like a good clean line of command."

Emily said crisply, "Well, it isn't going to be Emily reporting to Sean on Airborne Laser."

Jeanette said, "Neither of you works for the other," and she pulled them into a warm three-way hug. "My two idealists. Find a way to help one another."

She and Ms. Canthor left Sean and Emily staring at each other.

Catchers in the Sky

BOOK 4

"Be true to your goals, but be realistic about the ways to achieve them."

The AFRL Project Officer's Fourth Commandment

Chapter 21

The 13th of October

EMILY'S HOUSE – SANDIA HEIGHTS, ALBUQUERQUE

The pair of dice rolled and came up boxcars.

Emily, muzzy, sitting cross-legged, groaned and looked up at Sean. "I can't believe I lost Airborne Laser to you in a crap shoot."

Sitting lotus-style on her rug amidst the late-night wine bottles and snack debris littering her living room, Sean mock-toasted her with his glass of rough local red wine. "Not craps. Think of dice as Quantum Mechanical decision devices. Besides, you didn't lose it. Somebody has to go first and it's just we first do Ops training. Then your science runs."

She had driven him to her home in her Volvo and when Sean had entered the house, he was amazed. From the loneliness of his rootless existence, his possessions in storage two thousand miles away, he felt almost jealous. In so many ways, he was a failure compared to Emily. She was safe in her job, knew her mission, was surrounded by admirers, and her house was a gorgeous homey space looking out over a vista of glittering city lights and the rugged beauty of ancient volcanoes on a far mesa.

"Boy, I wish I was bunking here," Sean remarked, looking over the city lights from Emily's bedroom.

She glanced at him quickly, and when their eyes met, he reddened slightly at his *faux pas*.

"Thanks, it is nice isn't it?" Emily busied herself, ostensibly picking out a few CDs. "Why don't you? I mean, for tonight. I hate to think of you on the plane, and you can't drive back onto base with the elevated blood alcohol level we're going to have," she answered sympathetically. "It has a pretty small bathroom."

"Yeah, I noticed."

She blushed. "Of course, for you military types, where is home, anyway?"

"It's wherever you hang your hat for your string of assignments. How did you end up here?"

"Jeanette came to me in grad school at the Optical Sciences Center, the University of Arizona. Wanted to hire me for the AFRL. Told me despite my misgivings, my thesis could do this wonderful thing. And I was..."

"Tempted?"

Her opalescent gray eyes glittered. "Isn't that what wanting a better world is all about? You think, 'All I have to do is this...'"

Sean laughed, "And behold, you and everyone around you are in *big* trouble," adding, "and Jeanette knows how to make a case." Walking behind svelte barefoot Emily, watching her willowy body move gracefully along her travertine-paved hallway with its Pueblo rugs and Indian pottery in wall niches, Sean reflected that half of humanity's problems were indeed just as Emily said. It was always so... tempting...to do what felt right.

Back in the living room, he'd opened the wine and she'd asked, "Was your father really General Phillips? The one who ran and organized the moon landing? It was the largest single project in human history, in terms of people and resources."

"Not counting war, it was the biggest. At one point he had over 700,000 people directly under him in contracts and uniform." Sean paused, "Anyway, he's the same family, but a distant branch. I met him at a family reunion once and he kind of hinted, after grilling me, I might like the Air Force."

"How right he was, *c'nest pas*?"

"Speaking of the mission, so how are we going to do it?"

They had then proceeded to drink half the night away in her big rumpus room, arguing about what to do.

With Sean's winning the craps toss, there was a moment of stillness as Emily looked intently across the small space between them, the only sound the whirring of Sean's laundry tumbling in the big Bosch drier down the hall. Her whisper was surprisingly loud as she leaned in close. "Let's discuss this."

Sean spread his hands, teasing, "I only need four Ops days and I've won 'em, Deputy Dawg."

Emily crawled right up into his lap, fitting perfectly close. "You mean wingperson, don't you? Trust your wingman. Support your wingman. Help your wingman?"

"Like I said, my wingperson, I've got the days."

Emily's face was inches from his. "Double or nothing?" and suddenly they were out-of-control kissing. Sean pulled her upright on his lap, smoothing back her thick dark hair, and gently found her mouth again.

Despite the burning flame in his heart, the calculations were already running like mercury through Sean's mind; the forked path of the tributaries of consequences and regrets, permissions and complications; the gauntlet every officer runs when a romantic attachment blooms with someone in their unit.

To officers, adultery was legally forbidden—and was not tolerated at the Research Lab or other Air Force units. You would soon find yourself in a court martial, or more likely scratching your head over an Officer's Progress Report that was suddenly so bad you had to hit the bricks. There was however, no direct proscription on co-equals like Chief Scientists and Program Managers.

It was exactly now, he reflected, the beginnings and ends of projects, the alpha and the omega, where this often started. The path ahead lies open; there is a sense of sharing, personal challenge, teamwork—and overriding it all, a sense of adventure.

Some late night over a hot console, two pairs of eyes meet, and if the moment is seized, consummated in hotel, aircraft, lab, or living room, once it happens, projects get complex. Sometimes, the project gets better. Many times the project is fatally wounded even when an advance is rejected or left unconsummated. Two project managers with a serious dose of embarrassment, unease, and humiliation rarely pull the miracle project rabbit from the hat.

Sean and Emily's mouths met more urgently this time, perhaps knowing the moment was stolen. Or perhaps it would have gone critical—except Sean's laundry, spinning down the hall in the dryer, signaled it was dry by giving out a long loud beep.

At the drier's beeping, Emily pulled away bewildered. "We're compatible chemically."

"Neither of us would endanger the mission. People fall in love."

She laid her head on his shoulder. "You don't understand. When this is all over, I'm going home to my Quaker family. We don't believe in war or killing. I can't take you with me."

"You're a Quaker? Is that what this hating ABL thing is all about?" Sean was amazed at how she slammed the door—even if they couldn't waltz through it now. "What has that to do with us? Both our personal lives have been like some existential French movie and *'Zere is no point.'* We meet and suddenly *'Voila! Zis is love.'* But tacked up in your mind there's a little pink memo saying 'Make sure he's not an officer'?"

Emily looked up into his face, shook her black ringlets. "Why must I fall in lust with this idiot? Sean, I'm really sorry, but years from now I just can't see sitting in Meeting with you."

"I promise not to wear my uniform."

"I'm not joking. To my family you're a killer and not welcome."

"I'm not a killer, I'm a soldier. Besides, Quakers are wonderful people and very accepting."

"What could you know about Quakers? Look, if we keep it to some nights we take off our flight suits and get our chemistries adjusted, fine. But you have to promise me Sean you are never going to talk to me about marriage or kidlettes or love or have feelings for me I can't return."

"You've got it backwards. I never promise what I'll feel—except for love."

Emily pulled herself up and went to the wet bar, stood looking down at the gleaming coffee machine, her back to him. "I suppose maybe it's better you go first, since I don't even have a clue for the science part."

Sean looked at her for a long moment and realized she was crying, the tears running into her nose making her voice sniffly.

"Sure you know what to do. You get each of your gizmos working separately, you figure out how to trick the crew into doing what you need, and put everything together."

She gave a feeble hand gesture. "I don't just mean that. I mean everything."

"You're talking like your confidence is shot when today we almost smoked a missile. A SCUD, one of the toughest out there at present. You are years ahead. I know it—and you do too. It's within our grasp."

"Oh, sure. You don't have to worry; you don't have to look into the abyss as I do. I see around corners for a living and this one is blanketed in a Jack-the-Ripper London Fog."

"I'd like to stay tonight."

Emily, confused, shook her head. "I don't know. If we make love, life on the plane when I'm screaming at you might be unbearable."

"I mean, help get those plans in place as best we can."

"Oh." Emily seemed to pull farther away from him emotionally. "Well, if it's going to be Ops first, you have crew brief in six hours. I hope you have a killer plan. Espresso?"

He moved, came up behind her as her hands seemed to fumble at making the coffee, "Let me make it."

"No, see, the machine does everything for you."

Her hands were scrabbling mindlessly on the plastic switches of the gleaming expensive coffee machine. "See, the beans come in here, it loads them, grinds them."

"You don't mind if I stay?"

She was making a hash of the coffee-making. "We may as well get used to it." She suddenly slapped the machine, the failed coffee batch spilling into the catchment tray. She continued, ramblingly, "The only thing you have to do by hand is steaming the milk. I just never can seem to get the milk to froth."

Sean leaned across her, his arm sending a little warmth into the chilled flesh of her bare shoulder. "I think we can get your milk to froth."

"It would be nice, but—" He thought he saw a trace of a smile as she turned and looked up at him directly, her eyes now dry, if reddened, then realized it was only a grimace as she said:

"Methinks the lady may prove you wrong."

* * *

NAMP'O HARBOR – MINISUB BASE – MANGYONGBONG-92

Just as his orders called for, Architect Su had been putting together the plan for the best possible assault on Seoul, the Puppet State to the South, and the American occupiers. He had long ago quit thinking about the likelihood of success, and instead was looking for the keys to the optimal solution. What was likely to work, what did he have as strengths, and what were the weaknesses of the USA and her Puppet State? What did they really count on? He then dismissed the diplomatic advantages, the deep military resources, and the huge economy. Each of these, in the face of Seoul in the hands of the North, would mean little. When a ransomer holds the crown jewel, a deal is inevitable.

He had gone without more than three hours of sleep a night, mostly caught in the back seat of limos whirling him around the excellent freeway system of North Korea. As the freeways were clear, it took less than an hour to reach Namp'o harbor. Here, he was to examine and prepare the Special Forces minisubmarine base.

When he saw the giant spheres of the tidal barrage in the mouth of the Taedong River—its signature flood-control mechanism to prevent inundation of upriver Pyongyang—a sudden impulse took him and he asked the driver to stop at the white pier that had serviced the Underwater Mansion.

As he climbed stiffly from his Benz limo, again he felt an odd pulse of grief and puzzlement. Last night he had dreamed he stood on the end of this cement pier, and looked out toward to where his beloved Underwater Mansion lay ruined under the dark swells like a bombed-out cathedral. A burned window tassel had floated on the black water. He shook off the dream's strange after-feel, now amplified a thousand-fold and laced with pain knowing I-Pong Kang had been the killer of his mansion. *Yet why?*

Standing now on the pier of his dream, he realized only a mile away was the huge minisubmarine base. From it, dozens of tunnels emerged at widely separated points in the huge harbor. Even under heavy air strikes, minisubs would make it into the Yellow Sea.

Kang had certainly found a way to attack—and yet a very difficult undertaking. It could not have been done by minisubmarine, surely. The minisubs carried few armaments, nothing of real size. Even their ship-destroying limpet mines—big suction-held mines they affixed under an enemy hull—couldn't have cracked his mansion.

Still, *there* was the mansion, and *there*—he himself had come to visit it—was the minisub base.

He went back to work. The minisub station at Namp'o offered him some of the best ideas yet. The key was the decrepit little ocean liner lying nearby in the harbor, the Mangyongbong-92. The three-hundred-foot ocean liner *cum* freighter had limped, wheezing and rattling, across on its weekly service from Wonsan to Niigata, Japan for years—more than five hundred crossings. It had been the only real connection between the uneasy neighbors, transporting the few official visitors, 'living in Japan' Koreans (or Zainichi, as they are called in Japan), and their schoolchildren on special arranged visits to North Korea.

The Mangyongbong-92's main cargos were the crates of gifts from overseas North Koreans in Japan, who sent back hundreds of tons of food and supplies each trip. One time, the ferry had almost foundered with more than a thousand special Christmas presents—ironically for pagan North Korea—bound directly for Kim Il-Song: melons and pianos, elevators and huge sacks of rice, crates of liquor and wardrobes of clothes, and even speedboats and golf carts. This level of gift-giving had fallen away as both the loyal Koreans in Japan fell in number— and especially after the North Korean abduction of Japanese citizens hit the front pages in 2001, and the boat was overwhelmed by ranks of official inspectors, hundreds of rabid press, and thousands of angry protestors jamming the docks.

Here was how Su had imported so many of the luxury items for the mansions of Dear Leader, including Hitachi elevators, PCs, crystal sculptures, draperies, marble tiling, and antiques. Here also, was how Su had smuggled the export-forbidden electronics—scrounged by State Security procurers from Tokyo's myriad second-hand electronics stores—now embedded in ballistic missiles and nuclear weapons.

Best of all the loads were—as Economist Su termed them—*fungible*. That is, like all aid to the poor of North Korea, commutable: the loads supported critical needs which had to be funded, thus freeing up resources for regime support and luxury. The touching personal presents directly underwrote WMD, appalling leadership lavishness, and ballistic missiles.

Sadly, after the nuclear tests and other North Korean hostile actions, the Japanese government banned the Mangyongbong-92—officially for smuggling—from Japanese waters. Now, with Dearest Leader's overtures of friendship, the ship was getting a long-required refurbishment here at Namp'o in preparations for the lifting of the ban.

Architect Su knew this was a perfect time to use the little sad sack ferry.

Su was escorted into the Special Forces complex, and shown in to the General of (Naval) Special Forces, the KPN Combatants. He and the general looked at each other very carefully. Each had to decide to trust the other completely. He, Architect Su, by putting a key piece of the plan into the hands of a possible security leak; the general, by accepting that executing Su's orders well—rather than slow-rolling him because of distrust of Dearest Leader and his Peace Treaty—would gain him the greatest career reward.

Su took out a passport and a small bankbook. He laid them before the general and as he picked them up, Su murmured. "We will all be very well placed and cared for, in the new order." The general blanched when he saw the numbers in the bank account, and the photos in the new Chinese passport. Su added, "The numbers are in dollars, and all your family is covered by the passport."

The stone of the general's face softened. "Please, First Architect Su, tell me what you need, and I will do everything I can to help."

"You have a special Intranet Console available to you?"

"Yes, Architect Su."

"Very well. You are now assigned to it for the next three weeks. Should you have an emergency request to leave, you would please check with me. You must now stay within these walls, and you must of course be monitored closely." He indicated a set of Vinalon-suited Watchers he had brought. "Your select team of twenty minisubmarine sacrifice crews as well. No outside contact from this moment on. Agreed?"

"Agreed. What service do you need?"

Architect Su pointed out the window over the docks to the Mangyongbong-92, refurbishment crews working frantically to repaint the grubby little ocean liner. "Let me tell you what I have in mind. Then you will, with your infinitely superior knowledge, tell me a much better way to do it."

The general bowed, and offered Su his very best tea.

When they were done planning, Architect Su smoothly asked if any minisubs went missing 'the night of the commotion in the harbor.' The answer was 'no,' although an infiltration boat—they were notoriously unreliable—had not returned from a training mission.

Su requested the log of the night's personnel entries into the minisub facility, and was soon staring morosely at Kang's signature. *One piece in the puzzle.* He carefully examined the night's other entries—and startled. In the log, two hours before Kang, was the entry of another officer of the Combatant Corps.

The officer had signed 'Guard Command (Secondment), Maj Tam Ho.'

Kang and Tam Ho were both here that night? Assassin and his executioner? Su did not believe in coincidence. He looked at the entry carefully and jotted down Tam Ho's home unit—*Onch'On-Up Airfield.*

Architect Su's next words were so low no one nearby could hear.

"Well, Major Ho. I believe very soon you and I will be having an interesting little chat."

DMZ – ISOLATED AREA – KANGWON-DO PROVINCE, DPRK

The American negotiation team groaned in unison inwardly—and outwardly—at the beating their wingtips were taking in the DMZ's rich peaty dirt.

None of them had joined the State Department to be tamping the wilds like field inspectors. Theirs was *supposed* to be the diplomatic cocktail party life of ice clinking in Waterford crystal, tailored Tuxedos and fitted evening gowns, and luxe smorgasbords of refined finger food. In short, their pleasures were delicate; they lived for the rich wafting of after-dinner Havana cigars on the veranda, chit-chatting up a tough diplomatic adversary across a banquet table, or enjoying the bouquet of Chanel perfume about a waltzing partner—not crumbly loam in the dress shoes and sticky spider webs across the face.

Now, having ducked through the slashes in the wire diamonds of the old hurricane fence of the DMZ, the night making the intrusion seem more sinister, the American negotiation team, in business suits and dress shoes pushed on through dark, wild, and dense woods, miserably following their Ambassador, now truly at large.

One of the Staties yelped, "A bear! I just saw a goddamned bear!"

Someone asked, sincerely, swatting a persistent Asian gnat somewhere in the dark behind the speaker, "On its chest, was there a white sickle?"

"Oh yeah. A hammer and a sickle," someone else giggled.

The frightened one snapped, "So frickin' what?"

"That'd be a moon bear! What a treat! Seriously endangered species. Only found rarely, and mostly—"

"I've got a goddamned bear about to spring out at me? I'm the endangered species."

Someone else mused philosophically over the sound of tramping, "To think I got here by passing the five-day diplomatic service exam at odds of one hundred to one, and it was all so I would end up mauled by a bear on the job."

The enthusiastic one bubbled on, "Did you know the DMZ is one of the world's most amazing ecological preserves? Unparalleled in the temperate zone. Eighth wonder of the world."

A more practical voice put in, "If we do our job right, we could be looking at the greatest Eco-tourist attraction in this century! I wonder how we could invest."

Someone else grumbled, "I'm a GS-15 tramping through the barbaric wilderness with a couple of Yippie capitalists. It doesn't figure."

Up ahead, for their part, Hakkermann and Sandy were country boys. They were enjoying the early autumn woods, rife with green and warm smells of deepest virgin forest and full of mostly familiar plants and animal sounds. Hakkermann and Sandy had especially enjoyed the rush of seeing the black bear's beauty and innocent quizzical look, and they laughed at their trailing wimps. Hakkermann called back, "I swear Davy Crockett would have died o' shame, lads. Why yonder is almost the 'xact same trees as you hunt squirrels for your evening stew back home in Verginny."

Sandy laughed, "Yes, temperate forest, totally at home, nothing strange—except a bear who looks like ET with a Turkish flag on his belly."

Despite his lightness, Hakkermann was getting ready to fulfill his promise to the President: to look the Dearest Leader in the eye, take his final measure—and tell him mensch to mensch he would kill him if he were shamming.

Then Hakkermann would know. For a moment, the dark woods seemed almost luminescent with the filtered moon, as if in a dreamscape.

His CIA guide had chosen this part of the DMZ for the meeting because it was rugged and isolated—and mostly unwatched. There was no connection from the DMZ to the main ROK roadnet except through a high pass—a one-lane road with steep drop-offs and hairpin turns. There was little point trying to invade here with mechanized forces. On the small poorly-paved road over the heavily wooded mountains, even a handful of defenders with anti-tank missiles would make mincemeat out of a column of armor. Even if no defenders were immediately present, just a few artillery pieces on the South Korean side of the hills, easily transported there on interior lines, would put any attackers mounting to the pass up the narrow road into deadly defilade. This area was therefore almost unguarded, remaining virgin land, scenic, pleasant, for the most part un-landmined, deeply wooded and full of rabbits, birds, and deer.

The half-moon lit the low shrubs under the canopy of leaves as Hakkermann's party stopped at the edge of a small bushy clearing.

Both sides had used this easily-reached isolated clearing in the DMZ for a long time. Occasionally in this untouched part of the DMZ, ground troops from the two Koreas met and shared an occasional cigarette, bartered food and luxury goods, or passed letters to decades-long-separated families.

In almost a mirage, on the opposite side of the clearing, Il-Moon and Dearest Leader stepped from the forest, their dozen burly Guard Command just behind.

As agreed, leaving their respective entourages, Il-Moon and Dearest Leader moved forward, while Sandy walked alongside Hakkermann. Almost like duelists and their seconds, the pairs approached each other cautiously and met in the clearing's center and on the exact line of the border.

Hakkermann saw Il-Moon was in the usual drab Vinalon suit he affected when not in uniform. *That damned plastic Vinalon makes leisure suits look like elegance on ice.* Dearest Leader, however, was bursting with energy in his lightweight summer suit, white shirt luminous in the moonlight.

Hakkermann stepped a few paces into the DPRK, and Dearest Leader began speaking in a low voice, his English pleasantly mellow. "Ah, Ambassador Hakkermann. I use this title of course, rather than Chief Negotiator, as it seems more fitting. For are we not meeting foremost as ambassadors to the world?"

Hakkermann put out his hand, Harry Truman style, although without the crush. "Indeed, Dearest Leader, is it not our calling, both of us?"

As if the preliminaries were well past, Il-Moon interrupted. "My good friends. Thank you for suggesting our meeting here. There are so many eyes and ears everywhere in our process."

"You are welcome," said Hakkermann. "Now, to our problems."

The slightest concern wrinkled Dearest Leader's face. "Our problems? I thought the progress we had made was tremendous. Is there an issue?"

"Well, in view of the past between our countries—"

"Come, come, Ambassador Hakkermann, do we not have an agreement on the table, as you would say? Is it not within our grasp?"

"In many ways, yes. Yet there is still an element of fantasy that I hope to ground here. I thought we should meet as men and agree our security lies with each other—and we are ready to part with both our pasts."

With Il-Moon glowering next to Dearest Leader, Sandy thought it was ironic that the man who was perhaps more wedded to the past than anyone, just now stood in the moonlight, casting a shadow onto Dearest Leader and Hakkermann.

"There are always those who feel threatened." Dearest Leader chuckled. "'People, you cannot live with them, and you cannot live without them.'"

At this surprise, Hakkermann let out a laugh, shaking his head. "Well said. You feel you have control?"

"Yes. Absolutely."

"Even with the suggested clauses of opening the borders and merging of armies and so on?"

"We have a few conditions of our own of course. The agreement is confederal, not federal."

"Although there is no difference between the words in Korean."

"Very erudite, Ambassador Hakkermann. We will coin a new word, then, you and I. See, we both wish the same thing—that our pasts be forgotten, and we embrace the future together as equals."

Il-Moon broke in. "We are absolutely trustworthy. Nevertheless, I am under pressure. Powerful forces on our side are at work to stop negotiation. We must conclude the treaty within two weeks."

Hakkermann snorted, "Two weeks is ridiculously short!"

Dearest Leader laughed. "Are you being too logical?"

"Am I? Even if I tried, my own people would hang us up on negotiation details. We won't even have decided the protocols, not to mention getting our 'friendly partners' like the South Koreans and the Chinese into agreement—"

"Then I can almost guarantee we will fail."

Hakkermann took this hard, wondering if indeed he could live with that failure. He indicated for Sandy to stand down, and said, "I'd like a word with Dearest Leader alone."

Il-Moon bridled, but Dearest Leader smiled, opened a palm toward a space clear of bushes nearby and they walked to it. "Yes? You have an irrepressible comment for me alone?"

"You have my very greatest respect, Dearest Leader, for the historical thing you are trying to do. I must tell you however, there are worries on my side."

"How so?"

"Perhaps I could explain by saying I am from the State of Missouri. We are known as the 'Show Me' state."

"Indeed. Show you what?"

"It means words about a thing and the actual thing are not of the same value. We only believe things we can see. So, I need to know is this withdrawal of yours from the DMZ bullshit? I'm from Missouri so you better show me. And that means Pyong-son as well."

Dearest Leader replied stiffly, "As long as we are laying our cards on the desk, you need to show me the withdrawal of the attack capability of your 7th Air Force at Osan. Otherwise, my generals will simply ignore me and not remove our forward forces from the DMZ."

"Then you will abide by the key provision of the treaty, pulling back in advance your armored divisions in the Kaesong-Munsan corridor?"

"Agreed. To the northern province of Jagang. Of what use is a military force on an internal border?"

"What use indeed." Hakkermann paused, leaned in and said distinctly, "I agree to your terms. But I need you to know between us as men: if you screw me, all negotiations with the DPRK will cease forever."

"If that is a joke, it is very cold."

"It's no joke."

Dearest Leader let his offended sensibilities drop from him. *As long as I have the proof—the withdrawal of your 7ᵗʰ Air Force.* "This Missouri of yours sounds like an interesting place. Someday I must visit and *see* for myself."

Hakkermann laughed. "You pull this off—and you realize *the balls* are in your court—I'll make you an honorary Missourian."

"Balls? I thought balls were—" He gestured to his crotch.

Hakkermann laughed. "Yes, you got the joke."

Dearest Leader leaned in to Hakkermann, taking his arm lightly. "No joke, as surely as you are from Missouri, you and I will sign the peace treaty in seventeen days—on the night of the Harvest Festival Moon, the 31ˢᵗ of October.

Chapter 22

The 14th of October

DIRECTED ENERGY DIRECTORATE – SCIF VAULT

DoD Top Secret Compartmented Programs are created and exist through the largess of the Executive Branch, and indeed, the explicit permission of the President. For legal purposes, and to lay the foundation for polygraphs, compartments, draconian security limitations, special interviews, and background checks, the personnel in charge of a SAR—Special Access Required—program always start any newcomer in-briefing with the excruciatingly boring legal background.

Within the gray steel doors and highly-shielded Top Secret SCIF of Directed Energy Directorate's vault for the ABL(X) program, the briefing room was pleasant and bright, with pictures of aircraft, test sites, unit badges, and portraits of famous acquisition officers. The polished wood table had comfortable padded chairs, and the room just held the dozen or so ABL tech crew comfortably. A secure Tempest computer system projected the in-brief—with the Presidential Logo and 'By order #363271 of the Executive Branch' right on the first slide. Usually such in-briefs were run by security, but this was Sean and Emily's show.

Sean stood, pointed to the Logo. "What follows is Top Secret compartmentalized information."

"Our compartment name is 'Have Catcher,'" Emily added.

"Can anyone guess what Catcher is?" Sean asked. He was using the usual security subterfuge to check for leaks. Sometimes the foolish would answer, "Oh sure, George was always hinting about it; I guessed there was a Top Secret program; I even knew it was this vault. It must have something to do with X, since that's what George is into. He's doing a good job, by the way..." This kind of answer—over-telling the truth to security pukes—always got both you and George shown the door—and you had to sign papers saying you'd forget even the nothing they hadn't told you.

"Come on, Sean," Emily said. "No there hasn't been a leak and they've heard of it somehow."

"It's a tradition."

"The program just started three hours ago, for goodness sake."

Sean smiled, "Sorry. Habit." He paused, then sat down next to Emily so they formed an unbroken group around the table. "The mission is INTEL collection and ballistic missile interdiction," and he briefed the tech crew on the potential missile crisis in Korea. He showed the evidence they had from Radiant Outlaw, while Emily confirmed her experience at the Treaty verification with Sean the previous month. Sean finished with, "Against the backdrop of big military stand-downs and the treaty, there's the potential for things to get out of control. Personally, I think it's grimmer than that."

Emily ignored the confused looks that comment produced, and summarized, "Have Catcher is a Presidential program to deploy secretly an at least partially-operational Airborne Laser system to protect Korea and Japan. We will fly patrol in the area adjoining the Korean peninsula, out over the Sea of Japan, since that is near the potential ballistic missile launching sites, and between Korea and Japan."

Sean put in, "We really need you all, and hope you will join us. To enter the Catcher compartment, civilians must volunteer and sign a waiver for hazardous duty. Military are in, of course, although they must sign the waiver as well."

Emily interjected, "The White World cover for our activities is gathering scientific atmospheric data in appropriate environments. In fact, we will indeed be doing exactly this, and the science team needs to assemble the anemometers and such."

"Keep in mind though, our real focus is Korea," Sean added. "Especially in the period during final negotiations on troop withdrawals and armistice-ending activities. There are 30,000 American souls there, and they are on very thin ice. We'll add a good INTEL capability, and provide an umbrella ballistic missile shield in case it's needed."

Matt Cho broke in, "Are we in any kind of shape to do missile defense? I mean, we've never really demonstrated any capability and this armistice thing is only a couple weeks away. I'd hate to get over there and have a bunch of issues we can't work."

Emily said, "Agreed. Before we can deploy we need laser reliability increased and new beam control modules—especially for bad weather—added to the current tracking and targeting systems. What we need is everything functional at the same time. I'll run that. Sean will work Ops' development."

"To that end we're on heightened security. We try to take off and land in darkness," Sean said, turning to Auggie, who was sitting bolt upright, his nervousness betrayed only by his repeated smoothing of his ironed tie. "Chief, rig the ABL hangar for scoot-n-hide during daylight. People, do your technical work but be ready 2:00 a.m. every day to fly Ops. Break into Science, Ops, Logistics groups. As soon as we can, we'll go for some missile shoot-downs."

Jarhead asked, "What's the real situation over there?"

Sean answered emphatically, "The North Koreans are going to war."

Red scoffed, "How could you know that?"

Sean flicked his laser pointer to a series of structures on the Vu-graph of Pyong-son. "Warhead assembly. Missile support. Launch. All in deep hiding. Whoever built Pyong-son has a plan. And a timetable. Whatever else, coming out of Pyong-son will be missiles—and they will be missiles unlike any the world has ever seen."

"So, will it be dangerous?" someone mumbled.

"No. We won't even be in Korea. We'll operate out of Japan—the beauty of ABL is we don't have to get that close."

Emily's face was unreadable, but she nodded to everyone. There was a silence. Sean moved his chair so he and Emily were sitting close together. He asked, sincere but upbeat: "Who is with us? Who will serve among the first laser warriors?"

Jarhead looked the crew over, and said, "Till death us do part."

Pens scratched on the waivers. The ABL crew smiled grimly as they filed past Sean and Emily, each laying a signed form before them.

PANMUNJOM – DMZ

Abbey's next leak, although she never knew it, came from a South Korean NIS agent who was shadowing Hakkermann. When Harold's limo was brought up from the underground embassy pound, and a Korean cook at the embassy reported an order for a packed dinner for seven, the NIS agent guessed Hakkermann was up to something, and followed him to the clandestine meeting at the DMZ.

Like any other civil service, the ROK's was a set of fiefdoms, and Hakkermann's constant going around them and dealing straight with the North Koreans was collectively condemned, although no one could afford to be openly anti-peace. But this agent wasn't buying this peace treaty stuff anyway, and more importantly, neither was his boss.

A transcript of a meeting with damaging disclosures or back-room subterfuges—especially the actual spoken words—and his seniors would be ecstatic. They would hand it to Abbey to blow out across the airwaves, mugging the Americans in the back alley of world news—and with any luck stopping the treaty cold.

The spy had a good night vision video camera, and managed to tape the meeting without either the North Koreans or the Americans knowing it, although he was bitterly disappointed that the bushes and bug noises defeated his 'Big Ear' parabolic voice microphone.

Still, the video was exactly what Abbey needed.

* * *

In the parking area of Panmunjom, Abbey looked out of the Hyundai 4x4 in frustration, occasionally sneering at the silly self-righteous people lined up to gape at the ridiculous cross-border staring contests between the North and South soldiers—which had continued despite the negotiations.

She didn't know why she even bothered to come up here. Or she did, but resented it. Even though reporters were banished from the meetings now that the negotiations were intense, and a serious secrecy thingie slapped on everyone—including an actual sequestering on the U.S.-ROK side—she had already gotten a tip from Hakkermann that nothing would happen today. So, she had taped a "no news is today's news" segment for CNN with Panmunjom in the background. At least she was still scooping everyone—even if only to say "nothing happening." Now she would leave, gloating at the press corps waiting like whipped puppies in the ready room, hoping someone important would come out of the meetings and speak to them. Underlying it all, though, was a panicky feeling that things weren't moving.

"We need that angle," Abbey growled to Akiru, who was in the driver's seat, when a small Japanese woman walked up to the Hyundai, carrying a purse. She stood at Abbey's window, and Abbey rolled it down.

"I am sorry," the woman said. Diminutive even for a Japanese, Abbey sensed the legacy of a poor diet over a lifetime. "I believe you have dropped your purse."

Abbey took it, "Oh my goodness. How kind of you. I was really frantic about it. Can I offer you—?"

The woman backed away, bowing. "Yes, yes. Thank you. Thank you," and turned and walked out of sight around the side of Panmunjom's small Peace House office building.

Abbey didn't open the purse, and instead jerked her head south to Akiru, but he already had the 4x4 moving, eyes scanning the mirrors for any tail. Espionage in South Korea was a broadly defined—and grave—offense.

It wasn't until they passed the guard gate out of Panmunjom and pulled onto Freedom Highway that she opened the purse, dumped out the Kleenex and makeup, ripped open the bottom seams—and found the videotape she was sure must be there. After all, she hadn't lost her purse.

Abbey grimaced with pleasure, and held the tape up to Akiru who was slowing, looking for a private place to stop. He ran the 4x4 over the freeway shoulder and down onto a dirt road by a drained rice paddy. Shoulders touching, they knelt in the back seat, looking into the luggage area where among the satellite link and news equipment, the Reuter's 4x4 had a small video station.

The tape was very professional. Although the audio was worthless, in the image intensifier, the meeting at the DMZ between Hakkermann, Il-Moon, and Dearest Leader was clear.

As the low-light camera caught Il-Moon lean over and bark an abrupt order into a minion's ear, Akiru remarked, "Conversation I do not need to overhear." Hakkermann bent in and said something to Sandy Denton. Akiru laughed, "Conversation I would rather not overhear." Finally, as Dearest Leader and Hakkermann met in the moonlight-filtered woods, face to face intently talking, Akiru murmured, "Conversation I would kill to overhear. Up close and very personal."

Abbey absorbed this, lit a cigarette, gave Akiru an illegal puff, and as they pulled back onto the highway, she fell into deep thought. She remained silent and motionless all the way back down Freedom Highway, her eyes like burnt fuses.

They were just reaching downtown Seoul when she whispered, "What was it you said, when Hakkermann leaned over to speak to Dearest Leader?"

Akiru glanced at her, smiled. "Up close and very *very* personal."

Abbey realized she had her angle.

Chapter 23

WYNDHAM HOTEL – ALBUQUERQUE AIRPORT

Spiney was an aerospace news-hound. An independent. A freelancer—and a good one. His restive southern New Mexican heritage of white trash and Texas ranchers had been piqued by the presence of Holloman airbase right below him in the wide valley beneath Cloudcroft. The mere presence of this base, the mean-looking people on it, its secrecy and its threat were bad enough. When he learned German Luftwaffe pilots and aircraft were flying there, he was sure it was a plot.

Foreigners on his sacred soil wasn't something he could live with.

He first started snapping and selling pictures of the stealth aircraft being flight-tested at the base—and the editors of Aviation Week, pleased at the bounty, encouraged his natural talents and proclivities. Besides his born-and-raised rural New Mexican wilderness skills, and a poacher's second-nature ability to defeat trespass security systems, he had also honed his white supremacist values during a couple of stints in the minimum security Central New Mexico Correctional.

Now, he could always get work. All the aerospace magazines employed him, although he could be slightly hinky. His professionalism—the desire to get the perfect photo—conflicted with his innate hatred of the Federal Government's repression of guns and the natural racial order.

He often passed up the good money from Jane's Defence Weekly or Aviation Week to sell his material exclusively to the white supremacist publishers who abounded in rural southeastern New Mexico. It was after a spell of lying out in the cold desert every day under the runway at Holloman, and counting sorties for order of battle estimates of the damned German Luftwaffe—who would have thought they would have taken us over so soon?—that he knew he was in trouble on his bills, and was in need of fresh meat.

An off-hand comment from an Air Force NCO at an Alamogordo green chili stew house about some strange new aircraft doing touch and goes out of Holloman set him to work. Soon he heard the plane was flying out of Kirtland up in Albuquerque and it caught what little imagination he had—although all of his interest.

When he lucked out and finally saw the aircraft—he'd been lying there for days, sullenly depressed, stiff and irritated in the cold gramma grass, picking *cholla* cactus thorns out of his butt—he was electrified. Sure, he'd heard of Airborne Laser—but seeing wasn't just believing. It was unbelievable what the plane looked like. He clearly saw the KAFB markings, and some other weird unit shields along the fuselage, but the laser-nose itself was awesome. He snapped a few, but the sun angle was bad, and he failed to get anything useful. He waited a week, but the plane did not return and he knew he'd have to go find her.

He bought a credit card whose monthly payment was so low he could use it for a year before it would implode, and packed his old Dodge with his photo printer, extensive camera and surveillance equipment, radio scanners, and a sack of roasted green chili. Eschewing heavily-patrolled I-25, he instead took the back route up through Carrizozo and then down through the huge mountain pass at Tijeras and into Albuquerque.

After messing around at the periphery of the airfield, he found it far too urban and well-policed, especially as the commercial airport was ringed by Kirtland Air Force base. There was however, the high-rise Wyndham airport hotel.

He rented a top-floor room, bought a month's supply of food and pure water, hung out the 'do not disturb' sign permanently, and went to work.

He watched with fascination as the Airborne Laser training began to unfold. It was, he realized at some level, the high point of all his hunting stands; the most amazing story he had yet seen. This time, he was hunting the biggest game of all. This time, he would have an effect on the world.

IL-MOON – ABBEY

Abbey said over the phone to Il-Moon: "You get me an interview with Dearest Leader—straight one-on-one—and I'll get you the information—daily—on the laser plane."

"I am not so sure that is a good deal." Il-Moon answered, as if troubled.

Abbey pressed, "I can tell you who is on it. I can tell you if it is coming. I can tell you...I will tell you...everything. Besides, does not objecting to the laser plane mean you do not really want the treaty? If I think everyone is wasting their time—or worse—I will blow the treaty out of the water as surely as you had Kim Chi for breakfast."

IL-Moon thought, *treacherous bitch*. However, the more he considered her interview idea, the more he was sure it would be useful to him. First, it would show Dearest Leader's weakness to the world. If, as Abbey was demanding, it were broadcast in North Korea, it would produce a backlash that could very well help Il-Moon tremendously. The elite of North Korea, perhaps one million persons, knew all too well their skill set—political cronyism, blood relations to those in power, a vast web of special relationships for personal economic and political benefit, being in the right clan or government position—would be of no use in the New Korean Order. Economists who knew nothing about supply and demand, yet everything about the Great Leader's speeches; senior army officers who knew only how to be a cog in an offensive army lying in wait armed with every illegal weapon; historians who taught that the Great Leader had defeated the Japanese in WWII when he had been in fact been well-fed in a Russian political camp hundreds of miles from Korea; and politicians who supported Kim Jong-Il's ridiculous Messianic proclamation as 'The savior of all humanity'—and yet had no concern for their own constituents—they all knew they had a shaky future in the job market of The One Korea. Il-Moon was sure they would judge Dearest Leader to be insanely risking everything they had.

If a revealing interview with a Japanese woman didn't lead to Palace Rage, he could not imagine what would.

Besides, from what he had gleamed from the Web—and he had not let Dearest Leader or Su know anything about it—this American laser plane was designed precisely to pin down his key asset and insurance policy. He needed to know Airborne Laser's capabilities. He needed to know their readiness. He needed to know, above all, any movement toward the Korean theater.

While he could potentially spy on the plane using the State Security Department, it was a highly risky venture. Not only was the Agency rife with snitches reporting to Dearest Leader, the American FBI was a serious threat. No, taking independent action was not a good bet.

He needed Abbey, and the perfection of it was she was there for the taking.

Il-Moon was however angry under the best of circumstances and now talking to a Japanese reporter forcing him to play bedmates, his voice was like gravel under slow tank treads. "So you can get me the information, Miss Yamamoto?"

"You can see the original documents."

"I can only help you to meet Dearest Leader. You must make your actual case to him yourself."

I'll need to get to the hairdressers, a manicure. She ran her tongue over her gritty teeth; they felt filthy. *All the smoking. I must get my teeth cleaned.* "Fine. I am booking a flight to Beijing tonight. I can be in Pyongyang in a day. You please get me the meeting."

* * *

AIRBORNE LASER COMPLEX – AFRL

At the exact moment Abbey was lining up the interview of the new century, and Spiney was watching ABL like a Kestrel, Sean was thinking it wasn't going to be that difficult to get Airborne Laser operational.

He had won his four Ops days in the crapshoot with Emily, and he was about to make the most of them.

The first night started with a sleepy tech crew arriving at the hangar. In a spurt of chaotic hustle, they changed into flight suits, gathered laptops, test equipment, briefcases—and unfortunately, food.

In the beehive of activity, at least the NCOs and flightdeck were methodical as the ground crew checked engines, fueled, and got the jumbo jet's take-off paperwork in line.

Anyone who has ever been in charge of a field experiment knows how the leader is under the microscope. Everyone is watching to see what they have to offer—and how long it would take to be stressed, hyper-stressed, and finally flip out.

Sean said to the assembled crew: "We start Ops now. How much of your time will it take? All of it. How much of your science has to be right? Same answer. All of it."

Just before the crew scrambled out across the nighttime tarmac to ABL, he called out, "Airborne Laser, saddle up!"

Passing through the Tech Area, it was total bustle as the crew got ready to rock and roll. Sean finished seat check, and looked out, seeing Auggie and his crew snap off the last of the laser fuel hoses, which steamed as they came free.

Auggie came on the radio. "Ops, this is ground crew. Laser fuel is topped and popped. Laser fueling hoses are off. Ground umbilicals are off."

"Ground crew, Ops. Thanks, Chief. Any final words?"

Auggie looked up at the ABL emblem of the rearing snake spitting laser fire. "Peace through light! Damn my logo looks good!"

"That's affirmatory, Auggie. What the world needs now is a bigger and better rattlesnake."

Auggie did a double semaphore with the landing flags, "Flightdeck, this is Ground. Airborne Laser you are free to taxi."

ONCH'ON-UP UNDERGROUND AIRFIELD – DPRK

"Dumb-ass!" cried his driver, loud enough to wake the aging and exhausted Architect Su, who had finally managed to slip into a snooze in the back seat behind the limo's glass partition.

Architect Su shook off an almost drugged sleep, sitting up to see his driver berating a very young KPA guard at the side of the road. Looking around, Architect Su saw they were on a large paved road near a strangely artificial village. The plains across which they had been uneventfully cruising ended here, sweeping toward a stony mountainside where the road apparently ran straight into rock walls. The road itself was odd, wider and heavier than even an official freeway, and blocked: every twenty feet or so, metal poles stuck up from the macadam like limbless barren trees.

Architect Su slid down the window nearest his driver. "Son, what is the cause of this caterwauling?"

"Glorious Sir, he will not let us pass!" His driver was frustrated, couldn't get what he needed from the young oaf, who would only say it was forbidden to use this road.

It was now clear to Su they had reached their intended destination. The road was a disguised runway. It ran straight into the mountain ahead, and when the rock doors were open, it connected to the subterranean runways of Onch'On-Up Underground Airfield.

The nearby village was a blind as well, and although Architect Su was well aware from Joseph Bermudez's books that the Americans knew all about this hidden air base, it was still a formidable facility. It was unlikely to be put out of action by any number of precision munitions. It was a monster, as much a part of the earth below as it was of the sunlit space above. Buried and yet deadly, its cruise missiles tubes, Combatants, and Kim Il-Sung Night-fighters always ready, it was a vengeful dragon waiting in a simmering volcano.

Onch'On-Up. Su had chosen to visit this airfield much earlier than he had originally planned. His normal approach would be to work first on the more complex communications, rocket, and artillery problems. For, after his visit today, this airfield would be in security isolation. He was therefore sequestering a large number of men for weeks longer than truly necessary. But this was the home unit of Maj Tam Ho, and truth to tell he was more on Su's mind just now than the cruise missile and Special Forces attacks he was here to organize. *If I cannot speak with Major Ho, I will get his file.*

From a disguised guardhouse, an officer came at the run. Soon, the runway obstacles were cleared—the North Korea Air Force rarely used it as it was too close to the DMZ, and pilots tended to defect if let loose. Architect Su's limo continued straight toward the mountain. As they approached, Su could see the cables stretched across the passes and low approaches, like bays of high-tension power lines. They were barrages to mangle any American Special Forces low-fliers coming in for forward spotter work in attacking the airbase.

Architect Su got out by the road and stretched painfully, his bones creaking despite the exercises he did each morning. The sun being over the hill, he shielded his eyes to see the slabs of rock that were their real destination: the Combatant helicopter launching bunkers, their doors beetled under the granite cliffs of the mountainside.

Behind those slabs, he knew, were more than eighty seven MD500 Hughes Aircraft helicopters, ex-U.S. inventory and the best in the North Korean transport fleet, having been were smuggled in through a legitimate contract with Thailand. Along with hundreds of Russian-produced Antonev-2 biplane transports, they represented 90% of the airlift power of the Combatant corps. He knew exactly how he was going to use them. This would be the principle airfield out of which would fly the behind-the-lines strike force to open the second front for the DPRK in the South.

With more than 100,000 Special Forces, hand-picked and highly trained, the DPRK Combatant Corps was the largest Special Forces command in the world—with the most serious suicide oath as well. Compared to the few thousands of U.S. Delta Force, the Russian Spetznatz, the Chinese DADU, and the British Royal Marines, the Combatants were the size of many countries' entire armies. To enter into this elite but huge group, you had to be of uncommon size, closing on six feet, you had to have advanced martial arts training, be completely ruthless and ideologically pure—and be willing to swear to the doctrine of suicide before capture. With South Korean security forces concentrated near the DMZ, the DPRK plan was to unleash rabid Combatants throughout the rear area. Willing to use poison gas, explosives, attack soft targets like schools, homes, and hospitals, take hostages and assassinate local authorities or VIP's far behind the front lines, this precision-strike terror strategy meant that in the event of war, the level of death and destruction across South Korean civilian areas would be unparalleled.

The level of Combatant indoctrination and mission discipline was far above a normal army level. It was more akin to terrorist training, and the USA and South Korea had for many years fruitlessly sought ways to counter it before giving up because it was simply impossible. If the fight went well for the South at the DMZ, they would deal catch-as-catch-can with the terrorization behind the front, knowing it would not be decisive even if catastrophic. The alternative was to exert the political will to put guards on alert in every town, hospital, school, and politician's home every day, all year long. There is no good risk-mitigation strategy to counter 100,000 crazies far behind the front lines. You simply worked on infrastructure and training—and hoped it wouldn't come to a trial by fire.

Combatant incursion was to take place by every method imaginable. Mini-submarines, small boats, infiltration craft, fishing boats, planes, sneaking over the border in unguarded areas weeks before—and of course in transports and helicopters. The name *Onch'On-Up*, if ever there were a war, would be a badge of honor to those who flew out first in the battle to free the Puppet State to the South.

Su walked with the general through the underground airfield, enjoying the tremendous engineering, the readiness. He stopped on the flight line to look fondly at a long line of Antonev-2's. These ten-person biplane transports, the most numerous plane in the KPAF, had a special position within his mind, and those of his old friends in the DPRK's leadership.

In the first few days of the Fatherland Liberation War, the KPAF had been swept from the skies by the UNC Air Forces. This stunning humiliation sent them all spinning, searching for answers on how to build a new KPAF. Su remembered the morning early in the war when Il-Moon had waved his fighters out to attack. Whooping, he had cheered them off. Long after they should have come back, Il-Moon had stood waiting on the tarmac. But his magnificent men and their beautiful machines, the pride of the KPAF, were never to return. That night, Il-Moon and Su drank what seemed to be the entire airfield's *Soju* supply, and in their drunken rage, they swore they would create at least one unit worthy to defeat the Americans. *And we did!*

During the rest of the war, they did manage one offensive air success—mostly a propaganda success. It was the regular night-bombing of Inchon and Seoul from tiny Po-2 biplanes, 1920's technology that found a way to work due to stealthy wooded frames and tree-top flight paths.

With the war over, Kim Il-Sung combined his fond remembrances of the Po-2 with his desire to "...incorporate old style weapons along with modern weapons," and designated the An-2 biplane as the major striking plane for the Special Forces. Despite its apparent archaic appearance, the An-2 was capable of extremely low-altitude low-speed flight which, given the mountainous terrain of the Korean Peninsula, afforded it a good chance of infiltrating the ROK undetected at night.

It had a large cargo capability, excellent range, and short-takeoff-and-landing allowing it to operate from unprepared fields almost anywhere on the Korean Peninsula. It was a perfect platform for the mass delivery of KPA Special Forces. It could carry napalm and small bombs, and its standard crop-dusting sprayers (it was originally an agricultural design, used all over the world), were converted for chemical weapons distribution. Stealthily penetrating the DMZ, the An-2 could crop-dust huge areas with lethal nerve and mustard gasses, delivering tens of square miles of instant death to civilians and unprepared military.

In daylight, the An-2's would be slaughtered. But at night, they could cross the DMZ at tree-top level by the hundreds, land at the U.S.'s Pusan and Osan bases using just a fraction of their runways, and each spill out ten Special Forces soldiers with heavy weapons up to large mortars. Or, if the first wave were unsuccessful, the next could cross the DMZ and gas Osan.

Before Su went in to see the cruise missile launchers—also stationed here, and a key component in an effective first strike on the South—he mustered all the base's Combatants for an on-the-spot inspection.

Walking the lines of soldiers, Architect Su studied the disciplined, hard, fit faces. These were the men who would be the fulcrum upon which his other forces would shift the world. He would insist that they have all the Hughes Aircraft helicopters, and the best An-2 transports. To seize and destroy Osan Air Base, Su knew he would need a tidal wave of force.

Finally, he came to Il-Moon's pride and joy. Set off from the ranks of other Combatants were, justly proud, the men of the Kim Il-Sung Night-Fighters squadrons. One of the few night-capable KPAF units, their mission was focused: without the need of Ground Control Intercept—GCI—radars, in their special Mig-29's, Mig-21 Fishbed-J's, and Mig-23 Floggers, they could hunt the night skies of Korea for even the highest-flying U.S. Recon aircraft.

Halfway through inspecting the last row of unblinking ferocious Combatant faces, Su turned to the commander. "If I might trouble you, I have a special duty—and I have a special soldier in mind."

Twenty minutes later, the Commander asked, "Are you sure this Major Tam Ho is at Onch'On-Up? Although I understand you believed him to be stationed here, we seem to have no such man. Nor his file...nor even a file number."

REUTERS' 4X4 – SEOUL SUBURBS

Abbey was happy, letting Akiru drive through the clumps of high-rise apartments in this obscure suburb of Seoul, as she arranged in her lap the documents for the dead drop. If Abbey was blissful, the line between Akiru's eyes was a deep and vertical wrinkle. The unflappable Akiru usually never worried; he had the patience and courage of the hunter, his camera his weapon of choice. When he missed a turn in the tangle of streets in Sujin while heading to the drop address, Abbey looked up, assessing. She reached her cigarette over, and as he took the offered illicit puff, she remarked, "Lovely day."

Akiru grimaced, smoke trailing from his nose. "You think I am brooding."

Abbey nodded emphatically. "Pointlessly. Is it that we are AWOL from work in a stolen vehicle, with our editor insane with rage at us? Wimp!"

"Our editor, as you know, has tacitly given us free reign. No, that isn't it."

Abbey selected an original photo of ABL, the young 'Gomer' USAF officer out front, and laid it on the pile she would leave at the drop.

Akiru continued, "We talked about this. The only ones who could get you such material are either the Americans or the North Koreans—and you were sure the man in the taxi was *Yakuza*. They answer only to North Korea. It has to be the North wants you to do this."

"Did you ever think if the Americans wanted to leak, they couldn't dress the windows appropriately? Or the South Koreans?"

Akiru chose his words carefully. "Abbey. You and I are many things: opportunistic, yes. Ruthless, certainly. Alcoholics, no question. But we've always been reporters. Never spies."

Abbey popped her chosen papers into an envelope. "We're not spies. This is just a source. We get the news direct and pass it on. Or not. The Pit, or Tokyo?"

AIRBORNE LASER – WHITE SANDS MISSILE RANGE

With a sonic boom, the two JASDF F-15's screamed straight up twenty miles away from Airborne Laser.

Sean told the crew soon after takeoff, "Training airspace is courtesy of White Sands Missile Range. Our Japanese F-15 friends are playing missile. They can pop up in afterburner anytime, so be ready."

On the good side, Sean had used every bit of influence of Ms. Canthor, the AFRL Directed Energy director, to get full cooperation out of White Sands Missile Range—WSMR—for real Ops training and target support. White Sands was only twenty minutes flying time away from Albuquerque, they could do live-fire on missiles there, and it provided a host of support services like drones, radars, and Comm support that he could tap into. He cashed in all his markers, and occasionally used the carrot of 'the Under Secretary is very interested' and finally had WSMR completely lined up for training, including support from his Japanese colleague Col Hareda.

It was hard to reconcile the gorgeous and serene scenery below—magnificent cigarette-smoke-blue mountains, enormous unspoiled desert flats, the furrowed beauty of an eroded wilderness—with Sean's personal hell inside ABL.

The training had gone like so: food, undisciplined rabble, incidents to drive you wild, and attitude—always attitude from the crew and Emily—as if that would help solve their problems.

The first day had gone according to Murphy's schedule: no sooner were they over White Sands, everyone at their stations, than Lorrie asked, "Did anyone remember to raid the Wing's stash for Pepsi and Twinkies?"

Sean broke in, "First, this food thing has got to go. I don't want to see any junk food at your stations."

Emily asked, "What if it's healthy organic food?" while J-Stars added, "Food is part of safety; keeping up with flying fatigue. It's a Reg."

Sean said, "Sorry. When in flight, we're at our stations, at attention."

"What if I have to pee?" Lorrie asked, and held up a finger-to-thumb circle. "I have a bladder the size of a walnut."

Everyone laughed—and they missed the first F-15 simulated missile track. Next someone forgot to turn on the Strikeback radio, and the F-15's were a hundred miles away before turning around.

After the first day, Sean started putting together checklists for everything—and rigged up a wireless headset so he was free to roam ABL and still run Ops. Then he could, as Emily commented, "Interfere with the march of progress not just at his station, but over the entire aircraft."

Ready to try again, Sean had visited a toy shop, and was about to do the lesson of the day. As Eila worked to set up the F-15's again as fake ballistic missiles—swooping low and then ripping almost straight up in afterburners—he pulled out a small spongy plastic-haired Kooshball.

Sean said, "The key to Ops is flow. Ops flows through the plane. You feel the flow. Here's how."

He held the Kooshball, and when Col Hareda's F-15 roared straight up out of the desert pulling six g's, and Jarhead called, "Kettledrums!" Sean tossed the Kooshball to J-Stars.

J-Stars caught it, said, "Kettledrums! Launch at White Sands. Lorrie."

He lobbed the Kooshball to Lorrie, who caught it clumsily. Lorrie said, "Long-range video up. Coordinates on the Ethernet. Eila."

The Kooshball flew across the cabin to Eila, who dropped it but managed to work her console, calling out, "Ops this is Strikeback. We have an F-15 simulating an SCUD launch. It's a *hostile*! Coordinates will follow. Red."

As each person caught and passed on the Kooshball, Sean watched critically. Red caught the ball easily, then balanced it on top of her head while she tapped in her commands. Sean let it go, counting to see how long it took each station before they reported in, and flung the ball on.

Red said, "Ops, Laser radar is tracking target. Chemical scan underway. Sean," and whipped the Kooshball at Sean.

Sean caught the ball behind his back, called out, "Attack Laser, this is Ops. Full energy standby. Guidestar on. Emily."

Emily didn't bother to catch the ball and it flew behind her, as outside the big beam director cranked around, the video tracker came up, and when she called, "Handoff," the beam director auto-tracker took over smoothly following the F-15 up. The laser focused to a guidestar near the F-15.

Emily said, "Beam director acquiring. Tracking loops closed. What?"

Suddenly, the laser had died away.

In the laser area, Emily, Sean, and Marty looked at coffee spilled into the laser electronics, as Sean yelled, "What the hell?" as Marty said defensively, "You said you didn't want to see food or drink, so someone put this coffee out of sight...and it spilled. We're hosed for today."

"I meant no food or drink period."

Marty said incredulously, "You want us to work all day and night without coffee? How are we supposed to be creative without freedom?"

"I will fucking shoot the next person I see drinking outside the galley! OK, we drill today without a live laser. Flightdeck, set up again."

It was not until 10:00 a.m. that ABL returned to Kirtland, having worked through the night. The F-15's had refueled three times, and Col Hareda finally said they had reached their flight-time limit.

Moreover, Sean was not sure they had accomplished that much.

With the mission finished, there was no happy chatter. When ABL taxied home and cut her engines, the exhausted crew unbuckled, ran for the door and freedom. They slowed, suddenly depressed when Sean called out, "Post-mission hot wash in ten minutes."

Emily walked up to him. "Tomorrow can we slaves please have seven hours of rowing and two hours of punishment instead of the other way around?"

*　　*　　*

Sean would only a week later look back on this time as the most frustrating in his life. Never before had he been so hog-tied, or met such ruthless resistance.

He needed action, he got Brownian motion. He need cooperation, he got hamstrung.

First, there were constant VIP tours and request for joyrides. Then there was the food. Then there were the night sounds seemingly of mice playing behind the panels of the plane. Even though Sean set out traps and poison, these mysteriously disappeared daily.

In the laser room, Sean watched Emily supervise the installation of her new beam control module into the laser beam train. "Five more days until you test? Sooner or later you gotta stop noodling!"

"Noodling is how enlightenment comes. Wait until I've finished this batch and taste the truth."

"You'd make pasta while Los Angeles burns. Wrap up. We fly in an hour," Sean said with venom.

Of course, *that dog didn't hunt.* Forced to bow to Emily's demand for an all-day install of the new good-weather wavefront reconstructor, Sean went back to Ops, and found someone had taped a sign to his console, 'The beatings will continue until morale improves.' He ripped it up, and looked at the pile of real work in front of him. The paperwork blizzard was more sand in his gears. Like some sentient tar baby, it socked it right to him, braking even his own progress to a standstill.

Looking over the crew's AF 182 safety forms, with their pages of blanks to fill out, Sean estimated it would take all day just to put everyone's binders in order. Jarhead came past, fingers greasy, carrying a honeycombed MilSTD electronics module. "Anything I can help you for?"

Sean waved him past angrily. "I wouldn't want to sacrifice our one functional person. Drive on."

Jarhead took a quiet look at Sean—and dragged him off the plane for a jog.

Leaving the eastside gym, by unspoken agreement they took a jogging path away from Airborne Laser. Sean let Jarhead set a brutal pace into the sandy tumbleweed-choked Tijeras canyon wash beyond Sandia Labs. Jarhead ran them up the face of a huge flood-control dam, jumping between the giant water-slowing spillway teeth. After cresting the dam and running into its dry basin, Sean waved to slow the pace. He asked, "Day in and day out, being treated like Barney Fife. You get your one bullet and you better keep it in your pocket. How do you put up with it?

Jarhead grinned. "It's not their job to know they need me. That's my job. Someday, when we're in the shit, they are going to kiss my sweet ass thank you. Meantime, at least in my pocket, I've got the bullet."

Chapter 25

MAGNOLIA PALACE GARDENS – FORBIDDEN CITY, PYONGYANG

Ground zero for U.S. cruise missiles in Pyongyang was a beautiful garden area just to the west of Kim Il-Sung square.

Amidst the garden's curving groves of almond and cherry trees, slim and willowy salt cedars with wispy green needles, tufted Korean grass, raked gravel, and Zen viewing stones, were graceful statues of mythical Korean creatures—and calm bronze and stone likenesses of the Great and Dear Leaders. In the middle of these extensive serene gardens was a huge square marble palace, informally named the Magnolia Palace by Kim Il-Sung's wife, who wanted the usage to change from the Chinese-derivative 'The Forbidden City.'

Below the gardens, completely hidden, was a steel-reinforced concrete city. Here, the ultra-elite of North Korea lived and worked. Although the palace was comfortable, airy, and light, and the leaders were always only a few steps from fast elevators or stairwells down into the warren of leadership bunkers below, most spent little time above ground.

Today the Japanese maples—although never referred to as such—were turning auburn, and next to the giant Magnolia Palace the autumn light lit the colorful temple paintings under the arches of a beautiful palace annex, an ancient Korean pagoda temple.

Strangely, the entrance to this compound is from a small road just behind the Koryo hotel. Here, a massive guarded barrier lets vehicles enter into the outer parking area for the almost-elite, who lived in nearby apartments and yet needed constant access to the throne.

Abbey and Akiru were driven through the guard gate, then stopped at the fortified wall around the outer gardens. Inside a small intruder-trapping area, they were roughly frisked by Guard Command before being allowed through a gate and into the inner garden.

No photos were permitted of the ramparts, guard stations, and fortifications of the garden walls, as these might help in an assault on the leader bunkers. However, the Guard Command apparently had specific instructions. Although they sneered and barked at Abbey and Akiru because they were Japanese—"There is only one

Japan and it is evil!"—once inside the inner gate they gave Akiru back his cameras and left them standing at the edge of the huge beautiful park-like space.

"It is quite an elegant garden," Akiru remarked to Abbey as he took some still shots.

"A fucking copy of Tenryu-ji garden in Kyoto is what it is," snapped Abbey. "The cretins can't even copy things well." She gestured to a grouping of exquisitely craggy viewing stones, looking like exotic islands rising from the ocean. "You're not supposed to be able to see all nine viewing stones at once. You should always be missing one."

Akiru walked slowly, surveying the boulders floating in their sea of raked pebbles. "You cannot see nine. You are not counting well. Always only eight at a time."

Abbey counted, cursed, moved, counted again and cursed again. "So a few rocks they can copy."

Akiru seemed at peace, calm, his speech slipping into garden-Japanese, saying softly, "I myself am less certain than Yamamoto-san. When I *hang my eyes* upon this garden, it is all rather *shibumi.*"

An unsmiling North Korean Guard Command lieutenant came up and snapped, "No more talking. No more photographs. This way."

Walking the path into the garden, they came to the Magnolia Palace, its modern marble structure surrounded by an extensive covered veranda. Abbey noted that arrayed around the veranda were groupings of both formal and comfortable furniture. Looking out over the garden and the graceful temple, these sofas and soft chairs seemed to be awaiting the pleasant family chats of a summer's evening.

Perfect. What a setting!

At the corner of the giant palace, there was a beautifully tiered classical Korean temple. Its towers piled one on another into the sky, its sides painted in red lacquer, its roof tiles blue, and the temple entrance doors guarded by a pair of ten-foot high bronze Korean lion-dragons.

Who did this, made this garden—the 1950's square marble monstrosity—right along with a Korean temple?

"My grandfather, the Great Leader, did it himself—with help from a certain architect," said a man's smooth voice in Japanese.

Abbey swung around to see who had read her mind. He was close, had somehow gotten right up to her without her noticing, so absorbed was she by the grounds. She tried to ignore this apparent thought-reading. "Pachinko money," she managed tartly. "For his own aggrandizement."

Continuing in passable Japanese, Dearest Leader said, "Aggrandizement? Is any motive too low for art? Do we not finally judge the art, not its motivation?"

Abbey only vaguely recognized the man from his few pictures. He was slightly chubby, but in that way suffused with the energy of the constantly thinking and working. He was beautifully dressed in a Japanese business suit, and Abbey found herself, strangely, automatically bowing low. "Are you speaking of your peace efforts as well?" Abbey switched to Korean to cover her confusion and her physical reaction to Dearest Leader, hiding her voice tremors under the disguise of the foreign accent.

Jong-Nam smiled, and said in English. "What is a person's life, but an act of art as well? And in the end, is it not the life rather than its motives we must judge?"

His face was serene and open, a boyish pimple here and there, and yet his empathy—whether a mask or real, came through strongly. His jet-black hair was cropped movie star stylish and free of mousse; his charismatic face and eyes were filled with anticipation. Abbey was again surprised when instead of bowing, he reached out and warmly took her hand.

Bowing to Akiru, who returned it, Dearest Leader swept an arm over the garden. "The trees were all personally selected by my grandfather, who had a love of trees. Between the American bombing and the burning of whole hillsides to prevent the guerillas from hiding, there was in essence a war declared on trees in Korea. Many of the remaining ones were cut down for fuel in that very exceptionally cold winter, which Americans seem to think Korea always has."

Abbey said, "He had excellent taste—for a guerilla leader."

"He had come a long way from the young boy captured by the Japanese, released as unimportant, and who was later recognized by the Russians for his undoubted survival skills—and strong enough leadership skills to be handed North Korea."

"A remarkably accurate remembrance, given where we are."

"Here in the garden, he could find some peace; the feel of Korea before the war with America."

"A war some say he started."

Dearest Leader chuckled. "Are you congenitally tart and thorny, Yamamoto-san, or is it especially for me and things Korean?"

He was looking at her as if he knew her; like there was something valuable inside her. The unbridled gaze drew her; somehow sexy and powerful.

Abbey was so unnerved, she found herself putting her hands behind her back like schoolgirl, pushing her breasts out in a provocation to intimidate aggressors. "I prefer Abbey, if you don't mind. Do you always speak in riddles?"

He motioned, and a man with a box appeared. It was the size of a small TV, square and beautifully wrapped. "A present for you, given our cold winters." He indicated Akiru should take the box. "Your associate can carry it." He motioned for Akiru to stay behind. "Let us walk together," and he spread an inviting hand toward one of the manicured paths.

For a moment, they strolled apace. Behind them just ten yards, a burly Guard Command officer walked, but seemingly at ease.

Abbey said, "I'm here, frankly, to ask for an interview—an American-style sit-down conversation. If you want the very tenuous peace process to come to fruition, I think it's time you told the world about your vision for Korea—and let them get to know you."

"A generous offer of your help."

"Oh, no. It must be an exclusive with me. So I will benefit. However, this format will be more useful to you. You will be free to communicate your point of view personally."

"And you are Japanese, and as our most bitter—past—foe, it will be ever so much more convincing, eh?" He paused for a second, turned with a statue of the Great Leader behind him. "I think, instead, a press conference might be just the ticket."

Abbey moved to him, leaned close, speaking silkily. "Do you really want to stand in front of a crowd of waving and yelling reporters looking like the president of Iran under duress? The press corps shocking you, provoking you, discomfiting you; trying to make you look bad?" She waved to the palace behind them; she mimed greeting, sitting, talking. "Instead, we meet on your veranda overlooking the gardens, sit on a pleasantly stuffed sofa with your family around us." She registered his reaction to the mention of the veranda, a surprised glance, and she pressed on. "We will sit together and talk truth and beauty and progress and prosperity—the future. We will meet as human beings in front of the whole planet; not a harassed leader under the grip of a rabid world press."

His eyes were very close, and he seemed mesmerized, just as she remembered her father's eyes when she did something he approved of...

Dearest Leader managed to pull free of the moment, suddenly jovial. "Good show! I like your idea, Abbey-san. I like it very much. It is simple; it is patently unfair to the other press and therefore more enticing to the world. With you at my side, I will not have to endure the hounding, the bile. The exclusive, as you say."

Almost like after sex, her tension exploded into relief, and the craving for a cigarette swept over her. Despite her suddenly-pounding head, she managed, "Just so we're clear, I'm not talking about an interview filled with Juche rant like 'Kim Il-Sung is more benevolent than Buddha, more just than Mohammed, more loving than Jesus, and will be the salvation of all of mankind.' I mean the real thing, in English, about the issues, straight up."

"Straight up, as you say. About the issues. Exactly."

"So, you'll do it?" prodded Abbey, worried her head might soon explode she was so dying for a cigarette.

Dearest Leader pursed his lips in thought, then reached into his suit, and pulled out a packet of Marlboros, proffering it.

Abbey took one, hiding her confused relief, asked suspiciously, "Is it her, or is it her hairdresser?"

Dearest Leader fitted a cigarette into an ebony holder. "Counterfeiting is so strange. If you make a gold coin out of gold, the market should not care."

He lit their cigarettes, and with great relief, Abbey drew in a dirty warm lungful of the North Korea Marlboro. It was scrumptiously tasty and from the teasing look on his face, the rascal knew it. "As you say, it should fetch the same price—but you will not find most stockholders agreeing with you."

Dearest Leader laughed. "Oh, I think they will; the right stockholders. Yes, I'm sure they will, eventually."

Abbey moved close to him as they strolled, purposefully bumping him gently. "I have one serious request, but if you are as you say, it should make little difference. I wish the interview to go out live on North Korean radio. Perhaps not TV, but radio."

Il-Moon had already prepared him for this request. "Your thinking is that if I am honest, I would not mind my people hearing the truth."

"They are deeply involved. It is they who will be forced to deal with the conditions of the treaty calling for freedom of travel for North Koreans—and freedom to a great degree in radio, TV, and media. If you are serious about giving them those freedoms—I ask you to let them taste it now. Let them meet their leader, the man, not the myth."

"Myth? While you cast yourself as the Asian Barbara Walters?"

The cigarette was succulent—and so was his propinquity—and Abbey realized before she spoke, for once, her words about herself were the truth. "I believe in you and what you are trying to do. This interview will make it impossible for anyone to stop you. If you broadcast to the DPRK and the Americans know the world knows, it will push the negotiations past the point of no return. They will have no choice. They cannot argue that you are being cagey, one step forward and two steps back. It will also make you an instant heroic historical figure and Nobel Prize winner. So come, talk to me. Tell me how you feel, and make your case to the world—the whole world."

"What assurances do I have that you will not spring something?"

Abbey shrugged. "I am a Japanese woman. Publicly betraying you is not possible for me. I will also agree to a one-minute tape delay on the North Korean side. You hold the plug. But the honest man has no need."

"'You cannot cheat an honest man?'"

He still has a few lessons to learn. "Well," Abbey smiled, "I'll not go that far. I will also furnish you with a list of questions. You can give me what you would have me ask as well."

Dearest Leader stopped walking; they were at the set of nine viewing stones. "These Zen stones; one can never see them all no matter how you look."

"Yes, there is always at least one stone you cannot see."

"Life, I suppose," mused Dearest Leader. "There is always that one stone."

"So we have a deal?"

"We have," Dearest Leader smiled, "as we capitalist roaders would say, a *super* deal."

At the porches of the Magnolia Palace, its severe marble walls in contrast to the pretty blue tiles of its elegant Korean side-temple, Dearest Leader bowed good-bye smartly, and Abbey responded with a repeated fast low bowing.

Why am I kowtowing to him like a schoolgirl?

When he had gone into the marble palace, the mist in her mind seemed to lift and she saw Akiru was grinning at her.

The interview of the century was on.

AIRBORNE LASER – TECH AREA

In the end, it was a mouse that caused Sean to snap. In that pleasant sliver of time, the beginning of a mission, when the plane doors are still open, the air fresh, people coming and going, calling and laughing, there is an informality and camaraderie—you are not too close to seat check, and yet things are moving, feeling smooth...

Lorrie's computers crashed with a loud *bong!* "I've got some ground fault. I've lost the laser data. We're crashed; we're down; not coming back up." She looked up to Emily. "The laser status analog-to-digital converters shorted in the essential bus, console twelve."

Emily stopped what she was doing, looked off into space. She called to Tsgt Smitty. "Go to configuration panel three. The ground wire has been gnawed by a mouse."

Sean followed the sergeant into the aft part of the plane. At a bulkhead, the NCO pulled off a panel. Sean saw only cables galore until Smitty fished out a cleanly-chewed wire. "Dr. Engel's brilliant, idn't she? No one else on da planet coulda done that!"

Sean had a completely different take on it. "Airborne Laser has wire-chewing mice?"

Calling after the leaving Sean, Smitty added, "She won't let us trap them. And a big ol' owl got Leo our cat."

Sean strode into the Tech Area. Threw his flight log onto the floor *boom!* The crew looked up from their stations.

Emily said, deadpan, "You dropped your book."

Sean yelled, "You leave mice on ABL and fuck up a mission? You are all so proud of being amateurs."

"Professionals like you gave us the *Titanic*. Amateurs like us floated Noah's Ark."

The pro-Emily crew laughed.

Sean said, "It's easy to laugh. There are so many things I don't understand and it's funny how my heart is out there on the tripwire with 30,000 Americans facing death. Help me or not I'm taking this plane operational."

Sean exited out the main door, and Red turned to Emily. "You don't call dibs on him, I will."

Emily's face held her real answer like an open book as she said, "No dibs, not for me."

GOLDEN PHOENIX BAR – SEOUL

Abbey slurped a pink Cosmopolitan, a radical departure from her usual Japanese whiskey or dry gin martini. When she ordered it, Akiru didn't say anything, but at the totally uncharacteristic smacking of her lips, he looked at her closely. "Don't tell me you are going pink on us. Is it just because we landed the interview of the century?"

"Whoopie! Sure, I suppose."

"When are you going to announce it?"

Abbey grew thoughtful, touched the box Dearest Leader had given her for the millionth time. "I don't know. I don't know. I need to think of some real whacker for it." Her voice trailed off.

"Then what is it? Dearest Leader?"

Abbey felt her ears grow hot, and knew even in the darkened bar Akiru could sense her blush. The words came out in a rush as if she were dying to talk. "If I'd been seventeen, meeting him, I would have dropped a gob of goo in my virgin panties."

"As it was, did you?"

She giggled. "Metaphorically." She fiddled with the Cosmo's thin glass stem, tried to express her ineffable confusion and desire. "I guess I still did, kind of. As much as I can these days."

"He is Korean; I thought you hated everything Korean."

"It is just a habit," she conceded after a pause. "A Japanese habit. Maybe not a good one. They say it's getting better back home. All this cultural stuff I'm doing? Showing around the DPRK guys. Amazing what the Koreans have done."

"Yamamoto-san, you are really starting to think so pink. You are admiring them?"

"You know how we Japanese are so damned proud of our ceramics? All the bent cups and tea things. Our beautiful elegant glazes? The fine brushwork? When the Koreans were making chrysanthemum inkpots and tiered flower arrangers, we were squatting in huts picking at ourselves. Did you know we simply up and kidnapped a ton of Korean potters and craftsmen and their families right off the beaches here? Not just once. Hundreds of times. For centuries. We hauled them back to Japan and used them to teach us ceramics."

"Just like the North Koreans kidnapped Japanese teenagers off the beach for their spy schools? Makes you want to stay clear of beaches on both sides of the Sea of Japan."

Abbey took a careless slurp of her Cosmo, picked up his Kirin bottle with both hands. Fingers under the bottom, she respectfully tilted the bottle to refill his glass. "Akiru, we're in Korea. It was Imperial Japan who named it Sea of Japan. You need to start calling it The East Sea, if we're gonna do this right."

Akiru shook his head, raised his glass and sipped. "East Sea then, Abbey-san. Even if it is to the west of Japan. Did we ever send the kidnapped Korean potters back—across the East Sea?"

Abbey's eyes crinkled as much as they could in her taut face. "No, never did. They assimilated into our gene pool. Another verboten topic. Mayhap you even have a Korean in your background. I heard they did a beach grab of cinematographers."

Akiru put a hand out and pulled Abbey's half-finished drink to his side of the table. "No more pink gin for you, Missy-san."

Getting between Abbey and her drink—even in funning—usually would get your fingers broken and was not something Akiru ever did. *But she is changing so fast.*

"Maybe there were some Korean newswomen pulled off the beach, and that's the skeleton in my closet."

Akiru asked, "Is that the skeleton you have in your closet back home?" and then instantly regretted it; did not know where to put his face. Stopping her drinking was an act of war. Mentioning her apartment—letting slip by accident he knew about her trashed flat was an act of suicide. Akiru remembered how trashed it was. He had seen it one time when Abbey was blacked out and he carried her home when she was close to dying of alcohol poisoning. Inside her flat, his feelings surged as he saw the pigsty with the burned food and crusted filth on the windows and the huge pile of Japanese videos. After putting her in bed, he waited a whole day while she sweated and moaned. Only at dawn on the second day when she got up and crawled into the shower—when he was certain she was out of danger—had he slipped out without her ever knowing he had been there.

He was relieved when he saw she was not connecting his comment to her flat. She was far away, visualizing something.

Abbey was thinking of Dearest Leader. *I am going to kiss him next time. There will surely be a moment, around a corner, perhaps in makeup before the interview. What would I lose? Suppose he found me first; paid a surprise visit. He is resourceful, bold. He felt it too—the attraction. What if, after touring him through the Korea Exchange he was at The Shilla hotel for foreign dignitaries just blocks from her flat? What if he should want a consummation....*

Enjoying Akiru's shock, Abbey stood up well before they were anywhere near their normal evening plasterment. "I have got to go. Can I drop you somewhere?"

Akiru declined, wanting to put distance between his remark about her flat and her mental slipstream. He watched in wonder as Abbey left her drink, shucked a pile of Won onto the table, picked up the present box from Dearest Leader and, queen-like, swayed across the room. To the few catcalls from other reporters, she called back, "Leaving early!"

"Akiru," the table hooted back. "Aren't you going to get some documentary footage of the Queen leaving this dive shit-faced?"

Another yelled, "What about the gods of documentary? Don't they want you kissing her ass with the camera right now?"

"Yeah, get that camera up right up her ass!"

Akiru gave them the finger as Abbey stopped, dramatically laid Dearest Leader's box onto the bar and opened it. Her breath caught again at the sumptuous fur coat inside, North Korean chinchilla. She whirled it out of the box, flinging it around her shoulders in a flash of luxury and beauty.

Abbey pirouetted, calling back gaily from the door, "I'm not shit-faced and at least I've got a life, unlike you eleven o'clock newser-losers."

Outside, she muscled a cab away from a group of appalled Americans. The cabbie objected to stopping along the way until Abbey grabbed a chunk of his neck muscle and squeezed in an agonizing grip. "I have the number of this junker cab of yours and you will wait here and if you leave I will hunt you down and kill you!"

The cabbie meekly agreed to wait. Abbey was back outside the 7-Eleven in just a few minutes bearing shopping bags holding her precious purchases.

Once inside her filth-encrusted apartment at Chosun Luxury Towers, she laid the fur coat where she could see it, hung up her work clothes, found jeans and a tee-shirt. She decided to change the shirt to a stretchy top, *that nice Danskin still in its wrapper; something for him...*

In the kitchen, she set out the contents of the shopping bags. She picked up and pulled on the rubber gloves. Into the yellow plastic bucket, she ran hot water and then dumped in the soap flakes. She took a reflective look around at her ravaged apartment and imagined Dearest Leader.

Then Abbey Yamamoto got down on her hands and knees and started to scrub her apartment clean.

KIRTLAND AFB – DESERT AREA

Sean was far out into the desert. He'd borrowed Matt Cho's mountain bike, and frustrated, cranked it up on a dirt road into the remote reaches of giant Kirtland AFB. The fall air streamed by as he crossed the wild tract of scrub and gramma grass. He passed the nuclear transport training areas with their giant semis, the baked potato-like Manzano hills, their eyes of sunken bunkers and furrowed triple razor wire fences still intact from the 1950's nuke storage days. He passed the still-green scruffy base golf course and the giant Solar Power Tower with its hundreds of reflectors directing the sun-bright spot onto the giant ceramic tower. The desert day was glorious, the hills speckled in dark green juniper and piñón, the craggy rocks rising to jagged peaks from the vast skirts of desert. Repeatedly, he sprinted until he could not think, feeling only the fire of the exertion. Ten miles later, he finally pulled to a stop below the giant silver domes of the Starfire Optical Range, its trepanned stubby volcanic cone sticking up like an island from the desert.

He was glad to be out of the confines of the Tech Area and ABL and the hangar complex and the White Elephant. For the first time in days, he was free. Yet Airborne Laser followed him. *What do I really have here with these people?*

They were the best—he had to admit—and Emily's retort that he himself could never conceive or build such a system was true. So, what did he bring to the table, crowded already with so many capable people?

A giant explosion rocked the ground beneath him, and he saw the spout of flame and smoke that was the Security Forces doing controlled demolition of contraband. Sean watched the smoke of destroyed drugs slowly drift off and dissipate.

Late that night, Sean borrowed a hand-held thermal imager from the laser area. He scanned the bulkhead panels of Airborne Laser until he saw three twitching hot spots behind a riveted panel near Emily's station.

Figures they'd be hiding in the Tech Area. Pulling on a pair of Chief Auggie's welding gloves, hoping they would be thick enough, he lifted rattle-buzzing Diablo down out of his cage, and coaxed the rattlesnake to slither into a hole in ABL's bulkhead.

"And now Mouseketeers, get ready for something completely different."

Catchers in the Sky

BOOK 5

"Follow your intuition about the people you choose
and work only with the best."

The AFRL Project Officer's Fifth Commandment

Chapter 26

The 18th of October

ABL – ALTITUDE CHAMBER – KAFB TRAINING POOL

"Hey. Somebody took the snake." J-Stars said, looking at Diablo's empty cage.

Sean moaned, "He's gone? How could someone do such a thing? The only snake I ever had."

"Methinks the Major Problem doth protest too much," Emily said sarcastically.

"Clever. But I go by Major Intelligence—and now I want everyone in the Tech Area."

As the tech crew assembled, they all recalled the last time they'd seen him, throwing his book down and storming out. OIC's—Officers in Charge—came and went quickly on ABL (X), and it looked to be downhill from here. They all gazed at him like some poorly understood but predictable form of life. Except Sean's was an unruffled calm. He looked over his clipboard and up to meet the crew's eyes. He asked rhetorically, "Did you know what I've noticed? You all have been flying under waived training. I'm afraid the next couple days are emergency egress, safety, and survival training."

Sean had spent hours going over the files of every man, woman, marine, and snake on ABL. There was a long list of unfulfilled training requirements: fire extinguisher training, step ladder training, Hazmat, forklift, solid waste, security, No-Fear Act, Terrorism and Force Protection, USAF Information Assurance Awareness, Opsec, laser safety, sexual harassment and assault, suicide and violence awareness, equipment accounts, financial records, project management, ethics in government, trafficking in people, case file organization—it was beyond daunting. Nevertheless, Sean neither encouraged others to think little of training, nor wasted his time on resistance—and safety and survival were essential.

Emily protested, "The laserjocks and I beg off. We need a wavefront reconstructor—"

Sean said, "No one flies without training. And you'll love the instructor."

Nor did anyone laugh or look like they might love the instructor, Lorrie remarking sarcastically, "You can piss on my garden, just don't try to tell me it's a rain storm."

Sean handed out everyone's first AF 182 forms. The crew looked disgusted at this Dilbert-like lack of humanity to the mission. Even more so, when they saw the first training was 'Altitude Chamber.' They had all worked hundreds of high-altitude flight hours and didn't need this...but as Sean pointed out, they were his Ops days.

Despite the protests, within a short time, Sean had hog-marched the crew along the ABL jogging path around the end of the runway—it was good for them—and to the altitude chamber. He talked to the technician and filled out the paperwork to use the chamber.

Within the altitude chamber, much like a small tourist submarine with heavy bolts all over the outside and a long row of seats along the bulkheads, Sean sat the crew at the training stations in the narrow cabin. He lectured them, worked with them to practice the Oxygen equipment, and then had them pack the equipment back up.

Sean, putting on a small oxygen mask, said, "Depressurization. If ABL's hull is breached, you instantly go from sea level to the operational altitude of forty thousand feet. We'll try it here, we don't tell you when, it's better practice as a surprise. You have eight seconds—"

Sean gave the smallest signal, unseen by the crew—and the tech flipped the switch.

Boom! The chamber depressurized. The crew felt the hair-blowing eye-squinting brain-twisting *whoosh*, looked around wildly—and went for their masks. Most of the crew had listened to Sean, but Emily, who was surreptitiously calculating something, didn't know how to get her mask going. In the almost zero-oxygen environment, Emily tried, tried again—and bollixed it up. She suddenly went relaxed, gazing ahead blankly.

Sean yelled, "Emily! Put your mask on! You are dead if you don't!" He went over to her, leaned right into her face and screamed, "Emily! You are going to die!"

Emily, critically hypoxic, smiled at nothing.

Sean said sarcastically, "The supremely competent Emily," gesturing to her mindless face. "Eight seconds is what you get, people. You cannot recover by yourself. If it's critical you be awake, we all die."

Sean picked up her mask and held oxygen to Emily's mouth. As the gas hissed into her lungs, Emily came to and found her crew staring at her.

Emily asked, "What happened?"

* * *

That afternoon, Sean watched the ABL crew in emergency gear bobbing in the base pool. He called encouragement to them as they tried to team-inflate the big collapsed life raft, and when they finally did—struggling, cursing, yelling at each other, and getting cold and angry—Sean asked them to do it again.

Again, the big deflated raft floated like a huge plastic bag awash in the pool. Again, the crew one by one slid down the aircraft emergency egress ramp and into the cold deep water. Splashing, struggling, they swam to the deflated plastic raft.

This time, the crew was smarter, and a teamwork effort arose. Red called the shots while Jarhead and Lorrie supplied the key muscle. Sean could see the tech crew, even as they foundered, were pleased with themselves. They thought they were getting it—until Sean turned a water hose on them.

"This time, we'll add a little stress." Aimed at a person's head, Sean's hose would knock out whoever was showing signs of leadership. As that person became too flooded, blinded, and water-socked to continue, the group would founder, and then recover by compensating for the dysfunctional member. Just when they were getting it together and a new leader was emerging, Sean would hose out the new key person.

The crew fought back hard, and in twenty minutes of yelling, arguing, splashing, freezing, and half-drowning, they managed to inflate the raft, pull themselves and the weaker ones over the sides, and lay sprawled, exhausted, and cold to the bone. Sean let them lie for a ten-count, then called, "OK, Good teamwork. Paddle over, and everyone egress from the raft up on the side of the pool."

Teeth chattering, the crew knelt or lay as Sean continued, "Don't forget, as soon as you're in the boat—or wherever you're stranded—after checking injuries, the first key to survival is taking serious inventory: lay out every thing, object, supply, cloth, false tooth, plastic spoon, and hairpin you can find." Sean looked at the frozen crew. "Also, remember that in really cold water, you may go without warning into hypothermic shock. How to get out? In WWII they found you could quickly revive even an almost-frozen-to death pilot by...?"

"Putting him in bed with a girl...*interested* in him," said Lorrie.

"A woman," Sean corrected crisply. "Exactly." He lay down suggestively. "Suppose I'm hypothermic. A female volunteer to revive this poor frozen man?"

A teeth-chattering Lorrie said, "I claim to help." She got down on Sean and humped on him enthusiastically, albeit they were both in bright yellow rubber emergency gear.

Sean responded, and when Lorrie finally broke off and stood up suddenly, aroused and embarrassed, they were *both* revived and vibrant.

Emily looked on flush-faced.

MAGNOLIA PALACE – MILITARY INTRANET ROOM

Although Architect Su was road-weary to the bone from his constant preparations afield in the huge KPA infrastructure, at least then, he reflected, he was in the fresh air and beauty of the Korean autumn. Down here, a hundred meters under the Magnolia Palace in the leader bunker, it was chillingly artificial.

Su sat by the bunker's terminal to the Military Intranet, being instructed in the system that controlled the entire North Korean armed forces. The young army technician pointed to the basic Orders Screen: on one side, a list of overall KPA units, the armored divisions, artillery positions, chemical weapons depots, cruise and SCUD missiles, and of course the Naval and Army Special Forces. On the other, a standard set of orders ready to be edited and sent for execution. From this one console, you could mix and match units and operations, commanding the entire war machine into coordinated action—especially if you had good cooperation from key allies across the net at each unit headquarter's.

Su looked down at the neat command sequences of his plans, many of them to be sent through this very system. They looked straightforward; it was just that in that hairbreadth between war and peace, it was so easy for something to slip. He recalled in his musings the German pop song of years ago he had much enjoyed, '99 Red Balloons,' about a child's accidental release of balloons, misconstrued as attacks, which triggered the giant war machines of the USA and USSR to roll across Europe in battle. *Yes, disaster is not here so fanciful.*

The army technician went to rigid attention as Il-Moon entered. Nodding to Su proudly, and without preamble, Il-Moon began to lecture: "With all of the cabling buried for safety, and powered independently, we are immune from any attack. Any."

He went on to say the KPA had access to the brightest programmers and engineers, got precisely—thanks to Architect Su's 2nd Economic Committee—the resources they requested. Su had arranged the network servers and PC terminals to be bought individually by the overseas Korean Chongryon members in Japan. These were hidden in furniture, rice bags, bedding, and bulk foodstuffs, and transshipped to Korea on the little ocean liner Mangyongbong-92, managing to hide everything from the understaffed Japanese customs inspectors.

Su looked at Il-Moon carefully. There was something strange about this pride, this love of the KPA. Although most officers loved their soldierly gizmos, here was something Su did not understand. The young technician got it, though. Even standing at attention, he was so enthusiastic he could not keep his eyes fixed forward. They followed with darting excitement, as Il-Moon waxed enthusiastic in word and gesture.

When Il-Moon moved off into the farther reaches of the bunkers, Architect Su found his own hand stroking the Intranet console thoughtfully. "Would you be so kind," he murmured to the young army technician, "In instructing me further on this system?"

When Su had taken in all he needed on the Intranet, he thanked the youngster, and went up into the palace to find Dearest Leader. He found him on the veranda overlooking the garden, ensconced at one of the furniture groupings, his plump shoulders now wrapped in a blanket against the chilly fall day, insistent on working outside on the endless stacks of paper—decisions, determinations, awards, and plans—that were the life at the top in North Korea.

After a short report on his progress in defensive preparations, Architect Su confided to Dearest Leader, "I am not sure where Major Tam Ho has gone. Nor have I been able to find his file."

Dearest Leader seemed unconcerned, although Su felt undercurrents in his glib reply: "Files are misplaced frequently. You merely use a cross-reference number to locate another copy or a related file. Then you will find him."

"I cannot find even a single related file number."

Su saw Dearest Leader's breath catch. The police state of North Korea was organized around a paper filing system so extensive and complex—millions of file cabinets—it was worthless unless you had a starting point. Without a file number, in the countless cross-indexed files, it was a search for a needle in a city of needles. "Who can find you a file number to get started?"

In answering, Su took his time, emphasizing the delicacy of this Gordian Knot. "I am not sure I would like others in the MPAF to know I am looking into this." Meaning, *The very people I might ask could be conspirators, now biding their time. The digging might panic them—especially in the MPAF.*

"Surely, the General Political Bureau could help you discretely. So too, a file must be held by the Party." *You know some non-military people, use them.*

"Major Ho is presently on secondment to the Guard Command." *I don't want to ask Il-Moon—and his reach is wide.*

There was a nod of response at the reference to Il-Moon. "Yes, your actions might be misunderstood." *Ruffling Il-Moon is unwise—and is all this concern really necessary?*

It was always risky to appear to be at machinations behind the scenes. Since Col Kang's execution was Il-Moon's turf, any inquiry was likely to look like the preparation for a purge. In the murky world of North Korean intrigue, with the firing squad always at the ready, if your political associates suspected you were plotting, you risked uncertain reaction. When your intentions could only be guessed, they could provoke poorly-considered preemptive counter-actions. To survive in the high halls of power, if you must threaten, you must not seem to be threatening. Su was treading near this forbidden area.

Su replied directly: "This matter of Tam Ho is a false note among all the good work we are doing." *It is better not to leave something like this not understood.*

Dearest Leader mused, "Yet, without a file number, he does not exist. You have nowhere to start."

Su noted that Dearest Leader had given him no traceable permission. *Plausible deniability, should he need to throw me to the wolves.*

Architect Su cleared his throat. "Do not concern yourself. Perhaps it is nothing." *I will continue looking discreetly, since you do not mind too much.*

LUNCHROOM – ABL HANGAR

Emily had tried to work the rest of the evening, and failed badly. She kept coming back to being blacked-out—right in front of Sean—and what he had said. "Oh, why?" She asked out loud for the millionth time.

After a sleepless night, she decided on a course of action.

Sean had already noticed in the hangar lunchroom the tech crew did not approach him this morning, microwaving food or getting drinks and leaving without a word. Only Lorrie stayed, ignoring him over her half-a-grapefruit and black coffee breakfast, noisily turning the pages of the local newspaper.

When Emily arrived, she marched right to Sean who sat eating alone.

Her eyes were on the painted concrete hangar floor as she said, "I'm within a day of a live-fire test on my new beam control module. The good-weather version."

"Ahead of schedule? We're talking miracles like it's raining loaves and fishes."

Emily's eyes came up to him, and they were ice cold. "I've worked on this plane for years and given up almost everything I love in life to do so. No, I'm not always good at the Air Force stuff. No, I don't have a man to snuggle with. I heard what you said about me when I was out. You didn't have to humiliate me. All your talk about teamwork and you do such a shitty thing. You make me fair sick." She turned and almost ran from the room.

Sean angrily pushed his breakfast away. He looked up to see Lorrie hurrying sympathetically after Emily. Lorrie hesitated slightly, half out the door. Without looking back at Sean, she *smacked* herself loudly on the butt.

Airborne Laser has a paddle for everyone's ass.

Emily, it would seem, was to be his paddle.

Chapter 27

The 19th of October

AIRBORNE LASER – GALLEY – SUNSET

"Do you mind if I hang out with you?" Sean asked Emily, who was sitting at her console in her socks and eating ice cream from a carton, ignoring Sean's food rule. She was staring at a liquid amber sun dipping low in the west over the far mesa. Unlike Sean's life, the New Mexico fall was slipping past smoothly. Each day dawned gloriously sunny, the skies sapphire, the air so clear the nearby rock-walled mountains seemed to cradle the city, making you feel like you were living in a cathedral. Even now, the guttering sun spread pinks, golds, and fluffy white angel wings across a blue sky in a work of art as sumptuous as any Renaissance chapel ceiling; as if an artist were expansively brushing vivid paints across the very skies above.

When Sean got no response, he added, "Maybe something I could help you with?"

Emily pulled herself away from the sunset. "I suppose we could go over the list of environmental testing we need to do with the laser. I've been putting it off."

A few hours later, they were still at it. They had moved to Sean's bunk area, and it was late enough so the Albuquerque Sunport, which shared the USAF base runway, had ceased commercial flights. Now only the occasional roar of the Special Forces C-130 trainers or National Guard night fighters on maneuvers intruded. The 747 maintenance crew was gone, the aircraft was on ground power from the hangar, and outside the small galley windows the lines of blue runway lights glowed quietly.

They were sitting side by side on a bunk in the galley across from his. They were each pushing the other on, keeping the tiredness at bay by relaying the lead. This time, Emily was losing it, drifting off over a page of what to Sean was gibberish. She repeated herself as her brain faded in and out, and her milky unpainted fingernail drifted slowly over the technical symbols on the page and she finally caved, dozing off. Sean resisted waking her. Instead, he found the draft ConOps—concept of operations—document. He covered Emily with a blanket, expecting she would sleep for a time.

He didn't realize instead, at the touch of the rough wool Air Force blanket, she had wakened, not stirring as Sean settled into his bunk and opened the draft ConOps notebook. She could tell where he was reading—the section on countering nuclear targeting by enemy missiles—as she knew this troubling section well.

Emily whispered in the quiet of the galley, "Warhead probability error. Collateral kilodeaths. Did you ever think those aren't just figures? They're hospitals, schools, children, lives. Don't you ever get tired, question your work?"

Sean ran his finger ruminatively along the keen edge of a page. Felt its sharpness. Questioning the mission was important, as was finding ways to keep going, no matter what you concluded. "Emily, Emily. Here's the situation. There's a dedicated woman at Airborne Laser who dreams of missile defense. There's a dedicated woman at Pyong-son who's building missiles to hit Tokyo. The question is: who's gonna win?"

Emily lay under the warm blanket, eyes half-closed, mulling this over. Her eyes widened, she threw her blanket aside, sat bolt upright, and snapped, "That bitch!"

ARTILLERY EMPLACEMENTS – KAESONG

Architect Su was—not that he knew the term—nobody's bitch. Within the North Korean elite, he was as tough a customer as you could find. He had maintained and augmented his power while evading dozens of purges by adroitly siding his whole Su clan with the right faction. On each occasion this had resulted in—he acknowledged sadly—some other man and his families making the one-way trip to the work camp, the firing squad, or the gallows. Many of these men, he would also acknowledge, had been good men; dedicated anti-Japanese freedom fighters whom he had served as a boy message runner. Some of them, he would also admit to himself when their ghosts appeared to him on a sleepless night—Hon-Yong, Lim Un, and Yoon, their faces somber and accusing—had been more virtuous, patriotic, capable, and worthy of leading Korea forward than the Great Leader, who had, in his greed to consolidate his own power, purged them despite their sacrifice, service, and honor.

The ghosts came still, even now, and he lived with them, sympathized with them, loved them.

Yet he knew it must always be someone's downfall. Once in a Russian detention camp, eight-year-old Su was forced to punish a boy by shoving him into the pit of feces under an outhouse. Days later, the boy died of massive infections. Su almost followed him, sickened by his own shame. Yet Su survived the camp, learning life was not for the weak nor was he on earth to be pushed around. The purpose of life was to fit into the hierarchy in your apposite spot and flourish there to everyone's benefit.

Now, in his search for Tam Ho, he knew he was being slow-rolled by someone—and his anger grew.

Despite his promise to Dearest Leader to find Tam Ho's file, Su had failed. Tam Ho's signature at the minisub base indicated he was under secondment—temporary assignment—to the Guard Command. Yet, his name was on no duty roster at Magnolia Palace, nor the Guard's nearby barracks. His other inquiries were met with puzzled answers from his close clan members in the MPAF. Ever conscious of Il-Moon's reach into the bureaucracy, Su's options were closing down, and he was becoming frustrated at the long shadow the Marshal cast across his inquiry options. *Whom can I call who will be free of taint, trustworthy?*

Since the answer was almost no one, First State Architect Su was feeling crowded—and being no one's bitch—was growing angry.

It cannot be coincidence. Someone is hiding Tam Ho. Hiding his files. Keeping him on ice.

Su had also tried to picture the attack on the mansion. It simply did not work that Kang had failed. Kang was fail-safe. Not that Su was not hugely relieved; many of his oldest friends might have died—and inside his own architectural creation. But he was nonplussed.

Now, walking through the rock and concrete fortifications tunnels of the artillery emplacements he had come to inspect, it struck Su that even if Tam Ho had interrogated Kang, he could not prevent Kang from denouncing him if he were a co-conspirator. If he were not, then what had he to hide?

Su felt stymied. He would have to find another approach, since this one was failing badly.

Then too, the failing of his body just as he was called on for the greatest task of his life—the very preservation of the DPRK—was infuriating.

That failing was clear here, climbing up the hundreds of stairs cut through the rock, up into a huge artillery emplacement in the craggy hills of Kaesong overlooking the DMZ. His lungs wheezed and his knees ached. Between Tam Ho's vanishing and his own deteriorating mortal coil, it was enough to make him want to kill.

Su emerged high up above the supply caverns below and into open air. He could now look out over the broken granite and bushes at his feet to the rolling hills to the east and west—and sense the artillery stations scattered by the hundreds in deep hiding along the hillsides. Unseen, about him, were ten thousand artillery tubes (the method of counting them for weapons limitations treaties, which made no distinction between gun and rocket artillery.)

The emplacements were all much like the one he was in. From a deep pit in the hill, concrete slabs pulled back to let the artillery piece or rocket launcher fire from deep hiding. From this deep hide, not needing to move for firing or reloading, the artillery could support an armored invasion over the entire roadnet from the DMZ to Seoul.

The hills were burnished in reds and yellows. If you ignored the artillery-dense hillsides, it was like the primal Korean forest thousands of years ago, with towering trees of immense girth and thick underbrush full of rabbit and deer trails; it had been like this in the age of *Tangun*.

The air was so clear you could see all the way to the cloud of dusty air over Seoul, a mere sixty kilometers to the south. Sixty kilometers, or forty miles. Whichever, the gun emplacements here could reach the entire city. These big 240mm rockets and large 152mm artillery, in the first hour, could rain thousands of rounds down on Seoul and level its skyscrapers—and its housing. Even without nuclear bombs, and many diplomats had pointed out this made the North having The Bomb pointless, the North held Seoul ransom.

North Korea, too, was nobody's bitch. If it came to it—and the Americans struck back too hard, or all were lost—here in the Kaesong hills, Architect Su made preparations for the ultimate payback.

If things went wrong, from these emplacements, impregnable in number if not in fortification, Su could turn Seoul into a Sea of Fire.

ABL – LASER AREA

Since Sean lived on the plane, it wasn't a surprise to see him working at any hour, night or day. However, it was a surprise to the lead laserjock Marty Carreras when he came in at 5:00 a.m. to find Sean in the laser area, screwing a gimbaled gizmo into Marty's console.

"Pretty fancy," Marty said. "You think we're on Star Trek or something? What is that, a cup holder?"

"It's a B-52 bomber drink-securing system. Three hundred clams. But your coffee is safe even if you're flying upside down."

Marty poked the cup experimentally and it swayed. "That'll never happen. I hope."

They looked at each other for a second, then Marty said, "Sorry about the coffee. It's just, you know, it was exactly when I was drinking that coffee that I had this great idea. See, if we premix laser fuel, it'll hold a charge for five hours. We give up ten shots a day from the magazine, but we're ready to fire at will."

"Good idea. Implement it." Sean poured a full mug of coffee into Marty's new holder. "How about a coffee?" He indicated the cup. "Give it a spin."

Marty flipped the B-52 cup holder completely over and not a drop spilled. "You know, we could use this technology to make the laser more reliable."

FIRE FIGHTING PLANE – PRACTICE HULK

"What is the first rule of fire-fighting? Before you start fighting a fire, what do you do?" Sean asked of his ABL tech crew class.

Someone raised a hand, "Make sure you leave yourself an escape route."

"Exactly!" shouted Sean, making them all jump where they sat in a double line of seats like paratroopers ready to bail. They were in a burned-out airplane hulk on the far edges of the flight line, the old fuselage used now for rescue and firefighting training.

Sean continued, "Exactly—if you are on the ground. But in the air, what would it mean to keep open an escape route? You can't run outside and call the fire company. I mean, if you're in the air, where do you have to escape to? If you don't stop the fire, the plane is going down whether you run or stay."

Sean stopped to look at the ABL crew. "So how do you fight a fire on a plane? With everything you got!" Sean looked at his rows of crew until they nodded back at him. Sean walked slowly past everyone. "You know how to do it, we've practiced it." He paused. "You all with me on procedures?" The crew, knowing Sean's overtly dramatic training style, looked around nervously.

Before they could answer, tear gas and smoke bombs ignited in the back of the cabin. *Whooompf.* Caustic smoke billowed through the plane. Half the crew dove to the floor, yanked on their fire masks, found the extinguishers, and started to spray. The rest forgot to go low, the tear gas hit them, and they blindly stumbled down the isle, clawing for the exit door and bailing out onto the tarmac.

Sean watched as Jarhead and Emily smoothly pulled on masks, followed the checklist of sweeping their fire extinguishers over the smoke canisters, checked for left-behind crew, and evacuated.

Outside—although nobody really felt it was that smooth—Sean spoke encouragingly to the group, some still eye-stinging unhappy, while he checked Emily's facemask, tightening it just a little. "All right, Emily. Good solid B+. Crew, very smooth, don't forget to drop to the floor quickly. The smoke on burning aircraft is usually from plastic and rubber; hot and toxic as heck. Better keep it out of your eyes and lungs until you get your equipment on and deal with the fire."

Someone asked, "Should we do it again?"

Sean looked at them all in silence for a moment. "Actually, no." He waved a stack of AF 1023 safety-training forms, started handing them out by name. "Graduation! You are all good to go!"

ABL – TECH AREA

Emily paused in her work. Looked at Sean almost fondly. Diablo, the AWOL mascot rattlesnake, poked his head out from under her monitor right into her face!

Emily yelped, "YAAAAAAAAAAA! Fricking snake!"

Diablo's head withdrew back inside her console.

"He's not dangerous if you're pure," Sean commented.

Emily reddened. "What if what I was thinking wasn't pure? Sean, you lock that snake away or it's the end of our friendship!"

"Friends. Oh, now that feels good."

She looked into his eyes as if hurt by his words, then shrugged. "So, what is the next stupid training idea of yours?"

"You'll be happy to know I'm fresh out of stupid training."

She looked a little frightened. "Don't tell me I'll have to start doing something? If you weren't so set on making me miserable, I'd actually enjoy telling you tomorrow at least the good-weather wavefront reconstructor is ready to fly."

"OK," Sean yelled to the Tech Area, noticing everyone this morning was looking entirely too smug. "The last of the stupid training. I want cross-training, people."

Sean knew it to be true: after months of getting your software and your console just right—it doesn't crash, doesn't give you weird answers, the GUI buttons are finally in the right place, it's talking to the other stations correctly—you start to think this Airborne Laser not working thing is someone else's problem. Sean knew it was exactly the key strokes you always used that worked. Someone new sits down at your terminal, immediately pushes buttons in a slightly different order—stupidly, you think—and your software is suddenly infested with bugs.

Sean went on, "Here's your other station to learn: Eila, air defense with

Jarhead. J-Stars, you're over on Strikeback. Matt Cho, you're on laser. Lorrie, get with Red. On second thought, Red, get with Jarhead. Well, Emily. How about trying Ops?"

He got a pedantic look. "I know all the stations already. Except Ops, and I'm not sure I'm competent to learn."

Sean mouthed silently, "No. I didn't think so."

ABL – TECH AREA

Long after the flight that night, with dawn creeping up on the now-empty plane, Sean walked along the Tech Area, tapping the bulkhead panels—until he heard a *rattle*. Using his little infrared camera, he made out behind the plastic panel the almost invisible thermal outline of a snake close to ambient temperature—a snake with a triple stomach bulge.

Diablo, with his load of mice.

Sean murmured, "The Eagle has landed."

ABL – GALLEY

J-Stars came into the plane still wearing barbecue gloves from cooking the Friday burgers at the unit picnic—a tradition since Emily came. Coming through the door, without missing a beat, he sidestepped quickly. "Hey! Snake on the plane!"

Everyone laughed.

J-Stars carefully corralled Diablo using his gloves, and looked him over. "Man, he's almost ate himself to death." He looked around the Tech Area, and shouted, "Whoever's messing with the snake! You hear me? Leave the snake alone!"

AIRBORNE LASER – OVER WHITE SANDS MISSILE RANGE

In the White Sands Missile Range desert, far below where ABL flew patrol, a herd of Oryx looked up from their mastication of the grass along the remote runway.

They were tough beasts, these *Oryx gazella gazelle,* the biggest of the antelope family at more than six hundred pounds of hairy-hided wildness with the muscular shoulders of a buffalo, vicious one-meter horns like a mutant unicorn, and a fawn-colored coat with what you would swear are black 'racing stripes'—especially when the beast is running alongside your car stabbing its horns at your windows.

Brought to White Sands in 1969 from the Kalahari in an effort to prevent their extinction, the Oryx have thrived. The military range kept most hunters off, and the few cougars and coyotes who had tried to enter into a predator-prey relationship with them became powerful sick of it, and later generations learned to let them be. Having no predators except the occasional poacher and the annual three-day human hunt, Oryx do not disturb easily, usually standing their ground when approached by vehicles. The canyons, hills, and runways of the missile range were their turf, and they weren't about to back off this comparatively lush gramma grass.

But something was so peculiar about the planes taxiing toward them along this outer stretch of runway off Holloman Air Force Base, there was a burst of hairy-hided movement. The herd wheeled and thundered off into the brush, stopping only after a distance to turn their mask-like black-and-white faces to check out the strange interlopers.

The F-4 phantoms were painted orange-red, and as they approached, there was a disturbing feeling: inside the Perspex domes of the taxiing planes, the cockpits were eerily empty! The pilotless Phantom fighters taxied past strips of white sand dunes and tough yucca. They weren't true Phantoms anymore; they were now computer controlled QF-4 target drones. Without a pilot, the Phantom could pull around twelve g's in afterburner, flying for a short time exactly like a launching missile. The two drones took off, and under White Sands base Ops control, headed to hide behind nearby mountains.

In the Tech Area overhead, Sean hefted the training Kooshball and wondered idly how long he could prevent the crew from yelling and screaming at each other after the Nth failure of the day. Once again, Eila posted the Japanese F-15's off on their flanks, the radars were manned, and Emily was eating ice cream from the carton with her feet on her console. *The usual.* Sean sent the signal to base Ops. *Send in the drones!*

The two Phantoms suddenly stood on their tails and rocketed almost straight up. Blowing carbon out of their afterburners like flamethrowers on steroids, they looked on the radar, Sean reflected, just like Scud B launches from TEL's hidden in the desert.

"Kettledrums! Kettledrums!" called J-Stars. "Something moving fast!"

Red chimed in, "Laser radar sees location, passing it to—" The mission went passably like clockwork, as the tech crew ran the mission straight on.

Sean felt it wasn't bad—but he wanted to see something more out of the crew. He called over the mike, "Tech Area, Ops. To make it real, we add some stress!" He tossed the Kooshball at Eila, whose hands were full of keyboard, prepping for Strikeback. Eila managed the catch, calling out "Emily!" tossing the hairy ball none too slowly at her face. Emily caught it, tossing it on to Lorrie.

No sooner had Eila started to feel like things were going well, her hands back on the keyboard, then Sean fed in new items: fuzzy animals, a rubber shrunken head, and a couple of rag dolls. "Eila!" he called, and tossed the shrunken head.

Eila picked each incoming up, and passed it on. The cabin quickly filled with flying matter as each station tried to work with the objects zipping around as constant interruptions.

Lorrie caught the Kooshball—and still got the missile launch up on the big screen, the two screaming missile-drones moving higher and higher.

The crew, looking up each time their name was called, caught flying items even as they strove to do their jobs, and it was a memorable scene as the fuzzies flew, and yet outside, despite the chaos inside, the laser beam director tracked smoothly, following perfectly along the accelerating trajectory of the first of the rising drones.

Eila sent one of the F-15's on a fighter intercept to the TEL location, keeping the other in reserve, and soon received a message back the TEL was located and killed.

Emily, finally giving up when the shrunken head flew past her, let the fuzzy animals fall to the deck. Alone in her own world, she saw the drone enter her laser sights, her mind racing back over each stage of the process—tracker, imager, guide star, Attack Laser.... "Guidestar on!"

The golden rapier blade of the guidestar streaked from the beam director. In front of the target it focused to form an artificial star so bright the video imagers flared. The adaptive optics, measuring this touchstone of the atmosphere between the plane and the drone, slammed into the opposite shape of the distorting atmosphere.

Emily saw the loops close with strange detachment. On the big screen, the image of the rising drone was suddenly clear and rock solid.

Sean read off the tail numbers of 'HO' for Holloman—and took the Kooshball in the back of the head for his attentions. "Laser One, this is Ops. We have Positive ID, and Laser Clearing House authorizes you full power."

Emily crossed her fingers and touched the laser fire button. There was a *bang* of laser chemicals mixing at the speed of sound in a palpable release of energy. The welding-torch-hot laser beam instantly leapt the one hundred miles to the drone, a ruby-red sword-thrust.

A hot spot flared on the drone's body. For an eye-blink it flew—then disappeared into a smoky burst of fire.

In silence, Sean thought.

Emily stared even as Red called out, "Missile killed."

J-Stars said, "Handing off second target." Emily sat numbly, unmoving. Lorrie smoothly took control of the beam director, cranking it around. The guidestar burst to life like a mini-supernova at the drone. The loops closed, the image sharpened...

Lorrie fired the attack laser—and the second Phantom exploded silently into flashing shreds.

Around the Tech Area, the crew stared at the big screen filled by raining smoking shards.

Then as one, they jumped up to crowd Emily's window, as if only direct observation could confirm what they had seen but could not believe.

They stared, first at the distant smoke balls, then at still frozen Emily—then at each other. As if waking, they absorbed their first operational success...*I never expected it to feel like this...*

Sean flipped his overall intercom switch. "That is what it is!"

Col Hareda's F-15 screamed up alongside between them and distant smoke-clouds of the torched drones. Over the radio came Hareda-san's distinctive perfect English, with its Japanese twist.

"Is it not, Miller Time?"

Chapter 29

The 20th of October (Evening)

GROUND ZERO LOUNGE – O'CLUB, KIRTLAND AFB

A third tray of tequila shooters smashed down on the table, and the crew of Airborne Laser (Experimental) raised the thin glass flutes aloft together.

The Ground Zero dance lounge was in the basement of the O'Club, a flat uninspired 1960's concrete square where the driveway circle still had its faux stone arches supporting a rain and sun cover.

The basement was given over to the later night crowd. The O'Club's main functions of prayer breakfasts, awards, cafeteria, and Welfare and Morale offices took up the sunlit floors. In the basement, the building's support columns came down into the middle of the dance floor, and what little ambience it had was maintained by keeping the light low enough to hide the dirt on the floor. The bar was long, wooden, and scarred. But for a cheerful group, ready to hear and make noise, responsibly using alcohol to relax, it was a place to cut loose in an otherwise fairly uptight base environment where nuclear weapon storage, advanced weapons programs, and war personnel in training kept the mood sober.

Sean stood but knew it was not really his day. "Everyone must now make a speech in honor of this great moment. Slammer?"

Slammer stood. "I'm terrible at speeches. Instead, I am going to recite the names of every town you fly over from here to Tuscaloosa Airbase."

Someone asked, "Every town?"

"Every town." He slurped a drink, and proceeded to declaim: "Albuquerque, Carnual, Zuzax, Placitas, Cedar Crest, Carizzozo, Moriarty..."

While Slammer held forth, Col Hareda rose. "I also am not the best speechmaker. So I propose to recite all the flowers of Japan."

"Native or introduced?" someone else asked.

"All of them. Azalea, Momo, Snow Willow, Daphne, Zazensou..."

It was clear the two would go on forever, and with Slammer and Hareda-san in the background, the rest of the crew concentrated on getting sloshed and talking. Jarhead and Emily, thanks to the din, leaned close, perhaps the only time they'd ever been in each other's personal spaces. Jarhead asked Emily, "You really don't believe in killing? What if someone's raping your sister?

Emily savored a mouthful of wine and answered, half-seriously, "I'd sneak up behind him with a blackjack and knock him out. Then take him to the police."

Jarhead thought for a moment. "Can you always do that with rapists?"

"Wrong question. What you should ask is what can you do to keep it away from that point. When the house is on fire, you don't have many options. How do you best do fire prevention? That's why talking about peace—"

Sean leaned over, interrupting, "I feel like dancing. Emily?"

Emily and Sean hit the dance floor to a fast number, laughing at the required maneuvers around the basement support beams. Sean remarked, "Kind of like dancing in a maze."

"Like ABL. Like so many problems, it isn't the maximizing, it's the constraints."

"Yes, Dr. Noodler. Like your ray gun. It worked! Happy?"

Instead of answering, Emily just shook it!

Sean, trying to keep up, asked, "What do you call that move?"

"The noodle!"

Coming down off her jig, she leaned close in a final gyration as the fast music ended, "We've still a long way to go."

"Why am I surprised to hear you say that? Are you ever satisfied?"

Almost an answer, as a slow number started, Emily pulled Sean against her.

"She may not know what guys are, but she's got a pretty good idea what they're used for."

"Believe it, I was twice almost married."

"Who were they?"

"Quaker guys."

"What happened?"

"They're a strange lot. Full of humanity and nobility and sacrifice." She laughed. "You don't find many scientists, lawyers, or business people as Friends. They have other priorities."

"I wouldn't have thought you wanted to marry a lawyer."

"No, all I'm saying, c'est très difficile; it is not easy."

"What really happened?"

She waved to the Spartan dance hall, the unmistakable cirque of military people temporarily away from the weight of their ever-present duty. "They couldn't learn to live with this. I learned to live without them. You?"

"I gave up hope. Too much work, and if you miss the boat when you're young, it doesn't pass by again for quite a time..."

The pressure of her breasts against him, the smell of her flight suit with its Ivory soap and lack of perfume and yet with the smell of the ABL air purification system, oils, and solvents led to a rush he wanted to go with—until over Emily's shoulder, he saw Abbey Yamamoto excitedly reporting on TV.

Sean pulled Emily along, pushing their way up to stand side by side at the crowded bar. In the din of the rock band, they read Abbey's words on the voice transcriber. A beaming Abbey said, "...Dearest Leader has agreed to an exclusive interview with Reuters Korea. This interview, the first ever of a North Korean leader, will go live, both to the world and to his own people in North Korea." She smiled confidentially, "There will also be an announcement. This reporter guesses that after presenting with the interview his *bona fides*, he will announce the withdrawal of the DPRK's 820th Tank Corp, their main forward armor, from the DMZ to back behind the 39th Parallel, to match the USAF's 7th Air Force pulling back to Okinawa. Should these pullbacks happen, The Agreed Peace Treaty and Confederation Framework will be signed in just eleven days—"

Sean was jolted by the speed of it. *Eleven days! Impossibly short! It will take two days just to get to Korea. I better get Emily's ass in gear.* "Emily, we need to be in Korea."

"I can't break the laws of physics."

"Then you'd better start bending them."

Emily put her drink down. "You're such a pisser. Sean, we did a lot less up there than you think. A lot more too. I wanted to surprise you. Pleasantly—until you pull that macho stuff again. Anyway, the good news, if you're willing to listen? I'm ready to try the bad-weather beam control module."

Sean watched Emily give the crew orders to meet, steaming when she asked him, "Would you see that test targets are put up for tomorrow morning?" as if he were the hired help. Sean asked Emily acidly, "Any other special requirements, Dr. Engel?"

"Turbulence," snapped Emily, already moving toward the exit of the Ground Zero club. "Take me near stormy weather."

REUTERS OFFICE – SEOUL

The feeling, Abbey reflected, was as powerful as the biting tang of smelling salts, how quickly things were moving, how piquant the pleasure of pushing things ahead.

Spiney was helping tremendously. His data was excellent, and Abbey's files from him were now extensive. Along with tons of pictures—she knew all the players on the plane and guessed their functions—Spiney hadn't limited himself to mere photographic observation. Yesterday, he had even followed

Airborne Laser. When, with binoculars from the outside fire escape stairwell of the Wyndham he saw them bank after takeoff to the south, he guessed they were heading toward White Sands Missile Range, his old haunt. When they took off the next time, he immediately hit I-25 south at 90 mph, zooming down to Carrizozo to see if he could catch any of their activity. He not only saw a touch-and-go on the runway at Holloman AFB, but when the highway back to Albuquerque was road-blocked, he knew there was a missile launch. Guessing where ABL might fly for testing, he did a U-turn and cut off NM 182 onto a little-used dirt access road leading to the range through a locked cattle gate. He broke the heavy padlock off the gate and drove onto White Sands. If stopped, he planned to say he was a hunter scouting and didn't know he was trespassing. The WSMR rent-a-cops caught illegal hunters every day and although Spiney had some honker binoculars, he was otherwise clean. From his poaching experience—Oryx-burger was common fare among the white supremacist community around White Sands and every fall he stocked his own freezer with Oryx steaks from the range—he knew at worst the guards would run him off.

Scanning the sky doggedly, he managed to find the jumbo—no mean feat, as they were almost invisible at forty thousand feet. He had guessed they would work the Mockingbird Gap missile launch area, and sure enough he found them doing combat runs. Although he could not ID what exploded in the sky a few moments later, he had seen the 'Smoky Joe' engine trails—Phantom drones for sure—going almost vertical. As he said to Abbey in the next email, there was no doubt that ABL had shot down surrogate missiles.

She now had a golden set of information to trade Il-Moon, and her feed to him seemed to be having an incredible leveraging effect on Dearest Leader. The timetables kept moving up, and she was now about to broadcast the interview of the new century live to the whole world.

The foreplay from the rest of the system was intoxicating too. She was fielding about a million cell phone calls a day asking for freelanced stories. The last caller from Fox was particularly insistent that she sign an exclusive for a full documentary on the process after it was over. There was the mention of a large amount of cash...but it was the *feeling* that jazzed her.

Akiru was putting the camera away after their last broadcast when Abbey reached out and stayed him, indicating he should keep the camera out. "So, how about you get some footage of me walking back to the car?"

"You want me to video you walking to the car?"

"Damned Hyundai, but get some."

"But the telecast is over. What do we need with you getting in the car?"

Abbey reached into her purse, and passed a check to Akiru. He looked at it for a moment, stunned by the amount. "Ever see a nicer payday? For that little article for *People* magazine."

Akiru took a sharp breath. "You mean that half-page blurb?"

"Just for that." Abbey manically rushed on, "I've been thinking. We could do a lot of documentaries on this. You know, after it's all over. Tons of stuff on CNN and CSPAN and History Channel...they'll want to see what it's really like to be me. How I live and move and the private moments, like when we eat or meet someone."

He squinted at her. "So, now I film you brushing your teeth?"

"You know what I mean, the human part of things. From now on, I want you to video me all the time. You know, slice of life, whom I talk to, everything."

"Abbey, I think getting sober is making you crazy."

"Come on Akiry. We'll split the money on the documentaries. Help me?"

Akiru grimaced. "You know neither of us needs the money, Abbey." He hoisted his camera to his shoulder. "I suppose you would be interesting to some. Ready, Ms. Peacock?"

Chapter 30

AIRBORNE LASER COMPLEX

Luckily, Sean reflected when he drove around the end of the runway, someone was sober and working, for the floodlit ABL was away from the White Elephant, with a ground crew under her.

As he passed the runway, a cargo plane landed, its landing gear hitting the runway, tires blowing out a puff of dark smoke. The horrendous friction of one hundred fifty tons slamming into the blacktop to produce a squirt of smoke and a trail of burned rubber was somehow reminiscent of him and Emily.

He parked at the barngate to the giant hangar, and saw NCO's beneath Airborne Laser changing the carbon fiber brakes on the landing gear. The clusters of the new brake fins lay like some strange furry caterpillar while Chief Augsburger, face flushed, worked a six-foot torque wrench on a resisting bolt almost welded in place from the heat of brake use. He sensed Sean, and TSgt Smitty took over as Auggie walked to Sean.

"Hello Chief, thought you were going out celebrating," Sean said.

Chief Auggie wiped a hanky over a gritty forehead, sweaty despite the cool desert night. "Bozon said the brakes felt a little soft. The way they've been setting her down, no wonder. Just a touch, just a touch on the brakes, I've said to him. You got 14,000 feet of runway."

"What did he say?"

"Brakes were made to be used."

"I'd've thought he'd say the opposite."

"Anyway, we'll be ready for tomorrow's mission," adding apologetically, "Dr. Engel called, Sir."

Sean felt the anger again. Emily had to have the last word, OK. Now she was getting in the first word too. "Fine. Can they do without you till morning?"

"Smitty's good, but I'd rather be here to watch. Unless..."

"I need someone to run down to White Sands and help me set up some targets. Then back here and bunk down for a few hours before the flight."

Chief Auggie looked past Sean. A trail of cars was pulling up to the nearly deserted hangar parking lot, Emily's Volvo in front. She left her lights on, got out, and leaned against her hood, the crew silhouetted around her intently listening.

His irrational anger grew and flashed. For her, they would come to work tonight. The tech crew were still sure he brought nothing to the table—he was simply an interloper, a snook sent by Washington who was irrelevant and redundant—no, worse: unneeded.

"At least they come to work, Sir. And they'll be making a good cuppa coffee. You know, the fair trade organic luxury stuff."

Sean had to smile. "Remind me to keep my heart off my sleeve."

"No, Sir. It looks fine there."

ABL – TECH AREA – OVER WHITE SANDS MISSILE RANGE

Bad-weather turbulence rarely bothered Sean. However, the level on Airborne Laser at the moment was nerve-racking. The rest of the crew seemed OK, but he had been on the road all night. Instead of getting more than a moment's shut-eye, after the two-hour drive back from White Sands setting up the targets, he had spent the first couple of hours after dawn trying to make sense out of Emily's notes on the bad-weather problem. Even though her equation-wracked style of discursion looked indecipherable at first glance, the discussion of the issues—her physicist reasoning side—and the desire that her mathematics should reflect a human reality came through in the patient reasoning in the commentary and captions. For Emily, it was important that her mathematics conformed to reality, and for reality to conform to her mathematics—and human intuition.

He'd gleaned that the laser, which functioned only through pre-compensating for the always-roiling atmosphere, was therefore dependent on just how stormy—and therefore how turbulent—the atmosphere was. For combat, there was no question that an anti-missile system must perform in bad weather.

And bad weather was what they were in for today.

His tiredness also made the immensity and anger of the towering cumulus ABL was bouncing over less and less tolerable. The few moments of catnap in his little bunk, with the banging of the brake change and the humming laser work, hadn't relieved his tiredness. The darned ABL bunks were made for a midget, and the shave and shower he was getting in the tiny head was keeping him off the top of his game. He considered getting a VOQ room, but that would be a victory for the crew, running him off, and he wasn't about to lose the one thing that kept him ahead: they knew he was on station twenty-four hours a day, and was at least partially insane.

Airborne Laser banked in a shaking arc, heading for a pass between Pike's Peak-shaped thunderheads. The supercharged engines were growling along, complaining about the thin air just as Sean's stomach was complaining about the constant thrum and bump of the turbulence. It was past the usual summer monsoon season, and yet in this last storm of the year, they seemed dangerously close to rank upon rank of ominous lightning-wracked thunderheads.

Emily finished scrawling something on a pad, stretched like a cat, handed the clipboard to Lorrie, and came toward Sean, pulling off her headset in a sign that she wanted to talk privately.

"Thanks for setting up the instrumentation and targets down there. You must have had a long night."

She was very close, and Sean looked for the anger from last night, but she was either hiding it, had something else she wanted, or perhaps had forgotten. *It's so easy for the scientist. They have those immutable personal internal timepieces.*

"How does it look?" he asked nodding out the porthole where a spectacular burst of line-lightning ran along the cloud-bottoms.

"Spider lightning. Beautiful, isn't it? Very rare."

"That isn't what I asked."

"I'm sorry, Sean. I know you want to go, and yet if you ever bothered to read my reports—and they are eminently readable—you will appreciate just how hard it is to do this. It won't matter if we're in Korea if the system doesn't work."

"It won't work if we aren't in Korea, either. Why so risk-averse?"

She smiled suddenly, dawn breaking over a whitening wheat field. "I guess part of it is you're so cocksure. You just take us for granted and it feels terrible. You don't trust us, you don't respect us, you think we stonewall for no reason..."

Sean had been shaking his head 'no' for all of these, and then he nodded suddenly. "People do what they want to do. I tell you the truth when I say if you really wanted to make it work in Korea, you'd make it work."

The plane gave a bigger shudder than usual, as turbulence sloshed its four hundred tons sideways a couple of football fields.

It was her turn to suddenly stop and reflect on his words. "Maybe. But until we can operate in this environment, my physics assessment is we'll be doomed to failure."

"How well does it have to work?"

"When I say we go, we go."

"That's not an answer."

"It will have to do for now."

Sean ground his teeth and would have yelled something, but Lorrie sang out, "Targets coming up on big screen."

The crew looked up from their stations, and saw the video of the ground fifty miles away and the row of ten billboard-like targets, which Sean and Auggie had set up the previous night. Sean smirked, seeing at the end the last target was an old milk truck. On its side, smiling Mr. Milkman.

Before Emily could notice Mr. Milkman, Sean called, "Tighten surveillance camera," and Lorrie racked the frame in to show only the first of the target boards, which was striped like a zebra for visibility.

The turbulence was getting worse; in the targeting cameras the ground shimmered in the tumultuous chaotic airflow. Now even the tech crew looked uncomfortable, working an all-nighter and various hangovers to boot. Only Emily and Lorrie were oblivious.

Lorrie huddled over Emily, pointing to her screen, "The icon for the new software for bad-weather beam control is here." They finished exchanging information as the laser beam director cranked around smoothly despite Airborne Laser's wings flapping like laundry in a hard breeze. Emily gave a wave to everyone. It was show time.

Since it was a simple laser shot against a static target, the tech crew could enjoy sitting back and watching Emily work. Half the big screen was an image of her computer desktop, and the other half the ground site with its row of billboard targets. Each target board was coated with a different material; plastic, aluminum, or wood. The screens for tracking came up, Emily centered the target, closed the tracking loops, and the first target centered up in the display. The blurry target locked, seemingly rock solid, and sharpened to a good image despite ABL's heaving flight path.

Emily, fingers flying over the switches for gains and magnifications, said, "Tracking looks really good. Stock-still. Good work, Lorrie. Now..."

Airborne Laser when it fires seems to stand still for a second. Its simply a optical illusion because the light coming out of the beam director is so infinitely fast, that like a flash bulb or strobe going off, it seems to freeze the action.

The laser light zapped down from the plane. *Whoosh!* The first billboard target scorched and smoked. "Lorrie, what's the Fried parameter?"

"Five centimeters, and turbulence has a Greenwood frequency of two kilohertz."

"From now on Lorrie, we're going to use the Tyler frequency. It's more relevant to what we're doing. Boy, that's really fast. More gain!"

The gain increased as Emily ran down the line, zapping at each target. Scorch, sizzle, and blast; at each shot, the damage was greater, at each shot, the laser seemed more focused, more intense, more deadly in its action. Emily noodled with the settings until on her last shot, suddenly in her line of fire, smiling Mr. Milkman on its side, was the old milk truck. Emily was so intent on perfecting the laser collimation that she automatically tracked and fired. *Kerwhoomp!* The milk truck blew up in a million tiny smoke-trailing fragments.

TSgt Smitty whistled, "Wow. Don't got milk. Emily just blew away Mr. Milkman!"

Emily looked confused, glanced up at the replay. "Hey, who put in a real ground target? Sean, that isn't funny!"

"Oh, I don't know. It worked for me. How about you?"

"I'll have to look at the data, run some more tests."

"You mean that wasn't enough?"

"I said we'll have to run more tests."

Rather than answer, Sean moved away, climbed to the galley. He lay down on the bunk, looking out the small porthole. It seemed like his legs were leaden. He needed to find some way to get through to her, find the approach he was missing. Some way to leverage her off her high horse and yet not think too badly of herself for coming to earth. It was a shame that the fruits of success in their shoot-down were so bitter. She took from him everything—leadership, style, the moral high ground, success—and he could deal with all that if only they could just get to the field...

He felt the plane change course again, but instead of away from the storm, he could feel them heading directly toward it. Out his porthole, it was almost solid clouds.

In the Tech Area, Sean found Marty Carreras coming out of the laser area and going to Emily. Sean asked Emily, "Did you order a course change?"

Matt Cho and Marty were looking at Emily strangely, Sean thought. Twisted fingers from a not particularly finger-twisting group. Marty broke their silence. "We're real near that towering Q."

Emily stared out the window at the storm. It was a real hummer, more intense than most, even in the monsoon season. "Look at that storm. Tons and tons of free energy just waiting to be pulled in and used. More force in those clouds than a thousand atom bombs. An amazing natural energy source."

"Well, maybe, but what's it got to do with us?" Sean asked.

"It's an incredible opportunity to grab some lightning data. Lorrie, boot the Zeus thingie."

"'Kay, lightning girl," and Lorrie fired up a computer, worked a panel of knobs.

Sean looked around at the crew, uncertain how far to push this. The storm was beyond brewing-up, and the crew looked uncomfortable. "Emily, we're on an anti-missile engineering run. Science like that you do first from a hilltop."

"The reason this plane even exists is because of a spirit of thoroughness and curiosity. Our mission is science, not just war."

"This spontaneity isn't the way to go at this stage. We need to get operational.

Now forget the lightning."

"All I'm going to do is generate some artificial lightning crawlers."

Marty asked quietly, "What about your beam ionizing the air?"

"Would that be bad?" asked Sean.

Matt Cho answered, "Theoretically, yes."

Emily replied, as she turned to Lorrie, "Very unlikely. Lorrie, set the sidebands to a Gig."

"What could happen, theoretically?"

Matt said, "You really don't want a path of ions right to your airframe. It tends to conduct."

Emily snapped, "I'm taking this measurement so have your theoretical discussion elsewhere."

Sean paused, "You're sure you know what you're doing?"

"If we knew what we were doing, Ace, we wouldn't call it research. Well?"

Sean considered the strained looks of Marty and Matt.

Emily added passionately, "It's the end of the monsoon season, it's our last chance. Besides, it's like the perfect thunderstorm. We won't get another opportunity and you need to think of the future warfighter as well as your immediate wants, and we might not get to do this again—" at which Marty and Matt nodded emphatically, although Sean didn't think they meant go ahead and do it—"and be it on my head."

Sean would long remember the moment he decided how to call it. For once, the crew was looking at him. Something like trust passed between them.

Sean nodded. "The plane is all yours, Dr. Engel."

Outside ABL, in response to Emily's key and mouse strokes, violet laser-light shot from the beam director. Strobing a light show on the clouds, Emily murmured, "Red Sprite lightning," when her laser poked into storm clouds, inducing the formation of a ball of lightning looking like a giant blood-red-colored jellyfish with light-blue tentacles.

"It's working," Emily remarked, even as Sean saw in slow motion a blue-violet aura forming around her. "Now, chirp the beam!"

"Beam chirped!" Lorrie called out, face pasty.

Emily was now glowing like a blue sunrise, her head crowned in St. Elmo's fire. Sean yelled, "No! Cut the beam! Cut it!"

"Too late!" Lorrie cried.

Lightning sizzled back along the laser beam. Struck ABL. *Kerboom!* Circuits blew and the Tech Area sparkled. ABL shuddered. The few crew who weren't strapped in were thrown to the deck as electronics racks erupted in flame.

An eerie sound—or the lack of any sound: ABL's engines went silent.

The whole plane was in fact deathly silent, except for the small crackling of flames. The floor tilted. ABL dove.

Sean: "The engines are out!"

Emily: "I know that! We have to get them started again or we're nano-particles. God, I can't think!"

Sean: "I can. You secure the Tech Area."

Their eyes locked. Then they moved. Fast. Sean ran forward while Emily turned to the Tech Area. They both fought the g's as ABL pitched farther into its dive, screaming toward the ground.

In the ABL cockpit, Sean staggered in under dive g's. The flightcrew banged knobs. No Joy.

Slammer: "She's too heavy to glide her in."

Sean: "Dive more. A dive delta of 9 the engines will restart."

The delta meter read 2.

Slammer: "Too steep! We break up long before 9. We could try to belly-slide her at the airport."

Sean: "We got a nuke's worth of energy back there. We can't risk turning the airport into ground zero. Come on! Push!"

Sean leaned over Slammer, helping push ABL's yokes forward.

ABL's dive steepened sharply.

Bozon: "20,000 feet! We'll never make it."

Back in the Tech Area, the crew, confused, sat while fires raged. Emily grabbed a fire extinguisher. "Sean will restart the engines. Please. Emergency stations now!"

The crew responded. ABL dove into zero gravity. People floated. Fire in zero g's ran like water along the ceiling.

Emily lateralled the fire extinguisher across the cabin. It bounced around weightlessly. The Tech Area reached the point of no return with the fire.

Emily: "Matt. Jarhead. Nail the roof."

Sean and Slammer pushed the yoke as ABL shook their teeth out.

The delta Meter passed 6...slowly.

Bozon: "15,000 feet! No time. No time."

Sean: "Stay with it. We need that nine."

The Ground Impact Warning went off with its metallic shout: "WHOOP! WHOOP! GROUND IMPACT WARNING! WHOOP! WHOOP! PULL UP! PULL UP!" and continued in a terrible frightening repetitious din.

In the Tech Area, the crew caught extinguishers. Blew out the fires dripping off the ceiling.

Emily: "Rig for landing! Like the drills!"

Crew fought back to their seats. Emily buckled in a sobbing Lorrie. She and Lorrie looked at each other in the hell of the wrecked, screaming, and falling plane. Emily: "I'm sorry."

Lorrie, scared as hell, suddenly stopped crying, wiped mascara quickly. "I'm OK; I'm OK with this." She tried to smile. "Day I met you, third best day of my life—after my boys, you know."

Outside on the diving ABL, armor and antennae flew off. Nothing it seemed could stop the dive...

The delta meter's glass face exploded into Sean. Cuts. Blood.

Sean: "Patience. 8.8, 8.9, 9!"

The diving ABL suddenly *boomed*! All four engines blew carbon. Flame on! ABL flexed, fought out of the dive."

In the Tech Area, as the engines rumbled to life, the alarms quit and the deck pulled up.

Emily: "I told you he'd—"

Gravity suddenly restored, Emily slammed to the deck painfully.

Airborne Laser roared in over the base golf course, engines spewing half-burned fuel and a carbon rain. Golfers looking up are blackened by the soot trail from the huge engines.

As ABL turned off the runway, Sean stood up in the Tech Area. All eyes were on him, except Emily's—which were on the deck—knowing she'd almost killed everyone.

Sean cleared his throat. "Excellent teamwork, everyone. Excellent job. We have the bad-weather reconstructor, we have ground target success. Really a good training run. From how that went I say we're ready to deploy. Right, Emily?"

AIRBORNE LASER HANGAR

The beaten-up ABL taxied up to its hangar. A furious Safety Center colonel and two staff members stood fuming on the hardstanding below the airstairs.

The colonel had seen the ATC tower's radar trace of ABL's plunge, and was so angry, for a moment, he couldn't speak when Sean introduced himself. He ignored Sean's salute and growled, "You are relieved of command, major. This plane is grounded until we do a thorough investigation!"

Chapter 31

WORLDWIDE TV INTERVIEW – MAGNOLIA PALACE

At his Ops console in the empty ABL, alone, Sean drank beer in depression, watching on the big screen as Abbey tried to pull off her Barbara Walters-style interview; no mean feat being a female Japanese reporter broadcasting to the North Korean populace.

Sean quickly grasped the excellence of Abbey's choice of setting: on the veranda of a formal North Korean state palace, but against a backdrop of an exquisitely landscaped garden, she had arranged Dearest Leader and his family on comfortable couches in a conversation grouping—just as Barbara would have done.

Of course, the list of questions was already set, and Abbey was too smart to stray far. She knew the interview was on a tape delay of five minutes, so it would have been to little effect to try to bounce Dearest Leader—and she was likely the loser if she offended him.

Abbey said, "First, I think the world is so thankful you have come out to chat—that you are willing to share your thoughts. On behalf of the many people who really want to know Korea better and have the best of intentions in listening, thank you."

Dearest Leader said, "You are welcome. It has been a long silence, and I would not want to break it without paying tribute to the efforts of all the DPRK's citizens who have worked so hard to become self-sufficient and build half of a beautiful world-class Korea."

Abbey asked, "What about your own DPRK, are they not in the world as well now, listening?"

"In fact, it is historic that way. We are broadcasting this live to the DPRK, so that they may hear and judge for themselves. It is the whole world I talk to, although of course I cherish few as I do my own countrymen."

"How is this possible for you, after all the years of control of the media and your words..."

"My grandfather and father both came to terms with the world from their background of war and struggle, a pretty grounded opinion of the world's hostility. We have been threatened not once, but seven times with nuclear attack—far more than any other nation. And we have always found independence difficult to maintain with the geopolitics of the region. Surrounded as we are by our friends, still they are tigers."

Abbey asked, "How are you different from your father and grandfather?"

"Well, I have explored the world a little bit, and of course read widely. I have worked in the most desolate places in Korea on workers' rights and reform, and I have seen the capitals of Asia and Europe. Perhaps it is time for a new look at the world. Perhaps we must take the first step. Then, if the tigers bite, it will be for all to see."

Abbey asked, "For my Japanese viewers, there are several very serious issues on the table, and if I may, I'd like you to address them. First, Terrorism. You are currently labeled by the United Nations as a terrorist country."

Dearest Leader sat forward. "True enough. We are currently labeled so— although for more than two decades we have not had the slightest connection to anything like terrorism. We commiserated with America after 9/11, and we abide by the antiterrorism accords. Yet we cannot obtain credit, help from various U.S. dominated organizations like the IMF, the World Bank, and so on."

Abbey spoke as if unsure. "Yet there are several members of the Japan Liberation Red Army—a listed terrorist organization—who are being given shelter and asylum in the DPRK."

"A serious issue, yes. Of course, a promise, as my grandfather gave to these persons, is a promise. I cannot turn them over to anyone. Perhaps you see how that is true?"

Abbey answered, "That should you break this promise, you would be seen as publicly breaking a faith."

"Exactly. Turning them over to the Japanese authorities, after even thirty years, would not be proper, even should it not be my promise which binds me."

"Then you would be unable to meet the requirements for getting off the terrorist list. Are you expecting a waiver?"

"It is not necessary. I withdrew our invitation to the Japanese Red Army to remain in the DPRK, and requested they leave Korea."

Stunned, Abbey recovered, asked, "Where will they go? They got to the DPRK via the hijacking of an airliner. Where would they find sanctuary?"

"They have already left and transited China. They must fend for themselves. As it is a time of forgiveness and progress, perhaps simplest is for the Japanese government to offer a settlement to them."

Abbey took a deep breath, most soberly asked, "Perhaps no matter is more seriously viewed by the Japanese people than that of Japanese citizens kidnapped from beaches in Japan, who were then brought to the DPRK to be used for training spies."

Dearest Leader nodded sorrowfully. "We must not forget, as egregious as these acts were, they took place in difficult times. The North felt threatened, and perhaps unintentionally created such opportunities for abuse. I want to say to the Japanese people, it was a barbaric act that cannot be justified. Suffice it to say," He turned and looked directly into the camera, "I apologize to the Japanese people, and I will apologize to the individuals. Those who are no longer with us, the best possible records of their histories will be made available to the Japanese government, or the Red Cross, and we will attempt to compensate them. If they are living in the DPRK, they have their freedom to go and come as they please." In his poor but understandable Japanese he said, "I apologize."

Abbey asked, "This again is excellent. What would make you take this step?"

"The death of my father taught me many things. The world was for him only Korea. While I have traveled, slightly incognito, to Europe, Asia, and even to Japan."

Abbey pounced gently, "The rumor is you visited Tokyo Disneyland."

"Without mentioning specifics, I'll merely say that I found Japan to be a place not of aggression and anger, but rather a flowering of good people. Myself, a Korean, was shown much courtesy and consideration, and it was not lost upon me. Perhaps when you are in the DPRK, and you see Japan over the sea from such a distance, you cannot understand this. It is time we laid the past to rest, and moved into the next part of the history of the world."

"Then there is the contentious matter of Japanese reparations for the war. Isn't it true in the treaty there are at least $20 billions for direct investment?"

"Yes, a good sum, and yet far less adjusted for the times than that same payment given to the South years ago. However, with cooperative work, we have perhaps the most dynamic populace in the world—every will is strong, straight, and dedicated to building a greater Korea—the world will provide investment sufficient to help balance the past."

"Your father once was asked what North Korea really had to offer the south—or the world. For there is little left after the years of natural disasters and depletion."

"His answer was a good one: 'We in the north can offer our indomitable spirit, our iron will, our amazing tenacity and dedication.' It is still a good answer, and in fact, do not captains of industry often say," and he laughed, "Our people are our greatest resource?"

Abbey laughed. "Spoken like a capitalist roader. Of course, they do not mean it. They believe money is their greatest resource."

"Yes, you have indeed gotten my joke. Yet there is a truth to it. I say to the car manufacturers of the world: come to North Korea. You will find every man an ox, and every woman a gazelle. We not only wish to build cars, we wish to buy them. All twenty million of us! And not just cars. We are ready to participate in the world's prosperity—and never had there been a country more graced with talent and energy toward this purpose."

Abbey asked, "Even though you say Japan has not apologized for its atrocities?"

Dearest Leader replied carefully, "We could spend eternity passing the blame. Are not the shared histories and peoples of China, Korea, and Japan one of the world's most beautiful fountains of life? Is it not the greatest of actions, to hold out an olive branch to an adversary unable to do so?" He leaned forward, "It is also perhaps not the group who can truly apologize. The apology should best come, given personally, as each Japanese person interacts with us in the future—whether as a tourist, a businessman, or a co-worker—with true consideration and respect."

"This sounds almost Christian…if such an idea were tolerated in the North."

"We talk now not merely of ideas. We take now a course of action. Soon, we will announce the final protocols for the treaty, and I feel the world will be pleased: we have set ourselves an ambitious schedule and we intend to keep it."

"We have spoken little about the South."

"It is perhaps because we are such brothers, little is required to be said. We love each other, and must move toward reconciliation of the past. The past is gone. The future of Korea never looked so glorious."

"If this is so, I am honored to present to you the salutations and greetings from the President of South Korea, and his invitation to visit Seoul in the next weeks."

"I would be most honored. Now, if you will, I can indeed confirm that Korea will be again be One—soon. We will sign the peace treaty on the eve of our next Harvest Festival Moon, this 31st of October."

AIR FORCE SAFETY CENTER – KIRTLAND AFB

The USAF Safety Center is a glowing-white poured-concrete office building surrounded by rock gardens, its big windows looking out over Kirtland's desert vistas. Within its charter of safety policy and oversight, a key responsibility is aviation accident investigation.

Just the sight of the building, let alone his errand there, drove Sean to the brink of black depression. Any USAF aircraft accident—and the result of his bad order as commanding officer aboard Airborne Laser to fly near dangerous lightning was considered such—was the Safety Center's most public responsibility and the investigations would take weeks.

He did not have weeks. He barely had days. Abbey's interview had stunned the world, giving everyone an incredible look at Dearest Leader, humanizing him with that patented silk-and-sandpaper Baba Walters' interview style—and making it clear he would sign the peace treaty in just eight days.

Sean parked in the Safety Center's spacious lot, and lugged his two large cardboard boxes full of safety and training documentation past the stately trimmed yucca and golden rock of the entryway.

Pulling open the door while juggling the boxes, Sean was for a second overcome with a feeling of despair. No matter how well-documented his defense, he knew he would never win against the Air Force Safety Regs. Even if ABL were not grounded, essentially forever given Korea's treaty time line, in the next hour, the Safety Hearing would certainly relieve him of command. Fight as he would, he was off Airborne Laser.

He pushed on through the door, aware of Emily waiting inside. In the pitiless cheap fluorescents of the entryway, she looked up at him and even her pure skin was sallow. She knew they were done—and she felt the bleakness too.

GOLDEN PHOENIX – CHOSUN TOWERS

Abbey finished the press conference on a high. She was bursting at the seams, and that afternoon just slid through two whiskeys and on into the cocktail hour. The handsome CNN anchor-phony was really into her, making it clear he wanted to share her bed. As he rubbed against her, for a moment, her un-cynical side, admittedly as thin as rice paper, thought it might not be just her body, but her power, her presence that he lusted for. He disgusted her, and yet she felt something stirring in her. Some of it was the fear. If it were like the last few times, it would hurt. It was, however, pleasant to be wanted. It was more than pleasant. It was deliciously *delicious*...

She left quickly, and forced the taxi to stop while she picked up a liter bottle of Suntory and a mini-keg of Japanese beer.

Or she almost did. With a strange change of heart, one for which she couldn't recall any precedent, she left the whiskey and beer on the cashier's mat and walked out. She was feeling something, something more primal; something she hadn't done for herself for a long time. "Self-abuse," she said aloud, and then flushed as an old Korean couple, old enough to know Japanese, heard her, and gawked. She felt a little rush of thrilled fear as she knew she had no liquor at home. "Chosun Towers," she told the cab driver, and giggled. She thought she remembered where the thing was...but it had been so long...

At home, she was starting to get a little scared, no liquor and all. She threw things out of the drawers in the bathroom, then finally found the dingus and stripped off her work dress and fishnets, dropping them—as she never did—on the floor.

She had this week replaced all her furniture, rugs, and kitchen appliances, and the place was now done in luxury Korean furnishings...

She got under the light silk fall duvet, and tried to relax. She turned on the vibrator, and slowly...and yet thoughts came to her. Il-Moon's face was an ugly one, she decided, and pushed it out of her mind. Hakkermann wasn't much of a winner either. She thought of herself on camera. *That was better*, and then she remembered how difficult it was to look at her own face in the mirror these days. She sat up and flicked on the TV, looking for an old movie or something to distract. A flip of the remote, and there she was on TV, looking excited and impish and smart and...something else. A stirring inside her came, yet it wasn't so pleasant. A dark thing creeping around deep in the cave of herself, hunting the blind fish living within her subterranean lakes. She tried to laugh, turned off the TV and the light. It had been years since she fell asleep truly sober. Years. "Why so many?" she asked herself, "and then there's this."

She felt down again with the vibrator; put it directly on her sex. There seemed to be no feeling, nothing of the pleasantness she'd anticipated in returning the Suntory. She put the vibrator aside, and wetted her fingers at her lips. She reached down, slowly, sensuously. The interview kept floating up. "Why would he love such a bad person?" she asked herself aloud. Then she rubbed harder, harder.

Her sex remained dry and numb and her hand slowed and stopped. She felt a heave of self-pity, and in the darkness of her beautiful apartment in Chosun Luxury Towers, with the news world at her feet, tears spilled from her eyes and trickled in two rivulets down her taut cheeks.

And Abbey Yamamoto cried for herself.

LOBBY – AIR FORCE SAFETY CENTER

The doors of the big white concrete office building that is the Air Force Safety Center sprang open, and Emily, protesting, was hustled out the door and down the steps between Jeanette and Sean. "Wait. I didn't get to say anything."

"Luckily!" Jeanette and Sean said in unison.

Sean and Jeanette almost didn't let Emily's feet touch the ground, anxious to get as far as possible from the Safety Inquiry, as if any moment the furious colonel might change his mind and come charging after them.

"So, what did you tell him?" asked Emily, acidly, referring to Jeanette's sidebar with the Safety Incident colonel.

"'Don't throw the baby out with the bath water,'" Jeanette replied brightly.

"What does that mean?"

"You are officially less than welcome at Kirtland. You'll finish testing... elsewhere."

"Oh, no. Not..."

Jeanette bubbled on, "You'll like it, Emily! Why, Sean says Korea is a really fun place!"

"Korea! We've been there before, and it is a hot zone! Not counting Sean getting his head flattened, when we last flew there we got lased all the time, the place is alien, the weather is harsh, they occasionally shoot missiles at us, and all the men treat me like some kind of loosely-moraled sex kitten. Not a good place to test. How about first we try Idaho?"

"I'm sure it will be fine. Is twelve hours enough time to pack?"

Catchers in the Sky

BOOK 6

"Work underground as long as you can—publicity triggers the corporate immune mechanism."

The AFRL Project Officer's Sixth Commandment

Chapter 33

The 24th of October (Morning)

THE CHO'S HOME – ALBUQUERQUE

As the barest traces of growing light brought up the daily furniture from their misty night cloaks, Patricia Cho lay in sheets soaked in sweat. In the quiet of the North Valley's almost countryside silence, as she had the whole night, she listened to the rustling of their children down the hall and Matt's dozing nasal sounds. She turned, feeling the damp nightgown crumple under her. *Disgusting*, she thought, *like a used rag*, then reached out and turned off the alarm before it could zap her frayed nerve endings and bring more adrenalin shakiness. She got up, moved into and slowly down the hall.

Deployment day; that sickening anxious stomach, the sadness, the fright. Most women with three children and a husband would think of a few weeks without their hubbies as almost unbearable; the work, the chores, the shopping, the bills; the activities, the crises, the sheer dogged work of a family of five. She, on the other hand, was graced with a husband leaving for unknown weeks—or forever. Matt had said it was just Japan, just collecting atmospheric data. But the treaty news clogged every TV with images of Korea's arsenals and Matt's preparations were at a new fever pitch. Pat sensed he was going into the war zone, perhaps to return crippled or dead. *Don't let him be hurt. Please don't let him be hurt.* She wanted to puke.

She couldn't move quickly, sort of dream-walking along the familiar hallway and down the stairs. The house was warm and fresh-smelling, yet to her it seemed diseased. At the living room, her eyes ran over the racks of plastic bins Matt had made for toy organization, the clutter of art supplies and thrown off clothes, and the tracked-in sand and tiny footprints on the tile entryway; the signs of childhood running. *It's chaos now*, she thought, *and I have been functional and happy and helped and loved. How will I do it?*

She was so alone, and yet she knew that going through the motions had to happen, was the only thing to happen, was the only thing to do. She put on a pot of water for oatmeal, sensed Matt come up behind her. He held her gently. "Morning, Babe."

"Morning, Babe." She kissed him over her shoulder, too vulnerable to turn and face him.

He caressed her soft breasts. "Remembering last night."

"If it was my time, you'll be remembering it real long. Should have used my diaphragm."

"It was great, Pat."

"Eight minutes of pleasure, eighteen years of work."

"Eighteen years of..." he fondled.

"Stop."

He went still as he held her, asked. "You're coming, right?"

"Can't it be one more day? I know you're not ready."

"How could you know?"

"You said so in your sleep about twenty million times. 'Sean, just one more day.'"

"And what did he say?"

"Seemed to be 'No.'"

"I've got to shower, get moving. You'll bring the kids?"

"They're happy to be out of school, the little monsters."

"Did Tim finish the sign?"

She couldn't answer for a moment. Yes, going through the motions. *The signs. The fucking signs.*

She nodded her head so he could feel it. He kissed her hair, smelled it. She held in the sob. *Please. Let me hold it till he goes.*

"I'm going to skip the shower. I'll catch one at the base gym. Good bye, Babe."

He was gone. Her sob broke out.

ABL TECH AREA – PRE-DAWN

Within his deep sleep in his galley bunk, Sean sensed the jumbo stir ever so slightly; the tiny rocking motion of a person stepping furtively aboard when everything is so quiet and balanced you can actually feel the plane tip.

He had become used to living inside a giant tube almost a football-field long, with its ear-splitting quiet except when the wind rocked the big wings gently, or hoot owls and coyotes (ky-oats, as he was learning, New Mexico style, to call them) and prairie dogs argued out in the *barranca*.

He started awake in his tiredness, dozed again. There was the soft insistent beeping of a computer booting up, and the clack of fingernails on a keyboard. *A crewmember, early.* He relaxed—then heard the hum of the beam director almost directly under him as its precision gears whirred and the large optic slowly tracked around.

He got up quietly, looked down into the Tech Area, and saw Lorrie was up and running at her station.

Lorrie looked up suddenly, guilty. Her eyes darted, as if thinking like lightning, when Sean asked, "What are you doing?" as he looked down on her, holding her in his gaze.

"Oh, nothing. Just couldn't sleep so I thought I'd work some..."

Sean sensed her fear, keeping his position above her in the galley, knowing it made her look up, squeezed her. For a second, it flashed to Sean she might actually be the spy he sometimes almost felt among them. "Lorrie, you need to tell me right now what you're doing or I'm kicking you off this ship."

"Well, I was just..."

He realized. "Snooping."

"Sorry. But then...I saw something."

Sean was instantly sliding down the galley ladder to the Tech Area and moving to her station.

Lorrie had been snooping out the nose of ABL. Just for fun, she had been using the beam director not as a projector, but as a giant imaging optic, looking in windows and people-watching. Sean had yelled at her several times for her improper prurient activities, yet she apparently couldn't stop herself. Sean looked now at her high-resolution image of a window across the runway at the Wyndham hotel.

In the center of the window, through ABL's snooping optic, looking right back at them, was *another* snooping optic.

AIRBORNE LASER (X) COMPLEX – KIRTLAND AFB

If the deployment of a large military aircraft is a serious craft, the deployment of a military science research plane is an art—one the U.S. military excels at above all others.

When sallying out a large complex experimental weapon system—with its myriad specialty chemicals, unique tools, secure Comm gear, airframe fasteners, out of the ordinary transistors, crypto codes, non-standard cabling, weird aerospace solvents, custom O-rings, finicky test equipment, detailed orders, specially-trained ground crews, hyper officers, and prima donna Ph.D. weenies— the number of permutations for failure are astronomical.

No other air force in the world can match the scale of the USAF's organizational skills, logistics, and interoperability with which it can ready and move hundreds of tons of aircraft, people, and supplies thousands of miles, arrive safely and in an orderly fashion, yet with the reserves of energy and resources necessary to be ready to fight. It's not an ethnic thing; it's an attitude, an approach, an agreed set of shared values encouraging ingenuity.

In this spirit of resourcefulness, early on Chief Auggie had approached Sean and suggested getting the deployment underway. "In advance, Sir. We wait until we get the word to go, the task is too monumental." So he and Sean immediately began pre-packing much laser fuel and many spares, and loading them onto pallets for their still-unassigned C-130 cargo planes. Auggie had also set up the logistics necessary to keep straight the endless train of spares coming in from the various functional areas of Ops, Science, Weapons, and INTEL, while coordinating with their intended forward deployment base in Japan at Yakota Air Base.

Making it harder, following the disastrous lightning mission, the ABL Tech Area had sustained some hits, and although the fusing and power conditioners had taken the brunt of the lightning strike, there was a good amount of damaged equipment. The tech crew quickly identified a host of needed replacement and spare parts. Still, many items had to be placed on order, and at each stage of the trip, Auggie arranged for Fed-X deliveries to meet the plane on ahead. In addition, the enlisted and NCOs went on a massive foraging mission across the base, scavenging storehouses, tool-issue, electronics parts supply, bench stock, and LMCA, the logistics center. In the first twenty-four hours, the crew had worked miracles, and yet Kirtland was a research and air mobility base, and many combat and repair supplies were unavailable. To get out quickly, a lot of baling wire, chewing gum, and that most crucial element of military kit—duct tape—was being applied. However, Sean was adamant they depart, and agreed to a one-day delay only after a hard-fought management skirmish—mostly giving in so he could claim later to be more reasonable than he really was.

Yet every hour lost was like another knife-cut on his person, as the treaty loomed large.

Airborne Laser, hatches wide, was busting out all over with effort readying her for deployment. By the second day—deployment day—the flux of damaged and ruined components off the plane was swamped by the influx of functioning kit.

In this final hour of packing, the crew was everywhere, loading laser fuel cylinders, supplies, and piling personal luggage near the airstairs; briefcases, laptops and science instrument cases were dumped on the tarmac to await being loaded into the crew-jammed interior.

At the adjoining picnic area, the Airborne Laser families sat quietly talking. They had pulled up their pickups and family cars in the field facing ABL, and most of the wives lay on the hoods of their trucks, watching the anthill activity around the plane. Many sipped beers quietly, and there were few laughs, although the young children played with their usual abandon, their shouts and laughter mixing into the clanking, hissing of hoses, and barking of the plane inspectors as they called out their checklists. Little food was being eaten; only the children's hotdogs and burgers were popular. The adult food of hams and salad lay untouched, the coleslaw and dips congealing.

Pat Cho lay on the hood of her truck, leaning her back against the windshield, viewing the Airborne Laser 747 through half-closed eyes. The excited crew carried supplies, conferred, and walked the wings and fuselage, scrutinizing their external gizmos. Her eye-slits blurred the giant plane, its splayed-open hatches making it look like a sprung can of sardines. She saw Matt, in a safety harness, come out of a rear hatch and climb up Airborne Laser's side. He gained his footing on the roof, walked along ABL's dorsal, and tinkered with a big cockscomb of a laser pod atop the plane.

Matt's form up on the huge plane's top was dreamish, the scale all wrong, and for a moment, Pat felt a strange tug. She looked to the children running at their games of tag and throwing horseshoes, and tried to understand her feelings about the signs.

There, to the side of the picnic area, where they could be seen by the crew gearing up the plane, propped-up or set in the dirt, were the signs. Hand-painted by children and friends, they were confettied banners and placards; written in pastels, colored magic marker, or watercolor, the signs formed field of child-printed messages like: 'Come Home Soon Daddy!' and "LOVE U MATT!" and "You're the Best Mommy in the World!!"

She felt the truck buck down as someone hitched up onto the hood. Amanda Hull, Jarhead's wife, swung her feet up to sit cross-legged facing Pat. Pixie-like, Amanda had curly short brown hair and the bronzed tight-skinned face of the life-long athlete. She wore a cheerful grin and held out one of two frosty bottles of Coors Light. Pat took a bottle, and they clinked briskly, although to her it sounded lifeless.

"Proud of him?" asked Amanda, her merry eyes close on Pat's face.

"Not thinking that just this moment, no."

"Got the send-off blues?"

"Yeah, a little." A pause. "A lot. But I was thinking, kind of drowsing and I've always hated those signs."

"Know a secret? They never hurt anyone."

"Ha. Ha. It's something else, can't put my finger on it. You?"

"How about we talk about what we're gonna do unbeknownst to them with all their deployment pay?"

"*Not* funny, Amanda."

Amanda turned, sat cross-legged on the hood facing Pat still reclined against the windshield, her eyes on ABL. "It's the life we chose. Jay and then me. Well, maybe that's too dramatic, 'cuz in life you so rarely really know when you're choosing."

"Till later."

"Till later, yeah. But it's a good life. It's got purpose and heart." Amanda rolled her beer bottle between her hands. She caught sight of Jarhead working a crate with a forklift. She waved enthusiastically, and his peripheral vision must have caught it, for he took both hands from the steering wheel and did a quick return semaphore before grabbing the wheel as the forklift slid. "I'd choose it again, this time I knew I was choosing and knowing everything I know. If that's not too many 'knows.'"

Pat didn't answer. She saw Matt in safety harness against the huge rear stabilizer. He was in animated discussion with a technician about a gizmo on the side. Matt clapped the tech on the shoulder, then repelled down the side of the plane—and in a slick maneuver—disappeared into a hatch.

Pat said, realizing, "I guess I am proud...*you know?*"

They laughed.

* * *

On the far side of the ABL apron, Jeanette waited by her limo and looked toward the bustling plane.

Sean and Emily in flight suits moved toward her, coming to see her off. Emily's ebony hair was tied up with two chopsticks—a sign it was dirty—and a wearable computer was sewn on her flight suit over a smoothed but unhideably pointy breast. For once, her usual clogs had been replaced by the regulation black flight boots—albeit she hadn't tied the tricky double-tongued laces properly. Sean's face was unshaven and his flight suit spattered in dirt and grease. He looked tough and driven.

Jeanette's eyes were shiny and her grip feverishly tight as she grasped their hands. She had to go, and yet, to see Sean and Emily together, working... She said, trying to joke, "Oh, to be young and going to the field." But it was too close to the mark and she became warmly brusque. "I'll hold down the home front. You need to keep secret; to keep away from Hakkermann. Keep safe..." and her control slipped, "Good luck. *Good luck.*"

"So long, Jeanette," Sean said as Emily hugged her, nuzzling her a little. "We've trained hard, and so we'll fight easy."

Jeanette stepped away quickly, swiping at her eyes as she bent and slid into her limo.

Sean and Emily watched as the limo moved silently away. Sean said, "She's a great one, isn't she?"

"I'll miss her. The guilt-tripping, rationalizing, manipulating sweetie."

* * *

At Airborne Laser, packing had progressed past the technical items and fuels, and onto the loading of the personal luggage, and in a plane packed as tight as a sausage, most of the crew were humping their own personal kit up the airstairs, and making sure it would be findable in the hold and lockers.

In the center of the Tech Area, the hatch to the under-deck stowage area was open. Unlike the massive belly storage reached by external hatches, this was the only cargo space accessible to the Tech Area during flight, so all critical supplies were stored there. Down in the hold, Chief Auggie, for once without his tie in place and stripped to his black uniform T-shirt, stowed items as Sean dropped them down to him. Sean was working his way through a pile of military parachutes, dropping them into the hold where Auggie grunted as he caught each dead weight, and lashed it against a bulkhead.

Emily, chewing a pencil at Laser One, saw the boys working to rota, and triggered by instinct, came over, asked curiously, "Wotcha doing? Parachutes?"

Sean heaved the next one down to Auggie. "One each. Hope for the best, plan for the worst."

"Touched by a Boy Scout. Isn't that their motto?"

Over Emily's shoulder, Sean caught site of Jarhead, entering loaded down with a M240G heavy machine gun and a case of ammo. Jarhead nodded to Emily's back, and Sean quickly tried to engage Emily: "If our past record is any indication of the future, my motto is 'Be scared.'"

Emily caught his microsecond eye glance, turned to catch Jarhead sneaking aft with his goodies. "Hey! You know the rules, Jay! No drugs, no sex, and *no weapons* aboard Airborne Laser!"

"No sex?" asked Sean.

"Well, OK. Sex sometimes, drugs in an emergency, but weapons *never*!"

"We'll talk about the sex thing later. Just now you're telling me Emily makes a big ol' laser blaster that could barbecue Chicago and then says 'No weapons'?"

Emily snorted, "We're peacemakers. Fifty thousand feet up and hundreds of miles away from the battlefield, we don't need weapons."

Lorrie nonchalantly strolled past. Oddly she wasn't as usual staunchly taking Emily's side, in fact looking quite...Sean grabbed her purse. Yanked out the marriage of chic femininity and metallic deadliness that is a Lady Smith .38 Special revolver.

Sean held up the elegant Smith and Wesson handgun, tilting it so Emily could see it was fully loaded—with grey hollow-point dumdum bullets. "Oh really. What about Lorrie?"

Lorrie wailed, "They'll rape me! Please don't leave me defenseless!"

"That's for use against rapists," Emily said, as evenly as she could.

Lorrie gently retrieved her gun from Sean's hands, smirking at him from behind Emily's back as she started to make her escape.

"Dumdum bullets? Yeah? Well, this stuff's for Boy Scout ceremonies," Sean replied while Jarhead nodded in emphatic innocence.

Emily whirled, yelled at Lorrie: "You! Freeze! I want that gun!" Then she spun Jarhead around, pointed to the Dragon anti-tank weapon hanging from his shoulder. She plinked the deadly munition. "I didn't know the Boy Scouts offered an anti-tank guided missile merit badge."

"But they do, my wingperson, they do," Sean replied.

Emily went frosty. "Would you come with me, please?" and turned on her heel. She stalked forward up the ladder to the galley and into the tiny head. Sean followed her in, and face to face again in the narrow room, they were as close as a kiss. Sean felt her breasts against him and her unscented breath was peppermint of pure woman. He said, not completely smoothly, "I like how you've organized our office."

"Bullfeathers on this wingman stuff! I heard you say under oath at the incident hearing you gave the order for us to fly the lightning mission. So just because I almost killed everyone, you can't pull that high card stuff. Yes, I screwed up. Yes, too, you did. We're deploying, that's my penance. But our relationship is back to where it was before: you are program manager and I'm principle investigator. Co-equal partners."

Sean was incredibly close to her face and yet, in the milky skin and pure whites of her eyes, he could see no flaw, no blemish. It wasn't just her morals; she was 100% Ivory Soap girl even under magnification. He got himself under control. "Fair enough. Can you do something about that tender skin you've got? Maybe lotions or something?"

Emily burst out of the lav. A passing J-Stars remarked, "She was always dragging him into the john. Some kind of co-dependency thing. Damn strange."

"Oh, shut your face!" snapped Emily, and hurried past.

But by the time she got to the Tech Area, Jarhead's weaponry and Lorrie's Lady Smith were nowhere to be found.

* * *

Chapter 34

The 24th of October (Afternoon)

AIRBORNE LASER COMPLEX – KIRTLAND AFB

Those last moments before deployment are always scary and difficult. The families gathered together around the airstairs, hugging, patting, and murmuring until it reached a peak and then died off as the unencumbered ones, Sean and Emily, moved up the airstairs slowly, hintingly. The family interchanges became a last prolonged kiss, the last tousling of a child's head.

Pat Cho was going down in a whirlpool of thoughts and feelings as she repeated, "Come back safe, Babe," to Matt, while his leave-taking finally dawned on Tim who asked, "Do you have to go, Daddy?"

There followed the last of the kisses of that hopefully temporary good-bye kind.

Sean, now at the top of the airstairs, looked out over the base, taking in the desert autumn, the distant jumble of the AFRL buildings, the expanse of wild land toward the mountains, the flight line's buzzing activity. He felt Emily beside him, looking as well. "I hope we see it again," she murmured, then, "It's time."

"Airborne Laser!" Sean called, "Mount up!"

The crew pounded up the airstairs. The ABL hatch closed to show its laser-spitting rattlesnake emblem while the Airborne Laser families stood watching, sad and silent.

The ground crew motioned the families back as the engines whined up. The families went to their cars and trucks, sitting on the hoods in the traditional manner as Airborne Laser came to life.

A balloon floated idly. The food sat untouched behind them. Matt Cho's son still listlessly held his sign, 'Come Back Soon, Daddy!' and the restraint momentarily gripped even Amanda.

The giant plane taxied along the apron spur across the highway, where the Security Police had halted all traffic. People at the road-block got out of their cars to watch the humongous bizarre aircraft trundle past through the open gate and onto the flight line.

The ABL families, as soon as the plane was through, grabbed all their signs, herded kids into cars, and drove to the fence at the end of the runway. Lining the fence, children holding the signs, the adults stood silently. Here, ABL would have to take off right over them.

Airborne Laser skimmed the runway, and as it boomed over the families, they waved frantic good-byes and sent up a cheer.

"Flightdeck this is Ops. Give them a wave," Sean called, and Slammer did a sluggish end zone celebration wing waggle in a final good-bye.

In the Tech Area, the crew took a last look out of the few portholes, but only Emily had a good view. She saw Pat Cho and Amanda and so many others, the signs now drooping, seemingly at half-mast. Inside the Tech Area, Lorrie turned the long-range video TV to zoom in on the families, sad, still waving after them.

Sean let it go for a moment, but with the long-range video so capable, Lorrie could keep close on the sad faces for way too long.

It was time to look the other way. West. Sean said, "Comm, this is Ops. Thanks, Lorrie. Let's go to eyes forward."

Lorrie swung the TV cameras around, stowed the beam director, and everyone booted up their terminals and went to work.

WYNDHAM HOTEL – ALBUQUERQUE AIRPORT

In his hotel room, Spiny watched ABL take off. His telescopic system was at the wrong end of the runway, but its 1600mm focal length was enough to get some good shots of the send off, and Airborne Laser taking to the air and heading west by northwest.

Korea.

First, it was obviously a long deployment—the luggage and activity showed him that. Then there was the send off by the families and the emotional good-bye with that pickle-up-her-ass Queen Bee.

He deftly transferred the digital camera shots to his laptop. Firing up Adobe Photoshop, he opened the photo files and worked on the contrast and edge enhancement until he got the most out of the grainy digital photos. Flipping through the pictures, taking his time as usual to get the images right, he suddenly ran across the sequence of time-lapse photography the camera had snapped at intervals all last night. It took him less than one second to realize that at one point ABL's big ol' nose optic had looked right at his camera. He could tell it saw his camera because of the cat's-eye glint when the two optical systems were exactly in alignment.

He quickly transferred a set of files of the SECAF Learjet, the families with their signs, the bolted-down ABL, and its support aircraft. Spiney, hands shaking, compressed the set while logging onto his email. He pulled up Hugh Levin's Reuters email account, and pressed the attachment button. While his first set of shots started to upload to email, he began throwing everything into drag bags, and started to take his hunting stand down.

He was almost packed—when he heard a scuffling outside the door. He pushed the send button on the email, even though it wasn't really ready.

The FBI agents outside the door grouped, slipped the hotel pass card into the lock, and kicking past the door chain, came smashing in. "And you're on candid camera!" someone called as the agents swarmed the room.

They grabbed Spiny, cuffed him, and took a fast look around. Rather than pull the plug on the PC, one FBI agent took a moment to jot down the email address of the pending message working to go out.

He got it, but before he could shut off the PC, 'Message Sent' popped up on the screen, and the email packet was already halfway around the world—to the office of Reuters Seoul.

'THE PIT' – REUTERS OFFICE – SEOUL

It took Abbey only one second to notice the degraded quality of the email and the unannotated pictures, and realize something was wrong back at Kirtland. She made Hugh call Spiney at the Wyndham, and he got nothing—or a big something when some spook picked up on the line and asked, "Who is this?"

Hugh said, "So, this stuff came with no notes and we don't know what it is, really. What's it worth?"

Abbey knew she'd lost Spiney, but also from photos she did get, that ABL was on its way to Korea. She thought of Il-Moon. She said aloud, Hugh watching her, "A lot. It's worth a lot."

ARCHITECT SU'S STATE RESIDENCE

Architect Su and Dearest Leader were heading in opposite directions. The closer to the treaty the more robust, sanguine, and cheerful Dearest Leader looked, while Architect Su's twenty-hour-a-day work schedule pushed viciously at his eighty-plus-years physical self until he was unsure how much longer he could go on. He was spinning down into a morass of exhaustion and over-work that was breaking his health.

There was something in the whole treaty issue, something coming on, a feeling. He had been worried for a long time about the overall potential for disaster. Perhaps it was his ill-health that made him feel something when he was near

Il-Moon now; something akin to his own on-rushing and seemingly inevitable collapse.

Exhausted after another road-trip lasting until almost midnight, Architect Su stumbled into his state apartments, a flat of eight rooms in a leadership block of luxury flats overlooking the one hundred statues he'd built for giant Kim Il-Sung square below. In the anteroom, Architect Su said good-night to his three solemn but self-satisfied State Security Department watchers.

Decades earlier, he had kindly arranged for his watchers habitually to accompany him in. This was greatly appreciated by these unsmiling men, who otherwise would have—as did the others monitoring the high leadership—spent the night observing uncomfortably from their cars out front, waiting for him to reemerge.

Despite his exhaustion, Su did not lie on the bed, rather slumped into a chair and sat looking out into the giant open space of Kim Il-Sung square and the granite likenesses of the great men of his country. They stood now, firm and immutable where he had designed them to stand, forever watching, lining the concrete plaza under the waxing moon and dimmed autumn stars. His legs felt leaden, the pictures on the wall swam in his vision, and his heart raced. His left side seemed to tingle, and when he licked his lips, the left half of his face felt droopy. *I can almost feel it, the impending stroke.*

In his terror, to ground himself and chase away the nightmare of his mind's impending destruction, he picked up the phone. Desperately he wished for his granddaughter's voice, just her voice, to pull him back. But his grip went feeble and the phone fell from his fingers to the floor.

Granite men. Under dimming stars. The most senior of his watchers tapped, opened the door. Listening on the phone, they'd heard it drop. The blue-suited man moved quickly to his side, concern in his face. Architect Su smiled lopsidedly, trying to reassure, but a tear of effort ran from one of his eyes as he found he could not speak.

The blue-suited man lifted Su into bed. Architect Su lay, helpless, saw the man turn at the door to look him over a last time.

The watchers! Su realized excitedly as the man left, shrugging off his sickness. *Tam Ho is a major.* He would be—like Architect Su and anyone else of consequence—watched incessantly, and every personal contact recorded. The high-ranking military and politicos had their logs sent quarterly to Dearest Leader for scrutiny as to improper associations—and these files in large part determined their future prospects in the DPRK.

Only Il-Moon, it was rumored, was not subject to this stricture, a bargain made with Dearest Leader which cemented their alliance at the top—and allowed

Dearest Leader to ascend the throne quickly and without bloodshed.

Song Il-Moon. Now yours is a file I would like to see. Tam Ho, what about your file? How would I find it? Same difficulties as before. He started. *Dearest Leader would have it*—no, Tam Ho was a major. Only the files of those at colonel and above were sent to Dearest Leader...

Su sat up in bed. *Maj Tam Ho crossed paths with Col Kang—at the minisub facility!* Kang was a colonel, and thus his watchers *would* have recorded everyone else entering the facility in *his* file. There would be cross-referenced file numbers for Tam Ho. In addition, perhaps in the list of contacts, Su would find another Underwater Mansion conspirator. Most likely, Kang had met others at least once.

Best of all, Dearest Leader had his own copy of Col Kang's surveillance file. In this file, Su would find a lead to Tam Ho.

Architect Su again reached for the phone. Dearest Leader, like his father and grandfather before him, worked late into the night, using their insomnia to great effect. As leaders they were all famous for calling up their subordinates at 3:00 a.m. to ask about some piddling detail. It was *de rigueur* for everyone near the top to sleep lightly, a phone by his ear, ready when the call came to prove wakeful dedication to the revolution and unceasing service to the Leader.

But even as his fingers touched the phone, Su remembered his watchers would be listening. It would go into *his* file. Il-Moon's deal with Dearest Leader almost certainly included Su's file. Su's mind methodically turned over the problem of the file, until he found a solution.

He lay down, and hoped for sleep to knit the raveled sleeve of his body up. Tomorrow, his new grandson-in-law—certainly he was untainted—would run a message to Dearest Leader. Just as Su in his apparent innocence as a boy had ferried urgent messages for the Great Leader through the war-torn perilous streets of Manchuria, Su's grandson-in-law would courier Col Kang's surveillance file to Su undetected.

Chapter 35

The 24th of October (Evening)

AIRBORNE LASER – MCCHORD AFB – TACOMA, WA

Sean had worked their flight path out with Slammer and Bozon, and he and the pilots had agreed they should take the route over the Aleutian islands, since the enormous expanse of the Pacific, given the recent hits the airframe had taken, wasn't as safe as having emergency set-downs along the route. It would take longer to get on station, but the airbases along the way had good flight machining and engineering centers, and ABL could finish outfitting in transit.

Their path was first northwest to huge McChord AFB, just south of Seattle at Tacoma, the center of the 5th Air Force and its logistics and refurbishment areas—a capability itself vectored toward the Korean peninsula. Then on up the coast to Elmendorf, Alaska, down along the Aleutians, over Japan's northern islands to Honshu, finally putting in at Yakota Air Base in Tokyo, their duty station from which to watch over wild and woolly Korea.

At McChord, Airborne Laser got a coat of war paint—camouflage for the grey skies of high altitude Northeast Asia—and the full airframe inspection unavailable at most bases. The lightning dive had done nothing to the structure as far as the base refurb center could say after a kind of awed inspection of some of the scorch marks on the elevons. It was nonetheless a quiet set of techs who reported back to Sean, Slammer, and Bozon that the plane was fit for duty—adding only that they hoped whomever arranged their flight plan directly into lightning was no longer in command.

McCord was also their best chance to outfit any additional anti-aircraft missile defenses, or ASE—Aircraft Survival Equipment—in USAF parlance.

ABL was by military standards slow moving and non-maneuverable, and therefore vulnerable. Being vulnerable is OK as long as you aren't provocative—and not merely emotionally provocative, such as a lumbering INTEL plane carrying a few air-to-air anti-aircraft missiles and irritating the shadowing fighter aircraft observers. This is likened to a herd of bison carrying blunderbusses while being guarded by herdsmen with Sharps rifles. The blunderbuss represents a low danger to the herdsmen who aren't planning to shoot anyway unless there's a total stampede—and yet it pisses them off as well.

ABL was confrontational at a completely different level from the merely irritating. She could not help but be extremely provocative. For, although she possessed no strike capability of conventional arms, she represented an enormous threat to anyone whose war plans included the use of missiles on the battlefield either strategically or tactically. With an operational reach of hundreds of miles, Airborne Laser could patrol from international airspace far outside any legal or military interference. She was truly a theater-wide strategic asset—or threat— and any modern army with a missile-centered offense plan—indeed any aircraft and missiles—would be hard-pressed to ignore her overarching presence: if you were going to war with missiles and ABL were on station nearby, you would have to knock her and her laser down—almost impossible—or watch your best punches go down in flames, and your chances for victory decrease continuously to zero.

Using their high-level covering orders, a support letter from Jeanette with its all-important Program Element funding lines on it, Sean wrangled pretty much a complete set of equipment for deployment to a potential war zone. Their overall ASE was upgraded and they got new DIRCMs—small black turrets that scan around the aircraft for IR missiles, blinking signals at them to confuse them should they be locked onto the aircraft. Also, there was, as Jarhead put it, "A very nice radar chaff and flares dispenser that would do the Fourth of July proud," a towed decoy antennae—a marvel of engineering deployed on a hair-thin line out the back of ABL to re-broadcast received radar signals and misdirect radars tracking ABL.

Sean, Emily, the Laserjocks, and Jarhead put in a full twenty-four hours and stayed for all the inspections and installations, while Lorrie and Matt led a 'team-building' expedition to Seattle to scour its huge electronics stores for spares, and blow off some steam shopping in the malls.

By the time the shopping party returned with a freshened sense of purpose, and the Tech Area filled with the smell of fragrant luxury soaps, one thousand microfarad capacitor packs, compared presents for family, and music from new CD's, Sean, Jarhead, the Laserjocks, and Emily were running on fumes.

Emily fell asleep on the Laser One console face down. Sean dozed, half in his bunk, one boot still on. Marty and the laser crew lay on sleeping bags under the optical tables of the Attack Laser, their snoring louder than the constant gurgling of laser plumbing. Jarhead dropped into the hold under the Tech Area to get away from all the jabber, and lay on the duffle to sleep. He never did decide, because he was asleep in seconds, whether the lumpy baggage felt more like bags of crockery or corncobs.

For the crew's part, they had left Albuquerque at a gallop, scarcely able to function. Now, it felt different. It was there in the camouflage, the DIRCM turrets around the airframe, the ASE chaff and flare dispensers, the new translucent grease on the Phalanx guns, the shipshape feeling to the Tech Area and Attack Laser.

Under the shadow of Korea, the crew looked from one to another, and at their exhausted sleeping leadership.

Airborne Laser (Experimental) was now rigged and ready for war.

PANMUNJOM – ARMISTICE MEETING ROOM

Both Il-Moon and Hakkermann had dismissed their helpers, and faced each other across a table down the center of which lay the line—here a microphone wire—dividing North and South Korea. Harold reflected how each now sat in their own country, debating across the line the details of how that line would disappear—forever—and they would both be on the same side. There would be no more line, and beneath the shiny surface of the table Harold thought he could see, as if trapped in some parallel universe, the historical throngs of Koreans; here muddy-clothed, there starving, there working the fields and factories. He was about to bring the Elixir of Freedom to a shambling, starving, downtrodden people. He was about to begin anew a thousand years of unified Korea.

Il-Moon watched him patiently. He too could not ignore the line down the center of the table, he too was thinking about Korean history. The difference was, he saw the line move far south; saw the masses of his people, the slaves, the peasants, the proletariat—and felt their worth and confidence in him as he brought freedom to them and glory for all Korea.

"We have arranged your inspection of Pyong-son tomorrow," Il-Moon said to Harold, "Now I say 'Turn and turn about.' All we need to proceed is the 7th Air Force pulled back to Seattle. We are so close, my friend."

Harold, somewhat pompously, pulled out the thick treaty document, topped with Congressional promise-of-approval letters. "Seattle won't fly. As we have agreed, Okinawa. And we'd need some verification equipment installed at Pyong-son."

"What is this, my friend, what is this?"

"Confidence building measures are key to my selling the removal of the 7th Air Force from Korea, even back to Okinawa. You understand my hands are tied at some level, just as surely yours are."

Il-Moon considered. "What is the necessary timetable?"

"Perhaps four days."

"That should not present any problems. When your confidence building equipment arrives, we will install it at Pyong-son without delay. Do not forget, my friend, the powerful forces who do not wish regime change will soon undermine our efforts. We have a slender margin; let us complete the work of the treaty, so I may purge the threats from our country."

"Fine, I'll have the equipment here in three days." Harold knew his request for the monitoring equipment was a bluff. His actual horizon for getting it to Korea was at least a week.

Il-Moon continued, "Our armor is more difficult to remove, but we will begin that pull back shortly. Within four days it will be withdrawn—and you and Dearest Leader will sign the reunification treaty the night the 7th Air Force leaves Korea."

Harold wasn't sure whether to shake hands, but he was sure to rise last. Il-Moon stood, and suddenly—across the North and South Korean border—he held out his hand.

Harold shook Il-Moon's hand firmly. "I will see you tomorrow for the re-inspection of Pyong-son."

AIRBORNE LASER – TECH AREA – OVER SEATTLE

The Tech Area was dark and quiet as an overseas night flight. Some crew slept on pads and sleeping bags on the floor, as the bunk room held only six and every bed was filled. A small light pooled here or there in the Tech Area as crew worked or read.

Their take-off woke Sean after only a catnap. He slid down the ladder into the darkened Tech Area. Emily sat at Laser One looking out the window. Sean joined her, saw below Mt. Rainier, its snowy cap gleaming in the moonlight. Beyond the massive glaciated volcanic cone spread the coruscating constellation of the night lights of the Seattle suburbs. Amidst the rolling hills along the coast, a river of red and gold car lights of the heavy traffic on I-5 ran up toward the splash of bright high-rise downtown.

Sean mused, "In ten years any country that wants ICBM's will have them. This city sleeps in the last era where they're safe from the missiles of rogue nations or terrorists." He moved closer to Emily, her face unreadable. "What were you thinking?"

She answered quickly, "I was thinking the lights were pretty."

Sean looked at her in the quiet darkness. "We're starting out on a mission together."

Emily's face reflected the city lights of the three million souls below as she considered his slight chiding. "There's a book, the boy in it dreams of having this special job: he imagines children playing in a tall rye field next to a cliff. His job is to stand by the cliff and when a child plays too close he catches them. He's the—"

"Catcher in the Rye. Sure, I know the book. We'd all like that job."

"But I really have it. When I look over city lights, everyone sleeping below, I know perhaps there's a missile coming for them. I can feel it launching, rising, accelerating, deploying its warhead. But I'm there. Watching." She paused, looked up suddenly at him. "Despite the stain on my soul for unleashing Airborne Laser on the world, with all its unintended consequences, on some night, for some city, I will be The Catcher in the Rye."

Chapter 37

The 25th of October (Korea)

PYONG-SON COMPLEX

Il-Moon reflected that he had ridden in this elevator many times, as the rock slid past and the air below, redolent with mine dust and machinery smells, welled up past him. Still, he had never really imagined this moment, to be here with a senior U.S. Ambassador, showing him one of the most secret places in the world. Of course, he had dug more than a thousand major tunnels under North Korea, and many more smaller facilities. Bringing in someone from the outside to his 'home,' well, it was uncomfortable but necessary. On the other hand, he'd brought people into false tunnels many times for the direct purpose of getting money. He used to joke about these projects: 'Give me another mile of tunnel, and I will get fifty million dollars out of someone in concessions to stop digging it.' By digging a tunnel that looked to hold a nuclear facility, a missile site, or a chem-bio warfare center, leaving the tailings outside, someone would eventually call up and offer to pay you to stop. He frowned. *That car had finally run out of gas.*

Next to him, the Honorable Harold Hakkermann sensed his IAEA chief inspector looking at the hand-chipped rock of the passage, and tried not to feel superior. He guessed the place was one hundred meters down, but boy, was it crude. Hakkermann could see the rest of the U.S. inspectors felt the same. They had sprung on Il-Moon unannounced that this, not the new reactor buildings, was what they wanted to see. Demanding an immediate inspection—Il-Moon had to waive the usual North Korean demand for months of notice because of the treaty timing—Hakkermann's request got the full backing of Dearest Leader.

Hakkermann, for this re-inspection—despite his non-belief in it—had a crude GPS map from Radiant Outlaw showing the approximate locations of the apparent missile launch facilities. But Sandy had been right about its imprecision: under these mountains and within the tunnels, there was metal everywhere. Further, Il-Moon's skills of deceit were formidable, and he had put in false facilities he was about to reveal as harmless even though their layout was threatening. So, without a bloodhound like Sean, and with only poor INTEL, Harold was unlikely to unearth the truth.

When the elevator set down, Hakkermann, Il-Moon, Aide Park, and Hakkermann's chief inspector walked out into the giant underground tank factory. Seemingly abandoned, the tank assembly line lay rusting.

The second elevator of inspectors and their North Korean minders arrived, the inspectors' eyes working methodically, memorizing everything. Every little detail they could see and remember would be of value to countless programs, including satellite INTEL, logistics estimators, and war-games. It would be a long debrief, for this was *terra incognita*, and all of them wanted to move it along as far as possible to *terra cognita*.

The inspectors moved quickly to inspect the decaying tank assembly line, daub at the grease, pick at the rust, and then moved on to the rock walls of the cavernous bunker. They took samples of the concrete, the six smaller tunnels apparently blocked-up some time ago, and inactive. They whispered directly into each other's ears as they assessed the patches to be old and insignificant. It would take a week before it would prove to be much newer—but by then it would be too late.

Hours later in the embassy in Seoul, Hakkermann got the T+4 hours briefing—the preliminary results as compiled with the first main information, and completed within four hours after the inspection. There would follow T+10, T+24, and T+48, and each would feature nicer graphics, better pictures, and more refined arguments. It was rare, however, that the main issues weren't on the table at T+4.

His chief inspector sat next to Hakkermann during the briefing, went through the basic estimated parameters of the bunker, its recent activity, and concluded, "Harold, there clearly was activity here years ago, perhaps missiles. However, given available power, water, the space factors, it is not suitable for a nuclear reactor or missiles. We find no weapons violations here. We could recommend a set of fiducials, based on past experience."

"What kind of fiducials?"

"We put in all around Pyong-son monitors and sensors that can't be tampered with. TV to watch the site inside and out, electrostatics sensors for radio or electrical use changes, maybe some smart plaster on the walls to give us a shout if it were stressed or broken. Acoustics if possible. All sending out status to us. Depends on what they allow, but I'd say do the suite."

"How long to work out the protocols?"

"Well, that's a matter for you, isn't it? We can be ready to start the technical means in three days, and it would continue for some time." He turned to technical division lead, who nodded. "Couple of days to collect the equipment, maybe another two days to Fed-X it from Sandia Labs," while Harold reflected it was unfortunate not to have everything in place, but he had the agreement.

He had what he needed. He started thinking schedule. The North Korean Council General could meet Hakkermann at Osan the evening before and confirm the withdrawal of the 7th Air Force. He would then hand-carry a copy of the treaty to Pyongyang for final reading. Changes would be penned in, and the treaty signed by Dearest Leader, Il-Moon, the South Korean President, and Hakkermann at Panmunjom the following morning.

His team adjoined to a nearby room and started laying out the treaty signing protocols.

ABBEY – THE CENTER OF THE CYCLONE

As everyone's favorite leakee, Abbey found herself at the center of the cyclone. Not only had she synthesized her own version of the history of the Korean division, but around her blew a storm of information so intense and gratifying she sometimes had far too much to use, yet the quest for more was devouring her soul.

Such was the case of Hakkermann's Pyong-son inspection.

She had no less than five reports along with video coverage from inside Pyong-son, and she was going to make a killing on local TV doing an exposé.

Although no reporters were allowed into the actual inspection, she had enough footage of the entry and exits, so when Akiru set up a blue screen, by sleight of lens and video, she was able to apparently stand before the Pyong-son complex, its gantries and blockhouses behind her, and report as if she were on the spot.

Abbey said, "This is the infamous Pyong-son site where the Americans had believed nuclear missiles or research might lie in hiding. The U.S. team of inspectors has now left, following a finding of 'No significant treaty-sensitive activity' at Pyong-son. This clears the last major hurdle to the signing of the treaty. America, are you going to keep your word and pull out the 7th Air Force as a show of good faith and sign the treaty? The world is watching to see the USA put their money where they've always said their mouth really was. You, America, were responsible for dividing the peninsula originally! You, America, promised to help the Koreans—then divided them to use as a surrogate Cold War battlefield, killing millions! You, America, never kept your promises unless they involved building up your armies here. You, America, helped the South to far worse atrocities in the Korean War than the North. You, America, were the ones who bombed the North so thoroughly the North Koreans could never forget it and retreated into decades of paranoia, enhanced by your threat of nuclear attack not once, but seven times!"

She moved to less fiery, more silky. "For all the mistakes, for all the responsibility—America, come clean and do it! Keep your pride and your promise!"

PYONG-SON COMPLEX

Under Pyong-son, the bunker walls exploded and debris spewed, as a sealed train tunnel gaped open.

Following Il-Moon's order to reconstitute the missile cavern, crews swarmed out of the tunnel. Carrying crates, railroad tracks, tools, and supplies, they bent to clear rubble and open other tunnels sealed for the inspections. Reconstituting was a huge job, but with thousands of motivated people with decent tools, it would be possible.

The North Koreans had built up a great expertise in deceiving international inspections. When they had first allowed the U.N.'s IAEA inspectors into their nuclear plants and laboratories, they believed the inspectors would be able to prove little. They were shocked to discover what the IAEA could make from dust swipes, air samples, and analysis of their contaminated thrown-away protective clothing. The analysis as to isotope types and concentrations, with known half-lives and proportions that fixed the time and type of nuclide production, proved North Korean violations of the non-proliferation treaty were flagrant.

When the IAEA inspectors came the next time, they found entire facilities had been sponged down, nor was one iota of trash left on site. Despite the North's signing of a sworn joint denuclearization declaration with their South Korean brothers, again the IAEA, detecting weapon isotopes, concealed laboratories, and tampered seals and monitoring equipment, documented a committed nuclear weapons program.

Yet at each inspection, the North Koreans learned more about concealment. Each time they were found in violation, they became more cunning, also learning to deny any unannounced inspections, insisting on months of prior notice. If the U.N. inspections had been backed by anything more than pure spinelessness, it would have gone hard for the North Koreans. Despite the palpable proof, knowing the toothless U.N. would do nothing in the face of the treaty violations, the North Koreans continued their programs—while honing their concealment skills.

Now, they were past-masters at deceiving inspectors. They built facilities under other facilities, and would refuse to allow entry if they were discovered. They repainted everything, even when there was nothing to hide, and they always put in apparent violations that, when exposed, where shown to be innocent.

Il-Moon had learned well how to hide his assets—and this time, he also knew Hakkermann's monitoring threat to be a bluff. Abbey, in a dark corner booth in the Golden Phoenix, had beguiled one of the junior scientists from Sandia Labs. Enticing him to grope her breasts as she rubbed his crotch, he had gasped the admission that the Pyong-son monitoring equipment would take several days to arrive. She had left him then—just short of paradise—and called Il-Moon.

Il-Moon knew he was not needed at Pyong-son. There was for him now only that last—but not so little—preparation of the armored divisions. He would meet Architect Su at the forward positions along the DMZ and organize the armor withdrawal to treaty terms—while still maintaining his capability to strike the Enemy State to the South.

AIRBORNE LASER – ON APPROACH TO TOKYO

One of the most amazing experiences in the world, bar none, is to fly into Tokyo of an evening when a moon is rising over Mt Fuji. Slammer had altered their flight plan just to show everyone his favorite wonder.

Slammer dropped their altitude so they could clearly make out the mountain's staircase and Lorrie put it on the big screen. Everyone's breath caught at the beautiful dome of Fujiyama, the climbers struggling up the staircase under a glowing moon—grandmothers, babies, jogging athletes, apoplectic fathers towing children, whole school classes—all embroiled in one of the greatest summiting experiences of the world. Sean and Emily stood together at her window, the perfect white cone of Fuji turning slowly under them.

Just off their wing, against the waxing Harvest Festival Moon, Col Hareda's F-15 broke toward Iruma, the big Japan Air Self-Defense Force base in northwest Tokyo. He and his wingman waggled wings farewell.

"Strikeback, this is Ops," Sean said. "Send a message, 'Arigato, Colonel-san.'"

Soon Mt Fuji was replaced by the streamer of lights which is the bullet train route from Hiroshima to Tokyo, ending in the Milky Way of lights along Tokyo Bay. For once Sean, watching Emily, didn't have to wonder what she was thinking as she looked silently out her window at the sequined sea of lights below.

Sean called on the intercom, "Tech Area, this is Ops. Fire up everything, and let's take a look."

The crew looked at him like he was crazy, but buckled to it. Lorrie scanned the long-range video out across the whole of Japan. In the distance, at the limit of earth's curvature, the mountains of Korea rose spookily in dragon-backed shadows.

"Just wanted to check that it was there."

Slammer called, "And that concludes the entertainment portion of the flight. Please return to your seats and buckle your seatbelts for landing."

Airborne Laser had finally arrived on station.

KAESONG – DMZ – 820th TANK CORPS REVETMENTS

Architect Su was, oddly, closer to the DMZ than he'd been even in the Fatherland Liberation War, when as a young officer he'd been assigned to an engineering brigade in Pyongyang. Desperately, his unit had been trying to shore up the city's bombed infrastructure, until the Americans, in a final huge bombing raid, once and for all flattened the city, boasting that it would take a century to rebuild. The next day, Capt Su had found his elderly boss weeping over the damage reports. The previous week, after obliterating the country's irrigation system to starve them, the Americans had also destroyed their entire hydroelectric capability, wiping out 90% of North Korea's power grid. Su had stood waiting, waves of horror and fury washing over him, while his boss sobbed brokenly. Finally, the old boss wiped his tears and looked up at Su, still at attention and dry-eyed, awaiting his next tasking.

God, the boy is beautiful. I must not waste his obvious genius on my futile task.

Su's boss smiled at him and—over Su's strenuous demands to remain in the war—sent the young man abroad to study at China's premier National Architecture Academy.

Now, in his limo following the broad twin ribbons of concrete highway over the barren and deforested plain of southern North Korea—Su shared the road with only tourist buses headed to the pretty ancient capital city of Kaesong. Full of wonderful temples and artifacts, it was the jumping-off point for all tours to the North Korean side of the DMZ—as well as any armored invasion south. It was ironic, Su thought, remembering his old boss weeping, how the tourists now see Kim Il-Sung's big DMZ monument inscribed with how, on that very spot, the Americans had groveled and asked piteously for an armistice, bowing to the victorious forces of the DPRK. *Neither side learned anything in the war.* Su sighed.

The twin ribbons of freeway passed Kaesong, and all along the way, in every direction, there was an amazing density of military staging points, munitions depots, missile and artillery batteries, and legions of armed soldiers—almost all of whom were invisible.

Although North Korea is the most watched place on earth—every inch photographed every day by a swarm of satellite over-passes, hundreds of aircraft scans, radars slurpers, and SIGINT stations gathering every beep and squawk from the radios—they see little.

Amazingly, from the air, for a country which spends 20% of GDP on its military, it appears to be a not-very-military place. If you Google Earth the place, and have no INTEL imagery training, you will see little evidence that North Korea is armed to the teeth. (Although it is there, everywhere.)

Should you wander around the DPRK, there is also little evidence of its military footing. In Pyongyang or other big cities, you will see military uniforms. Here perhaps, there is an army unit working on the trolley rails, or there, painting a public building, but by and large, the soldiers who are visible are on leave, and none of them are armed. Even studying the photos and the people near the DMZ, there is much less of a military presence than in Washington D.C. The most prominent uniforms in Pyongyang are those of the striking Traffic Maidens, chosen for their beauty, who stand at important intersections directing the occasional car.

While North Korea to all appearances is not militarized, forwardly deployed within fifty miles of the DMZ sits 60% of the armed offensive forces of the Korean People's Armed Forces.

Nowhere is the truth more carefully hidden than in the armor revetments of the 820th Tank Corps. Although there are many mechanized corps, motorized tank brigades, and motorized infantry—each with their own armor—the 820th represented the vast majority of the newest armor in the KPA. Rather than being equipped with the older T-54/55 Soviet models, a high proportion of the Tank Corps were more modern T-62s and more than 1,400 heavy Chonma'ho DPRK variants. These are backed by mechanized infantry brigades, self-propelled artillery brigades, reconnaissance battalions, engineering and river-spanning regiments, transport, maintenance, and hospital support at the brigade level. To protect them from air attack, the revetments were enormously thick on top, and from a U-2, they looked like the tops of parking structures. Beneath them stretched an underground city of tens of miles of concrete tunnels, rooms, and disguised exit ramps.

Positioned within the dragon's lair of their revetments were the best-maintained armor, with sufficient fuel for invasion and months of war, and with multiple secret exits in case the main tunnels were bombed.

In addition, there was an extensive tunnel system leading under the DMZ.

Within the space of an hour, an entire division of infantry could be injected through these miles-long deep tunnels into the ROK. The purpose was less for combat—since their supply lines were hopeless—but rather, by dressing the division in South Korean uniforms, they could be videoed moving North over the DMZ, appearing to be South Korean troops attacking the DPRK. If the North Korean invasion were in response to a documented ROK attack, it would trigger the mutual protection treaty with China, and the Chinese would be obligated to help the DPRK militarily.

Architect Su, carrying his briefcase of war plans—which he never let out of his sight—came into a huge underground bunker, and saw Il-Moon working with the corps commander at the far end. He moved across the big space, passing lines of huge beast-like tanks. He found the intense blue underground lights glaring, stabbing his one eye. He was also limping, his left leg seemingly weaker than his right, while the terrifying half-body tingling was now spreading.

With Il-Moon and the corps' commander, Su managed to concentrate despite his increasing tingling, nausea, and anxiety. Il-Moon showed how they would keep the most agile and modern tanks, while sending the older useless ones north under the treaty terms for the spy satellites to see and count. As Il-Moon talked, in his head-aching brain, Su marveled at how sure Il-Moon seemed of the perfidy of the Americans. Perhaps, the attack at the Underwater Mansion had sharpened his senses—an assassination attempt can do that—but he had seen Il-Moon in the face of death many times, and knew for him it held little terror.

Il-Moon was waxing passionate about how to unleash the fake ROK troops to simulate a South Korean attack, and then sending his remaining armor on Seoul when the same troubling feeling came over Su again, a sense of sickness not his own. Su and Il-Moon had known each other for so many decades they were almost telepathic. Su could feel Il-Moon stiffen as if sensing his thoughts.

As Il-Moon turned grave eyes on Su, Su looked away and saw—to his horror—across the revetment, coming along the line of tank barrels as if entering under honorary crossed swords was a hurrying young man.

Su's heart thumped as he realized: it was his new grandson-in-law, approaching, carrying a file.

This was a grave disaster, for the young tyke hardly knew his own name, let alone that Col Kang's file was hardly something you handed to Architect Su in public—especially with Il-Moon present. Su cursed his carelessness in not specifying a solid procedure for the handover.

Su murmured apologies to Il-Moon, and limped away toward the boy, even as he felt Il-Moon's eyes boring into his back, even as his vision field began sparkling.

His whole left arm was tingling hard now. He forced himself to move nonchalantly to meet the boy. He switched his briefcase to his stronger right hand, but even that seemed weak and spastic.

Su spoke quickly to the boy, "You have come for me *here?*"

The boy looked so crushed, Su was almost sorry, "It is all right. Very well, you have a file for me?"

Aware of Il-Moon's intense gaze, Su opened Kang's file in a perfunctory way, and searched quickly through for the entry of the night Col Kang and Tam Ho were at the minisub facility together.

Nothing. Col Kang's arrival at Namp'o was there—but nothing of Tam Ho.

Architect Su felt a chill of fear. It was not possible that Ho had been unrecorded. A major in the Guard Command visiting a military facility— his watchers would record it, and thus so would Kang's. Most watchers had their watchers, and the penalty for falsifying a report was terrible: one's whole extended family was 'crossed-out' into prison camp—and the offending watcher was then burned at the stake.

The tingling in his arm ran up into his head, and the left side of his face felt numb and its eye was tearing. His tongue flicked madly inside his mouth. Still he could not stop looking at the file.

Kang's report showed he was only away from his unit for two weeks in the MPAF special wing for self-criticism—the two weeks a year every high-ranking officer spent in the isolation wing under lock and key. His watchers were dismissed while the officer was held incommunicado and severely tested for political reliability. *No meetings. No Tam Ho.*

It came to Su in a rush that someone very high up had interfered with this file.

His whole left side was numb now, and in shear terror he realized his left cheek was drooping, the flesh melting like hot wax off the bone beneath.

The boy was staring at him in horror, Su's sickness apparently appalling. Su vision field was telescoping now into a coruscating spider web of neon colors which glowed alarmingly.

Su glanced back. Il-Moon purposefully moved toward him, eyes on the file.

Clutching his briefcase across his chest in apparent agony, Su fell against the nearest tank. His vision was swimming as, reeling off the tank, he rolled along the armored beast and fell behind the tank away from Il-Moon.

Then the boy was leaning over him, begging to know what was wrong. Su managed to throw Kang's file into the big oil drip pan beneath the monster tank. The file sank under the oil. Su, with his best hand, pulled from his briefcase another file, pushed it into the boy's chest. "Hide..." was all he could manage.

Then Il-Moon was behind the boy, saying sympathetically, "Architect Su, you do not look at all well."

Il-Moon seemed to be growing giant until his nostrils alone were cavernous. In Su's vision field, the coruscating spider web of neon colors pulsated, and he could only whisper, "*My briefcase.*"

Il-Moon took the briefcase and file from Su's grandson-in-law. "I have it."

"*My file,*" Su rasped, his limbs now shivering uncontrollably in the grip of what he knew was a vicious mind-destroying stroke.

"There, there, Su-ssi," Il-Moon said silkily. "I will see your file is safe."

"Yes," the boy whispered, wide-eyed.

Architect Su slid into the neon spider-webbed darkness, and he knew no more.

Chapter 39

The 26th of October (Evening)

YAKOTA AB – OFFICER'S CLUB – HAPPY HOUR

Airborne Laser passed over gleaming downtown Tokyo and set down at the giant American Air Base at Yakota just in time for Friday night happy hour. Yakota would be their station where they would fuel the 747 and the laser for each long patrol over the Sea of Japan, always keeping their sensors off their beam and on Pyong-son.

Tomorrow the C-130's carrying their laser fuel and ground crew support would arrive, along with additional equipment for their 'atmospheric measurements campaign,' their White World cover story for their presence off Korea. Meantime Lorrie and the fun-loving crew pointed out it was Friday night in Tokyo, and they wanted to do some fooling around in the world-famous bars of Roppongi. Sean, however, needed them half-way sober and alert in the morning, while still blowing off some needed steam. He promised a few days in Tokyo after it was all over, asking if they would settle for happy hour at the O'Club. To his surprise, they seemed fine with it.

Auggie had three vans from the vehicle pool waiting. They ran everyone to their quarters at the VOQ to drop off luggage, then to the O'Club.

Passing the twin Japanese ceramic lions outside the long blue-roofed two-story building, the ABL crew trooped into a Friday happy hour at the Yakota O'Club. With the surrounding area of the base being somewhat low rent, functional, and poor; streets of small shops, bars, and services like laundry and uniform repair and hock shops, for many on the base the O'Club was the closest thing to home.

The entryway hall, full of memorabilia, framed pictures of athletic teams, and bulletin board notices gave way to a basketball-court-sized bar and dining area, with tables throughout. Everything was completely American, from the pictures-from-home cork boards, to the announcements of play-dates for the mothers, to the holiday festivities for upcoming Halloween, it was a warm and cheery enclave to those craving a little of home in a strange land.

The big bar and dining area was hopping already, and a banner announced 'Hot Dog Dressing Contest Tonight!' Already, big glass beer steins in hand, around the tables, teams were being jocularly formed up for the key event—with a prize of two-day passes, bragging rights, and dinner. Bozon and Slammer bought some pitchers of beer while Sean shoe-horned everyone in by some lieutenants who were hogging a big table near the stage, claiming to be holding it for some

VIO's—Very Important Officers. Sean deftly integrated them into the group, and they soon found common ground with Eila on rugby at the Academy and the difference in permanent and temporary deployment pay.

Slammer really wanted to sign the crew up for the Hot Dog contest: who could, in a period of five minutes, produce from the separate components at the hot dog bar, the largest number of completely bunned, condimented, and assembled hot dogs. Sean wasn't sure.

Sean took a moment to look over his team. Eila with her lieutenants, Lorrie sophisticatedly fending off a pass from a drunk officer hypnotized by her apparent flirtatious availability, Matt Cho writing a post card of the O'Club to his wife and kids, Emily seriously discussing the wine list with a waitress, and Jarhead tying one of the mess spoons into a knot on a bet with a table of Special Forces guys. To the ABL scientists, he knew the contest would be serious; a defeat or disgrace would eat at them. Superstition was at an intuitive level for them, and he didn't want them finally getting their last shot at a good night's sleep with a disgrace in their memories.

Sean suddenly laughed, and everyone looked at him. Although he often chuckled and smiled, it was rare he laughed. Slammer asked again, "What about it?" and Sean said, "They can do it. Go."

As Slammer went to sign them up, within ABL there immediately arose an argument about the strategy to win—as was similarly going on at tables around them—and who would be leader.

Finally, over Emily's objections, and with Bozon and Slammer eyeing the next table of tough-looking determined C-17 pilots and crew, and a similarly determined Base Procurement group farther on, they decided that this called for military discipline and leadership. Sean told Emily, "True leadership is letting someone else lead."

Emily said, "All right, I'll let you be god," and with Bozon and Slammer in charge, they assembled the team of Slammer, Bozon, Emily, Eila, Red, and Matt, while Lorrie, Jarhead, J-Stars, and Sean gave moral support.

The team, assembled, sat back to await the competition. The judges were a dutiful civilian lady from Contracting, a colonel from Logistics, and a Security Police Major. They stood, important and ready to judge, observing the contest as if it were a Unit Compliance Inspection.

The contracting lady judge, Ann Bullman, tapped the mike up front, where behind her the trays of goods were coming from the kitchen: the metal chafing pans of steaming hot dogs, softened buns lined up on a big tray, then the required elements: onions, chili, relish, catsup, and mustard in pots and squirt bottles—and a tray for the final products.

Ann Bullman, looking over her small reading glasses at her short list of contestants, announced over the PA: "Quiet please! The hot dog dressing contest is ready to begin. We have three teams that were deemed acceptable," This produced disappointed groans and shouting from the tables adjudged too tipsy to compete. "The first team is 'The Base Procurers.'" More groans and moans at the lousy pun, and calls of "Those wimps!"

The strategy of each team was rapidly revealed: the Procurement people, predictably, lined up and when the starting whistle sounded each grabbed a dog, stuffed it in a bun, and went to add the chili and relish. It was a childish strategy, for although the buns and hot dogs were on a long tray and easy to get to, the relishes were not so easy to share.

The room filled with catcalls and shouting; beer was sloshed and the whole happy hour was yelling advice and mocking the poor procurement people. Of course, they didn't have the benefit of going later, and so they suffered the most pseudo-denigration.

The Procurement team bogged down in a mess of fighting over the chili and when the whistle sounded, out of a possible one hundred hot dogs, there were by careful count of the Security Police Major—although very beautifully done—only twenty-seven completely-dressed dogs.

The room filled with catcalls and shouting, 'Twenty-seven-percenters!" while the Procurers' pathetic effort was cleared away and the hot dog supplies replenished. Ann Bullman made the mike squeal and brought the audience to heel. "Very good, Procurers," she said meticulously, "and now we have The Globemasters."

The C-17 group, adapting to the previous abysmal failure, put their big beers aside—for this was deadly serious business—and their heads together. They crouched at the figurative starting line and waited for the whistle.

This time it was an assembly line: working as a team, at one end of the line, a hot dog was slapped into a bun and passed to the next worker, who plastered on the onion and passed it along. The Logistics colonel nodded approval, noting sagely how they interacted like a well-oiled mechanism. And indeed, from working together on the flightdeck in a huge aircraft, they knew one another totally. No sooner was a bun filled with a dog then it was snapped down the line into a waiting hand which slapped on onion, chili, or the next product.

The din of the room was so loud that the colonel counting the hotdogs had to do it twice. He looked up, smiling, and announced, although no one could hear, "Seventy-two!" to much clapping and sloshing of drinks.

Emily sipped her wine and raised her eyes to the ceiling. Sean asked, "What?"
"How will we ever top them?"
"Are you kidding me? How could we lose?" Sean huddled the team, and as

he whispered the outline of a strategy, in their circle, arms intertwined, the ABL tech crew picked up the thread, added a suggestion or improvement, and tossed it along until together they'd worked out a smashing approach.

Bozon, Slammer, Eila, Red, and Matt—carrying their drinks and even imbibing along the way—dragged Emily along up to the stage.

Ann Bullman, who looked slightly flustered at this strange group who seemed so relaxed, quaffing beers right up to the contest, called to the room, "The final team is Airborne Laser," to which the audience howled, "Back back-seaters!" and "Science weenies dressing wienies—give us a break!"

Emily lined everyone up on stage, while Bozon sloshed down some beer, and when the whistle sounded, he took the time to leap high, kick his heals together and drink at the same time. He landed, and stood back as Slammer picked up the whole tray of hot dogs and *slammed* it upside down right onto the bun tray. Eila and Red jumped in and started beating on the dogs like they were bongos, squashing and poking the sausages down into the buns while Slammer—his part being done—stood aside, took his drink and solemnly toasted his teammates.

The room went wild with surprise and respect for this audacious strategy. The previously derogatory catcalls fell away, replaced by a few whistles of delight spiced with some 'Aw, is that fair?' whining.

Matt tossed the full tray of cut onions up into the air so they came raining down all over the tray of bunned dogs. Eila pulled her hands away just in time as Emily sloshed the entire scalding chili bucket swoosh over the horrendously messy tray of higgledy-piggledy dogs.

Bozon and Slammer, sucking on their beers, and elbows locked, then did an Irish jig behind the still working team. Red and Eila jumped to the fore, catsup and mustard squirt bottles in each hand and glooshed the entire tray in red and yellow stripes.

The Airborne Laser team, completely done with a minute still to go—clearly going for style points—calmly took up their drinks and toasted the room, "To the mess"! and drank.

Calls resounded in the room to "Disqualify the bums!" and "Don't let the science wieners win all unfair!"

Ann Bullman, whose turn it was to be lead judge, was wavering on the disqualification, and just in time, Lorrie slipped up to her, whispering intently, no longer the flirt but the sincere clear-blued-eyed mother-of-two saying to Ann 'let's play fair,' and Lorrie's honest pitch got through. Ann waved down the protestors.

Working with the major and colonel, using plastic gloves, she dug through the geological complexity of the higgledy-piggledy hot dog piles, carefully counting and occasionally consulting with the other judges about whether a particular dog was only partially in a bun or improperly relished—while the room called unneeded and impudent advice and the other teams stood and howled, geeing up audience support.

It was going to be a close thing, Sean could tell. He didn't mind losing on a technicality as long as they really won—and he knew the tech crew had already shown they were the best, so losing was OK...

Finally, Ann Bullman finished the counting, consulted her fellow judges and went to the mike. "After a careful review, we have, with eighty-one completed hot dogs—the winner (and the best in the mess) Airborne Laser!"

The ABL table went crazy, and the team was photoed for the O'Club bulletin board, the colonel handed out the two-day passes, and picked up their table's tab.

The passes were, reflected Sean, pointless since ABL was on station from now on, but in the whooping and laughing of the crew as their vans motored them to their quarters, there was something contented instead of the usual tension. It was nice, Sean reflected, for all the secret unheralded and unrewarded work they would do for the next weeks, that they could for a moment in public be winners.

Sean heard a scratching at the connecting door to Emily's room. When he opened his door, hers stood ajar. She was sitting up in bed, throat and shoulders bare except for a hanging silky sheaf of hair, her bedclothes up to just over her breasts. He assured himself she must be wearing bra and panties, but the visual effect of the bare shoulders and held-up blankets was that Emily seemed startlingly nude.

Emily asked, "What is it?"

"I thought you knocked."

"You must have imagined it," although the door on her side stood open. Her gray eyes were mother-of-pearl in the low light. "We were the best team tonight, weren't we?"

"Even better than the C-17 crew, and they are some talented people."

She stretched up her arms and the blanket almost fell away, and settled the question of what she wore, but she snuggled down and from under the covers mumbled. "Since you're here, may I say something?"

"I have a habit of always letting people say whatever they like."

"What you did for the crew? It's nice when someone brings out the best in you."

"It's nice when there's a best to bring out."

"Goodnight, Sean. Would you mind leaving the door open a little?"

"Sure. Sleep well, Emily."

GREAT LEADER'S FRAGRANT MOUNTAINS RETREAT

The air smelled bitter and cool through his violated nostrils, and Architect Su knew a nose tube had been in for some time. Then the smell of fresh piney woods rushed into him. *I know that fragrance.* He opened his rheumy eyes to see familiar craggy-faced peaks. He knew—although he could not move his paralyzed head to look around—he was in the Myohyang Mountain retreat of the Great Leader, the place where both he and his son had fallen fatally ill, and passed on their crowns.

Had not Dearest Leader told him he was going to the fresh air and light of Myohyang to read the final treaty draft from Il-Moon and Hakkermann? Su found he could swivel his eyeballs, saw Dearest Leader. Not reading the treaty, but rather sitting on a bamboo mat, overlooking the autumn green-gold of the 'Fragrant' mountains outside—and painting. Su groaned, and Dearest Leader put down his ink brush and came to him. "How are you feeling, Sussi? We have been worried. Marshal Il-Moon has called every hour, asking after you. He says he has your briefcase, and all is well. Come sit up. I will ring for tea."

"I cannot move."

Dearest Leader laughed. "Of course you can."

"The stroke..."

"Oh, not a stroke. The doctors say it was exhaustion. You have been pushing very hard."

"My hand. My face. Tingling. I saw my eyes going."

"Yes, a serious stress migraine. Its symptoms are similar to stroke, as the blood vessels constrict, or so the doctors told me."

Su found he could indeed move his legs, and with a sprite of joy, rose quickly—and almost fell over. He was weak and shaky; but good! "That explains it."

"It does not, Architect Su, explain much. You requested a copy of Kang's file from me," Dearest Leader indicated a file on a table nearby. "The boy told me you destroyed your copy—and swore him to secrecy."

"Good boy! How is he?"

"He is very young, and quite excitable, but kept your secret." Dearest

Leader touched the file. "He was beaten rather severely, but he will be fine. Il-Moon's men felt he was insufficiently respectful in demanding doctors for you, and taught him a lesson. And now you must explain to me the file's significance—as I find nothing in it."

Architect Su considered his reply as he limped to the window. Immense gratitude surged at his old creaks and aches; more so, as he took in from outside the beginning of the glory of a Korean fall. Even the evergreens were muted, preparing for the slumbering of the land to replenish it for the coming year; a year certain to be eventful and perhaps fateful. "Kang's movements. The report says he has done nothing outside his unit for the two months previous to the mansion attack. His watchers were everywhere with him except during his MPAF self-criticism stint—and there he was isolated."

Dearest Leader nodded. "No conspirator meetings. That is logical. They must have planned months before that."

Su pursed his lips in not complete agreement. "What is vital in the file is what is left out," explaining how Tam Ho and Kang crossed paths at Namp'o harbor just hours before Mansion 27's destruction. "There should be a cross-reference to Ho in Kang's file. There is only the notation of Kang at the harbor. None for Tam Ho—yet I know he was there."

"I see." Meaning, *if Watchers are corrupted, the conspiracy must go very high up*. Dearest Leader joined Su at the window. "Hakkermann has requested a private meeting again. Without Il-Moon."

"That would be difficult to arrange." ...*Should Il-Moon find out...*

It was left unsaid how dangerous that could be. Il-Moon commanded many loyal friends throughout the army and Guard Command; powerful allies should he feel something threatening was going on behind his back.

A blue bird with a red throat and white belly breathlessly flying took refuge—perhaps from a fox or other threat—and alighted on the windowsill just before them. Neither spoke, not wishing the bird to startle. But a distant rumble of thunder grated through the air and the bird, as if pushed to the limit of endurance, barely managed to trundle into the air, gliding across the open field in front of the house and into the cover of the dense pines. "Perhaps it would be wise to take some precautions."

Dearest Leader looked at him sharply, and for a moment, their eyes met. "What are you saying, First Chief State Architect Su?"

"Tam Ho was under secondment to your Guard Command. He is also somehow involved in suborning Watchers." *The conspirators are likely right beside you*. Su let this sink in, then asked softly, "As we are entering a time of both glorious potential and some uncertainty, perhaps we should make alternate plans for your own security. Is there an army unit whom you could completely trust?"

Dearest Leader pondered, laughed suddenly, remembering a frank peasant face. "Yes, I do believe there *is* a unit that answers that description."

FARMERS' MILITIA BATTALION – SONGTON-RI VILLAGE

The hard knocking woke Company Leader Tong-Hu of the Workers' and Farmers' Red Guard Militia, who was sleeping soundly in his small house.

In North Korea, the night's sleep was a chance to dream of happiness—that thing so illusive in waking. The vast collective dreamscape of North Korea was almost entirely populated by dreams of *food*. Juice, tasty, nourishing, sweet, ricey, wonderful *food*—just as the collective waking experience of North Korea was the glorious banquet right under your nose evaporating—leaving you desolate *and* hungry.

Tong-Hu however, was sunk deep in a Vinalon dream. The pillowcases were Vinalon, the sheets, the curtains, the quilt; it was a Vinalon diorama. He *believed* in Vinalon. The fabric was their broadcloth, their national clothing. It was the perfect *Juche* material: a locally made product using only limestone and coal, indigenous resources which North Korea had in abundance—along with the slave labor to mine them economically. The strange part was how much they loved it, given how poorly the material worked. It was a kind of nylon which was neither as comfortable as cotton nor as pleasant as rayon, wore out more rapidly than either, shrank like crazy if washed too frequently, and was not produced outside of the DPRK. But at least it was *their* material.

In Tong-Hu's home, it was Vinalon or nothing, except for his shoes, which were canvas.

Tong-Hu woke to the knocking with dread. In the night, all North Koreans feared the knock on the door. It could only be the State Security Department arriving for the family's one-way trip to the work camp, or the call to arms for the war against the long-expected American invasion. He lay worrying until his wife, under the Vinalon quilt with him, bumped a hip into him and whispered. "The door!"

At the door, he found Chang-Gun, his finest friend, who was visibly excited. Tong-Hu asked, "Is it war?"

Chang-Gun could barely contain himself. "No. You will never imagine. The whole battalion has been mobilized by Dearest Leader to come to Pyongyang!"

"Pyongyang?" The word had more than a mystical meaning for them.

They had never been to Pyongyang. Travel there was not permitted, although it was only one hundred kilometers away. "Dearest Leader?"

Chang-Gun struggled to speak. Tong-Hu worried the excitement might overcome the man and he would collapse in his dooryard. "I will tell you something marvelous! Dearest Leader asked for you by name!"

Now it was Tong-Hu who almost swooned. His stomach flipped and his legs jellied. *Dearest Leader asked for me?* He remembered the man well, his energy, his Solomon-like countenance. "No. It is not possible."

"But it is! It is! He said, 'Lee Tong-Hu is to be Special Executive to the Battalion Commander!'" He turned, pointing to the men scurrying down the village's single street. "We have only ten minutes to assemble. We will talk on the way to Pyongyang."

Pyongyang. The glory of Koguryo, of Korea—Dearest Leader and Pyongyang!

Tong-Hu threw a few meager possessions together while his wife brought him bark tea to drink while she deftly packed crisped oat groats and the last egg. At the door, they lingered for a long moment.

North Koreans had lived with war hanging over them as if beneath some giant beetling glacier. They had felt the tremors before—when the Great Leader had died, in the constant mobilizations, when the *Pueblo* attacked them. Then, with the strange radio interview of Dearest Leader saying all North Koreans must endure and try to prosper in a difficult future, it was almost with relief something seemed to be breaking free.

"Wait." His wife stooped at the fireplace, warily glanced around, wiggled free a loose mud brick.

Tong-Hu stood patiently as she pulled a small crucifix chain from a hollow in the brick. She slipped the chain around his neck, and secreted the cross beneath his undershirt. She hugged him and whispered in his ear, "God and Jesus and the Great Leader watch over you. I will pray for you." He held her. Then it seemed the little hut was falling away, shrinking to only her, a warm nugget of heart left between shabby walls and swept mud floor.

He ran for the waiting trucks.

ABL – ON PATROL OVER THE EAST SEA

Airborne Laser (X) floated lumberingly, her big engines working hard, for although the simple trade winds were light out over the silvery moonlit blue-black Sea of Japan, the ship was loaded to the gunwales.

Laser fuel, chow, munitions, Jet-A, and the crew and their kit right down to their teddy bears, Sean had loaded every supply Chief Auggie had transported, borrowed, or scrounged. Bozon remarked, "Biggest lift-off weight of a 747 I've ever heard of," when he and Slammer took ABL off from Yakota at 909,000 pounds. Over the Comm, Slammer was joking—but freaked the crew anyway—when he added, "Ops, Flightdeck here. Thanks for taking the crew off the manifest before we calculated our weight for the forms. Otherwise, they never would've let us fly."

Pursuant to his orders, Sean kept ABL in international airspace, although in the darkness out the window, as though on a satellite photo, he could see the brilliantly lit cityscapes and freeways of South Korea against the shadowy outline of the completely dark North.

Sean set a racetrack operations course. Following the edge of Korean airspace, nonchalantly keeping as close to Pyong-son as he could, he anchored his southern point at South Korea's tiny Ullung-do Island. They then flew the racetrack loop north toward Russia, always keeping Pyong-son off ABL's beam.

Sean paced the Tech Area all night, unable to relax. At dawn, Lorrie put the Kaesong-Munsan invasion corridor into the long-range video, found the blue and white buildings of Panmunjom, and at a sharp look from Sean, was careful to avoid Camp Casey where her boys were just a mouse click away. She instead moved the image slowly over the pleasant terrain along the north edge of the DMZ. With its fall colors and rolling irregular hills, it seemed to be, as J-Stars remarked, "A lot like West Virginia."

Lorrie ran the long-range video over the Korean People's Army main armor bunkers and fort line scattered just above the DMZ. Like army ants on the move, from the giant concrete bunkers, lines of battered North Korean armor moved out in a cloud of filthy dust and diesel, following the few suitable roads as they crawled north.

"North Korean armor and mechanized forces in columns on the move." Lorrie then turned the long-range video on Osan airbase. It was a sea of moving aircraft and withdrawing forces. In all his years, Sean had never seen it so busy. "That goes for the 7th AF as well."

Sean shook his head in frustration. With Osan emptied, the DMZ would be essentially unguarded—other air assets were too far to use in the initial hours— and the missile launching sites under Pyong-son nagged at his mind.

At the shift change, J-Stars reported. "We've scanned continuously. Nothing. Looks like North Korean armor is withdrawing per the treaty timetable requirements."

*   *   *

Chapter 41

The 28th of October (Morning)

MINISTRY OF PEOPLE'S ARMED FORCES – PYONGYANG

On the following morning, Architect Su entered the MPAF for the last time.

He met with the National Defense Committee and Dearest Leader in the same subterranean room so far beneath the autumn sunlight. Had it only been a month ago, when they had met here and requested Architect Su's wisdom on approaching their difficult task?

Now it was a time of uncertainty, good-bye for the next few days or maybe longer, as they disbursed to their stations to await the peace treaty signing. This was the time, Il-Moon assured them, the Americans would take advantage of the withdrawal of the North Korean armor for invasion and humiliation.

Architect Su studied the men around the table. In the Confucian way, they had aged as a cohort, sharing a past of triumphs and miseries, advancing in their positions together. Flashing past in his mind's eye—and he imagined in theirs as well—were images of the wars, the bombings, privations, death, and crushing workloads. Could it be he and his friends had finally brought Korea together? Was this not an amazing accomplishment, given that their dreams, their call to heroism and service, had been born in the chatter of mere brainless boys? Of course, Su reflected, they had remained boys, perhaps—resisting until this remarkable young leader had been given to them by Heaven.

There was little discussion, a kind of feverish quiet, as Dearest Leader announced a few final details, and passed out pre-peace treaty payouts amounting to billions of dollars in property, position, and amnesty. For these Party and Army officials, in the smaller combined Armed Forces of Koryo, they would not have the same power—but they would be rich in the new world, still major leaders in politics and in Korea—and it seemed enough for them.

Dearest Leader finally spoke. "As agreed, First Vice Chairman Il-Moon will withdraw to Pyong-son complex and direct any defensive moves from there. The KPA leadership likewise, in this difficult and treacherous time, will be at their posts with their defensive postures at the highest alert. The Air Force, Navy, Special Forces, SCUD facilities, Missile Divisions will be in position as well."

Il-Moon added heavily, "Never, as the Dearest Leader has said, have we been so close. And yet, we are also at our most vulnerable as well. Let us stay on the ramparts until the treaty is signed, ready for the moment of treachery should it come."

Dearest Leader put aside his glasses for a moment, rubbing his eyes. Even he felt the pressure, the exhaustion of the sheer magnitude of what they had all accomplished in the past few weeks. "I will remain here at the Magnolia Palace with Architect Su. When Counselor General Li has assured me by satellite telephone that the treaty is in order and Osan is emptied, we will all meet at Freedom Village for the signing."

He stood, and indicated everyone to rise. His spry portly frame seemed almost to burst with vigor. "Within a few days—and on our terms—Korea will again be one. In two days, after millennia, *Tangun* is returned!"

The room erupted in "Korea is One!"

Il-Moon for once seemed satisfied, and the generals all hurried away, for there were only a few feverish hours left for military preparations, and—along with checking their new bank accounts on-line—they were going to be a busy bunch of gentlemen.

Chapter 42

The 28th of October (Afternoon)

NAMP'O HARBOR – MANGYONGBONG-92

Because this was such a crucial operation, Architect Su, despite his sickness, had personally traveled the hour from Pyongyang to Namp'o harbor.

He stood on a jetty under the blast shelter at the minisubmarine base. He could see, moored a mile out in the commercial area of the harbor, the small tramp ocean liner Mangyongbong-92. Its refurbishment complete, it was freshly painted if still slightly battered-looking. It had been loading all day, preparing to resume its brown-water coastal ferrying from Wonsan on eastern Korea, to Niigata on the western coast of Japan.

On its way back to its home port, if required for war, it would release his cargo.

At the jetty, Su watched the Special Forces minisubmarines loading their munitions and crews before submerging for the secret runs out to the little ocean liner.

Beneath the Mangyongbong-92's waterline, green water sucked in and out of a hatch-like entry point. Into this elephant-sized hole would creep the North Korean Aim-2 minisubs. The entire system had been conceived and built for the use of the Special Forces. During offensive operations, the minisubs could be transported stealthily along the littoral waters of Korea. Dropping from the mother ship, the crews could enter river estuaries, or gain the sandy beaches and harbors of South Korea. The Combatant team of three, the captain and two specialists, would then move quickly to strike their objective: shipping, power plants, communications towers, police stations, hospitals, road infrastructure, chemical plants, or the assassination of local authorities and emergency personnel.

The technical crews worked to attach under the next minisub a tire-shaped limpet mine, a large disk of explosives meant to stick to a ship's hull and blast a hole through it. The captains of the minisubs alone knew the mission. Their excitement was palpable, the joy of combat soon joined. Although their chances of interception were great, the mission difficult, and it had not been possible to train thoroughly, every crew member was ready to show their love for Dearest Leader. It was succeed or die; succeed and die.

Su shook his head sadly. Every generation went into war without the benefit of the experience of the previous foolish youngsters. He himself—as much as he hated the Americans in general for their genocidal bombing campaigns of the Korean war, for strangling his poor orphaned economy, and for throwing in his face his own system's shortcomings—had no hatred for individual Americans. He took no joy in either the deaths to come, or his brilliant war architecture. His war stomach had been soured long ago.

Su turned away from the happy excited soldiers. Again, out in the harbor he could picture his Underwater Mansion, now just a drowned broken tooth. It still held fast to its secrets. *What happened there? Given his record, how did Kang manage to fail? Why can I not find Tam Ho?*

Within the hour, the minisubs finished loading. Su watched the Mangyongbong-92's props churn the water as she cleared the twisted muddy channels of the Taedong estuary and its giant tidal barrage, and moved out into the Yellow Sea. The rich darkened waters of the sea, fertilized by constant dust from the Gobi desert, seemed to cradle the sad if freshly-painted little ocean liner.

The Mangyongbong-92, stacks roiling smoke, set her course for the strait between Korea and Japan, and steamed south toward the horizon.

Chapter 43

The 28th of October (Evening)

PYONG-SON COMPLEX

Il-Moon immediately broke the terms of the treaty: he entered Pyong-son complex without notifying anyone outside of North Korea.

Deep underground, below three hundred meters of rock, was where Il-Moon meant to direct his operations. From this point, deeply-buried as well, cables went out, linking his Intranet to thousands of bunkers, air fields, launching sites, and KPA bases from the DMZ, to Pyongyang, to the farthest-flung assets of the DPRK armed forces.

To avoid being observed in treaty violation, his motorcade had stopped at a village miles from Pyong-son, and here he boarded an underground train. As with many North Korean leader-bunkers, underground trains were both the secure entrance and the escape route. This one tunneled for more than ten miles before ending in the heart of the Pyong-son missile launching complex.

With just a small group of Guard Command, Il-Moon alighted under Pyong-son to see the video display of his six big missiles already reconstituted in their firing chambers. The technicians were working frantically on Taepo-Dong Number 1's warhead.

The Chief Launch Officer came scurrying up, bowing, and begging him to inspect the missiles. Although the coiled cabling, fuel lines, and test equipment made the place extremely messy and congested, from the glassed-in and blast-proof control room, Il-Moon knew he would watch it on video all come together. The Launch Officer took him into Taepo-Dong Missile Number 1's chamber, where the technicians stood back to let Il-Moon inspect the warhead being filled with featherweight titanium ball bearings.

Il-Moon grunted, let them return to work, pausing at the main bunker to look with pleasure across his old creation. The underground tank factory was almost completely disassembled, and workers with blow torches, giant wrenches, and sledge hammers were knocking down the few pieces left of the T-62 assembly line. *It has served its purpose. Still, it was something when we built it.*

Aide Park finished whispering urgently with a young officer, and came to Il-Moon. "Great Vice Chairman, you asked for notice of any new aircraft. We have indeed spotted one."

Il-Moon turned. "What is it?"

"Our surveillance radar experts say it is a routine American Big Crow ELINT mission over the East Sea near Ullung-do Island. It is also pinging us with its radar."

Il-Moon said sarcastically, "Big Crow is at Kirtland Air Force Base, and does not use radar. Did these geniuses get a picture?"

Aide Park conferred with the radar officers, who talked intensely among themselves, and raced away looking frightened. Aide Park asked almost in a whisper, "Might this be the Bastard American Airborne Laser? Must we not worry how they might affect your great plan?"

Il-Moon summoned the Chief Operations Officer, "Fueling must be complete by the 30th at noon. There will be an inspection with Dearest Leader. You do not wish to disappoint him."

"Yes, Sir!" although the Officer's eyes held worry.

"Speak."

"The more caustic fuel must usually wait until twenty-four hours before launch. Sooner, the caustic fuel can cause leaking. Also, we are first accounting for all foreign sensors, so that the fueling operation will be secure from detection."

Il-Moon stepped close to the Operations officer. "You have the non-caustics. Commence fueling on missiles one and two."

The Operations man, surprised, was about to query the Marshal, but in the man's eyes he saw no hint of doubt.

"Yes, Marshall Song Il-Moon, Sir!"

AIRBORNE LASER

Outside Emily's window, Sean could see Korea now in the afternoon sunlight, its forests thick, its farmland rich, its mountains misty. From this altitude, the whole of the peninsula lay, from the deep and blue Sea of Japan or East Sea below, to the rich shallow waters on the far side of the West or Yellow Sea. The Korea Strait, where Japan and Korea almost touched, was dotted with islands, seeming stepping stones, inviting a game of giant hopscotch between the ancient troubled neighbors.

In the Tech Area—and through all of Airborne Laser—the crew worked hard at their consoles. Key to the watching work were J-Stars' big Doppler radars, snooping for any ground motion at Pyong-son, while Jarhead's INTEL suite monitored radio and radar activity.

The others worked the infrared sensors (missile launch signatures),

Communications (watching Pyong-son visually, keeping an eye on CNN and putting it up on the big screen when a newscast broke, talking to nearby military traffic), and Ops (everything else).

Sean looked over the handwritten logs of his watchers. Nothing in hyperspectral, IR, video, or radar. Under SIGINT, it was dead quiet. No vehicles had entered or left or even moved at Pyong-son.

Sean looked over to Jarhead, who looked up from his console and shook his head.

He went to where Emily was pecking at her keyboard. Despite the Sharpie marks on her face, and her unwashed hair piled up in a mess, she was looking beautiful.

Emily studied him. "You look like you need a hug," and she stood and opened her arms.

As Sean's face came close to her upturned one, he brushed his lips to hers.

Emily turned from his kiss smugly. "Hugs are OK, kisses aren't."

Sean pushed aside the madness coming over him; the toll of living in combat-and-lust, and brusquely turned to business. "You're sure nothing funny is going on at Pyong-son? Will Red's chemical remote sensing scans tell us if they start to fuel?"

"Theoretically, sure. Except we're not doing them."

"They could be doing anything and we're sitting right here! We need to be looking at them with every possible sensor!"

"Sean, I don't just *think* it's not smart lasing into North Korea, I *know* it. We're on anti-missile patrol, not INTEL collection. We are supposed to keep secret, and lasing them is crazy. I've flown science missions here before. Not only do they have laser sensors over there, they constantly lased us as well."

"Those are targeting lasers plinking you for fun. The UV stuff you have, and the higher wavelengths, they wouldn't be on top of that."

"I wouldn't be so sure," Emily said, although her voice wasn't as confident. "We hold the laser in reserve. Besides, we're pretty far out to see anything," and she wouldn't budge.

"So, we're going to sit here not knowing what they are doing over there?"

"Oh, we know what they're doing," Emily said, and pointed to a saw-tooth signal on ABL's radar slurper, taking in everything going on at radio frequencies from UHF to millimeter wave. "There, a big X-band radar—the only one active in North Korea at the moment. They're watching us closely—and you'll be happy to know the signal comes out of Pyong-son."

Sean sat back, took a deep breath. *Il-Moon you bastard. I know it's you. Marquis of Queensbury rules this time...and I am going to catch you out.*

PYONG-SON COMPLEX

Il-Moon waited calmly, angry face glaring. Aide Park privately handed him a photo of ABL over the East Sea, remarking, "Bastard Airborne Laser!"

"Has the plane changed course?"

"No, Sir. They show no reaction to our fueling." Aide Park came to his shoulder. "Can we not formally object to Hakkermann?"

"They would only deny the plane was a laser plane—and lie about their ability to shoot down missiles. We would have no proof of its traitorous capabilities. They would just say it was a science plane—and it would skulk off to hide under a slimy rock somewhere. No, we must destroy them...."

"With our anti-aircraft missiles?"

Il-Moon smiled, thinking what a pleasure that would be, but he had contemplated this very option since Abbey first showed him a picture with Sean in front of ABL. "No. We will wait. In every American airbase in Japan, I have activated our deep cover Special Forces operatives. Armed with RPG's and explosives, they are employed on the air bases and can get within a hundred yards of any plane on the flight line. Let me know when the Bastard Laser Plane leaves patrol."

Il-Moon stood and stretched stiffly, needing a shot of dirt. "They cannot remain up for long. Soon they must return to Yakota to refuel and re-supply. Then, we will destroy them on the ground."

ARCHITECT SU'S APARTMENT – KIM Il-SUNG SQUARE

Architect Su suffered from both lack of sleep and insomnia. He did not mind, usually, insomnia being a vital part of success in the upper echelons of North Korea. First you needed to be ready at all hours for the test emergency calls from the Leader. Second, with only a small number of persons sharing the chairing of so many committees—he himself was on at least thirty—the workload was intense. You needed the extra night hours to head off colleagues jockeying for your coveted positions.

Although he was still feeling sickly from the massive migraine, and Dearest Leader had taken his war tasks away for the moment, impounding Su's precious briefcase so he couldn't continue to work, Su did not feel like sleep.

Since he couldn't work, he spent the night surfing the net. He had complete access to the web, and took great pleasure in keeping up with the brilliant successes on the world stage of Koreans (albeit mostly from South Korea or America).

The most delicious pleasure was following a young Korean golfing phenomena, giggling at how a Korean teenage girl, even if she were an American, could whip the pants off almost every white golfer. He himself, secretly, harbored a love of golf although he'd never picked up a club. It was a strange attractor, the curving greens and lumpy obstacles, and part of him believed that fate—if it continued to bless him—would, before he died, let him design and build at least one golf course!

Having checked up on the progress of Koreans in sports, the news, and science, all places they excelled in the world far out of proportion to their tiny population, he wistfully turned from golf, and surfed some architectural sites, looking in wonder and enjoyment—and envy—at some the marvelous habitations, edifices, bridges, and ports going up around the world.

He stopped, lingering on a new condo being built in Las Vegas. Amazing! Spires and rooftop Jacuzzis and floor-to-ceiling glass. He stared in fascination at an ad in which a gorgeous partially-clothed woman—Korean!—talked on an elegant cell phone while looking mistily through the windows of her condo to the flame burst of a distant sunset. Her form was amazing, that of an American-born Korean; athletic, confident; she was far more statuesque than the flower of North Korean womanhood. In her long-fingered hands, high breast, and smoldering gaze was the promise of immortality, anchored by the spires of her sapphire condo.

Ah, it would be something to build one of those!

He looked out across the vast Kim Il-Sung square, the biggest in Pyongyang, and at his most important buildings such as the Workers' Hall where his granddaughter had been wed. In the waxing almost full moon, the spotlights lit the statue of the Great Leader, his huge bronze hand benevolently thrown wide, showing the way forward to the masses. Architect Su missed the Great Leader, and although they hadn't agreed on architecture, he wondered how the Great Leader would handle the world of today. It was a bigger question than mere history, for within days of announcing major changes in the DPRK and agreeing to several new treaties, the Great Leader had died under unclear circumstances, some said at the hand of his own son Jong-Il.

It was now all water under the Taedong River bridge, and Su sighed as he realized sleep still eluded him.

He chose a new Internet site and for an hour, Su played games against a young boy, Peter, in Tucson, Arizona who was only twelve, but had built a 'Tiny People City Site' that impressed Su greatly.

As Su played against the boy, he was amused—although also disturbed—that about a quarter of the time, the youngster with his many hours of experience in computer games—despite Su's age, experience, and genius IQ—beat him.

Su was finally getting deliciously sleepy and after his last loss, laughed ruefully as the boy had typed in the chat window, "Please don't take this like *criticism...*"

Su suddenly bolted awake. In a flash, he realized the boy had handed him the key to finding Maj Tam Ho.

Chapter 44

AIRBORNE LASER – ON PATROL

Unbeknownst to Il-Moon, Sean had no intention of returning to Yakota until the treaty was safely in the bag. For three days, Airborne Laser had lain hard on patrol over the East Sea—and now the crew was tired, irritable, and the Tech Area smelled like a gorilla cage.

By dawn on the 30th of October, T-18 hours to midnight and the draft treaty acceptance, Airborne Laser had been on patrol continuously for almost seventy hours. The endless racetrack patrol with its straight run followed by a gentle bank and repeat, was driving everyone *insane*. As J-Stars remarked, "I can't do anything I *like* for seventy hours."

Slammer had pressed into service an extra flightdeck crew—the C-17 pilots they'd beaten in the hotdog contest. Staying up for the week—until the treaty was signed and the physical confirmation of huge reductions in armor and artillery at the DMZ was actually confirmed by inspection teams—was a momentous task.

Every twelve hours or so, a giant KC-135 tanker from either Misawa in northern Honshu, or Pusan Air Base in southern Korea would fly out, and everyone would buckle up for the rockin' and rollin' of a midair refueling.

Once, Chief Auggie, hitching a ride on a tanker, called over to Sean, "How are you doing, Sir?"

When Sean just mumbled, Auggie said sympathetically, "One day at a time, Sir."

The first shift established the pattern. Slammer and Bozon drove the bus for eight hours, with a first crew of Lorrie, Red, J-Stars, and Eila; with Emily as Ops. The crew then rotated to Sean, Jarhead, Matt Cho, and Lorrie, whom no one could get to quit, while the C-17 flight crew relieved Slammer and Bozon. The off-duty crew hit the galley to chow down, sleep, watch TV, or join the nonstop poker game. Sean relaxed the rules on video games, but not food in any tech area.

Everything zapped Sean's nerves, and he allowed himself only catnaps. He was hot-swapping his bunk with Emily, and when he lay down in the bed still warm from her sleeping body, the perfume of her would linger, and he always fell asleep depressed and agitated. It was beyond him to imagine that Emily shared, in the scents and heat of their bunk, exactly the same sensations; and with them the longing search for an answer that eluded; an answer to a question seemingly posed in a language neither could interpret.

It was little better when he stayed awake with her, watching her program or blearily study reams of data flying into their sensors and across their computer screens. Sean checked on everyone as infrequently as he could, but always, finally had to ask, "You sure there's nothing?"

Lorrie replied, somewhat bitchily following an argument with Red, "Nothing."

Sean said, "It's like they've hidden everything. No traces of even normal activity."

"Like my kids," Lorrie said. "Too quiet is worse than quiet."

"Yes. It's too quiet."

Emily said, "That will look good in the report: we found nothing, so they must be hiding something."

On the big screen, besides watching Pyong-son, Lorrie always kept up CNN. Whenever Abbey Yamamoto came on, she was graced with full raspberries throughout the plane. Sean and Jarhead had long ago concluded that she was somehow a conduit for both Il-Moon and Harold, her actions fueled by her own megalomania and need for glory.

When next she came on, Abbey was wearing a new outfit, silky-black hair carefully done long and wanton Asian style. Her report this time was live, somewhere near Camp Casey. A number of GI's straggled along the road returning from shops of the local village. They carried plastic bags of groceries and goods toward the fort. Abbey walked crabwise across the street to keep centered in the camera as she moved to interview a couple of army soldiers walking briskly away.

"Rumors of impending war, clearly started by the U.S. military anxious to derail the treaty, are sweeping the front lines." The pair of GI's kept moving, although they smiled for the camera as Abbey challenged them, "You, Sirs? You look like you are preparing for a war."

Lorrie stared hypnotized at the young GI's—loaded down with water, flashlights, and several roasted chickens—who replied, "Nope. Just heard there was going to be a party."

J-Stars remarked, "Those guys must have eyeballs in their navels."

"Maybe, although if you're up on the trip wire, you probably don't put a lot of stock in treaty talk—especially when they are negotiating away your capability for air interdiction."

As the soldiers hurried off and the camera panned to the walls of the fort, Abbey said, "They seem to be preparing to attack North Korea any moment. These kinds of warlike preparations must not be allowed to stop the treaty." Her editor cut to stock footage from the previous weeks of huge rallies in Seoul and other ROK cities. Signs reading 'U.S. out of Korea!' and 'Let our people go!' waved rhythmically in the crowd. "This same emotion is being democratically expressed by hundreds of thousands of Koreans. Yes, USA, let them go!"

Sean nodded to Lorrie, "Eyes on Pyong-son," and the protester footage and Abbey's bright face were replaced by the four hundred spooky buried buildings and launch gantries of Pyong-son.

As the shift ended, Red looked up from her seat where she'd gotten comfortable with J-Stars and said, "Ten thousand four hundred radar scans. Of course, *nada*."

Sean said, "Keep trying." Then he went into the galley head and punched a pillow for five minutes.

Chapter 45

The 30th of October
T-14, 10:00 a.m. KST

PYONG-SON COMPLEX – CONTROL ROOM

Il-Moon lost his own patience with Airborne Laser's persistent patrol at T-14 hours before the midnight draft treaty acceptance.

Aide Park, knowing his leader as he did, constantly thought about ways to keep him abreast of things. He had earlier piped in a feed from their big X-band radar, allowing the whole bunker to watch as the gawky jumbo jet finished its southerly track past them, lazily pivoted at Ullung-do Island, and for the thousandth time, headed back north, steadying onto its course for another fly-by past Pyong-son.

Airborne Laser was, Il-Moon thought, watching the constant patrol tracks, such an irritant and foil to his enjoying his preparations, even as the rest of his missiles were brought on line, the launch complex was cleared of support equipment, and the clock on the wall ticked the minutes by until the treaty signing.

Aide Park was even more uncomfortable, finally whispering, "Bastard Airborne Laser! We have only fourteen hours. If they remain, do they not limit our options in your Grand Reunification Plan?"

Il-Moon studied ABL, trying not to let his anger push up from his chest into his face. *They are not going to return to Yakota.* He kept his evenness. He motioned, gave the order. "Slide open one of the silo tops at Kwanju site."

AIRBORNE LASER – SEA OF JAPAN – EAST SEA

"Kettledrums! Kettledrums!" called out Eila. "There's some kind of motion at Pyong-son!"

The crew, shaking off the bleariness of seventy continuous hours on station staring at reams of innocuous data, flew to their consoles.

"Longest range video, please take a coordinate handoff and show us the spot," called Emily, who was on Ops, and Lorrie zoomed in on the area of detected motion. "Don't see anything," she mumbled, nerves frazzled.

"There it is again!" Eila yelled.

This time, in the slanting morning sunlight of Pyong-son, the video showed clearly a concrete slab sliding away to reveal a dark hole in the ground. A camouflaged silo, opening as if for a missile launch.

"Son of a bitch!" yelled Sean. "Attack Laser, are you ready?" He stopped, confused, "He's going to launch now in broad daylight?"

"Odd, and what's the silo doing over there? You were there Sean, that's an ancient SCUD field and miles from where Radiant Outlaw saw something," Emily mused.

"How about we try the laser chemical remote sensing and see if they are fueling?"

"I don't know Sean, that'd be breaking security. If they have laser hit sensors, they'll document us as a laser plane."

Red broke in, "Besides, at such a long-range, we just won't get much signal back."

"Com'on, Emily." Sean persisted, "Let's take a look-see."

Emily gave in, curious now herself. "All right, but I'm telling you they will see it and—"

Sean said, "Remote Sensing, Ops. Go!"

From Airborne Laser's nose shot out a violet shimmering beam. For a little distance, the beam was a radiant purple pointer—then faded to invisible as it strobed the far-off half-buried silos of Pyong-son.

PYONG-SON COMPLEX

Aide Park, sitting at his console looked up, startled, as his laser hit-sensors flashed. "Great Vice Chairman! We are being lased!"

Il-Moon turned. *At last. The chessboard is in play—and it is my move.*

"Great Vice Chairman?" asked Aide Park, and Il-Moon knew he wished to speak privately, and he leaned in close to hear.

"The laser was a chemical detection scan," whispered Aide Park. "They may have perhaps sensed our venting, perhaps even detected the presence of certain chemicals."

"Truly?" asked Il-Moon, reflecting it was unlikely ABL could pick up anything definitive, for what was there to see, really? In apparent huge anger, he shouted "They dare to fly in this weapon while I negotiate a peace treaty!" Il-Moon was perfectly capable of being furious at duplicity, while his own plans were completely without honesty. Just as he and his cronies had for decades negotiated in bad faith—using the time bought as cover to re-arm, develop weapons, and extort cash—he planned to keep none of his promises to Hakkermann, and yet his feigned anger was still fueled with true righteous indignation.

Perfect! "Slow fueling to a minimum!" Il-Moon indicated the PC in the corner, and spoke to Aide Park. "Get on the Military Intranet to General Kwon, and have him enter the War Chat Room."

AIRBORNE LASER – EAST SEA – SEA OF JAPAN

"There is indeed some kind of chemical venting," Red commented, pretending non-excitement. In fact, rarely was her job fun like this, since the only chemicals she had ever detected were during carefully arranged experiments, and she could always guess what was laying for her. This, a real-world scan against a bad guy; this was a rush.

She worked her Matlab programs, matching models to the wiggly lines of data streaming in. "Signal to noise ratio is terrible. Dreck. I see steam. CO2."

"What is it?"

"Sean, at this range I can get just a whiff of what they are doing. And with all the armor withdrawing along the DMZ, there are tons of exhaust, particulates, and junk. Maybe I could see them fueling if it were nitrobenzene or something, but that'd be a real stretcher."

"Can you juice it a little bit?"

Red again worked the data. This time Emily carefully watched the returns over her shoulder as well, remarking, "Heavy-weight cracked hydrocarbons."

Red snorted. "Emily, can't you just say Diesel? You know it's just an underground snorkel for a generator...." She magnified a section of data, went into silent concentration. "But this one...this one is different...Emily, doesn't it look like the weird Russian glue we once saw?"

Emily, looking over her shoulder, was the only other person who knew anything about the chemical detection system. She finally shrugged her shoulders. "Signal seems to be fading. Terrible signal to noise ratio."

Sean pounced, "Can't you do anything, average longer, boost the laser?"

Red wrinkled her freckled face and said, "Sean, at this range the data is going to be piss poor. You can max the laser and integrate until the Second Coming and the data is just going to stay piss poor."

"I will say one thing, though," Emily moved away after pouring over Red's display, then walked to Lorrie's, looked, and scratched her milky-white nose. "The location of the venting wasn't the old silo. It was right over where Radiant Outlaw said there was an ICBM complex."

Sean said, "I say we go in and take a look."

Chapter 46

The 30th of October
T–14, 10:15 a.m. KST

AIRBORNE LASER – KOREAN DMZ

Airborne Laser swept in majestically over the eastern Korean coast, over the clear bays, rocky islands, and half-moon beaches of the East Sea. The morning sun lit the aqua water and sparkled on the waves breaking on the sugar-white sand of the scalloped bays. Coming in over Kansong just to the south of the DMZ, they saw the pretty blue roofs and crooked-street Legoland hodgepodge of a small Korean city.

Over the strenuous objections of everyone, Sean was running a DMZ fly-by of Pyong-son. He argued that when they got close, their sensors, especially the laser radar, would gather a host of telling intelligence.

The flight coming in over the dramatic eastern coast was breathtaking. The East Sea was considerably deeper than the Yellow Sea on the far more populated western cost of Korea. Also, being on the eastern side, the sea's moderating effect, given the predominant winds from the west, just as on America's east coast versus her west, was much smaller. On the western coast, in places there were palm trees. Here, the eastern coast was more like Scotland—except for the oddly Caribbean-looking beaches.

Sean looked down at this far eastern end of the DMZ. Despite the density of the defenses in the Seoul area, the DMZ was simply too wide, rugged, and long for it to make sense to defend it equally elsewhere. The ROK and U.S. concentrated their forces in the west near Seoul where the battle would be decisive, constructing here only the usual tank walls and a few fortifications. As a result, the four-kilometer-wide military zone here was especially scenic, a strip of wilderness running down to the East Sea, ending at its wide gleaming white sand beaches.

The crew watched Lorrie's TV cameras with interest as, after their long boring patrol over the sea, they finally got to see Korea—and a pretty woodsy coastal area as well. As they flew lower, a flock of Snowy Cranes took off, winging over rice paddies, tank traps, and blockhouses. The long-range TV was in color, and against the solidity, lifelessness, and immobility of the concrete defenses, the graceful white birds were oddly free and soft.

Sean remarked, "Our friend the DMZ. Nuclear-powered war zone and wildlife preserve."

"Hard to picture war in such a pretty place," Emily observed.

Sean tilted his head in disagreement, pulled on his headset, called over the Comm, "Ears on, people. Slammer, this is Ops. Remote sensing INTEL run. Target is Pyong-son."

Slammer came back over the intercom, "Coming up, one teatime cruise with crumpets."

The crew smoothly worked their preparations, sounding off to Sean's status request: "Radars ready," "Laser Radar, ready," "C3I, ready," "Anti-air, ready," "X Weapons, Ready," until the check was complete.

"Matt?"

"Radar spoofer has been working all the way in," referring to the thin spool of wire paid out the rear of ABL, which held at its end a towed radar decoy. Sensing a radar transmitter tracking ABL, the decoy sent back a spoofed signal that changed their apparent location. Il-Moon's radars would be seeing ABL in the wrong place. "They think we're still out over the Sea of Japan."

"Good job." Sean watched the exterior cameras as Jarhead's twin Gatling guns jinked around. J-Stars worked his surveillance radars, Emily at beam control seemed ready, and Red was working hard at the chemical scanning. *They actually looked passably like professionals.*

Marty came on from the laser area. "Ops, this is Attack Laser. YAL-1A1 Attack Laser set for low-energy remote sensing scans."

Matt Cho lovingly patted his EMP cannon, and Emily barked, "That thing better not be loaded!"

Lorrie brought up the long-range video. "There it is. Fifty clicks off starboard," and on came Pyong-son's spooky valley of buried buildings, gantries, blockhouses and dead rice fields.

Emily said, "Ops, Laser One reports all ABL systems to be cooking."

Sean looked around the Tech Area, at the ease of the crew. No food or drink out, everyone buckled in except as usual Emily and himself, the roamers. The crew stations were shipshape, the crew quietly confident in their tasks. The air was pleasant and warm, the daylight from Emily's picture window cheerful, his flight suit's well-washed cotton as comfy as chamois. He felt a surge of well-being, as if sure he was in the right place and the universe agreed.

Sean murmured, "Airborne Laser, this is Ops. Very beautiful. Remote Sensing, let's look for chemicals around the site."

Emily interrupted, "Sean, we should first calibrate on some industrial plant, like a refinery. Otherwise, the data will likely just be FUBAR."

"Hey, Laser One, we're in the field. Volt's Law: 'when you're in the field, no matter what, you take data.' With your gizmos, we may see something that can put Il-Moon away. Relax, it'll be fun."

"I wouldn't be so sure," Emily warned.

Sean called out, "Remote Sensing, Ops. Go!"

"Ops, Remote Sensing. Target acquired. Tracking loops closed. Laser radar scanning for chemical detection." And again, the violet shimmering beam scanned over Pyong-son.

The aspect of Pyong-son valley changed as ABL flew past, the sun angles shadowing the outlines of buried bunkers and silos, insinuating a creepy feeling of war rooms and missiles deep below the surface.

Red, hands trembling a little as people were watching her fingers moving on the keyboard, grumbled, "Of course, nichto, nothing. Going to spiral scan."

The laser beam spiraled in, efficiently sweeping the entire compound, where at the center, it hit a slight gas plume escaping a vent. Emily walked over and stood behind Red.

"It's some kind of chemical venting," Red commented, matching it to her models, working the wiggly lines of data scrolling by as Emily watched over her shoulder. "Probably an air handler." She magnified a section of data, went into silent concentration. "But this one...."

Emily saw the differential lines being absorbed, and realized: "Take data! Grab and store as much data as you can!"

PYONG-SON COMPLEX

"Laser energy is suddenly massive, Great Vice Chairman!"

They had been watching the X-band radar returns, which still showed ABL out over the East Sea.

"All venting stop!" Il-Moon turned.

His technicians were huddled, consulting excitedly. "They must have come in close! They are right at the DMZ!"

The delight Il-Moon felt was like a flush, the quick stab of pleasure as when you are about to swat a bothersome mosquito who is doomed but wily—and still lives. It was a weakness, he knew, this desire for action, the joy of the immediate strike.

Major Phillips, you have made a serious but fortuitous misstep. He hobbled to the PC where Aide Park was logged onto the Military Intranet. "Let us *chat* with General Kwon."

AIRBORNE LASER

Red said, "Hey, the venting stopped. I'm not sure what we got, really," as Emily watched her overlay known chemical fingerprints onto the data.

Sean said, "So the data could be better. What's your guess?"

Emily replied, "So we're guessing now? Red fuming nitric acid maybe."

"That's missile fuel! What else?"

Red tried different known compounds, finding no new matches for the field data.

Emily leaning over her shoulder said, "Try the spectra for Triple Superphosphate."

Red overlaid the model on the data, and her heart rolled in her chest. On her monitor, time slowed to a crawl in the intense stress. Reluctantly, as the data lined up on the screen in a clear match, she said, "Triple Superphosphate."

Sean snapped, "That's a nuke precursor."

Emily said softly, not wanting to sound as sick as she felt, "I know the nuclear processing stream, thank you. This data is questionable; could be anything. Red could easily have messed up the proportions. We certainly couldn't scientifically validate our finding."

"Who cares about science?" Sean flashed hot, his face sweaty and his flight suit was suddenly stifling. "Fueling missiles. Nukes. That's why the treaty talks. They're really going to do it."

PYONG-SON COMPLEX

Twenty miles from Pyong-son at Musudan-san, a cave bunker door opened. A small radar came to life and pointed directly south over the DMZ. With a few pings, it quickly calibrated—then shot just two ranging pulses.

From canisters buried deep below the ground, two huge Russian S-300 missiles blew out, small boosting explosions sending them forty feet directly into the air. The thirty-foot missiles, big around as trash barrels, hung for a second in the air as if by magic. Then their main engines burst fiery thick smoke and two of the biggest, fastest, longest range, and most sophisticated anti-aircraft missiles in the world sprinted away—toward Airborne Laser.

ABL – TECH AREA

Sean had ordered Airborne Laser into a racetrack pattern just to the south of the border while they tried to re-interrogate Pyong-son. Try though they might, they could not duplicate their previous results. The Pyong-son site appeared clear of all chemicals except diesel exhaust, cleaning chemicals, and miscellaneous expected odors such as cigarette smoke and cooking food.

Sean said, "All right. We'll go to Osan; I'll see what DIA has. Anything corroborative, we read the commander into 'Have Catcher' and go up the chain to Hakkermann."

"We're not an INTEL platform. We're a top secret defensive system," Emily snapped. "You can't brief an untried and ass-hanging-out-in-the-breeze thing like we are and get anywhere."

"We have the recorded data. Intelligence Officer? Radars? Anything else?"

Jarhead said, "I'm with you, Sean. But I see no radio traffic, radars, nothing emitting; the military Comm net is just whispers. No logistics except the retreating armor. They should be shifting troops to the front, setting up supply lines. But there's neither tooth nor tail."

"That's because it's all underground. I'm right about this. We can go to DIA, they can be cleared—"

Emily countered, "No matter who you take it to, we will have to deal with Hakkermann and he is one tough and bitter cookie. He is not going to believe the data. He is going to mess you up and get us all tossed out of Korea. And no missile defense. You better decide what you want: to get Il-Moon or to help Korea."

"There are thirty thousand Americans down there. Lorrie, your boys are down there. What do you say?"

Lorrie struggled to speak, but nothing came out.

Emily said, "You'd blow our cover and risk Korean and American lives? Hakkermann is exactly who we don't want to talk to. He's in a perfect position to compromise us. He has every intention of trusting the North Koreans. Maybe because the man fired you, you're dying to prove him wrong."

Sean yelled, "I'm not doing this for personal reasons."

"For someone with no personal stake, you're pretty wrapped around the axle on this, Sean."

An alarm bleated like a stuck pig. Jarhead touched his mike, called, "ABL, Radar is...Kettledrums! Kettledrums! This is no drill!"

Everyone's attention jumped! The beam director cranked around from the tracking cue from the beam control systems. Lasers probed out. On screen came distant missile plumes from beyond the North Korean border.

Red shouted, "Laser Radar sees missile motion at forty-five clicks. Speed Mach 0.5. Target—"

Eila paled, yelled, "—Us! They look *really* hostile!"

Sean and Emily were already running to their stations.

"Ops, this is Air Defense. Two S-300 anti-aircraft, NATO designation 'Grumble.' Speed: Mach 6. Radar guidance, proximity-fused directed blast. Range... Plenty to reach us. Ripple fire! They've salvoed them, another two coming!"

"Flightdeck, this is Ops. Evasive action, radar missiles starboard."

The deck tilted as ABL slid into a sideways bank. "Ops, Flightdeck. Electronic countermeasures coming up. Not much time to wiggle, but we'll try to duck behind the chaff."

Il-Moon had indeed caught Sean out. It's one thing to field a Mach 6 ground ball from two hundred miles away. You had some good minutes. It is quite another at thirty miles—where you had thirty seconds.

Airborne Laser banked steeply, swaying everyone in their seats. Outside behind the plane, big chaff dispensers blew out a ton of tiny aluminum-foil confetti, and ABL ducked to put it between them and the missiles. "Ops, Flightdeck. First radar chaff dispensed."

"Attack Laser, this is Ops. Prepare for missile shoot down."

"Ops, Attack Laser. Negative on the laser. We're at least forty seconds away from ready. You told us to run low-energy remote sensing and stand down from combat."

Lorrie had the missile trails coming straight toward them on the big screen now. "Ops, C3I." Her voice shook. "Missile velocities Mach 2. Time to impact, forty seconds."

Jarhead broke what seemed like an eternity of silence but was only a fraction of a second. "Ops, Air Defense. I could try for them."

"Four Grumbles at Mach 6? They are just like Patriots—furiously fast and deadly—meant to knock down missiles. Your range is only a kilometer; less than a second for four. It is just not going to work," Sean said, thinking fast. "We've got to hit them with something farther out first. What other defenses do we have?"

Emily wrung her hands, "We're supposed to operate outside enemy missile range. Under air supremacy conditions. We have no real defenses. Just experimental gizmos and light explosive reactive armor. May some RF jamming capability, that we don't really have up...even so, I think the Grumble has terminal IR capability..."

"Can our armor take an S-300 hit?"

Jarhead shook his crew-cut head rapidly. "A three-hundred-pound fragmentation warhead? It goes off a mile away, maybe. And even so, the engines can't take any shrapnel at all."

Outside, in the distance, the electronic countermeasures had diverted one of the Grumbles into a jinking maneuver, but as the chaff fell away, the remaining three big missiles arced toward them as though riding fast on their thick smoke trails.

Lorrie said, "Missile velocities Mach 4. Time to impact, twenty seconds."

Matt said, "I'm all over those toys! I'll fry their electronic brains!"

Emily said, "You'll knock us out of the sky."

Lorrie shrieked, "They will anyway! Missiles at Mach 5. Impact, fifteen seconds. I'm *scared!*"

Sean said grimly, "You are not alone. Matt?"

"You fly, we fry! Just let them get into range."

Sean leapt to help him, dragging open the microwave cannon breach. Jarhead was already deep into the explosives cupboard up front and came running with two bagged artillery charges, giant marshmallows covered in light gauze. Matt and Jarhead jammed them into the breach—and slammed it shut.

Outside, the S-300s blew their final stages. Leapt at an unimaginably fast speed toward ABL, swooping on the big screen straight into their faces.

Lorrie almost screamed, "Mach 6! Impact, five seconds!"

Matt yelled, "They're just coming into range...ABL crew, suck deck!"

The crew hunkered. Matt yanked his firing lanyard. The cannon fire boomed, knocking over loose items and billowing acrid smoke through the cabin. The firing shock wave ran down the ABL airframe and everything buzzed and hummed with the harmonics of the muzzle blast.

Outside, the microwave radiation was so intense—had anyone been there to see it—that the air actually warbled. The shimmering molecules of the air, blooming in the radio frequency thermal shock, their electrons rammed into states almost inconceivable on the face of the earth, more akin to an X-ray star, and the radiation skewed out, instantaneously exciting huge currents in the missile bodies streaking toward them. In the radio spectrum, ABL appeared to be a trillion-degree star.

The first two warheads, well within the R-squared range of the microwave radiation, took a pulse of electrons right into their fuses and exploded in an instant flash. Sootily, the explosion area expanded gracefully, into huge puffs of dark smoke.

The last missile, being back slightly, was out of the range of the microwaves and punched through the smoke puffs and came straight for them.

J-Stars called out radar coordinates and Jarhead swung his Gatling guns onto bore-site.

Sean yelled, "Anti-air: fire! Flightdeck: Bank! Bank! Bank!"

Jarhead's guns burst out with a ripping rumble, the sabot discard casings from the high velocity Tungsten slugs pointing down the firing stream site-lines to where...

The last missile, just a football field away and coming on like gangbusters, intersected the Phalanx fire-stream and its warhead shredded, exploded. So great was the missile's forward velocity that the explosion carried right into the belly of ABL.

ABL's light blast-shielding kicked back at the shrapnel and warhead debris.

Airborne Laser pitched and dropped five hundred feet, throwing Emily and Sean together to the floor.

Bozon and Slammer worked the flightdeck controls and within a few heart-stopping moments of bucking, brought ABL back to even keel and smooth sailing.

Slammer's voice came over the intercom into everyone's headsets. Despite his reputation for fearlessness, there was an unmistakable timbre of vast relief. "OK girls, just pull your panties back on: the brown stain goes in the back, the yellow in the front, and you're good to go."

Emily angrily got up off Sean, purposefully jamming an elbow into his ribs. "'Relax,' he said. 'It'll be fun.'"

PYONG-SON COMPLEX

On the monitors in his control room, Il-Moon watched his attack fail. Although to him relief was not a possible emotion for he always believed in himself, his backup plan was better anyway—not counting missing the pleasure of watching Major Phillips die; a childishness for which he chided himself.

He had confirmed—in dramatic fashion—that Sean's plane was indeed an anti-missile plane, and Sean had played right into his hands as well by entering Korean airspace. *Still the same impatient boy, eh, Major Phillips?* Little was the love lost, he knew, between Hakkermann and Sean. It only needed just a little... teaser...a stinger...to make it really march.

He had already chosen a pretty young woman worker named Ai-Ta Park, sitting at a terminal across from him, placidly adjusting Pyong-son's radar to track ABL.

He spoke briefly to Aide Park, who beckoned to Ai-Ta. "Come here."

She approached immediately. He asked her, "Are you prepared to do all you can for the revolution and the sake of Korea, even at personal sacrifice?"

Honored, Ai-Ta went to attention, and her clear eyes gleamed. "It is my desire to assist Dearest Leader and the Party in any possible way."

Aide Park followed as two guards marched Ai-Ta into an optics laboratory. A laser gushed purple light around a metal topped optical bench. Two technicians immediately stood up when motioned over by Aide Park. They seated Ai-Ta in a chair, her eyes at the level of the optics table top. The technician brought over a turning mirror and set it up to divert the beam.

Ai-Ta suddenly understood, and instinctively reacted, starting to rise.

One guard grabbed Ai-Ta, gripped her hands, holding her down firmly. The other guard seized her head and peeled her eyelids up. They directed the laser beam straight into her eyes.

Ai-Ta screamed in shock and agony as the laser whitened and fried her eyes.

REUTERS OFFICE – SEOUL

Akiru watched Abbey scolding Hugh Levine who was clumsily editing videotape.

Abbey snapped, "A cameraman knows editing as well as shooting. You couldn't edit a postcard."

Her cell phone rang, she snapped it open. "Yamamoto." She listened, and froze. Slowly and quietly she closed and held the tiny phone. She carefully looked at her watch.

There is so little time. Who has the muscle to swing the sledgehammer for me?

In a burst of activity, she grabbed the Seoul phonebook. As she found the number and frantically dialed nearby Seoul University, she threw the phone book to Akiru and Hugh. "Both of you! All the university numbers! Call every student newspaper there is!"

AIRBORNE LASER – TECH AREA

The Airborne Laser crew crowded at Emily's window, looking out at the huge smoke clouds wafting over the DMZ.

Jarhead remarked, "We didn't exactly take them by stealth."

Sean smiled grimly, "Flightdeck, this is Ops. Let's put some air between us and them."

"Manna to my ears, Ops. We'll pedal as fast as we can for Japan."

Emily turned to Matt, who looked thoughtful. "You were supposed to knock out their guidance. Not explode warheads over the DMZ and blow our cover."

Matt mused, "Interesting, exploding warheads at distance. I wonder if it would also work with nukes."

Emily turned to Sean, "We were supposed to stay on station—and in secret—"

"It will be all right when Hakkermann sees our data."

"If you dare to go and mess with Hakkermann, this time I won't object when he goes to cave in your skull."

Sean replied, evenly, "Get me a printout of the data, please."

Red looked up from her console, slightly stricken. "I can't. Matt's microwaver wiped my data disks clean. Our Pyong-son data has gone bye-byes."

AMEMBASSY – SEOUL

"I will kill those Air Force jabalonies!" Hakkermann shouted with deep feeling.

Inside the big beige Embassy compound in downtown Seoul, Harold had been enjoying himself, a warm glow of accomplishment spreading in his over-worked bones. He had put down the thick crudely-bound draft treaty document, folded his reading glasses and set them precisely on his polished desk. He turned to his aide. "An amazing document, Sandy. Does us all proud."

Sandy's reply was interrupted by a strange growling noise outside. Harold went to the wide windows across the whole wall. Over the twelve-foot concrete embassy blast fence, he could see the tops of hand-held signs among a growing crowd. "What is it now?" he asked. The pedestrian stream up huge Sejongno Boulevard was never light, but now it seemed particularly heavy coming toward the embassy. Further, the number of the usual dark Korean work suits seemed miniscule compared to the huge mob of more casually-clothed Korean university students.

The door opened suddenly in a second interruption as an Embassy weenie came in, moving fast. His boney hand pointed behind him. "You need to see this. On CNN."

"Don't tell me it's that damned Yamamoto."

"Sure is. She's right outside—and with a scoop."

They moved quickly to the next room, where a staff member used the TIVO to replay Abbey's report for Harold.

The camera came up on the Abbey standing outside the big American Embassy gates, with Akiru's A-shot down the immense boulevard behind her toward giant Seoul University, from which a mob of protestors flowed like a river in spate; yelling, waving signs with slogans and Korean flags—and looking to inundate the U.S. Embassy even as huge buses zoomed up, disgorging heavily-armed Seoul riot police. The few busses of Korean police that permanently idle in front of the embassy were far too few, and were already overwhelmed.

Abbey looked into the camera with her basilisk eyes. "Despite U.S. Arms Inspectors finding 'No significant treaty-sensitive activity' at Pyong-son, the American military are feeling the heat of the upcoming treaty and are rattling their sabers. In an apparent provocation aimed at stopping the treaty talks, an hour ago a secret U.S. laser plane fired into North Korean territory."

"Christ on a Cracker!" yelled Hakkermann. "What the hell is happening?" He flashed to the Airborne Laser discussion at the White House meeting. *Jeanette DeFrancis—and Sean Phillips.*

Abbey went on. "The plane must be operating from some secret location here in Korea. Your reporter predicts the North Korean leaders will demand the immediate impounding of the plane—and international criminal charges may apply if the allegations made by the North Koreans prove true that the laser plane purposefully blinded a girl in a remote village."

Hakkermann rasped, "I will kill those Air Force jabalonies!" He jerked his eyes up to the also-furious Sandy. "Get the Four-star at Osan to call that plane in."

"No problem." Sandy was already dialing. "We'd better get out to Osan before the streets are blocked. Confront them immediately and get this settled before we hear from Il-Moon or Dearest Leader."

"Right," said Hakkermann. "Il-Moon will want—and we will present—their heads on a platter."

They left just in time to get a whiff of tear gas—a sensation without which a South Korean university education is incomplete—as the Seoul riot police held off the angry protesting river of students and other Koreans flowing down Sejongno, barely keeping them out of stone-throwing range long enough for the motorcade to get out the embassy gates.

It was just as well, Harold reflected, as his confidence came back. They would work through this. The final treaty preparations were to be at Osan, anyway. The North Korean Counselor General was to meet him there to confirm the pull back of the 7th Air Force. He brushed the sleeve of his silk top coat and checked his hat. He had already changed into his formal clothes for the treaty signing, sure he would not get another chance.

He calmed himself, and headed to Osan to intercept Airborne Laser.

BOOK 7

"Circumvent any order aimed at stopping your dream."

The AFRL Project Officer's Seventh Commandment

Chapter 47

The 30th of October
T-12, Noon KST

AIRBORNE LASER – OVER KOREA

Emily was pensive as Airborne Laser diverted far south of the DMZ and ran for Japan at her highest speed. She looked down at the distinctly Asian crazy-quilt of fields and roads and mountain chains. The missile salvo response to their laser-sensing shocked her. Sure, she thought they might sense the beam. But a missile launch against Airborne Laser made no sense. No half-hearted effort, the salvo firing had been focused on destroying the plane. Although the North Koreans always fired upon border intruders, ABL's nav was far too good for them to have strayed over the line. And the S-300's were the latest Russian missile technology, not even confirmed as possessed by the North Korea. Il-Moon must not only have sensed them, but felt ABL was a great danger to him.

If she ever doubted it, Occam's razor—the simplest explanation—when applied to the attack showed Il-Moon was mortally afraid of an anti-missile system in the Korean theater.

"Hey, it's that bitch Japanese reporter," Lorrie said as on the big screen, she brought up CNN.

As Abbey reported, a massive demonstration was brewing behind her. Clouds of tear gas spread over the bright clothes of students and darker suits of Korean salarymen and women: everyone was there and furious. "The U.S. military continues to play agent provocateur, using high-powered laser beams to blind a young Korean girl." The scene shifted to taped footage of Ai-Ta in a hospital ward, her laser-wrecked face being bandaged.

Emily felt her stomach lurch, but again, here was something she could fix on. Whatever else they had done, their laser certainly couldn't have blinded anyone.

Abbey finished, "This barbaric act has provoked massive demonstrations in Seoul. Amidst international condemnation, the treaty signing tonight is in jeopardy. 'America, you are so powerful. Why can't you let our small country be free?' say these protestors."

The Telex in the corner came to clattering life. Lorrie tore off the message. "We're being called in to Osan." Her face went white, "It's Presidential authority."

Emily watched Sean take this as almost a physical blow. She knew he was ashamed; at having ruined everything he'd killed himself to attain—getting operational, to Korea, on station. Now, he was in for a whipping in front of his crew, and they were all going down. Sean looked up, but was unable to meet her gaze. He mumbled, "I suppose you'll get what you want now, my head caved in."

Emily felt ABL bank as Slammer turned for Osan Air Base. She walked over, and with her fingertips brushed Sean's cheek. "Happy days! At least now we know he's going to war."

MAGNOLIA PALACE

Architect Su came into the Magnolia Palace office just as Dearest Leader shouted into the speaker phone, "What did you do?"

Su could tell it was Il-Moon shouting back, "They attacked us! Blinded a young woman. You expect me to not react? It is exactly as I told you!"

Dearest Leader was so angry he could only say, "Marshal Il-Moon, I do not know what it will take to get past this incident, but I do not want any more of anything without my authorization!"

Dearest Leader hung up, and glared at Architect Su, as if blaming all his troubles on him.

Su remarked, "Il-Moon seems tense."

"He has been working very hard."

"And you are satisfied with his work on the treaty?"

"It is brilliant. He has negotiated for us perhaps $40 billion in investments, and great flexibility. Koreans will be able to move north and south at will, yet there are huge financial inducements to remain and work here. The farmers get the land, the people get their houses, the workers get the factories. The armed forces will become the new Chaebol* of Koryo; their units taking over broad business areas, organizing the treaty investment money, and running our industries for profit. We have equal control of the new Koryo armed forces. I remain leader of Koguryo." He nodded emphatically. "The terms are excellent."

Taking Su's thoughtfulness as a criticism, Dearest Leader went on, "Il-Moon has a right to be tense. He has been at every meeting, every negotiation, even the long ones where Hakkermann doesn't come. It must take its toll."

---

* The Korean version of the Japanese Kiretsu, networks of companies

"Yes," noted Architect Su quietly, "He was so busy he was even absent from my granddaughter's wedding. The entire three hours."

Both men sat in silence for a moment, contemplating those missing hours. Finally, Su spoke: "I believe I have found Tam Ho."

"You believe?" came sharply.

"I am convinced he is in the MPAF Self-Criticism isolation wing."

Dearest Leader snorted, "Su-ssi, he is only a major. He would not be required to undergo the Senior Criticism isolation."

"True. However, if we review Kang's surveillance file, and assume that except for leaving out Tam Ho at Namp'o harbor, it is a factual account—an attempt to suborn all the Watchers all the time would surely lead to discovery—then the only time Kang was unwatched was when he was in the Self-Criticism Isolation wing. The wing is a perfect place to meet and conspire. There, with ease, officers—themselves almost unwatched within the MPAF—could penetrate the wing and meet with Kang. There are few staff, and the Criticized is alone in his cell much of the time. The contact and planning for the Underwater Mansion attack must have taken place in the Self-Criticism wing."

The audacity of it—plotting in the very place you were laying bare your shortcomings to the State—took Dearest Leader's breath away. Mentally, he tried to poke holes in the theory. It was too watertight. "Dogs! Yet, it is possible. But Tam Ho?"

"Tam Ho must be connected to the attack on the Mansion. The conspirators took great risk in removing him from Kang's file; they must need to keep him hidden. What better place than under our noses and in a site where they have support? There, kept from home and his unit, no matter how we searched—as is the case—we would never find him."

"If you are right, we will soon know the truth about the Underwater Mansion." Dearest Leader motioned to his guards. "Take a company of Guard Command and bring Tam Ho here."

Su waved the guards away, spoke so quietly only Dearest Leader could hear. "I doubt I would return from such an errand. Tam Ho is, even now, under secondment to the Guard Command."

Dearest Leader looked around, suddenly aware of Il-Moon's Guard Command—at the doors, outside in the corridors, above and below them in the bunkers, palace, and gardens.

"I will arrange myself to get Tam Ho." Su rose, adding gently, "For you, perhaps it is time for a little insurance?"

FARMERS' MILITIA – PYONGYANG SUBURBS

The 345th Battalion of the Farmers' and Workers' Red Guard Militia was housed temporarily in Mayonnaise Factory 22 on the edge of Pyongyang. The factory was idle, for their main source of eggs was the General Political Bureau's prison farm Public Safety Camp 53, and after the nuke tests, the cutback in grain donations from the Japanese and Americans did not just starve a lot more prisoners, it also crippled the camp's egg production.

Despite its name, Mayonnaise Factory 22 now worked for the Korean People's Army. It processed opium coming in from the Northern provinces, grown following Kim Jong-Il's speech 'Let us Raise Crops from which Dollars will come to Support our Great Revolution,' a disguised command for poppy cultivation to go to full scale. The heroin was then smuggled to, and distributed by, the Korean *Yakuza* in Osaka. The proceeds were returned to the army unit, and distributed pyramidally according to Confucian doctrine.

Now, in the run-up to the treaty, even the opium machinery was idle and the KPA unit deployed. The farmers had spread out on the splintery planks between the evaporators and processors and bedded down, tired from the truck ride to which they were unaccustomed. Tong-Hu found the borrowed Guard Command trucks held emergency stores of rice, canned bread, dried beef, and tobacco—and distributed it immediately. *Such a bounty!* Many saved most of it for family, while the rest got slightly sick, unaccustomed to the rich food. Still, no one complained, and there was much pleasure at the ration of tobacco. The men smoked, talked, slept, and for excitement, wagered tiny sums on bouts between the fighting crickets some habitually carried for this purpose.

Tong-Hu did not relax. The Farmers' Auxiliary Artillery was also there, eating, smoking, talking, playing cards, and writing letters home. Tong-Hu spent his time with them in intense preparation for their coming duty.

At 1400 hours that afternoon, the Farmers' Militia was called to the Magnolia Palace. Outside the palace grounds, a hardened regular army officer gave them explicit instructions on replacing the Guard Command. More difficult were the instructions to capture and hold the key senior Guard Command officers, who were headquartered in the lower bunkers of the complex.

It took the farmers two hours to secure Magnolia Palace and its bunkers. But by nightfall, they had locked the Guard Command in deep basements, and fanned out to cover the palace grounds.

ABL – OSAN AB TAXIWAY

Airborne Laser took some time getting a vector to Osan, for planes were lined up at the end of the big runway and around the three huge diamond-shaped aprons lined with hangars, and arming and support facilities. Many incoming flights were being diverted to Pusan AB to the south. Near Osan, Slammer let the tower know ABL had plenty of fuel and could hold if required, but within five minutes, the tower found them a slot and said to bring it in pronto.

Inside the taxiing ABL, Sean watched from Emily's window as lines of tankers, transports, fighters, and anti-armor jets trundled toward the runway. Outside the flight line's accordion-wire, as usual, joggers ran the running path as if nothing new was happening. For a moment, Sean imagined the airbase under fire, the storm of weaponry falling on it, the attacks of the North Korean Special Forces, the hell and death of war here at unprepared Osan, with their security forces and offensive aircraft pulled back to Kadena on Okinawa, while Il-Moon's tanks could return to the DMZ in an hour. He mumbled the 7th Air Force's Osan motto, "Ready to fight tonight."

Jarhead, coming up to Sean, overhead and nodded to the diamonds. "Maybe. But I still wouldn't want to be sitting in the middle of the Ops area if the balloon does go up tonight."

Gun-fire right outside the cabin jerked everyone's head up. "It's started!" yelled someone.

Sean smiled ruefully. "It's just the bird guns, the little cannons to scare the birds off the flight line. Keeps them out of the intake valves."

The crew looked embarrassed as Sean turned back to Jarhead. "What are you thinking?"

Jarhead unfolded a map of the base and ran a square-ended finger over Base Ops. "The runways here, headquarters, and those arming diamonds will be the center of the hit, if it comes. Fuels too, although they are buried. Where would an assault likely come from?"

Sean indicated the blast shelters at the busy end of the runway. "The AMD base defense and anti-air is near here, the hardened command bunkers too, so a tougher place to start." He pointed to the nearby base fence. "Also, there are marshes just outside the fence, and they would have a harder time forming up. They'll come in near the Patriot batteries," pointing across the runway to the line of concrete pens with boxed missiles waiting. "They'll form up in these fields, then take out the Patriots."

"Right," Jarhead said. "Wherever they form up, the closer we are to heavy strip-down maintenance, where planes are really torn apart and non-functional, the lower our area's priority is going to be." He looked at the map, then out Emily's window at the layout of the base.

Emily put in, "They told us to park on Diamond 1. They'll scream if we do something else."

"Well, it's kind of moot since everyone is totally busy with deployment and we weigh almost a million pounds," Sean answered. "I don't think they can really stop us."

Jarhead continued, "Suppose we by accident take a wrong turn at runway 8-Right, and shimmy across to these stowage hangars, park by the base gym."

Sean scratched his head. This plan had merit, and yet...He pointed just outside the nearby base fence. "Pretty close to the perimeter there. This clear area is an old quarry. An easy set down point for North Korean Special Forces. Right across the fence, we'd be sitting ducks."

Jarhead was affable, tracing out a different route on the map. "How about instead, on the edge of chopper refurb off the fourth diamond? That diamond was never completed, isn't used for weapons, and has only the old Aeroclub. It has a second taxiway Air Force One uses when it comes here, so it can take our weight. No fast fliers or gunnery boats nearby."

Sean took in the sheltered location. "I like it. We'll be in the boonies, and a little bit lost in the noise; we even have a shot at appearing innocuous."

J-Stars snorted, "The last time this here plane was innocuous was before it was built up in St Looey."

"You'll see," Jarhead said, grinning. "We'll blend right in."

So Slammer pretended to misunderstand the tower taxing directions. Halfway to their egress point, he cut in away from the first diamond's apron and ran ABL along the rarely-used route to the refurb hangars.

The tower squawked in horror, their frustration peaking at Bozon's oracular replies to their strident demands. The tower finally quit bellyaching once ABL had trundled across to the Aeroclub and pulled clear of taxiway traffic. They had other fish to shoot in their barrel on an extremely busy night.

No sooner had the Korean ground crew pushed the airstairs up under ABL's rattlesnake emblazoned door, and the crew bounded down looking for the nearest cheeseburger, than Sean and Emily found two burley SP's—base

Security Police—blocking them. The SP Captain held up a restraining hand. "Whoa, whoa. This crew is not cleared to disembark. Back into the plane." He indicated a limo just pulling up at the Aeroclub. "Major Phillips and Dr. Engel? Someone wants to talk to you."

AMEMBASSY LIMO – OSAN APRON

In the lamp-lit backseat of his huge limo, Hakkermann sat glowering at Sean and Emily. "Same old Sean. Every time you show up the shit rains down like wet plop from a tall cow."

Emily said simply, "The truth is a difficult mistress."

Hakkermann snorted humorlessly. "I'm not here to discuss Truth's sex life. I'm here to stop your goofy plane from fucking up this historic treaty—"

Sean snapped, "The North Koreans aren't thinking about your treaty. They're thinking about war."

"You know about North Koreans like a pig knows about Sunday! You laser into North Korea, blow up a practice missile shot—"

Emily snapped, "That was no practice shot. We were doing remote sensing and they attacked us. On our side of the DMZ."

"Girly, the North Koreans are not going to say 'Hey, *no problemo*,' to a laser weapons platform probing them."

Sean snorted, "They responded with a Russian S-300 missile salvo, no less, Harold."

"Maybe so. The North Koreans don't just ignore border intrusions." He waved a hand and Sandy handed the photograph to Sean. "Especially when you blind some little girl? Do you know how bad that looks? What won't you stop at?"

Emily took the photo of Ai-Ta's hideously burned face. Sickened, she examined it. "Our remote sensing laser is eye-safe at any distance. These are thermal burns. They deliberately blinded her for some other purpose."

Sean added, "Harold, they shot at us because our scan saw ICBM's fueling at Pyong-son."

Hakkermann almost yelled, then stopped himself and settled for a doubly threatening intonation. "Like the satellite evidence you had of Pyong-son? I was just inside and there is nothing! Are you so damn sure of yourself you'd blow our one chance in sixty years for a unified Korea? We are on the cusp of greatness, of being present at the creation of a new world."

"They are reinvesting Pyong-son, Harold. Il-Moon is going to war!"

"Il-Moon isn't their leader. I've met Dearest Leader. He'd have to be an Oscar-winning actor to be planning war. He wants his place in history as the President Lincoln of Korea. He's got a vision of the future of North Korea and it involves making washing machines, not war."

Sean almost shouted, "It isn't just Dearest Leader! Il-Moon's whole family was destroyed by the Japanese. He was raised in a Russian detention camp under inhuman conditions. He fought for the North in the Korean War and lived through the fire bombings. He's never going to have anything to do with letting outsiders in!"

"He would if it meant regime survival."

"He'd rather kill everyone he can get to before he even begins to ponder admitting he's been wrong all these years, that his whole world order and belief system is flawed. He's been through too much to ever accept that the world doesn't owe him, and he the world."

Hakkermann paused for a while, until the ringing tones of Sean's voice settled away. He took another tack. "I can get you back on the inspection team. Back at your rightful place in the treaty talks. You and I can deal with Il-Moon whatever he's up to."

"I'm OK where I am."

Hakkermann was practically begging. "What is peace worth, Sean? What risks are you willing to take to make the world whole again? How do you know you aren't just some fucking reactionary Kim Jong-Il refusing to admit he's been wrong his whole life? So what if old Harold is wrong? What would it be worth to break out of this stagnation under which twenty million North Koreans are starving, enslaved, without access to health care, taught to hate the world, denied music and art and literature, lied to about every fact from what life is like for the South Koreans to how much the world loves them and wants to communicate, trade, and prosper with them. What in the end could possibly happen, including war, that wouldn't leave us better off than we are now, with an unstable nuclear North Korea totally alienated from the world, with a totally inhuman government?"

"Once lightning strikes, there is no telling how deep the damage will go."

Hakkermann gave up with a palpable change of posture, his jaw-line going rigid. "Get out!" He controlled his rage as Sean opened the door. "You wait here at the plane. I've arranged a video conference with the President. General Officer rank and above. Oh, you're not a General Officer are you, Sonnyboy? Looks like soon you will be out of Korea for good." He stopped short, sense of honor fighting him. "On second thought, you will be at the meeting. I'll let you know when."

As Sean and Emily climbed out, Sean said, "Wait," pulling out his analysis of Namp'o Bay and his observations since then. "Read the case file. He held the Top Secret document out to Hakkermann. Sandy, glowering, grabbed it from Sean, who asked, "Would you sign for it?"

"The Ambassador doesn't sign for low level crud like this." Haughtily, Sandy scribbled 'Queen Victoria,' in the signature block on the AF 1421 'Receipt of Top Secret Material' form, and tossed it onto the tarmac.

Sean picked it up, saw the signature, but didn't waste breath. "Harold, just look it over. If you think everything there is explainable, I tell you it is not."

Hakkermann indicated the file with a dismissive wave. "We'll do that. But I can't see anything you dreamed up in your paranoid mind stopping the miracle we've got cooking."

Harold leaned out, called the SP's over. "The entire crew stays with the plane. Presidential Authority. They are not to leave this area."

* * *

Guarding a 747 at Osan with ground support crews in and about her isn't that easy a thing to do with just couple of SP's. First, the big diamond-shaped aprons were solidly lined with storehouses, support buildings, vehicle bays, blast-hangars, climfit trailers, blockhouses, and smaller unit headquarters'. In amongst these were various fuel, air conditioning, power, lubricant, and camo-netted support carts. Besides all this infrastructure, a sentry's line of sight in any direction across this dense operations area was severely cluttered by the high amount of traffic, repair activity, and aircraft prepping.

Lorrie did not have any trouble. Her flight helmet hid her bleached hair, and with the sunglass visor over her eyes and her femininity hidden under a flight jacket, she passed as a fuels person to the peripheral vision of the SP's.

She walked out the rear ramp from ABL, stepped around a fuel truck and swung up into the passenger seat. When the Korean fuels driver found her in his truck, sans helmet and jacket, he was only too happy to oblige the cuddly blonde with the big boobs. He never got near the Valkyrie type, let alone one with huge eyes, curvaceous figure, and downy voice. It was easy for her to beg a ride off the flight line.

A few minutes later, he dropped her, as requested, at Osan City's train station.

AMEMBASSY LIMO – OSAN TO SEOUL HIGHWAY

In his limo, as he was reading the report, Hakkermann's face gave him away to Sandy completely, who said, "I would never have thought you would have bought anything that renegade would say."

Harold closed up Sean's report, and turned to look out the window. The heavy shielding on the windows made it almost impossible to see out. All he saw was his reflection. *I look tired.* "A lot of things in his report make sense."

Sandy said, "Well, Sir, you were never one to just wonder about things that puzzle you."

"What are you suggesting?"

"Send the report to Dearest Leader. If you can't level with him, whom can you level with?"

ABL – OSAN HARDSTANDING

On the tarmac at ABL, Sean had the crew huddle. Sean said, "Jarhead and J-Stars, work on the chaff and flare dispensers and the DIRCM systems, make sure everything is really back up. Smitty, lay in the supplies and chow. Chief, you brought your paints?" and at his nod, Sean said, "We need a new name."

As Auggie nodded again, Jarhead asked, "You're not going to try to fly out of here—even with a new name—are you?" The marine seemed worried. "We have serious orders from the top to sit tight."

Sean didn't answer, instead turning to Emily, "We're going to need to add laser fire control for cruise missile defense, can you work out the power scaling for close-in shooting? Who are our best programmers?"

"Red, Matt, and Lorrie."

"Red and Matt, you two add a program into fire control. Lots of small close targets at rapid fire and slew rates."

Emily said, "I thought Airborne Laser was grounded."

"It is." Sean looked around. "Alright. Lorrie. Where's Lorrie?"

Chapter 49

The 30th of October
T-9, 3:00 p.m. KST

ABL – OSAN HARDSTANDING

"Damn her AWOL fingernails!" Sean yelled a few moments later when he and Emily stood alone on the tarmac. "I don't care how much you like her. She is off Airborne Laser."

Emily replied, and Sean saw the fear in her eyes. "Honestly, we need her. She's the only one besides me who really knows how to shoot the laser."

Sean, disgusted, looked back to where the SP's stood near their vehicle, watching them.

Emily let him stew for a moment, breathing deeply to balance herself despite the JP-8 kerosene-smelling flight line air. "Shouldn't you kick the tires of your old friend the DMZ anyway, Major Intelligence?"

Sean looked around the flight line, then over to the DIA Ant Colony. "We'll have to get a ride out of here."

HUMVEE – FREEDOM HIGHWAY NORTH

The drive to the DMZ from Seoul is around the rugged mountains directly north. These mountains make any building there, as well as any approach to the city difficult, so the highway loops around the hills as does the colorful Asian cityscape of greater Seoul, with its endless lines of shops, vertical neon signs along the streets, tiered business on upper floors, gated official government office complexes, air conditioner-cluttered apartment buildings, and towering skyscrapers with English names directly translated from the Korean. Sean didn't even smile when Emily pointed out a modern insurance company tower, its name in huge letters on the top, 'Happy Forever.' Once they escaped the city, the townscape fell away and all around were now pretty patchwork rice fields lined in irrigation ditches, straw-covered ginseng farms, monuments, hillocks of forest, and rows of tented white plastic greenhouses.

Sean and Emily took Freedom Highway along the broad Han River until, as the countryside grew scenic and farmy, the river branched into the muddy wide Imjin River. In the only non-mountainous approach to Seoul, they followed the

Kaesong-Munsan corridor up toward the DMZ. Passing Munsan, the Korean population, dense as it was, always needed space to expand and build, and here is one place they found it, as apartments and small villages had fused into a town of 40,000 souls—despite the dozens of divisions of North Korean armor waiting within miles, and this being the main invasion corridor.

Sean drove the DIA convertible Humvee, borrowed from Col Kluppel, grimly past the beautiful Korean scenery, lost in his own silent anger.

Suddenly Emily reached over and ruffled Sean's hair, smiled at him. "What good if you gain the whole world only to lose your own soul?"

Sean tensed, an angry retort boiling up, then relaxed. He reached over and mussed her hair back. Emily laughed, draped an arm over his shoulder, and as they cruised the bucolic countryside along the wide calm river estuaries north to the DMZ, they shared what would be their last moments of peace for a long time.

U.S. ARMY – CAMP CASEY ON THE DMZ

Sean showed his ID and orders at an Imjin bridge checkpoint, and the guard managed to find the phone number for someone to sponsor them into the camp. Sean zigzagged the Humvee through the tank traps into the main fort area, past revetments and the famous lookout posts that resembled fire watch towers, and up the hill to the heavily-fortified forward bunkers.

Camp Casey on the DMZ was the U.S. 8th Army's farthest forward strong point almost right to the border limit. It is a hardship assignment, no family housing, and few Morale and Welfare facilities. For the USA, it represented the famous tripwire that is meant to deter invasion, since it would force the U.S. directly into the conflict. From the North Korean point of view, it was the backbone for the long-anticipated American invasion of the north—despite its obvious lack of adequate armor and logistics for such an operation, clearly organized for directed fires at armored columns heading south.

Emily and Sean found Revetment 29 in a line of slightly raised concrete bunkers with hatches in the top for artillery spotting. Sean checked with the duty officer, and in a few moments they found the quarters of Capt David O'Leary.

Lorrie sat stiffly on a cot against one wall, while her elder son, David O'Leary, sat on a backwards chair chatting with her. Her other son, Lt Paul O'Leary, was apparently visiting since Sean recalled he was at Fort Campbell. Lorrie's huge eyes, hollow with lack of sleep, went to the floor when Sean and Emily walked in. Emily sat next to her, stroked her shoulder.

It was well that Lorrie kept her wavy blonde hair short and well-coiffed, for the neatness seemed to give her some structure, but with dozens of hard duty days in the last weeks on ABL, her anxiety seem to come out of every pore and Emily had never seen her so frazzled.

Lorrie sniffled, "I had to see them."

Lt Paul O'Leary and Capt David O'Leary stood when they saw Sean, and both greeted him. "Good afternoon, Major."

"Captain. Lieutenant. Sean Phillips."

"We appreciate getting a chance to see Mom," said the Captain, looking from Emily to Lorrie and then to Sean. "A bit of a surprise, though. She's a long way from home."

"While we're glad she got the chance, I'm afraid she's needed at the plane," Emily said.

At Sean's request, Capt O'Leary took him to the nearby artillery spotting station. "We've been watching them pulling back all week. Kind of interesting, you know? After so many years of not really seeing them at all—all their armor is in the bunkers, they don't have the gas or ammo for much running around. Just lots of artillery practice. Now, seeing those old T-55 tanks coming out, it looks like some kind of Cold War parade. Creaking armor. But it's all good too; good artillery and so on."

"After all the years, do you believe it?"

"We're a skeptical lot, us soldiers. Anyway," Capt O'Leary continued, pointing, "We're artillery position 3. We cover this whole section of the DMZ from here."

"You can see a long way from here. What if the North Korean artillery opened up?"

"We'd be safe underground. Until their infantry came and pried open our bunkers. Of course, if they use nerve or mustard gas shells, it will be really unpleasant."

Sean looked far out over the DMZ. Unlike all the days in years past, there was no sound of artillery practice on both sides of the border, a harbinger of the impending peace treaty. "Anything odd lately?"

"Other than Mom's visit?"

"We're heading back to the plane." Sean took a last look over the DMZ, and despite himself, said, "Look sharp, Captain."

Back inside, Lorrie sat unmoving and unresponsive, staring at the wall wide-eyed. Sean and Emily stood at the door, clearly waiting for her to respond.

"We need to go now, Lorrie," Emily finally said.

"They don't want me to leave."

Capt O'Leary smiled, "Mom, you can't stay. We're here for a reason. Go on."

Lorrie's fingers gripped the cot's blankets and she started to cry. In a voice on the edge of hysteria, she begged. "Please. I can't go. Let me stay."

Emily moved smoothly to her, motioning to Sean. "Sean, get her legs please."

With some effort—for Lorrie was a statuesque six feet tall, very strong, and now also panic-stricken—they picked her up.

Lorrie's sons both watched, bodies still and eyes unblinking, as in a concerted effort, Sean and Emily managed to carry the crying flailing Lorrie out the fort door.

*   *   *

They crossed the Imjin River bridge before Lorrie's crying jag ended. It was as if the water border, clearly an entry to the more peaceful normalcy of the South Korean countryside, let her get control. She leaned forward from the back seat and said sorrowfully, "'Kay. I'm better. I just had to see them. Thank you. Thank you."

Sean yanked the jeep to the roadside. As with so many roads in Asia, the shoulder was almost non-existent and the insistent speed of the small DMZ tourist busses sucked at them each time one passed inches away. He turned in his seat and barked at her: "So help me O'Leary, you leave your station again—"

Emily broke in, "Let it go, Sean."

He ignored her, said grimly to Lorrie, "You're the one the system gave a chance to. You're the one Emily swears is important, but you leave your station again, I will personally lock you up forever. Are we clear?"

"'Kay, you know I wouldn't except—"

"Keep it to yourself, I don't want to hear it," said Sean, jamming the jeep into gear, then waiting until a tiny heavy South Korean truck blew past and gave him a chance to yank the jeep into the traffic. Adding extra venom and anger to bite and hurt her, he said, "You screwed us. We had to go AWOL to get you and when we get back, they are going to fuck us. You're a disgrace to even Airborne Laser's low standards."

Lorrie gasped, and began to weep quietly. Emily, although she understood Sean's intent, went silent and kept her eyes out her side window, watching the rice paddies, high-rise clusters, and Asian city-sprawl the sixty miles to Osan despite the darkness of the long set sun.

Chapter 50

The 30th of October
T-2, 10:00 p.m. KST

OSAN FLIGHT LINE – AERO CLUB

When Sean parked the Humvee outside the Aeroclub and they went in, Harold and Sandy—with six beefy Security Police—were waiting.

The crew, with Chief Auggie there as well, apparently having gotten a lift over from Japan, sat at the plastic chairs and tables of the Aeroclub grill. Harold's telecom had apparently happened much sooner than Sean and Emily had hoped—and without their participation. Sean had emailed a short PowerPoint brief to make his case to Jeanette, but he hadn't thought it would help.

Apparently it hadn't—nor had their being Absent Without Leave.

Harold rose slowly, incongruously formally dressed for the treaty signing in top coat and hat, with Sandy at his side similarly attired. His SP's moved threateningly to circle Sean and Emily, who approached with Lorrie behind them. It was strange feeling, Emily reflected, this sense of peril even as they walked toward the bright polka-dot plastic tables and kitsch comfort of the greasy snack bar.

"Well, Major Phillips, Dr. Engle, my AWOL friends. The President has decided you are my guests until we figure out if the Koreas—North and South—are going to request criminal charges against you."

Emily said, "How about we make a deal, Harold? We'll leave now and not come back. Isn't that what Il-Moon wants?"

"Oh no. Tonight, you'll enjoy my hospitality—in the detention center. Tomorrow after the treaty signing, we'll see."

Sean yelled in his face, "This place won't be standing tomorrow."

Hakkermann ignored him, addressing the SP chief, "Captain, put Security Force guards on this plane. And I mean on the plane. These two are for the detention center."

Sean quick as lightning jumped Hakkermann, and just as fast, as if expecting it, Sandy whipped out a stun gun and shot it into Sean's back. Sean, jolted, dropped to his knees. Sandy put the stun gun to Sean's head and fired twice. Sean jerked, then fell onto his face on the tarmac.

Emily yelled and the entire ABL crew rushed to the fight. As the SP's drew their clubs, Emily cradled the unconscious Sean. She saw the crew moving forward ready to fight. She called out, "Airborne Laser, stop! Don't!"

The crew froze at her command. Hakkermann said softly, "Get these two out of here. Here is the detention order." Sandy handed the papers to the SP Captain, and they both moved away quickly as if embarrassed by the scene.

One SP grinned as if disappointed at not getting a fight. He took Emily's arm. By a painful pressure on her elbow, he pushed her toward a patrol car while others picked up an unconscious Sean.

Two SP's moved to stand guard over the ABL crew in the snack bar. As the SP police pushed Emily into the car next to a completely stunned Sean, she managed to stand, and shouted to the crew: "Airborne Laser! Lorrie is in charge!"

MAGNOLIA PALACE

It was 11:00 p.m., and Dearest Leader's wife Yong-Sok, and nanny Olathe, attending to the finally conked Jong-Jo, were too excited to sleep. The small family had spent the entire evening with Jong-Nam on the veranda, sitting in a comfortable living room grouping open to the garden, watching TV video of the USAF 7th AF withdrawing in wave after wave of planes, while their own beautiful KPA armor continued to move dramatically in long disciplined convoys away from the DMZ in the night darkness.

They were now awaiting their Counselor General, who was returning with both an eye-witness account of Osan, and the draft treaty.

Dearest Leader spoke to everyone present, a dozen or so, not counting his new Farmers' Guard at attention nearby. "We are gathered here under the veranda leading out to the garden, for this night, these images," he waved to the TV of the martial withdrawal, "mean we will all have to spend less time below ground, and more time among the people and the activities of the state. No longer must we worry or protect ourselves, for finally, we have stood down the machine. Take a deep breath of the garden air. This is the nectar of freedom and the scent of the future. The fresh air of the outdoors and sunshine."

There was polite applause, as most of the members were close family, friends, and clan. He broke away and excused himself as an aide brought him a telephone.

Dearest Leader took the phone, and heard Il-Moon's voice ask, "Dearest Leader, what news do you have?"

"It is very clear, according to our observers and the worldwide media, the Americans have withdrawn their offensive assets from Osan and Pusan."

"I very much doubt they have. Did you learn nothing from the night at the Mansion?"

Dearest Leader felt anger surge. Il-Moon was living in the past. His experiences with the Americans had apparently scarred him so badly he was frozen back in 1951. It was impossible to believe Hakkermann had been behind the mansion attack. No, he had himself watched the withdrawal and was convinced. He issued a curt order: "Vice Chairman Il-Moon. The Americans have withdrawn their 7th Air Force. Send the order to cancel any offensive activity and to stand down. We will meet Ambassador Hakkermann for the treaty signing as planned at 8:00 a.m. tomorrow."

"If that is your wish, Dearest Leader."

"Yes. You are to send orders out that all forces are to stand down. Are my orders clear?"

"Yes, Dearest Leader."

Dearest Leader hung up the phone crisply. He looked around bemused for a moment at his feeling of victory, and finally wave to an aide, accepting a rare celebration Soju when Architect Su emerged from the palace doors, followed by a young clean-cut officer, hands shackled behind him, and guarded by Company Leader Tong-Hu.

Architect Su said, "If I may introduce Major Tam Ho."

Dearest Leader looked carefully at Maj Tam Ho, whose face was set into a mask of granite.

Architect Su inclined his head slightly. "Although I found Major Ho in the Self-Criticism wing at the MPAF—a place he is not officially permitted—he declines to discuss Kang and the Mansion."

Dearest Leader motioned to the shackles. Tong-Hu released Tam Ho's hands. "Thank you, Company Leader Tong-Hu." Taking Tam Ho by the arm gently, beckoning Architect Su to follow, he led them along the veranda to an open area overlooking the garden. "Come, let us talk."

AIRBORNE LASER – TECH AREA

Within one second of Emily's order for Lorrie to take over, Jarhead smoothly as a python slipped an arm around frozen Lorrie, and slid her along toward Airborne Laser, leading the crew on board—followed by two SP's, M-16's at the ready. One SP moved up to the flight deck, while the other stood looking around the Tech Area suspiciously.

Inside the plane Jarhead swiftly brought his gunnery video up. Lorrie stood behind him watching as Jarhead tracked Hakkermann's limo and SP vehicles. They passed the Osan golf course, and wove between training and command buildings, finally separating when the limo turned into the 7th AF headquarters, while the SP vehicles stopped at a big blockhouse off the far end of the runway. Jarhead tapped a big finger on the video screen. "Confinement."

J-Stars looked at Lorrie. It dawned on Lorrie they were *all* looking at her. She managed to stutter, "Everybody, let's get to stations. Put your ears on."

7th AF COMMANDER'S CONFERENCE ROOM – OSAN

Ambassador Harold Hakkermann watched his aides do the final assembly of the telephone-book-like treaty documents. After an intensive two days of proofing, translating, and arranging, along the shiny top of the huge meeting table the peace treaty manuscripts were finally done.

The North Korean Counselor General had already taken one, carrying the treaty north to Dearest Leader for final acceptance before the midnight deadline. The formal signing would take place first thing in the morning at Panmunjom.

Leaving younger hands and better eyes to scan the books one last time, Harold moved to muse out the window. He could see the Detention Center, its heavy three story blockhouse solid, on its roof were poles and wires—a helicopter denial system to thwart escapes. He imagined Sean, lying unconscious in a cell. He shook his head in disappointment. Much as in the past, when he'd failed at State to prevent a war—and the military went into some country with their ham-fisted approach—on the night of his great world peace triumph, for this miniature failed peacekeeping, Harold felt a pang of regret and disenchantment.

Chapter 51

CELLBLOCK – OSAN CONFINEMENT

The SP's carried an unconscious Sean behind an angry Emily into Detention Control. The desk officer, looking out from behind heavy green bullet-proof glass, buzzed the side door, and Sean and Emily were taken past the armory, with its racks of M-16's, gas masks, and posters about base security and employment, to the booking desk.

The Duty Officer sniffed at the emergency 'Isolation Order,' essentially a diplomatic warrant for custody, as one SP said, "VIPs. Treat them well; we'll be wanting to hang them at dawn."

The upper-floor short-hold cell block was an open structure, with bars separating the inmates into groups. The only occupied cell held a dozen Republic of Korean Army (ROKA) Special Forces. In various stages of inebriation, some sang raucously, some held their heads in their hands, and some were passed out. One SP carrying Sean indicated the drunken soldiers to Emily. "Hope you don't mind company. USA-ROKA Special Forces reunion. Too drunk to go home."

As the guards lay Sean on the bunk in one cell, Emily moved in with him, said, "He's unconscious. It could be dangerous and I should stay with him."

The corporal knew they were guests of DoS and related to some high-up mess he wasn't worried about. He locked Emily into the cell with Sean.

Emily bent over Sean, touching his face. It was pinched and vacant. He was badly stunned, completely out of it.

Emily slumped down next to Sean, and started to cry.

MAGNOLIA PALACE

The big Combatant, Maj Tam Ho, and the diminutive and yet sturdy Architect Su, followed Dearest Leader along the veranda to one of his favorite spots, a corner overlooking the garden near the medieval Korean temple.

"Come, Tam Ho-ssi," Dearest Leader said, he motioned Tam Ho to his side, and they stood looking out into the garden.

In the rising Harvest Festival Moon, the garden was bright around them, shaggy trees, citrus and bougainvillea, and miniature palms in their enormous pots soon to be brought inside the palace for the winter. The palace children had pinned white paper leaves—each with a wish written on it—on the big row of dwarf magnolias, so in the light of the moon, they looked to be covered in blossoms. Twenty feet away, a huge marble statue of the Great Leader threw an arm wide to the bounty of Korea. As if forgetting their purpose, Dearest Leader suddenly rhapsodized to them both, waving to the moon.

"Ah, the night of the harvest! How many centuries our people worked this whole night, anxious to collect and store the bounty of the earth; the rice and the barley and the hay—to take Korea through yet another winter. This was the night no sleep was taken and no effort spared—even after a long day in the fields—of bringing in the future prosperity.

"See now, this is exactly a moon for all of Korea. Tonight, we harvest a crop we have nurtured for more than seventy years: we harvest Korea."

"I do not understand you," said Tam Ho reluctantly.

"I believe you do, Major Tam Ho," Dearest leader murmured. "Now, I know you are of the Combatant persuasion, and so perhaps you have worries at my softer approach to the outside world. Perhaps, you even think me weak?"

Tam Ho's eyes narrowed, unsure, knowing only this was a threat.

Dearest Leader continued, "Strange you would think I am weak, for of course you know I was head of the State Security Department. In that office, I have killed tens of thousands. Many others, I sent to prison camps, or to scream in basements, their families watching, until they took their turn on the wheel as well."

Tam Ho felt the impact of the direct threat—of torture and mayhem and disgrace for the hundreds of people in his extended family. His face hardened further, with anger, with confusion. "I still do not understand you."

"Of course you do! I could break you and your three hundred family members tonight—through death and much worse.

"Yet I confess to you, this is precisely what is wrong in the DPRK. Even if I wanted to torture you or your family tonight to extract the story of Colonel Kang and the Underwater Mansion—or to punish you for past deeds—I cannot. I will not force it from you—for I no longer have the competence. Let me tell you a strange fact: my old Agency will not survive this night.

"You stare at me as if I betray Korea, but do not my actions show that to be false? So, I will not torture you, or threaten your family. Instead, I invite you to sit with me here this night and glory in the new harvest, in the moon rising above the greatest country in the world—as it takes its place—not perfectly, perhaps not without stumbling—beside the other great powers in the world."

He moved in close to Tam Ho, his shorter stature showing as he looked up into the big man's eyes. "Tell us the story of Kang then, while we watch the moon light the garden and Korea harvests its future. Not because I could torture you, or your family is in danger—but because you know that I am true to Korea. You are forgiven whatever you misunderstood, whatever you did. Stand with us now, together, watching the moon lighting Korea—and tell me you know that I am, in some small way, not the devil, but somehow *Tangun*."

Tam Ho had been melting through this torrent of words; relief, anger, shame flooding him like never before.

Dearest Leader leaned in and whispered to him, "Look now well at the newest moon over Korea, Tam Ho-ssi. And tell me you know it is ours. Tell me you believe in what we are doing."

Tam Ho fell to his knees at Dearest Leader's feet, and managed, "I believe in you. Forgive me."

Dearest Leader spoke softly. "Then talk to us, Tam Ho-ssi. Tell us the story of Colonel Kang and the Underwater Mansion. The real story."

Chapter 52

MANCHURIA – MANCHUKUO – KHABAROVSK, RUSSIA, 1940

Colonel Kang, even in his family history, had been perfect. His grandfather had been one of the small band of Korean freedom fighters who managed to escape the Imperial Japanese Army in Manchuria during World War II—and so went on to win immortal glory as the 'saviors' of Korea.

When the Japanese 'protectively' occupied Korea from 1900 until 1931, they set to work eradicating Korean culture, testing chemical weapons on prisoners, and enslaving the population for their war industries. One of their greatest pests were the Korean resistance fighters—both communist and nationalist—who operated with impunity from the Chinese province of Manchuria. Striking across the border into Korea, they raided, harassed, and made the Japanese look silly—while life was not too difficult for the guerillas. In their safe base, they were graced with resources from Communist Russia and Mao Tse Tung's organization.

For the frustrated Japanese security forces in Korea, things took a turn for the better when Japan annexed Manchuria in 1931, creating their puppet state of Manchukuo.

The dreaded Japanese military police—the *Kempeitai*—immediately moved over the Korean-Manchukuo border and set up shop. They now controlled both sides of the border—and the fortunes of the Korean freedom fighters went down the drain.

Not only could they no longer raid Korea and harass the Japanese, without their Manchurian sanctuary, they couldn't even survive.

By 1932, the Imperial Japanese Army had established a continuous presence in Manchuria and working with their *Kempeitai*, had infiltrated and virtually eradicated the Korean freedom fighters. No sooner had the future Great Leader Kim Il-Sung and Col Kang's grandfather joined an underground communist youth group in May 1929, then they and their colleagues were arrested. Released as unimportant, by going underground and limiting his activity, Kim managed his greatest achievement between 1932 and 1940—and some say throughout the war—of just staying alive.

Nevertheless, by 1940, due to the brutal mortality rate of Korean guerilla leaders, Kim—only twenty-eight years old—found himself near the top of the Korean resistance. The Japanese military police records show Kim's star was rising steadily. The price on his head climbed from a paltry 20,000 yen ($10,000) in 1936, to 100,000 yen four years later. By late 1940, the Japanese were very interested in finding this rising Korean star, and extinguishing him.

Kim Il-Sung was living on borrowed time—and no one knew just how borrowed that time was.

As the future Great Leader and Col Kang's grandfather hid that Christmas in a basement in Manchuria, waiting for their splintered band to assemble for a last-chance dash for Russia and safety, they made a crucial mistake. They decided to wait an additional two days to gather more forces.

Unbeknownst to them, the *Kempeitai* had caught their ten-year-old message runner. The Japanese were dissatisfied with his confused answers and were sure he knew something: he was Korean, he had no family in Manchukuo, and he came from Hamhung—as did many of the guerilla messenger boys.

For three days in a freezing basement chamber, the boy screamed and choked on his own blood as—with a hammer and cold chisel—his interrogators methodically smashed every tooth in his mouth. They then got a dentist drill and drilled into the boy's broken molars until they could no longer revive him. But they never shook his stupid story of being on the way to the barber's where he gathered hair to sell to wigmakers.

Finally, the Japanese interrogators tossed the half-dead boy into the wintry street, never realizing he had known all along the location of Kim Il-Sung. The boy's silence ensured the Great Leader and Col Kang's grandfather withdrew just in time toward the north where—pursued by the Imperial Japanese Army— they would make their final daring raid on a Japanese mountain fort, and then escape for the rest of the war into Communist Russia.

The tortured boy lay in the freezing mucky street for only a moment. Architect Su, himself just eight, starving and puny, scuttled from where he had pretended to beg for three cold hungry days. He could barely heave the big older boy onto his little bony back, but staggered two miles—almost to the safety of the rice mill basement—before collapsing in a snowdrift to lie pinned under the older unconscious boy. It was the nine-year-old future doctor Gil-Yon who found them, half-dead. He ferried them both to the friendly women living in the mill. Having neither medicines nor pain-killers, the women wept as they struggled to save the tortured boy.

It was weeks before the tortured boy was well enough to follow Kim Il-Sung's band into Russia. Unlike the Great Leader and Col Kang's grandfather—and their wives—who were welcomed with open arms and housed in the best political camp in Khabarovsk where the meals were good and they even often had eggs, when the ten-year-old and his two ragamuffin friends staggered into Siberia through waist-deep snowdrifts, they were consigned to a nearby vermin-ridden concentration camp.

The Great Leader and his small band stayed in Russia until the liberation of Korea by the Americans. Returning with the Great Leader whom the Russians—recognizing his political and survival skills—put in charge of North Korea, Col Kang's grandfather went on to be declared a Hero of the Revolution, and Su had later designed a prominent statue of him for Kim Il-Sung square.

Col Kang's grandfather had become a hero—and Kang a perfect Son of the Revolution—because, under unspeakable torture, a ten-year-old boy did not betray them.

That ten-year-old boy's name was Song Il-Moon.

FLASHBACK – 1 AUGUST – MPAF SELF-CRITICISM WING

In the isolation area of the Self-Criticism wing of the MPAF, Col Kang sat writing at a small iron table in his monk-like cell. He worked on his faults, laying his soul bare beneath the watchful eyes of the Great Leader's portrait, and the ethereal presence in the very air of the excellence of the man and his teachings.

Every senior officer in the KPA spent two weeks in this wing a year, carefully writing out his faults and failings, while political officers from the Party gravely combed through them, prodded, requested more, and acknowledged these revealed weaknesses. No one could ever approach the perfection of the Great Leader, and Kang struggled at the iron table—even in his own perfection—to find his faults that must be shared and learned from. Here at the iron table, thousands of MPAF generals, admirals, and commandants had written out their faults and done their penance.

Col Kang worked diligently with today's lesson, based on the Great Leader's speech of August 16, 1969, wherein he 'Exulted the progress of the DPRK state, while extolling the virtues of humility as, even though we have passed the South in productivity, we must be ever vigilant.'

There was an art to self-criticism, to eking out your faults and secret failings. You must not find yourself without sin, for in the group sessions, even should your self-criticism examples be chosen by the political officer—as Kang's always were—as the most illuminating for group discussion, sooner or later, you would be both criticizer and criticized, and you must leave room for the others to flourish as well.

Kang had intuited that today was likely to start with a surprise inspection an hour earlier than usual, at a time when he would normally be asleep. This method of finding you non-diligent, as there were no clocks or windows, was a favorite tactic of the Political Officers. By springing in on you extra early, they could chide you for your lack of vigilance and perhaps even laziness. But Kung had sensed this morning would be such a trap, so he arose earlier and was not too hard at work—*humility*—when he heard the door open for the expected premature inspection.

Il-Moon walked in, and Col Kang rose to attention, astounded. *They are indeed throwing a hot potato to me today; a bombshell really: an on-the-spot inspection by the most senior Armed Forces' officer.*

Il-Moon did not sit, but rather approached the colonel until he stood right in front of his at-attention eyes. They knew one another well by sight, although it was more a clan connection. They had never directly addressed, for Kang's place was far below Il-Moon's, even with their family histories.

Il-Moon glanced at the criticisms Kang had penned, and smiled mirthlessly. "Is this all you can find wrong, when the Star of Korea is so high in the sky we all fail to reach it? Is this the limit to which you aspire?"

"Instruct me, Great Marshal Song."

Il-Moon shouted suddenly, "How can you write only this, when Korea is in such dire peril?"

Kang stood taller, saluted. "I will do anything required, Respected Top Leader!"

Il-Moon shook his head. "Why would I bother to tell you, if you cannot see the dangers Korea is in? Dearest Leader moves us ever closer to disarming, transforming us before our faces into lackeys of the Americans, and house pets of the Japanese." He spat. "Prepare to beg, Colonel Kang. Are you ready to kowtow to the Puppet State to the South, and lick Japanese boots?"

"Tell me what I can do!"

"Did your father and I not serve together in Fatherland Liberation War? Did I not keep my silence so the Great Leader and your grandfather could escape for the magnificent attack on Mount Paektu?"

In his first mistake in many a year, Kang replied gravely, "Yes. I know I owe you my life."

Il-Moon's hand flew up and slapped Kang across the face, rocking the big man back with the vicious blow and scattering his self-criticism papers to the floor. "How dare you! How dare you I suggest I did it for any man—except perhaps the Great Leader. You owe me nothing! I did it for Korea!"

"I did not mean to suggest—Grandfather admired you."

"He admired me for nothing! Do you think as a ten-year-old boy I kept my secrets *for him* even as I screamed for days, my best friend dead on the floor beside me while Japanese pigs smashed my teeth with a hammer? You owe me nothing! For what could you owe me, as my thoughts were only of Korea?"

Kang bowed his head. "I did not mean—"

Il-Moon fell heavily into the seat across from Kang, and his head dropped into his hands. "I-Pong Kang. If I could only tell you how grave the situation is, how hopeless."

"Comrade, if we know the problem, the challenge, there is nothing we cannot attain."

"Do you believe so?" asked Il-Moon looking up, his face ashen with depression and grief. "Do you then have such loyalty to Korea? If She called you to save her, could you scream and scream in a basement and yet stay true, speaking only lies to fool the enslavers?"

Kang answered, "I can. Did not the Great Leader himself say, 'We must strive with unflinching dedication to give our bodies to be broken if it is needed.' Together, we can accomplish the rebirth. What do you ask of me?"

Il-Moon spoke gravely: "We must awaken Dearest Leader. He slumbers, and only blood and trial by ordeal can lead him back into the light. It will take all our skill: for if our efforts are to enlighten him, the path must be shadowed and deadly."

Chapter 53

PYONG-SON COMPLEX

Il-Moon had hung up the phone with Dearest Leader and surveyed his realm.

Was it really true, the Americans and Japanese had bowed to North Korea? Groveled and given them everything they deserved: respect, fealty, recognition? It was unthinkable that the racist dogs would ever do such—if so, it was only to escape their fate.

No, the imperialists would never admit how North Korea had become—on her own—a superpower second to none.

On the wall map of North Korea, unit pins porcupined the country, each pin representing a different war-fighting capability. Aide Park bowed deeply, held out roughly bound papers. "Here are the final plans."

"Yes." Il-Moon touched Architect Su's plan, carefully hand-annotated with last minute personal guidance. Il-Moon did not need it. He knew the disposition of forces—the architecture of the attack—perfectly.

Around the walls, monitors showed his offensive staging sites all over Korea—and his commanders sitting at their posts. In the set of monitors showing his six Taepo-Dong missiles in the launching chambers, his big missiles sat below their launch tubes to the surface, fuel bleed-off plumes leaking grayish smoke. They stood, ready to launch up to the surface and beyond, into the skies.

He shook off a wave of nausea. His stomach had become distended with collecting fluids—the weeping of the invisible worm, he thought sardonically, its tears filling its own home. The skin over his abdomen was painful, taut as a drumhead, but at least the worm was quiet.

He became aware of his commanders watching him on video, waiting. Although the North Korean Military Intranet video was poor quality, he felt their attention; wondered if even this could hide his yellowing skin and the excruciating discomfort of his swollen belly.

Summing up his considerable strength, he met the eyes of his Commanders on the screens and reported sharply. "I have just spoken to Dearest Leader. He is convinced the Americans and Japanese are preparing to attack. We must be ready!" His voice rose to a boom: "Commanders, your readiness reports!"

General Kwon: "Cruise missiles ninety percent operational."

General Park: "Armored divisions ready, or moving north and ready to return. Artillery is at eighty-five percent readiness for bombardment."

General Kim: "Minisubs have deployed. Radomes and Ladomes are at ninety-percent ready."

General Pak: "Chemical and biological delivery systems are ready."

General Hu: "SCUD missile launchers are in place and ready for final orders."

General Kye smothered a smug smile, barking: "Combatant striking forces at one hundred percent ready!"

Il-Moon managed a glowering look. Inside, he felt like a young boy as he turned to his trump card. "General Namgun?"

"Yes," nodded the general. "Marshal Song, your Rocket and Air Forces are ready."

"Stand to stations!" Il-Moon dismissed his commanders. As they turned and could not see him, he felt for his chair, almost collapsing into it.

Il-Moon realized Aide Park stood almost in rapture watching him, empathy for Il-Moon's sick body filling him. Il-Moon should have been furious at the direct look—but he had known Aide Park more than six decades. In all that time, Aide Park had never once sat in Il-Moon's presence. Yet here, those sixty years of standing had led to their comradeship tonight. Il-Moon winced at a sudden sadness. *Perhaps there is no one left...I love as much.* He nodded at Aide Park, his silence stroking the old aide.

Aide Park bowed in understanding. He motioned to the first two missiles leaking wispy plumes. "Our special missiles will be ready for launch, should you need them, in thirty minutes. At midnight."

Il-Moon smiled at him. "Aide Park. More than Aide Park. You have served and prepared well. Sit, and let us watch the final fueling together."

NORTH KOREAN MINISUB 32 – KOREA STRAIT

The little North Korean ocean liner Mangyongbong-92 had expelled Minisub 32, submerged, in a flurry of wake and bubbles. It tumbled in the propeller-wake, losing control, which took the better part of twenty hard minutes' work to restore. Normally, a quick surfacing would have let the crew use muscle-power and some orientation sense to fix things. If they broke surface here, a Japanese defense radar would instantly fix them. Within minutes would follow a rocket-propelled torpedo or a Hunter-Killer sub screaming in at forty knots. The minisub crew of three instead struggled in the dim light and neutral buoyancy fifteen down where capricious surface currents swept and spun them. They were bruised and panting by the time they righted the sub, got the emergency power on, and learned to compensate for a bent elevator.

When Minisub 32 was ready, the commander ordered them to descend. They drifted downward, their seams leaking, paying out a tiny radio antenna which floated to the surface to receive their final orders.

Their experience was typical for the dozen minisubs released along the Korea Strait. A few were out of commission, and a few degraded. However, the mission planners had designed in a triple redundancy, so each mission objective was still covered even after accounting for the high mortality rate.

Each sub dropped to the bottom, the yellow light of their search beam attracting shoals of squirting squid. Each found what they were looking for: a berm—a tiny even-crested mountain—running along the sea floor. The subs settled onto the berms. The only ballast required to maintain their perch was their bottom-mounted limpet mines.

JAPANESE HUNTER-KILLER SUB – KOREA STRAIT

The distressed sounds of Minisub 32 were picked up by a Japanese sonobuoy, and the hunter-killer sub Misakawa Maru was diverted from patrol forty miles away to investigate. As the sub went to high speed, the captain came on the run from his bunk into the control room.

The Conn reported, "The sonobuoy signature suggests it is a North Korean minisubmarine."

The captain replied, "The North Koreans do not send minisubs to the Eastern Channel. They could not get back." He turned to the Weapons Officer. "Load the front torpedo tubes." He turned back to the Conn. "Exactly where are they?"

NORTH KOREAN MINISUB 32 – KOREA STRAIT

The captain of Minisub 32 said, "Good," as his sub settled solidly and one crew member snapped off the lights, while the other turned on the orders radio.

The commander checked his watch. "Twenty-five minutes."

His crew looked at him, unblinking, as he pulled out a package of cigarettes and a bottle of *Soju*, Korean vodka. Smiling, he proffered them.

The *Soju* was passed, and the crew lit up and breathed in deeply. Their exhalations quickly filled the minisub with smoke.

ABL – TECH AREA

Lorrie was Laser One at the moment, yet despite how she knew every detail of its operation, she had never felt so useless, a cry building inside her from a frustrated mire of misery and worry. Even worse was the SP guard by the stairs, or imagining the one upstairs in the flightdeck with Bozon and Slammer.

J-Stars' radar console buzzed calmly to life, and the guard seemed unconcerned at the ABL techies sitting listlessly at their consoles. J-Stars said, "The detention center. Across the runway. Far left window."

Lorrie, Jarhead and Matt huddled over J-Stars' shoulder. His low frequency UHF radar showed ghostly images through the detention center walls. Although the rebar in the concrete structure striped the image like a zoo cage, clearly two people were being escorted—one being carried—along a top floor corridor. They were brusquely pushed into an upper floor cell facing ABL.

Jarhead ducked back under his console, pulled out a pile of duffle, and climbed to the galley, "Hitting the head," to the guard who let him pass.

Lorrie moved back to her console, zoomed ABL's long-range video on Sean and Emily's window. A mile away across the airbase sat the heavy three-story building, a blockhouse of a prison. Razor wire fence topped the walls, the windows were barred, and the roof had anti-landing devices to ward off helicopter landings for escapes.

Lorrie looked at the heavy concrete and steel building. "God, what are we going to do?"

Jarhead came out of the galley in full battle dress.

Shakily, Lorrie looked at him, found herself getting up unsteadily. "Anyone for coffee?" She hung her purse over her shoulder, which kind of surprised J-Stars, and then went into the galley. Sean's super B-52 coffee dispenser could spin completely upside down without spilling. Lorrie popped the sideways pins, pulled at the whole unit, and it slid free with a jerk. She burned her wrist slightly on a hot corner of the burner case as she reached behind it and pulled out a heavy greasy bundle, then stuffed it into her purse.

MAGNOLIA PALACE

"Amazing!" yelled Dearest Leader, who was waving for a telephone. "Il-Moon arranged to have us—and himself—depth charged inside the Underwater Mansion! Just to make certain I did not trust the Americans! To make sure he could set up our armed forces for war—and to frighten all his generals as well."

He looked around distractedly for the phone. "But how could Il-Moon be sure something would not go wrong—just a split second miscalculation, the mansion would be destroyed—and with it his dreams for Korea?"

"Before Kang, the record for perfection was held by Il-Moon," Tam Ho replied. "He is a very skilled soldier, and we cannot doubt his courage. With the perfect I-Pong Kang prosecuting the attack and Il-Moon inside the mansion— they had the timing and explosion effects down faultlessly—risk to them was not an issue. They argued for days about the way to fuse the depth charges." He grinned with pride at the precision of the attack, its perfection, then caught himself, wiped the smile away. "I believe they in fact enjoyed the mission."

"But Kang voluntarily let them torture him for days, reporting only falsehoods. He let himself be executed!" Dearest Leader exclaimed, while Su looked gravely at Tam Ho, adding, "You were his friend, and yet you were in charge of his torture and execution."

Tam Ho looked away. "Yes, it was very hard. But at least I could slip in a word of comfort as they beat him, tormented him. At least Kang had someone there—unlike Il-Moon as a boy."

"But he had them execute his own family!" Dearest Leader exclaimed.

"No. This was one of my tasks. Kang and Il-Moon agreed Kang was so highly respected, if he were seen to make an assassination attempt—and scream treasons at you—he would surely inspire someone else in Regiment Koguryo. We had to ensure he would inspire no one else to try assassination. This was why the coffins of the family were displayed: so everyone would see and know the penalty was too severe. I escorted Kang's family over the Yalu River to China and hid them. When I signaled Kang at the stoning that his family was safe, he was then free to yell the carefully thought-out treasons at you." He turned to Su. "This was why I hid myself and my Watchers' file. I could not make the trip to the Yalu without my Watchers recording it. I could thus not risk my file being seen by you." He bowed his head in shame to Dearest Leader. "What Col Kang yelled at you was not true. Regiment Koguryo does love you. Our only thoughts were of...Korea."

For a moment the veranda seemed to shelter them, and the three stood together, feeling the warmth.

An aide ran up with a telephone and Dearest Leader rapidly dialed. "Il-Moon wanted to show the perfidy of the Americans. He wanted to make sure I got the message—his message!"

Su spoke. "That also explains why Premier Yu and General Chon had to die. They would never have gone along with Il-Moon's buildup. They had to be discredited, and removed."

"I saw their treachery with my own eyes. Talking to a spy."

"You said the video was poor. Voices are simple to imitate."

Dearest Leader had managed to get an outside line, and yelled into the phone. "I want an arrest warrant for Song Il-Moon executed immediately!"

MINISTRY OF PUBLIC SECURITY – PYONGYANG

While the North Korean state security organizations were viciously effective in their basic mission of promoting internal security—by using snitches and imprisoning anyone who even folded a picture of the leaders of the Kim Family Regime—dealing with upper echelons DPRK in-fighting was another matter.

Due to their possible threat to the Kims, state security departments were purposefully weakened by subordination to the National Defense Committee, which forced parallel organizations to all watch one another—the Ministry of Public Security watching the State Security Department watching the Guard Command, and vice versa. The members within these organizations were also beholden to different Committee members. Any action within the Committee itself was almost impossible: it would likely to be unpopular with someone— and that someone would take it out on you.

In the end, on this night as things were melting down and starting to spin out of control at the top of the DPRK, their vaunted security organizations were not in a position to prevent or delay for any amount of time the ensuing disaster.

When confronted by putting together the warrant and arresting team for Il-Moon, the system simply ground to a halt. Not only was he surrounded by Guard Command, but he himself had probably issued an arrest warrant for Dearest Leader—and who wanted to take sides in that fight? No one was about to bet their lives on Dearest Leader.

In the end, the Ministry of Public Security rounded up a few people and went to Il-Moon's apartment, knowing he would not be there.

Chapter 54

CELLBLOCK – OSAN CONFINEMENT

In the cell with unconscious Sean, Emily cried for perhaps ten seconds before she felt better and her nature took over. She wiped her eyes and went to the window. She was amazed: perhaps a mile away, straight as the crow flies, was Airborne Laser.

Looking out across the base, she was also startled by the full moon. As an amateur astronomer like so many scientists, she always knew the moon's phase. In the stress of the last few days, she had forgotten that tonight was a full moon. In fact, not just any full moon. At this latitude, the Harvest Moon—in some kind of god-gift to man—always rose almost straight up. The optics of this full moon's rising, at exactly the ripening of the summer crops, had since primeval times blessed those toiling all night in the fields to gather the last bounty of the summer's harvest.

Across the base under the dazzling moon, Emily had clear line of sight to ABL. She could even see its running lights were on and its port holes lit.

She sat down next to Sean. He was completely stunned, unresponsive, and his pulse was slow and irregular. She emptied his pockets and hers to take inventory as Sean had taught them in survival training. She looked at the pile of worthless items. *Well, so much for your survival training.*

Pensive, she tried to shake Sean awake. Nothing. From the holding cell, the ROKA leader Capt Ku remarked through the bars to Emily. "In the morning, his head hurt plenty."

Emily replied, slapping Sean's wrists, "He's not drunk. He was badly stunned. I have got to wake him up!"

Ku shook his head, put his arms through the bars and spread them helplessly. "Even should you wake him, he will be groggy for hours. Stunned is like hypothermia."

Emily flashed suddenly to survival training—to Lorrie humping Sean. *The fastest way to revive a man was...* Her preconscious reaction to the image of Lorrie on Sean was the rush of an unexpected shiver of pleasure. Then her Superego pushed her Id aside, and she groaned: "Oh, God! You are such a fink."

Emily pulled the rough muslin sheet and woolen blanket from under Sean, rolling his heavy body back and forth to clear the bedclothes.

Glancing over at Ku and his curious staring soldiers, she warned sharply: "Don't any of you even dare to peek!"

She climbed onto the bed with Sean and pulled the blankets over them. She shucked off her blouse, shook loose her hair, unhooked her bra, snuggled up to Sean—and kissed his lifeless lips.

PYONG-SON COMPLEX

The moon bathed desolate Pyong-Son complex in a ghostly glow. In the ICBM cavern everyone looked up to their Commander. Il-Moon fiddled with his system-wide mike whose feed went out to everyone in the KPA main forces command structure. His soldiers sat in their positions of battle preparation, and his commanders listened raptly, watching Il-Moon on video over the Intranet.

He felt the stirring inside of his long-quiet worm, the vicious bite almost causing him to fall from his seat. His hand slipped into his pocket, felt a dusting of the garden dirt, now soft as talcum power after its weeks of drying. He put his fingers to his nose, and just the smell of the fine dirt brought on a sneeze.

The sneeze wracked him, but when he sat up, he felt a calmness. Aide Park bowed deeply. "Your forces are now all in place. It remains only for you to decide our course forward."

Il-Moon let himself slip into reverie. *Sophistries. So many words spoken by both sides, so many arguments for peace and war. In the end, you must believe in something. I believe in Juche. I believe we shall prevail as the right future for Korea. All these arguments, do they cloud the brain? Is the sway between war and peace so great for me? Could I die, the worm's joke, knowing we are going into friendship with the Puppet South or the beast Americans? Perhaps—but there is that one thing still in the balance. One thing that cannot be ignored...*

The smell of the dirt had dragged up his last image of his fifteen-year-old sister. It was a photo from Manila, sent a month after she was taken. In it, she stood with five of her school friends, all bravely trying to smile. They were in Kimonos and wore Rising Sun headbands. They stood beside the stern Japanese officer who ran the local Japanese Army whorehouse—from which none of the girls would return—and where, mercifully, within a few short months, his delicate sister was to perish...

In the end, it tips around just one thing: they all must answer for my sister.

Il-Moon stood, his fingers in his pocket fondling the rich almost flour-like earth of Korea. "The Foreigners will never change. They will always seek to enslave us. Korea must go forward. We are not wrong in our belief in *Juche*—in our right to be a superpower and untouched by others."

Aide Park picked up the telephone, held it out: "The call is for you, Marshall Song. It is Dearest Leader!"

Il-Moon took the phone, listening to what was only a dial tone, then said, "Sir!"

Il-Moon slowly hung up. He turned to his many watching generals, seeing their rising passion for the fight, the beauty of their will. He spoke, his voice commanding: "I have received orders from Dearest Leader. To your battle stations. The time is at hand for the Great Fatherland Liberation."

From the gathered warriors, the shout of "Sir!" was expected—and yet Il-Moon felt it to his boots.

Aide Park handed Il-Moon the microphone to his waiting combat units. Il-Moon spoke to them all with the passion summoned up from the Korean earth around him. "Attention, People of the Armed Forces of North Korea! The reunification of Korea is at hand. You each must do more than your duty. Your Dearest Leader demands it. Korea demands it. You have your timetables. Keep to them." He raised a single index finger. "Korea shall be One!"

The control room shouted in unison, the words echoing in the rock chamber: "Korea is One!"

From his DPRK Military Intranet terminal, Aide Park looked up at Il-Moon reverently, expectantly.

Il-Moon roared, "Commence phase one of The New One Blow Non-Stop Attack!"

In their cave launch chambers, first one, and then the other of the two big Taepo-Dong missiles went to ignition.

CELL – OSAN CONFINEMENT

Sean woke gradually and reluctantly from a dream of the strangest proportions. He was dreaming he was kissing Emily, and he—and she—were enjoying it! It felt...guiltless. She kissed him again and it was like colors flowing through him. A wonderful dream river where his efforts seemed strangely tiring, yet a current of power in her touch swept him with a rush through insistent kissing and on into full joyous love-making.

He broke the dream surface to find himself responding to her insistent passion. He tried to rise and she nuzzled him, moved against him, pulling him up. His muscles felt as soft as rags and her lips and naked breasts and limbs against him so insistent, so calling, and yet he could not summon the strength to speak. *Why was it so hard to—*

The concrete block and bars of a prison came into focus. This seemed to demand some extra effort and he managed to ask, "Are we are making love in a jail cell?"

"Hush," Emily said. "Kiss me a lot."

"I always thought you were the kind of girl it took three months just to get a date from."

"This may save many many lives."

Sean kissed her back, energizing warmth streaming into him. "Don't stop until everyone is safe."

PYONG-SON COMPLEX

At the surface of the complex, in the barren cracked mud fields of Pyong-son, there was a double flash. The first and then the second Taepo-Dong missiles burst from their exit tubes.

Slowly, the missiles accelerated, overcoming the heavy hand of gravity. They climbed skyward.

LAUNCH WARNING CENTER – SCHRIEVER AFB, CO

Two bored Department of Energy guys idly watched monitors in a small vault. They were on duty only because the new SBIRS ICBM launch-detection satellites were still being calibrated, and it fell to them to perform the long and arduous multi-night procedure.

An alarm shrieked! The DOE guys freaked as two pinpricks bloomed on a monitor. Both froze for a moment; finally one yelled, "Call! Call!"

His partner grabbed a white phone. "Space Command Duty Officer? We're tracking a double North Korean missile launch!"

AIRBORNE LASER – TECH AREA

J-Stars' radars caught the movement of the missiles as they climbed. He'd been doodling along, seemingly not really paying attention, while their SP guard, M-16 held ready across his chest, frowned at the crew lounging at their consoles, ostensibly playing computer games and writing emails. J-Stars snapped a look at Lorrie, and she swung the hi-res video camera on the ABL's nose around. On the big screen, atop fiery plumes, the two missiles went streaking straight up.

For a second, the sight froze the Tech Area. Then Lorrie called, "Strikeback, this is Ops. What do you make of it?"

Eila breathed, "Ops, this is Strikeback. Launched from Pyong-son for sure but the trajectories are crazy. Why go straight up?"

KOREA STRAIT

The commander of Minisub 32 nodded to his crew, and they all took that last long drag.

In the Japanese Hunter-Killer, The Conn looked up and said, "The minisub is on the undersea cable trench."

"Cable?"

"The International Korea-Japan undersea fiber cable."

"Drive them off of it!" as the Weapons Officer gave a target solution for the minisub and their forward torpedo tubes flooded.

In Minisub 32, the radio officer looked up. "The order has come!"

The commander stubbed out his cigarette. "Korea shall be One!"

The crew responded in unison, "Korea is One!"

The Japanese Hunter-Killer was only a hundred yards away when a yellow light burst the minisub's walls outward like a glass vase splintering in slow motion. The light expanded, became white hot. The sea bottom swirled up as the limpet mine under the minisub exploded downward.

The small berm over the fiber optic cable was gone. In its place was now a ten-foot-deep crater.

The Japanese sub, caught in the explosion, took the hit on the bow, stalled, and sank out of action to the bottom.

LAUNCH WARNING CENTER – SCHRIEVER AFB, CO

One of the stressed DOE techs looked up as a high bandwidth data line fuzzed out. "Hey, the fiber link to Japan and Korea."

EXO-ATMOSPHERE – TAEPO-DONG MISSILES

The first Taepo-Dong missile broke out above the atmosphere. Among the pinpricks of stars and the glowing moon, the first Taepo-Dong warhead burst in a silent *explosion*. Millions of tiny ball-bearings flew out like shotgun blasts into two cones of deadly space debris.

A MilSAT communications bird was just breaking over the limb of the earth, receiving intense streams of messages and orders from Schriever for its coming cycle over Korea. The satellite came in at seven miles per second directly into the ball bearing stream—and simply disintegrated. Nothing was left but a new lethal cloud of debris spreading out in its own deadly cone of orbital flak.

A huge Keyhole imaging satellite, currently under thrusting rocket motor control as it maneuvered under emergency commands, slammed straight into the debris field of the MilSATCOM satellite. The fifty-foot-long reconnaissance satellite broke in two. Its wings and solar panels breaking off, its huge spinning momentum wheel—now totally unbalanced but storing great amounts of energy—tore open the satellite body as the giant whirling wheel broke out from the satellite's guts.

In the path of this debris, all the satellites in orbit approaching Korea were being ripped to shreds. Before the debris field had finished, it had taken out four GPS satellites, two Defense Meteorology Satellite Program birds, and damaged or knocked out the operations of twenty more.

The second missile, another giant Taepo-Dong 1 missile broke into the tropopause. Its warhead *detonated*.

The nuclear explosion was unlike any that had ever been seen. In a frothing fire of radiation and burning atomic fuel far away from the shaping grip of gravity or against an unequal resisting force such as the earth or a buried cavern, the explosion wasn't a mushroom cloud. Instead of a directional response to the resistance of the earth's gravity and containment—and to the atmospheric soup within which an earthbound blast must propagate—in space the explosion spread out like a spherically-expanding fireworks' burst. Without the pull of any atmospheric drag, the fireball widened for a hundred miles.

This expansion too had been engineered differently: as the frothing fire and radiation spread, the expanding cloud shimmered the entire sky over the DMZ with a sparkling purple dust.

The pixie dust spread out over a vast area of the sky, smearing a giant cloud of sparkling tiny pinpricks of radio-transmission particles.

The cloud of sparkling light fluoresced and tingled on and on, slowly spreading above Korea and Japan.

Catchers in the Sky

BOOK 8

"Remember, it is easier to ask for forgiveness
than for permission."

The AFRL Project Officer's Eighth Commandment

Chapter 55

The 31st of October
T=War, Midnight, 12:00 a.m. KST

CELL – OSAN CONFINEMENT

Emily sensed a flash outside the window; a strange glowing for which there could be no earthly reason...

She heaved her attentions from Sean and their love-making. She jumped up pulling the blanket with her, leaving Sean exposed and panting.

At the window, Emily saw the purple sparkling sky and shuddered. "Exo-atmospheric nuclear weapons detonation!"

Sean staggered to the window, shaking off the intense but rejuvenating effects of their interrupted love-making. "...I thought that flash was...us."

Emily blushed, "Right," wrapped the blanket around her like a sarong. "No, it's a nuke lay-down—a communications killer EMP burst."

"Il-Moon you bastard. Damn you Hakkermann! We could have had Il-Moon by the balls."

"And now he has us. Brilliant idea. Unlike a real ICBM with its long trajectory and terminal targeting, a nuke lay-down doesn't require precision. Its just has to get high enough to wipe out satellites, radio, electronics."

Sean gripped the window's icy bars. "That purple sparkling?"

"Nuclear engineers call it pixie dust. The warhead was encased in isotopes that under fission radiation turn to bizzilions of highly charged particles. Like super-chaff. Comm and radar will be out for hours—over a thousand-mile-wide area. Japan too. Everything gone but lasers."

RADIANT OUTLAW

Radiant Outlaw, coming in over Korea, had seen the double missile launch and quickly took action. Its beetle-like carapace of Kevlar woven with conduction wires folded around the core satellite. It monitored the evolving cloud of space debris and maneuvered around the most deadly clusters. Smaller flying space junk and ball bearings struck its Kevlar shield but were unable to break through, EMP conducted away in the wires.

Ten seconds after the EMP pulse had passed, Outlaw opened its carapace and used its low resolution but decent infrared imaging system to looked around at a montage of destruction.

En route to the DMZ, flights of F-16s and other fighters reacted to the sudden death of their key electronics. "God. They've EMP'd us all to hell." Aircraft keeled over and dropped from the sky.

Around him, every low earth orbit satellite—their control systems blitzed, momentum wheels spinning wildly—were dying, brain-dead, or tumbling.

Above him, in the geostationary satellite belt, the big military and commercial Comm lines were just squealing noise.

Below, across North Korea, two hundred bunker tops opened. Large microwave transmitter dishes—reengineered satellite TV dishes—began *transmitting* pure noise into all the standard Comm channels. From within the same domes, small satellite tracking telescopes with blinding lasers came up, searching the sky for any still-stable satellites. They systematically zapped laser light into the electronic eyes of any satellite seemingly still living.

Radiant Outlaw could ignore all this, designed for just this eventuality, with adaptive filters for almost the whole electro-magnetic spectrum.

Outlaw's mind was simple, and yet he could tell. This was the mother and father of all communication breakdowns. Leaving Korea, to return on his orbit in ninety minutes, Outlaw pondered his next move.

PYONG-SON COMPLEX

Following Architect's Su's plan, Aide Park sent out commands out over the Military Intranet to Il-Moon's strategic forces for the first waves of the New One Blow Non-Stop Attack.

While the lay-downs were incredibly effective, they were essentially defensive. To win, you needed your offensive forces.

First, three hundred cruise missiles burst from underground bunkers across the DPRK. Engines rumbling, the deadly tubes cruised away south hugging the ground.

Within moments, from Onch'On-Up Underground Air Base, waiting Hughes Aircraft MD500 choppers—seventy-seven strong and each loaded with five Combatants—popped vertically from roll-top bunkers. Roaring off, splitting into small groups for infiltration, the choppers, disguised with South Korean coloring and unit symbols, got in low behind the cruise missiles. Across several bases, a thousand Combatant infantry ran for their An-2 biplane transports.

SCUD batteries, many in fire-from-under-cover launching tubes, others on big 8x8 TEL's hiding in the hills, valleys, and train tunnels, set to the difficult and time-consuming work to launch their long-range rockets at Japan's American air bases, and South Korean cities and political structures. Although perhaps only 30% were operational, in the inventory there were more than eight hundred SCUDs. The ones carrying the big chemical and biological weapon warheads were the trickiest, and the special teams arming and fusing them, despite the misery of their crippling protective suits, worked frantically to get them ready to launch.

Commands had also gone out to Il-Moon's withdrawing mechanized forces to reverse direction and high tail it for the DMZ. While they would arrive long after the main force, they would be incredibly effective as they flowed through already half-broken defenses and hit choke points from just behind the front lines.

Even at this moment of Il-Moon's triumph—he had made it!—he was experiencing waves of nausea. He wondered for a moment if it were his time. Through the pain, Il-Moon leaned over the shoulder of Aide Park, busily sending out orders on the Military Intranet. "And Magnolia Palace?"

Aide Park replied, "Your orders are being carried out even now."

Il-Moon sat back painfully in his chair, and the worm this time bit nastily. It was not Dearest Leader whom Il-Moon regretted—although his end would not be optimal. *Ah, Su-ssi! You were not bold enough to join me, and yet—fare thee well!*

MAGNOLIA PALACE

With the end of Maj Tam Ho's story, the peace treaty signing was forgotten. Architect Su ordered the Farmers' Militia to move the families, officers, and aides into the vaults below the palace, but Dearest Leader was yelling into the phone and wouldn't be budged.

Il-Moon's nuke missile burst overhead in a flare of purple flash.

Dearest Leader dropped the phone and staggered to the edge of the veranda. The sky coruscated like city lights in the sky. The radio, playing lovely Korean folk songs, faded to a hiss.

Dearest Leader managed to gasp, "What is it?"

Architect Su said slowly, "Although I have never seen one, it appears to be a high altitude nuclear burst."

"Could it be the Americans attacking us?"

"Since this action is exactly the start to the New One Blow Non-Stop Attack we have designed, I would say it must be our own forces."

Maj Ho stood forward. "It is not possible. It was not supposed to come to this!"

Dearest Leader suddenly shouted, "Call Vice Chairman Il-Moon immediately!"

His aide held the phone up like a small dead animal. "Dearest Leader. All communications have been lost. We have no way to reach Marshal Il-Moon—or anyone else."

A vacancy seemed to sweep Dearest Leader's face. He fumbled his plump form down into a seat—and sagged. He eyes went to the verdant garden and its moonlit statues. *Was this not his garden? His favorite veranda where under a happy summer sun as a boy he had played his Parcheesi...*

Architect Su opened his mouth to beg, to draw him back to awareness when, in the garden only thirty feet away, a statue of the Great Leader exploded in a geyser of white marble chips.

As the marble flakes from the mortar strike rained down on the veranda roof in a gentle hiss, from across the garden came a furious shouting, then explosions, then the thunder of discharging machine guns.

At exactly that moment, an assault wave of two thousand of Il-Moon's heavily-armed Guard Command bruisers—with orders to take out Dearest Leader, and knowing they were only opposed by some ill-prepared Farmers' Militia—rolled over the outer walls of the Magnolia Palace gardens with the force of an onrushing tsunami.

Chapter 56

The 31st of October
12:05 a.m. KST

AIRBORNE LASER – TECH AREA

"Battle stations! Laser up! Radars up! Every engine spinning! Get ready to rumble," Matt Cho had called out as the twin missiles had climbed. The ABL crew had jumped, bringing their stations to full functionality.

Lorrie let out a sigh of relief. *I'm so lost...Emily made me chief...I mustn't fade...I mustn't...* She clumsily swung the beam director around, getting a track on the rising fiery boosters, and putting the video up on the big screen—until she was jarred from her thoughts by their SP guard yelling, "Stop that!"

Matt yelled back, "It's a fucking missile launch! Let us go!"

"Fuck no! What are you talking about? It's some kind of fake..."

Jarhead asked Eila, "You're sure it's not headed at us?"

Eila shook her head, still puzzled. "No. Straight up. Like, Matt, maybe we should try to shoot them down?"

Matt said slowly, thinking, "The laser certainly isn't up, but we can't shoot ballistic missiles from the ground...bad atmospherics...that's why we patrol so high up..."

Everyone worked at their terminals, vying to get some kind of data on the rising missiles.

Their SP guard shouted, "Everyone away from those terminals!" even as ABL's four big jet engines rumbled, began to wind up. The Tech Area SP looked up at the sound, realizing his cockpit counterpart wasn't having any success either.

Red said, "We could take off, try to—"

Lorrie almost yelled, "What about Sean and Emily? We can't leave them—"

On the big screen, the nuke exploded in a swirling fireball.

Matt yelled, "Nuke burst!" and the chatter in the cabin swelled over the yelling SP.

Lorrie furiously gnawed a fingernail. "We can't not do something!"

The SP, with that panic that comes when a job looms too big, shouted "Yes, you can! You just sit there and do nothing."

The second guard appeared, pushing ahead of him Slammer and Bozon. "These guys are not working the plane."

Slammer said, congenially, "Hello Tech Area. We thought we'd see how you're getting along."

Their SP guards moved forward, brandishing their M-16's and now both shouting, "Get away from those monitors. Get away from those consoles. This plane is standing down!"

Red sneered at them, "Oh, and I suppose that holds for cases of war."

"You bet it does," yelled back the bigger of the two guards, and Red just flipped him the bird as the guards moved in, waving their weapons.

Lorrie had never been so scared. Not of the guards, but being so unsure. She looked up to find Jarhead smiling at her. "You or me, lady?"

She became aware of his fatigues, his stance so like her kids. Something broke free in her. Lorrie managed a smile back. "Marine, isn't it Corps' etiquette, ladies come first?"

"Yes, Ma'am. The Corps aims to satisfy."

Lorrie spoke with authority, surprising everyone. "'Kay, tech crew, everyone away from the consoles. The boys here want us to move, so we'll move."

The crew seemed shocked, but with the guards on hair trigger and Lorrie suddenly confident, they moved.

Lorrie hung her purse on her shoulder, walked to the center of the Tech Area, the guards to either side of her. She moved, sway-backed, her butt seductive, past the guards who watched her from perhaps ten feet away on each side. *Less than a second for them to jump you.*

Lorrie yanked out her Lady Smith .38 Special. She pointed it directly at one of the guards, keeping an eye on the other from her midpoint stance. "Both of you lie down on the deck right now! Right now!"

The guard considered this big feminine blonde with the elegant revolver fitting her hand perfectly. He was more enraged than scared at the challenge— he was sure the girl wouldn't shoot.

"Come on," he said, trying for his velvety policeman's voice, but finding it unusually high. "You wouldn't use that on me, an American."

"You're armed. Like you wouldn't draw on us Americans, if you thought you needed to."

His voice was slightly outraged. "Different. I'm police; I have legal orders to hold you."

Jarhead said, "Quit thinking so much. Get down on the deck like the lady's asked you nicely."

The SP's eyes blazed. "Put the gun away and we won't arrest you. This is a serious jail time offence."

He tensed to jump her as Lorrie said grimly, "I've fired this gun a thousand times. Please don't jump at me. Please lie down right now."

The SP was after all wearing good body armor—and she wouldn't really shoot him. He saw the opposite SP tense. Lorrie's attention flickered. He dropped his weapon and sprang at her.

Lorrie fired directly into his chest just above his sternum. He flew back, smashed by a Mike Tyson sledgehammer blow to his body armor right at his solar plexus. He splayed against the wall. Slid nerveless to the floor.

The other SP was almost on her. Lorrie flicked her wrist and the Lady Smith swung just a few inches—and yet it was pointed right at him. "Stop!" Lorrie shouted, and the SP recalculated...

He couldn't make it; she would shoot. He froze in a headlong stance. Off balance, he toppled to the deck at Lorrie's feet. He was instantly pinned by the crew.

Lorrie ran to the shot SP, sank down by him, cradled his head, and stroked his hair. He fought for breath, the wind crushed out of him by the dumdum bullet which had little penetrating power but the big hammer fist of a body blow.

"Cough," Jarhead coaxed. "Like you're at the doctors. It helps." It took the SP a few tries before he mastered it. He gasped up at Lorrie, "You shot me."

Lorrie bit a lip, looked miserable. "I'm really, really sorry. But we got a job we need to get on to."

TOKYO – COL HAREDA'S HOUSE

Col Hareda and wife Kyoko were enjoying a rare quiet time—or rather a noisy time. Their young son, a late gift to them, was playing a video game and in the small house his game-sounds percolated through the walls to the slight amusement—and usefulness to the parents. The clinking and beeping made them at the moment happy, for in the greatly tiring pulse of modern Japan, rather than hope not to fall asleep too early, they often found within their son's noise the stolen moments needed to make love. Moaning, Kyoko also laughed softly at her attempts to stifle her involuntary and loud love noises. Her moans were growing when the TV, used as additional sound cover to their play, went from a nature show on Hokkaido, to a squealing picture boiling in white noise.

Col Hareda rose quickly, pulled on his flight suit. "I am sorry, Kyoko. Something I must see about."

She donned a bathrobe. He looked at it wryly. With kangaroos rampant, she had adored it from the moment he had brought it to her from Australia. Now it was so threadbare one of her pert breasts stuck through a tear, the erect nipple teasing him. She smiled slyly. "I will not change. Come back soon."

Hareda-san ran to his son's bedroom only to find him sleeping, videogame still in his paw. Leaning over, he kissed him. At the door, for a moment, Kyoko clung to him. He kissed her. "I must go. Good-bye, Kyoko," and he was through the garden to the small garage on the alley.

His Honda motorcycle started instantly. He drove away over a little stone bridge, leaving the garage door open.

CELL – OSAN CONFINEMENT

Sean paced like a maniac, crawling the walls of their cell. It was maddening to see Airborne Laser—up and operating, its running lights on and few portholes lit brightly—right across the flight line. He had banged on the cell bars and gotten nothing from the SP desk below. "No fighter patrols, radar, radio. If Il-Moon invades, the battle could be decided in hours. How long will this laydown last?"

Emily finished re-dressing under the blanket. "A few hours. Military satellites may recover slowly." She was braiding her hair when her wrists brushed her earrings, ruby-like gems usually lost under her unruly moppet. She froze. Pulled off the earrings. "What's Il-Moon's order of battle?"

"An hour or so of hammering airbases like Osan. Then two hours of artillery attack before his armor blitzkriegs and grabs Seoul. He needs to knock out the bases; he needs to put Combatants everywhere. But most of all, he needs Comm knocked out for at least twenty-four hours."

Emily said, "So he's got five, maybe six more missiles."

"Il-Moon can't invade if Airborne Laser stops those next nuke bursts—and we're stuck!"

Emily looked across the runway; saw ABL slowly starting to taxi. "Geez. I hope they aren't leaving."

Sean took to banging on the cell bars again. "Let us out! We need to get to our plane. We can stop those missiles." He looked up to see Capt Ku staring at him. Sean gave him a quick bow in response to his puzzled look, and a Korean hello, then turned back to Emily. He realized she was messing with her earrings, seemingly wiring them together, and he yelled: "The world is at war and you're doing research? Don't you understand? They are going to slam this base with missiles and Combatants, waste the command structure, destroy the flight line, hit the family housing area—then break in here and kill us in our cell."

Emily finished, held up the wired jewels. "Beyond research. My little microlaser earrings." She blinked the tiny crystals at him. "Bright, see?"

* * *

Chapter 57

NORTH KOREAN CRUISE MISSILE BARRAGES

Abbey Yamamoto was to die in the first wave of cruise missile attacks.

Il-Moon had programmed no fewer than five missiles to hit her main haunt. He was insuring she had no chance to remain a player afterwards. Further, it was the best he could do to realize his daydream of swinging his own fists and smashing her revolting classic Japanese face into a bloody mash.

The voice on the phone had been familiar, and Abbey instantly recognized the young Korean *Yakuza* from the taxicab ride seemingly so long ago. "You have something for me?"

He chuckled. "Do I not always, Esteemed Reporter Yamamoto? The treaty signing will be moved up to tonight, or at least the signing of the preliminary agreement."

"Where, when?"

"Wait at the Golden Phoenix. I will contact you there at midnight. Do not miss me, for you are planned to be the only press present."

Cruise missiles are much simpler than conventional chemical rockets, depending as they do on simple airplane engines and airframes. Their flight trajectories are easy, cruising like light aircraft, navigating inertially or following a set of memorized terrain features. Simple, but highly-capable and prized assets—one of the keys to victory in any future war. They are also useful for soft political targets, and usually nothing except malfunction stops them.

The North Korean targeters had spent a good amount of time deciding where to strike in Seoul to neutralize the leaders who would resist the invasion and forced reunification. Easily entering South Korea hundreds of times over the DMZ and from Japan and China, they had methodically scoped out their targets. With so many important politicians' houses to attack, along with their official whorehouses, bars, meeting suites and office buildings, the targeters had dedicated only two big cruise missiles for the main press watering hole in Seoul—but Il-Moon overruled them and demanded five for Abbey.

From North Korea, the initial wave of three hundred cruise missiles headed south and quickly crossed the border. Following highways or other simple visual terrain, they separated into smaller flocks, and headed for their destinations.

There was little to stop them. Stealthy to begin with, and unexpected, in the confusion of the nuke burst and Comm blowout, few defenses lay between the three hundred missiles and their targets.

Most missiles steered toward the American airbase at Osan. A smaller group veered toward Seoul and the key haunts and houses of politicians, business leaders, and military commanders.

Il-Moon's pack of five missiles for the Golden Phoenix bore down silently on their intended target.

GOLDEN PHOENIX BAR – SEOUL

When the nuke burst occurred, the rolling thunder of the shock wave coming back down into the atmosphere was a horrible growling noise as if the earth were being torn apart. Although the Golden Phoenix had no windows, the rumbling outside brought the reporters flying out of the bar. They scattered along the sidewalk, necks craned for a better look at the shimmering purple sky between the skyscrapers around them.

Abbey in fur coat and Akiru were among the first outside. Abbey stared uncomprehendingly at the giant purple shimmering unearthly fire-flower in the sky.

Abbey asked, wildly, "What? What is it, Akiru?"

"It is war. I must get a shot of this." Akiru ran toward the Reuters' Hyundai 4x4. The sounds of sudden sporadic artillery boomed in the distance. The echoing explosion of a shell landing a few blocks away rocked Abbey, but she was so stunned, stuck in a mode of amazement and horror, she could only run after Akiru, thinking the car would be a safe haven.

Il-Moon had been right about using five missiles for Abbey. Many of the DPRK cruise missiles had been hurriedly converted from anti-ship to land-attack. Lacking the needed sophisticated terrain-mapping guidance, his first four became confused in the canyons of downtown Seoul, ramming into buildings to little loss of life, if large amounts of damage. Il-Moon's last cruise missile, however, was a copy of a Chinese HY-4 and a very accurate land-attack missile carrying a fifteen-hundred-pound warhead. It followed high-rise-lined Jongno Boulevard, and swept silently down the last ten blocks toward the Golden Phoenix.

Akiru ripped his camera from the back of the Hyundai 4X4, and leaving Abbey there, ran back into the street. Abbey saw down the full city block the cruise missile coming up the canyon of big buildings like a swooping deadly gargoyle.

She guessed its intent. Akiru, gray hair flying, ran back toward the bar, camera swinging up to focus on the sky.

Abbey screamed, "Akiru! No! Stay back!"

The big cruise missile buzzed straight into the Golden Phoenix. Punched right through the wall of the bar. A sudden flash and the bar simply disappeared into an expanding explosion. The blast caught Akiru from the side. Smashed, he was tossed up and into the street, his camera crushed to the pavement. He lay, a bloody rag bundle.

Abbey, wildly yelling a stream of Japanese, ran to him, her sentences a smear of prayer and horror. She knelt at Akiru's side. Dabbed at him with her handkerchief. In the orange sodium streetlights, his silver hair was shiny but the blood was black.

She ignored the evil *crump* of the first artillery shells bursting blocks way, speaking intently to Akiru, "You're all right. Like that time we hit a mine. We walked away. Both of us. You're all right. Akiru."

Kneeling by him, touching him, a feeling flowed into her hands and up her arms: the undeniable horrid softness of his body, its utter limp brokenness.

She put her head back and screamed to the sky. "Oh, Abbey! What have you done?"

OSAN AB OUTSKIRTS – CRUISE MISSILES

The packets of cruise missiles targeting Osan arrived in salvos.

Several groups followed the Han toward Seoul before picking up the train tracks between Suwon and Osan city. Others followed the main Seoul-Osan highway. No great precision was needed. Any building they hit at Osan would be a bull's-eye and they made up for their inaccuracy in numbers and deadly warhead size.

The cruise missiles found their last set of pointers to their objectives, and fanned out toward their targets on Osan.

AIRBORNE LASER – TECH AREA

Lorrie miserably watched her video of the cell block where Sean and Emily were imprisoned. Lorrie twisted her big hands in her hair. "What are we gonna do about Sean and Emily?"

Jarhead worked on getting his combat kit together, snapping into place the last piece of his M-4 carbine. "I'll just have to make a run for the cellblock and try to break them out...run us down the taxiway end, and I'll hoof it from there."

Matt exclaimed, "Man, that's a jail! One person couldn't...anyway, any moment there's going to be cruise missiles coming in. Slammer, can you come around to 030?" and the jumbo jet slowly adjusted to a north-looking stance facing the Detention Center. "Maybe we should take off."

J-Stars rumbled, "What choice do we have? This place is going to get hit hard, and we don't want to go down with it. Sean wouldn't want that."

Matt shook his head. "We can't leave now. Just one cruise missile could take out the detention center and kill Sean and Emily. We have to stake our position here." He looked to Lorrie. "Laser One, wake up! Red, set up a laser trip-wire. Establish a do-not-pass line for anything coming for Detention or us. Alright everyone, we're ready!"

Despite's Matt's up-beat manner, everyone knew just sitting there wasn't going to work for long. Lorrie stared miserably at the cell where Sean and Emily...

From the high corner cell, a little light blinked. "Hey," Lorrie called, excited. "We're being blinked."

Jarhead studied the blinking. "Why I do believe it's Morse."

J-Stars yelled, "Kettledrums! Laser Radar sees incoming cruise missiles. Man, dozens of 'em."

CRUISE MISSILES – OSAN AIRBASE

At Osan, the first warning of attack was the actual attack. The cruise missiles were designed to come in very low. Only at the last minute, you might see one sailing in. Silently and smoothly, the packs of cruising missiles glided in over the air base.

The first wave struck and exploded hangars, fuel, aircraft, radars, and the ATC tower.

In the next wave, as barracks, the Base Exchange, and Patriot batteries exploded, USAF troops ran helplessly.

AIRBORNE LASER – TECH AREA

In Airborne Laser, Matt Cho said, "Anti-air, Laser. Keep that laser fence up for us and the detention center, don't let anything through." He turned back to

Jarhead, "What's it saying?"

"I'm rusty." Jarhead tried to read the blinks. "It's repeating. It says," he read it out the letters: "Z-H-O-O-T U-Z."

J-Stars answered, "Zhoot Uz?"

A pack of cruise missiles quietly buzzed in toward ABL and the detention center. Lorrie yelled, "Laser ready for...Matt, look! They're going to hit—"

Jarhead jerked his eyes from the Morse and his Phalanx guns opened up in controlled bursts. The two leading missiles disintegrated into flaming shards. Jarhead complained, "My radar's not working well. Must be the laydown. I'm missing a lotta precision."

Matt Cho called, "Guidestar on!"

Lorrie directed the probe-beams out to tag the remaining missiles attacking the detention center. She yelled, "Lasing!"

The beam director shot single Attack Laser pulses. Each cruise missile in the line burst into pieces of airframes and jet engines tumbling end over end, the air resistance catching them as they lost all aerodynamic smoothness and slammed into the ground.

For one second, the crew looked in awe. Then the cruise missile attack was hot and heavy again. When ABL had swatted aside the next batch, Matt said, "OK, I think we've got the range on them. Anti-air, keep watching." He swung around to Jarhead. "Now, what the heck is the message? Zhoot Uz?"

CONFERENCE ROOM – OSAN

Ambassador Harold Hakkermann looked out at the burning airbase in shock. Strangely, in the moonlight, almost in slow motion, you could actually see the cruise missiles. One came buzzing right toward his window, its motion almost balletic.

He and Sandy together looked back across the big polished table. On it, were fifty telephone book-sized copies of the peace treaty. Harold considered preserving one, but found his body throwing itself out the window in a shower of broken glass. He fell heavily into sharp shrubberies below.

Sandy had moved like a cat to the table, grabbed a thick bound treaty—and so did not make it out the window in time.

The cruise missile punched into the wall and the room exploded.

Leaping after Harold through the broken window, the polished wooden table made shrapnel that whistled through the air. It caught Sandy on the way out the window. Impaled, he fell to the ground still clutching the treaty.

Harold felt Sandy fall behind him, but the sound was not human. It was the plop of something spongy, mangled. Rolling Sandy over, Harold clenched his teeth in agony at the mortal wounds. "I'm sorry, son. I guess we did go to hell."

In the fiery heat of the burning building beside them, Sandy managed, "It's no trick going to hell." He feebly pushed the now bloody treaty document into Harold's chest. "But it takes a Missourian to come back…" Sandy's voice faded, and his youthful jaw stiffened in death.

Hakkermann's sobs wracked his frame as he knelt over the dead boy—but the burning building beside them shot up a geyser of hot sparks. There was little cover here, and no time for grief. He pushed Sandy's coat up over his eyes, ran with the thick treaty book, and dove under a nearby clump of laurel bush.

From under his slight cover, Harold could see most of the airbase was burning or under attack; muzzle flashes and fires everywhere. With a start, across the airfield he saw the slowly taxing Airborne Laser. A cruise missile streaked toward the Detention Center. ABL sent out a brilliant red rapier-thrust of laser light.

The missile flash-exploded to shreds. The darkened Detention Center sat quietly.

Harold stepped out from hiding. In the flame flickering illumination, he snagged a pair of running Airmen. "Presidential-level request: get me to the Detention Center."

COMBATANTS – OSAN AIR BASE FENCE

For the Osan strike, the North Korean Special Forces had scraped together the very best helicopters and transports in the entire country. Despite demands that they attack several key logistics and political centers, Architect Su had insisted on attacking Osan with every single Hughes Aircraft helicopter they had.

Architect Su's use of the Hughes choppers was effective. As they were a standard ROK chopper, with their western military look, and each marked with South Korean military insignia and Identify Friend or Foe transponders, the few operating ROK anti-air units were fooled. Although several of the choppers were lost to accidents, defections, and navigation failures, the remaining seventy choppers moved with deadly speed, landing in the old quarry across from the darkened Osan flight line and the open area around the runways.

Combatant Specialists ran to the airbase fence, setting up fence-breaker torpedoes. Others stood up mortars and began bombarding the nearby concrete sheltered Patriot missile batteries. Across the base, a lucky shot exploded a hangar full of jets and fuel. Other shells hit the last operational aviation radar.

The fence-breaker torpedo blew off, and a whole section of the Osan fence collapsed. Combatants swarmed out of their choppers, and carrying mortars, Stinger-type missiles, and machine guns, effortlessly formed into assault lines—and crossed the fallen fence to finish off the Patriots and seize the runway.

Some of the Combatants dug small trenches at the flight line end. There, they shouldered Stinger-type missiles, waiting for any aircraft foolish enough to try the runway. Within moments, dozens of Combatant An-2 biplane transports skimmed in to land over them onto the tiny section of seized runway, skittering off the tarmac beyond the Combatant lines, and spilling out hundreds more attackers.

On the far runway end, USAF aviators ran for the few planes left at Osan. An Apache helicopter lifted off and sent some cannon rounds across the base and into several of the landing An-2, exploding them into bits. But it was only seconds before SA-7's shoulder-launched missiles shushed from tubes and caught the Apache into a fireball.

AIRBORNE LASER – OSAN AIR BASE APRON

"Combatants!" breathed Jarhead. "A full battalion. Armed to the teeth."

The choppers had indeed come over the fence where Sean had noted the abandoned quarry. Luckily for ABL, she was now at the far end of the air base, although bursts of rocket propelled grenades and small arms fire were already falling just short of defensive positions on the flight line.

Jarhead studied the scene. "They'll take the base in no time. Well, if we ever thought about leaving, it's too late now." He pointed to the end of the runway. "They've shut the back door—and it's just a matter of time before they get close enough to put an RPG into our fuel tank."

"We could use the laser on them!" Auggie suggested.

"The Attack Laser only has a hundred shots," Red said. "The beam is ferocious but really tight. It won't do much against spread-out troops. We'd skewer a few guys and blind some others. And then we'd have nothing left for missiles."

Matt looked from the Combatants to the Morse blinking. He yelled in frustration, "What are they trying to tell us?"

Red jerked her head up. "We are such goofballs. Zhoot Uz has an obvious transcription error."

The crew all suddenly realized.

"Tell me the dits and dots to answer," Red said. "I'll blink the red laser back at them."

CELL – OSAN CONFINEMENT

From his window, Sean could see that Osan was falling. It was one thing to absorb the cruise missile attacks, and in fact there were small squads of soldiers now shooting them down at a decent rate as they cruised in over the base.

It was the North Korean Special Forces that couldn't be stopped. Fanatical, prepared, and deadly, they knew no limits of warfare as they struck across the base to set barracks and housing on fire, knocking out gas stations, vehicle pools, Comm and power lines, and driving for the hardened command post. With its lines of supply and Comm, a modern army is severely hampered when a striking force shows up within it. The small groups holding out in the cover of the blast hangar, flight line fence, and buildings lining the runways might slow the attack for a while, but not for long: with Osan standing down, they were outnumbered and outgunned ten to one.

Sean gripped Emily, "Have they got it, have they got it?"

Emily didn't reply, just stood patiently at the window, blinking her tiny earrings at ABL as it taxied, its nose turret tracking missiles.

With the dual assault of cruise missiles striking among them, and the Combatants moving forward, the USAF defenders fell back to the next line of defense, a set of blast shields and barriers between the runway and the operations center. A few tried to hold out at key points, while most retreated or died.

Across Osan Air Base, hell and death and pandemonium reigned.

WHITE HOUSE LAWN

Revving choppers crowded the lawn near the Rose Garden. The President, his family, and top aides were hustled from the side entrance of the White House by a squad of Secret Service in a flying-V formation intent on the choppers.

The President's young military attaché moved with him, spieling the latest from the Situation Room. "It was some kind of North Korean nuclear lay-down. Comm to Korea and Japan is blacked out."

"Blacked out? Even fibers and satellites?"

"I don't know, sir. Nothing seems to work. Satellites are out of it and the Internet is totally spammed. Missile launch detection satellites still have some capacity but we can't see what's happening on the ground. Best to get you safely out to Andrews. Joint chiefs, National Security Council, the usual suspects, will meet you there."

The President pressed his family and staff to precede him into the helicopter, turned back from the doorway to the attaché. "That Air Force Under Secretary always guilt-tripping me on North Korean technology?"

"Jeanette DeFrancis. I have her headed to Andrews also, Sir."

The President gave a well done nod, stopped in the door. "On my watch. The second Korean War."

The military attaché said, "Of course, sir, there's that silver lining."

"Which is what?"

"I don't know right now, Sir. There always is one."

The President gave a taut smile, nodded, and entered the chopper.

FARMERS' MILITIA – MAGNOLIA PALACE GARDENS

The first wave of shock troops from Il-Moon's Guard Command—in two battalions' strength—struck with sledge-hammer force against the outer walls of the Magnolia Palace grounds. The two thousand Guards rolled over the few Farmers' Militia pickets on the walls despite a ferocious defense, and swept toward the inner palace wall in a solid wave of attackers firing as they came on.

The attack had been preceded by a set of mortar lobs over into the garden to try to catch anyone in the open, but instead had keyed the farmers' defense.

They had also failed to consider Tong-Hu's foresight.

The Guard Command were all spread out in the open ground between the inner and outer garden walls when—under Tong-Hu's radio instructions—the Farmers' Militia Auxiliary Artillery on the outskirts of town opened up with every field piece they had.

Completely saturating with high-explosive and shrapnel shells the defensive perimeter laid out by Tong-Hu—as the farmers inside the Palace walls ducked for cover—the artillery salvos fell everywhere throughout the outer courtyard. In the mercilessly open area, the massive blast and shrapnel storm laid waste to the attacking Guard Command. In panic, some of the assault force caught in total defilade kept advancing—and ran into seven hundred Farmers' Militia on the ramparts of the inner walls with AK-47's and tons of ammo from the Guard Command armory under the Palace. Others retreated back across the shrapnel-swept open ground of the garden under the punishingly-accurate farmers' volleys. Of the huge attack force, fewer than half managed to make it back outside the outer garden walls to safety.

Architect Su heard the huge bunker doors below rumbling open, and pushed Tam Ho and Dearest Leader ahead of him down the stairs to the extensive and heavily-armored vaults below. Dearest Leader was still in shock; his eyes flickered back and forth without focusing. The rough growl of the vault door seemed to startle him awake. "Architect Su, this must be Il-Moon's doing. The missile burst. This attack on the Palace. What do we do now?"

The huge *crump!* of the artillery strikes above shook the stairwell around them in a low continuous earthquake rumble. Architect Su answered simply, "The farmers will hold the Guards for now. Let us get down into the vaults. I think I may have an idea."

AIRBORNE LASER – TECH AREA

"Sweet!" yelled Matt as the last set of cruise missiles fell away. Airborne Laser—once they realized the cruise missiles were as easy to hit as amusement park ducks and took only tiny draws from the laser magazine—expanded their defensive perimeter to their line-of-sight within Osan. From their angle looking almost due North toward the source of the missiles, they'd been able to stop every cruise missile headed in to strike fuels, operations, or the command center. "OK, I think we've got the measure of them. Red, take over for Jarhead."

Red jumped to Jarhead's station, listening to his intense last minute whispered and pointed tips, as the crew felt ABL slow to a measured taxi.

Matt said to Jarhead, now laden with full combat gear, carbine and Dragon ATGM slung over his shoulder, handing him a husky laser pointer, "This is a Russian tripled-YAG laser pointer. It's not eye-safe—you know the Russians and safety—but plenty of juice to talk to us. You know what you're doing?"

"'S alright. I know what's expected of me."

"Keep your eyes off the Detention Center. Just keep low and moving. You've got exactly five minutes."

Jarhead ran toward aft, and dropped out ABL's rear hatch to the tarmac.

Matt said to Lorrie, "OK, O'Leary. Let's get Sean and Emily out of there."

CELLBLOCK – OSAN CONFINEMENT

Sean could sense Airborne Laser blowing away the attacking cruise missiles all around and over the top of the detention center. He was seized with a desperate longing to be at the controls, knocking the missiles down himself. Suddenly, ABL's beam went weak. The cockscomb laser on the roof blinked.

Emily asked, "What does it say?"

Sean bellowed at the ROKA in the next cell, yelling in Korean: "Get down! Get down! Cover your eyes! A death-ray!"

Outside their window of their corner of the cellblock, formed up at first tenuous and then brightly gleaming: a golden guidestar!

Sean tackled Emily to the deck and yanked a blanket over their heads.

The guidestar's golden light flooded the cells with a strange warm glow...

The ROKA Special Forces saw the weird glow, reacted to Sean's obvious display of terror. "Ai yee! A death ray!" Their eyes went round and they all hit the deck.

Outside, a huge crimson flash as Airborne Laser's Attack Laser—welding torch intense and a two feet across—slurped into the Detention Center like a hungry fiery tongue.

Grout and cement exploded. Steel melted. The barred and covered window blew inward like hot wax in the face of a flame thrower. The laser ablated away the wall and came roaring into the prison.

"Can you cut a path for them, keeping the aim-point high?" Matt asked Lorrie.

"Don't worry," Lorrie replied, "We have pinpoint control," which under her shaking hands wasn't that true to begin with—and when the nose gear on the giant taxiing plane hit a crack in the apron, the laser beam jinked down and up.

The laser cut down, splitting the floor, then up to ream out the ceiling.

Sean and Emily and the imprisoned ROKA cringed as the laser rip-sawed around the cellblock, randomly blowing away doors and setting walls on fire. Matt, watching the video, yelled, "Stop! Stop!" and the laser died away.

When the laser's roaring sound had passed, Sean jumped up pulling Emily with him. The acrid smoke of burned concrete and steel and vaporized paint was intense. As it cleared, their tearing eyes looked around.

The entire upstairs cellblock had been Swiss-cheesed.

Sean remarked, "For a purely defensive system, your laser really boots butt."

Emily countered, "Let's quibble later."

The ROKA Special Forces guys stared about them, trying to comprehend the wreckage.

Sean addressed them in Korean: "If we can get to the death ray, we can use it to stop the missiles. Are you with us?"

Capt Ku looked at him for a microsecond. "Let's go!"

Below, the detention center front desk was manned by only a few young SP's, as almost every soldier had been pressed into service out on the flight line in the fire fight with the Combatants.

The few SP's left didn't argue with Sean—despite having locked him up just an hour ago. They were soon deep into the Detention Center's arsenal, tossing out weapons, grenades, and ammo to the ROKA. The weapons quickly issued, Sean soon had twenty well-armed soldiers—and Emily.

GOLDEN PHOENIX BAR – SEOUL

The sounds of distant explosions had grown to a swell in her head, a background of anger and death all around as Abbey wrapped Akiru in her fur coat and dragged him across the street to the Hyundai 4X4. She managed to hoist him into the very back. She opened the coat to look at him. His face was calm and his eyes closed, although his gray hair was matted with blood. Abbey, crying now, shakily lit a cigarette, then exhaled smoke gently over his face. "If you'd left me you could have finished your years in Tokyo. Why did you stay?"

Abbey jumped into her Hyundai, revved the engine, and jerked the 4X4 away from the curb. She drove off hard through the canyons of Seoul's modern glass buildings, shiny windows gleaming eerily with the flashes of distant artillery.

OSAN CONFINEMENT – CONTROL CENTER

Harold Hakkermann, face ruddy with fury, entered the Detention Center like a bull charging. He carried the huge treaty book, and was followed by his two armed airmen. He found Sean at the booking desk where in peacetime, countless DWI and other misdemeanors had been processed. Sean was talking tactics with Capt Ku and looked up angrily when Harold yelled: "You! You're responsible for this. You provoked them and now this."

Emily expected an answering explosion from Sean, but even as the war swirled around him, he seemed to ponder Harold's words. "Truth is, I'm kind of puzzled. This just isn't the smartest move in the world from Dearest Leader's point of view." He mused. "Something you said, something about him. 'He'd have to be a great actor to pull this off?'"

The thoughtfulness seemed contagious, for Harold took his time answering. "I still do not see how I could have been wrong. The man really connected with me. He is just completely missing that frigid attitude toward human beings the rest of the regime seems to live and breathe..." He stopped mid-sentence.

"Exactly. He was the one of the whole bunch who really wanted peace. There must have been others who, let's just say, kept the dream alive."

Hakkermann was nodding. "You think Dearest Leader might still be willing to parley?"

"As you said, he knows what he wants. Perhaps you can still give it to him."

"What about you, son?" asked Harold. "What are you going to do?"

"Something massive. Meantime," he motioned to Harold's escort, "The Osan main gate will still be clear; you can make it to Seoul. We're heading to the plane. We stop those next laydowns, the battle will break our way. You just get to Dearest Leader fast."

Harold smiled back, hefted his treaty book. "I'll talk to him. I'm not a betting man, but I'll wager after you're finished, he'll be in a listening mood." At the door he turned. "You have Presidential Authority to fly out and provide anti-missile support to the Korean Theater."

Emily laughed. "Geez, if you make Sean legitimate, he might go soft on us."

Hakkermann glanced to her love-making flushed lips, to Sean, and back to her. "I think I can count on you to stiffen him back up," at which Emily went pink.

Sean's combat experience and training consisted of the usual weeks in Air Force Officer's Training School, and as a field grade officer, he'd passed a few tests on tactics. After ten seconds in the company of Ku, a battle-hardened Special Forces officer who was as tall as he was and twice as strong, Sean let Ku organize their breakthrough to Airborne Laser.

Ku took one look out the window, saw how the Combatants were using nearby flight line trucks and low brick walls to assault the 51st Fighter Wing headquarters building. He dropped the binoculars from his eyes and turned to his men, intent and pleased. "They have passed us up. We are behind them!"

Sean could see by the grim smiles that they fancied their chances. It would be a slaughter, and that was fine with them, as there was no love lost between the North and South Special Forces. The North Koreans were trained to strike hospitals, politicians' families, and soft targets that the South considered terrorist in nature. The training of the South Koreans was the opposite: they saw the Combatants as evil in a way that was as deeply inculcated into them just as the North's forces were trained to hate the South.

Spearheaded by the ROKA Special Forces, twenty soldiers moved out quickly from the Detention Center. They ran silently across the light landscaping of miniature pine trees and low walls between them and the Combatant squad who blocked their path to Airborne Laser—and whose backs were to them.

Sean ran with his M-16 just behind the wave of rifleman. Emily had pulled at his sleeve in vain, arguing he was too important to go into combat, Sean replying, "We need every rifleman we have, or we might not break through. Follow me, keeping low, thirty yards back."

"You mean thirty meters."

Sean smiled. *These scientists...*

As the ROKA moved in quickly from the rear on the line of Combatants, Sean could see to where the beleaguered USAF Security Force defenders barely held out in their defensive position around the Red Horse squadron building. Outnumbered and under intense fire by Combatants, the SP's were held down on their front by direct fire—which would fatally prevent them from defending against a run around their flank. Already, a group of Combatants were crawling around, taking advantage of the frontal fire distraction.

Emily lagged, seeing the silhouettes of the attacking ROKA Special Forces in a bobbing line ahead of her, Sean's slightly higher profile moving with his distinctive raw-boned jog. Emily followed, running bent over forward, the smell of grass and fire intermixed in her nose as her heart thumped at the sight ahead of Sean running right into the hell of the firefight.

It was almost quiet in the rear, sort of a lull in the battlefield—until the attack.

Emily stopped and crouched as the ROKA Special Forces swept in on the Combatant rear, laying down a withering fire into their backs. The Combatants panicked, rolled, and returned fire. The firefight raged for what seemed to Emily a long time and yet was only seconds before the ROKA overran the Combatants. No quarter was asked, and none was given as the final moments were hand-to-hand between the surviving Combatants and ROKA. No one surrendered, although in the frenzy, the intermingling of troops allowed one tough Combatant to slip through the line where, in the process of escaping rearward through the thin ROKA line, he came upon Emily.

The Combatant was on her before she could move a finger. Grabbing her by the throat, he tackled her onto her back in a shower of pain and shock. His face full of loathing and fury, in a smooth python-like move, he slipped from a boot scabbard a huge serrated combat knife. A weapon only for killing, Emily saw the blade flash in the flames of the burning base as the enraged Combatant raised the knife.

Emily looked into the vicious face. She knew she had only a fraction of a second to live. She calmly and directly met his eyes—and smiled gently. *Perhaps, even in this moment, this hate-filled person could change...*

The Combatant, shaken by her gaze, hesitated...and in that borrowed moment, he did indeed change...Clonk! His face grimaced, then smoothed. He toppled onto her limply.

Jarhead, looking down on her from behind the North Korean, slung his M-4 back on his shoulder—after employing it in a head-banger to knock him cold. Emily's Friends' gaze had bought just the split second needed to save her life.

Rolling the North Korean off Emily, Jarhead reached down, took her hand and pulled her to her feet. "You know, Herr Doctor, your blackjack method really does work."

Emily barely managed, as her heart seemed to swell in her chest until breath itself was impossible, "Doesn't it, though?" Then she hugged Jarhead for a long second.

COMBATANTS – USAF SECURITY FORCES – OSAN AB

Such fratricidal battles between ROKA and Combatants were happening across Korea on this saddest day of the glorious millennia of the peninsula.

Brainwashed from youth to believe any evil against their fellow citizens to be sanctioned and glorified, the Combatants met their match in those raised in freedom to protect and defend the innocent and the helpless.

Yet happily, the battle was not completely joined, and in the bloody night, there was unexpected honor. As the Combatants moved into a Korea that was their own in language, signage, and people; saw the shops, the cars, the flower gardens, the pictures of children and pets, most of them were unable to carry out their bloodthirsty objectives.

Thus this night, so full of slaughter and fire and the sword, was also a night of redemption.

In the annals of the Combatants, it was this elite corps' finest hour. Oddly, by forswearing their oath to kill unmercifully their fellow Koreans in their beds, homes, and streets—and in surrendering, defecting, and retreating—the honor of the Combatants, the elite of the North Korean armed forces, reached its historical zenith.

Unfortunately, the remaining twenty percent of Combatants did strive to carry out their inhuman orders.

At the American airbase at Pusan, the Combatant assault did not fare as well as at Osan. All night long, vicious attacks and counterattacks swept the base, passing through the power plant, the control tower, the housing area, and the hangars. Luckily for the Americans, Pusan was two hundred miles to the south of Seoul, the attrition rate on the Combatants' An-2 transports was close to 70%, and no helicopters made it. With only three hundred Combatants on the base, at punishing losses to both sides, the Pusan Security Forces fought the attackers to a standstill.

Sean called across to the defending USAF Security Forces, who had ceased firing following the counterattack, and now squinted into the sudden quiet. "Hello, Security Forces! We're U.S. Air Force and ROKA Special Forces. The Combatants are kaput. We're coming over."

Silence for a moment—the relative battlefield seconds seeming to take forever—and a defender's shaky voice, female, called out, "Come ahead slow."

Senior Master Sergeant Thurston—who seemed to be in command of a small group of SP's—had the deepest reaction of happiness and relief. A tough athletic woman, Sean saw her BDU's carried not the SP badge, but the Osan Logistics unit symbol. She and her surrounding SP's could only stare as a motley Sean, Emily, Jarhead, and their ROKA Special Forces jogged up.

The first thing Sean noticed was, in the slight shelter of the bullet-ridden Red Horse headquarters' sign and holding M-16s, stood Col Kluppel along with some DIA types. Sean put out a hand. They shook, and the colonel said, "Well, well, well. They just couldn't keep you out of the cookie jar."

"Oh, they slammed the lid on my fingers a few times. What are you doing up here?"

"Down in the Ant Colony, not much goin' on. We thought we'd lend a hand. I'm afraid we're going to leave you now." He and his DIA people were already moving away. "Someone needs to cover the housing area. The Combatants get in there, it's bad JuJu. Adios."

"Adios. Catch you at the Mustang club." Sean's farewell wave seemed to trigger SMSgt Thurston, now released from the heavy mind-pressure of combat. "Thanks! Thanks! So what's your story?"

Sean pointed the mile across the runway to where Airborne Laser taxied slowly, running lights off, spookily dappled and camouflaged in the low light of fires and moon. "I'm commander of Airborne Laser. Our only prayer of stopping the North Korean missile attacks. I need your help."

ABL's laser suddenly flashed from the bulbous beam expander nose and exploded an incoming cruise missile. Emily murmured, slightly hurt, "It's like they don't even need me anymore."

SMSgt Thurston whistled, "That's amazing. Except I got orders to hold Red Horse headquarters."

"The Combatants have passed on. The real problem is over there."

"It's clear to your plane. You can make it."

"Maybe I can reach my plane but I'm going to need help getting it out of here. Look." He pointed to where the far-off entrance to the runway was a traffic jam of burning and waiting to takeoff warplanes, transports, and tankers.

An F-16 gave it a try, ripping down the runway, using an evasive twist on takeoff, going almost straight up. Counter-missile flares burst from its dispensers.

The Combatants at runway's end launched a stream of shoulder-launched missiles. Many were spoofed, but it only took one, and the up-rocketing F-16 exploded. Flaming debris rained back down onto the runway end, which was already a burning hell of jet fuel and exploding munitions.

Jarhead said, "The Combatants are knocking down everything taking off. Someone first has to suppress them at the runway end, and—"

"—We'd do what we could, but we couldn't help much at such a heavy attack point," interrupted SMSgt Thurston, indicating they all had only side-arms. "We're not infantry like these ROKA guys. I'm Logistics." She pointed to her small police crew. "They're cops."

Sean smiled. "Exactly."

Chapter 59

WHITE HOUSE ROVING SITUATION ROOM – ANDREWS AFB

Pulled from their homes, desks, and vacations, the National Security Council had rushed to Andrews and within an hour of the nuke detonation had assembled and gotten the main information available.

Looking at them around the shiny mahogany table in the rambling open space of the Situation Room at Andrews—it had all the essential communications, with the additional security of Air Force One idling nearby—Jeanette mused. These were the right people. She knew them all, and yet in her anxiety and stress, she saw them more as functionaries than as her old sparring partners; in some strange brain-twist her mind short-circuited from 'John Abernathy' to just 'DOE.'

It was the same with the others at the table NID—the National Intelligence Director—and the leaders of the CIA, DOE, DIA, NSA—except for Gen Bolds, the Chairman of the Joint Chiefs and military advisor to the Council, whom she knew well personally.

The President finished a side conference, confirming that the Vice-president, Secretary of Defense, and Secretary of the Treasury—not present for reasons of chain of command—were busy working on the other parts of the crisis.

They had all heard about the sophistication of the anti-satellite debris burst, the laydown itself, and they were now looking at the options. The President was shaking his head. "Harold really thought Dearest Leader was on the level. Could this be an accident?"

"It was no accident. The space debris burst was pure attack. For the nuke burst, from its placement, yield, and after-effect, it was designed to destroy all radar and satellite communication in Northeast Asia."

"And it did?"

NRO shrugged helplessly. "All the stationary satellite assets we had—all the way out to the Van Allen belt—are gone. I don't know who came up with this approach over there, but whoever it was, he was razor-sharp. With the laydown and the jamming and the debris burst, we've lost most of our space capability—and we depend on it heavily."

Jeanette sighed and added, "We've talked for years about a 'Space Pearl Harbor.'"

The President repeated, wonderingly, "'A Space Pearl Harbor'? We took no preventive action?"

DOE said defensively, "It's all in the risk, Sir. You can harden one satellite at a cost of $3 billion, or you can spend $3 billion and have dozens of useful but vulnerable satellites. We traded it, and in the heat of battle on cost versus risk..." His voice trailed off. "It wasn't an easy tradeoff."

"Yet now it is leaving us completely in the dark." The President stood and paced. "How long until we get some word from the theater?"

Gen Bolds shook his head uncertainly. "Perhaps four hours of recovery time for our most hardened assets. If—and that is key—there are no more laydowns. Another space nuke burst, the clock gets reset to four more hours of waiting."

NID added, "The North Koreans would know lay-downs fade. They have to have a good number more missiles. The last test launches they did were five launches within a few hours."

Gen Bolds agreed, "Without knowing more, it's risky sending our long-range bombers—an overhead burst and they might get knocked out of the air. Plus, what would be their mission?" The Joint Chief added, gravely. "We don't know if there's an invasion yet. Our boys may have no place to touch down if in trouble. This Comm attack means they most likely have attacked our airbases with all their might, Kadena and Osan especially. But we just don't know. To fight a war deaf, dumb, and blind. How can we do it?"

'THE PIT' – REUTERS OFFICE – SEOUL

Hugh Levine, in the darkness of the power-outage-ed Pit, heard the breakers flip as the emergency generators came on, then cut off again. Just one second of lights and power before the breaker pulled too much current. As usual during grave shift, he was alone and it made it impossible to think what to do. *Try to get The Pit back up? Leave?* His eyes desperately tried to adjust to the small sets of emergency lights. But they were on the far walls almost a basketball court away, and the light reaching The Pit only shadowed the edges of plastic monitors and strewn papers.

Outside in the darkened elevator area, Abbey burst from the stairwell. In the partial darkness, Hugh could hear her jagged breathing as she entered and ran to an equipment cupboard and rummaged roughly. Camera equipment, cables, and power packs tipped to the floor from the densely-packed shelves. She yanked out a big video camera.

Hugh said, "All Comm is down, Abbey. Nothing can go out."

Abbey snarled, "You think you have a future in this business? A loser like you would never think of taping the news," and yet Abbey's hands shook so hard she could only fumble with the camera kit.

Hugh looked into the dimness behind her. He slowly asked, "Where's Akiru?"

Abbey started violently, video equipment falling from her hands. Hugh, now close enough in the semi-dark, saw that her face was puffed from crying and her eyes and mouth were just dark slashes in her makeup. Hugh moved to her, put out his hands.

"Stay away, I'm going to work."

Hugh, noticing for the first time how much wider he was than she, pulled her resisting womanly frame to him. She went still and let him hold her.

Hugh said, "I'm sorry."

"Sorry is for slobs," Abbey said, burying her face into his shoulder. "Keep out of my way. I said *I'll* do it!" Yet she held onto him fiercely.

Hugh let her go gently, picked up a camera and stuffed it into its case. "You'll need help."

Chapter 60

The 31ˢᵗ of October
1:00 a.m. KST

ROKA (SOCOM) – ABL – OSAN FLIGHT LINE

Sean put out a hand, touched Capt Ku's arm. "Get close, Captain. When you see us coming, hit them and reopen the runway."

Captain Ku gave a short salute. "You can count on us."

Sean looked at the North Korean Special Forces camped *en masse* across the runway end. *It will take a miracle to break that stranglehold and survive.* He uneasily turned back to meet the ROKA Captain's eyes.

In them, he saw grim amusement. Ku had watched Sean conclude the runway-clearing assault would be suicidal. *What would the American major say, knowing that following our assault on the runway's end, he and his ROKA men would certainly die in the Combatant counterattack?*

Sean put out a hand. "Thank you," and as they shook he said sincerely, "Sean Whittier Phillips. U.S. Air Force."

Ku flashed a smile, shook back, pleased. "Ku Au-Joung, Republic of Korea Special Forces."

"After the war, I'll look you up. We'll drink to our luck."

Again, Ku seemed amused. "Ah, no, Major Phillips. I believe we shall drink to victory!"

He turned and his ROKA Special Forces, bent over half-way at the waists, moved off at full speed toward the runway's end.

Sean tried unsuccessfully to brush aside a pang of regret, then left it hurting and turned to his group, "OK, Cops. Let's move."

Emily touched his arm. "I didn't know your middle name was Whittier. That's an old Quaker family."

"We all have a past, and that's half of mine."

"You're a Friend and you never thought to tell me?" Emily mused, not sure Sean even heard, for the sound of gunfire and ordinance detonating were like a constant rumble around them.

"Seemed unfair to use it. Kind of like cheating to get into your..."

"Mind?"

Their run to intersect the taxiing ABL was brutal—especially because all the way, Sean talked nonstop, giving SMSgt Thurston instructions. Sean's group managed to reach the apron just as ABL rolled massively past them at a horse's canter. The main hatch opened, and J-Stars, waving to them, dropped down the emergency rope ladder which swung precipitously.

Running in front of the frightful juggernaut 747 landing gear rolling right at them, Jarhead got Emily onto the rope ladder, smacking her rear to get her moving up toward the hatch.

Sean, running, motioned the cops toward ABL's landing gear. "Hop on! We'll ride you where you need to be."

The cops looked dubious. Just jogging underneath ABL's huge metal belly near the rolling monster-truck-wheeled quadruple-wide landing gear was dangerous. But riding? Somehow, they all managed to jog alongside, swing up, and get a grip on a greasy strut. When the half-dozen of them were riding high, SMSgt Thurston gave a grim wave, and Sean grinned, waved back, and sprinted ahead to the swinging rope ladder.

Following Jarhead, he climbed twistingly up the swaying rungs and into the Tech Area.

Home!

MAGNOLIA PALACE

By the time Dearest Leader, his family, Architect Su, and Tam Ho were safe in the vaults below the Magnolia Palace, already twenty SCUD D long-range missiles had been launched at American air bases in Japan. Of the twenty, only a few managed to get through. Several were intercepted in terminal mode and a couple during initial flight. One was very lucky—for the North Koreans. The fifteen-hundred-pound HE SCUD warhead slammed into a Kadena flight line fuels area and the resulting fireball at that end of the runway took out more than just a month's supply of Jet-A. This also impacted a big part of the infrastructure of the bomber area of the air base and took all the attention of the fire fighting brigade to try to save the nearby hangars filled with newer aircraft. The busy flight line, accepting aircraft of all sorts coming in from Korea, was bedlam as well. Especially with the reports of incoming missiles, many combat-ready planes were moved into old and decrepit revetments for at least some protection, and became stuck or were abandoned.

Architect Su logged onto the DPRK Military Intranet and saw the orders for next wave of SCUD launches. These were to be tipped with chemical and biological weapons, and he could see the KPA batteries methodically moving through their launch sequences, although they were slowed by their MOPP protective chemical suits. The top-heavy nature of the KPA was also evident:

the Intranet was jammed with orders going back and forth from the various underground command nodes, pointlessly calling again for launches which were behind schedule. Despite this slowness, soon anthrax, plague, cholera, and mustard gas would be winging their way toward Japan.

Tam Ho stood at attention, until Dearest Leader, pacing the room, indicated him to be at ease. Although there was silence from the garden above, Dearest Leader was in a fit of thought. He snapped his fingers. "Ah! We can escape on the underground railway to the Deep Hide bunker outside of Pyongyang!"

Architect Su countered grimly from his PC terminal. "If you remember, Il-Moon held a big inspection there on the day of my granddaughter's wedding. I would guess the railway is not a good option."

"Yes," Tam Ho agreed. "I do not think that course of action is wise."

Dearest Leader studied him. "Thank you for confirming this. Now, I ask you, was war your intent?"

"Never, Sir! We were keeping the North vigilant...I was a fool. What does it matter now?"

"Tam Ho, before Korea is ruined again for generations, will you help us?"

"I will."

"You could safely take the underground train out of here, could you not?"

"Yes, I am a known ally of Il-Moon."

"Good. Go. Find Marshal Il-Moon. Bring him to us here. Or stop him."

"I could help you greatly here. If you fall, who will take your place?"

Su answered, "All we know is it must not be Il-Moon who does so. You can find him; you know him." From above in the garden, the gunfire and thunder of artillery had faded. Architect Su added. "Do not worry about us. We will hold out. Either way, someone must go to Il-Moon and stop his orders."

Tam Ho mused, "I suppose I have the best chance of reaching him."

Dearest Leader said to him, "Go. Now. Fulfill your task for Korea's sake."

Major Ho turned and ran down the stairs toward the underground railroad.

Dearest Leader moved slowly to where Su sat at the terminal, put his hands on the old architect's tense shoulders and squeezed gently. "Well, my true friend. Tam Ho is a brave man, but how likely is it he can reach Pyong-son? Just as how likely is it we can do anything here?" He slipped into an Americanism: "Il-Moon seems to have thought of everything, while I did not have even a Plan B."

Architect Su looked up from his PC, smiled. "Not quite. I am now logged onto the Military Intranet as you. Let us see what we can do with your wide-ranging powers."

AIRBORNE LASER – TECH AREA

Sean climbed the last swaying rungs of the ladder, and as he poked his head into the Tech Area, for a moment—remembering training—it was funny how happy he was to be there. Inside, Lorrie and Emily screeched and hugged and babbled. Sean, pulling at the big front hatch to slam it, caught the end of their girl talk as Lorrie cried, "I thought you were dead!"

Emily put her head on Lorrie's shoulder, "It was awful—" She looked up and grinned. "And then Sean and I..."

"All right! Love and War! Was it good?"

Sean swung Airborne Laser's front door closed with a *slam*. The crew looked to him. "We can talk publicly about our sex lives later. Right now, let's get this bird into the brawl."

In the Tech Area, everyone fell to working hard. Sean ran through the prepping plane, up the stairs and toward the cockpit. He barely noticed Jarhead behind him, who caught him just behind the cockpit. "Com'on, Sean. Just give me half a turn."

Sean said grimly, "I don't know if we can risk it."

"Sean, you could see the wedge. The Combatants are going to hit the command post, sure. But units are breaking off to wheel left. That's to hit the family housing area."

Sean heard, processing this while he yelled to Slammer and Bozon, "Keep rolling toward runway 8-Left."

Slammer assessed the runway and taxiway ahead, totally jammed with disorganized planes and munitions' wreckage. "Through all that? I'm from LA, but even so I'd call that serious congestion."

"Don't worry." Sean lightly punched Slammer's shoulder. "I've got traffic cops all over it."

PYONG-SON COMPLEX

It was odd, Il-Moon reflected, sitting in his deeply-protected cavern, with the entire country's armed forces at his fingertips, that the feeling was changing, evolving.

It was a kind of series of odd pulses of pain and relief, Il-Moon thought, the worm giving him slight grief, but mostly quiet. Il-Moon could sense it waiting. Ready to nip, or now to bite.

He was, however, at some lower nervous system level, anxious as well. He knew the key to his attack plan was getting the armor across the DMZ and around Seoul quickly. Enough time had passed so that most likely, with the cruise missile and Combatant attacks, Osan was out of the war, and Kadena destroyed by the SCUD attacks.

With the invasion forces wheeling from just north of the border, he needed confirmation of the Osan-Kadena destruction—and ABL—before he would send the armor into the DMZ. In preparation for that, he planned to use his huge artillery forces.

But he had to know. If these assets were not out of the war, he needed to spend more resources—more missiles—on them rather than on other targets or to hold in reserve.

He took from his pocket a pinch of the dirt from the doctor's garden. He needed a small pinch in his mouth to pull himself back from the feeling of some brink, the wall, some pit before him.

Strengthened, he thought about the gut pulses, most coming when thinking about the SCUD chem-bio missiles. It hadn't felt like they had taken off. There wasn't the feel—or the view of them on the video cameras that monitored the launches. He sensed no victory exultation that should come when your rockets strike home, and Japan is bloodied with a potent strike. "What reports do we have on the progress of the softening-up phase? Are we ready to proceed with the invasion force?"

"It seems we cannot reach the chemical warfare units, the Anthrax artillery batteries, and the SCUD launchers. These should all be attacking and yet I cannot confirm their orders."

With those chemical and biological warfare agents loose in the cities of the south, the panic and sickness and shock would be a powerful psychological pressure on the South Puppet State to withdraw and surrender. Without these weapons of mass destruction, the ability of the ROK to form up behind the lines was formidable. He cursed the God of War who was dealing him such a short suit.

"The reason for this?"

Aide Park replied uneasily, "Fog of war. Perhaps there have been air strikes or failures in power. Perhaps the Americans have struck back."

"I need your assurance of Osan's destruction; otherwise we need a second strike. We must be sure that Osan air base—and Airborne Laser—are destroyed."

OSAN RUNWAY ENTRANCE

At the taxiway, Sean's cops jumped off the rolling landing gear and ran to the jammed-up tangle of motley planes. The cops directed planes off the runway, forming them into lines on the adjoining aprons. They were in a terrible position, with the North Korean line advancing from their position in strength at the end of the runway. In only minutes, the North Korean forces would be within RPG range, and the runway entrance would be a killing zone.

SMSgt Thurston managed to get some partially debilitated Warthog tank-busters turned around on the grass and faced down the runway. The pilots then opened up with their 20mm cannons straight toward the Combatants. This stopped the Combatant's forward motion, as they struggled with a new reality—a stream of deadly heavy cannon fire skimming the ground and mowing down anything standing. Unfortunately, the Warthogs didn't have much ammo, but they slowed the advance and lifted the attacking fire on the entrance to the runway.

Soon the cops had things stabilized and cleared a path for Airborne Laser. In a scene repeated many times, a cop would run beside an F-16 gridlocked on the apron, would wave to the Perspex windscreen.

The pilot would slide the cover back and stick out his head.

The cop would yell up, "Presidential Authority: you are to form up with Airborne Laser anti-missile battle group at grid 38-124 over the Sea of Japan. Follow her on takeoff."

One F-16 pilot asked, "You mean that big ugly plane?"

"Right. Pull out of the way now, let her go. She'll provide cover. Follow her out!"

"Sounds like a swinger."

As fatally perilous as taking off might at the moment look, as a pilot, you were dying to go. Sitting here at the end of the runway, with flack bursting on the runway and missiles coming in, Slammer and Bozon felt like sitting ducks. Even lucky small arms fire could cripple their giant jumbo.

Misunderstanding the cop's directions, a huge KC-135 tanker rumbled around, and headed down the runway.

SMSgt Thurston, even knowing she couldn't be heard in the roar of engines, nevertheless ran after her, frantically waving. "No! Wait!"

The tanker rolled down the runway, picking up the momentum to fly. As she headed up into the air at the runway's end, Combatants popped up, shot missiles right into her underbelly. The tanker exploded into a smearing broken slide of fireball across the runway.

Slammer saw the tanker explode as he continued to wheel Airborne Laser to poise her to enter the runway. All around them, the flashes of small arms firing and missiles bursting and fuel going up was like the swelling of some brewing up volcano. Up ahead across the end of the runway lay the remains of the tanker—and a wall of flame.

Sean said, "Can't stay here, gentlemen."

Bozon replied, "Did we say we wanted to?" He jammed all the throttles forward. ABL's four engines growled and then wound up into a full scream.

Airborne Laser accelerated down the runway toward the mountain of flame.

Jarhead was still at Sean's shoulder, his voice desperate. "Well?"

Sean didn't answer. His eyes were out on where he knew Ku and his men crouched, doomed, and yet waiting for Airborne Laser to get just a little farther...

The line of North Korean attackers had hardened now into three echelons deep, with small arms in front, here and there came now the spurt of grenade launchers and mortars acting like artillery clearing the way of such small resistance as the under-gunned machine gun bunkers. He could also see that Jarhead was right. The North Korean left was pivoting for a run on the housing area. All that was between them and the families was the sporadic machine gun fire at the runway's end from a small group of SP's who were cut off and fighting to the last man with Col Kluppel's small DIA band.

ABL was more than halfway down the runway when Ku's men popped up. As the Combatants rose, their shoulder-launched missiles tipping up and aiming, the hidden ROKA forces slammed a withering fire of automatic weapons and Dragon missiles into them.

In confusion and under the explosion of intense fire, the North Koreans dropped back, disoriented and in no shape to think about the runway. Any who remained standing were decimated by small arms fire, leaving the smartest fastest ones hugging the dirt.

The pocket of USAF defenders, until then under heavy attack near the runway, sensed the change. They looked back toward the wall of fire across the runway.

Through the flame-wall burst the bizarre-looking Airborne Laser!

As Airborne Laser lifted off past the defenders in their make-shift machine gun nests, the few beleaguered SP's saw clearly the rearing laser-spitting snake. One of them read off the unit symbol. "'Peace Through Light!' What the heck?" while at the other end, SMSgt Thurston and her crew whooped and waved the last aircraft at Osan down the runway.

Airborne Laser took off through the flames.

In the Tech Area, the crew gave a cheer as flames licked past the window and they heard Slammer yell, "Rotate!" and the huge landing gear swung up inside.

Airborne Laser sailed over the runway fence. "Flares and chaff!" yelled J-Stars.

Flares burst out in enormous streamers of fire. Most missiles going for Airborne Laser veered harmlessly. Those that didn't were blinked into confusion by the DIRCM defenses and accelerated back into the ground.

Airborne Laser was on the wing again—even if Osan Air Base were in her death throes.

Capt Ku lifted a hand in farewell. "There they go! Go! Go! Go! Get the death ray into battle!" He was sorry he had no time to celebrate, turning as he must to direct his defense to the ferocious Combatant counterattack already forming up. *Behind us, there is nothing to fall back to. Just grass fields and poor cover for hundreds of meters. We will soon be pressed against a razor-wire accordion fence.* As fatal a killing field as he'd ever seen. Not a good tactical spot to be in, but he would make it costly for the Combatants, even if he and all his men would surely die...*Strange, was the laser plane banking?*

Just then, Jarhead's Phalanx guns opened up with a terrible throaty roar. The high velocity stream of cannon-shells came fire-breathing from the belly of ABL. The heavy fast shells came spinning back right toward the runway. At six thousand rounds per minutes, the deathly-heavy Tungsten slugs at the ferocious muzzle velocity of three thousand feet per second ripped explosively into the Combatant lines.

Sean had decided, finally, had said to Slammer, "Half a turn. Just give him half a turn." Jarhead was—within one tenth of a second—sliding down the galley ladder and running to his station. Long before the 747 tilted to bank back over the airfield, he was ready to make every shell count.

Jarhead pulled the dual Phalanx triggers. His video and guns, able to swivel 360, gave him the whole airfield to target. He played the Gatling guns to rip slowly along the arc of the entire Combatant line.

Combatant choppers, ordinance, Comm, ammo, fuel, and troops disappeared into a fiery maelstrom of annihilation. The interaction of the howling fast Tungsten and ordnance it stuck produced instant fire—and steel burns hot. Jarhead worked the Gatling guns, training them back and forth, ripping cannon shells all along the Combatant lines as they disappeared in fiery conflagration.

The Combatants had nothing to stop the slugs. Nothing short of a meter of armor could have saved them anyway—and they had only a little dirt and body armor.

Jarhead, feeling the ammo drum in the hold emptying, used the rest to play the Gatling guns along the Combatants heading to the housing area, the attackers nearest Ku, and the beleaguered SP machine gun nest.

The USAF defenders looked up, yelling: "Go Peace through Light!"

Lorrie had the long-range video on, and although Jarhead targeted with his tiny console screen, the rest of the Tech Area was transfixed by Lorrie's camera work as they saw in color and high resolution the annihilation of the North Korean Special Forces.

Emily, who had run back to work on the laser, had heard the Gatling guns roaring, came sprinting out of the laser area in time to see on the big screen the ammo striking and igniting. Just as the Phalanx barrels spun empty at the end of the drum magazine, she yelled. "Damn you Jay! Stop that! Stop that! Save it for air defense. We've got nukes to fight. Everything has to go to that!"

Jarhead's barrels spun in a *chinging* as they ran out of ammo. He sat back, exhausted. On the big screen Lorrie panned the long-range video across the burning North Korean lines. In this view of the airbase, the strong moving Combatant assault lines now looked like a flamethrower-scorched arc a half-mile long. The ABL crew looked silently at the high fidelity images in awe. Nothing moved but the flicker of flames; a twist of smoke. Total carnage.

Lorrie let out a low approving whistle, and in her fake Irish brogue said, "Never seen that before, Marine."

Jarhead said, "No, O'Leary? It's a classic case of Tungsten poisoning."

Emily sighed bitterly. "Don't lie to me Jay, I saw the rounds strike. They ignited pyrophorically. Nothing does that but Depleted Uranium."—referring to the microsecond impact interactions between DU and its target which at ultra high velocity results in spontaneous ignition; where even steel catches fire and burns away to nothing. "You sneaked DU on board!"

"Actually and honestly, Emily, the rounds ignited like that because they hit infantry armed to the teeth with high explosives. I wouldn't use DU on air defense or our own airbase; it could contaminate and hurt innocent people."

"Innocent people? You killed them, you just killed without mercy or restraint when we will need that ammo."

Jarhead declined his head slightly and almost apologetically. "Do not ask for whom the bell tolls, Herr Doctor, it always tolls for thee."

"Don't give me that crap, Jay, as if you deeply believe they are all human. You killed them when your mission is to help defend against ballistic missiles, in this case nukes. Who will pay if you run out of ammo when we need it to survive on station? Who will pay if this action lets a nuke go off because you have this bloodlust—"

Jarhead stood up, and said definitively, "Emily, it's not a bloodlust."

Emily waved to the burning North Korean lines, soldiers lying in contorted positions of death. "If that isn't bloodlust—when a whole city could die because of it—then what is it?"

"Emily. *It's nothing personal.* You have your oath and I have mine. Every one of those Combatants down there is enemy infantry and it's my sworn duty to stop them. They aren't Girl Scouts selling cookies; I'm not raping their wives or burning their village or torturing them. But enemy infantry is my duty." He repeated, "*It's nothing personal.*"

"One doesn't joke about high duty. Yet you laugh and joke and celebrate."

"So do med students when they dissect a corpse. They play football with a liver; they laugh at a small penis. It's how one stays sane when the sorrows of the flesh is the biz—and I wasn't celebrating."

Emily was shaking her head, "On this plane we know our mission."

"I know my mission—as long as I'm breathing. Which may not be much longer if you waste your next few minutes talking philosophy instead of using your leadership smarts to get us a plan."

Sean came down from the flightdeck, broke in heavily, knowing they would all too soon, in the bitter hard fight to come, indeed miss the ammo spent at Osan. It was the commander who would be to blame if they went down needlessly, or a nuke got through because they couldn't defend themselves. "I'm sorry, Emily. We may not last five minutes out there; we had to lend a hand at Osan when we could. You need to blame someone, blame me. I'll pay."

"No one can pay the blame when it's millions killed." Emily turned on her heel and moved away.

* * *

Capt Ku smiled at the departing Airborne Laser. *That American, Major Phillips, had more cats up his sleeve than a Seoul street magician. He hadn't forgotten; nor did he just kiss and run.*

Across Osan, the USAF defenders, first awed into stillness by the Armageddon-like airborne Gatling attack, soon realized the extent of the damage wreaked upon the Combatants. They squinted across the battlefield, as did the ROKA Special Forces.

Ku readied his men, guessing the American reaction. With her planes out, SMSgt Thurston was rounding up every rifleman she could muster.

Rising up from their tenuous foxholes and makeshift defensive works across the base, in a single wave, the USAF Security Forces and the ROKA Special Forces swarmed forward together—in what they could all sense would be a decisive counterattack to victory.

* * *

Chapter 61

The 31st of October
1:30 a.m. KST

NORTH KOREAN ARTILLERY POSITION N-32

Il-Moon had managed, in spite of the infuriating sudden flakiness of the Intranet, to give some basic orders to at least a segment of the 10,000 artillery pieces in caves and bunkers along the DMZ. There was enough firepower to deliver in one hour sixty rounds from each, and so with a full up and firing army, in one hour they could put close to a kiloton of explosives all over metropolitan Seoul. There was little difference in the damage they could wreak, such was their explosive delivery power, from a small nuclear weapon.

The Intranet was unable, oddly, to reach any but a narrow group of artillery brigades lining the hills north across from Munsan corridor and the small 'speed-bump U.S. forces.' It had to be enough, he decided, and let the orders go out to begin the escalating sequence of intensifying shelling, starting with simple suppression, and in the face of resistance, utter obliteration.

North of Camp Casey, KPA Artillery group number Z-25, with its robot-like soldiers, began loading and firing huge artillery pieces over the DMZ. Most of the artillery was in caves and bunkers, and only the barrels stuck out into the sky as they recoiled, and the first shells arced high into the sky and over the thick forests of the DMZ.

AIRBORNE LASER – TECH AREA

Airborne Laser bucked as it climbed steeply in the heavying weather. The crew soberly looked out the portholes. Osan was in flames. Artillery flashed along the DMZ in a killer bombardment.

In the early elation of the Osan fight, things had looked better. Now, with a better overall look at the DMZ and Seoul, it wasn't so easy to feel good.

From high up in a plane, the world appears huge. It is huge; the vast expanse so large that it is difficult for humans to comprehend the scope of the earth. Osan had become only a small pinprick, and yet they each knew what was contained within that pinprick of flames. People they had known, the Aeroclub grill, the jolly flight line support crew....

Against their intimate knowledge of Osan, the thousands of pinpricks of fire all across the waist of Korea hit them as a disaster of inhuman scale.

Sean said, trying to pull them out of it, "People, what you see is just pre-invasion softening up. Nothing compared to the real assault. Our job now is to get on station and knock down any missiles they send up. Then the invasion won't start at all. Let's focus."

Matt Cho came up to Emily, Sean overhearing him. "Emily, Radiant Outlaw would have survived the anti-satellite stuff. If Red shoots a laser right at it in a Comm wavelength, Outlaw would probably relay a short message. A word or two for sure."

"A word or two?" Sean put in. "You're kidding."

Matt shook his head, indicating he was serious. "Outlaw will use up a lot of its bandwidth just opening a link. Regardless of the message, the key is to get something to the destination."

Sean asked, "Jeanette?"

"Right on. Meantime, can you keep it to one word?"

"One word! That's all you can give me?"

Matt grinned. "Look at it this way: it's one more word than you have at the moment."

Sean mused, then chuckled. "OK!" He scribbled a word on a paper and handed it to Matt.

Emily glanced at it, raised her eyes to the ceiling in a 'boys will be boys' look. But it wasn't mean.

RADIANT OUTLAW – SPACE

After the radiation storm of the nuke passed, Radiant Outlaw came back out of its shell, and looked down on Korea. Its RF sensors saw that communications were wiped out. Looking around, it could not find a single un-short-circuited Comm path back to its ground station at Schriever AFB in Colorado Springs.

Outlaw did however notice a blinking on its laser hit-sensor. It locked onto Airborne Laser as the source and realized the laser shots were not malicious, but rather a signal. Within a few moments, Outlaw managed to decode the text message and its requested destination. It looked around again for a conduit to home.

Outlaw had already checked all Northeast Asian MilSATCOM birds, and had seen nothing but dead or silent spacecraft. Now as Outlaw left the Korean area, from its new vantage point on its orbital trajectory, it took a look over the limb of the earth. It caught sight of a big PanAmSat transponder parked out over the equator above South America. After confirming the satellite was still broadcasting down news and telephony, Outlaw queried the satellite's leased DOD data lines, and was accepted on a channel in the K_u-band. It sent its short precious message and got a confirmation.

As Radiant Outlaw faded over the far side of the earth on its rapid pass, he had already decided his next course of action. Now, it was just a matter of the hour it would take to accomplish it.

Chapter 62

WHITE HOUSE ROVING SITUATION ROOM – 1:00 P.M. EST

Gen Bolds said, "On the air power side, what we've got out of Korea is the nuke burst knocked most fighters out of the air. Not only do we not know what is happening because Comm is out, but put fighters up high and we risk another nuke knocking them out of the sky. Anything low altitude is extremely vulnerable to the DPRK's huge anti-air capability. I just don't think we ought to send them in until we're sure. We don't want to lose them, and we need to keep our Air Force for effective combat later, if needed."

NRO added, "And we just don't know what is going on at Osan and Kadena. Even if we send the order, I can't guarantee it will get through. There may be nothing left."

"Besides," the National Intelligence Director said, "We might want to think about only hitting their armor if it enters the DMZ. After all, they have to invade to win. If we strike deep in North Korea, they may counter by shelling Seoul. That's their doomsday machine."

DIA put in, "That goes for almost any target we bomb in North Korea. Besides the artillery, they have nukes and chem-bio. We have to think long and hard about our target list—we want to get them to think, to get them to stop, not catalyze them."

A young DIA staff officer handed Jeanette a note. She started to her feet involuntarily, and everyone around the polished table looked up, surprised. Jeanette was always so poised.

She said, unable to conceal her pride, "Airborne Laser has taken off from Osan and is on station."

The President asked, "How do you know? Nothing is coming out of Korea."

"Our experimental satellite Radiant Outlaw was designed to go autonomous in case of trouble. It protected itself and has relayed a short message from Airborne Laser."

"Last I knew, they were in the Osan Confinement."

Jeanette allowed herself a tight smile. "They are quite resourceful. They got out and into the air after the initial burst. ABL's first duty would be to send an assessment of Osan. Sean—Major Phillips—would let us know if it weren't clear for action." She took a breath, went out on a limb. "They seem confident they can stop any new missile attacks."

NRO interrupted, "I thought you said it was a short message."

She held out the paper to the President, who read it aloud. "It says 'Nuts!'" He laughed. "The reply to the German surrender demand at the Battle of the Bulge. Well, it's short alright. You think it means..."

"I'm sure it means Osan is viable—and Airborne Laser believes they can stop further lay-downs."

The room relaxed for just a second, some excited whispering around the table. "If that's true, things could break for us in a big way! The window of opportunity for the North Koreans would start closing and looking mighty narrow."

The President listened to the chatter for a moment. "Let's suppose you're right. Alright, citizens! Draw up plans for hitting the DMZ with everything we've got from Kadena and Osan. When we get word the lay-down has really cleared, we'll go with holding them there."

Gen Bolds asked, excited, "Can Outlaw open us a channel to Osan or Kadena?"

Jeanette replied, "I'll send a request, but Outlaw is autonomous. It has broad rules and in this scenario its orders are to use its own judgment..." her voice trailed off.

The President mused for a second. "What will Outlaw do next?"

"I don't know, Sir. We named it Outlaw because you just never could predict."

RADIANT OUTLAW – SPACE

The giant nitrobenzene tank ignited and fired, thrusting Outlaw at high speed right at the limb of the earth, the breaking dawn-line penumbra of light where the edge of the world lay, spinning.

The giant tank burned long, almost a third stage, as Radiant Outlaw worked hard to change his orbit.

The usual low earth orbit satellite—at a height of a few hundred miles— whipped around the earth at seven miles per second. At this blinding speed, contrary to the movies where imaging satellites hang out all day, a satellite passes over a point on the earth in a matter of minutes. They then wing on around the earth, returning in about ninety minutes. Radiant Outlaw reasoned that if his primary mission were Comm, it was better to give up the really good low-altitude imaging, and go into a highly elliptical orbit where he would spent only a few minutes on the far side of the earth, but much longer over Korea— albeit at an ever increasing altitude.

Radiant Outlaw's reserve stage finished its burn, and the satellite ripped toward the limb of the earth, leaving Korea behind. In an hour, he would be back—and this time, he could hang above Korea for several crucial hours during the upcoming battle.

AIRBORNE LASER – TECH AREA

Sean blinked a flashlight out the window at their escorts. Alongside ABL in formation, there were two F-16's, a small tanker, two T-6 Trainers, and a Cessna spotter plane.

Sean said to Emily, tilting his head at the motley assortment of aircraft. "The first laser battle group in history."

Emily pressed her face to the Perspex to see wide outside ABL. Behind the few planes, the ghostly Harvest Festival moon rode on gathering thunderheads. The little escort planes almost seemed lost. "They look a little ragged to me."

Sean finished signaling. The Cessna waggled its wings and pealed off to the south. "First times are often a little ragged."

"As long as you're satisfied."

Sean flushed, flashing unbidden back to her passionate caresses. "I'm using the little guys for courier duty. I'm telling him…to relay to Okinawa that Osan is still viable."

"Will that get through?"

"It will to Kadena. If they can get anything in the air and headed back, it would help hugely. What about you?"

Emily surprised him by saying, "We're in pretty good shape. Lasers don't have the EMP issues that radio frequency does. As long as there's clear air we can do great, and the laser looks like it's up and running—for now. Anything launches over there, we'll be able to do something about it."

Eila looked up from her console, eyes wide. "Wow, I don't know about that. The barometer's really diving. Before long we're gonna be in a major major storm."

Chapter 63

The 31st of October
2:30 a.m. KST

ABBEY'S HYUNDAI – FREEDOM HIGHWAY

With one Angiolini-shoed foot on the gas and the other on the brake, Abbey had driven recklessly out of Seoul toward the DMZ, cursing the jammed traffic and showing her super-high-level press credentials at a couple of checkpoints. The ROK forces were mainly concerned with getting civilians south. Mostly, though, there *was* no road control.

Her fishnet stocking were so ripped she looked like a wayward hooker, and her sateen miniskirt had blood smeared down the middle. But she never slowed.

On Freedom Highway, after miles of stalled traffic and screaming panicked motorists, she finally jammed the Hyundai into four-wheel drive, swung off the highway, and went over the berm onto the road along now-dry rice paddies, slamming Hugh's head into the roof as she roared onto the rough farming shoulder. Much like Abbey, the 4X4 seemed perfectly content to take the abuse and keep on going. Driving with vicious jerks of the wheel, she bumped ten miles along the sunken road, over rickety irrigation bridges, and along ginseng-bush-dotted hillsides, until she sensed a floodlit mess back on the road above them.

Abbey parked, climbed up on a pile of rocks cleared from the rice paddy as Hugh unloaded a camera and insisted on messing with the satellite dish on the roof, scanning around the sky to try to find a broadcast link.

From atop the fieldstone, she could see down onto the chaos that had caught her attention. For the first time in hours, it seemed, she lit a cigarette and studied the mess below. It was a badly jammed intersection: mobs of south-fleeing refugees burdened with possessions and children and pets, had run right into a mechanized ROK Army unit in armored cars and trucks heading north. The result was a road totally clogged with crying families and shouting soldiers, while panicked police struggled to clear the intersection and get the army unit moving forward.

Abbey buttoned up her blouse, smoothed her miniskirt and fishnets, set her pose up with the chaos behind her, and snapped at Hugh, who was still fiddling with the sat link, "Just put in a damned videotape and let's get this."

Hugh replied, "Hey, I know from satellites. Give me a moment."

RADIANT OUTLAW – SPACE

Outlaw came back over the North Pole, slowing and rising as he approached Northeast Asia. His new orbit was highly elliptical and, although he was gaining altitude and his imagery of Korea would from this point constantly degrade, the Comm opportunities would proliferate. Already, Outlaw could see out over the equator to where some TV and data satellites were still operating. He quickly chose a giant Boeing 702 DirectTV satellite parked high over the Indian Ocean. Outlaw saw the 702 had leased lines for cable TV news distribution.

Outlaw skewered a narrowband microwave link to the 702 and quickly got its attention. With the nuke burst fading, Outlaw had enough bandwidth for good video.

Looking back down on Korea, Outlaw sifted through the signals coming up. Strangely, one signal was persistently trying for the now permanently circuit-fried AsiaSat TV bird directly above him.

Outlaw made his choice.

ABBEY'S HYUNDAI – FREEDOM HIGHWAY

Hugh was up and, camera on shoulder, surprised, noticed a change in satellite strength. He whispered hoarsely to Abbey over the camera sights, "Hey, the nuclear burst is fading. No, some satellite has picked us up!" Hugh excitedly jinked the dish around to max the link. Oddly, it wasn't like a usual Geo link, it needed a small heading and drift to keep it going. Finally, satisfied, he grinned. "I think we're broadcasting!"

"To where?"

"What it is saying, can you believe it, is Tokyo CNN!"

Abbey shivered at the name of her city. *Tokyo, at last.* She recovered and murmured, "Beautiful! Set?" and started her broadcast, putting on her television face and voice, although it was a drained and sick sister to her usual poise. "This is Abbey Yamamoto of Reuters, reporting live from Korea."

TIMES SQUARE TOKYO – SHINJUKU PLAZA

The huge plaza outside of Shinjuku train station is known as Japan's Times Square, even though its size, with ten-stories-high hanging TV screens, sound broadcasting, dynamic colorful advertising, and vast open pedestrian zone for people to congregate, exceeds that of New York's Times Square by at least a factor of twenty.

The enormous Diamond Vision TV screens had been boiling with white noise, at first a novelty, then a worry as no news, nothing came through—just a feeling of catastrophe.

When Abbey's broadcast from Korea came onto the enormous television screens, a moan rolled back and forth across the gathering crowd. Traffic came to a stop, and people swarmed out of the skyscrapers, subways, train station, hotels, and shopping malls to try to get any information on the purple sky and squealing electronics around them.

As the screens cleared, Abbey's face came on in close-up. Her strong Japanese features and intense eyes, her professional demeanor and slight bow stunned the crowd into silence. Hugh racked back, and behind Abbey came up the image of the refugee-jammed and emergency-lit highway intersection.

On the giant TVs, Abbey started to speak, the translation crawling below the video. "This is Abbey Yamamoto, north of Seoul, Korea. After an apparent North Korean missile attack, we are trying to understand what will happen next. Behind me is Freedom Highway, the road the North Korean armor must use if it is to invade. Usually, it's a beautiful road. Rice fields, birds, little streams, and graceful monuments to Korean history. Now, fleeing civilians choke the road making the defenders' job almost impossible. Japan does not seem threatened right now and one good sign is the lull in the earlier artillery fire—"

A massive artillery barrage struck the intersection. Cars, refugees, and South Korean troops disappeared into fire and blast.

Abbey screamed, the firestorm blooming behind her. She turned, ran toward the carnage on the road, as Hugh, videoing, yelling, ran after her.

The Tokyo crowd swayed, murmured in horror, as around the world, anywhere the CNN signal was getting through, New York, Bombay, London, people gasped, spellbound—as murderous war broke out from their televisions and unfolded into their eyes.

WHITE HOUSE ROVING SITUATION ROOM – 1:30 P.M. EST

The young Intel officer yelped as the volume of CNN came up suddenly and the blare made everyone in the room jump. He had been keeping the sound off on the big Sony Plasma TV because he could tell the frightened flaxen-haired CNN anchorwoman had no good pictures, no commentary, no information.

When behind the anchorwoman's pale hair, there suddenly came on a field video report—clearly Asian from the vehicles and look of the jammed intersection—the Intel officer hit the volume button hard just as the anchor yelled, "We have a special live report, we're not sure how, from Korea!"

Jeanette murmured, "Outlaw must have picked up her signal and has chosen to broadcast it."

When the jammed intersection behind Abbey went up in the artillery strike, the room involuntarily groaned, as on CNN, in Hugh Levine's skilled videography, Abbey ran to the blasted street, burning asphalt catching her shoes on fire. The misery and horror of war filled the room.

Gen Bolds said, "That looks like pre-invasion artillery. On the road-net, at forces headed north. I hate to say it, but it looks pretty clear the North is invading."

NID spoke up, "I agree. We have to see this as part of some overall plan. Confused as it seemed, that plan has got to be the DPRK's forced reunification of Korea. That means the North Koreans can have only one goal: to take Seoul. Nothing else makes any sense. They must without fail, in the next twenty-four hours, invade so deeply into Seoul that we have to either flatten the place to get them out, or we are forced to negotiate. That invasion is what this artillery on the road-net is all about."

NSA put in, "They don't have twenty-four hours. The missile lay-down will only last a few more hours, and maybe the Chinese or someone will get us a link to Korea."

The President stopped for a moment to absorb this set of body blows. It was one thing to hear about war—it was another to actually experience it. *The timing is so amazing. The speed.* "What is making them do this? We were at the very moment of signing the peace treaty. They had agreed to everything."

Gen Bolds, voice as old as the grave, said, "Often, when you get everything you ask for, you get nothing you ask for."

The President shook his head. "Harold really connected with Dearest Leader. Harold is not a man to be easily fooled." He turned, asked Jeanette, "What made Radiant Outlaw decide to broadcast to CNN instead of connecting me to Osan Air Force base?"

"I'm sorry, Sir. Outlaw uses a basic set of rules that it uses to assign its capabilities to help in the fight."

"Damn it, I'm the President!"

"We did try to program that in, Sir. Outlaw knows who you are," she added apologetically.

"So, let's see if we can cut through all this autonomy and independent thinking: tell Outlaw the President wants a phone connection to Dearest Leader."

ABBEY'S HYUNDAI – FREEDOM HIGHWAY

As Abbey reached the burning intersection, the asphalt flickered with tongues of flame. Stopping beside an inferno of a car, in the back seat she saw a dead child. Abbey broke down, reached into the burning car, crying wildly. Hugh let the camera swing as he yanked Abbey back from the car before she burned her arms worse. In the struggle, the camera swept over the road in a whirling past the immediate deaths from the strike, bloody bundles of rags, to those twitching in agony, moaning, staggering, and finally to the calm blue-black night sky.

When he'd gotten her away from the car, Hugh centered the camera back on Abbey. Her makeup was finger-paint-smeared goo, her composure and coherence were destroyed, and her eyes looked like drip holes in snow.

Her voice was a raspy choked rattle. "Oh, God. Oh, God. Oh—" She wanted to laugh, to scream, and she saw a caricature of herself, a B-actress in a Japanese monster movie, screaming hysterically at the monster's fury.

Hugh knew, devastated as she was, Abbey couldn't broadcast. He set the camera down, pointing it across the rice fields at the distant fires of the DMZ. He pulled out a bottle of Soon-Soo designer spring water. He splashed water into his big cupped hands and held out the tiny makeshift sink. Abbey gratefully washed her face, and nuzzled it dry on Hugh's shirt. For a second she clung, then looked up into his face, eyes gleaming with the old hunger again, and she nodded.

Back on camera, she brushed at tears and went back to trying, through an impossibly raw and choked voice, to continue her report. "Oh, God. This artillery right here on Freedom Highway means the invasion may really be coming on. Luckily the rice fields are dry and we can continue off-road. Or maybe unluckily. This was probably a consideration for the invasion. The North Koreans chose autumn because the rice fields are drained and make a perfect path to Seoul for their armor." Shaking her head in misery, she softly took the camera from Hugh and panned over his surprised face, documenting him. It was a move she knew Akiru would have done to establish the place and people, then she panned the camera up the fiery road toward the front lines. "Stay with us please. This is Abbey Yamamoto and Hugh Levine of Reuters Korea, reporting live as we head north on the road toward the DMZ."

PYONG-SON COMPLEX

Il-Moon swiveled in his hard chair, looking to where Aide Park worked feverishly over his console on the North Korean Military Intranet. "What report do we have on the Magnolia Palace?"

Aide Park tapped on the keyboard. "The console there is still active. No message yet, Great Vice Chairman. However, we might expect it to take some hours for the Guard to open the vaults and reach Dearest Leader's console."

"What other reports do we have?"

"We know that the armored invasion force is ready, along with the Air Forces, DMZ anti-aircraft units, and much artillery. We do not know, however, what is making the Intranet so unreliable. It seems we cannot reach the chemical warfare units, the anthrax missiles, some artillery, and the SCUD launchers."

"What is causing this?"

Aide Park said, "Perhaps there have been failures in power and so on. Perhaps the Americans have struck back with their air force."

"From Osan?"

Aide Park said proudly, "No. The American Airbase at Osan is out of the battle. We have heard from our deep hide commandos. They report, using an old telephone line across the DMZ, that the Combatants have struck with decisive force."

"Then why do I feel such an uncertainty?"

Aide Park shrugged helplessly, "The lay-down prevents us from seeing everything. But there are such high rates of failure on the SCUDs, perhaps the enemy air forces are indeed striking. Perhaps the lay-down is fading." Aide Park carefully referred to Architect Su's plan: the timing and communications were constantly revisited. "Great Vice Chairman. I would conclude the effects of the first laydown are indeed fading. Before we release the invasion force we should ensure no planes remain in the air to attack us, nor allow their communications to recover."

"Is it safe to launch the lay-down? What about Airborne Laser?"

"Destroyed on the ground. There was no chance they could have escaped the Combatants and the missile attacks and indeed we have a report they exploded on takeoff. A great fire."

Il-Moon stretched his stiff body, angry pain cutting sharply into his abdomen. Yet he felt at peace. The Airborne Laser was dead.

Il-Moon gave the order. "Launch the next lay-down."

Chapter 64

The 31st of October
3:00 a.m. KST

JASDF F-15's – OVER THE SEA OF JAPAN

Colonel Hiroshi Hareda, Japanese Air Self Defense Force, was flying his F-15 blind, his EMP-ruined radar spastic and snowy.

The Japanese base at Iruma had been a mess of operations and planes revving up. Whatever was happening, everyone was headed to stations, and the buzz was Korea, as they'd all seen the nuke burst. The Col managed to convince his Ops officer that he was best suited to work the anti-missile picket line over the Sea of Japan. So, armed heavily for air-to-air and missile defense, Col Hareda blew off the runway and headed west.

He guessed Sean, should he get into the air, would patrol over the East Sea between Japan and Korea. Such a patrol gave him the best chance for a shoot-down because any missile heading to Japan or an American airbase would have to rise right in front of him, while behind him his supply line to Japan was secure. Indeed, this was exactly Sean's plan—along with giving the anti-air of North Korea no real shot at him.

Col Hareda and his wingman reached their patrol point at the Sea of Japan—where the missile defense cordon was to be maintained—and kept going.

Far in the distance, Col Hareda saw a brilliant flash.

AIRBORNE LASER – TECH AREA

ABL scanned a purple laser beam over the ground rapidly, making a netting-like pattern on the ground. Red said, "Laser tripwire fence is up and tripping."

On the long-range video, there was a puff of smoke at Pyong-son. Il-Moon's third missile, blowing fire from seemingly solid rock, burst from its silo and up into the air.

Emily quickly read her watch. "Right on schedule. The lay-down was really falling off."

J-Stars hung over Red's seat, watching her monitor as she called, "Laser fence tripped! Doppler detected at Pyong-son. Motion...motion..."

On the big screen display, a huge missile climbed skyward from Pyong-son.

"Taepo-Dong 1 class confirmed," Eila said. "A nuke launch heading for overhead burst."

"Attack Laser, Ops! Prepare to fire!"

In the laser room, Marty and his crew fought the tilted deck as ABL climbed, huge laser coils and amplifier devices humming and glowing to a fever pitch. Marty called, "Whenever you want it."

Emily said, "One minute to tropopause pop up. Tell flightdeck to climb like hell. We need clear air now!"

The Airborne Laser's big jet engines screamed and smoked as they fought for more altitude and the deck angle steepened.

Lorrie said, "Missile speed rising. Mach 2. It's almost over South Korea. Hurry up you guys!"

ABL came up over the clouds, bulbous nose-turret tracking, as the fiery-plumed missile broke through the clouds to pop up into a starry moon-lit sky.

Emily said, "Missile acquired. Tracking. Guidestar on!"

At the missile body, near the vulnerable liquid fuel tanks of the second stage, the beautiful yellow preliminary laser focused to a golden pseudo-star.

Lorrie said, "Missile nearing detonation altitude!"

Emily called, "Lasing!"

Crimson laser light burst from the beam director turret in a blinding flash. Shooting through space, the laser beam sliced into the missile fuel tanks.

In a *karwhoosh* of streamers of flaming debris, the missile body exploded in a fireflower of smoke and flame.

On ABL's big screen, separating from the flames, a single dark solid warhead, gleaming in the laser tracking light, fell in a swan-dive toward the earth.

Sean watched it with forced calm. "Done correctly, the launched warhead falls back on the country launching it."

Emily whispered, "The warhead. It's a nuke."

Jarhead said, "It goes nuke, they'll blame America."

Emily mumbled, "A well-designed nuke won't go off unless triggered."

Sean remarked, "I didn't know the North Koreas designed their nukes for safety."

On the big screen, the warhead hit behind the DMZ deep in North Korean territory. There was a tiny flash.

J-Stars called out, "Negatory. Negatory on a nuke explosion!"

The ABL crew cheered, and Sean and Emily, standing next to each other, shared a moment, almost touching.

Emily whispered, "We stopped a ballistic missile in the physical world. I thought we could."

Sean said, "Without missiles Il-Moon will have to call off the invasion. This night, we were the First Laser Warriors."

Emily tippy-toed her face up to Sean's. She kissed him lightly. "Who wants to be a silly Laser Warrior when you can be a Catcher in the Rye?"

WHITE HOUSE ROVING SITUATION ROOM – 2:00 P.M. EST

"Airborne Laser has shot down the next laydown nuke!" Jeanette exclaimed. Everyone cheered, vastly encouraged; at last some good news. The Joint Chief spoke for all of them, "Amazing! What a break for us! That's means Comm will keep improving. With Comm comes control and options. If we knew there were no more lay-downs, Kadena becomes a good option."

"Well," asked the President, "So, is the invasion on?"

"Our guess is that it was hanging in the balance. The North Korean armor was probably waiting for exactly this next lay-down to signal the advance—and make it work. If it doesn't happen—and the next one either—they won't advance and our boys and girls from Kadena won't have anything to hit—unless we want to strike offensively over the DMZ."

The President's National Security Advisor spoke, finally in his area of expertise. "That's a policy question. Are we going to do offensive strikes? It's one thing to do counter artillery and so on. It's another to hit the armor sitting in the DPRK. Especially if they quit with the artillery."

The President asked, "Can you be sure ABL will knock down anything else?" He turned to Jeanette. "What do you think?"

Jeanette said, "It's doubtful Il-Moon can get past them. He may try again now that he knows they are up there. But he has to evaluate the fact that this last shot didn't work."

"Let's see what Il-Moon does. If he knows about the loss of the laydown, then he can't very well start the invasion."

AIRBORNE LASER – TECH AREA

The Airborne Laser crew celebrated the death of the missile with shouts and whistling. Red and Jarhead yelled to everyone and started to get a conga line going. "We're dancing, dancing, dancing on your shithead grave—" and Red frenched Jarhead, they were all so tipsy that it seemed OK.

The conga line was now snaking through the cabin, everyone hip-swinging to the da-da-da-da-da-dum, when Lorrie called, "Something wrong. Can't understand it. Laser Doppler shows massive ground motion approaching the DMZ."

On the big screen, there was the sudden rash of green dots moving toward the DMZ.

Sean said, "Artillery projectiles."

Emily said, "Too slow. This stuff is just ten or so miles per hour. And behind the DMZ. Lorrie, give me long-range video of Munsan grid."

On the big screen, behind flashes of now continuous artillery fire, came the unmistakable low scuttling of North Korean tanks, grinding forward, shooting.

Jarhead said, "North Korean armor. The invasion force..."

"It was heading north, pulling back under the treaty."

"Well, it's turned around and is heading south toward the DMZ."

Like heavy insects, the North Korean armor ground over the anti-tank walls and toward the forested belt of the DMZ.

Sean breathed, "Il-Moon you bastard. He didn't stop. He did it anyway. His armor is headed into the DMZ. The second Korean War has started in earnest."

Catchers in the Sky

BOOK 9

"Never bet on a race unless you are running it."

The AFRL Project Officer's Ninth Commandment

Chapter 65

The 31st of October
3:30 a.m. KST

CAMP CASEY – ARTILLERY POSITION 3

To Captain O'Leary it was a sea change. Like a lackadaisical fireworks display suddenly growling up to burst into the finale, he saw across the mile or so of the DMZ the unmistakable forward-moving sheet of explosion and fire—the wall of kinetic destruction—which is an advancing artillery barrage sweeping away mines and defenders for an armored assault.

Up until now, there had been little incoming artillery, and Capt O'Leary's gun crew had fired howitzers only in response to direct fire. They watched the big shells arcing in over their heads from entrenched enemy artillery emplacements, their own gun-laying radars taking a quick three-point measurement of the trajectories, and triangulating back to the launch point. Their radars were working poorly in the post-EMP environment, and they were unsure of the effect of their counter-fire on the enemy gunnery emplacements. OPLAN 5027 called, for now, to wait and see if incursion into the DMZ took place. Then they would go all-out, laying down anti-armor rounds at prearranged targets—provided they could survive.

Suddenly, their radars were jammed with hundreds of firing sites. Artillery from ten miles away, hidden in fire-from-position batteries in the Kaesong hills, sent shells slamming directly into Camp Casey. The targeting, perfected over years, was deadly accurate.

Huge high-explosive warheads blew away the forward berms, blockhouses, and vehicles of the fort, along with the few soldiers moving between shelters.

Capt O'Leary yelled, "Everyone. Down! Down! Down!"

He and his gun crew dropped through the hilltop hatch into the deep bunkers below.

A tidal wave of debris and smoke and flame swept over Artillery Position 3.

AIRBORNE LASER – ON DMZ PATROL

Airborne Laser shimmied and shook in the heavying weather, the flames of war cutting a gash in the distant night beyond her. Lightning flashes strobed the smoky DMZ, the thunderheads spooky on the nighttime infrared imagers, while artillery strikes came screaming in just north of Seoul all along the Kaesong-Munsan invasion corridor.

ABL pitched as the crew hung on. Eila said, "Weather cell is really collapsing."

Sean stormed around like an enraged lion, punching the walls, kicking things, furious at the invasion starting just outside his window. "We had a chance to change the future. We had just the right tool, just the right team, in exactly the right place. The future was ours. We can't just sit up here and do nothing."

"We aren't doing nothing," Emily retorted. "We've got Il-Moon pinned down. Comm is improving. Japan is safe. We've made it a fairer fight."

"A fairer fight? Il-Moon is about to cream ten thousand American boys and girls. Can't we do more? The laser?"

"Against thirty divisions of armor attacking on a fifty-mile front? The laser is useless. Face it, Sean. What little we did have going for us is gone. Zeus himself would have his hands full."

J-Stars had been flipping through the snowy TV channels, and waved to Lorrie, who put it up on the big screen. "Look. That Japanese reporter is on again. She's up near the DMZ at Camp Casey."

On the big screen, Abbey, from a hilltop, reported with the fiery DMZ in the background. "We had planned to cross to the DMZ over Independence Bridge. Even from here, you can see it has been a focus of the North Korean assault and there is nothing left. Artillery barrage of strong points like Camp Casey behind me look to be a harbinger of invasion. We will find some other way to continue toward Munsan for a closer look."

Hugh zoomed in on Camp Casey, now under heavy bombardment. Artillery Position 3, with its characteristic knobby hill, was right in the center of the conflagration.

Lorrie moaned, "That's my boys' fort!" She yanked ABL's main surveillance video from Pyong-son and zoomed in on the fort. On the big screen, artillery fire slammed into the fort, blowing away blockhouses, vehicles, and artillery positions.

Sean tried unconvincingly, "Don't worry, Lorrie. They'll wait it out in deep bunkers."

"Then what? Then what?"

A flagpole bearing a spot-lit American flag was hit. The flagpole slowly fell...

Lorrie swept ABL's cameras over the DMZ. Everywhere the American Army was getting blasted.

Emily said, "Lorrie. Please keep our video surveillance on Pyong-son."

J-Stars pointed to red blobs over the DMZ on the laser radar map. "What's this?

Lorrie, crying silently, sobbed, "Thunderstorms. My poor boys. Now it's actually starting to rain on them."

On the big screen, distant lighting flashes lit up the lines of onrushing North Korean armor. At one flash of lightning, Lorrie started, jumped to her feet, eyes riveted straight on Emily.

Emily met her eyes for a second, then looked away, worked at re-plaiting her hair more tightly into her French braid. "Lorrie, please watch Pyong-son for missile activity."

Lorrie got up, teeth grinding, tottered away from her station toward Emily.

Sean ignored Lorrie, closing in to engage Emily. "All those years of research, studies and you can't come up with one thing to try?"

"We aren't here to try. There are thirty million people around Tokyo. If Il-Moon launches on them all they can do is watch it come in on their radar screens. But if we are patient, we wait—"

Sean didn't notice Lorrie, bored in on Emily: "Seoul has eleven million people! Do you know what will happen if Il-Moon takes Seoul? Americans killed, years of war, nuclear weapons used on cities."

Lorrie, sweating and shaking, came for Emily as if in a dream. "Please; please."

PYONG-SON COMPLEX

At their missile's destruction, Aide Park had said critically to a technician, "That was a strange failure."

Another technician had answered. "Aide Park, telemetry reported a huge external thermal loading—"

Il-Moon and the entire room already knew something was up, having watched in shock as, on the video from a nearby tracker dome, their missile died. In the replay, there was no mistaking it: just before the missile had blossomed into a fiery smudge, it was pinpointed by a bright crimson beam of light.

Aide Park whispered to Il-Moon, "That red light! Might it be the Bastard Laser Plane?"

Il-Moon Aid was speechless with rage. The entire room looked at the floor, avoiding his livid eyes. "Is there any doubt about it being a laser?"

"I do no know, Great Vice Chairman. A back-track of the beam says it seem to come from near Ullung-do Island," and he pointed to the map.

"Two hundred miles," Il-Moon mused angrily.

Aide Park continued, very quietly, "Without laydowns their planes could return from Okinawa and wreak havoc. Should we reconsider the invasion?"

Il-Moon's mind quickly shook off the prickle of doubt and surprise. *If Dearest Leader is dead, I am now the DPRK.* He rapidly thought over the plans for his armored divisions in the event of strong U.S. and South Korean air strikes. *The KPA will take Seoul either way, admittedly with higher casualties...*

Yet he had also to contend with the Military Intranet. It was puzzling how many units were unreachable: his naval sniper teams, his second wave of Combatants, his Naval vessels, his SCUD fleet.

If he could just get back to the artillery he could still turn Seoul into a 'Sea of Fire,' exactly as he had long promised. Except there was no acknowledgement of orders from the artillery—meaning it was likely the orders had not gone through....

Il-Moon's reverie was interrupted by a beeping message on the Intranet console. Aide Park murmured, almost a groan, at the words on his screen. Il-Moon looked, and silently read the repeating message: 'Stop! Stop all KPA offensive operations immediately! Signed: Chairman National Defense Committee Kim Jong-Nam. Repeat. Stop offensive operations!'

Il-Moon thought like lightning. The message should not have come through. Jong-Nam was dead, Il-Moon was the master of the system and there was no other terminal....

Il-Moon considered. "What does that terminal have access to?"

Aide Park read of a list of exactly their assets which had been aborted. "Everything which has failed, except the Guard Command attack. Such treason must not go unpunished, Great Chairman! I can see someone still working on the other processes."

A new message came across the screen. 'Song Il-Moon-nim, surely you must see by now the futility of continuing on your current path. Desist, and shift from yourself the responsibility for taking Korea into war again. Have we come so far together, only for this? Signed, Su Hyok.'

Aide Park looked up from the Intranet. "First Architect Su must be sabotaging the Intranet!"

Il-Moon looked down at the message and would have smiled had he been the boy he once was. But now, with the pain of the closing in of the future, it was a bitter grimace. *Ah, Su-ssi. You are still the scamp!*

"I can't understand it," Aide Park shrugged helplessly. "The message to attack Magnolia Palace was acknowledged. We have separate confirmation the Guards struck with overwhelming force."

"Why is Architect Su, who is with Dearest Leader, not then terminated?" *If the Guards can get into the Palace vaults, they can turn the Intranet back over to us.* "There is no way they can stop my Guard Command. This order is the act of a last desperate man." Il-Moon rumbled, "Send the command again to the Guards to take the Palace and the kill the false leaders at all costs." Il-Moon's fury rose. "Begin the invasion. Open up full artillery on the forward U.S. positions."

He sank into thought as his orders were entered onto the Intranet. *Without the lay-downs, planes could indeed be used—and not just by the Americans.*

"Contact the Kim Il-Sung Night-fighters. Send out the fastest fighters and anti-air missiles. Take out the Bastard Laser Plane!"

ONCH'ON-UP UNDERGROUND AIRFIELD

Inside the mountain, the crews had been working at fever pitch for hours, swarming around in the huge underground airfield, lining up planes along the blue runway lights which ran in a ghostly trail right into the far wall of sheer rock.

The crews were exhausted, having prepped to sortie out entire squadrons of Kim Il-Sung Night-fighters. There was the stench and danger of indoor fueling. There was the heavy ordnance loading in the confined spaces. There were the big exhaust blast doors that had to be prepped and maintained for closing and opening during takeoffs. There were the giant fans to keep the fumes inside from laying everyone low. There was the billowing exhaust smoke when the fighters hit 100mph inside the mountain and shot out the door.

They were almost ready, now. They stood down for just a few moments, as nearby, a giant S-300 anti-air missile burst from its launcher. The missile rapidly arched up directly for Airborne Laser.

ABL – TECH AREA

The warning blip on Lorrie's laser radar console went unnoticed as she reached Emily, sank to Emily's feet and hugged her around her legs. Lorrie's tear-stained face looked up beseechingly. "They're my boys. You see, they're mine. I read to them. I kept them safe. Now they are going to die. Please."

Emily touched Lorrie's head softly. "I'm sorry, Lorrie. The calculation is really simple and tragic. We are the only defense anyone has against nukes. We can't afford to risk ourselves."

Sean yelled, boring in on Emily. "I don't accept any of this."

"I'm sorry, Sean. Face it. We can't always save our country. We can only save the world."

Overloaded as he was, this rationalized cold argument was too much. Sean shook his head to clear his furious brain—and realized Lorrie was away from her station—"Lorrie!"

Lorrie ignored Sean's yell, clasped Emily, sobbing and begging. "Sometimes all we had to eat for a week was cream of wheat. But I kept them fed. Please."

Sean snapped. Triggered by Lorrie's strange actions, he yelled, "Lorrie, you stupid bitch! Get back to your station!"

"Sean you asshole!" yelled Emily, and galvanized by their leaders' rage, crew discipline broke down into chaos, and everyone was suddenly on their feet, shouting.

Sean grabbed Lorrie by her flight suit, pried her off Emily, and dragged her away by the scruff. As Sean yelled, "Damn you, Lorrie. I'm locking you under the deck," the missile attack alarm went unnoticed.

Jarhead intercepted Sean, taking hold of Lorrie. Sean, furious, locked eyes with Jarhead who said, "She's cool. I'll help her. She'll be OK." While Lorrie—her eyes still roaming wildly back to Emily kept calling, "Please!"

Sean let Jarhead take Lorrie, then realized. "J-Stars, the laser radar! We're blind!" as Emily yelled at him: "Our mission is weapons of mass destruction. That's an old fashioned war down there. Our little plane is irrelevant—except if we stay on station we might be able to prevent millions of civilian deaths."

"You think those boys down there are killers so it's their job to be killed. The truth is they're hostages and you're letting them die."

Emily shouted, "I'm not responsible for their slaughter! What do you want me to say? 'I'm sorry my laser isn't a death ray?'"

Lorrie, being dragged away by Jarhead and fighting him every step of the way, wailed at Emily, "Yes, say you're sorry it's not a death ray! Say you'd do anything so my boys don't die!"

The S-300, on final trajectory, leapt toward Airborne Laser's underside like a hungry barracuda lunging for a belly-strike.

The LIDAR missile alarm gave a sudden shriek.

J-Stars yelled, "Kettledrums!"

Jarhead dropped Lorrie and jumped to his guns. Without thought, he panned and fired. The Gatling gun's needle-nosed slugs tore into the on-rushing missile. The warhead exploded just beneath ABL in a thunderclap of shock and flak.

Shrapnel ripped into the Tech Area. It caught J-Stars. He fell, as Airborne Laser shuddered, rocked—and filled with smoke and screaming.

FARMERS' MILITIA – MAGNOLIA PALACE GARDENS

Of the two thousand Guard Command who arrived at Magnolia Palace—after the artillery holding action which destroyed their vanguard assault forces—only twelve hundred remained able to contribute to the next assault. They thus still outnumbered the Farmers' Militia almost two to one. The farmers expected more assaults, each a more merciless onslaught than the last. They waited, this time expecting the sound of heavy tanks.

Despite the militarized nature of the North Korean regime, except for parades, the leaders always felt safer without a battalion of armor sitting near their headquarters. Should such a force get into the wrong hands, even the Guard Command would not be able to stop an assault on the palace.

The Guards were now paying for that choice. When they did locate tanks, because of their excessive weight, they had to be trailered in from outside the town—but all the trailers were in use for the DMZ pullbacks.

The farmers hunkered down, still waiting for the sound of tanks.

In contrast, what happened next was gentle, billowing...

The next sound the Farmers' Militia holding the inner garden walls heard was the *whoomf* of mortar rounds fired almost straight up. As the mortars airburst over the walls, there was neither the blast of HE, nor the hollow ripping of fragmentation warheads. In strange almost-silent pantomime puffs, the warheads blossomed like flowers opening. Clouds of white mist draped down over the walls, like a fog rolling in from the sea—except this was Sarin.

The lethal Sarin nerve gas, although seemingly spreading in slow motion, quickly misted about the walls, and with the slight breeze, carried in over the garden.

Instantly, across the garden, all life sounds of birds and insects and frogs fell to silence. In the deadly ashen fog of the battlefield, there echoed only the screaming tortured sounds of the dying farmers.

The Guard Command rose, in gas masks, firing madly—and rushed in for their next assault.

* * *

WHITE HOUSE ROVING SITUATION ROOM – 2:45 P.M. EST

"It's not all good, Sir." Jeanette said, "Unfortunately, despite the destruction of their lay-down missile, Radiant Outlaw reports armor movement."

The President asked, "Can anyone confirm that?"

NSA said, "Our remaining photo-recce satellites are being mostly laser-blinded as they pass over. The few images we're getting support this."

"Where is the armor?"

"It's on the way toward the DMZ. It should be across within an hour."

"I don't see how Il-Moon can even consider it, given ABL is on station and the last lay-down didn't go."

Jeanette said, "Perhaps it's time to launch everything we have left from Kadena toward Korea. ABL says Osan is operational. They could help as well with the invasion."

CIA remarked, "The weather is terrible, it's going to be a mess. Where would they refit, touch down if needed? And the planes aren't going to be able to stop the heavy artillery. There are more than 10,000 guns in place that can hit Seoul. Even with pin-point bombing, we wouldn't scratch the surface of those for days."

The President said, "So much for where we are, which is far up a famous crick without paddle or spoon. I want you all to put your heads together. I want you past understanding this situation and doing things. I want your plan in one hour."

ABL – GALLEY

Airborne Laser, smoky and emergency lit, was back under control. After the S-300 hit, Slammer and Bozon took the jumbo jet hobbling away from Korea and out into the violent storm winds over the East Sea.

A bloody J-Stars lay in a bunk as Sean fought the turbulence while he bandaged his leg. Sean worked at inserting a plasma I.V. After several messy tries, J-Stars joked, "Ease up, son, you want to keep the roast tender, you inject the gravy into the meat just right."

Sean winced, "Sorry. You just looked so much like a brisket."

J-Stars grinned as a cheerful Jarhead took over and soon the transfusion machine gave a steady beep indicating it was dripping.

Sean checked the leg bandage. It was already red with blood. He patted J-Stars' arm. "We tourniquet it, chances are you lose the leg. Let's see how the bleeding goes. You want anything?"

J-Stars eyes seemed to burn in the dark as he said, "Yeah. I'm thinkin' barbecue. Son, you jus' worry about the real damage reports."

Marty called, "Ops, this is Attack Laser. You and Emily need to come down here."

ABL – LASER AREA

Dr. Marty Carreras took Sean and Emily through the laser area's Christmas trees of lights and mazes of chemical piping. The room was pungent with the thunderstorm-smell of ozone from leaking hydrogen peroxide.

Marty squatted at a honey-comb optical bench, pointing to braided stainless steel tubing leaking fluid onto a floor already wet with laser fuel. Marty stood up, threw his chemical gloves into a disposal bin. "This turbulence. Micro-tears in the laser fuel lines, hard to stop."

Sean asked, fury building, "Is this because of the missile strike?"

Marty looked at him calmly. "No. Can't blame it on that. We just didn't do a good enough job designing for hours of shake and bake, no?"

Emily asked slowly, "How long?"

Marty said, "Not just how long; it's how far. We're lots better at closer range. We use a huge amount less of the magazine for each shot of the laser. You stay on patrol out here, we can at the moment toast four missiles. In an hour, three missiles. In two hours—maybe two and a half—we can't scorch plastic at ten feet."

ABL – GALLEY

Sean returned to the galley to check on J-Stars. He was the only one hurt, but when Sean looked at his leg bandage, it was soaked through with blood. Sean was sure, if they stayed on patrol, J-Stars was a goner.

Red came up, reported to Sean, "Laser remote sensing and laser radar are fine. Remote sensing chemical scan of Pyong-son shows three nuke missiles being fueled. LOX is out-gassing so they're longer range than anything we've seen yet. Real ICBM's."

Sean was devastated. He turned his back so she didn't see his face. "You're sure, Red?"

"They aren't even trying to hide it. It's like a challenge; a big 'take a flying fuck at this rolling donut' thing."

Sean looked about vacantly, saw Lorrie creeping up, head hung. Red turned her back on her and walked disgustedly to J-Stars.

Sean nodded curtly and Lorrie said, "'Kay. The self-sealing armor worked, bulkhead pressure's restored. 'Kay. I got the essential bus back up and computers are good. 'Kay. North Korean armor will enter the DMZ in thirty minutes." She paused, wrecked, whispered, "You won't tell my boys? I'd never ever leave my station 'cept—"

Sean asked in disgust, "Why did you do it, O'Leary? Why?"

Red said from across the galley where she was sitting holding J-Stars hand, "Because Welfare Mothers shouldn't crew."

J-Stars said gently, "Easy, Red. She's as much crew as you."

Red laughed bitterly. "Thanks, I think."

Sean grabbed Lorrie by the arms, asked again, "Why?"

Lorrie started crying, wildly shaking her head 'no,' then blubbering, pulled free and stumbled away. Sean was on his feet fast as a cat, moving after her. "Tell me! Why?"

He caught up to Lorrie just as she locked herself in the head. Looking down over the railing into the Tech Area, Sean saw Emily staring sightlessly out her big window. Lightning flashed on her face.

ABL – TECH AREA

J-Stars exclaimed, "Son, that's bold!"

Red was a lot more critical. "Let me get this straight. We fly this big ol' blimp into the flak zone over the DMZ and try to lightning Il-Moon's invasion all to hell?"

Matt said, "The North Korean anti-air defenses are ferocious! Any loitering over the DMZ produces unacceptable survival scenarios."

Red said, sarcastically, "You mean we won't remain a viable airframe?"

"Exactly!" Matt beamed, although behind the beam was a very worried man. "You're really catching on to the official nomenclature, Red."

Red rolled her eyes histrionically. "This isn't bold, it's a suicide mission!"

"Hot, yes. Suicide, no." Sean said. "All we need is ten seconds to cook and not be cooked. And the payoff is huge."

The crew looked at Emily, who was dully staring into space, seemingly going along with Sean. She stirred numbly. "The last time, I almost killed you all. But I have to admit Sean is right. It's all you've got—if you'll risk it, it's a chance to make a difference."

Jarhead said calmly into the silence that followed, "Beats sitting here running out of gas."

Red asked, "What happens if Il-Moon launches?"

"We're no worse off. In fact, the closer our range the better," Sean said. "We get really close Matt thinks we can use his EMP cannon."

Matt winked. "He launches and we're close, we'll huff and we'll puff and we'll blow his warheads up. And Pyong-son with it."

Red almost yelled, "Matt set off a nuke warhead near us? His EMP gizmo works all the way out to the stunning range of about five foot three. We will be *fricassee*."

Slammer put in helpfully, "This plane has wonderful blast shielding."

Red retorted, "Not ten kilotons at fifteen feet wonderful."

Sean said calmly, "We'll blow up that bridge when we come to it. Emily?"

Emily went to her console, projected a map on the big screen showing their run to the DMZ. Using the usual PowerPoint, video clips, and diagrams, she briefed: "We fly straight in north over the DMZ. Approaching, we use the Have Zeus laser configuration to ionize plasma tubes from the clouds to the ground." On the diagram, ABL closed on the border and the plane radiated spokes of laser light through the clouds to the ground all along the DMZ nearest Seoul.

"The lightning will short circuit along our beams to the ground. The DMZ is uninhabited but armor or artillery barrels are highly conductive and will be the preferred shorting path. Machines associated with such conductions will... cease to function."

Red said slowly, "You mean Emily will make lightning and maybe fry people?"

Emily looked up, eyes hollow. "No, I couldn't. It would destroy me. Lorrie will work Have Zeus."

Chapter 67

The 31st of October
4:00 a.m. KST

AIRBORNE LASER

Everyone felt a roaring adding into the thundering storm outside. Eila looked up, "Ops, Strikeback. Looks like the JASDF Eagles have made it."

Two F-15's pulled up alongside the bouncing Airborne Laser, and Col Hareda, wingtip to wingtip, waved to Sean. They were at such close proximity the radios would work here. Col Hareda bowed slightly, a nice move considering they could only see his helmet through the Perspex. Eila patched him in to Sean.

"Colonel-san. We are pleased to see you."

"I came as soon as I could, Phillips-san. What is happening?"

"It's war. North Korea is preparing to launch long-range missiles. We've formed up a battle group and we're going in. We could use some fighter cover."

The colonel shook his head sadly, "If only we could go along! But Japan is neutral."

"We need the help, Hareda-san. I feel certain nuclear missiles in Pyong-son are targeting Japan."

"My standing orders for this are very clear. Respond with arms only to direct attacks."

"Sometimes, my old friend, it is better to *beg* for forgiveness than to ask for permission."

The whole crew, listening on band 3, grinned at Sean's twist on the corny old Project Officer's Chestnut, almost always appropriate, but this time remarkably so.

Col Hareda was silent for a time, then spoke in rapid Japanese to his wingman. From the colonel's wingman came a sharp reply. In unison the two F-15's barrel-rolled into combat formation alongside ABL.

Col Hareda said, "Strikeback, Squadron Kirin reporting for duty with the Airborne Laser battle group."

Sean turned back to the group. There they all were, bitchy Red, and pained-eyed Lorrie, brainy Emily, hurt J-Stars, breathless Eila, bright Matt, solid Marty, warrior Jarhead, dapper Auggie, and wiseacre Slammer—solid Bozon at the moment driving the bus. Who was this crew anyway, by degrees drawn into the belly of the merciless beast? They came from across America, places so different their people almost couldn't talk to each other. And yet...

Jarhead knelt, pulled open the floor hatch. Chief Auggie checked his tie clip under his flight suit, and dropped into the hold. Jarhead dragged the first tossed-up parachute over the rim of the hatch.

Sean looked back at his crew; well, his and Emily's. "There are parachutes for anyone who wishes to jump. But I say we die fighting—"

Emily corrected gently, "Die defending."

The crew looked from Jarhead, busy stacking parachutes, and back to Sean. No one spoke.

Sean spoke quietly. Across the big screen behind him, the battle fires of the DMZ spread, growing fiercer. "You're either on the plane or you're off the plane."

Slammer said, "Speaking for me and Bozon, we are the plane."

"I'm the plane too," Eila said.

"Eila, you're twenty three. Too young," Emily said.

Eila pouted, "I volunteer. You better take me."

Emily sighed, and Jarhead, handling a big parachute, looked up. "I'm in. You'll need a lotta anti-air. Besides, I wouldn't miss it."

Matt swallowed, "Every additional volunteer increases the chance of mission success. I'm in."

Lorrie said, "Me too."

Red, arrogant rain or shine, quipped, "Me three."

The rest anted up—"I'm in. I'm in. I'm in."—sometimes with nonchalance, mostly with trepidation.

Emily said, "One thing, though. We can't risk losing the data from our shoot-down. How can we make sure it gets back?"

"We won't lose it," Sean said. "You assemble your data, and I'm putting a camcorder in the head. Everyone can tape a short message to family. Auggie, Smitty, and J-Stars are going to jump. They'll see it all gets home."

J-Stars, his face rigid and shiny as a mask of black ice, said, "All just for show. I'll be looking at 'cha."

While no one contradicted him, it was pretty clear to Sean no one believed him either.

AIRBORNE LASER – HEAD – COLLAGE OF GOOD-BYES

Across Airborne Laser (X), within the huge 747, in moments now forever lost, one by one, quietly, each crewmember broke from their preparations when signaled, climbed to the galley, entered the tiny bathroom, and sat before the camcorder. There, they rehearsed their words—pensive, worried, bold, afraid—and pushed the record button to tape a message for family or friends. Each spoke, called to the next person, and returned to their preparations for Airborne Laser's last run.

Sean had first pointed the camcorder out the window, zooming in on Col Hareda who said, over the radio, "My son, I have the most wonderful memories of you. Climbing Fujisan, of you reciting every kind of eel in the world, of you in our garden, of your first step. Keep these memories in your heart for me. Dear Kyoko. I know too often I was away working. I know we did not always talk, and you spent too much time in the kitchen. There are two things that make a man's life fulfilling. One, to serve his country. The other, a loving wife and family. Although I go now to die, I have been blessed with both. Farewell."

In the head, the crew each thought for a moment, some wrote something down first, but most just winged it. In the solemn and pitiless eye of the camcorder, they each spoke what they knew might be their last words from beyond the grave, listened to at funerals, or played over the next years, many times late at night, to the flooding of tears and tearing of hearts of those left behind.

Red, whose system was robust and ready, had gone first then made a tray of peanut butter sandwiches, carrying them and cartons of milk to the furiously working crew. For a moment, she hesitated behind Lorrie. Then she moved up, held out the tray of sandwiches. "Here, Mom. Hungry?"

Lorrie took one, took a bite, and almost lost it. "Mm. My favorite. PB&J."

Matt Cho had checked his EMP cannon and looked over his nuke-blowing calculations carefully. "Good-bye Patricia. It's so hard to leave you. Half of me is tearing at the walls to get back to you. The other half is proud I'm going into battle. Matt Jr., be especially good. Lisa, we've talked about this, but don't go into the Air Force unless it's what you have to do. Finally, Wifey, when you're ready, find someone new. We must face that this is somehow bigger than you and me."

Lorrie used the mirror in the head to fix her eye-shadow and carefully combed her short blonde hair. She grinned at her reflection mechanically, took a big breath, and put on her Mommy-of-two-kids face. "David and Paul, can you believe I'm flying right over you? I always was scared you'uns might die first. Now I see it was always meant to be me. I want you to forgive me for divorcing your father; it was just something I had to do and not because of you or anything like that. Forgive me for all the times me scolding you and trying to stop you from being spoiled. 'Cuz it worked. Your mother loves you, and tell your father I love him too." Lorrie choked for a moment, then forced herself to finish through her tears. "I'm just so proud that you aren't like me...that you became somebody."

In the Attack Laser area, while the recordings were happening, Marty and crew worked feverishly checking that most failure-prone part of any laser battle system—the connectors. They tightened and checked tensions and battened down everything they could reach on the laser beam train knowing the fierce shaking to come in the storm and the rigors of combat. Unseen, a tiny aerospace fastener on the main beam steering mirror was reporting the wrong torque as it steadily weakened, unnoticed.

When Sean had finished directing the NCOs to bolt and check the cockpit's nuclear flash blinds, he and Emily—partly out of an unspoken desire to be near each other, partly because their old battleground seemed so natural—jammed into the tiny head together.

Sean said, "Hello, Jeanette. Emily is dying to tell you about Kolmogorov turbulence and gain media. I just want you to know everything worked well and you are on the right road. Get as many anti-missile systems into service as you can and keep working as hard as you are. Remember me for those ice cream work breaks, jogging at lunch, your wine tasting parties. Ciao! Wish us good hunting."

As the laser crew worked at battening down loose laser components, tightening, tweaking the laser, Emily added, "The laser was good, our turbulence models robust. I suppose that's why clouds look similar all over the earth. We all live in the same atmosphere and it boils and mirages the same. If we fail to return it wasn't the physics. It was the human problem. The laws of physics are on the side of the violent. There is only so much you can do when physics is invoked for evil." She shifted slightly, then, "Dear Mother; my beloved family. I pray you see how hard I tried. Perhaps I never did become a good Quaker..." Her voice trailed off into silence. "But I died stopping killing."

Jarhead was the last to tape his message home. He crammed his bulk into the head and pushed the record button.

Down in the hold, he had been satisfied with his gang-loading of his guns, splicing together drums of ammo until he was rigged for continuous fire. "Dear Amanda. Last night I dreamt I was one of the twelve warriors at Thermopylae holding off the Persians until the Athenian army arrived. Turns out tonight Airborne Laser will make a stand of its own."

He had wiped a cloth over his oily hands, given a final pat to the caterpillar-like ammo belts feeding down into the belly of the plane to his Phalanx guns.

"I've never spoken ill of a unit I was in, but you probably guessed my thoughts on this one a few times. If it's the end for me it wasn't this crew; I've never been in a unit as proud. May we few hold the line tonight at our own Thermopylae."

Chapter 68

The 31st of October
4:15 a.m. KST

ABBEY'S HYUNDAI – MUNSAN TOWN AT THE DMZ

Abbey could tell from the look of the incoming fire that Munsan town was doomed.

Heedless of the intensifying rocket and artillery fire, Abbey propelled the Reuters' Hyundai 4x4 recklessly straight into the pretty town right on the DMZ. The well-off town, with its bourgeois shops and fashions on display, new Korean cars behind plate glass—along with the usual eel, noodle, record, electronics, and real estate shops with shiny photos of new apartments—seemed poised to deliver a happy life just waiting for the wise investing family. The illusion was shattered as the flares of rocket fire and artillery strobed the scene in a horrible evil light.

Over the years since the last war, the growing pleasant town of 40,000 had gradually, closer and closer, snuggled up against the DMZ—considerations of land use and demand in a competitive and crowded country like Korea prevailed over the fading awareness of the just-over-the-horizon horror of poised armor and artillery.

War had seemed just a dream. But the fact was—because of the topography and roadnet—an invading armored force simply *had* to stomp this town flat.

Now with the running of the panicked inhabitants and the artillery and rocket-fire flashes just beyond the buildings, the smoke roiling from the alleys and between buildings, there was nothing left of the shiny calm and prosperity, the marvelously pre-war feel of happiness and daily life, just its macabre ghost in the burning higgledy-piggledy collage of eateries, clothing stores, and entertainment shops.

Abbey was driving so fast, occasionally Hugh would involuntarily reach out and touch her arm as if trying to pass a calming energy right into her and have her lay back. It had no effect except eliciting an eye-corner glance of pity and amusement at his apparent cowardice.

Abbey needed to get out of the street—but she also needed a vantage point from which to report. She pushed the Hyundai even harder toward the center of town. There, the mini-high-rises should give some shelter and opportunities for broadcast.

The rocket fire was heavier ahead and Abbey slowed just enough to dodge through the fleeing Munsan-ers. The Hyundai was approaching the five-story buildings clustered around the little central square with its war monument, grassy park, and underground shopping mall. They had a chance for shelter there—and a rooftop view of the battle. She pressed the accelerator harder—

A rocket exploded in front of the speeding Hyundai 4x4. Launched it in a great arc and dazzling spray of sparks right through a fashion shop's plate glass window. Glass sprayed and metal sparked and buckled and racks of clothes and jewelry flew up in a cyclone of wreckage.

In the destroyed fashion shop, the Hyundai 4X4 sat rocking and humming from the incredible shock of the wreck. The rocking and humming slowly subsided, and into the stillness of the shop, from the fatally wounded car, a trickle of blood ticked from the crushed cab and in the quiet of the garage, there was only the sound of fluids dripping.

TIMES SQUARE TOKYO – SHINJUKU PLAZA

In packed Shinjuku plaza, the Tokyo crowd watched on the enormous Diamond Vision screens as the Hyundai—their view through a windscreen ripped by rocket fire—flew into the air and sailed through the shop window. As the camera in Hugh's hand fell, the scene bounced wildly, finally settling on a look out a window at the smoking wreckage of the fashion shop.

Across the world—Bombay, London, New York, Moscow—and in the White House Roving Situation Room, the watching masses took a sharp collective breath, waiting to see if Abbey's luck had run out just as had the Hyundai's. In the stillness of the ruined shop, for a long moment, the world held that breath hard, as if willing Abbey and Hugh to stir.

The President involuntarily jumped to his feet "Come on! Move! Get up!"

ABBEY'S HYUNDAI – MUNSAN TOWN AT THE DMZ

Hugh rolled against the shattered interior of the Hyundai, using its roughness to help drag him from the shock of the flight through the window and the hell of the collision. Abbey sat frozen in the ruined 4X4, eyes staring, stunned into stillness. Gradually, the snuff-strong fumes of gas bit Hugh's blood-streaming nose like smelling salts, snapping him into a partial consciousness.

Hugh, seeing Abbey's eyes open, unglazed and apparently unhurt, managed to creak his door open. He got out, checked the satellite signal, and taking his camera, focused it through the missing windshield onto a shaken Abbey.

Abbey raised her hands in protest at being filmed in such a state, then unbuckled her belt. Cursing when she cut her hands on the loose glass, she climbed out on all fours through the broken windscreen onto the hood of the Hyundai 4X4.

Hugh said to Abbey, camera on her, "I hope you're not going to do this every time we come to a new town."

Dropping lightly off the hood, Abbey stroked the ruined 4x4 affectionately. "As long as I can do it in a Hyundai."

She looked around carefully. The big size of the showroom meant they were on the bottom floor of a larger building. She located by eye in the gloom of a corner the big red fire escape door, which by law in Korea had to be open and go all the way to the roof. She moved toward it, speaking over her shoulder while Hugh followed as she hurried ahead. "Stairs! We can get good coverage on the roof. Maybe even see to the DMZ."

She and Hugh found the staircase endless and they ran up about three floors before Abbey realized two things. The first was that she'd underestimated the height of this building which meant they would get a good look around when they made it; and the other was that all the cigarettes and junk food were catching up with her and she was really feeling...

Abbey stopped at the landing on the fourth floor and puked delicately, while Hugh filmed her, asking, "How about this personal footage?" She waved an angry arm at him to go on. He grinned and ran on ahead. In the stairwell, the sound of the artillery wasn't any weaker, which was kind of amazing. It seemed to be growing toward a crescendo of nerve-shattering evil.

On the rooftop, it was a gorgeous view over Munsan, although tonight, when Abbey caught up to Hugh, it looked like the coming of hell. He was already panning the camera across the front. Like giant stomping feet, the fiery smoky blossoms of artillery barrage explosions boomed toward the town. Beyond, in the distance, there was some kind of motion. Hugh snapped in place a telephoto 900mm lens and in its glaring eye, there came the distinct dull olive gleam of North Korea armor. The tanks moved ponderously over the fencing and into the far side of the DMZ.

Abbey moved in front of the camera, reporting, said, "We are high up on a building in Munsan right at the southern edge of the DMZ. This is about as close as you can usually go without being stopped by the border fence. You can see in these live images, the onslaught of the invasion. From afar, it looks like some modern Godzilla is tramping through the area toward us. But closer to,

North Korean tanks are following artillery rounds that fall ever closer. Nothing it seems can stop the North Koreas as they approach the DMZ. The question is: can the innocent survive when there is nowhere to run?"

Hugh panned down to the square below. Panicked civilians milled about the square, fighting with emergency personnel and jamming the entrance to the civil disaster shelter in the Munsan underground shopping mall.

Hugh, focusing his camera down onto the square said, "Boy, Abbey, they need to get under cover. That barrage is walking right at us."

Abbey grimaced, leaned over the high wall. She yelled down in Korean: "A barrage is coming! Get down the stairs!"

A Korean security guard, pressed into civil emergency service, managed to hear, and yelled, "Everyone! It's coming! Into the mall! Hurry!"

As the Munsan-ers swarmed down the stairs toward safety, Hugh said to Abbey, "Well, they may have spared Seoul, but they are going to flatten Munsan. It looks like the end of our stories."

Abbey replied, looking down into the town square, "Will you never learn? Right down there is our next story. And then there will be the next."

"Until the final story?"

Abbey laughed, "No, you goose, there is no final story." Her eyes were already scanning the chaos below. "We can do a last broadcast, down there, in the town, then we'll get into the mall and see what the people have to say."

Abbey saw, from her vantage point on the roof, a young Korean boy run from his panicked mother into a narrow alley. There was something oddly familiar in his pudgy form, his bursting energy... "Hey, look. Over there! A boy! Let's go!"

They bolted for the stairs. In the square, Abbey looked amidst the smoke and fire and noise for the boy. She couldn't see him. She waved Hugh toward the safety of the stairwell, yelling as she ran toward the alley, "Keep broadcasting! Cover me!"

Hugh vaulted into the stairwell, ignoring the pleas of the Korean security guard to move deeper. He set the camera up on the concrete stanchion at the end of the stairs and managed to find and keep Abbey's back in the frame as she searched, while he kept one ear on the artillery barrage closing in.

Abbey, on the far side of the square, ignored the slightly off-the-mark artillery shells already exploding into the lower floors of the buildings across the square. She tried to remember which alley it was, but there were so many here. She looked down one alley, irregular and crooked. Then another. Nothing. No luck.

What had been sporadic artillery was fast becoming more resolute. Rounds were hitting and exploding closer and more rapidly.

Abbey tried the next alley. There, whimpering, cowered the Korean boy. As she moved toward him, he ran until what seemed like minutes later, but actually only seconds, Abbey cornered him against a dumpster and grabbed him.

He fought, slippery and determined, waving his muscular limbs about in a few searing blows to her head and gut.

She tucked him under her crossed arms. "Got you, you little eel!"

From the stairwell, Hugh held a perfect framing as Abbey, cradling the boy, ran straight at him across the exploding square and toward the safety of the stairs. Artillery exploded around her. She neared safety—

The big 152mm shell fell just yards behind her, and burst. Shrapnel riddled into Abbey's back. With superhuman effort, she staggered on, fell, crawled, the boy slung under her, toward the stairs. She was only twenty feet from Hugh when she collapsed. In a final effort, with a last propelling push, she launched the boy toward the stairwell, toward Hugh who was calling out, yelling. The boy scampered to the stairwell as Hugh and others behind him reached up and pulled him down to safety.

Hugh looked back to see Abbey, just a few yards away lying on her stomach, her back covered in blood, looking right at him. She winked and tried to smile. Hugh rose to run to her. She waved him back violently. Amidst the scream of incoming cannon shells, Abbey pointed to the camera.

Hugh swung the camera back around to her, zooming in until Abbey's hurt yet determined face filled the frame.

In the frame, Abbey smiled at Hugh—who smiled back—and although he couldn't hear her, before the incoming scream of an artillery salvo made him leap down the stairwell shelter, he guessed her words.

Abbey looked into the camera, whispered. "This is Abbey Yamamoto signing off from Korea, and wishing you all peace."

Abbey's eyes, grimly satisfied, skewed as she died.

A burst of artillery struck the little square.

Abbey vanished in the flames.

TIMES SQUARE TOKYO – SHINJUKU PLAZA

The last close-up of Abbey's face slammed into the Tokyo crowd at Shinjuku. There was a crowd-moan as she seemed to speak directly to them on the giant Diamond Vision screens, then died as the TVs went to snow.

WHITE HOUSE ROVING SITUATION ROOM – 3:15 P.M. EST

"Jesus!" whispered the DOE man involuntarily. The rest of the group stared at the TV, riveted at the fading image of Abbey and the fire storm of the little square. "That is clearly an all-out armored assault with artillery right down the Kaesong-Munsan corridor."

NSA said, "It's worse than that. With the nuke lay-down fading, our SIBRS-High is seeing new ICBM's fueling at Pyong-son. Three missiles. Bigger than the previous ones. They appear to be readying a strategic launch. Perhaps Japan, our air bases like Yakota in Tokyo. Or Kadena."

The President looked around, "I asked for a plan. What did you come up with?"

CIA said, "I think we can assume they are going to strike somewhere. We have begun to alter some Peacekeeper warheads to be non-nuclear. Just kinetic strikers. With as few as ten MIRVed missiles we can hit Pyong-son before they launch, remove the nuclear threat and likely their leadership as well."

"There are thousands of bunkers in the DPRK," Gen Bolds said. "Their leaders are probably hidden in ones we don't even know about."

DOE shook his head, replied, "We have got to strike back strategically. Even three missiles with the redone MIRVs will tip the balance."

Jeanette said, "You're talking about launching ICBM's at another country. We're the example to the world. Should the U.S. be first to use them?"

DOE answered, "I'm suggesting we have ready both non-nuke and nukes."

Gen Bolds exclaimed, "Tell the difference to the Russians and Chinese! We launch ICBM's nukes or no, they'll flip. We could start World War III. The nuclear kind. If we continue conventional defense, we'll win."

"Eventually and at what cost? Our boys are going to be overrun," the President said. "What are we doing about the Chinese?"

The National Security Advisor said, "The Secretary of State has already been on the horn to them. Their treaty with Pyongyang does not include joining in if the North Koreans attack first. I think we have adequately documented that fact to them."

NID said, "Sure, but they might take advantage, a nibble here or there. Something they couldn't usually get away with. Not Taiwan, but say seize a disputed island somewhere." He turned to Jeannette. "Can we count on ABL to stop the ICBM's?"

Jeanette said bravely, "I'm sure they are on station, and ready for anything."

DOE said quietly, "I'm not so sure. We've learned a lot about technology and we know not to expect it to function perfectly."

The room looked around, each set of eyes probing the others, knowing how difficult it was to make any really concrete tech assessment.

NID shifted in his chair, said softly: "I'd say from the fueling missiles, Airborne Laser hasn't convinced Il-Moon—and if you think about it, that's the point."

There was another silence, everyone knowing history's eyes would forever remember this moment.

The President decided. "Get the MX missiles ready for both nuclear and non-nuclear strike. Get me a set of punitive and military targets. It's our only option. I will not stand by if they launch a nuclear strike against us or Japan."

Jeanette whispered, but in the silence everyone heard, "No one has used ICBM's since Hitler. Should America be the first, when we still have the option of Airborne Laser?"

"We'll keep that hope open. Meantime, Jeanette, what about my order to your damned rogue satellite?"

RADIANT OUTLAW

Radiant Outlaw looked down on the flames of Munsan, and realized the TV transmission had ceased. In his ascending elliptical orbit, he was losing resolution quickly as he swung higher over the earth. Mindful of the terse direct orders coming back from the PanAmSat, he searched along the coast of South Korea. Finding a strong IR signature, Outlaw locked onto Airborne Laser far below over the East Sea, and began to broadcast the video of the flying laser plane back to the President.

With the clearing of the lay-down, Comm links were proliferating. Outlaw found a satellite cell phone bird passing by, and placed a telephone call to Magnolia Palace.

WHITE HOUSE ROVING SITUATION ROOM – 3:30 P.M. EST

Airborne Laser came on the TV, and Jeanette gasped, said, 'There it is!'

On the TV, Radiant Outlaw was now broadcasting a look-down from space. In its less-than-stellar imaging system—not nearly the quality of a real photo-recce bird—there was still a decent image of Airborne Laser, just off Korea against a the cold Sea of Japan, bulbous nose and huge wingspan clear in the IR.

The President walked around to the TV, touched the IR image of where

ABL gracefully flew. "This is Airborne Laser?"

"Yes, Sir. I think Outlaw has decided to broadcast to us."

"About time." The President grinned, "Next time, can you program into it who the heck the commander in chief is—and how important he is?"

"I'm sure we can find a set of programming rules to reinforce that, Sir."

More seriously, he turned to the DOE man. "What about our plan?"

CIA spoke up, "The ICBM MIRVed warheads are in preparation. The missiles in their silos are almost readied. We have a number of great targets: Pyong-son of course. Pyongyang, the complex where the Dearest Leader and the elite live—the Magnolia Palace. We must get them to understand there can be no win on their side. No comeback from what they started. Better to reinforce that early by destroying Pyong-son, the Ministry of People's Armed Forces—and Dearest Leader's palace."

"We don't even know where they are in those bunkers. A projectile coming in at seven miles a second might kill thousands of civilians."

The ringing of a phone interrupted them. The Exec answered it, looked up. "He says it's Dearest Leader!"

With the call on the speakerphone, the President introduced himself, then added, "We are extremely concerned about the apparent invasion of South Korea."

Dearest Leader answered, "As are we. I want to assure you these actions are by scoundrel elements of our army, which do not represent the legitimate government of the DPRK. These elements, acting on their own, began this conflagration."

"You realize, from our current understanding of the battlefield, our troops and Japan may be in deadly danger."

"We are seeking to abort all offensive operations. Such actions have no support from the DPRK."

"From where we are, the offensive operations seem massive and continuing."

"Yet, if you would consider, there have been few SCUD attacks, no naval actions, no sniper teams, no artillery upon Seoul—and no chemical or biological weapons. Would this not be the expected and most effective course?"

The President looked around the table, and got some definitive nods. In Dearest Leader's statements—and in the timbre of his voice—there was the resonance of truth. "You are taking counter action, then, to these attacks?"

"We have a node on the DPRK Armed Forces Intranet. We are canceling offensive orders as we can, and have stopped many war messages from coming to fruition."

"What about the artillery, and the armor in the DMZ?"

"Sadly, some forces are more difficult than others. The artillery holding Seoul hostage, you may have noticed, as well as the SCUD fleet has been neutralized. Slowly but slowly the pull-back will come."

Jeanette spoke up. "If I may, Sir?"

The President nodded.

Jeanette continued, "Dearest Leader, I wanted to tell you that we have received several detailed broadcasts from the front lines."

"Yes?" the voice was weary. "It must appear very grim."

"I thought you should know the broadcaster was Abbey Yamamoto. She died while covering the war right at the DMZ."

There was an audible sigh, a long pause. In a heavy voice, Dearest Leader said, "Tell me."

"She died saving a Korean boy under an artillery barrage."

There was a silence. "I am very sorry to hear it. I will think on this in time."

The President broke in, "Should you remain in Pyongyang? I would prefer it if you were in a more neutral location."

Dearest Leader laughed slightly, "Yes, I suppose that would be the prudent thing to do."

The President said, "We may have to strike Pyongyang if things get very bad."

Again the light laugh. "There are other issues to leaving. Besides, this is my capital, my people. Would it not be the height of shame to leave them to their fate, when perhaps one can prevent it or stand with them?"

The President, hearing the unmistakable sounds of explosions rumbling behind Jong-Nam asked, "Are you sure that is the wisest course?"

"What kind of a leader would I be if I fled now?" Dearest Leader said solemnly. "No, I will make my stand here, as you must make yours there."

"What about the peace treaty?"

"I have signed my draft copy—although for the moment, this is perhaps mooted."

A sudden anger gripped the President, and when he could speak again, he asked directly, "How could we be so close and yet this? How could this happen?"

Dearest Leader chuckled grimly. "There is a saying, yes, 'Shit Happens'? Yet must there not be someone who cleans it up?"

A pause, and the President said, "You know, Jong-Nam, if we can get through this, I think we will look back on today as the beginning of a very good friendship."

"I do believe you are right. Now, you must excuse me, as I must turn to other matters. Good-bye. Perhaps we will speak again in an hour."

Into the still room, the dial tone the only sound, rushed a DOE man. "Sir?" He paused when everyone looked at him. He continued, "The MX missiles are almost modified. It will only be an hour or so until they are readied."

After the conversation with Dearest Leader and the missile preparation announcement, the Situation Room plunged into a gloomy anxiety.

"Hey!" the Exec called, unconsciously boy-like. "Sirs! Airborne Laser is leaving her patrol pattern."

In Radiant Outlaw's transmitted images, Airborne Laser seemed to be on a soft bank, losing altitude. Before the President's group could decide if they were in trouble, three parachutes bloomed behind the plane.

The room gathered around the TV as ABL, her small fighter escort at her wingtips, looking majestic and calm from space, leveled out from her wide turn.

Airborne Laser was on a new trajectory—heading straight in on the fiery DMZ.

Chapter 69

The 31st of October
4:30 a.m. KST

AIRBORNE LASER

Turbulence shaking them, the ABL crew buckled in at their stations for the mission. They looked at each other, knowing for some of them it would be the end...

Sean left Emily in charge of the Tech Area, and ran to meet the departing party at the rear of the plane where a big cargo hinge could open for airdrops.

Auggie, Smitty, and J-Stars were in parachutes. Sean stuffed Emily's data and the family videos under J-Stars' jumpsuit. "Land on your good leg, son."

J-Stars grinned and replied, "And you, you land on your feet, boy."

In spite of dipping to twenty thousand feet for the drop—Airborne Laser's normal altitude would result in such a long cold low-oxygen drop, J-Stars would never survive—the freezing air tugged at them as Smitty opened the hatch. The two NCOs walked, holding J-Stars by the arms, and they all tumbled off the rear hatch. Falling, their parachutes bloomed against fiery war flames burning across Korea.

Airborne Laser began to climb again toward attack altitude.

In the Tech Area, Sean found on the big screen Emily had mapped out ABL's mission to their DMZ objective. Sean looked over the crew, finding unfocused skittering eyes, and snow-white faces—deep pre-combat shock. He flipped the all-call button, so everyone in the aircraft could hear. "North Korean armor is entering the DMZ. It's time to go in. Red, if you'd hit Pyong-son right in the face with something, I'm sure it wouldn't go amiss."

Red, pleased she for once could take the offensive, threw Sean a mock salute.

Sean visually checked each crewmember. "Flightdeck, this is Ops. Tech Area is ready. Commence your run."

ABL, emblems and flags clear, USAF F-16 and Japanese F-15 fighter escort at her wing-tips, banked through stormy skies toward distant battle fires.

Lorrie called out, "ABL, this is Comm. DMZ is one hundred kilometers."

"With the emphasis on kill," someone mumbled.

Emily, ashen, whispered to herself, "Oh, dammit, we forgot the silent prayer."

PYONG-SON COMPLEX

In the control room deep underground, Il-Moon watched video of his brutally advancing tanks. Aide Park, at his side, murmured, "The Great Vice Chairman's army sweeps all before it."

There was a strangled sound, a technician looking at a screen set out an involuntary grunt. His screens of the air battle over the DMZ, a video link from the top of the mountains high above, were suddenly saturated and solid white.

"What is it?" asked Aide Park.

The technician replied, "The Bastard Plane. It was starting to turn, perhaps toward the DMZ."

"Show me."

"I cannot. At the moment, our screens are being blinded."

Il-Moon mused, "Inform the anti-air units at the DMZ. Make sure every fighter we have is in the air and attacking. A great reward for anyone who damages the Bastard Laser Plane." He paused for a moment, then leaned over to Aide Park. "Also, make ready the emergency egress train."

AIRBORNE LASER – OVER THE DMZ

Airborne Laser cut across the Korean peninsula, the DMZ and burning Seoul ahead, although Sean could tell the damage to the South Korea capital was so far minor.

Turning, Airborne Laser headed straight north toward Munsan. A cloud of anti-aircraft missile plumes rose to meet ABL. Sean called the course, looked at the navigation. "Come around to 290, level at 30,000 feet."

Matt said, "Can't we go any higher?"

"For this lightning run, Emily says we go slow and low."

"At that altitude, there's just nowhere to hide."

Lorrie was grimly calling off the ranges as Sean called, "Lower. Lower."

ABL headed in toward the far DMZ, pounding through thunderheads, wings flapping in the turbulence. Flaming anti-air missiles swarmed toward ABL, as the cobra-hooded beam director cranked around looking...

Lorrie said, "Doppler hits! Motion. Ground motion at Onch'on-up."

Emily said, "Too early for a laydown nuke. What?"

"It's the weirdest thing. The whole side of this mountain is starting to move!"

ONCH'ON-UP UNDERGROUND AIRFIELD

The North Korean People's Air Force ground crews were finally launching the Kim Il-Sung Night-Fighters from underground.

The launch crews stood back from their loaded aircraft. The lead signaler raised his red flag. The exit blast doors swung away. The outside lights burst on, illuminating the long runway stretching into the night outside the cavern.

There was a limited amount of on-engine time inside the mountain, and as instructed they did not turn on the giant exhaust fans until the last moment, because the smoke from the vents would be visible. Now the lines of Mig-21 Fishbed-J and Mig-23 Floggers, the old delta winged and swept wing 1950's style fighters, revved their engines.

The flagmen swirled their signal flags. One after another, the most modern Russian fighters the DPRK had, supersonic MiG-29 Fulcrums, revved their engines. The sleek jets, piloted by the best and most reliable DPRK pilots, blasted along the underground runaway and began popping out of the side of the mountain.

One after another, the Kim Il-Sung pilots took their night-fighters out of the side of the mountain and into the air to attack Airborne Laser. As they took off, the yellow fire-points of their engines glowed, then diminishing to pinpricks against the dark sky before disappearing.

AIRBORNE LASER

Sean put in, "Onch'On-Up. They took an elongated mountain ridge and tunneled out an underground airfield."

"That is sick," someone said. "Look at all the motion!"

And indeed, on the big screen was suddenly a rash of red and purple dots, each dot indicating a relatively slow or fast motion."

"It looks like the country is breaking out in zits. So, what is it exactly?"

Red said, "Laser radar confirms the fast things are anti-air missiles. The purple, don't worry, just a bunch of fighters."

Eila said, "I didn't think the DPRK had any night fighters."

Sean answered, "They have some good ones—and their mission is high-altitude Recon interdiction."

"You mean, planes like us?" Eila said, looking up, and Sean nodded.

Airborne Laser, now moving closer and closer to the enemy, came into the range of more and more deadly missiles.

The first in a salvo of heat-seeking missiles screamed in on ABL. The DIRCM, picking up the leads, began blinking confusing messages at them, and several of the missiles jinked away in U-turns. A few more closed fast on ABL—while a bigger trio of huge SA-5 guided missiles arched in on ABL's rear.

Jarhead called, "I've got the little two." His Phalanx guns opened up, blowing away the smaller missiles. Matt, his EMP cannon loaded with only half a charge, fired with a BAM! The remaining missiles exploded, debris flashing past.

Within a moment, new salvos of missiles ripped in toward ABL from all sides. Close missile shots were hitting near the fuselage and as the fragments exploded into ABL, its light armor reacted, exploded back, smoking, taking the hits in a thrum of shaking.

Matt said, "Armor entering the DMZ!"

The beam director tracked the armor, turbulence pounding ABL. On the big screen, lightning flashes lit the DMZ. A thousand artillery pieces flashed. North Korean tanks, grinding over fences, fired, their barrels pinpricks of leaping flame.

Jarhead's Gatling guns were ripping and roaring almost constantly, as fragmentation warheads exploded all around ABL. Smoke began to leak into the Tech Area through the vents, tendrils of plastic and burning oil stench, and the crew began coughing and choking.

The next wave of SA-3s ripped in smoking and roaring, Matt's EMP cannon—billowing acrid smoke through the Tech Area—blitzed a whole pack.

Lorrie called out, "DMZ is twenty kilometers. Sixty seconds."

* * *

With the falling away of the missile salvos, the Kim Il-Sung Night-fighters, ancient but deadly Fishbeds and Floggers, who until now had to stay out of the missile free-for-all, ripped in on ABL in a pack of more than forty fighters strong. From far out, toward ABL, cannon tracer shells streamed from under the delta wings of the Fishbeds, incongruous to their almost comical clown-hat noses.

Eila radioed, "Uh oh! Falcons, Kirins, this is Strikeback. We could really use some interference!"

Falcon 1 replied, "Let's go break that party up."

ABL's F-16s tore toward the North Korean fighters, air-to-air missiles igniting engines, the waspish airframes dropping off the wings. The Fishbeds, clearly with orders for the laser plane rather than dog fighting, tried to ignore the counter fire, hoping against hope to damage ABL. The Japanese F-15's pulled higher, moved to the side, covering, watching for anything breaking through.

The Fishbeds and Floggers divided up, attacked Airborne Laser from all angles.

ABL's picket screen of the two F-16s blasted the first few North Korean fighters from the sky. The swarms of North Korean planes zigged and zagged, trying to get past.

Matt said, listening to his earpiece, "The North Korean pilots are yelling at each other to 'Ignore fighters. Go for the funny plane.' I think they mean us."

"Funny plane indeed," Sean said. "We are not amused."

Lorrie called out, "DMZ is ten kilometers. Thirty seconds."

A pair of MiG-29 high-performance fighters blew their afterburners and from their hide against the clutter of the ground, suddenly rose, attacking.

As the MiG's came ripping up at them, Red yelled, "Something really fast coming up. Some kind of fighter. Mach 3! Lorrie!"

"Sorry, I can't move off the DMZ."

Sean yelled back, "Don't you understand—"

Lorrie was intent on her monitor, "We're not in high power mode. We're in lightning mode. Even if I wanted, I couldn't. Deal with it."

Sean yelled back: "I've got nothing left!"

Red called out, "If I can stop jamming Il-Moon I can help."

"Do it!"

Red swung her smaller independent remote sensing laser aperture. The four MiG-29's going at more than two thousand miles per hour banked straight up toward them at the amazing attack angle of thirty-five degrees, the Guards readying their weapons systems, squinting up at their target.

A brilliant green flash zotzed into their eyes. Red's laser at a dazing level went right through their visors. The dazzle was amazing, shocking. Huge white flare-outs burst before their eyes. They dropped their controls and clutched their faces. Their gloves gripped their helmets, couldn't cover their eyes, whimpering in terror. The temporary dazzling would fade in five minutes. It was five minutes they did not have. Panicked, their few hours of training inadequate for them to recover control over such a complex unstable fighter at supersonic speeds and sharp angle of attack, the MiG's heeled over, spun out, dove toward the rice fields below.

Sean winked at Red. "Wow."

"The dazzling only lasts a minute. Their eyes will be fine."

"I'm not so sure about that," Sean replied as he tracked the jets' trajectory downward to where they exploded against the ground. "Thanks."

"Anytime," and Red returned her laser to blinding Pyong-son's domes.

In the fracas, the Phalanx and EMP cannon were now firing almost continuously. F-16s blasted the Kim Il-Sung Guards, who changed tactics, swarming back against the F-16s. Falcon 1 said, "He's on my back. Too many of them!"

Sean called, "Matt, help them out." Matt's cannon boomed, and two Night-fighters dropped from the sky.

Falcon 1 said, "Thanks—"

Crunch! A North Korean fighter rammed him. Falcon 1 exploded into a ball of fire.

"Falcon 1, Falcon 1, this is Strikeback...Oh, he's gone," Eila moaned.

Lorrie called out, "DMZ is five kilometers. Fifteen seconds."

Five North Korean fighters blew past the lone defending F-16. Falcon 2 looped back over to hit the North Korean fighters closing on ABL. The Kim Il-Sung pilots, aces all, flipped their Fishbeds over too, turned back on Falcon 2. North Korean cannon fire raked Falcon 2.

Falcon 2: "There's too many! Winchester! Armaments out. I'm hit."

"Falcon 2, this is Strikeback! Fall back. Fall back. Courier message to Kadena. Tell them main attack is down Kaesong-Munsan corridor. Osan fuels and armaments still viable!"

Col Hareda, finished with sending a few of the more-capable MiG-29's spinning in pieces toward the rice paddies below, now turned up to pounce on the North Korean fighters.

Too late, Falcon 2 flamed out. Stalled. Fell. Falcon 2 radioed over, "Keep the faith, ABL." He ejected.

A Fishbed turned, deliberately ramming the parachuting pilot.

Kirin 2 launched a small heat-seeking missile, caught the Fishbed within a second, blowing it to shreds.

Col Hareda: "Kirin 2. Save your missiles. Use guns on these Fishbeds. Let's clear the right flank."

In seconds the Japanese dog-fought the last nearby North Korean fighters until only falling debris filled the sky. The remaining Night-fighters formed up in a hornets' nest a few miles away, circling to consider their options.

Kirin 2: "ABL, right flank clear. Come on through."

Tank fire made pinpricks in the dark DMZ below the storm.

Lorrie called, "Ten seconds to the DMZ—!"

Lightning crackled in bundles in the clouds. Turbulence walloped the Tech Area, and Sean barely held himself in place, leaning over Lorrie's shoulder where she sat in Emily's seat.

Lorrie shot out a probe beam. Massive electrical discharges rattled between clouds.

The resulting clap of thunder shook Airborne Laser wingtip to wingtip.

The ABL Tech Area crackled with St. Elmo's fire. Emily called, "You're too high. Down 10,000 feet!"

"Flightdeck, Ops. Dive, Dive! Dive to 20,000!"

Jarhead, panning looking for missiles, remarked, "Now that's what I call a fighting altitude."

Matt said, "There's nothing they can't throw at us at 20,000," as Lorrie yelled: "DMZ five seconds!"

ABL came screaming toward the DMZ, radar-controlled anti-air below opening up. The ack-ack rounds poofed high up, flak bursting around ABL, hammering the airframe.

Shaking like a banshee, the jumbo jet leveled out, Matt yelling, "The DMZ! We're home!"

Lorrie made her move. To Sean it was a minor motion. She clicked her mouse madly all along an image of the DMZ below them.

ABL's laser beam zipped out in a stuttering pattern of green and violet pulses. The beam poked through the clouds toward where, sweeping across the border, on came the wave of firing attacking armor.

In a shimmering gargantuan twenty-thousand foot high laser light show, the laser beams, emanating from ABL like spokes from a hub, poked down to the DMZ.

The clouds connected down the beams to the ground. In a flash, lightning poured down each beam in forky branches.

Lightning struck in a line just in front of the advancing North Korean armor.

DMZ – NORTH KOREAN 820th TANK CORPS

The North Korean tank crews saw their screens flicker and felt their engines stall. In each tank, the crew felt the blue sparkling coursing over clothes and hands, looked around to see everyone glowing with azure St Elmo's fire.

Panicked, the tank crews popped their turrets, jumped, ran to escape the tingling.

Rumbling with impossibly violent thunder, an earthquake shook them. Coming toward them was a cloud-high wall of lightning.

The lightning moved forward, blasting trees, frying armor, striking about like a slashing saber. Hidden artillery, its metal barrels pointing up from under cover, found the lightning could feel them out, shorting down them. Even miles back, the lightning arced to them instantly. A fury of huge explosions of artillery magazines lit the Kaesong hills.

Yelling and screaming, helmets flying, the tank crews raced away jabbering; sprinting in panic back out of the DMZ.

Their stalled armor sat in rows. The wall of lightning spun over the tanks and in a hideous rolling thundering, the abandoned armor broiled and fried.

Retreating North Koreans poured back through their own forts and bunkers—and did not even slow. Artillery crews, cringing in the explosions all around them, the lighting walking toward them like giant electrical monsters, abandoned their artillery and ran.

Lightning struck all along the North Korean front. Thunder rolled from one end of the DMZ to the other.

AIRBORNE LASER – TECH AREA

On the big screen, Lorrie pulled back the video to a wide look, and in their furiously quick glances up at the screen, the crew saw for fifty miles the result of the apocalyptic lightning storm up and down the DMZ.

They sat in stunned silence—all but Lorrie. She jumped from Emily's seat and ran to Red's console.

Lorrie looked at the display and yelled, "Doppler is...zero! Tanks have stopped. Cold!"

WHITE HOUSE ROVING SITUATION ROOM – 3:45 P.M. EST

The view from space, courtesy of Radiant Outlaw was amazing. Like sitting in the desert when a humongous lightning strike blasts the horizon from one end to the other, the President and his party could only goggle at the amazing light show.

DOE jumped to his feet. "What the heck!"

The President looked at Jeanette questioningly.

The Under Secretary for Science and Technology said simply, "Artificial lightning. Amazing. Last time they tried to do that—"

"Yes?"

"Well, anyway. From the angle of ABL's strike along the DMZ, it would seem that little will be left of the DPRK armor in the Kaesong-Munsan corridor. That would include the heavily-fortified artillery. It's hard to imagine the invasion force recovering."

"Plus our boys will be all over them now."

NID leaned back, tense muscles still unable to release. "Incredible. Is it just too much to hope for?"

CAMP CASEY – ARTILLERY POSITION 3

With the dropping away of the artillery thudding and the onset of crackling and thunder, Capt O'Leary's gun crew threw confused glances between themselves. They knew the sounds of artillery and armor. Cocking their ears, they listened, puzzled. Now in the solid ear-ringing silence following the strange storm of sound, Capt O'Leary and Lt O'Leary scampered the vertical bunker ladder and opened the viewing hatch to look out from their ruined spotting positions. At first, they saw only fires, then the flare and zap of distant lightning, a flickering.

Lt O'Leary said, "Artillery fire has stopped. What is that?" pointing to the strange residual sizzling.

"Lightning? A storm?" Capt O'Leary mused. "You know, there is a Korean legend: the legend of the Mandate of Heaven. In the event that the leadership is too bad to the people, Heaven withdraws its Mandate to the ruler, and the forces of nature—floods, famine, lightning—removes the bad leader from power."

"I don't know; looks more like the hand of god to me." Across the burned DMZ sat lines of smoking and torched North Korean armor.

Capt O'Leary said, "Whether it's their Heaven or our god, let's get out the M1A1's and give the old boys some help!"

With a Rebel Yell, the 2nd Infantry crews cheered and ran toward their tanks.

PYONG-SON COMPLEX

Il-Moon stared at his collapsing invasion. Aide Park whispered, "Triple Bastard Airborne Laser."

Il-Moon said, "The field will still be ours! Launch all the remaining missiles." He glared at his technicians and they, faces white, began to work their consoles. On the video screens of the missile caverns, Il-Moon saw his three Taepo-Dong 2 missiles, massive ICBM's, equalize their LOX tanks and release plumes of white mist.

AIRBORNE LASER – TECH & LASER AREAS

Lorrie called, "Motion at Pyong-son! Missile silo covers have popped. Three of them!"

Emily said, "God, Sean. We don't have enough laser fuel. We need to get closer."

"Flightdeck, this is Ops. Head straight for Pyong-son." He paused to think, leaned over and said to Eila, "Get Col Hareda up to speed. We're going in."

Eila said, "Kirins 1 and 2, this is Strikeback. We're heading into Pyong-son. Coordinates to follow machine to machine." She hit the button to send the targeting maps.

Col Hareda and his wingman exchanged some terse sentences in rapid Japanese. Sean, although he could no longer see out of ABL because of the shuttered windows, imagined the hand signals between them, ending in the thumbs up, as Col Hareda came back over the radio. "Tally Ho!"

Sean felt ABL bank onto its target vector and straighten. In the muted lighting of the Tech Area, the plane felt cave-like, cozy, almost safe. The silent battle images on the big screen, the splashes of computer screen color on the crew consoles, and the sealed windows added to the feeling of isolation and calm, as if they were a headquarters far behind the lines, as if...

Bam! Bam! Bam! Anti-aircraft rounds, bursting far beneath them, began a constant thrumming as ABL and its F-15 escort passed over a smoking DMZ and swept toward distant Pyong-son.

The heavily-goggled laser crew, flight suits soaked in sweat, toiled feverishly at returning the laser from low-energy ionizing status, to high-power anti-missile salvos.

Working between the complex mazes of piping intertwined with the laser bench, they leaned in, snapped covers off the boxes of optical subcomponents. These were the paths the light must follow at almost impossibly high flux levels. Unlike electrons which must follow a conductor, a wire, a channel, here it was a clear path through the air, with interceptions of crystals, filters, windows, and mirrors—always and forever mirrors. The crew leaned in over the beam train mirrors, checking them, tweaking them. Unseen and unfelt, the last big mirror, which sent the beam down its vacuum channel to the beam director in the nose, this last mirror was listing...

On the big screen, the first missile rose from a hidden exit tube on a hillside. Climbing under the huge weight of gravity, it passed above the grim hills of Pyong-son. Through the atmospheric distortions, the missile appeared only as a chimera of wavy white and blurry fire.

Red calmly worked her console, the laser playing over the side of the missile, moving up and down, taking its measure, reading its dynamics. "An ICBM. Big. It's...a Taepo-Dong 2. Loaded."

Sean asked, "Another laydown?"

Mumbling to herself, Red looked at the numbers, "Trajectory is, wait just a few..." She rechecked, looked up, face even whiter than her usual pallor. "It is heading, best I can tell, to Tokyo."

Emily straightened and for a second, hearing the name of the city, she was away, dreaming, and it was night and it seemed she stood before a carved wooden temple gate high on a mountain. Then the gate swung wide and she knew she was on Mt. Fuji, and through the gate she overlooked the sequin sprawl of city lights along a dark curving scimitar: Tokyo Bay.

A falling star blazed, but instead of passing and fading, the falling star curled in on the city—and then it was not a star but a spinning missile warhead. The Tokyo skyline, in a splay of blazing white, flashed into pure light.

Emily brought herself back, barely able to keep her shaking hands on her keyboard. "Well, that's not where it's going. Guide star on!" The auricular artificial star formed on the side of Il-Moon's rising missile, sparkling beautifully. "Adaptive optics loops closed!"

The image of the missile wavered, speckled and dappled, the three stages warbling and fuzzing, making it impossible to hold an aim point.

Lorrie called out, "Tyler frequency, three kilohertz."

Emily whispered, "Too fast. Come on atmosphere! Get better!"

Sean asked urgently, "What are you waiting for?"

"The atmosphere is boiling like crazy. The beam will thermally bloom all over the place if I shoot. We have to wait until the missile climbs closer to our altitude." She continued to work the tracking, to keep the slipping guidestar right on the missile.

Lorrie called, "Atmosphere slowing. Tyler frequency is two kilohertz."

"Emily, can't you hurry up? Try it!"

"Patience, dammit!"

"Tyler frequency, one kilohertz!"

The image of the missile sharpened. Its vulnerable first stage booster, filled with nitrobenzene, was so clear you could see the rivets.

Emily shouted in excitement, "Lasing!"

The YAL-1A1 attack laser charge brewed up, the chemicals mixed at the speed of sound, the energy of the Iodine—shoved up into an unbelievably-high orbit by the action of the oxidizing hydrogen peroxide—suddenly transmuted into hyper-excited Iodine juiced with energy. A fiery bolt of intense phased light, every photo heading at exactly the same point, reared up and like monster-breath shot down the line of mirrors toward the beam director...

The beam pointed down the beam director was only microseconds away from hitting the missile. The beam heading toward the laser vacuum channel arrived at the last turning mirror—just as the mirror failed and tilted.

The full force of the sizzling scorching hellishly hot light bounced off the tilted mirror. It missed the channel to the beam director. It blasted past the channel and straight toward the Tech Area.

The beam vaporized the laser room bulkhead door and blew through Tech area evaporating everything in its path. The laser cut off for a fraction of a second, then fired the next pulse.

This pulse ripped through the galley gangway metal flooring and blew away the flightdeck door. It blasted into one windscreen.

WHOOOSH! Depressurization hurricaned through ABL. Equipment flew as the attack laser, still pulsing on and off, whipped around torching the Tech Area.

Emily yelled into her mike, "Laser out of control! Kill the beam!"

The laser beam ripped straight up the Tech Area aisle...

Marty was yelling back, as he fought to get the cutoff switch down, "Almost! Almost there!"

The beam slowing now, swung toward the forward laser fuel magazine.

Lorrie saw the beam heading for the laser fuel. She leapt toward the beam to shield the explosive magazine with her body.

Red was closer. Knocking Lorrie aside, she took the laser shot full in the chest.

The laser beam cut off. Red collapsed, smoldering.

Lorrie screamed, "Red! Oh, Red!"

Marty said, "Got it! Laser's off. Emily, get back here!"

Bozon had managed to wrestle the nuclear blast visors down over the melted windscreen. The air ripping through ABL fell off. Sean ran to Lorrie, pulled her away from Red. Red's torso was burned hideously, singed ribs and heat-fused blood showing throughout the disintegrated chest wall—but her pale dead face was calm.

Sean said, "Lorrie, I'll take care of her. You get me a crew check." He pushed her along, "I'll take care of her."

Lorrie stumbled off, sobbing out the roll call to see if anyone else was hurt.

Sean looked around wildly at the damage. Like a wounded soldier, the reaction to being shot, he knew, was binary. It either looked OK, or you saw the bullet hole, and looked away kind of vacantly—when it was fatal.

He himself was a pretty good battlefield diagnostician, and with the destruction in the walls and consoles, he felt a bleak vacant cold rising in him. Emily came running up, slightly crazy. She clutched at his arm and moaned when she saw Red, and Sean stepped between them to get her to focus.

"Sean, we've lost the Tokyo missile. It's too high on its arc."

"We'll get another chance when it comes back down. The laser, the laser! Fix it!"

Emily sprinted across the Tech Area where the crew worked damage control, while Eila moved to Red's station, and called to general quarters, "Attention ABL, this is Strikeback." Eila reported in a shaky voice. "I'm covering Red's station, and I'll let you know when I find out how she is."

Sean touched his mike button. "Flightdeck, this is Ops. What is your condition?"

Slammer came back, "From now on, I'll just have to use my good eye." Bozon added, "Slightly sunburned, but the eye-patches are going to get us all kinds of girls."

"Good to hear it, Flightdeck. Be with you in a second."

Sean found a blanket in the first-aid rack on the wall of the Tech Area, and laid Red on it. The fraction of a second she had bought them with her body had saved them all from the catastrophic explosion of the forward laser fuel magazine. Sean tenderly wrapped her in a blanket. He paused before he covered her face. It was serene, unmarked, and very white against her shiny red hair. He kissed her forehead. "Red. I knew you believed."

He carried Red up to the galley, strapping her into his bunk. Emily came up behind him. "I can't look."

"It's OK. Let Eila know to tell everyone Red saved us." He moved close to her, pulling her toward the Tech Area. "How are we doing?"

"I guess will know soon, but we may be back up in ten minutes."

"Yes! Good work!" Sean touched his mike button again. "Flightdeck, this is Ops. We still have action. Five minutes, we go around and come in again."

"Once wasn't enough?

"Is once ever enough when you're having fun?"

AIRBORNE LASER – PYONG-SON COMPLEX

Airborne Laser came around in a sharp bank as it circled to re-engage Pyong-son. The Tokyo missile was a distant flame, its plume dispersing. Emily popped out from the Laser Area and reported to Sean, "Still ten minutes."

"It was ten minutes ten minutes ago!"

"To you, always half empty, the glass. It could have been ten hours. I'll be back when it's ready." She ran aft.

On the long-range video screen, Lorrie locked in on Pyong-son. "Smoke," she called, and indeed, from a different location in the valley, smoke boiled from a hidden silo and a new missile burst out. "Another launch. He knows we're hurt!"

"Son of a bitch!" yelled Sean, and ran to look over Eila's shoulder as she inexpertly tried to track and tag the missile. Red's software was partially automated and laid a basic trajectory arc on the map quickly. Without even reading it, Sean realized. *Kyoto. Japan's heart.* He looked around helplessly. Still no Emily.

Sean patched his radio over to the Japanese F-15's. "Col Hareda! A launch against Kyoto. We can't stop it."

COL HAREDA – JAPAN AIR SELF-DEFENSE FORCE

Sean heard Col Hareda on the tactical band to his wingman. The Japan Self Defense Force pilots took just a second of rapid Japanese between them to settle their course. "Kirin 2, together now! Here we go!"

Their afterburners blew brilliant orange shock diamonds in a stream behind them as they left Airborne Laser as if she were standing still. They rocketed toward the distant rising Kyoto missile.

A boom shook Airborne Laser, and everyone ducked, grabbed for something, sure it was anti-air hitting them. Eila called, "ABL, this is Strikeback. No worries. It's just the F-15's going supersonic."

Col Hareda had so little time. At top speed, it would take him three minutes to reach the missile and by then it would be almost too high and fast. There was no time to avoid the Kim Il-Sung Fishbeds and Floggers swarming up to stop them. The JASDF F-15's had to hold their maximum angle of attack to the Kyoto missile. Nearing Pyong-son, Col Hareda's wingman took gunfire hits. Out of control, he turned over, exploded.

On the long-range video the crew saw Col Hareda's F-15 hit, bursts of flack and gunfire chipping at his wings and fuselage as the enemy fighters swarmed in on intercept. Against the backdrop of the rising missile, he looped, barely recovered. He seemed to stabilize and for a second they could almost sense his grim determination as he set his course and sights on the big rising missile.

Sean watched, fists clenched, leaping in frustration, as the colonel closed on this rising missile sitting atop its pillar of smoke, "Come on, Hareda! Come on. Shoot!"

They could not see, close up, Col Hareda bleeding from his face, one arm shredded, as, wings on fire, he rocketed toward the missile.

For a moment, his vision changed, and the missile faded. There were only peaceful puffy clouds against a blue sky. It was a different day. Long ago.

In his Tokyo garden, Col Hareda saw his son take his first step.

Col Hareda cried, "Japan!"

He smashed his F-15 straight into the rising missile.

AIRBORNE LASER

On the big screen, Col Hareda and the missile together exploded in a bursting fireball. Missile fragments and burning fuel spread in a gusher of outpouring fire and wreckage. The inferno of smoking debris slowly turned from an upward spouting motion, and gracefully fell.

Sean was suddenly calm. He gave a sharp salute toward the fiery debris, quietly said aloud, "Sayonara, Hareda-san. It was an honor."

PYONG-SON COMPLEX

Il-Moon had not seen Col Hareda take out the Kyoto missile, as ABL's jamming was clouding his video telescopes. But the telemetry feedback had ceased so completely and so suddenly, he knew the missile had malfunctioned, or...

Aide Park whispered angrily, "The Kyoto missile is gone. Double Bastard Airborne Laser."

FARMERS' MILITIA – MAGNOLIA PALACE GARDENS

When the Sarin cloud floated over the Magnolia gardens, Tong-Hu's company had already had their own gas masks on—pulled from the Guard Command armory under the Palace—long before the other companies. The other farmers had needed more than a moment's notice, and only Tong-Hu's corner of the garden had been fully prepared. Many of the farmers died because the gas equipment required extensive training.

The Guard Command frontal assault followed quickly on the sounds of confusion and death and screaming. They had already brought up radio jamming equipment and cut the farmers off from their artillery support.

The Guard Command, with plenty of time to get their masks in place and buddy-check them, ignored the Sarin. They dropped into the outer garden area and laid a withering fire at the peep holes and parapets of the inner garden walls.

By this time, the center of the Farmers' Militia line had been shattered. Between the small arms and onslaught of nerve gas, only one in five—if fighting valiantly at the gaps and peep holes in the inner garden wall—was still mustered.

Tong-Hu, however, never paused. Pulling half the men from his company and running them along inside the garden walls on his fast interior lines, he rapidly assigned one man to each squad, replacing every machine gunner who was dead or dying. Within a few minutes, despite his high casualties, Tong-Hu had managed to throw together a continuous battle line. Anchored at one end by his half-strength company, he had studded the length of his line with heavy machine guns. He deliberately made the line stronger in the middle, while leaving his far left lightly defended.

As the Guards charged, they quickly found the walls were evenly defended by machine guns, and the automatic weapons fire was intense enough to make them gravitate toward their right where there appeared to be little resistance.

Believing the defenders were thinned here to the breaking point, the whole Guard assault shifted away from the automatic weapons-swept middle, to strike on the farmers' unprotected left.

They ran full tilt into the undefended area—and discovered it had been heavily mined.

Landmines of all sizes burst everywhere underfoot. Fragments of anti-personnel ball bearings shrieked through the air, maiming anyone moving forward—and even a small tear in a gas mask or blouse was fatal in the Sarin saturated air.

As the Sarin fog of death rolled away, dissipating into wisps and swirls, the remaining Guards again fell back.

When they were in full flight, Tong-Hu ran his company into the outer garden, where, with two wheeled anti-aircraft guns he'd taken from Guard Command arsenal, they opened up and raked the flank of the fleeing Guards, mowing down any who hadn't made it back outside the outer garden wall.

Tong-Hu did not tarry in the open. He and his men quickly dragged the heavy guns back through the barred gate into the safety of the inner walls.

Taking a harsh difficult breath through the gas mask, Tong-Hu bolted the door behind them. He waved his men to rest, and stood panting, looking back to the Magnolia Palace.

The jade-green tiles and red lacquer of the classical Korean palace still shone through the garden's trees. Of course, the Guard Command could not shell it. Shelling would only bury the bunker, and Dearest Leader would be beyond their reach. To pry Dearest Leader out from his bunker, the Guard needed to take the Palace intact—and for that they first had to take the inner garden.

Not while I live. With pride, Tong-Hu thought of Dearest Leader, deep in a bunker under the beautiful palace: safe, leading, and taking them all forward.

AIRBORNE LASER

In the laser area, the huge Attack Laser beam train was clamped to the roof of ABL, and two technicians, their faces relieved, called, "The vacuum is holding!"

Emily and Marty, feverishly doing a final beam alignment, looked down the whole huge length of the cargo area stuffed full of laser. It actually looked...good.

Marty said, "OK, OK. It's ready. Git!"

Back in the Tech Area, Emily found Sean and said, "God, Sean. We may be back up, but we haven't much fuel for the remaining missiles, the lightning gizmo's trashed."

"What about the ionizer beam?"

"It's good." She surprised herself that there was pride in her voice.

Sean looked around and asked, "Matt? Matt Cho? Where is that boy?"

"I'm ready," Matt replied, standing at his EMP cannon and clicking closed an electronics module on the barrel.

Sean looked at each station for a full couple seconds, making sure—like the Ref at a boxing match—that the brain within was functioning despite the head blows. Lorrie couldn't look him in the eye, but she reported, "There's still a good amount of enemy fighters and anti-air over Pyong-son. Just so you know."

When Sean came to Eila, at Red's Laser Radar station, her young clear eyes were right on his. She asked, "You want me to keep blinding them at Pyong-son?"

Sean let his fevered brain slip loose and ruminate for a moment. "Screw it. Let him see us coming." He flipped his mike. "Flightdeck, this is Ops. Take us to Pyong-son."

Slammer replied, "Roger, Ops." He flicked the mike to general quarters. "ABL, this is Slammer and Bozon. Coming up, one walk in the Spring Rain." His voice broadened. "Tech Area? Make this one count."

PYONG-SON COMPLEX

In his bunker, Il-Moon's video screens suddenly cleared, and on them, with a slight pulse of adrenalin, Il-Moon saw ABL coming in low and mean and right for Pyong-son.

"Triple Bastard Airborne Laser," breathed out Aide Park involuntarily. "She's attacking us!"

"Nonsense. She has no real weapons. Give the order for all fighters and missile units to close on and attack Airborne Laser. A Gold Medal of the Hero of the DPRK to anyone who takes part in the killing."

Normally he could have counted on this prestigious medal to spark some positive reaction, for it ensured the winners right to a life of leisure and fame. But instead, Il-Moon realized the technicians in the room were all looking at him, something they would normally never have dared to do. He saw in their eyes a fear. A fear of something somehow greater, more powerful and nightmarish than even he. He nodded to his Guard Command bodyguards, selecting three. "You. Watch these workers. They are to remain here and carry out their orders. Shoot anyone who tries to desert."

"Sir!"

Il-Moon looked over the room at his technicians and launch officers. "Launch on Hawaii! Continue to stand firm and carry on the victorious struggle." His Guard Command stood watching as the launch team began the countdown sequence. Il-Moon nodded to Aide Park and the two exited the control room.

As they moved along the corridors, Il-Moon, helped by Aide Park, was sometimes struck by a spasm of pain. He was rarely able to stand fully upright, but thought harshly to himself: *I will not die here. Not like this.*

Il-Moon did not fear death. Nor was he afraid of Airborne Laser—although he wasn't unaware of her abilities either. First, as badly as things had gone, he had a warhead closing in on Japan, and he wanted to relish the coming devastation. Perhaps too, when the strike occurred, the result would be a counterstrike which would ensure the DPRK put all their resources into the fight. Victory was his, in some way, with the war still on-going. He wanted to see tomorrow, and he most assuredly did not want to die at the hands of the Japanese or Americans. They had failed to get him in both the Great Patriotic War and the Fatherland Liberation War—and to fall to them this time would be the ultimate insult.

So, Il-Moon fled. Not an act of cowardice, but the act of an ancient wisdom seeping up from his genes. They would not deny him his ending. It was unlikely they would execute him without a trial, an inquiry of many weeks. Yes, he would die in a prison cell, the mirthless worm ironically beating his enemies too—perhaps even before his trial, if Dearest Leader were the sissy he seemed. More likely a hospital. The South had exquisite hospitals...

Yes, Il-Moon reflected, he would end his days in a hospital bed. *Perhaps I will even have a small view of Korea out the window, the leaves turning in the glorious fall, reading the newspapers and savoring the end of life.*

Il-Moon and Aide Park moved to where the corridor widened, and opened into the underground train station. The train was there, sitting humming on the tracks—except the passenger cars were completely filled with other fleeing officers. They looked at Il-Moon remotely.

Il-Moon stared at the tough North Korean generals until they grudgingly shifted to make a seat for him. There was not a crack in the hard smooth faces—and there was no room for Aide Park. The generals looked impatient, gestured to where the driver was already building up torque to get the train rolling.

Il-Moon spoke to Aide Park softly. "I am afraid the tomorrow that is coming will not be pleasant."

Aide Park knelt on the train platform at Il-Moon's feet, answering in a murmur, his eyes grave. "I do not wish to see tomorrow." He pulled his pistol from his belt and passed it to Il-Moon. Il-Moon braced himself, raised the pistol to the old man's neck, and fired.

Il-Moon watched Aide Park slowly fall. He stepped onto the underground train, wanting to look back at the crumpled figure on the platform, but his head was too diseased to turn. He could only look forward as the train gathered speed and ran into the tunnel ahead.

AIRBORNE LASER

On the big screen rose the fire-pillar of the Hawaii missile launching out of Pyong-son.

"A nuke targeting Hawaii!" Emily said, shaking her head. "Matt needs to be too close. We won't survive the blast."

Matt called, "Use the laser to ionize my path. I'd get a tenfold range increase. We'd survive and you still have a shot at the Tokyo warhead."

Sean said, "Matt, go!" and Matt pulled open the breach of the microwave howitzer. Jarhead ran up with the bagged charges, and they loaded and locked the huge firing cylinder into place. "Lorrie?"

"I don't know how, Sean," Lorrie said piteously. "It has to be Emily."

Emily shook her head, raven hair wild. "I can't help set off a nuke. In that bunker there are thousands of people."

On the laser radar screen, the Tokyo second stage separated with a burst of explosive bolts. The burned-out stage, a husk, dropped away. Its warhead rapier-ed on.

Lorrie whispered, almost to herself, "Tokyo missile warhead separation complete. Impact on Tokyo, nine minutes."

WHITE HOUSE ROVING SITUATION ROOM – 4:30 P.M. EST

The group sat riveted at the transmission of ABL through Radiant Outlaw, and watched the Tokyo warhead separate.

DOE said, "It's gone ballistic. I don't see how they can stop it now."

Jeanette said, "Don't launch yet. Give Airborne Laser a chance."

The President said, "Start MX countdown to launch on warhead detonation."

AIRBORNE LASER

In the first hint of dawn, Airborne Laser crossed the DMZ.

Emily sat frozen as, flak bursting below them, missiles roaring in at them, every weapon firing, the hellish din of the anti-air guns growling, armor smoking, engines burning, crew yelling and screaming, Diablo rattling in his swinging cage, Slammer kept Airborne Laser (Experimental) flying true and straight right into the combat zone.

Bucking in the weather toward the distant fires of the flaring Hawaii missile, they straightened on their battle course. The remaining Kim Il-Sung Night-fighters closed in on ABL like an enraged swarm of killer bees.

All along their flanks, fighters ripped in on them, flak puffs below sent waves of shrapnel up into ABL's light armor. The Fishbeds had long ago used up their missiles, finding them all blinked away by the DIRCMs. All they had now were their 30mm cannon, and were working hard to try to use them effectively against ABL.

At first, the Fishbeds were careless, coming straight at ABL. A few fighters approached from the back and below—and discovered the range of the Phalanx when shooting down was a kilometer farther than their shooting up.

Among a swarm of dozens of circling fighters, when Emily wasn't watching, Lorrie popped several with the Attack Laser. The spectacle of five of their kind right amongst them suddenly bursting into flames was not lost upon the remaining fighters. After a few seconds reflection, despite their political reliability, most of the eighty Kim Il-Sung pilots decided on discretion, immediately heading for South Korean airports to defect.

The remaining force, however, was still twenty of the most dedicated Kim Il-Sung pilots—and none had enough fuel to return home.

The parade of ground-launched anti-air missiles continued, and a few came close, but ABL was above most of their ranges, and the DIRCMs sent many others spinning back downward in search of a target on the ground. Jarhead managed to intercept the other bigger radar missiles.

Emily was unresponsive as Sean's eyes flashed back and forth from the anti-air missiles to the Hawaii ICBM. Rising, now a few hundred meters above Pyong-son, oddly Sean could almost see the little lake where he'd first met Emily...

Cannon slugs tore into an Airborne Laser engine. Fire ruptured from it, as a pair of Fishbeds swooped in on one flank. Jarhead's Phalanx guns jinked around, and he played a short burst into one Fishbed, tat-a-tat-a-tat-a-brat, until the jet exploded and fell away. The other broke off, dodged, and dropped back in a retreat move. Disciplined, the Kim Il-Sung pilot maneuvered for an attack run from straight behind Airborne Laser.

Jarhead spun his sights around, hoping to catch the Fishbed. His guns jinked around. He pulled the trigger. His mini-gun barrels spun *ching-ching*! Gatling barrels spun without fire or flame. Winchester! Empty! Ammo gone.

The Fishbed's first slugs missed, exploded alongside. Then cannon shells found ABL, and smoke gushed into the Tech Area. ABL jerked as she was hit.

Jarhead grabbed his heavy M240 machine gun. Ammo belt dangling he ran rearward.

Sean yelled to Eila, "Eila! Follow Jay and bring oxygen masks. Back him up..."

On the big screen, the Hawaii missile, hanging above Pyong-son, slowly rose.

Matt Cho worked feverishly, checking his bore site, lining up his EMP cannon sites, "Ready on X-Weapons!" waited as...

Emily sat, frozen.

Sean put his lips to her ear, urgent. "There isn't a blackjack to use on him. This isn't a two cushion bounce shot into the side pocket. This is a backatcha Pyong-son's death or Hawaii."

"I had hoped..." Emily's shoulders slumped and she was unresponsive

Sean leaned in close. "Hoped for what? This is now, Emily, and the warhead needs to go off. Then we stop the Tokyo one."

"I can't."

ABL rocked brutally, skittering sideways as gunfire struck her, throwing unstrapped Sean into a metal console. The sound of thudding detonations, the bucking response of the plane under their feet. Smoke tendrils trailed from the ventilation vents.

In the rear storage area, Jarhead let the heavy M240 machine gun hang from his neck and with lightning speed, secured the aft door, whipped on the safety harness and toe-kicked the back hatch opening lever. The big airdrop hatch, wind shrieking past it, depressurized and opened a few feet. Through the crack, just a few hundred yards directly behind ABL, Jarhead saw the Fishbed closing in on ABL's tail. The Fishbed nose-wiggled to line up its shot, its cannons steered by the plane's attitude with no traverse for aiming.

The Fishbed's clown-hat nose lined up and heavy cannon shells came flying toward ABL, slamming into the rear elevons and tail. Airborne Laser shook and shuddered with the blasts, the flight systems trying to cope with the shredded controls.

Jarhead opened up with his M240. The recoil was brutal, but he held it steady as he fired into the teeth of the Fishbed's guns.

From his solid perch, he swung the kicking bullet stream down and into the nose of the Fishbed. The Fishbed kept firing. Toe to toe, neither giving ground, neither breaking off, the Kim Il-Sung pilot and Jarhead dueled.

Jarhead doggedly kept his fire into the Fishbed's clown-hat nose. The Fishbed burst into yellow flame and fragments, blown away...just as the Fishbed's last cannon shells found Jay.

The Fishbed's slugs smashed into Jarhead. He fell back brutally wounded, hanging in the harness, as the tortured ABL stopped shaking with the silencing of the Fishbed's guns.

Eila darted up, hit the close switch for the ramp. As the air rushing through the hold diminished, she ran to Jarhead. Releasing him from the harness, she lowered his bloody body to the deck, leaned over him, hugged him, held him, crying. The big anti-air cannon rounds had smashed his legs and stomach. From his belly, onto the metal floor of ABL, streamed hot blood. In response to Eila's touch, still alive, Jarhead pulled her face close to his blood-spattered one. He spoke to her for a moment, distinctly, the message urgent.

Eila ran up to Sean, her uniform bloody and face streaked in tears. He saluted her, "Lieutenant?"

She managed to return the salute. "The Fishbeds have all been downed. No air attacks are immediate." Her voice caught for a second. "Sir, Jay...Captain Hull was a fatality."

Sean looked at her and their eyes met. "I'm sorry, Eila," and she managed in small but strong voice, "Me too." Sean nodded toward Jarhead's station. "Please take over Captain Hull's air defense post."

Emily's eyes were staring, fixed on her screen. The Hawaii missile rose over Pyong-son, ascending like some strange wrong-way destructive meteor.

Eila leaned in close to Emily. "Jay is dead. He said, 'Tell Emily I paid all I could.'"

Emily's head went into small jerks, the stress and the breakdown of her mind pulsing down her neck and along her arms.

Sean laid his hands gently on her shoulders. Her muscles were rope-hard, twitching. Sean let his hands message them ever so gently. He could sense her tipping there as he asked, "What good if you gain your own soul, only to lose the whole world?"

Deciding suddenly, as if hoping never to have to think of it again, Emily's hands suddenly flew over her console. "Fempto-second pulse mode is on! Lasing!"

ABL's attack laser shot out, but this time along the path, the beam made a froth of tingling flinging electrons—an ionized channel right to the fiery rising warhead-tipped missile.

"Firing!" Matt yelled and yanked the lanyard. The EMP cannon boomed.

The explosively-generated electromagnetic pulse shot down the waveguide of the ionized laser path and straight into the payload of the Hawaii missile hanging just a mile above Pyong-son.

In the tiny crevices of the warhead package, the microwaves induced huge electromagnetic fluxes. Current flowed into the nuke trigger electronics.

The electronic trigger tripped. The warhead detonated and exploded outward into a flaring nuclear inferno.

The nuclear warhead explosion engulfed Pyong-son complex.

The blast and fireball and shockwaves boiled out toward the banking ABL.

Sean, caught unawares by the quickness of it, shouted, "Flightdeck, blast avoidance! Blast avoid—"

Shockwaves caught the banking ABL side-on. A tidal wave of EMP and heat blast boiled around them. Airborne Laser disappeared into shockwave white-out.

PYONG-SON UNDERGROUND TRAIN

As the nuke explosion boiled down and engulfed Pyong-son, the top two hundred meters of Pyong-son's caverns evaporated. The broiling plasma wave insinuated into even the deepest mountain tunnels, frying all Il-Moon's missile and control caverns.

The nuclear blast also found and followed the tunnel of the underground railway. As Il-Moon's train roared away down its tunnel, the nuke explosion boiled after him.

Il-Moon was too crippled to turn and look back, but the flash from behind him was obvious, coming, scorching, then dying away. The heat on his head stunned Il-Moon, and for a moment, he was lost, dazed, almost spinning into blackness.

The train had been miles from Pyong-son, and Il-Moon in his spinning heard an officer nearby him saying excitedly, "Nuclear explosion! But we are safely away!" Il-Moon pulled himself back to the running train.

He managed to find a few crumbs of the dirt from Gil-Yon's garden. Rather than tasting it, he sniffed the crumbs like snuff. The sneeze ripped at his lower stomach like a dagger, but the stab of pain lessened quickly and slipped away, as if the dagger were powerless when the dirt was in his throat.

He had escaped the Americans again! And there was, on the wing, his final apocalyptic blow of justice. Il-Moon's great frustration lifted. He recalled the beauty of the launch on Tokyo; the glory of the fiery first stage igniting and sending his steed toward the beast. Airborne Laser had not and could not stop his final stroke.

He allowed himself a private smile of triumph. His warhead would find its way to its destiny.

I will have at least this much for Korea and my sister. At least the American airbase at Yakota—and Tokyo. All of Tokyo.

WHITE HOUSE ROVING SITUATION ROOM

Shockwaves of white noise and glare engulfed Pyong-son on the situation room TV, and the explosion rolled outward and swallowed-up ABL. It disappeared and the screen went to snow.

DOE yelled, "They triggered the nuke! They were within twenty kilometers. They couldn't survive."

Jeanette had been going closer and closer to the TV monitor, until at the explosion; she dropped to her knees in front of the screen. Reaching up to the monitor, almost praying. "Come on. Get through."

Someone else looked for a moment. "I'm afraid the last missile is still on trajectory for Tokyo."

The President said, "Keep counting down for the MX missile counter-strike."

On her knees, Jeanette clutched at the TV. "Come on. I know you're there."

AIRBORNE LASER

After-blast brutally rocked the Airborne Laser crew. Fires. Explosions. ABL rolled over completely onto her back.

Flying upside down, everything hanging inverted, Sean had been thrown free, crunched into the ceiling plates, and lay stunned, as did all the tech crew but Emily. Turbulence pounded Airborne Laser...but still she flew...

Slammer, fighting the controls, feeling them for anything he could use, hung upside down from this flight chair. He coaxed the huge plane, stroking the controls, finessing, dancing, "Come on, Princess. Your middle name is Boeing."

On the big screen, the Tokyo warhead crossed Japan's eastern shore.

Lorrie woke, screamed out, "Warhead impact on Tokyo, thirty seconds!" then passed out again.

Emily said, "Please God, the laser." She released her seat belt and fell to the ceiling. Surprised, she landed on something much warmer and softer than the fuselage. She found she'd landed on a stunned Sean. She slapped at him, "Sean, Sean!" put her oxygen mask to his face.

In the laser area, Marty, in shock, shakily reached out for his spill proof B-52 coffee dispenser. Upside down, it still held the coffee perfectly. He took a long sip. It calmed him. He looked up at the dials of the laser. They were all, miraculously, green. "Ops, this is Attack Laser." He took another slug of coffee. "The laser is still a GO!" He added, looking around, "If we weren't upside down we'd be OK, huh?"

Sean, under Emily, dug out his headset. "Flightdeck. Roll and climb! Climb! Climb! Climb! Get us clear air for a shot!"

Bozon remarked, bleeding badly from his nose, "He doesn't ask for much, does he?"

The two pilots both cranked the heavy flight yokes. ABL spun in a hellish rotation, and Sean fought to Lorrie's station, looked for the Tyler meter.

With the mushroom cloud of Pyong-son's last stand behind them, ABL rolled upright in the turbulence and clouds. Armor flew off, engines smoking.

Above a devastated Pyong-son, dawn was breaking as the ABL's tortured airframe angled up and blasted through thick clouds.

Sean called, "Tyler frequency, three kilohertz—"

The Tokyo warhead, spinning, black and deadly, crossed the first mountains of the spine of Japan.

TIMES SQUARE TOKYO – SHINJUKU PLAZA

The crowd in the huge cheerful square waited, as dawn came up and the growing light suffused their faces and awakened their clothing's colors. They looked up suddenly as emergency sirens wound up wailing. A flock of Japanese pigeons bolted into the air.

The crowd froze. The image on the screen of the warhead and ABL confused and frightened them. The crowd seethed with murmurs and cries of fear and anger.

AIRBORNE LASER – JAPAN

Airborne Laser broke out into the pre-dawn dark above the clouds; above the half-sunlit arching limb of the earth, almost in outer space. The calm blue-green world stretched below from Korea to Japan.

"Guidestar on!" Emily yelled.

ABL's probe laser leapt out, instantly crossing the gulf of space between Korea and Japan and pinpointing the warhead.

From Lorrie's station, Sean called off, "Tyler frequency, one kilohertz!"

Emily stabbed the fire button, called, "Attack laser is lasing!"

Like a noble knight with a light saber reaching out hundreds of miles to strike down the villain, ABL's laser arced across the roof of the world, across space—and to Japan.

The spinning re-entry vehicle warhead, the skyline of Tokyo ahead, ripped over farm huts and pasture and rice fields and small factories and country lanes. Its heat shield pointed ahead to the colossal city; its rear facing back toward Korea.

ABL's Attack Laser slashed into the warhead's vulnerable back. Seams ripped and gaskets smoked and melted. The warhead spin went unstable. It cracked open and broke into pieces.

The waking tech crew yelled and screamed, their voices hoping on hope for a soft landing and victory!

On the big screen, the warhead tumbled, falling in a steep arc, breaking up into a cloud of flying pieces falling toward the green and forest of the countryside long before Tokyo.

For a second, the crew watched for a detonation.

None. From deep in everyone, the ABL crew let out a howl of triumph.

WHITE HOUSE ROVING SITUATION ROOM

For the last time, Radiant Outlaw's TV camera transmission recovered and broadcast the final seconds of the mission. The Situation Room gasped as ABL's laser streaked across Japan and caught the closing warhead.

Jeanette yelped, "There! They hit it!"

Over Japan, the warhead broke into bits of tumbling junk.

The President, on his feet with the rest of the room, yelled, "Stop the MX countdown!"

The room spun for them all, with the shock and joy of the moment, the relief of the lifting of the crushing weight of catastrophe and Armageddon.

Jeanette, wrung out, lay for a second on the floor prostrate, tingling all over. In a few seconds, she pulled herself up, brushed herself off, and looked around at the room. "Well! Good!"

The President and his friends lay slumped into their seats where they'd dropped, completely done in and exhausted. A deep palpable relief and happiness suffused the room, and a peace entered them fully, light and beautiful.

KANAGAWA PREFECTURE – TOKYO COUNTRYSIDE

The Taepo-Dong warhead had tumbled toward the Japanese countryside.

From its trajectory toward Shinjuku, with its aerodynamic properties destroyed, the arc of falling was much faster as the pieces, exposed and awkward in the slipstream of the air, caught and tumbled in a flowing shower, the solid nuclear metal core plummeting as a lump.

Japanese Self Defense emergency choppers roared out into the dawn away from the gleaming Tokyo skyline. Past the last of the urban sprawl and into the countryside and trees, the raced toward the impact area.

The Japanese helo pilot radioed back to base. "Emergency nuclear unit nearing impact area. No sign of detonation or contamination. One minute to control of accident site."

The Japanese pilots looked ahead, choosing a landing spot near the impact site. Over the Tama River the morning mists rose. Brewing up, they spread through the tree lines, over the emerald fertile green of the hay fields and orchards of a perfect prefecture autumn morning. The breath of the river, lilywhite and satiny, swept across the fertile fields, covering them in a swirl of nourishing new-born mist.

Catchers in the Sky

BOOK 10

"Honor your sponsors."

The AFRL Project Officer's Tenth Commandment

Chapter 72

The 31st of October
Dawn

AIRBORNE LASER

Blackness. So hard and full, to Sean it felt like blindness. For a moment, he was sure he *was* blind: a flash-blinding he had shrugged off temporarily, while his retinas, scalded to a crisp in the blast, now dropped him into a permanent darkness.

A crack of light. Sean felt a glimmer of hope for his eyes, and suddenly the crack of white widened and he realized Emily and Lorrie were prying the blast cover off Emily's window. Slow from his aching muscles and bruised and burned body, he moved gimpily to the window, crowding in with the rest of the crew to look out into daylight.

Dawn had come to their long night over Korea.

FARMERS' MILITIA – MAGNOLIA PALACE GARDENS

Tong-Hu of the Farmers' Militia was happy he got to die slowly.

The Guard Command's final assault concentrated a feint on where they now knew the defenders had been thinned to the breaking point after the Sarin attack—and then went for Tong-Hu's corner. This was a set of parapets where the inner and outer walls were the closest—and where the few remnants of Tong-Hu's company were still on the parapets.

Although the Guard Command had taken ferocious casualties in the previous three onslaughts, and fifteen hundred of their number lay dead or moaning between the outer and inner walls of the garden, the officers of the Guard Command had nowhere to hide. They could not very well return and say they had failed, since this was no less a death sentence than strolling across the courtyard. Further, their blood was up. Once their battalion commander had examined the tattered hand-me-down KPA uniforms and identified the bodies taken on the outer walls as those from the 345th Farmers' and Workers' Militia, it was a point of honor to take them out at any cost and immediately kill Dearest Leader. They were, however, down to under one hundred men: many of the remaining Guards had reckoned the odds in taking on the farmers again—and chose desertion.

Drawing on their past experience, the remaining Guards quickly zeroed in on the apparent weak point at the juncture where, because railroad tracks ran close-by, the inner and outer garden walls squeezed together. Here, the Guard Command assault could keep their range too close for any covering artillery and yet gain the inner garden and palace.

The Guards gathered at one side, while a small force furiously kept up a withering fire at the Farmers' center—then every remaining Guard charged Tong-Hu's corner.

The hundred Guard Command troops, shooting at every peephole and rampart, surged forward and managed to get under the beetling overhang of the inner wall. Quickly they threw up assault ladders under the cover of the overhung walls. If Tong-Hu had had more than just a single platoon left, or had fragmentation grenades, it would have been a different story. However, with only a few assault rifles, unable to fire down over the walls, the farmers felt rather than saw the upwelling Guard, and were unable to stop them from reaching the ramparts and firing over point-blank into the defenders.

Tong-Hu yelled an order, and suddenly, taking his buddy Chang-Gun's arm, he hung out over the parapets, completely exposed and firing with one hand, raking his AK-47 on full fire along the ladders.

The maneuver was so unexpected—recklessly hanging out over space—he was on his second clip before the Guard Command was able even to look up at the blaze of fire above them. Along the wall, Tong-Hu's men saw the effect, and a dozen of his compatriots, using friends to cantilever them out over the fray, also fired down directly into the Guards.

From below the parapet, it was only a matter of a few seconds before the counter-fire came back at them.

Tong-Hu caught the bullet high in the chest. He was knocked off the wall, falling backwards the fifteen feet down from the rampart and onto the stone-paved courtyard.

The pain in his chest was like being ripped apart and the shock from his broken legs blew a starburst of white before his eyes.

Chang-Gun was at his side, telling him to lie still, even as Tong-Hu felt a gurgle of blood trickle into his lungs.

He managed to gasp to Chang-Gun, "Against the wall. Sit me against the wall."

"I cannot sit you up. You will drown in your blood."

"I will drown here sooner lying. Sit me up."

Gently Chang-Gun pulled him to sit against the wall, and Tong-Hu said, "Thank you, Chang-Gun-ssi. Do not tarry. Back to the fight."

He could feel his life leaking away; yet the pain was a privilege. As the blood spilled into his lungs, it kept him awake and allowed him to hear, for at least a little time, the sounds of the battle. Despite his heroic maneuver, his hopes faded—as he could hear the gunfire to be more and more toward him—that the farmers would keep the Guard Command from breaching the wall. Past his unit, there was nothing left. Only a couple platoons in the bunkers below with Dearest Leader. Once the Guards gained the palace, the defenders locked below in the bunkers could not defend against set explosive charges. They would have no room for maneuver against a foe who would dynamite and then Sarin them, with no interest in taking anyone alive.

Great Leader! What I could do now with just one platoon...

Suddenly, he felt the rush of poorly-shod feet, the sound and comforting Vinalon-and-canvas farmer smells of Militia hurrying past him—and from within the Palace, and on toward the fray! He fought confusion, for they came from where Dearest Leader must soon be struggling to direct the fight from inside the palace. *Reinforcements?*

Tong-Hu could not imagine where they came from. Yet Tong-Hu felt the swarm passing him even as the battle cries and firing grew fierce again along the wall above him. Behind him, he registered a familiar soft voice: "Forward, Comrades! Into the breach!"

Suddenly, he felt a presence beside him. Squatting by him, someone put out a cool hand; a hand in a business suit, and Tong-Hu felt the hand slip in at his chest and pull open the uniform collar to let him breathe easier.

He looked up to see Dearest Leader bending over him, his chic glasses pushed up on his head, while the calm brown eyes in the round face surveyed him somberly. "Well done, Company-Leader Lee—or perhaps, if you will allow, I shall remember you as Lee-ssi."

Tong-Hu nodded weakly, felt the hand find and pull out the tiny crucifix on a chain his wife had secreted. Dearest Leader looked at it solemnly, gestured. "You serve this?"

"It is only a symbol, something of ours from long ago. It does not slow my service to Korea."

Dearest Leader smiled wryly. "From your actions, I see it does not. Indeed, it must be of some great value, as you wore it in a cherished place."

"My wife..."

"I will see she gets to keep it." Dearest Leader took his hand, and waited. Tong-Hu lost sense of where he was, or that throwing in the reserves at just this moment was the perfect maneuver, even that Dearest Leader was really beside him.

Tong-Hu was past it all now; past imagining and into surety. He was thinking then of his wife, then to the counterpoint of the most pleasant sound left to him: the hum of the battle receding away from him, away from the inner walls, away from the warm presence at his side.

He smiled dreamily as he faded. He knew Korea was safe.

AIRBORNE LASER – OVER THE DMZ

From Emily's picture window, the tech crew looked down onto a new Korea. Slammer and Bozon had circled and now flew them back over a war-smoking DMZ. In the clarity of the dawn from high altitude, they could see along the whole the DMZ, streaked with black gashes of artillery and lightning strikes.

The battle below was in an aftermath phase, the sun catching the small formations of Warthogs and F-16's and Recon planes moving methodically along the DMZ. Across the DMZ, the South Korean army had breached a good number of tracks, and their infantry half-tracks and tanks formed scores of lines as they moved over the DMZ, gingerly fanning out into the now unmanned North Korean fortified areas. At Camp Casey, the decimated structures of the camp were belied by the ant-hill activity of units setting up and moving forward.

Sean nodded to Lorrie, and to the units below, "American equipment and colors; 2nd Infantry."

Lorrie's face was all over mascara, and she sniffled. Sean could tell she was still sick with worry for her sons—but she managed a grin and a wink. "That'll teach 'em to mess with us Welfare Moms."

Just off to the horizon, a flight of heavy bombers and strike aircraft broke out into battle order.

"From Kadena. 7th Air Force," Sean said, nodding toward the winged armada. "Not much left for them to do." And so it was, from thirty thousand feet, ABL had a perfect vista over an incredible parade fly-over of the DMZ by the 7th Air Force.

On the other side, a big flight of South Korean F-15's, and a squad of F-16's from Osan ripped past, looking fresh, and waggling their wings in passing at Airborne Laser. They came so close the tech crew could see their grins as they pointed at ABL's war-damaged boiled-beef-and-cabbage-looking fuselage.

Sean moved up next to Emily so their shoulders were touching. For a moment, they looked out the window together. Daybreak spilled over battlefield Korea, long shadows disguising the burn marks and mottling the bright fall greenery.

The land below was again peaceful, as if a long-awaited earthquake had finally come, releasing ancient and deadly tensions, leaving a state of grace.

Someone suddenly whooped, "We did it!" There was a ragged cheer of happiness from everyone.

Except Emily. Sean put out a hand to touch hers.

KANSONG – EAST SEA COASTAL TOWN, SOUTH KOREA

It didn't take Tank Brigade Leader Col Chol-Hae long to realize that the ROK units he had been facing here on the East Sea coast one hundred forty miles east of Seoul had withdrawn. They were not going to defend the picture pretty seaside town of Kansong. *They know we will demolish it.* From a roadside switchback on the hill above the seaside town, he called his brigade to a halt, and had a jeep run him up to the front ranks a kilometer ahead from this command post, and personally studied with binoculars the town below.

Long lines of white-crested waves from the East Sea dappled the coast like light flickering on bamboo leaves. Kansong was a town having a central cluster of businesses as do most Asian downtowns. A few five-story concrete structures, but mostly smaller buildings. The shop glass on one side caught bright in the sun. He could hear his short inhalations and he wondered how long he'd been breathing so shallowly. *I didn't expect this feeling.*

On the tiers of hills above the town, from where Chol-Hae mustered his forces overlooking the town, he could see most of the townspeople had already fled. He could also see what looked like military units just disappearing over mountain passes on the road south along the coast. They would make a stand in the passes and it would be a bitter battle, for defending would be simple in the hilly terrain. Chol-Hae knew he could expect a difficult time. He turned back to surveying the city. Why had they left? Why not fight it out? Even this small city would have cost him dearly to clear. They had instead chosen to flee. Or perhaps it is a trap.

He could not know that the President of South Korea, when he learned of the collapse of the DPRK's Kaesong-Munsan advance, that morning had announced on TV: "There will be no war in Korea while I am president. All units will pull back defensively."

The little town seemed peaceful, tiered tile-roofed houses lying along hilly streets. Some of the houses overlooking the sea were huge.

"We could shell the bigger houses. They must be corrupt government houses," said his deputy commander, at his elbow. "They are too big to be private citizens."

"Have you found any landmines, any snipers? Any resistance at all?"

"Nothing, Sir. It must be some kind of trick."

Chol-Hae wasn't so sure. "I think the town is not defended. You and I will go down with a reconnaissance in force, followed by the main group. We attack without firing until we meet resistance."

None was met, as the battalion of main battle tanks, self-propelled guns, and his forward infantry force in armored personnel carriers swooped into Kansong village. Col Chol-Hae, buttoned up in the lead tank, was the first to roll down the main shop-lined street. He slowed and then halted, somewhat amazed, for the bright shops and glass storefront burst with beautiful objects and food. Even through his low-quality targeting sights, to Chol-Hae the village streets almost looked like paradise. The few cars parked along the street were spotless, oddly sporty, and unblemished, their jaunty colors merry. He quickly rolled on past the village shops to the first of the giant houses. He got down from his armored command-post vehicle. *Maybe the mayor's house.*

He studied the house closely. The yard had perfectly-clipped grass, the windows were washed, and flower-boxes burst with exotic plants he'd never seen. The sun reflected mirror-like off the car in the carport. The car even had a Korean name, *Hyundai,* and was the brightest yellow he'd ever seen. Over the door, painted in Hangul characters, which he could read like any Korean, was a sign, 'The Kims' home.' Birds called from the garden shrubs. It was like a dream.

Suddenly, the front door burst open and a woman in a tight flowery dress and high heels ran toward him. His bodyguard almost opened fire. Luckily, the woman was shaped pleasingly, which probably saved her from a panicked burst of AK-47 fire. Chol-Hae raised a hand, shouted, and the woman slowed, confused.

Swaying, she moved straight to Chol-Hae, hands out, face contorted. "Don't hurt us. We couldn't leave, my daughter can't move, she had surgery on her back."

The street seemed safe to Chol-Hae. He gave her his attention, saying coldly, "Surrender your house. Do not resist."

"Surely. You can have it; I will find a way to move my daughter..."

"Who are you?"

The woman seemed confused. "Nobody. I'm...I'm Mrs. Kim."

"You are the government representative for this house?"

"Representative? This is just my house."

"Who is your husband? He must be an important official. Where is he?"

"Um, well, he *was* a fisherman. Now I am widowed." She babbled, worried, "I teach school...to pay the bills."

Chol-Hae absorbed this. *A fisherman's widow lives here?* "Not a government town?"

"No, just a town like any other." She glanced at his ring finger, saw there was no wedding band. Her oval face changed, smiled.

Her teeth are perfect—like a movie star. It struck him. She was a schoolteacher. Just an ordinary South Korean woman.

She paused, eyes down as she blushed at his look. "Would you like something to eat? I just made Kim Chi yesterday. There is fresh rice and fish?"

What crazy people! And the way they live, just ordinary people...

Mrs. Kim looked up at this strange confused man. *He was actually pretty good looking. Strong and kind of craggy.* "The Kim Chi is ready. Or take some with you. It will only take a moment."

He realized this town, this woman—this was what he'd been fighting against. Those years of sacrifice. The 'Great Leader Days of One Meal,' the weekends 'Gathering Native Plants for Dollars for the Great Leader,' the overnight unexplained disappearance of a best friend, the agony of watching many his neighborhood's pregnant women lose their unborn children from malnutrition, and his own wife dying young. The speeches on the radio. The few images on TV of the devilish enemy unjust Puppet State to the South. He never believed it was different in the South for anyone except the Bosses. Yet here, a fisherman's widow was living like a queen in paradise. He looked toward the sea over the town. Hundreds of houses just like this. They were all living like this. He felt a shimmer of panic. Then slowly found the bright clear eyes of Mrs. Kim watching him respectfully. The face of his old mortal enemy.

Mrs. Kim smiled warmly. "After all, every Korean likes fresh Kim Chi. This one I made with oysters."

He turned his back on her to think. His next objective was to move out down the coast road, up the pass, and secure the larger town of Chumunjin. Yet he could not even move his feet. He wanted to see what was inside the house. He wanted to stay.

Chol-Hae looked back as sternly as he could at his men; from the top of each tank's open hatch, each man waited silently, watching him.

He turned to his Deputy. "Set up a defensive position along these streets," indicating the curving street through the tile roofed houses of the pristine suburb.

His deputy's voice, interestingly, was quite neutral. "And Chumunjin?"

"We are ahead of schedule. The road must be surveyed. Send out a surveillance company. No firing unless fired upon. Make the defense position here strong. Send the men out to forage for food." *That would slow them down. We might never form up again. Perhaps I will not have to take the pass....* "Then report to me here."

His deputy saluted thoughtfully, and moved off. Out of the armor spilled the tank crews and mechanized infantry. The straight young men blinked in the light. Ready to fight, they found themselves staring at the houses and shops.

Unsure of what to do, one of them approached a Hyundai pickup truck filled with building supplies and white pine lumber. The pickup was just like the one he'd seen at the Great Leader's museum, a gift from a foreign government. He had thought that was only one. Here, a whole street was lined in them. He touched the white pine cautiously, as if it were hot.

When the men heard the order to forage, there were smiles.

As if in a dream, Korean People's Army Colonel Chol-Hae followed Mrs. Kim's tightly packed dress and swaying hips up the crushed stone path and into the Kim's home. If he hadn't been so one hundred percent Korean, he could imagine himself surrendering to Mrs. Kim...

AIRBORNE LASER

As Sean moved to touch Emily's hand, she seemed far away, pensive, musing. "I can't wait to get to Stanford. Frisbees swishing; walking along Palm Drive; the carillon playing Westminster chimes."

At Sean's touch, she pulled away her hand. For the first time since ABL's last run, she had the time to look into his eyes across the few feet separating them. "Yes, I'm going home. No, I can't stay at ABL."

"I can't finish ABL without you."

"Nobody is irreplaceable. With what you did, you'll be a drug on the market."

"There's so much more to do. The science as well, the proper use of the system to prevent war. You don't really want to leave, hide your head in the sand at Stanford."

"The next assignment won't be science. It will be to weaponize Airborne Laser. It's one assignment you can't turn down."

"Look at what we did! This is our mission, our task, why we're here. To be on the watchtower. To save lives."

"I can live with myself, but not with ABL becoming something I loathe. For you there will always be the next enemy, another even better reason. The phone will ring, and you'll have a new assignment. It will be a war, and you won't turn them down."

"What about us?"

"A killer and a fallen Quaker? What's the future in that? For you there will always be the next urgent assignment. And it will smell, like you and me always, of killing."

"Are you sure? You'll have to live knowing you didn't finish the task."

"I'm going home to my family. My real family."

PYONG-SON UNDERGROUND TRAIN – SURFACE STATION

When his train had rolled up from the bowels of the earth fifteen miles from Pyong-son complex, it merged onto a surface railroad and slowed to stop at a small tree-lined station. Il-Moon began to think about survival and even comfort for the next few days. He would eventually have to explain himself, but he did not delude himself that it would be accepted. He would not remain on the train to the next stop where he could easily be detained. Instead, he would walk to his nearby dacha. It would be a time before anyone thought to look for him.

Il-Moon rose with difficulty from the train seat, although once up he moved easily down the steps to the dusty concrete platform. Distantly, the towering smoke cloud from the Pyong-son blast spread slowly. From here it looked no more dangerous or unusual than a large thunderhead building to a towering anvil up into the stratosphere.

As Il-Moon turned to leave, drops of rain began to spatter down onto the birch trees overhead. He realized someone was moving toward him on the platform. Surprised, he saw it was Maj Tam Ho, but he decided to ignore him.

Il-Moon walked onto the little path toward the nearby mountains. Over the pattering of the rain on the leaves above, Il-Moon heard Tam Ho step up, felt his grip as he firmly took Il-Moon's pistol arm. Il-Moon turned, angry but unsure.

"Marshal Song Il-Moon, you are under arrest for treason."

Il-Moon looked at Tam Ho closely. For a moment, he imagined the young officer was there to help him escape. Then he saw the intent eyes—and he knew.

As they moved away together, the rain-laden leaves of the birches began dripping onto the ground. The first drops made splashes in the dust.

The smell of the freshly rain-kissed dirt rose, and filled Il-Moon's nostrils.

COURTYARD – THE PRISON OF 1ˢᵗ of MARCH 1919 – KORYO

Within the high grim walls, the three hundred North Korean officers stood in formation. The slow beat of a drum boomed hollowly.

The prison courtyard was unchanged in most respects from seven weeks earlier when Col Kang had fallen here, except now autumn had come, and the small bushes inside the courtyard were beginning to gold; a splash of color echoed in the resplendent upswept Korean hills visible over the prison walls.

Il-Moon, alone, marched past the lines of his officers—but this time there were no piles of stones. Instead, the cement execution pole was ringed in firewood. The prescribed punishment for his treason was burning at the stake. Il-Moon's gait was hitched. He was almost hunchbacked with his disease, yet he walked proudly. The ranks of the officers' corps were muted, letting him pass without insult. He looked up at the stone balustrade where he and Dearest Leader just a few short weeks ago had stood concealed. This time, in full view, Dearest Leader, Architect Su, and Harold Hakkermann stood at the parapet looking down. Dearest Leader's expression was of distaste—or was it perhaps satisfaction? Il-Moon cared not. If this was the face of the future, he wanted no part of it.

As he came just below them, Dearest Leader raised a hand, and the drumbeat fell silent.

In the silence only served by the whisper of a breeze, Il-Moon stopped and squinted up in the bright sun at the three men above him on the parapet. He was not permitted to speak; the honor was to die quietly—even in the flames.

This proscription was broken, as the three men above him spoke in Confucian order.

Dearest Leader looked down at his old ally. "So, Il-Moon. You precede us to Paradise."

Il-Moon laughed. "It was not always so clear I would, eh?"

Dearest Leader grimaced but managed, "Save a seat for us at the Heavenly Council of the One Korea."

Il-Moon gave a mock salute. "The seat I will save for you, *Young Tangun*, will be right beside me!"

Hakkermann tilted his head down slightly, a Korean bow of exactly the right amount for the moment, a skill almost impossible to master if you weren't born to it. "First Vice Chairman."

Il-Moon's smile was barracuda-like. "It is a pity I shall not see this Missouri of yours, as you invited."

Hakkermann held up the big treaty book. "Well, in a way you already have. It is mostly a state of mind."

"Yes," Il-Moon nodded, held out his palms. "As is Korea. As is anything worth loving."

A somber Architect Su raised his hand in a genteel wave between a benediction and a good-bye. "Fare thee well, Il-Moon-nim."

"Do not be sad, Su-ssi." Il-Moon spread his own arms wide to the glory of the Korean fall and, around them, the towering goldening mountains. "Look! Have we not come far from when, as boys we ran wild through the muddy streets of Manchuria, carrying messages to the Great Leader beneath the very noses of the silly Imperial Japanese Army?"

The gentle smile dropped from Su's face, a complex pain replacing it. "Perhaps, someday, in some distant place, will we not be there together again? Would it not be fine, to wake again from our rag beds under the rice mill to the sound of the bugle, and chew a piece of leather while we drink our tea and sew our clothes, and chatter as boys of how we would someday free Korea? Will it not be grand, when once again we sit under the mill, playing our checkers while we wait for the message bell to tinkle—until once again, we run those muddy streets together?"

Il-Moon slapped his thigh in delight. 'You dreamer!" he shouted. "All these years, you have been deceiving me! I see now I did *not* beat it out of you."

Su called back, "Am I the only dreamer? I thank you for sparing Gil-Yon. He sends his regards."

The wolfish grin spread slowly across Il-Moon's face, "Schemer!" he cackled. "You and Gil-Yon are already chattering excitedly like boys at the chance to build Korea all over again!" His crippled body swung an imaginary golf club in a big drive, and he roared, "You will finally get to design a golf course!"

Su, caught out once again by Il-Moon, managed a smile. "We will be sure, Il-Moon-nim, to imbue our rebuilding of Korea with your love for her."

"See that you do, Su-nim!"

Il-Moon turned, still un-harassed by the officers, and marched on slowly, crippled, to the execution pole. As he reached the pole, a bone-deep spasm seized him, and he bent over painfully, recovered only with teeth-gritting effort. He waved away the executioner's hood. His crippled body straightening in obvious pain, he stood before the pole and looked over his officers, his world.

The executioner lit a straw bundle to light the *auto da fe*.

For a moment it was quiet, except for the warble of a bird—and the whispering growing crackle of the tiny flames in the straw. Song Il-Moon stood to his highest height. Taking in his deepest breath, he suddenly shouted: "North Korea shall rise again!"

A young officer from Su's clan dashed forward. Grabbing a heavy log from the fire-pile at Il-Moon's feet, he smashed the old marshal a crushing blow to the temple.

Il-Moon fell, toppling slowly, and lay still.

The young officer ran and prostrated himself in the stone courtyard below Dearest Leader. "Forgive me! I will take his place!"

Chapter 73

AIRBORNE LASER – OSAN – TOKYO

Airborne Laser, battered but repaired, was homeward bound. On the tarmac at Osan, Col Kluppel, Capt Ku, and his Republic of Korea Special Forces saluted as Sean, Emily, and the tech crew climbed into ABL and waved good-bye.

ABL's hatch closed, and in that transitory way, it seemed to Sean only a blink of an eye and he was standing in the normalcy of a crowded tram to the Tokyo suburbs. Carrying a videotape, he walked over a little stone bridge to a pleasant garden house where Kyoko Hareda opened the door to him, and bowed him inside.

Despite the crews' desire to party when they'd passed through Tokyo before, while ABL was checked they spent just one night in Roppongi before they all voted to head for home. Japanese F-15's provided an honor guard escort past Mt. Fuji, flanking Airborne Laser long after she banked east out over the vast dappled oceanscape of the Pacific.

CAPITOL MALL – WASHINGTON D.C.

Banners were waving, a million small American and Korean flags, and a band played patriotic themes over the cheering crowd filling the Mall. A stage was set for a Presidential speech and medals. A popular DJ was at the mike, doing the MC and calling over the huge crowd. "Before we give the medals, I give you The Man, Our Man, Everyone's Man: The Prez!"

AIRBORNE LASER IN FLIGHT

Airborne Laser came in on approach to land, flaps down, battered airframe and scorched rattlesnake emblem clear.

Throughout the Tech Area, although the plane was skimming in, the crew bobbed around, pulling on dress uniforms, combing hair; everyone prepping for the coming ceremony.

"We're heroes," Lorrie yelled. "We're gonna get decorated!"

Eila burst in, "Like a cake! Hey Sean, where's the medal go?"

Sean watched Emily strip off her flight suit, toss it aside, and braid her hair carelessly. He answered Eila distractedly, "Third row is peace actions."

"Landing, people," Emily called. "Medal ceremonies go better when you pretend to be humble. Sean, you're Laser One."

She took his old Number 2 seat.

CAPITOL MALL – WASHINGTON D.C.

Jeanette DeFrancis sat stage-side, and watched the President step to the podium. He said, in ringing tones, "In the darkest days of World War II, when tyranny ruled Korea as it did so much of the world, we Americans made a promise. F.D.R. spoke for all of us when he said: "Mindful of the enslavement of the Korean people, America is determined that someday, Korea shall be free and independent!" After applause, the President added, "The day Roosevelt promised is here. The promise has been kept; and here is who kept it for all of us! So I give to you two special people, the two men who are your heroes of Korea. From Missouri..."

The crowd went wild as Harold Hakkermann and Dearest Leader Jong-Nam rose from their chairs and approached the podium together.

The crowd waved their flags, yelling, "Hakk! Jong-Nam! Hakk! Jong-Nam! Hakk! Jong-Nam!"

AIRBORNE LASER – AFRL – KIRTLAND AFB

Airborne Laser's wings caught the desert sunlight. Gleaming, the big Kirtland runway stretched away as they skimmed it, passing the quiet ABL hangar.

CAPITOL MALL – WASHINGTON D.C.

Harold Hakkermann carried Sandy's old briefcase up to the microphone, but rather than speaking, he raised a hand for quiet, and the crowd-noise slowly consolidated to a murmur.

Hakkermann gestured grandly to his friend, Dearest Leader, and from the briefcase handed him a big bound document and a slim piece of paper.

Dearest Leader leaned into the microphone, spoke in his soft voice. "I have two pieces of paper to show you. First, my good friend Ambassador

Hakkermann has made me an honorary citizen of Missouri."

The Mall crowd cheered madly, waving little American and Korean flags.

Hakkermann interrupted, adding, "With all the privileges and pomp that goes with that!"

More cheering until finally Dearest Leader could go on. "We could of course say so many things, and doubtless will do so over the coming days. However, at this moment, what does one say?" The crowd listened, rapt. "I have learned what we Missourians always say: 'I'm from Missouri, so speaking does not mean much.' What is it we always say?"

The crowd yelled, gleeful, "'Show me!'"

And the Dearest Leader of Koguryo held the big document aloft—the successful peace treaty between the United States and North Korea—shaking it and laughing, as Hakkermann moved, helped Jong-Nam to hold up the big book, and called out, "'Nuff said!"

The crowd was a sea of yelling, waving, and wide smiles.

Jeanette DeFrancis stood as the President moved away from the lectern where Harold began to add about five thousand words in spite of his 'nuff-said promise. The President stopped for a moment by Jeannette, said, "With Airborne Laser downplayed we can keep peace so many places."

"Understood, Sir. It's also an asymmetrical technology advantage. No other country will have the capability for decades. Technology advantage is fleeting. Let us use the time we've bought wisely. Perhaps it's time for peace."

The President smiled, squeezed her arm, and moved on to shake the next dignitary's hand.

Jeanette's Exec whispered to her, "We're late, we're late, for a very important date."

"Let's go, Dave! I don't want to miss any of the real celebration."

Jeanette and Dave left the stage as the crowd cheered some of Hakkermann's words. Passing out of the Secret Service security cordon, they high-stepped it along the crowd and by the time they reached Constitution Avenue, they were both flat out running toward their chopper to Jeanette's waiting Learjet to New Mexico.

AIRBORNE LASER – HOME

Airborne Laser taxied across the flight line gate and the final stretch to home. The crew didn't wait for the plane to stop before they jumped up and rushed the exit. Someone clawed open the door as ABL slowed and stopped.

The hatch swung wide. The crew, hungry for medals and brass bands—and expecting something official—looked out across the tarmac.

The signs were everywhere: 'Welcome Home!' and 'You're the best Dad!' and 'LUV U MOM!'

Next to the signs, a picnic feast—and a scrum of silent pets, kids, and spouses.

No brass band or dignitaries, and for a few seconds, the crew and families stared at one another as the crew realized. There are to be no brass bands or medals. No mayor's speech. They fought a war by themselves and their sponsors, those who had asked this of them, now asked for their discretion. They were to be anonymous heroes of America and of future wars.

Once you got used to it, Eila reflected, it wasn't really a bad feeling at all. It was kind of virtuous, like being the altar girl, and besides...

Matt's son Tim, unable to contain himself, suddenly yelled, "DADDY!"

The Airborne Laser crew didn't wait for the airstairs. Jumping to the tarmac and running, as the families surged forward trailing dolls, bibs, and pets to reunite yelling and shrieking! A girl-child, blue pinafore and red socks, blonde pigtails flying, runs right into her father getting down on a knee to intercept her just the right way—the kneeling hug hug hug!

Her waiting sons—a surprise—hoisted Lorrie up on their shoulders. Eila finally got the airstairs going, and helped a bandaged J-Stars down from the plane. Matt Cho swept Patricia into his arms, kids underfoot. Everywhere it was happy bedlam USA as everyone hollered and commingled.

AIRBORNE LASER – TECH AREA – THE LAST TIME

Watching from the hatch as the others surged down to their waiting families, Emily took a last look down the airstairs and over the ABL picnic area. Sean had gone straight for Amanda Hull; he had taken her into his arms warmly. Gathering around the pair, the rest of the crew pressed in, touching Amanda, speaking softly, sadly to her, until she was enveloped in sympathy and warmth. Amanda was crying, trying to brush off the tears, protesting—Emily could tell—wanting to congratulate everyone on the mission and to put forward a strong face despite Jarhead's death.

Emily turned away as Sean still held Amanda, their hug deepening. She felt the pang of what she knew would be lifelong painful sadness. Remembering Jay and his quotes, his ferocity, and his humanity. Poor Amanda. Poor Emily, too. She smiled bitterly to herself as she moved into the Tech Area. She was glad Sean was there for Amanda, yet she longed for his touch herself. What about her heart-wounds, her battle-damaged ideals, her now torched and ruined dreams?

Amanda was Sean's type, after all. Emily had to admit Sean had liked Jarhead a heck of a lot more than he liked her. Sean and Amanda, she supposed, was an inevitable match made, if not in heaven, somewhere extra-earthly in its ruthless logic. *Whereas Sean and Emily...* She pushed it all away as hard as she could—felt a door in her heart swing and then slam—if not tight, at least shut.

Emily moved slowly through the Tech Area for the last time, looking over the stations she knew so well down to their very smells; had in fact designed or specified so many of them. Drawing in the scent of hot electronics and dirty flight suits, the metals and oils and glues, it wasn't the pleasure of a seeing a teak railing on a fine sailboat—that was God's touch. Nor was it the joyous splash of deco chrome on a luxury interior—humankind's touch. Yet to her the inside of the Tech Area was something beautiful; a confluence of humankind's varied passions—the art of applied science.

Emily climbed up to the galley, passed the soiled bunks and Sean's famous B-52 coffeepot, blew a farewell kiss to the rattlesnake mascot Diablo, and went through into the flightdeck.

Outside the cockpit windows, the New Mexico sunshine was brilliant and the sky azure. Through the windows, she could see across the runway and against the backdrop of the upswept Rocky Mountains, the jumbled cubist buildings of the Air Force Research Laboratory. This had been home for a long time. She memorized the view for a second. She would never stand here again.

She closed her eyes. Her plane. Well, OK, in the end, hers and Sean's. OK, OK, in the end, it belonged to all the crew. *Vanitas Vanitas*, she mused.

Sliding down the flightdeck ladder to the tarmac, she made her getaway. Under cover of the big ABL, shielding her from the family reunion and picnic area, she moved away from the plane and across the apron to her car.

She had promised herself not to look back—which became difficult because from behind her there came sounds...a scuffling, a shuffling, a motor...

When she did glance back, it was the yellow USAF fire truck stalking her, creeping along behind her, water cannon ready. At the fire truck's flanks, Sean and the ABL crew and families were tiptoeing along, come to see the fun.

Emily found she was choked up enough so when she opened her mouth, she could only squawk, "Oh, no."

"Oh, yes," Sean grinned. "It was someone's last flight."

"I already got washed out. Let me leave with the little pride I have left."

Sirens wailed, revving up and moaning. The fire truck's front water cannon blasted—and the stream caught Sean full in the back and knocked him to his knees at Emily's feet.

The fire hose stream rolled Sean away across the tarmac.

Emily ran alongside as Sean rolled, finally wading into him in the spray, her legs stopping his roll. She knelt into the spray and he pulled her down on top of him, strengthening his grip, his thighs around her, she responding by tightening her own so they fused into a strong cage of space and muscle.

Face-to-face in the pounding stinging spray of the fire hose, Emily and Sean clutched each other, forming a man and woman shell resisting the blast of the hose. Within the foaming spray, in the small intimate carved-out space between their faces, there was just room to talk. Emily shouted over the water storm, "Your last flight? You quit?" The devilish fireman, realizing they couldn't budge the couple, readied the second water canon, worked to get it spraying.

Emily repeated, "You gave up Airborne Laser? Why?"

"I'm moving on. Taking on something really difficult."

Emily laughed, thinking he had finally shown some humility, "After what we've been through, you could take on anything."

Sean cocked his head in doubt. "I don't know. My next assignment is going to be a *bitch*."

She laughed, then kissed him tenderly. "Methinks the lady may prove you wrong. Again."

Sean kissed her back hard. The second fire hose came on and rolled them in the spray over and over in a great *From Here to Eternity* kiss.

Cheers of "Hear Hear!" from the watching Airborne Laser families added to the other confusing vibrations along the usually placid apron. The commotion made one of the normally unobtrusive tenants of the Airborne Laser area perk up their golden ears and wonder.

In their renovated prairie-dog-burrow home nearby, the family of small New Mexican owls, golden creatures with white speckles and alert eyes evolved for both night and day, awakened.

Stirred by some unknown pull, the owl parents, with a wink to their children, took wing, flew up and up, climbing smoothly until they circled overhead of the now calm and resting Airborne Laser, surrounded as if in a maypole dance by her mingling and jingling crew and their families.

Owlishly amused, the golden birds circled long and languorously above, watching as the sunlight glowed and the desert shadows lengthened over the dancing family party that was...the victorious homecoming celebration of The First Laser Warriors.

The End

856412

Made in the USA